Fiction

China and the West:

FROM A FAR LAND (1921–1952)

MANCHU (1624–1652)

MANDARIN (1854–1875)

DYNASTY (1900–1970)

A KIND OF TREASON

THE SEEKING

Nonfiction

CHINA'S RED MASTERS

THE DRAGON'S SEED

THE CENTRE OF THE WORLD

MAO'S GREAT REVOLUTION

MAO VERSUS CHIANG

THE GREAT CITIES: HONG KONG

FROM A FAR LAND

FROM A FAR LAND

ROBERT ELEGANT

RANDOM HOUSE NEW YORK

Library of Congress Cataloging-in-Publication Data

Elegant, Robert S.
From a far land.

1. China—History—20th century—Fiction.
I. Title.
PS3555.L37F7 1987 813'.54 86-27981
ISBN 0-394-56047-7

Manufactured in the United States of America

23456789

First American Edition

BOOK DESIGN BY LILLY LANGOTSKY

FOR HENRY FORD

and also for

MONICA AND FRANCIS CHEUNG

Is it not joyful to have
friends come from a far land?

THE ANALECTS OF CONFUCIUS

AUTHOR'S NOTE

From a Far Land is the story of the men, the women, and the extraordinary events involved in the development of today's China.

A novel should cast light upon reality as well as tell an exciting story. The author is therefore obliged to make his story very clear, particularly when a novel is set in a place unfamiliar to most readers and at some remove from them in time. Yet I feared that too much clarification would clutter the narrative of *From a Far Land*—a story of human beings amid great events. Therefore this Note, a brief outline of the chief forces affecting the troubled life of China during the first half of the twentieth century.

Confucianism then dominated the behavior and the thinking of almost all Chinese. That conservative political and moral code had been developed from the teachings of the Sage Confucius (c. 551–479 B.C.). It fostered authoritarian control within the home as well as the nation, and it militated against change.

Warlords were ambitious generals who fought each other for power over China after the Nationalist Revolution of 1911 overthrew the Confucian Manchu Dynasty. Warlord rule was usually rapacious, inefficient, and cruel.

The National People's Party of Dr. Sun Yat-sen struggled to sweep away the warlords and to create a unified, independent, and powerful Republic of China. Dr. Sun's policies were initially inspired by his Christian faith and his belief in modified socialism, both acquired abroad.

Strong foreign influence throughout China was exerted from *treaty ports* like Shanghai, where the outsiders governed themselves under their own laws, having exacted the concession of such *extraterritorial rights* from the Chinese by force. The foreigners were chiefly interested in fat profits and the soft life—for themselves, not necessarily for the Chinese. Some idealists—and some missionaries—supported Dr. Sun Yat-sen's Nationalists, but many foreigners wanted the lucrative disorder to continue.

Foreign ideas like democracy, science, feminism, individual liberty, and universal equality, however, inspired the *students* at China's new universities and colleges. They exercised political influence wholly disproportionate to their numbers because of the inherent Chinese reverence for learning, another legacy of Confucius. (The common people treasured even scraps of paper bearing the intricate Chinese characters, called *ideograms* because each expresses one idea.) Therefore, as the natural leaders of the nation, the young intellectuals played the decisive role in its transformation.

For decades, turmoil, mounting upon occasion to anarchy, wracked the world's most populous nation. Even after the People's Republic of China was created in 1949, protracted periods of mass violence tormented the Chinese people.

The People's Republic has, however, during the past decade put aside both its fascination with ideology and its propensity toward turmoil to strive purposefully and intelligently for the well-being of its people— and for a peaceful international order. That fundamental alteration is the most exciting—and most inspiring—political development of the latter part of the twentieth century.

R.E.

CONTENTS

PROLOGUE

SHANGHAI

MAY 2, 1952

The slender woman with the tawny hair twitched aside the curtain covering the limousine's window and peered out. She was determined to impale in her memory the dark tenements and factories of Shanghai, which loomed against the gray afternoon sky of May 2, 1952. The woman's face was pale, although her silk dress was the same festive scarlet as the pennant with the five golden stars that flapped above the chromium shark's-grin of the limousine's radiator.

She did not turn when the man beside her said, "Julie, I still don't see why you're determined to leave. But since you are, make sure you tell the world we did not drive you back to America. Quite the contrary! You know, I'm still wondering if I should let you go."

The woman sat still, apparently weighing his words. Finally she turned to the man in the elegant gray linen tunic and said, "Premier, I would stay if I could. The best of my life has been here. But I cannot stay, Premier."

"Why so formal, Julie?" The Chinese woman seated on the premier's left asked. "Among friends, formality cuts like a knife."

"I'm not cutting myself off from you, Rosamonde," the American woman replied. "But it *is* portentous . . . to me. Leaving means the end of so much! Almost everything for me!"

"It's because of Tommy, isn't it?" the premier probed. "Always Tommy."

"What do you think?" Julia answered.

"You can't forgive us, can you?" the premier persisted. "Though no one knows for certain what happened—not even I."

"If I knew, perhaps I could forgive. But as it is . . ."

Half a mile away, a pale man waited impatiently. His narrow eyes remote behind rimless glasses, he hovered on the fringe of the crowd of workers before the offices of the South Seas Spinning Corporation. Unlike those mill-hands, he showed no interest in the interrogation booming from the loudspeakers on the lampposts. In the muggy late afternoon, the mill-hands wore grimy singlets and baggy blue cotton trousers. The outsider smoothed the lapel of his pin-striped suit and nervously fingered the knot of his yellow foulard tie.

He turned toward the deserted roadway and, head cocked, listened intently. The loudspeakers were amplifying the voices of Communist cadres hectoring the owner of the South Seas Spinning Corporation. He waited for a different signal, rather than the harsh accusations and the feeble replies.

After several minutes, he smiled thinly at the approaching sirens. Surrounded by motorcycle outriders in the rumpled green of the Chinese People's Liberation Army, a black limousine turned the corner and bowled along toward the South Railway Station.

The man in the pin-striped suit wryly recalled that the ponderous Soviet-made Zil was modeled on prewar Packards, like the touring car he had owned when he was a graduate student at Georgia Tech. He nodded with melancholy satisfaction when he saw the scarlet pennant above the radiator, which confirmed the obvious. Since private cars had virtually disappeared after "liberation," a limousine could only be carrying a senior official of the New China.

The blue-uniformed traffic policeman at the intersection stiffened to attention, blew his whistle, and windmilled his arms to halt the nonexistent traffic. Other policemen officiously thrust back the crowd that spilled into the road.

The tall man slipped under their extended arms, his right hand thrust deep into his side pocket. Policemen fumbled with the wooden holsters of their Mauser pistols, and the bodyguard in the front seat of the limousine reached for the Tokharin pistol in his belt. But they were already too late.

Darting between the astonished motorcycle outriders, the man pulled a white envelope from his pocket and hurled himself at the heavy car. The impact flung him through the air. Despite screeching brakes, one wheel crunched over his body.

When the limousine halted, the premier knocked on the glass partition between the front compartment and the back and demanded: *"Shen-mo shih, Li?* . . . What is it, Li?"

"Wo kan-yi-kan, Tsung-li . . ." The bodyguard opened his door. "I'll check, Premier. But it doesn't look too dangerous. It's only one man."

"Another blasted suicide!" The premier's tone was sad, although edged with exasperation and sorrow. "We *must* crush the corrupt bourgeoisie, but . . ."

"Are you trying for a new record, old friend?" Julia spoke Shanghainese with a slight American accent. "Where is it all going to end?"

"What do you mean, Julia, a record?"

Chou En-lai, premier of the twenty-month-old People's Republic of China, imperiously governed more human beings than any other man on earth. But he smiled at that gibe. The woman in the scarlet dress had been his friend and ally for a quarter of a century. Glancing affectionately at her, he did not see that her mahogany hair now owed as much to art as to nature. Two years of "proletarian dictatorship" had not quite driven all the skilled hairdressers out of a metropolis that before liberation had been the most civilized—and most corrupt—city in Asia.

"What do you mean," he repeated when she did not reply, "by a record?"

"I was thinking of 1929 in New York," Julia said. "When you couldn't walk down Wall Street for fear of falling financiers. We've already had many more suicides in Shanghai than in New York after the stock market crash. And they're still going on."

"We do not *enjoy* it, my dear Julia!" The Chinese woman on the premier's right remarked softly. "I sometimes awake at night weeping. So *many* suicides. Sometimes I wonder: Are all these sacrifices really necessary?"

"Not only necessary," the premier replied, "but unavoidable, Madame Sun—ah—Chingling."

After two decades of friendship, the premier sometimes still addressed the older woman by her title rather than by her given name. She was a living monument. But her heart-shaped face was quite unlined, preternaturally youthful. Now sixty-two, she was a vice-chairman of the Chinese People's Political Consultative Council—and the widow of Dr. Sun Yat-sen, the great revolutionary leader, who had been dead for twenty-six years. Since both the Communists and their perennial antagonists, the Nationalists, venerated Dr. Sun as the father of the Chinese Republic, her prestige was unique.

"Perhaps suicides in protest are unavoidable," she temporized. "Perhaps they're also necessary."

"Do you really believe that, Rosamonde?" Julia, indignant, used Madame Sun's foreign name. "When you wake up weeping, do you really believe they're necessary? Are you convinced that driving hundreds of businessmen to suicide is unavoidable?"

The bodyguard slipped into his seat and nodded to the driver. As the limousine moved off, he reported to the premier. "The fellow was unarmed. Only this note. I found it near the body."

"No name, but he addressed it to me—by implication, at least." The premier smiled dourly. "I guess I'd better read it."

Chou En-lai could not allow himself to be disturbed by the wave of suicides among the capitalists of Shanghai, a city that had once been a capitalist's paradise. But today, for the first time, the campaign to stamp out "the five evil practices of the bourgeoisie" had touched him directly. Suicide before an official's door or under his chariot's wheels had for centuries been the ultimate Chinese protest against injustice.

Reading the note, the premier remarked defensively: "Nothing new. Only the usual complaints: The wicked Communists promised to preserve Shanghai; they swore the New China would not destroy capitalist enterprises. Now, he complains, we've gone back on our word. . . . What did the fools expect? The campaign to suppress the five evil practices, this Mr. Liu Zoongvee says, has destroyed him—as it has destroyed free enterprise in China."

Rosamonde Sun looked pained. Her porcelain forehead crinkled, and her plump hands smoothed the blue silk of her modest slit skirt. Although never formally a member of the Communist Party of China, she had concluded three decades earlier that the Communists offered the only hope for China's salvation. She was, however, upon occasion appalled by the ruthless regime she had helped bring to power. When she saw Julia's lips part indignantly, she touched her friend's hand and said in English with a soft southern accent: "It will be some time—perhaps a very long time—before we see you again. Please don't say anything you'll regret. . . . But here's the station."

The premier's party was greeted by a rank of uniformed railway officials drawn up before massed pots of azaleas. The American woman took Madame Sun's hand, and they followed the stationmaster into a waiting room banked with yellow and scarlet blossoms. When they were seated around a coffee table laden with bite-sized delicacies, the railwaymen withdrew.

"Of course the train's late again! Of course it's not ready for boarding." The premier's irony was strained. "I must do something about the railways soon—very soon."

"Even you can't solve all China's problems at once." Madame Sun soothed him. "But we must all try. And some day—"

"Don't wait for the train," Julia interrupted. "You're both far too busy. I can just about manage to get aboard alone."

"A compartment is reserved for you," the premier said. "But of course we'll wait."

"I really would prefer second class . . . leaving Shanghai after so many years. Second class is more fitting. Certainly not a compartment."

"Think of the face Chingling and I would lose if you traveled second class," the premier joked. "Besides, it's a long way from Shanghai to Hong Kong."

"And much longer from Hong Kong to America!" Rosamonde said. "Now Julie, why not tell us what is in your heart? Better not to part on a false note."

"Wo lao peng-yu . . ." Julia said slowly. "My old friends, my dear friends. I knew him, Liu Zoongvee, the man who just killed himself. Not well, but I knew him. He was a lightweight, a social butterfly, the son of a wealthy family, and a bit of a playboy. But he never did anyone any harm. And he was a first-class engineer. Does China have so much talent to spare? How many more trained people can you afford to throw away?"

When neither answered, she added with apparent irrelevance, "I still don't see why you wouldn't let me travel second class."

"It's the least we can do for a *famous foreign friend of China.*" The premier's tone was heavily sarcastic. "Do go on, Julie. I'm at your service."

"You promised, my friend. You promised to preserve Shanghai. And now thousands are dying. Not only is normal life totally disrupted, but you've gotten yourself into a wasteful war against the Americans in Korea. . . . Yes, I know the Americans are *very* dangerous. Particularly MacArthur. But war was *not* necessary. War helps only the Soviets. And you've purged your own officials only months after they took office—"

"They purged themselves, Julie," the premier interjected. "They purged themselves by intriguing, by forming anti–Party factions. Also by corruption, by misusing their power."

"Can't you see it?" the American woman pleaded. "Can't you see it's all unraveling before it's even properly begun? That's why I'm leaving!"

"You *could* stay, Julie," the premier suggested. "You're very welcome."

"You know it wouldn't work," she replied. "It's not just Tommy.
. . . The revolution is completed, and there's no place for me here."

"It's not nearly as bad as you think, Julie," the premier declared. "We
can't be soft—no more than we could while we were making the revolution. *You* weren't soft then either. We must be hard, but the results will
be well worth it all. You'll see."

"I am certain of one thing," Julia retorted. "You'll never change
Shanghai—not fundamentally. You'll never change its real nature.
Shanghai is too wild and wonderful, too wicked and too delightful."

"We hold Shanghai," the premier asserted. "And we will transform
Shanghai."

"You may succeed for a time—on the surface," the American woman
declared. "But in the end, Shanghai will defeat you!"

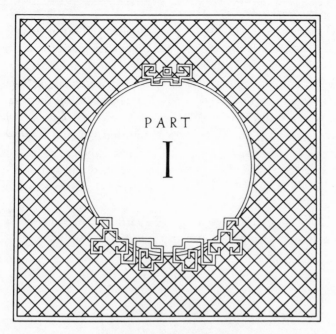

PART

I

ARRIVALS

1921-1923

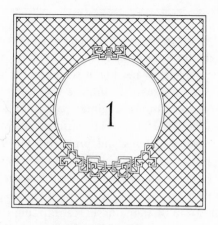

JUNE 21, 1921

The moored warships of five nations were lit by the setting sun against the low skyline of the embankment called the Bund. A young woman in a blue serge dress pirouetted across the cabin of an ocean liner and stretched a diaphanous scarf across the porthole. The turquoise butterflies and yellow crickets embroidered on the scarf seemed to hover frivolously over the stark men of war. A welcoming present, the scarf was quintessentially Chinese, the needlework so cunning that dewdrops appeared to glisten on the border of violets. The view of Shanghai through that veil seemed hardly Chinese at all, except for the junks with mat-sails on the dark Hwangpoo River.

Julia Pavernen caught her breath when she saw the Stars and Stripes flying from both a buff-and-white gunboat and an iron-gray destroyer. She shivered with pride at the flag, seen for the first time so far from her native land. It was reassuring to see other foreign flags on the warships. She reminded herself that Shanghai was not an unruly Chinese city but an International Settlement under the orderly government of Americans and Europeans. Yet Shanghai was undeniably in China— and still thirteen thousand miles from Philadelphia.

Julia identified the white ensign of Great Britain's Royal Navy flying on two destroyers and a heavily turreted cruiser. In the twilight, she also saw the tricolor of France, the radiant-sun of Japan, and the orange-white-and-blue stripes of the Netherlands.

No warships flew the flag of either of the two rival Republics of China. In late June of 1921, one had its capital in the north at Peking, and the other in the south at Canton. Those two regimes were the foremost contenders for power over China, but a number of other armed factions also fought for control of the world's most populous nation.

Julia reproached herself for her joy at seeing the foreign flags. It was wrong she knew for foreigners to impose themselves and their alien laws on China. Yet the Chinese regimes could not protect their own citizens, much less foreigners, from the warlords, the rapacious generals whose conflicts threatened lives and property. The foreign warships that patrolled China's rivers were a steel shield for Shanghai, the largest concentration of foreigners and foreign wealth in the Orient.

Behind Julia in the oak-paneled cabin, Emily Howe spoke vivaciously —and unintelligibly—in Shanghainese. Her buzzing z's and sibilant s's were echoed by her old nursemaid, Ven Jyeh, who had come aboard the *Empress of Australia* from the pilot boat at the mouth of the Yangtze River. Listening to their conspiratorial laughter, Julia suddenly realized that the young woman who had been her closest friend for ten years had another, and totally alien, life. Emily was called Yuelin by the old nursemaid—and she was indisputably Chinese. She was not another American college girl with exotic features but a daughter of the colossal and terrifying country that lay outside the liner.

"Are you in a trance?" Emily asked. "One minute dancing around like crazy, the next frozen stiff. What's wrong?"

"Nothing, Emily. It's just that . . ."

"I know exactly how you feel." The Chinese girl added reassuringly. "When I first saw San Francisco, I was scared stiff."

"But we're grown-ups now. Past twenty. I shouldn't be afraid, especially not with you around."

"Shanghai's almost as strange to me, Julie. Ten years is a long time to be away. I was only a child when I left—and China was still an empire. I'm just as curious as you about what Shanghai's like now."

"But you've hardly even looked out."

"Maybe I'm a little afraid, too. Anyway, we'll see it all later. Right now I've got to pick the right dress for the party."

"You'll never be packed in time," Julia warned. "Your things are strewn all over the cabin."

"Nothing to worry about. Ven Jyeh will take care of it. That's why she brought Ah Wong along, to help."

"Emmy, I don't understand. Two maids to meet you . . . us. But nobody from your family. It isn't natural."

"It's not *meant* to be natural. It's etiquette."

Emily joined Julie at the porthole, and they stood transfixed by evening's descent upon China. The foreign warships were fiery silhouettes against the Western-style buildings of the Bund: the British Consulate, the Maritime Customs House, and the Shanghai Club, among many others. They were the stolid façade of the foreign authority that ruled Shanghai's overwhelmingly Chinese population, making all those Chinese secure—and making some very wealthy.

Emily Howe wondered, Was she really coming home? Or had America become her true home? After spending ten formative years abroad, she was profoundly, perhaps fundamentally, altered. Was China still her home?

Perplexed by her own emotions, Emily explained, "Mom and Dad might have met me, even though it would scandalize their elders. The older generation doesn't come out to receive the younger. But they're giving that big reception this evening. They're thirty years married. They have to receive their guests."

"I was so afraid we wouldn't make it in time," Julia said. "All those delays—and your folks' only girl child *had* to be here."

"None of my brothers could welcome an unmarried young woman like you," Emily continued. "My sisters-in-law I've never even seen!"

"It sounds positively medieval," Julia protested. "But you sound so calm."

"Well, Ven Jyeh came. She practically brought me up, and Ah Wong's always been her helper. They *are* members of the Howe family . . . will be till they die."

"It must be nice to have such willing slaves," Julia said. "My dad's country parsonage in upper New York State just about runs to a hired girl."

"Your family's hardly poverty-stricken, Julie," Emily said. "Even if they don't have hordes of amahs. You know, I'll miss your folks."

"They loved having you stay, Emmy. Even if they did get scared that my cousin Bobby and you . . . Your folks would probably feel the same way. . . . Emmy, you're a mantrap, so demure the poor boys can't see the steel under the lace and perfume."

"In Shanghai, they'll probably think I'm forward. Also too tall— gawky and overgrown. What about your cousin Bobby? It was a flirtation—only for fun. I could no more think of marrying Bobby than you could, say, my brother Tommy. Fun's fun, but different races *are* different. But this talk is too serious. We've got to get gussied up for the party."

Julia turned reluctantly from the porthole as the *Empress of Australia* groped toward her buoy. The Bund, as Emily had said, was not only the gateway to China but the symbol of her country's subjugation. A Chinese-style customs house with red-tiled roofs and upswept eaves had once stood among the aggressively alien domed and pedimented buildings. It had been replaced by the present customs house with its crenelated clock tower, like Taylor Hall at Bryn Mawr. The foreigners, Emily had added angrily, wouldn't even leave the Chinese their own architecture.

You could never tell about Emily. Sometimes she was an ardent patriot, denouncing foreigners' influence and swearing to drive them out of China. Sometimes she sounded like a foreigner herself, remarking condescendingly that you couldn't expect the Chinese to be honest or clean or efficient. Taxed with her inconsistency, she would laughingly confess: "I guess I've got a treaty-port mentality. When the foreigners took over cities like Shanghai by shotgun treaties, they also took over our minds."

As the breeze died over the coffee-colored river, the oblong sails of junks flapped, and gray smoke rose from the braziers on their sterns. From the shore blew a musty odor, acrid with coal fumes and pungent with garlic. A gong boomed, firecrackers rattled, and a two-string violin wailed. Treaty port or not, Julia knew, she had come to China.

"Stop mooning, Julie. We'll be getting off soon. And just look at you!"

Julia glanced down. Her lightweight blue serge dress with its sailor collar and brass buttons was jaunty in the military mode inspired by the Great War. It was a traveling dress with flair. Although her father had grumbled, her mother had insisted that Julie's wardrobe, though meager, must embarrass neither herself nor her new friends on the other side of the world.

"What's wrong with my dress?" she asked. "Why you don't even have yours on yet!"

Although two inches taller than Julia's five foot three, Emily appeared fragile in the peach-colored slip that hung to her knees. Marveling at that lace-trimmed wisp of a garment, the maidservant Ven Jyeh lifted the hem to cluck disapprovingly at the long garters that kept gossamer silk stockings taut. Her delicacy was emphasized by the slip's narrow straps, for Emily's shoulders looked as if they would be bruised by the touch of a feather, much less an ardent hand. Her apparent frailty was accentuated by wide-set eyes and high cheekbones.

She had, however, been a robust forward on the Bryn Mawr hockey team. She was really as tough as old boots, Julia's mother had once declared, exasperated by the implacable will beneath the appearance of docile femininity.

"I'm just deciding which dress to wear. What did you think was in the leather trunk Ven Jyeh brought?"

"I didn't notice. I was too busy looking at the shoreline."

"Well, have a look!"

Julia lifted the red-and-gold lid—and gasped at the rainbow froth that burst from the trunk.

"There must be dozens of dresses here!" she exclaimed.

"For *both* of us to choose from. Some for you and some for me. We'll have a wonderful time with them later. Right now we've got to decide what to wear tonight!"

"I've already decided," Julia said. "My sailor dress is fine."

"You can't possibly wear that old thing to this party. Now just let me see . . ."

While Emily rummaged in the trunk, Julia continued her objections: "Your mother couldn't know my size. That tafetta-and-lace *is* beautiful. A pity I couldn't squeeze into—"

"I sent Mom a description of you. She didn't know exactly about me either. So she had the dressmaker run off outfits in several sizes. But Mom's frugal. She had him leave lots of material, so everything can be altered."

"Frugal! There must be thirty or forty dresses there! I can't possibly accept—"

"You can't offend my parents by refusing. Besides, I want you to look wonderful. Now let me see . . ."

Emily held up the tafetta-and-lace gown Julia had admired, but rejected it as too long. Ven Jyeh methodically folded the delicate fabrics, bringing order to the confusion her young mistress casually created. Just as deftly, she made minor alterations to the dresses the two finally chose and, with Ah Wong's help, did their hair. The junior officers of the *Empress of Australia* said good-bye at the gangway to two self-possessed young ladies.

Although tempted by the confections the dressmaker had whipped up from Parisian fashion plates, Emily had decided she must honor the occasion by wearing a Chinese-style dress. The circlet of pearls that secured her chignon glowed like the cream silk jacket with three-quarter sleeves. Adapted from the formal wear of the Manchu Dynasty, which had been overthrown a decade earlier, the collar did not confine her but rolled softly around her slender neck. Her skirt, which was a bell of tangerine silk, flaunted a border of antique embroidery.

After abandoning her resistance, Julia had also given herself to the delight of dressing up. She floated down the gangway to the launch in a finely pleated cream voile skirt with turquoise panels and sash. Despite her bold green eyes, Emily said, she looked ethereal because of her translucent complexion and the mahogany hair that fell to her shoulders.

Lost in wonder at landing in China, Julia was barely aware of the deference that greeted them. But no one could be unaware of the enormous motorcar that glowed emerald green beneath the bronze statue of Sir Robert Hart of the Chinese Maritime Customs Service. The Rolls-Royce Phaeton was bright with burnished brass, and its black canvas top was secured by leather straps.

A chauffeur wearing a peaked cap, leather puttees, and emerald-green jacket and breeches bowed before headlights as big as silver salvers. A footman in the same uniform held open the rear door. Julia inhaled the aroma of leather upholstery, sandalwood trim, and roses in cut-crystal vases.

JUNE 21, 1921

The footman seated beside the chauffeur was in constant motion, his head swiveling and bobbing. Although she was mystified, Julia did not like to ask her friend, who was gazing through the window. Her blasé airs forgotten, Emily was obviously fascinated by Shanghai, the home she had not seen for a decade.

Nanking Road, the chief thoroughfare, was a turmoil of glaring lights, ear-splitting noises, brilliant colors, and pungent odors. Enormous advertising banners flapped above a multitude of shops, and streams of pedestrians in strange clothes flowed beneath neon signs.

The throngs parted reluctantly before the "Hoo-oo! Hoo-oo!" of coolies trotting between the shafts of yellow rickshaws. Horse-traps commanded greater respect, and the people scattered for the trolleys' clanking bells. Fords and Morrises darted around the majestic Rolls at a foolhardy twenty-five miles an hour.

"Almost there now." Emily remembered Chinese courtesy to a guest. "We turn just a little way down Bubbling Well Road."

She was breathing rapidly, and her ivory cheeks were flushed. After all, Shanghai *was* home. She knew now that she belonged here. The focus of her loyalty was China, *not* America!

"Emmy, what's wrong with your footman?" Julia asked. "He keeps twitching like an epileptic."

Emily leaned against the red leather upholstery and smiled. "He's not a footman at all. He's a bodyguard who—"

"A *bodyguard*?" Julia was fascinated—and a little frightened. "What do we need a bodyguard for?"

"In times like these it's wise to take precautions against, for instance, kidnappers. Daddy's not exactly the poorest man in Shanghai."

"For instance, *kidnappers*? And what else?"

"Things are unsettled. No Chinese soldiers in the Foreign Settlement, of course. But the warlords are fighting all around us. If your Uncle Jack hadn't sworn up and down it was safe, I bet your folks wouldn't have let you come."

"If Uncle Jack hadn't paid the fare, I'd be back in Plattsburg right now. He swore there was no danger in the Foreign Settlement."

"No danger for you. But everybody knows that Daddy gives a lot of money to Dr. Sun Yat-sen. And Dr. Sun is fighting the warlords and the reactionaries, fighting for a modern, united China."

"Come off your soapbox, Emmy. So your father supports Dr. Sun. So what?"

"So some people would like to shoot Daddy. So a bodyguard always sits next to the chauffeur. There are also guards around the house."

The Rolls crossed Avenue Foch into Rue Pataro in the French Concession and turned into a lane shaded by plane trees. A red brick gate lodge stood beside a wrought-iron arch scrolled with the name HARMONY HALL. The gilt spearheads of the gates gleamed under paper lanterns swirled in scarlet with intricate Chinese writing. Other lanterns lit the gravel driveway that wound among phoenix-tail bamboos and towering rhododendrons bearing indigo-and-white flowers. Julia saw black figures amid the dark green foliage and assumed they were guards. After two minutes, the Rolls drew up before an enormous structure that was so brightly lit its outlines were indistinct.

"Don't be surprised by the way my mother walks," Emily warned. "She only unbound her feet after I was born. So she still hobbles a little, especially when she's tired."

Eurydice and Donald Howe, were receiving guests beneath the stained-glass windows of the circular entrance hall. The harsh light of the crystal chandelier glared on the checkerboard floor of pink and gray marble. The electric fans hanging from the vaulted ceiling were lacquered emerald green.

His features bland and his black-rimmed spectacles gleaming, Donald Howe bowed slightly to his only daughter, whom he had last seen a decade before. In his well-cut tailcoat, he was tall, imposing, and up-to-date.

But he did not move toward Emily. He was also an old-fashioned Chinese father who did not display affection in public.

Eurydice Howe's feet were concealed by her floor-length gold-striped skirt, and her plump chin was chafed by the stiff collar of her long Manchu-style jacket. Instinctively stepping forward to greet her daughter, she abruptly halted and stood stock-still, her torso slightly inclined and her square face devoid of expression.

Julia saw just how rigid Chinese etiquette was. That Emily's mother stood motionless although Emily had been so far away for so long seemed almost inhuman. Emily was herself motionless under the chandelier, her body bent in a deep bow. Her large eyes glistened, and her full mouth trembled.

"Jing-ai di fu-mu . . ." she quavered. "Esteemed parents . . ."

Donald Howe then moved almost as rapidly in his patent-leather shoes as did his wife on her crippled feet. Mother, father, and daughter embraced amid the rococo splendors of the hall, as demonstrative as a peasant family in a thatched hut.

"Hsiu nue-nue! Waw nue-nue!" Eurydice crooned. "Baby! My baby!"

A half minute later, the Howes once again stood apart. Their unrumpled clothing hung perfectly; their hair was unruffled; and their expressions were mildly benign. Emily's features did not alter as she presented her guest to her parents.

"Delighted you could come." Donald Howe's fluent English was distorted by a curious rhythmic intonation. "Glad to have you."

"You . . . are . . . very welcome." Eurydice Howe always claimed she understood English, but did not care to speak it. "I am . . . happy . . . you . . . come tonight."

Julia realized that her hostess was repeating the formula with which she had greeted all the foreign guests at this thirtieth-anniversary reception. The guest felt a surge of affection for the outwardly stolid couple who had momentarily displayed tumultuous emotion in welcoming their daughter.

"I'm so happy to be here, Mr. and Mrs. Howe," she said. "So happy you let me come with Emmy. I'm just tickled pink."

"Julie, honey, I'm tickled pink at seeing you." The voice was American, and the spare newcomer was dapper in a white linen dinner jacket. "You've turned into a mighty pretty girl—a fine little handful."

Her Oriental composure broken by that familiarity, Emily gaped like an American college girl. Julia, who was normally friendly to all, glanced at the newcomer frostily.

"But—but you must be my Uncle Jack!" she finally guessed. "You are John Pavernen, aren't you?"

His sleek black widow's peak, long nose, and cleft chin were not like her father's features. The small-town parson was much taller, and his remaining hair was still orange. But John Pavernen's piercing green eyes were exactly the same as her father's—and her own.

"None other, my dear." He held out his arms. "And how's my favorite niece?"

"Tickled pink to see you, too." She laughed in his embrace. "And very grateful for your talking Mom and Dad into letting me come to Shanghai."

"Julie, let's leave the Howes in peace to welcome their guests. . . . Where did that beautiful dress come from?"

John Pavernen tucked Julia's arm under his own. Still chatting, he led her down an emerald-green corridor to double doors that opened into a circular room so large and so crowded Julie could hardly see the walls. Beneath a glass dome, six many-tiered chandeliers cascaded hard light on the tightly packed throng.

"The ballroom," her uncle stage-whispered, "will just about hold the thousand-odd they're expecting. This is just the first act, mainly for *yang guei-tze* . . ."

"*Yang guei-tze?*"

"Sorry. *Yang guei-tze* means foreign devils. That's what the Chinese call us. The *big* bash next week, a gigantic banquet, is mainly for Chinese."

"Uncle Jack, what does Mr. Howe do? Emmy said her father wasn't poor, but this—"

"Donald Howe's not the richest Chinese in the Settlement. As for foreigners, the Sassoons or the Haleevies could almost buy and sell him. But Donald Howe isn't poor. He's maybe the second- or third-richest Chinese in town. His father left him a string of native banks. Silver shops, the Chinese call them. He's also a big property owner, and he dabbles in textiles and matches. I'm trying to interest him in some projects, but he's very conservative."

"Conservative? But Emmy says he supports the revolutionary Dr. Sun Yat-sen."

"He's conservative in business, Julie. Anyway, old Dr. Sun's no big bad Bolshevik. Maybe a touch pink, but no Bolshevik. He's even got a Christian wife, one of Charlie Soong's three beautiful daughters. And I'll tell you, Charles Jones Soong was no Bolshevik. He was a Methodist millionaire, practically an American by adoption."

"Then why does Dr. Sun want a revolution?"

"To get decent government going in China. Though I personally think . . . But hold on, baby. Later we can relax and talk, just you and me. I want to hear all about the family but this is no place—"

"Of course, Uncle Jack. We'll have lots of time to talk after I move in with you."

"Well, my place isn't really up to snuff yet. And Eurydice Howe says it wouldn't be right for a young girl to move in with—"

"With her own uncle? Really, Uncle Jack, I didn't know Shanghai was so strait-laced."

"Old Shanghai families like the Howes are *very* proper. So you'll be staying with them for a while. But, Julie, most of Shanghai's *not* strait-laced, not at all. You've got to be extra careful."

"I'll try," Julia responded dutifully. "Though I don't imagine Shanghai is any more wicked than Philadelphia."

John Pavernen laughed loudly and, recovering, said, "You've got a lot to learn, honey. Don't hold on to that notion. Shanghai no wickeder than Philadelphia! I've heard some good ones, but . . ."

Julia had not expected her deadpan humor to meet with such spectacular success. She was, after all, only half joking. The elite of supposedly wicked Shanghai looked sedate, self-important, and very respectable.

Manservants in ankle-length white robes were carrying silver trays through the chattering throng. Several tables against the walls were stocked with champagne, claret, whisky, brandy, and port, which stained the damask tablecloths as harried waiters filled fresh glasses. Before heaped lobsters, oysters, crabs, and shrimps, carved-ice dragons with flashing electric-bulb eyes guarded mounds of caviar, smoked eel, and pickled salmon. Other tables offered entire roast geese, ducks, pheasants, and suckling pigs.

"Not plopah Chinee fashion. Alle same *yang guei-tze* fashion walkee-walkee small chow," John Pavernen remarked and called out, "Boy, two cup *shahmpiyen.*"

"Uncle Jack, what *did* you say? I hardly understood a word."

"Manservants are called boy." Jack Pavernen grinned. "And I simply asked for champagne. Don't you understand straightforward pidgin?"

Julia remained prudently silent when he explained: "You'll learn pidgin soon enough. I also said the Howes were adopting foreign ways by serving canapes—which are, logically enough, called small chow. Chinese always sit down to eat."

"Very expressive . . . pidgin," Julia agreed. "Concise, too. All that in so few words."

"You'll do, Julie, you'll do." John Pavernen raised his glass to her. "Just remember: Shanghai is *not* Philadelphia. It's a *very* wicked town."

Although the louvers in the glass dome stood open and ceiling fans whirled, the ballroom was stifling. Still, more guests crowded in, while the chatter—and the drinking—grew more hectic.

A number of middle-aged Chinese men stopped to exchange greetings. Julia did not catch their names but knew she would not have remembered them anyway. All addressed her with profound, almost fawning, courtesy. She might have been a visiting princess rather than an unremarkable young woman from a country parsonage. Traditional Chinese politeness, she concluded, was obviously heightened by general esteem for John Pavernen. Her uncle must have carved himself a big niche in just three years in Shanghai.

When she congratulated him on his popularity, John Pavernen smiled noncommittally. No reason to tell Julia that *she* was the focus of respect —and curiosity. Not because she was his niece, but because all Shanghai knew she was the intimate friend of Emily Howe and the guest of Donald Howe.

Anyone that close to a throne, even a minor throne, commanded deference. Who knew when he might need a friend at court? Shanghai was no different from London, New York—or Plattsburg.

Julia and John Pavernen drifted into the circle surrounding an impressive foreign couple. The man was of medium height, his chest massive under his tailcoat. Miniature medals shone on his lapel, and the blue-and-scarlet ribbon around his neck displayed the cross of a Knight Commander of the Order of St. Michael and St. George. His nose was assertively curved, and his blue eyes were commanding above a silvered beard. The woman's blond chignon was clasped with a circlet of amethysts and diamonds.

Julia guessed that she was about fifty-five, five or ten years younger than the man. Her exuberant curves triumphed over the corset meant to flatten her bosom and her hips fashionably. Julia remembered seeing the evening gown in the latest issue of *Vogue.* The sprays of flowers on the transparent chiffon overdress with beaded cuffs and hem had obviously required hundreds of hours of painstaking needlework; the tiny sunflowers on her black satin evening slippers had white jade petals with diamond-chip centers.

"May I present my niece, Miss Julia Pavernen?" Uncle Jack was unwontedly ceremonious. "My dear, Sir Judah and Lady Haleevie."

Julia instinctively bobbed a half curtsy. Lady Haleevie reached out to clasp her hands, and Sir Judah patted her shoulder.

"We're delighted you've come, my dear." Lady Haleevie's accent was English. "Tell Emily to bring you to see us very soon."

"That's very kind of you, Rachel." John Pavernen was ingratiating.

"But you mustn't let Julie become a nuisance to Judah and yourself." Delighted at being permitted to call the Haleevies by their first names, he chatted animatedly while Julia accepted another goblet of champagne and a tidbit of crisp-skinned duck. A tiny linen napkin shielded the goblet, and the duck tasted of liquorice.

"The Haleevies are an old Jewish family, from Baghdad a long time ago," Jack Pavernen whispered after they had detached themselves. "Been in Shanghai from the beginning. Old Judah's so rich he can hardly count all his shekels. They're very orthodox, but they don't act like Jews. They're not just generous. They're extravagant in their charities—especially for the Chinese. Old Judah's also very shrewd and very tough. *Never* get on the wrong side of the Haleevies."

Many of the new arrivals were young foreigners in dinner jackets. Naval officers, all foreign, were dressed similarly in blue and gold, but the army and marine officers were gaudily diverse. Their scarlet, emerald, and royal-blue tunics flaunted silver aiguillettes, fringed gold epaulettes, and medals on rainbow-hued ribbons.

Confident that Julia would not be left alone, John Pavernen slipped away to pursue new contacts. She was very glad Eurydice Howe had sent these beautiful dresses to the ocean liner. Surrounded by the young men irresistibly drawn by a new female, she would have felt like a frump in her practical blue serge with the naïve sailor collar. Shanghai was obviously going to be fun, despite the scandalous stories she had heard about foreign bachelors and their Chinese floozies.

Repeatedly asked how long she was staying, Julia could only reply that she had no idea. She did not know whether she would want to stay more than a few months—or whether she could. However, she would not think about it tonight. Nor would she wonder about why her uncle was delighted to show her off but reluctant to have her as his house guest. Tonight she would just enjoy herself.

Frank male admiration was not new to her, but she had never attracted quite so many young men at once. She was impressed by the Howes's opulence and by their wealthy, powerful guests. Despite her first impression, the party was anything but stuffy. Whatever it might lack, Shanghai had glamour.

"Miss Pavernen, are you reading me?" The fresh-faced American with the cornflower-blue eyes was apparently not annoyed but puzzled by her inattention to his tale of piloting a Jenny biplane from Shanghai to Nanking. "You look a thousand miles away."

With an effort, Julie recalled his rapid-fire self-introduction and the visiting card he had pressed on her: Harrison Parker Smythe III ("Pronounced Smith," he'd said). He was a vice-consul of the United States of America, and he had trained as an aviator, although the armistice had kept him from France. Flying was now his hobby, an escape from the bills of lading, the distressed seamen, and the visa applications that filled his working days.

"Of course I'm listening," she protested. "You were over Chinkiang, the wind was rising, and Nanking still more than a hundred miles away . . ."

"Not as the crow flies. But I had to follow the railroad. My compass was way off, dusk was falling . . ."

Finally caught up in Harry Smythe's adventures, Julia was disappointed when he broke off abruptly. She had never liked cliff-hangers. But the vice-consul was staring across the ballroom.

"Now that is interesting," he mused. "Very interesting indeed."

"What's so fascinating, Mr. Smythe?"

"You see those two Chinese men? Over there with the beautiful girl in the pale blue *cheongsam,* the long dress with the slit skirt? The younger man, the one with the slicked-down hair and the round glasses, that's T. V. Soong. His father was Charlie Soong. Of course, you haven't heard—"

"Charles Jones Soong?"

"You're a quick study, Miss Pavernen. Just arrived, but you know about Charlie Soong."

"I only know his name. Also that he was very rich and had beautiful daughters. But who's the other man? And the young lady?"

A lean man in a checked suit inclined his head attentively to T. V. Soong's conversation. His eyes were set square in his face—and they crackled with authority. The young woman in pale blue, who listened without speaking, was almost too perfect. Her complexion was of matte ivory, and the slight fullness of her upper lip made her appear sensuous. But her square chin was cocked imperiously above her stiff collar, which was so high it brushed the black pearls in her earlobes.

"Very interesting!" Harry Smythe repeated. "I thought the general was safely tucked away in the sticks."

"I may be quick," Julia said, "but I don't have the faintest idea what you're talking about. Tell me, who is the young lady? And the other man?"

"She's Mayling Soong, T. V.'s youngest sister, a Wellesley graduate. Her Shanghainese isn't too good yet; she's having trouble, with those two chattering away so fast. The general is called Chiang Kai-shek. No reason for you to have heard of him, but he's a hobby of mine."

"Why is that, Mr. Smythe?"

"Chiang Kai-shek is worth watching. He's in his mid-thirties, a trained army officer, one of the few in China. He serves Dr. Sun Yat-sen, who is way down south in Canton."

"But you're surprised at seeing him here?"

"The general's mother died a few weeks ago. He should be home mourning, like the filial son he is. This meeting must be damned important."

"Why?" Julia persisted.

"Miss Pavernen, Sun Yat-sen is the best hope for decent democratic government for China," Smythe replied. "He's also the best hope for the U.S. You see, he went to high school in Honolulu. T. V. Soong is his brother-in-law and financial supporter—also pro-American, a Harvard man. If Sun Yat-sen can make himself president of China again, the U. S. will be in clover. General Chiang Kai-shek's bound to play a big role in bringing that about." The vice-consul paused, then asked, "Would you say the general's got his eye on Mayling? Miss Soong, that is."

"Really, Mr. Smythe, what do I know about it? But, offhand, I'd say your General Chiang is so wrapped up in what T. V. Soong's saying he hardly knows the lady's there."

"Well, you can't win 'em all. . . . Miss Pavernen, my apologies for digressing. Can we have dinner this Saturday, then? I'd like to show you Shanghai by night."

"I'd have to ask my hostess whether she has any plans, Mr. Smythe."

Shanghai ways, Julia reflected, were peculiar, if not necessarily wicked. Although she and Harry Smythe had not been formally introduced, they could, in these free postwar days, quite properly chat under the roof of a mutual friend. It would, however, be unthinkable for a young man she had just met in Philadelphia to suggest breezily that they dine alone.

"Harry," an English voice demanded, "introduce me to the lady."

Smythe complied with barely veiled antipathy: "Richard Hollings, one of our local newshawks. Miss Julia Pavernen. 'Bye, Miss Pavernen, see you Saturday."

"And will you?" Hollings asked.

"Will I what?" Julia asked absently.

"Will you see my friend Harry Smythe on Saturday?"

"Mr. Hollings, it doesn't really concern you, does it?"

"Not yet. But it will, I promise you."

"I didn't ask for any promises, Mr. Hollings."

"I'm sorry I've offended you. And equally sorry that I've confused you." He smiled, and Julia felt a slight fraying of her first dislike. "It's the language barrier. In England, 'promise' used that way means to guarantee."

"I don't see why my plans should concern you." She was flirting discreetly, in spite of herself. "Anyway, I don't want your guarantees."

"I'm crushed, Miss Pavernen, utterly crushed!"

He was clearly unrepentant, and Julia felt her interest flare. Cocky Richard Hollings looked more French than English. His hair and his eyes were dark brown; his manner was intense; and his movements were assured. A hairbreadth under six feet, he appeared completely at home in his body—and completely in control of himself. He was, she guessed, no more than twenty-three or twenty-four.

"You think I'm stuffy, don't you?" Julia asked. "Tell me, Mr. Hollings, why does Harry Smythe call you a newshawk?"

"An expressive Americanism, isn't it?" His dark eyes smiled. "Of course you're not stuffy, and I'm not a full-fledged newshawk—only a little nestling. I do write occasionally for *The Times* of London because *the* China correspondent prefers to pontificate from Peking. But I earn my daily bread on *The North China Daily News.*"

"How interesting. I've never met a real live newspaperman before. You must—"

"—meet the most interesting people," he said, completing the cliché. "Everybody says so. But this time . . . you . . . it's true."

JUNE 21, 1921

The wiry man in the checked suit did not linger in the bright doorway of Harmony Hall. General Chiang Kai-shek was annoyed at being bowed out only by a houseboy after Donald and Eurydice Howe had joined their guests in the ballroom. Stepping into a pocket of darkness among the rhododendrons, the general told himself that at least one of the host's four sons should bid a formal farewell to departing guests. The old courtesies were passing quickly! He did not see Thomas Tan-ssu Howe, the youngest son of the house, resume the post he had momentarily left to quell a squabble among the servants.

Despite his unattended departure, Chiang Kai-shek was pleased with the evening. Political necessity had forced him to attend the Howes' anniversary reception when he should have been mourning his mother at home a hundred miles away. He automatically used military terminology: Both the friendly forces and the hostile forces were in strategic flux, but he had just won a tactical victory.

The Provisional Government of the Republic of China, established once again at Canton only three months earlier, was in a precarious state. President Sun Yat-sen was too trusting. Chiang Kai-shek had struggled to convince his leader that he must be resolute toward avowed enemies and cautious toward professed friends. But the president was now relapsing, temporizing with deceitful enemies and confiding in false friends.

Meeting publicly with Dr. Sun's brother-in-law, T. V. Soong, had reaffirmed General Chiang's loyalty to his president—and had reminded T.V. of his own obligations. The millionaire, whose father had been Dr.

Sun's financial mainstay, now understood that he must urgently raise additional funds.

Alone in the secluded grounds of Harmony Hall, Chiang Kai-shek cautiously peered out from the cover of the rhododendrons. When his eyes adjusted to the flickering light of the lanterns, he saw no danger. But a rustling in the dark shrubbery across the driveway drove him back into cover. Although he expected no hostile action, his enemies were ruthless.

He was hoping to meet—and neutralize—one enemy tonight: Feng Yü-hsiang, whom the foreigners called the Christian General because he baptized his troops with firehoses. Tonight's meeting should conclude an alliance between that opportunist and the Canton government.

Chiang Kai-shek ran his sinewy hand through hair cropped short in the style of the Japanese officers who had been his instructors at the Tokyo Military Academy. Except for the Japanese, whom he could tolerate, he disliked all foreigners. The Americans were the brashest. T. V. Soong's sister Mayling had spent most of her life in America. Yet, she was a pleasant young woman, if a trifle flashy in dress. Still, her manner was modest and unassertive, the chief virtue in a woman.

The general trotted toward the bend in the driveway where the small Hupmobile that T.V. had lent him waited just beyond the rays of the lanterns. Although his surveillance had revealed no enemy lying in wait, he cautiously approached the boxy automobile from the rear. The chauffeur was asleep in the front seat, and his own uniform cap was resting on the ledge beneath the rear window.

The general heard the movement at the same instant a hand clamped across his mouth. Powerful arms dragged him into the rhododendrons. His whipcord frame stiff, the general threw himself forward to break away. Free for a moment, he groped for the small Belgian pistol given him by his blood brother, the secret-society chieftain whom men called the Green Dragon because they were afraid to speak his true name.

Before the general could turn to confront them, his invisible assailants tightened their hold. His hand was squeezed so hard that his pistol's grip cut into his palm. A blindfold covered his eyes, but he could still kick out.

"Ta ma-di!" His shoe sank into softness, and he heard a harsh voice swear, "Screw it!"

"I wear iron soles," Chiang Kai-shek gasped. "Are you blind?"

"I am not blind." That was the prescribed reply to the password he had given. "My eyes are brighter than yours."

The many-fingered grip relented, and the blindfold fell from his eyes. The general saw four men wearing cotton robes called long-gowns and wide-brimmed fedoras. That was the garb of Shanghai's toughs. The moonlight seeping through the rhododendrons lit the face of their leader, and the general recognized the Incense Master of the mother lodge. That secret society chieftain was immediately subordinate to his own blood brother, the Supreme Lord of the Floodgate Fraternity.

"Excellency, you were too fast," the Incense Master apologized. "We had no chance to give the password before you struck back. I deeply regret—"

"To wait till *I* spoke the words was slovenly. And why assault me? Surely an exchange of recognition signs . . ."

"Excellency, the Supreme Lord himself instructed us *not* to approach you. We were to seize you—so that any chance observer would not realize we were of one lodge."

"And your purpose?"

"Excellency, you must not keep your appointment with the Christian General. And you must not ride in that car. Your life is at risk."

Chiang Kai-shek was mildly irritated by the conspiratorial mumbo jumbo of the Floodgate Fraternity, which foreigners called the Green Gang. Always outside the law, even that powerful secret society had to maintain discipline by fierce punishment for disobedience. It had been three centuries since secret societies pledged to resist the Manchu invaders and restore the Chinese Ming Dynasty. Most were now glorified gangster bands with a taste for profitable interference in politics.

Assisted by secret societies, Dr. Sun Yat-sen's Revolution of 1911 had toppled the Manchus, but no one now dreamed of reviving the Ming. Although a few diehards still plotted to set a new emperor on the Dragon Throne, patriots fought to unite China under a president. Maligned by ignorant foreigners, the secret societies could help consolidate the Republic of China. Chiang Kai-shek therefore tolerated their criminal activities: prostitution, which he abhorred; extortion, which he despised; and narcotics, which he hated.

"Let's go, then," he said. "Doubtless my blood brother will explain fully."

"No need, Excellency," the rotund Incense Master replied nervously. "I can explain. But first send away your car."

Chiang Kai-shek emerged alone from the rhododendrons, slid into the back of the Hupmobile, and drew down the fringed window shades.

While the chauffeur cranked the engine, he slipped unseen into the darkness among the rhododendrons.

The engine caught, spluttered, and died. The chauffeur patiently resumed his cranking. The stout Incense Master handed Chiang Kai-shek a cotton long-gown and a battered fedora. Pulling the brim down to shadow his prominent cheekbones, the general became one more anonymous strong-arm man. After three raucous failures, the Hupmobile's engine clattered into life.

"Excellency, the Supreme Lord has charged me to convey certain intelligence." Slinking through the shrubbery, the Incense Master was still formal. "Quarrels among the warlords are, of course, unending. They are now clawing each other even more viciously for control of Peking."

"Peking is a symbol, not really the capital of China," Chiang Kai-shek declared sententiously. "The legitimate president of the Republic of China is Dr. Sun Yat-sen—the *only* president elected by the National Assembly."

"I am grateful for your instruction, Excellency." The Incense Master broke into the general's relentless didacticism. "But time is short, and I must explain."

"Proceed then!"

"I thank Your Excellency for his gracious permission." The stout man, too, restated the obvious: "The northern warlords are badly split. But they are united in hostility to the Canton government."

"Of course!"

"Feng Yü-hsiang, the Christian General, claims to carry proposals from a warlord group for an alliance with Dr. Sun Yat-sen. But his claims mean no more than does the fervent Christianity he pretends in order to gain foreign support. He is not sincere—"

"I do not expect sincerity," Chiang snapped. "Do you take me for a fool?"

"No, Excellency. Moreover, we have learned that the Christian General is a stalking horse. Peking has sent assassins to Shanghai. You are their target. He will lead them to you—knowingly or otherwise."

"I shall confront him—face-to-face," the general declared.

"Excellency, the Supreme Lord bid me say: *Your life is too important to hazard in random reconnaissance.*"

"As always, my blood brother is wise and prudent."

Chiang Kai-shek fleetingly wondered whether his blood brother, the Green Dragon, was also in touch with the northern warlords who had sent the assassins. But that suspicion was unworthy. Worse, it was naïve. Of course, his blood brother was in touch with the warlords. Only a fool would fail to keep all his lines open.

But the Green Dragon would not assist the assassins. If his blood brother was murdered in the Green Dragon's stronghold—the French Concession of Shanghai—his own power would be badly shaken and he would be reviled as a traitor. Chiang Kai-shek concluded comfortably that his blood brother's self-interest would ensure his blood brother's loyalty.

The five men in long-gowns trotted through the rhododendrons to the gate lodge. The Hupmobile rattled behind them, its feeble headlights looming around the bends of the driveway. As the Incense Master stepped boldly through the spear-tipped gates, he lifted his arms and joined his fingertips above his head. That gesture identified him to the guards, who were members of the Floodgate Fraternity. Chin down so that the brim of the fedora hid his features, Chiang Kai-shek followed. Behind the plane trees that fringed the narrow lane, they loped toward Rue Pataro.

When the boxy Hupmobile spurted through the open gates, its headlights' yellow beams cast black shadows among the plane trees. When the Hupmobile, the shades in back still drawn, turned jauntily toward Rue Pataro, the bright street lamps reached out to embrace it.

Chiang Kai-shek had dismissed the Hupmobile from his mind, much as he would a regiment withdrawn from battle. He was intent upon reaching shelter, where he could analyze this latest thrust in the constant intrigue that was Chinese politics in mid-1921. When a muffled backfire reminded him of the Hupmobile, he stepped into the roadway to see better.

Two stocky men, anonymous in long-gowns and fedoras, stood before the car. Elongated by bulky silencers, the Luger pistols in their hands spat at the windshield. As the Hupmobile swerved out of control, they shifted their aim to the back seat.

The peaked cap silhouetted in the rear window tumbled down, and the car hurtled toward the plane trees on the far side of the lane. Headlights glowing, it piled headlong into a moss-splotched trunk. When tongues of fire licked at the fuel tank, the assassins thrust their pistols under their long-gowns and disappeared down Rue Pataro.

Careless of the rising flames, Chiang Kai-shek tugged at the sprung handle of the chauffeur's door. He felt a heavy hand on his shoulder.

"Time to get out of here!" The Incense Master jerked his thumb at the chauffeur's slack form. "You can't help him, Excellency. He's dead."

Chiang Kai-shek's austere features softened, and for the instant he mourned another life sacrificed to unite China. The next instant he resumed his habitual stern expression.

"I was planning to meet the Christian General in uniform," he said inconsequentially, "so I left my cap in the back."

"They would have fired anyway. Pity about the driver."

JUNE 21, 1921

Tall and lean in white tie and tailcoat, both made for him in London, Thomas Tan-ssu Howe was saying good-bye to his parents' guests. Most of those to whom he rendered the half bow and the flowery farewell prescribed by traditional Chinese etiquette were themselves Chinese. His countrymen, the youngest son of the Howe family reflected, knew just when to leave a gathering. Foreigners were different, as he knew from his education in England. Aside from seasoned diplomats, foreigners considered even a reception for a thirtieth wedding anniversary an occasion for enjoyment, rather than the formal reaffirmation of mutual respect and mutual obligation between hosts and guests that it actually was.

With his palms he smoothed his black hair, which he wore in the English manner, a trifle longer than that of the closely shorn Americans. When he grinned, the severity that had momentarily clouded his narrow face vanished. His mother and father called him Tan-ssu, but all his equals, Chinese or foreign, called him Tommy. "Thomas," which was slightly forbidding, simply did not fit his personality. When in Shanghai on holiday, Tommy Howe enlivened the parties of the younger set with his humor and his generosity.

The other sides of his character he did not exhibit. He rarely talked about his devotion to China, which was a mainspring of his existence. He almost never talked about his medical studies or his professional ambitions.

"Hsieh ni lai . . ." he murmured to a rotund dowager wearing a dia-

mond necklace. "So good of you to come, Madame Yeh. I know my mother was so looking forward to . . ."

While the social patter fell from his lips, Tommy's thoughts turned to the trouble among the servants it had taken him twenty minutes to smooth over. If Old Woo, the Howes' majordomo, had not been supervising the service in the ballroom, the trouble in the kitchens would never have occurred. Although unaccustomed to the role of peacemaker, Tommy had finally imposed a sullen truce on the squabble between the Howes' three chefs and the two outside chefs employed for the occasion. The family's chefs were annoyed by the interlopers' bragging about the large sums they were to receive for one night's work and by their lack of experience.

"You're not fit to carry the stove of a wandering dumpling-hawker," the head chef had said scathingly. After that, the squabble had accelerated until cleavers and knives were flashing in the smoky kitchens.

There *was* something peculiar about the two temporary chefs, Tommy reflected. Their manner was not just self-confident, as became skilled Shanghai servants, but almost arrogant. Besides, they were obviously not skilled cooks. He would, he decided, look into the matter when the guests had left.

Tommy's attention returned to his task, and he bowed low to the frail chairman of the Silver Shops Guild. Although that ancient dignitary protested ritually, Tommy accompanied him to his waiting brougham.

Straightening from his final deep bow, Tommy saw a glow against the evening sky. Since the fire was so close, hardly a block away on Rue Pataro, he decided to investigate. He should, perhaps, remain at his post, but he was only twenty-three and the flames drew him. The majordomo, Old Woo, who had judged the chairman of the Silver Shops Guild worthy of his personal attendance, would take Tommy's place and bid ceremonious farewells to the departing guests.

Tommy did not sound the alarm. If the gates automatically clanged shut, carriages and motorcars could not leave the grounds of Harmony Hall. Besides, the alarm bells would disturb the remaining guests. No need to risk panic—or even embarrassment—when he did not yet know what the blaze was.

After speaking briefly to Old Woo, Tommy loped down the winding driveway, gravel crunching under his patent-leather shoes. He waved to the gatekeepers, somewhat surprised that they were all dutifully attending to their duties rather than gaping at the fire. After a minute or two he saw the Hupmobile blazing among the splotched trunks of the plane trees.

Despite the heat, he drew close to look into the car. There was, he saw, no need of a doctor—or even a medical student—to tell that the driver was dead. The steering column impaled his chest, and his blackened body, shrunk by the heat to half normal size, was crushed against the dashboard.

Consciously assuming a protective air of professional calmness, Tommy studied the burning car. Although most of the glass was missing, the holes in what remained showed that the windshield had been smashed by bullets. The car itself was familiar, although Shanghai already boasted more than a hundred motor vehicles. Surely it was T. V. Soong's new plaything, this small, angular Hupmobile. Yet Tommy recalled seeing T.V. and Mayling Soong leave a few minutes earlier in a big limousine.

The wrecked car, he concluded, posed no threat to Harmony Hall. The incident was puzzling, and the killing was deplorable. But the police would clear up the mystery. Above all, the Howes and their guests were quite safe.

Whistling meditatively to himself, Tommy turned back toward the family mansion. After passing through the gates, he ordered them closed. No harm in taking precautions, even though there was no visible danger—and almost all the guests had already left.

Troubled, nonetheless, by the mystery and depressed by the violent death, he walked slowly along the serpentine driveway between the tall rhododendrons. Most of the paper lanterns had burned out, and it was very dark except where the light of the crescent moon was reflected by the pale gravel. Annoyed by the gravel crunching under his thin soles, Tommy stepped onto the grassy border of the driveway. Although he was close to the enormous house, the night was silent except for the swishing of the grass under his feet.

"Nei-go geh fei-chu . . ." A grating voice speaking rough Peking dialect surprised Tommy. "That rich pig Howe, what's he look like?"

"Damned if I know," a light tenor replied. "They only told me he was tall. But we'll know him all right. Stands to reason, don't it? He's the father, the old man."

"And our two comrades in the house?" the first voice asked. "They know what to do?"

"They'll start a fuss to draw the others away and leave old Howe alone. Then they'll double back to help us."

"I'm not so sure." The grating voice remained uneasy. "Let's go through the plan again."

"Wang-ba . . . Son of a bitch, not for the third time," the tenor responded. "We can't fool around all night. The others did for old Chiang Kai-shek all right. Now it's this Howe fellow's turn. . . . Just think of the fat ransom. Let's go!"

Hidden in the shadow of the rhododendrons, Tommy had listened to the conversation of the invisible thugs with mounting wonder. He felt rather detached, almost like a spectator at a play. But the sharp command "Let's go!" forced him into action. The thugs' simple plan would probably work. Unless he acted, his father could be left alone to be snatched away.

"Lai lai, erh-tzu-men . . ." Tommy shouted. "Hey, lads, come to me. All of you. Help! Kidnappers! Help your father!"

Tommy moved abruptly when two black figures rose from the darkness no more than ten feet away. He moved toward them so that they could see his white shirt, white waistcoat, and white tie. Then he turned and ran away, calling again: "Lads, help your father!"

Deliberately sluggish, he drew them away from the mansion. He must not run too fast. Otherwise, they could suspect that it was not a man in his sixties they were chasing. Besides, he wanted them to draw very close for a moment. He circled back toward the house, his gait deliberately awkward.

Fingers grasped at his shoulder, and his pace was checked. Pretending to stumble, he let his assailants close with him. A violent thrust of his elbow doubled one over. Twisting out of the other's grasp, he ran for the mansion. Their blood up, the thugs would not notice the divergence between his presumed age and his fleetness. Their only wish was to catch him.

"Huo-dzai! Chiu-ming! . . ." Tommy heard the cries within the house. "Fire! Fire! Help!"

He hurtled through the bright doorway, the angry thugs following. Already startled by the fire alarm, the company froze in a silent tableau. His father was still bowing to Sir Judah and Lady Haleevie, who were his closest foreign friends. His mother, his sister, and the American visitor he had not yet met stood behind them still smiling.

His three elder brothers had apparently already retired. But he saw with relief the four young men in the corridor leading to the kitchen, where men were still shouting the fire warning. John Pavernen, Richard Hollings, and Harrison Smythe turned back. The fourth man, already moving toward him, was Joshua, the Haleevies' youngest son and his own particular friend.

In half a dozen seconds, the thugs were immobilized.

"And the fire, Tommy?" Richard Hollings asked. "Next on the agenda?"

"There is no fire, Dick," Tommy replied. "It was a pretext, a fake to draw you lot away. . . . Thanks for your help, by the way."

Julia Pavernen watched the byplay with a smile. The four younger men were striving to outdo each other in nonchalance. The evening had been exciting even before the dramatic appearance of the last young man. It was now becoming almost comical as the men self-consciously assumed casual attitudes.

Yet the newcomer loomed largest. Richard Hollings had called him Tommy. He must, then, be Emily's youngest brother, only three years older than herself. This disheveled young man, however, bore little resemblance to the elegant youth Emily had described. He was panting slightly, and his tousled hair hung over his forehead.

Still, he did resemble the photograph Emily had kept in the frame of her mirror. Not only authoritative but courageous, he was a dashing figure.

Julia smiled at her own speculation. All four of the young men were interesting, each in his own way. Besides, she had other things to think about than men—most of the time, at least.

JUNE 24, 1921

"We're still in Frenchtown, the French Concession. It's a gilded playground for rich Chinese and for foreigners." Tommy was eloquent. "And it's hell for the poor Chinese. That's the first target of all progressive patriots—the misery of the common people."

Feigning clinical detachment, he peered at the lice crawling in the matted hair of the coolie who lay in a half coma against the curb of Avenue Joffre. They were men of two different worlds. Tommy wore a starched shirt and crisply pressed tan trousers, while the dying man was naked except for tattered black trousers cut off above the knee. Though lean, Tommy was well muscled. The coolie's ribs were sharp ridges beneath his gray skin; his eyes were sunken; and his clawed hands twitched in feeble supplication.

Tommy's eyes snapped behind the black-rimmed spectacles of plain glass he wore to make himself look older and more scholarly, an effect accentuated by his long skull, his high forehead, and his stubborn chin. It was, Julia Pavernen reflected, a strong face and a pleasant face, but by no means a docile face. Although upper-class Chinese shunned the sun, he was also heavily tanned—evidently to demonstrate his solidarity with the common people, who could avoid neither windburn nor sunburn.

"Lucky it's summer," he said bitterly. "In winter you'd not find just one dying man on Avenue Joffre. Every morning there'd be a dozen— or more."

Tommy's English accent sometimes made his remarks hard for Julia and Emily to follow. He had acquired both his understated eloquence and his crisp enunciation at Radley, a school for the sons of the privileged, in Oxfordshire. Patriotic fervor, which his father called homesickness, had, however, driven him back to China after Radley. If he remained in England, he had argued, he would forget not only his native land but his native language. Donald Howe had therefore permitted him to return. He did not want his fourth son to become a deracinated treaty-port Chinese who spoke perfect English but was imperfectly acquainted with his own country's language and culture.

Now in his final year at Peking Union Medical College in North China, Tommy was enjoying the long summer vacation. He was also eager to show his sister and her friend as many of the innumerable faces of Shanghai as he could. Just three days since their arrival for the anniversary party, he was taking them to a meeting of the National Federation of Students.

"The Federation," he had said, "is a go-ahead setup with bags of political sense."

Constantly discovering new aspects of Shanghai, the two young women had already learned that it was not only businessmen and workers who flocked to the treaty port, so called because the territory had been ceded to the foreigners by the Chinese at the muzzle of a cannon. Artists and idealists were also attracted to the foreign concessions, where they could escape the harsh censorship, the police brutality, and the violent instability that blighted political, intellectual, and artistic life in China itself. Progressive political organizations such as the Students' Federation could also operate with relative freedom.

The International Settlement, under multinational administration, and the smaller French Concession together occupied no more than eleven square miles. But the foreign enclave was a thriving marketplace for new ideas, as well as goods, from abroad.

Although eager to get to the meeting at the Po Wen Girls' School, Tommy had paused on Avenue Joffre to point a moral. He discoursed like a professor of medicine while other pedestrians skirted the emaciated coolie who lay on his back with his arms flung out.

"You'll note the classic symptoms of malnutrition: emaciation, dull eyes, and a swollen belly," Tommy said. "Also, the strawberry rash of beriberi around the lips. Tissue tone is lost. If you press his skin, the dent will linger."

"Aren't you going to examine him?" Julia demanded.

"To do what?"

"Examine him, of course. You *sound* as if you could tell whether he'll live or die."

Julia was almost as surprised as Tommy by her outburst. She had never seen anything more horrible than the starving coolie who lay among dog-droppings, rotting vegetables, and foul rags on a pavement baked by the afternoon sun. In her horror, she had spoken like her astringent Aunt Evadne, who was the scourge of negligent parents and cruel pet-owners.

Tommy looked at Julia in fresh appraisal—with a flicker of respect. He could no longer dismiss her as a fun-loving American flapper, just the kind of pretty and mindless friend his impulsive sister would bring home. Behind her frivolous manner, the American girl apparently possessed deeper feelings—as well as the audacity to order him around.

Nor was she completely unattractive physically. Although most foreign women were repulsive, with their sickly white skin and their colored hair, her complexion was translucent and her hair a dark mahogany. Yes, Tommy acknowledged, she was not distasteful.

He dropped to one knee beside the wretched coolie. His movements were brisk and competent, in fact, professional, Julia felt. After laying his ear against the coolie's chest, he nodded again.

"What do we do now?" Julia asked.

"Do now?" he asked. "What do you mean?"

"We *are* going to do something about this poor man, aren't we?"

"Julie's right!" Emily interjected. "We can't just leave him here."

"Emily, do you know what you're asking?" Tommy turned on his sister the indignation he could not direct at their guest. "If every one of the sick and starving on the streets of Shanghai—"

"He's *not* everyone, Tommy," Emily insisted. "He's *this* one. We can . . . we *must* . . . help him. If we don't, Julie will think all Chinese are blowhards, forever talking about saving the country and the common people, but doing nothing about it. And Julie will be right!"

Tommy was shocked by his sister's tirade. Since her return, Emily had appeared light-minded and capricious, quite unlike the serious and tempestuous ten-year-old he remembered. Yet she was now haranguing him like a fishwife—an *American* fishwife.

"Well, we could call the Red Swastika Society," he conceded. "If we can find a telephone."

"I'm sure you can, esteemed elder brother." Emily was ponderously —and sarcastically—respectful. "The tobacco shop over there might have a phone. Can't you call?"

"Why me?" He resisted the renewed feminine onslaught. "Can't you manage a telephone call?"

"They won't pay any attention to a woman."

"I suppose you're right." He started for the tobacco shop but turned to grin at them. "You're a fine pair of harridans, you know. Is that what they taught you at Bryn Mawr—to bully your elders? You know, there are just too many people in China. So we forget we've got to help individuals, not just the collective masses."

"That *was* a handsome apology!" Julia said. "Emmy, I'm beginning to like your brother, even if he does think we're both shrews. And who runs the Red Swastika Society?"

"The Buddhists, I think."

"And people say the Chinese have no civic sense! Yet they can run a rescue service in a wild city like Shanghai."

"Julie, the Buddhists *run* it!" Emily stepped into the torrent of her friend's indignation. "But the funds, they come mostly from foreigners. You've got to realize—"

Her words were drowned by the hooting of a truck crammed with slight Annamese soldiers wearing the anchor of the French Army of the Colonies on their sun helmets. After the truck passed, the two were uncharacteristically silent. Emily was embarrassed by her own outburst, and Julia was learning how many layers of misconception, misdirection, and misunderstanding concealed the truth in Shanghai.

Emily, too, had been surprised three days earlier when her father released the captured thugs, rather than turning them over to the police. The two had readily admitted that they were secret-society brothers from North China who had been sent to Shanghai among a group detailed to assassinate General Chiang Kai-shek. Their leader had, on his own, decided to kidnap Donald Howe for ransom.

"We don't want to provoke a vendetta by jailing them," Donald Howe had finally decided. "Let them go free to prove the Howes' magnaminity—and to testify to the Howes' vigilance."

Their reflections—and the constantly changing street scene—occupied Julia and Emily until Tommy returned twenty minutes later. He was smiling, but his cheeks were flushed.

"Took me almost ten minutes to get through—and ten more to talk them into sending an ambulance," he said angrily. "I had to promise a donation on the spot. Now we'll be late for the meeting. That's what comes of meddling in other people's business."

Julia did not point out that the ideals Tommy professed made every one of his four hundred million fellow Chinese *his* business. He deserved praise rather than more hectoring. Very few Chinese men—and not many foreign men—would have yielded so gracefully to the pleas of two young women. Beneath his jocular air, which could be patronizing, Tommy was open-minded. Yet she had seen on the night of the reception that steel lay beneath the velvet of his amiable manner.

"Now, Julia, tell me why you've come to China," he asked. "Even Shanghai's no holiday resort, not to speak of the interior."

Julia frowned and considered the question, which she had thus far evaded even in her own thoughts, before replying slowly: "When Emily first brought it up, it sounded impossible. I only began to think seriously about coming when Uncle Jack offered to pay my fare. But *why* he did—"

"He's becoming quite a friend of the Howe family, isn't he?" Tommy's implication was unmistakable.

"If the Pavernens are crowding you out of Harmony Hall," Julia flared, "I'll leave tomorrow."

"Hang on a second," he protested. "I never said that. If the rest of the Pavernens are even half as charming as you, I'd be delighted to have a dozen of them. And you haven't answered my question."

"I'm not awfully sure I can. I'm very fond of Emily, and I did want to be with her and meet her family. Your parents are delightful—"

"But not her brother," Tommy interjected wryly. "He's a beast."

"Not at all. Just stubborn and opinionated. Nothing that can't be cured." Julia was astringently flirtatious. "It was also an opportunity to see a foreign country from the inside."

"You're stalling, Julia," he persisted. "Don't you know why you came?"

"Well, I studied comparative civilizations. And what other civilization is more different from America than China?"

"American civilization? What's that?" Tommy's mock hauteur dissolved into laughter when two indignant young women protested at once. "I thought you'd bite at that. And—"

He broke off when the ambulance of the Red Swastika Society came into sight. It was a somber black cart pulled by two coolies, who skillfully transferred the patient to a stretcher after extracting two silver dollars from Tommy.

Julia gaped when the eccentric vehicle trundled off into the stream of carriages, rickshaws, and man-drawn carts, its brass bell clanging peremptorily. Tommy wondered if the patient would reach Shanghai General Hospital alive, and what care he would receive if he did. The friendless and penniless coolie, he concluded bleakly, was unlikely to see tomorrow's dawn. He kept his own counsel while Julia and Emily praised him and congratulated each other for goading him to action. If his Americanized sister and her American friend wanted to play Lady Bountiful, he would not disillusion them.

Neither, however, would he deceive himself. If they had not insisted, he would have strolled away after using the dying coolie as the excuse for a political lecture. Like most Chinese intellectuals, Tommy reproached himeself, he talked glibly and abstractly about the suffering masses and the coming revolution. When it came to helping one suffering individual, he had hung back. But he was not too old to change!

Behind its concrete arches, the Po Wen Girls' School on Rue Bourgeat was pervaded by the musty smell of damp plaster—not because the school was new, but because plaster never quite dried in Shanghai's constant humidity. The classroom set aside for the National Federation of Students looked through grimy windows onto a littered courtyard. Though thirty-odd students were seated on the narrow benches at six forty-five, half an hour past the appointed meeting time, none of the speakers had yet arrived.

The young men and women waited with irritable expectancy, their patience abraded by the clammy heat. They were all well dressed and well fed, for they were all the privileged offspring of prosperous families. They were, Julia felt, a peculiar lot of radicals.

"Are they all students?" Emily whispered in English. "The three girls, too?"

"Girls can now attend universities," Tommy replied. "Quite a few do."

"But, Emmy, you said you *had* to study in the States," Julia interjected. "You said no Chinese university would take a female student."

"It was true then," Tommy said. "But Peking University finally admitted a couple of girls about a year and a half ago. Then others followed. Father believes the best education is still found abroad. There's also the snob value of a foreign degree."

"What about Peking Union Medical College?" Julia asked. "Why study there if it's inferior."

"That's different. PUMC is really a foreign school in China. Almost all the professors are foreigners, mostly Americans."

"Aren't you afraid of imperialist propaganda?" his sister teased. "Of corrupting your patriotism?"

"PUMC's nothing to do with politics, even if it is missionary-oriented. PUMC's only interested in medicine, unlike Peking University. It sometimes seems Peking U. is interested *only* in politics."

"What's that joke about Peking U.?" Emily said. "Oh, yes. It teaches reading, writing, and revolution."

"That's not completely off the mark," her brother said with a laugh. "Though you can't separate politics from education nowadays. . . ."

Tommy's attention was diverted when a heavy-set young man entered the classroom, his mouth working and the words pouring out. His thick hair was parted in the center, and was combed into black wings. The open collar of his homespun long-gown revealed a fleshy neck. His young cannonball head, was distinguished by a high forehead, heavy eyebrows, and a mole beneath a full lower lip. Swaggering toward the platform, where five chairs stood behind a trestle table, he looked around as if expecting an ovation.

"Mao Tse-tung, a student leader from Peking," Tommy whispered. "Actually, he was a library assistant. This next chap's much more important."

A second young man entered and nodded to an acquaintance sitting under the windows. Though he walked splay-footed like a peasant wading through a rice paddy, his innate authority was as evident as Mao Tse-tung's assertiveness. Taller than his colleague, the second student leader was also better dressed. Starched white cloth showed at the cuffs and above the choker collar of his dark-blue cotton tunic. His hair was close-cropped on his large head, and his deep-set eyes were candid above his heavy cheekbones.

"That's Chang Kuo-tao," Tommy whispered. "He was a real student —and he's been a leader of the progressive movement from the beginning. I'm really looking forward to hearing him speak."

Leaning forward, her tawny hair falling over her eyes, Julia listened intently. She was entering not merely a new country but a new world. The atmosphere was electric. It was thrilling but also frightening.

Violence was in the air. Women in China still fought for goals attained long ago in the United States, such as the right to attend university. Men as well as women were fiercely discontented with traditional restrictions upon their personal freedom—and with their country's near-anarchy.

The gathering fell silent; even the occasional cough stopped. The only sound was Tommy's whisper. Julia brushed her hair aside and saw that attention was focused upon the three of them. Mao Tse-tung was pointing at them, and every eye in the room was staring at her.

"Na-go nü-di . . ." Mao shrilled in Mandarin, the language of Peking, and Tommy murmured the English equivalent: "Who is that female?

Who has dared to bring a foreigner, a capitalist spy, to our meeting?"

Tommy replied in Mandarin, which the radicals were determined to make the common language of all China: "I am Hsia Tan-ssu, a student at Peking Union Medical College. This is my sister Yuelin. The foreigner is our American friend—our American sister. She's no spy. I vouch for her."

"And who are you to—" Mao began hotly, but his colleague tugged at his jacket, and he finally conceded: "Comrade Chang Kuo-tao tells me your guarantee is acceptable. Myself, I still wonder! The son and daughter of one of the biggest foreign-oriented capitalists . . . But Comrade Chang says it's all right."

"A fine welcome!" Emily snapped. "Just because Father is rich, are we not Chinese? Only ignorant servants think all foreigners are devils. This Mao Tse-tung also sounds convinced that all women are stupid! Why, I could—"

"That's enough, Emmy!" Tommy was emphatic. "You're holding up the meeting. Few understand you, but they're all fascinated by a Chinese girl who spits out her anger in English."

Decorum restored, the secretary of the Shanghai branch of the National Federation of Students introduced the visitors from Peking. Beginning in Mandarin, he was soon enmired in that alien language. He switched with relief to Shanghainese when another student volunteered to interpret for the visitors.

"They're both in their mid-twenties—at most," Emily whispered behind her brother's back. "Mao, the soft-looking one with all the hair, could be a few years older, maybe close to thirty."

When the preliminaries ended, Mao Tse-tung rose and began to declaim, his high-pitched voice soaring and plummeting in the cadences of traditional Chinese oratory. Tommy interpreted the slurred Mandarin. Eliding phrases and interjecting his own comments, he produced a staccato effect quite unlike the speaker's long, pompous sentences.

"I bring greetings to Shanghai from the Chinese people. [*Who does he think Shanghailanders are?* asked Tommy. *Abyssinians?*] Shanghai is a scandal, a reproach to the Chinese people. [*He's pretty scandalous himself.*]

"Shanghai is a reproach because its heart, where we now stand, is ruled by foreigners. How ironic that Chinese patriots need foreign protection to speak out for China's future. The foreigners live here under foreign law, spitting on Chinese sovereignty—on Chinese soil."

Emily spoke sharply to her brother when Mao Tse-tung paused to sip tea from a porcelain mug, and Tommy promised to cut down his caustic interjections.

"The foreigners of Shanghai ruthlessly exploit the Chinese masses— helped by their Chinese lackeys," Mao Tse-tung declared. "Industry prospers in Shanghai with sweated labor. Elsewhere, there are hardly any factories.

"In less than a century, Shanghai has far outdistanced the rest of the Motherland economically. Yet an industrial and trading city has little connection with the real life of China—the peasants on the land. [*Does he want us all to go out,* whispered Tommy, *and wallow in pig manure?*]

"Some two years ago, on May 4, 1919, the students of Peking University rose against the spineless acquiescence of the warlord government in Peking to the outrageous demands upon China made by the Japanese imperialists," Mao Tse-tung continued. "On that day, a new era opened. We live in the era of the May Fourth Movement, and we students can decisively affect political developments. We are now becoming the masters of China. We . . ."

Tommy's boredom was chiefly apparent only in his fingers' restless tapping the bench. After almost two hours, however, he whispered, "The end is near—finally."

"Comrades, we must overthrow the warlords! We must drive out the foreign imperialists and punish their Chinese lackeys," Mao Tse-tung exhorted. "We must struggle above all against Japanese imperialism. We must create a new China and a new Chinese people—unselfish, hard-working, dedicated, clear-eyed!"

"Well, you get the flavor," said Tommy. "I reckon he'll run dry in ten minutes or so. Thank God!"

Tommy was wrong. It took twenty minutes for Mao Tse-tung to come to the end of his speech.

Despite his harsh comments, Tommy was eager to introduce Julia and Emily to the student leaders. Both men smiled pleasantly, but neither acknowledged Emily's attempt to speak a few words of Mandarin. Yet neither displayed toward Julia the antiforeign ferocity that had pervaded Mao's speech.

The long twilight was just giving way to darkness. At ten in the evening, while they walked back to Harmony Hall, Tommy extolled the assembly he had derided while it was in progress. Though the National Federation of Students had no more than a hundred members throughout China, he declared, it was uniting all progressive elements. Both

Chang Kuo-tao and Mao Tse-tung, he added casually, were avowed Socialists, probably Communists.

"Why didn't they say so?" Emily was indignant. "They didn't say a word about socialism or communism."

"Well, they wouldn't, would they?" Tommy smiled. "Not at this stage."

JUNE 30, 1921

The backbone of the International Settlement was Nanking Road, running from the Bund to the Racecourse, which had once been on the Settlement's western boundary. There, the avenue became Bubbling Well Road, named after the sacred spring that now marked the western boundary. Densely commercial Nanking Road was lined with banks, department stores, and many retail shops. Bubbling Well Road transversed more open and greener territory, though the trolley tracks continued unbroken.

Jade House, Sir Judah Haleevie's mansion, stood in its own park on Bubbling Well Road near the border with Chinese-administered Greater Shanghai. Nightclubs, dance halls, and restaurants that catered to foreigners and to Westernized Chinese clustered around the beginning of Bubbling Well Road. Among those haunts of pleasure, a blue neon sign on a clapboard bungalow recalled mortality: RAFFERTY & SONS, MORTICIANS AND UNDERTAKERS.

Just after ten on the last evening of June 1921, Emily Howe gazed out the car window at the glow from Rafferty's display window. Illuminated by four arc lights and a rotating crimson spotlight, a coffin lined with white satin appeared to float in the darkness. Emily shuddered and looked away. Emily's grandmother had kept her canoe-shaped coffin under her bed, ensuring that she would make her final journey in a fitting vessel. But Emily was too Westernized. She found the spectacle macabre.

Her brother Tommy nudged her and pointed at the magenta-and-black motorcycle revving beside their emerald green Rolls-Royce. Despite the heat, the Chinese astride the saddle wore a serge tunic with a choker collar, serge knee-breeches, and leather puttees. The foreigner in the sidecar wore a white shantung dinner jacket. His gold teeth glittered more brightly than the burnished brass radiator of the Rolls when he smiled and raised a hand in benediction.

"Jeff himself!" Harrison Parker Smythe III, the American vice-consul, said from his perch on the jumpseat of the Rolls. "Jeff Jehosophat Geoffreys barreling toward his new domain."

Julia Pavernen looked toward Richard Hollings for enlightenment, but the Englishman was staring through the other window at a U.S. marine in crisp khakis bestriding a second motorcycle. A slender young woman in a black-sequined evening dress was riding pillion, her long blond hair streaming behind her. Julia was astonished when the blonde turned her head, for her features were wholly Oriental.

"Only in Shanghai, a blond Japanese." Hollings chuckled. "I'm told Suzuko's wig cost two hundred dollars. But she's a very gifted tart. . . . I do beg your pardon, ladies."

Neither Julia nor Emily had been offended, since neither knew what a tart was. Tommy Howe, who knew very well, grinned and muttered in a mock-Cockney accent, "Watch it, mate!"

Hollings replied cheerfully in the same accent: "Wash me mouf out wiv soap."

A Delage runabout that glowed the midnight blue of a star sapphire stood before a striped awning on which brass letters spelled out ST. ANDREW'S CAFÉ. Tommy Howe's heart contracted in envy. His father insisted that a gentleman would no more undertake the menial work of driving his own automobile than he would pull a rickshaw. Nonetheless, Tommy stared covetously at the red leather upholstery, the hand-buffed brass headlamps, and the miniature body that came to a point in the rear.

Sir Judah and Lady Haleevie's twenty-nine-year-old youngest son, Joshua, stood beside the Delage, his light blue eyes laughing. When they left the dinner party at Jade House he had complained that the runabout's lack of doors made a footstool necessary as a mounting-block for lady passengers. Since the minute Delage could not accommodate even a footstool, the Haleevies' chauffeur often followed in the Haleevies' Marmon limousine.

Tall and dark-haired, Joshua was unaccompanied this evening. Julia's eye had been caught by the splendor of his tailcoat with the two rows of miniature decorations won as a captain in the Royal Berkshire Fusiliers. His understated humor was appealing when he gestured with ostentatious resignation at the vehicles that flanked—and dwarfed—his tiny Delage: Jeff Geoffrey's massive Daimler-Benz sidecar-motorcycle and the Harley-Davidson the U.S. marine rode. All three motor vehicles were brutal intruders in the balmy Shanghai night. The stench of motor oil and rubber tires was alien to the fragrance of incense, wood smoke, and jasmine.

Tommy Howe, black-rimmed spectacles discarded, was a sleek man-about-town, quite unlike the rumpled patriot of the Federation of Students meeting. His shawl-collared dinner jacket had been cut with cool precision by Kilgour, French of Dover Street in London, for Tommy disdained Shanghai's master tailors. He would never wear a white double-breasted dinner jacket like Harry Smythe's or Richard Hollings's.

Emily, who had never seen a nightclub, knew that her mother would have been appalled at two young ladies' visiting the St. Andrew's Café, even with four protective escorts. Alighting from the Rolls, she was glad she had discarded her yellow straw cartwheel hat with the pink roses. Her pleated yellow voile dress and moiré sash were still too ingenue. The girlish look was popular, but Julia and she were quite young enough without affecting sweet-sixteenish costumes. Her friend was wearing a Lanvin model like the one she had chosen for her first night in Shanghai, with a long skirt that exploded into ruffles and a tubular bodice with clusters of red roses. They looked, Emily realized, like bridesmaids, rather than women of the world!

"You'll go upstairs, ladies and gentlemen?"

Jeff Geoffreys attempted a suave continental bow and waved them up the spindly staircase. Discreetly hidden by live plants and glass-bead screens, favored patrons of the former sergeant of the U.S. 15th Infantry Regiment could look down from the gilt-filigree balcony onto the glass dance floor. Through broad-leafed ferns, Emily Howe finally glimpsed the forbidden glamour of her native city.

She could have been anywhere on earth. Only the waiter's sharp features and knowing glances were obviously of Shanghai. Beside the gleaming dance floor nine young women wearing low-cut evening dresses in glaring electric colors sat at four round tables near the orange-and-yellow bandstand. From above Emily could see only their glossy black hair and the restless scarlet-tipped fingers twining around their wineglasses. Among the musicians in the violet-and-gold uniforms of operetta cavalrymen Emily identified Filipino, Mediterranean, and Scandinavian types, as well as Chinese. The band could have been pumping its slide trombones, caressing its saxophones, and flaunting its clarinets anywhere in the civilized world.

With sudden revulsion Emily wondered why she had longed to return to Shanghai. The city was a hodgepodge of the peoples, customs, and languages of a dozen nations. Shanghai was not China.

Yet this international community lived on Chinese energy and Chinese talent. The foreigners wrung her fellow Chinese dry and cast them aside—like the dying coolie on Avenue Joffre. A few Chinese like her father could enrich themselves, but most Chinese were mercilessly exploited.

Yet the great majority of Chinese living in China itself were even poorer than the poor Chinese of Shanghai. Foreign rule provided employment, stability, and a measure of liberty, as even the revolutionary firebrand Mao Tse-tung acknowledged. Until a Chinese government ensured security and opportunity in China itself, Chinese would continue to flock to Shanghai.

Shanghai was also vilely corrupt, a paradise for unscrupulous adventurers. Every imaginable perversion was practiced within its eleven square miles: from child prostitution, male and female, through live shows displaying torture and bestiality to the soul-destroying trade in narcotics. The human debris of those enterprises was finally shoveled into mass graves.

". . . you care to?" Hearing those words, Emily looked up. Leaning toward her, Joshua Haleevie repeated: "I was wondering whether you'd care to dance."

"I suppose we did come to dance," she replied tentatively. "But I wonder if I really should . . ."

"Why ever not, Emmy?" Julia demanded. "Why not, if the boys want to dance?"

"The ladies on the dance floor . . ." Emily began in confusion. "The dancing . . . ah . . . partners, you know, they're . . ."

"They're not angels, Emmy, that's true." Harry Smythe's innocent blue eyes apologized for his mildly risqué words. "But each has her . . . ah . . . special friend, and they all behave . . . ah . . . decorously in public. Jeff Geoffreys wouldn't permit anything else."

Emily hesitated, and Richard Hollings declared: "Certainly she won't dance! It's one thing to go slumming, to see the seamy side of life. Quite another for respectable . . . innocent . . . young ladies to appear on the same dance floor as . . . ah . . . taxi-dancers, no matter how well-behaved. I don't believe any of us—"

"Oh, come on, Dick, be a sport!" Julia knew she was being mischievous, perhaps offensive, but she was irritated by his pomposity; he evidently assumed that Emily and she required firm masculine control. "Let's all foxtrot."

Richard gave her a dark look. But he brightened when Emily smiled her thanks for his concern.

Men in dinner jackets rose from the candlelit tables rimming the dance floor and swarmed around the hostesses. The band was playing a tune Emily half recalled. When the hostesses rose, she saw that they were all Oriental. Most were Chinese, though she recognized a Vietnamese, a Japanese, and a Korean as well.

The Filipino bandleader stroked the saxophone hanging around his neck and entoned, "Please don't be offended if I preach to you a while. Tears are out of place in eyes that were meant to smile."

Emily recognized the tune sung at every college dance that year: "Look for the Silver Lining." She laughed when Richard Hollings whispered behind his hand, "And do forgive me for preaching to you."

The bandleader threw back his sleek head and crooned, "Look for the silver lining, whenever a cloud appears in the blue. Remember somewhere the sun is shining, and . . ."

Emily was half-mesmerized. Indistinct forms whirled on the dance floor amid spirals of smoke that were shot through with the rainbow light of the mirrored globe rotating above their heads. An exceedingly tall Chinese man in a black silk long-gown stalked stiff-legged across the dance floor, his small head cocked awkwardly on his thin neck. A hostess in an ice-blue evening dress with a plunging neckline raised her head and stared at him contemptuously when he spoke to her.

Emily blinked in surprise. Under the blue-black hair, which was drawn back in a chignon, the young woman's features were quite beautiful—and unmistakably European. Enormous dark blue eyes dominated her broad, low forehead, her marked cheekbones, and her small, square chin. Her skin was so white it appeared tinged with blue.

When the hostess rose, contempt apparent in her rigid posture, Emily saw that her dress was daring but old-fashioned. Her figure, too, was old-fashioned; a graceful abundance of bosom was displayed by the V-necked bodice supported by silver straps. Like the bodice fringed with tarnished silver tassles, the hobble skirt was slit to the knee, revealing delicate ankles in black stockings above scuffed silver pumps.

Although tall, she barely came to the shoulder of the very tall Chinese man when they stepped onto the dance floor. She took his hand mechanically, and his arm encircled her waist. Her right hand crept reluctantly to his shoulder. As they danced, she leaned backward, straining away from his insistent embrace.

Emily watched in fascination from the balcony. She had never imagined that there were poor foreigners living in Shanghai, much less a European woman so impoverished she was forced to become a dance hostess.

When the band segued into a tango, the tall Chinese leaned down and spoke insistently. He pulled his reluctant partner closer, his big fingers splayed possessively on her naked back. She stiffened, snarled up at him, and spat out a few words. The man shook her violently. Her head flopped like a rag doll's, and her tarnished silver pumps almost slipped out from under her.

Bracing her clenched fists against his chest, she pushed him away. But she could not break his grip on her shoulders. In retaliation, he shook her even more violently, while other couples danced around them unconcerned.

Her eyes wide, the hostess thrust her hand into her bodice. Her scarlet-tipped fingers emerged clutching a pearl-handled penknife. She flipped the blade open and stabbed up at the eyes so close to her own.

The big man's bony hand closed over hers. His mouth went slack with pleasure as he twisted the shining blade toward her face. The silver point descended inexorably, already describing in the air the crescent he would carve on her soft cheek. Displaying his yellow horse-teeth in a malicious grin, the tall man deliberately prolonged her terror.

The woman's nails raked the back of the hand that still grasped her shoulder. Startled rather than hurt, the man loosened his grip—and she broke away. Turning to flee, she slipped on the slick dance floor and stumbled.

The tall Chinese bent and grasped her shoulders again. Jeff Geoffreys moved between them, his shoulders and fists swaying and bobbing. Two stocky bouncers grabbed the assailant's arms.

Slipping down the staircase as the scuffle spread, Joshua Haleevie swept the young woman up in his arms. Without apparent effort, he carried her up to the balcony. He was setting her down at a vacant table when Emily directed: "Bring her here. We can't leave her alone."

The young woman smiled wanly. Her extraordinary dark blue eyes flickered from Emily to the waiter, who poured vodka. Resting an elbow on the table, she tossed the liquor down and smiled again.

At close hand she was unquestionably beautiful. Her hair fell in two crow's wings over her forehead; her nose was arrogantly arched; and her long-fingered hands were expressive.

"It's very good of you." She spoke in a cultivated English accent, though Richard Hollings's sensitive ear caught a hint of a burr. "Truly, I wouldn't want to be alone."

"Everything will be fine now." Striving to put their unexpected guest at ease, Emily wondered if her tea-party courtesies might not ring hollow. "More vodka? I hear it's a great pick-me-up."

"Just wonderful under the circumstances!" The young woman's smile was feline. "To your good health! *Nasdroviya!*"

"You're Russian?" Tommy asked. *'Nasdroviya'*s the only Russian I know. My name's Howe. Thomas Howe. Tommy, actually."

"Delighted, Mr. Howe. I am Elizaveta Alexandrovna Yavalenka. My nanny called me Liz."

"Your nanny?" Joshua Haleevie asked. "And where was that, if I may ask?"

"Of course you may, my gallant rescuer." She was humorously flirtatious. "In St. Petersburg in the old days. Her name was Annie, Annie MacCrossland. You've probably guessed she was Scots."

"I had somehow suspected from your accent," he said, grinning. "By the way, I'm Joshua Haleevie. And I'm called Joshua, not Josh."

"What else?" Elizaveta smiled.

"Was it terrible for you just now?" Julia asked impulsively. "You were so brave."

"Well . . . you all know what he wanted." She smiled. "And I snapped back. I was a little impolite, you might say. But he *was* objectionable. Then I thought he'd shake my head right off my shoulders. At the least, break my neck."

"How did you come all the way here from St. Petersburg?"

Frankly inquisitive, Richard Hollings noted with amusement that Vice-Consul Harrison Parker Smythe III was sitting primly erect in his cane-backed chair. The American's posture proclaimed his determination to remain aloof from the shady adventuress.

"Originally to Siberia with the Whites, the White Russian Army," she replied. "My brother Sasha was a major of Cossacks. Naturally, he was killed. He was his gallant father's son."

She added almost belligerently: "Does not even one of you know of Count Alexander Sergeiivich Yavalenko, the great Ukrainian millionaire and philanthropist? Have you not heard of his White Knights Sugar Corporation?"

When blank eyes and placating smiles confirmed their ignorance of her famous father, Elizaveta resumed her story. Her rhetorical pauses and dramatic gestures showed that hers was a tale often told: "I got to Siberia with a few poor jewels and a steamer trunk full of my mother's dresses. Paquin 1914, this little creation is. Finally I found myself alone in Vladivostok. The jewels were almost all gone. I had only a handful of depreciated imperial rubles and some evening gowns, all prewar. The Whites were almost finished. They had no discipline and, even worse, no luck. So I bought a ticket to Shanghai. Getting out of Siberia was the best way to celebrate my twentieth birthday. And here I am."

"Then you must have had some money." Julia was touched by the tale—and intrigued by the glamorous Russian refugee. "And now?"

"*Had* is the operative word," Elizaveta replied. "When I arrived, I hadn't a red cent left. That's why you find me at this trade. Taxi-dancing, they call it, but it's awfully hard on the feet."

"Surely you could find something more suitable," Richard Hollings declared suspiciously. "In a city the size of Shanghai, there must be something else you can do."

"Yes, of course. I could live on my dividends," Elizaveta snapped. "But, unfortunately, the bank's gone bust."

"Now, Richard, that'll do," Joshua warned. "And, Miss . . . ah . . ."

"Countess Yavalenka, actually. But it would sound rather silly for a taxi-dancer at Jeff Geoffreys's St. Andrew's Café to call herself Countess. Just call me Liz."

"Liz, then," Joshua continued. "If you're seriously looking for work, I might find something a little better than this for you to . . ."

The young Russian woman looked inquiringly into her empty tumbler. After the waiter replenished her vodka, she rolled the tumbler between her palms. This time she sipped the vodka, rather than tossing it down.

"I'd be grateful," she said. "Mr. Haleevie . . ."

"Do call me Joshua."

"All right then, Joshua. You know, there's no reason you lot have to look after me. I'm a big girl, and I—"

"Please don't deny me the pleasure of trying."

"I'd be most grateful, but I don't have much hope."

"Why ever not?" asked Emily, who did not totally share Julia's impulsive sympathy for the stunningly attractive refugee. "As Richard says, surely there are other jobs you can find besides this . . . ah . . . this work. Though I'm sure it's well paid."

Tommy cast a pained look at his younger sister. The kitten had sharp claws, it seemed, but he could hardly intervene to defend a stranger.

"Don't even dream of taking it up, my dear." Elizaveta unsheathed her own claws. "You're pretty enough, but I doubt you've got the stamina. Besides, it's not profitable at all. Not unless you . . ."

Elizaveta stretched out her right hand, displaying a small ring set with a single garnet, and abruptly clenched her fingers. Her unspoken meaning was clear, even to those innocents Julia and Emily.

"Precisely what have you tried?" Joshua asked gently.

"Mine are conventional feminine talents," she said. "Before the Bolshevik revolution, no young lady was taught to earn her own living. But, of course, languages: French, German, and Italian, as well as English. Otherwise? I can sew a fine seam, paint a fair watercolor, and play a little Mozart on the piano. Not tremendously marketable skills, you see."

"How do you know?" Richard Hollings demanded. "Have you tried? Really tried?"

"Indeed I have—time and time again," she replied equably. "I'm actually a rather good seamstress. But how can I compete with thousands of skilled Chinese women who'll work for tuppence a day? A little English teaching, since there's not much demand for Russian nowadays. We Russians are rather out of fashion. A little tutoring in French, too, but my lady students either gave up or decided they'd prefer not to have me about. I was—"

"Too much of a threat, I suppose." Julia supplied the missing words, and Elizaveta smiled gratefully before resuming: "And the gentlemen? Well, *they* did want me about. Too much so, if you take my meaning."

"And that's all you've tried?" Richard persisted.

"I'd like to see you in the same fix, Mr. Hollings." Elizaveta's temper rose to meet his antagonism. "I don't like your cross-questioning. But, yes, Joshua, I have tried other ways. I was governess for a time to a pair of the most objectionable French brats anyone ever saw. Fortunately or unfortunately, the father was transferred to Saigon. I've also worked in shops and at an hotel as a receptionist. But, again, I simply couldn't compete with the Chinese. I can't compete and earn a living wage."

"Let me see what I can do, Miss . . . ah . . . Liz," Joshua insisted.

"I'd be very happy, Joshua. Most grateful, although, as I said, I really don't—"

"What can you possibly do, then?" Julia's concern was genuine, but her tact was abysmal. "What're your plans? I see how hard it is for any young woman to make a living in Shanghai."

"Sometimes it seems there's only *one* way." Elizaveta ignored Emily's visible shock. "But quite simply, I plan to live. I plan to survive."

JULY 9–12, 1921

Chang Kuo-tao flicked the sweat from his forehead with his fingers. The tall radical leader with the heavy cheekbones, had appeared imperturbably self-assured at the meeting of the National Federation of Students. He was, however, now upset, recalling his father's reiterated criticism when he last visited his home six weeks earlier.

"You're only twenty-four," his father had said. "But you talk and act as if you had a monopoly on wisdom. You despise me for being what I am, a moderately well-to-do landowner. Of course, you happily took my tainted money for your schooling at that radical pest-hole Peking University. Everything you learned there has made you obstinate, opinionated, and reckless. You'll never amount to anything, you and your gang. You're all just children—adolescents playing at politics and revolution."

The remembered reproach stung sharply. Why should he be wounded by the angry words of a middle-aged reactionary? Yet, like all Chinese he felt an ingrained reverence for his elders. When would he sweep away the remnants of that reverence, which was a barrier to progress?

Today, this very day, he would liberate himself from his superstitious respect for his father's antiquated prejudices. The two middle-aged foreigners who had been sent by the Communist International in Moscow were acting just like all fathers: They were condescending from the heights of superior experience, and they did not hide their doubts regarding his group's prospects of success. He would show them, too!

Although the Communist Party of China was just coming into formal existence at this First National Congress, Chang Kuo-tao already knew beyond doubt that it would soon become the most powerful force in the nation—and would, in time, rule the nation. As acting chairman of the First Congress, he would take the lead in transforming China into an independent, powerful, industrialized, and just nation.

Meanwhile, there were the two troublesome self-invited guests to deal with. Best to get this unwanted session over as quickly as possible anyway. The heat was brutal in the French Concession just before seven on this July evening.

Fear of discovery by the police had impelled the delegates to transfer the congress from the nearby Po Wen Girls' school. For secrecy, a green baize curtain was drawn across the door to the minute courtyard, which was mottled with heat. Since the front door was bolted shut, the men choosing stools at the long table were already dripping with sweat. Intermittent thunderstorms made the atmosphere even denser, for steam rose from the baking pavements.

Twelve of the fourteen men in the small living room of the Spartan three-room house were Chinese, the eldest among them just thirty-four. All felt that this session was not only superfluous but also hazardous.

The Chinese were offended by the superior airs of the Dutchman and the Russian. Those unwelcome guests were resentful at having had to plead for a belated invitation to this special session. The foreigners felt they should by right have participated fully from the first day of the First Congress.

Chang Kuo-tao reflected: I'd also call myself Maring or some such if I'd been born Hendricus Sneevliet. It did not occur to him that the Dutchman might have found his name ridiculous if he had known its meaning: Chang Kuo-tao, Mr. Chang-the-Light-of-the-Nation—indeed!

The Communist International's chief representative was heavy-set and powerful. He looked like a middle-aged Prussian general with his square face and cropped hair. Despite his sympathy for the masses who were oppressed by both foreign imperialists and native ruling classes, Maring sneered at the backward Asiatic races.

In the shadow of that formidable personality, the second foreigner, a Russian known as Nikolaevsky, was almost invisible. Small and dark, he rarely ventured an opinion.

Acting Chairman Chang Kuo-tao knew that his own colleague Mao Tse-tung would prove troublesome. Shortly after addressing the Students' Federation, the twenty-seven-year-old junior delegate from Hunan Province had invented urgent business to lure the senior delegate away. The dozen or so members in Hunan were now represented only by the aggressive young man who held such a high opinion of himself. Pale and intense, Mao looked like a fanatical monk in his long-gown of gray homespun. Although he knew little of Marxism, Mao was immensely self-confident, shrugging arrogantly and smiling contemptuously.

While the delegates reluctantly took their seats, Maring shuffled his notes and instructed the interpreter who would render his English into Mandarin. In the Dutchman's eyes the chief purpose of the special session was clearly not the progress report he had demanded. It was his own speech, which would tell the young delegates how to conduct their affairs.

Acting Chairman Chang Kuo-tao glanced around again. Since everyone was finally seated, he rapped the table to call the meeting to order. The sooner they began, the sooner they could get out of this sweatbox.

Before Chang Kuo-tao could speak, the green baize curtain over the rear door twitched. A small man poked his head into the room. His features were obscured by the brim of his fedora, but his head swayed from side to side like a watchful cobra's. Without speaking, he appeared to be memorizing every face.

"Oh, I'm sorry!" he finally apologized in Shanghainese. "I must have come to the wrong house."

The curtain closed as the stranger withdrew. Sitting stock-still, the fourteen delegates listened to his felt soles' sighing retreat across the stone courtyard.

"Get your papers together!" Acting Chairman Chang Kuo-tao commanded. "He could be anyone. We've got to get out of here!"

After his decades of conspiracy, Maring was decisive. He rose, banged the table with his fist, and said: "I propose that the meeting adjourn. Everyone must leave separately!"

No discussion was necessary. The two foreigners in the lead, the delegates scuttled through the back door into the alley. A minute later, Chang Kuo-tao was the last to depart. Only two Communists remained: the tenant of the house and his close friend, who had offered to stand by him.

Ten minutes later, when they had barely set right the disorder left by their colleagues' hasty departure, the front door crashed open. The intruder had returned with a French inspector of police and five Chinese detectives in plain clothes. Crestfallen at finding only two men where he had seen fourteen a quarter of an hour earlier, the spy insisted that he had discovered a suspicious assembly.

"Why else were two foreigners present?" he demanded. "Why else did they disperse so fast?"

The French inspector interrogated the two remaining men. He was insistent, but he was correct. His threats were implicit, and his manner was courteous.

"What was the purpose of the meeting?" he asked. "Who were the twelve men who left? Why did you break up so abruptly?"

"We are a small cultural society," the householder replied. "We were discussing new trends in literature. The foreigners contribute another view. The subject may be a bit abstruse for a practical police officer. But it's of great interest to scholars and artists like my friends."

"Why did they run away so fast?" a Chinese detective reiterated. "What are they afraid of?"

"Their wives, I suppose." The tenant smiled. "Somebody said they'd catch hell if they weren't home on time. A new opera is opening tonight at the Great World Theater, and the ladies are eager to see it."

Although frightened by the detectives' persistence, the householder appeared serene. The friend who had stayed to provide moral support trembled with fear, and his hangdog look virtually proclaimed guilt. While the detectives ransacked the house, his expression became ever more woebegone.

Nonetheless, the inspector left when his men failed to find any incriminating evidence. However, the French Concession police would obviously abandon neither their suspicions nor their surveillance of the house.

Acting Chairman Chang Kuo-tao congratulated himself and sidestepped a handcart heaped with newspapers. He was satisfied that he had attracted no untoward attention. Having for once allowed enough time, he sauntered toward the waiting train. Puffs of steam and the snorting of air brakes confirmed his conclusion: Everything was turning out very well indeed!

The police intrusion upon the special session three days earlier had been an apparent ill wind that blew auspiciously for the Chinese Communist Party. There was no need to invite the overbearing Maring and his gray shadow Nikolaevsky to the closing session, since they could not make the railway journey without making themselves conspicuous. The Dutchman's sole contribution to the First Congress was to remain his formal motion to adjourn a session that had not yet been formally opened.

Waiting for the 7:02 express to depart, Chang Kuo-tao inhaled appreciatively. The air was still fresh, not yet fouled by the stenches of high summer. Slipping through the throng around the tea vendors, the bun salesmen, and the fruit hawkers, six delegates had boarded the train individually. All were inconspicuously dressed, and all behaved discreetly. Even Mao Tse-tung had refrained this once from strutting like a knight errant in a provincial opera.

The acting chairman munched the fried breadstick he had bought on the platform and sipped his green tea, which would be repeatedly replenished with hot water during the two hours it took to cover the fifty-odd miles between Shanghai and Kashing on the South Lake. Although most of the First Congress's work was completed, the journey would allow him to look over his papers undisturbed. He opened a file and began to read. But his chin sank slowly to his chest, and the pages remained unturned. When the conductor shook him awake at Kashing, he was astonished to find that he had slept.

Chang Kuo-tao felt secure when he stepped off the train. The Chinese police of this lackadaisical resort town were unlikely to be in touch with the police of the French Concession; besides, they would hardly act on the vague suspicions of the foreign police. Moreover, no one could approach a houseboat unseen, and no delegate could leave before the session was over. Security was perfect for the largely ceremonial closing session of the inaugural First Congress of the Communist Party of China.

As if on a pleasure outing on the balmy mid-July day, the young men embarked on the luxurious houseboat on the South Lake. Although he had been assured that the cook and the waiter were reliable, Chang Kuo-tao was pleased to find that they spoke their local dialect, but not the national language, the Mandarin that was the common tongue of the delegates. Security was impeccable.

The beauty of the scene was, however, a distraction. Arched tile roofs peeped through the spruces on the hillocks, and the shore was obscured by bullrushes and pampas grass. The houseboat itself was also a distraction. The carved rosewood panels and the gilded ceiling diverted the eye, and the padded couches and soft chairs sapped their will. The young men drifted for a time, captivated by the traditional charm of old China, which they all loved, although they hated the old China's traditional exploitation of the masses.

When they finally got down to business, the delegates progressed rapidly. They were ratifying decisions already discussed. After they approved the draft constitution by a show of hands, they agreed that the labor movement was to be the foundation of their own power. They not only would recruit working-class members for the Communist Party but would organize their own trade unions. Second, there was no need for a large administrative apparatus, because their movement could as yet count no more than sixty or seventy firm adherents. Instead, a respected professor who was unavoidably absent was named secretary general; the oldest among those present was given responsibility for propaganda; and the energetic Chang Kuo-tao was made chief of the Organization Bureau.

The acting chairman then delivered the closing address. The new Communist Party, he said, would neither affiliate formally with the Communist International in Moscow nor limit its freedom by accepting the financial subsidy Moscow offered. Chang Kuo-tao then declared the First Congress closed as the bright lights of the fishing boats began to flicker on the still waters of the South Lake.

8

AUGUST 14, 1921

Tommy Howe's bachelor apartment on the sixth floor of a dark brick building on Kiukiang Road was far more attractive since his sister Emily and her friend Julia had softened the severity of its makeshift furniture with rainbow-hued cushions and Japanese prints. Even Tommy acknowledged that the loft was now more comfortable, although he disliked changes in his surroundings almost as passionately as he desired political change.

"It's only a pied-à-terre," he had originally objected. "And I'll be going back to Peking for my last year at medical school any day now. Why bother tarting the flat up?"

Ignoring his objections, the two young women had made a livable apartment out of the enormous loft with the minuscule kitchen and the two tiny bedrooms. Fortunately, the bathroom was already more than adequate. Tommy was addicted to shining porcelain and hot water, after being deprived of those comforts at Radley, one of the miscalled "public" schools where the English ruling class trained its sons by Spartan deprivation. Otherwise, Tommy was, like any other Old Radleyan, largely indifferent to his surroundings—as long as his surroundings did not change greatly.

As Tommy's guests, Emily and Julia were now enjoying the fruit of their labors. Emily's enjoyment was wholehearted. But Julia was uneasy at deceiving Emily's parents, even by omission. The Howes did not know that Richard Hollings would be present. Tommy had reluctantly agreed to the pretense that the two were visiting him alone. Otherwise, Eurydice Howe would certainly not have permitted her daughter and her guest to leave Harmony Hall unchaperoned after six in the evening.

Tommy was himself untrammeled, since a young man was expected to sow his wild oats. He was, nevertheless, in revolt against traditional Chinese restrictions on personal liberty. Although he had, therefore, agreed to the deception, he felt that women had to be protected—and, usually, told what to do. After enjoying the freedom of Bryn Mawr, his sister Emily could not entirely be forced back into the traditional mold of feminine docility. Yet it was better for her to see her admirer under Tommy's brotherly eye, rather than alone.

Besides, Shanghai was Shanghai. The city was vibrant and cosmopolitan, not stodgy and inward-looking like Peking. But why, Tommy wondered, did Emily have to encourage a foreigner? There were dozens of suitable young Chinese men in the Howes' circle.

Obviously untroubled by such misgivings, Emily posed dramatically in the doorway leading from the small kitchen into the loft. She steadied the blue-and-white teapot on the slippery lacquer tray, unaware that the sunlight spilling through the skylight backlit her brilliantly.

Julia stifled a gasp of surprise. The sunlight outlined Emily's body under the sheer white voile dress with the slit skirt. Noting Richard Hollings's gaze, Julia resolved to warn Emily that the Englishman's interest was not confined to her intellect and her local knowledge.

Tommy had already reproached his sister privately for the sheer fabric and the clinging cut of her new dress, which she had expected to please him by its distinctively Chinese style. Actually, he had snapped, it was not Chinese at all but inspired by the riding coats of the nomadic Manchus, who had been the alien overlords of China from the middle of the seventeenth century until 1911.

After that confrontation, brother and sister had been curt with each other, though they lavished charm on their guests. But Tommy grinned when Emily stooped to place her tray on the coffee table, which was a packing case covered with a lilac Indian shawl.

"One thing is obvious from your *cheongsam*," he said in rapid Shanghainese. "You are mistakably nubile, my dear sister."

Emily replied in the same language: "You were a dirty-minded little boy. And now you're a dirty-minded big boy."

"You've always been an exhibitionist," he retorted. "I remember at Auntie Vi's house on the beach at Woosung. You were always running around with no top—and usually hardly any pants."

"For God's sake, I was a baby, only six," she said. "And you were naked as a jaybird all that summer. Little boys can show their equipment, but not little girls."

Richard Hollings leaned forward from the cushion-padded barrel that was his chair. His brown eyes shone in amusement, and he pushed his brown hair off his forehead.

"They sound like fish peddlers, don't they?" he said to Julia. "I'm sorry I took advice to study Mandarin instead of Shanghainese."

"Last week," Julia answered, "you were bragging about all the Shanghai swear words you know."

"Just a few, Julie," Richard countered. "Not like your friend Joshua. He talks Shanghainese like a native. The only foreigner I know who can."

"Well, he did grow up speaking the lingo," Julia said. "Just wait, though. I'm going to be almost as good some day soon."

Brother and sister were still speaking rapid Shanghainese to each other. Although the harsh sounds made it seem that they were still quarreling, they were now reminiscing about their childhood. Julia could make out only an occasional word—"uncle," "dumpling," and "pony." She could, however, already distinguish between a quarrel and a chat by their tone—a feat that evaded most foreigners in Shanghai forever. Besides, Emily impulsively embraced her brother, resting her forehead against his shoulder while laughter burbled from her lips.

"It's infuriating not to understand." Richard was watching their by-play so intensely he might almost have been jealous. "Speaking of Haleevie, he's seeing a lot of that Russian poppsy we ran into at St. Andrew's Café. . . . It's not love, I'm sure. And she's no more a countess than I'm a royal duke."

Hearing that remark, Emily abruptly switched back to English. "And they say women gossip! First my darling brother criticizes me like a maiden aunt, and now Richard repeats filthy rumors. It's all beastly male condescension."

Julia was amused—and moved—by her friend's ardor. Less than two months in Shanghai had transformed Emily from a demure mantrap into an ardent feminist. She was appalled by the severe limitations on their actions that most Chinese women took for granted. When Julia nodded emphatic agreement, Tommy threw her a superior glance; he might as well have told her aloud not to bother her pretty little head with grown-up worries.

Richard persisted: "Come now, you're only defending that Russian woman because she's female. Why she's an obvious fake. Some countess! Working as a taxi-dancer and, for all we know, worse!"

"But we *don't* know, do we?" Emily pointed out. "So we could, at the least, give her the benefit of the doubt."

"If she really speaks all those languages, she's no fake," Julia said. "How could she have gotten the education if her father weren't a rich man? Why not, then, a count?"

"She does talk them all," Tommy conceded. "Before Joshua tried to find her work, he checked."

"You see, Richard, she's definitely not a fake." Emily scored off her admirer before addressing her brother: "Tommy, you didn't tell me you'd seen Elizaveta again. Did Joshua find her a job?"

"I haven't seen her," Tommy said. "Only Joshua has. But there was nothing doing. Sir Judah put his foot down before he even heard her name. The old boy hates Russians like poison. Because of their anti-Semitism, their Jew-killing . . . He couldn't know how infatuated Joshua is—infatuated or bewitched."

"I'd like to see Elizaveta again," Julia said. "She's fascinating. But we're so hemmed about in Harmony Hall . . ."

"And a good thing, too," Tommy said. "Otherwise, God knows what you two would get up to. . . . From what Joshua says, this Elizaveta is very temperamental, sometimes wild. How he puts up with her moods, I don't—"

"Maybe it's love," Julia suggested slyly. "It happens, you know."

"I've a pretty good idea what it is," Tommy replied, laughing. "And it's *not* love. But she's so temperamental . . ."

"Beloved elder brother, you couldn't put up with a living Kwan Yin!" Emily defended all women by defending Elizaveta. "Even the Goddess of Mercy would be too temperamental for you!"

Julia almost protested, but it would be foolish to intervene between brother and sister. Yet Emily's condemnation was unfair, for Tommy was extraordinarily patient with his fiery sister. He also knew his own mind, although he was not yet twenty-four. Tommy was a strong person—and by no means unattractive.

Julia had never before thought about any Chinese as a desirable man. In the United States, she had liked some of Emily's male Chinese friends and disliked others, but she had never even considered them *that* way. Yet Tommy was unquestionably attractive in a very masculine way with his strong jaw, his square hands, and his level gaze.

She was just speculating, Julia assured herself. There could never be anything serious—not only because of their different races but because of their utterly different backgrounds. Under the gloss of his English education, Thomas Tan-ssu Howe was obviously Chinese to the marrow of his bones. He would never be happy outside China. Besides, she could not imagine spending her life in exile from her own country.

Julia reproached herself for her light-mindedness. She was mooning like a sixteen-year-old who thought every man she met was smitten by her beauty. Tommy was certainly not smitten. Quite obviously, he tolerated her only because she was his sister's closest friend.

When Richard rose, Julia saw again why Emily was so taken with him —and also why Emily took such pains to ensure that her parents did not learn of his existence. With his dark hair, dark eyes, and olive complexion, he looked more like a dashing Latin than a stodgy Anglo-Saxon. And his intensity was very exciting.

A shade under six feet, Richard Hollings wore the tan summer uniform of a lieutenant in the Shanghai Volunteer Force. A russet Sam Browne belt crossed his chest, and two small stars, which he called pips, shone on each shoulder strap. He was only a pressman, as newspapermen were contemptuously called by the *taipans,* the senior businessmen who ruled the Settlement and Frenchtown. But he was also an officer, for he was the special correspondent of *The Times* of London, which was a bulwark of the established order. He was also a public school man, having, like Tommy, passed through one of the institutions that trained the sons of the British ruling class.

Although she might rail against male domination, Emily had not abandoned the feminine wiles she had perfected on hapless American college men. She rose to stand beside Richard, laid her hand on his arm, and smiled up at him. Her wide-set eyes and the minute indentations below her fine cheekbones combined to make her appear mysterious and vulnerable.

"Come on, then, Lieutenant Hollings," she said. "We mustn't be late for the Volunteers' reception."

The door closed behind them with a clashing of the chains and bolts prudence dictated in the business district just off the Bund. Tommy grinned in self-derision, took off his spectacles, and diligently polished the gleaming lenses.

"Whew," he exhaled. "She's done me properly this time. Walked all over me."

"She always wins with men." Julia laughed. "She's so beautiful and so feminine she always gets her own way—no matter how she may carry on about men dictating to her. But what's bothering you?"

"The way Hollings and she just waltzed off. I thought we were set for a quiet evening at home—all four of us. If I'd known they were planning to leave, I'd never . . . It's very awkward."

"Yes," Julia agreed, "it certainly is."

She was suddenly aware that she was stranded with Tommy until

Emily reappeared and they could return to Harmony Hall together. He was, of course, a gentleman, although Chinese did have different ideas. She must seem either forward or foolish to allow herself to be trapped alone with him in his apartment. Even headstrong Emily and her Richard would be in a public place among many others.

"Very awkward." Tommy dwelt on his own concern, which was different from Julia's. "Suppose someone who knows Emmy sees them —and it gets back to the parents. There'd be the devil to pay!"

"Emmy thought, with such completely different circles, there's no danger. I'm only sorry you're stuck with me till she gets back."

"That's no hardship, Julia. A great pleasure, if truth be told."

Tommy's gallantry was automatic, the response any gentleman would feel obliged to make to her self-deprecating remark. His next words, moreover, proved that he was hardly aware of her as an individual—or a woman. He spoke with the same appalling frankness he might offer a stranger he had met on a train and would never see again.

"It's this damned foreigner business," he said. "Naturally, Emily's having a hard time settling back into Shanghai. And, of course, she couldn't have the same free-and-easy relationship with a Chinese man. She's obviously not put off by the differences—the fundamental, irreconcilable differences—between foreigners and Chinese. It looks as if she's actually attracted to foreign men, probably recapturing her university days. . . . It's Hollings now, but it could be any foreigner. I'm a chump to help keep the parents in the dark. It'll end in tears."

"Not just any foreigner!" Julia hotly defended her friend. "She has no time for Harry Smythe—or a dozen others we've met at Jade House. Emmy can look after herself. She's a pretty tough cookie! Anyway, I've seen her like this before. It's a passing thing—quick and intense, but not deep. She keeps a guard on her heart."

"Does she indeed?" Tommy responded. "Even so, she's got to get over her morbid fascination with foreigners."

Julia looked hard at the tall young man, who was wearing a cream linen sport shirt with a soft collar. Informal as befitted the enlightened 1920s, he nonetheless spoke like an old-fashioned bigot. She looked hard but could see no rancor in his impersonal candor. He evidently did not dislike foreigners, for no racist passion inflamed his words. And, rather humiliatingly, those words had nothing to do with her personally. It was a practical issue: Emily Yuelin Howe would do well to turn her interest to men of her own race and nation.

Tommy's detachment when discussing a matter of the emotions was slightly chilling. Julia assessed him again. He was appealing—lean, tanned, and nonchalant. He was also a challenge. Some day, some woman would draw from Tommy the same passion he now gave to politics. But that was one challenge she, Julia Pavernen, would not take up.

"Any rate," he finally resumed, "Emily's not as emancipated as she thinks."

"It's funny," Julia said. "At Bryn Mawr we thought Emmy was a bit passive. Too docile, almost like a Victorian miss—until she lost her temper. But here she seems—"

"Too ladylike for Bryn Mawr is practically shrewish in old-fashioned Chinese. . . . I know Emmy thinks I'm radical in my politics, almost a Bolshevik. That's nonsense, though I can claim to be an advanced thinker. But even I am still old-fashioned in some ways. I admit I'm rather conservative about young ladies and their . . . ah . . . behavior."

Julia saw that Tommy was neither as distant nor as self-assured as he might appear. Behind a façade that altered bewilderingly from raffish to grave, he actually seemed shy.

His black-rimmed spectacles lay on one of his treasured leather-seated folding chairs in the style of the Ming Dynasty. Like his glasses, those chairs were theatrical props intended to enhance his dignity. His gravity was, however, laced with humor that was no more respectful of himself than of others.

Julia impulsively decided to take up the challenge posed by Tommy Howe. She would, however, go only far enough to break down his remoteness—not an inch farther. Deliberately wide-eyed, she asked, "Young ladies' behavior?"

"I mean with regard to . . . ah . . . personal relations." His words were slow and precise. "In China, there must always be something aloof . . . mysterious . . . about a lady. Being remote, that's the essence of feminine charm, feminine magic. So, naturally, we expect that ladies will preserve themselves . . ."

He emphasized the care with which he was discussing the undiscussable by slipping on his glasses. His expression intent, he spoke delicately of the traditional Chinese reverence for virginity. Though he looked like a playboy with his deep tan and his short-sleeved shirt, Julia saw that he was truly an old-fashioned Chinese gentleman.

Tommy had hardly even touched her arm, though an American medical student to whom she had given the same opportunity would have tried to paw her. The American would have stopped when rebuked, but he would have tried. Tommy had not even tried to hold her hand for an instant. Perhaps, Julia wondered with a stab of dismay, he did not find her attractive!

"Penny for your thoughts," he said.

"I was just thinking," she prevaricated, "about . . . really nothing much."

She *was* attractive, and he *was* attracted. Julia reached that gratifying conclusion after considering herself severely. Although she had to protect her sensitive skin from the brutal Shanghai sun with broad-brimmed hats, her complexion had acquired a golden glow. Her shoulder-length hair, the color of tawny port, was set off by black silk lounging pyjamas with green beadwork. She had been afraid Tommy would think they were too daring. But he had earlier pronounced those pyjamas "smashing!" adding "snazzy!" to show off the American slang he was picking up.

"Don't you find it all terribly strange?" he asked abruptly. "A bit of a strain?"

That was the first wholly personal remark Tommy had ever addressed to her. He had paid her conventional compliments, and he had joked with her. But those two questions were the first indication that he was aware of her as an individual human being with her own hopes and fears.

"China, you mean, and Shanghai?" Julia said. "Well, it's not Plattsburg, is it? . . . Yes, Tommy, I do find it strange, very strange. A little frightening at times, but fascinating, too. I wouldn't be anywhere else on earth."

"At least you're old enough to be resilient . . . to bounce back. You've not been pushed off to a totally alien—and terrifying—country when you're too small to know what's happening. And with no possibility of escape, none whatever . . ."

Tommy's words trailed off, and he looked down at his meerschaum pipe. Embarrassed by his revelations, he busied himself stuffing tobacco into the white bowl and searching for matches among the litter on the packing-case coffee table.

"Not quite that, Tommy." Julia chattered compulsively while he recovered his poise. "But my first year at the George School was terrible. Daddy was so ill and Mother sent me away and I thought they didn't want me anymore. Sometimes I still do. . . . It was hell until Emily came along. Poor dear, she was even more adrift. So we comforted each other."

"You, too, abandoned?" he said. "But you knew the language. You weren't a foreigner with a strange complexion and peculiar eyes. . . . Did they call Emmy Chink at the George School?"

"Until I stopped them! Then they called me Chink, but I only laughed. Still, I have some idea how you must've felt."

"No, you don't, Julie! You can't imagine what it's like being odd boy out at an English public school!"

He lit his pipe with great care before resuming in a level tone: "Public schools are meant to make you tough—by suffering. They certainly made me tough. Beatings, canings, and constant fights. Beastly food, and I was always cold, wet, and hungry. I couldn't really speak English, though I thought I could. All that when I was barely ten. . . . Funny thing, I finally got to like the English. . . . Masochism, I suppose. . . . Worst part was being the only Chinese. And they all laughed at China."

"So that's why you care so much about China."

Julia had heard similar plaints from Emily, but never so vehement. Still, Emily had not suffered as sorely as had Tommy. When all was said and done, girls were kinder than boys, more gentle. Or at least there was little physical violence among girls.

"I suppose so," Tommy replied slowly. "I suppose the taunting made me realize that I was Chinese. But those memories hardly trouble me nowadays. I know what I am. And I know what I want to do—what I will do."

"Yes?"

"First, I'll be a good doctor," he replied. "For everyone who needs help, not just the rich. China's got so few doctors, every one man can make a big difference. And second, I'll work with others to make China strong and respected. Also help China get shot of foreign influence. No one will laugh at my country anymore."

"I see." Julia felt she was penetrating his defenses. "And how—"

"But you?" he interrupted. "What do you want to accomplish?"

Julia pondered, twisting a lock of her hair around her index finger, before she finally answered: "I'm not absolutely sure, Tommy. The usual things girls think about, of course: marriage and a family. But something beyond that, too. It's wonderful to be here in Shanghai—so different, so exciting and stimulating. I guess I want to really know China, understand Chinese civilization. Some day I hope I can help people a little. Maybe also change the world a little."

"I'd almost forgotten: your major in comparative civilizations. There's lots to compare. . . ." Tommy's tone was again impersonal and his manner distant, as if he regretted the tentative confidences they had been exchanging.

"I'll tell you a little story about China, Chinese civilization in the year 1921," he said. "Then maybe you'll see why it's going to be a job changing China—and also why we'll surely succeed. The story may sound a bit childish, but that shows the raw material we have to work with."

Julia leaned back in the rattan chair and watched Tommy's sensitive mouth as he spoke with the open passion he apparently reserved for politics: "You remember that tall chap at the Federation of Students, Chang Kuo-tao? He told me this story. . . . Just across the Hwangpoo, just across from the Foreign Settlement, lies an industrial slum called Pootung. And in Pootung stands the factory of the British-American Tobacco Company—the biggest plant of the world's biggest tobacco company in the world's best cigarette market. You've seen what heavy smokers Chinese are. BAT makes a fair penny, and BAT pays its directors, shareholders, and managers lavishly. All the top men, of course, are foreigners.

"But BAT doesn't spoil its Chinese workers. They put in twelve-to-fourteen-hour days. Tens of thousands in the countryside are just panting for regular work in the city. So wages are abysmal, and working conditions are appalling."

"You're leading up to the strike at BAT earlier this month," Julia interjected. "I thought the workers won."

"They did, and I'll tell you how," Tommy said. "Chang Kuo-tao is boss of a setup called the Labor Secretariat, which is tied up with the new Communist Party of China. The BAT strike was a golden opportunity for the Secretariat to move into the labor movement—and to build strong unions. Ten leaders of the strike came to see my friend Kuo-tao. He showed them how to organize a real union and how to unite all the workers behind demands for higher pay and better working conditions.

"Kuo-tao candidly told the strike leaders he was a Marxist, but that didn't bother them. Their spokesman said 'Every man is entitled to practice his own religion.'

"The strikers' biggest problem was BAT's senior foreman, who's high up in the Floodgate secret society. He was forcing the men to go back to work."

"Tommy," Julia interrupted, "what has a secret society to do with labor unions? I thought secret societies were half-political and half-gangster outfits."

"So they are—and the secret societies control the Shanghai work force. The chief foremen and the chief clerks of every major Shanghai firm are secret-society elders. They're interested only in enriching themselves—and in exploiting the workers for the management.

"For all those reasons, the foreman at BAT was determined to sack all the strike leaders. But Kuo-tao had an answer.

" 'You're already on strike,' he told the strike leaders. 'And the foreman already wants to sack you all. So things can't get any worse. I'd go for a mass meeting to mobilize your workmates' support. Then you can break the foreman's power.' "

Tommy paused to relight his pipe, and Julia put a Chesterfield into the long dragon-carved ivory holder she had found at a curio shop. When he offered her a light, she inhaled—and coughed at the unfamiliar smoke rasping her throat.

"At the mass meeting," Tommy continued, "four hundred workers listened in silence—and then drifted away. Chang Kuo-tao was discouraged, but the strike leaders were jubilant. Not one man had gone back to work, despite the foreman's pressure."

"What happened then?" Julia demanded. "Your strike is beginning to sound like a Chinese opera—no climax."

"The climax came minutes later." Tommy smiled. "While the foreman was threatening secret-society vengeance against every striker, a worker appeared with an enormous watermelon. He upended it over the foreman's head—and ripe, stinking night soil poured out.

"Drenched with human excrement, the great man was instantly transformed into a clown. He lost all face—and all power over the workers, just as a Taoist idol loses its potency when thrown on a dungheap. After that, the foreign management couldn't cope with the union's aggressive tactics, and it soon gave in to the workers' demands."

"And the moral?" Julia asked. "It's terribly interesting, but . . ."

Tommy took off his glasses and said, "There is a moral. In Shanghai today modern capitalism and modern Marxism, medieval superstition and ancient pride of face—all are muddled together. In the interior of China, it's far worse. But radical change is on the way—sometimes by means as strange as a watermelon full of night soil."

Julia was puzzled—and a little let down. Tommy had told the story well, and she could see its point: the primitive confusion on which the new China had to be built. But he had also dragged that story into the conversation as if anxious to choke the budding intimacy between them.

She was further disturbed by its antiforeign undertone. Tommy said he was not antiforeign, yet one of his goals was to drive foreign influence out of China. How much of a personal element was there in his ostensibly political motivation?

Tommy's strength and dedication drew Julia, as did his evident need for simple kindness. He was also an enigma. Outwardly sunny and relaxed, he was, nonetheless, a driven man.

Although she was intrigued, Julia vowed that she would not get further involved. Tommy was far deeper than his sister Emily, and he could entrap her. She had not come to Shanghai to have her heart broken by a fascinating, volatile, and alien young man. Beneath his jocular manner, he was too serious for casual flirtation. Yet anything more than casual flirtation would be dangerous. His power to attract— and to wound—was great.

"It's all very interesting," she said primly. "I wonder when Emily will be back."

9

Julia lifted her hand to hail a yellow public rickshaw but let it fall back to her side. When the rickshaw puller, who was eager for a fare, looked at her plaintively, she murmured, *"Fu yeo-lo . . .* I've changed my mind. I'm very sorry."

Placated when she gave him twenty cents, which would have commanded his services for an hour, the rickshaw puller trotted away between the shafts of his two-wheeled chair to find another fare—or another foolish foreigner. Julia set out with long strides down Rue Pataro toward the sidewalk café where she was to meet her Shanghainese teacher. She still preferred not to ride in rickshaws, although Emily pointed out quite practically that the rickshaw coolies would all die of starvation if everyone in Shanghai were as squeamish about being pulled by a human being.

Julia was happy to be alone for a time. Emily was not only her closest friend but her eager, if sometimes ill-informed, guide to the wonderland of Shanghai. She did love Emily, but she needed to be by herself from time to time. Emily's moods could be tiring, as could Emily's enthusiasm for the tart-tongued Richard Hollings. Fortunately, Emily had gone off in the Rolls with her mother on an obligatory family visit, leaving Julia to enjoy the first faint tang of autumn that spiced the sodden Shanghai air in the first week of September.

Despite that pleasure, Julia soon felt limp, and she wondered whether she had imagined that autumnal crispness. Although her dress was light cotton, perspiration trickled into the small of her back. But she stubbornly walked on, marveling at the wide boulevard, the leafy plane trees, and the stuccoed walls behind which rose the mansions of the wealthy. The scene was identical to photographs she had seen of French provincial towns, even to the wooden blinds let down over the second-story windows as the mansions closed their eyes for the afternoon siesta.

The fashionable residential district of Frenchtown was normally less crowded than the bustling Bund, and the afternoon heat had further thinned the pedestrians on the broad sidewalks. Nonetheless, Julia felt a quiver of unease. It was as if someone was dogging her footsteps. When she turned, she saw a figure in a long gray dress keeping pace with her on the other side of the boulevard. Conspicuous among the Chinese pedestrians, the woman flaunted long blond hair like a young woman's, but she moved with none of the elastic grace of youth.

As if drawn by Julia's gaze, the gray figure darted across the boulevard, just missing a low-slung Citroen. Ignoring the chauffeur, who leaned out the window to swear at her, the woman waved peremptorily.

Julia waited. She had been warned of the perils of Shanghai. But what injury could she possibly suffer from a middle-aged woman with the bleached hair and an arthritic walk?

"Miss Pavernen?" the woman asked in English with a heavy but indefinable accent. "You are Miss Julia Pavernen? . . . I'm so glad I caught you. I am Mrs. Schifferblatt."

"How do you do, Mrs. Schifferblatt."

"You do not know me," the woman added unnecessarily. "I am coming from . . . for Miss Yavalenka."

Julia must have looked blank, for Mrs. Schifferblatt said urgently, "Elizaveta Alexandrovna Yavalenka. You must remember. You met her at the St. Andrew's Café, oh, months ago."

"Yes, of course. And how is she?"

"Not well. Not in the least well. This is why I come to see you. There is no one else."

Before being sent off to school at the age of ten, Julia had been forbidden any more pets because she grieved so desperately when a guinea pig died or a kitten hurt its paw. She asked with ready sympathy, "What's the matter with Eli—Miss Yavalenka? Can I help her?"

"That's what she said," the woman muttered cheerfully. "Go to the one with the beautiful tawny hair! That one looks very kind. . . . Elizaveta is very sick, Miss Pavernen. Someone must help her, but she will take no help from her . . . from Mr. Haleevie."

"Does Joshua . . . does Mr. Haleevie know she's so ill?"

"No, and she will not let me tell him. She says he must not see her as she is now. She is more worried about keeping him away than she is about her sickness. She makes up many excuses—or I just lie for her."

"What can I do?" Julia asked.

"I am very worried about Elizaveta. Not eating and, now, this sickness. You? You can come see her. I tell you, though she must not know I tell you, she has no money, none whatever. I am her landlady, and she owes nearly two months' rental. But I am not asking."

"Has she seen a doctor?"

"No, Miss Pavernen. There is no money—and she says she does not believe in doctors."

"Well, the first thing then . . ." Julia mused. "Mrs. Schifferblatt, what's the address?"

"Kiangse Road, number 278. And please do not be too long."

The middle-aged woman hailed a rickshaw and was trundled rapidly down Avenue Joffre, her extravagantly artificial hair blending with the rickshaw's chrome yellow. Julie stood stock-still in thought while the stream of pedestrians flowed around her. She would first have to leave a message for her language teacher and then decide what to do about Elizaveta.

Her qualms forgotten, Julia hailed a rickshaw. Curiously, a man pulling that wheeled chair could go much faster than she could on her own healthy legs. The motion was not unpleasant, a slight swaying broken by slight jolts when the wooden-spoked wheels hit a bump. It did not occur to her that she could ignore the summons to help the young Russian woman, whom she had met only once. Elizaveta must be both friendless and desperate to turn to a passing acquaintance.

The trouble was that Julia had virtually no money of her own. Although her uncle, Jack Pavernen, gave her a few dollars each time she saw him, she was reluctant to take his money. She disliked being treated like a child, and she knew he was having business difficulties. Little point, therefore, in going to Uncle Jack. Her decision was made without further conscious thought: Tommy Howe was her best hope.

She had seen Tommy only twice during the three weeks since their long—and somewhat strained—chat while they waited for Emily to return from the Volunteers' reception. He had seemed very distant. Still, she could hardly expect him to display warmth amid the forbidding splendors of Harmony Hall.

As the rickshaw approached the dark brick building on Kiukiang Road, Julia saw Tommy standing at the curb. He was wearing a cream linen suit and carrying a small canvas holdall. While impatiently flicking a squash racket against his leg, he was hopefully scanning the traffic. His face brightened when he spied her rickshaw. He had evidently not seen Julia, who was sitting well back under the folding canvas hood to escape the sun.

When the rickshaw stopped, Tommy started to step in. He drew back with an apologetic exclamation when he saw Julia, obviously recognizing her only an instant later.

"Julie, what are you doing here?" he asked.

When she told him of Elizaveta's plight and her own concern, he waited only an instant before saying, "And you want me to take a look at her? In that case, I've no choice, do I? Old Joshua will just have to miss our game of squash. I wonder if it's . . . Just wait here with the rickshaw. I'll be right back."

He darted through the heavy front door, returning no more than five minutes later breathing heavily. "Faster to climb six flights than use the old lift." He proudly displayed a brand-new brown leather Gladstone bag and added, "I had to get my medical bag. A present from the parents."

After her reservations about Tommy, Julia was pleased by his immediate response. She was also mildly embarrassed by the forced intimacy of the rickshaw. Crammed together on the slick oilcloth seat, she felt his thigh hard against her own. He did not try to speak over the jolting of the big wheels and the clatter of the traffic in narrow Kiangse Road. She became even more sharply aware of his nearness when, without asking permission, he eased the pressure of his shoulder against hers by placing his arm along the top of the seat behind her.

She felt his warmth and smelled the fragrance of his tobacco. Realizing that she was virtually snuggling against him, she drew as far away as she could. Since she could not insult him—and make a fool of herself —by perching stiffly on the edge of the seat, his partial embrace was unavoidable.

Mrs. Schifferblatt looked oddly at Tommy, evidently surprised at seeing a Chinese doctor. The landlady led them up five creaking flights of stairs covered with worn sisal matting to a varnished wooden door with cracked panels.

When Mrs. Schifferblatt opened the door, Julia saw Elizaveta's crow-black hair spread on a pillow. Despite the heat, she lay under a heap of shabby counterpanes and coverlets.

The other furnishings were an ancient wing chair covered with dingy brocade, a petit-point screen, and a small alcove with a gas fire. Dust furred the dingy linoleum; soiled dishes stood on the cracked bedside table; and a cheap towel hung over the screen. The small bed-sitting-room was saved from total squalor by the rainbow of evening dresses hanging from the picture rail.

Elizaveta turned slowly at the creaking of the door and said something muzzily in Russian: "*Kto tam?* . . . Who's there?" Her eyes opened, and she said in English: "Oh, it's you, Miss . . . ah . . . Pavernen, and . . . ah . . . Mister . . . the medical student. Hello!"

As if muffled by cotton wool, her voice was heavy; her complexion was ashen; and the fine bones of her face jutted harshly. She blinked and said, "So terribly kind of you. I prayed you'd come, but, after all, you hardly know me. So terribly kind . . ."

"Hush!" Julia said. "You'll be all right now. You mustn't tire yourself talking."

Tommy glanced with approval at Julia and said with the gruff kindliness affected by the medical profession, "We'll just have a look at you, young lady. . . . Mrs. Schifferblatt, if you could leave us alone. Julia, you'd better stay."

He took off his jacket and washed his hands at the basin half-concealed behind the sleazy petit-point screen. Taking a stethoscope from his Gladstone bag, he directed, "Turn over on your front, please."

When Tommy placed the stethoscope's black horn between Elizaveta's shoulder blades and tapped authoritatively, Julia suppressed a smile. An instant's hesitation had given away the medical student's reluctance to examine his patient's chest. Finally he did so, sliding the horn decorously over the satin of Elizaveta's nightdress. After taking her temperature and blood pressure, he looked at her eyes and throat and declared with synthetic optimism, "You'll be fine! Just fine!"

Drawing Julia into the far corner, Tommy said softly, "As I feared. I shouldn't have let you come, Julie. In theory the bedclothes should be burnt, though what possible good . . . You've heard of Spanish influenza?"

Julia nodded. Coming like a scourge of God after the Great War, the disease had scythed tens of thousands in Europe and America in 1919 and 1920 and then vanished as abruptly and mysteriously as it had appeared. She was afraid for Elizaveta—and also for Tommy and herself.

"Same sort of thing, though definitely milder," he said. "Influenza's only a name. We don't know what causes it. She's not in acute danger, I'd say. Though she would've been if left untreated. We must get her into more salubrious surroundings. She needs light and air and better care. Pity I've got to leave for Peking in a couple of days. . . . Look here, I'll have a word with the landlady."

After hesitating a moment in fear of infection, Julia took herself in hand. She straightened the bedclothes and fluffed Elizaveta's pillows before carrying the dirty dishes to the washbasin. Eyes brilliant with fever, Elizaveta gratefully followed those movements. While Julia was washing and drying the dishes, Elizaveta said weakly. "I owe you a great deal, Miss Pavernen . . ."

"I'm Julia. Surnames are ridiculous at our age."

"Julia, I owe you more than I can say. But I was at my wits' end. . . . And I am still planning to survive."

That flash of humor and the intimacy created by their use of first names impelled Julia to say, "There is Joshua Haleevie. Why not ask him? Mrs. Schifferblatt says you won't even see him—or let him know you're ill."

"That's true, Julia, but what would you do?" Elizaveta said. "I'd hate to have him see me looking this way. Drawn and wan may be fine in lyric poetry. In real life it's not very beguiling. Besides, he would insist on helping . . . giving me money. . . . I *can't* take money from him. What would that make me? There's still some old-fashioned Russian pride left in my bones."

Julia was pleased. She was feeling protective, and Elizaveta's reply proved two points: Elizaveta might be Joshua's mistress, but she was certainly not the common prostitute Richard Hollings had virtually labeled her. Moreover, Elizaveta must be the daughter of aristocrats. She would otherwise not have maintained her Quixotic pride on her sickbed. That reasoning might seem quirky to others; by Julia's intuitive logic, it was irrefutable.

"I'm sure you'll be fine," she said. "Just as long as you keep fighting, you'll—"

A knock heralded Tommy's return. Professionally energetic, he declared, "All fixed up now. Mrs. Schifferblatt has a big room with a view over the back garden she's delighted to let you have. All I had to do was ask. She's also found a young amah who's happy to come in and look after you. Do some cooking, if necessary. But for the next few days, what you really want is lots of rest, two aspirin every four hours, and lots of liquids. If you're hungry, all to the good. But light meals: boiled chicken or fish, not foie gras or smoked sturgeon. . . . I imagine Julia will be happy to help you move. Leave everything except essentials. Mrs. Schifferblatt says she'll keep this room for you."

He briskly left the squalid room. While helping Elizaveta draw on her threadbare bathrobe and get her toilet articles, Julia smiled to herself. Tommy's imitation of a hearty family practitioner was not without dramatic merit. He was obviously camouflaging his nervousness at treating his first patient—who happened to be a beautiful young woman with an intriguing reputation.

"Will she really be fine?" Tommy repeated the question as they walked away from the boardinghouse. "Hard to say, but I think so. No need to get a qualified physician. No one really knows about flu. All we can do is wait. I'll drop in again, but I might as well be an Iroquois medicine man for all the actual good I can do her."

"How much did it cost you?" Julia asked. "Changing her room and so on? The landlady was worried about her overdue rent. Maybe also about Elizaveta, but I suspect the rent's the reason she decided to find me."

Tommy studied the pavement, as if he suspected that a trap had been set for their feet. Only when Julia repeated his name did he reply, "Well, the old crow's got her back rent. It's all cost only a pittance, I assure you. By the way, I know a pleasant convalescent home out Jessfield Park way. I'll fix that for her as soon as she can be moved."

"A pittance to the Howes. But not to Elizaveta—or me. You're very generous, Tommy."

"Well, in that case, let's spend a little more of my father's wealth." He screened his embarrassment at her praise behind the feeble jest. "The ill-gotten treasure of the Howes must be redistributed to the masses."

"Is that conscience or conviction speaking?" Julia fell in with his mood. "Are you feeling guilty or expansive?"

"Both—and it's just about the cocktail hour. What say we drop in at the Renaissance Café?"

The man walking beside her, Julia felt, was quite different from the Tommy Howe who had been alternately confiding and distant when they spent four uncomfortable hours in his loft apartment waiting for Emily and Richard to return. He was now candid and high-spirited, apparently untouched by either political or racial doubts. Having dealt very competently with the medical problem, he had also undoubtedly spent far more than a pittance on Elizaveta's welfare.

Without thinking, she slipped her hand into the crook of his elbow. He still looked straight ahead, but a brief pressure of his arm welcomed her touch.

Moved and, despite herself again speculative, Julia felt she was perverse. She should unreservedly be enjoying this new Tommy, who had cheerfully given up his afternoon to a mission of mercy at her request. Was it, she wondered, really for her sake or because he was drawn to Elizaveta?

"Mustn't tell Joshua about this afternoon's work," Tommy said abruptly. "I'll have to think up some excuse for missing our squash."

"Why that?"

"It stands to reason," Tommy replied. "If she wanted him to know, she would've told him. It's up to her what tale she tells to account for her absence—traveling or whatever. So long as she doesn't mention me. My friend Joshua can be jealous for no good reason."

Julia saw that she had an instant earlier felt irrational jealousy toward Elizaveta. That wayward emotion told her something about her own feelings, though she was not quite sure what. Her spirits soared in sudden gaiety but fell as abruptly. She had just realized that Tommy would be leaving for Peking in a few days' time—and even Shanghai would be a little bleak without him.

"At least Liz will get much face from the Rolls," Emily said complacently. "There aren't many around here."

"More likely Mrs. Schifferblatt will raise her rent," Julia replied. "Oh, Em, I hate to let her go back to that squalid little room—and, I suppose, to taxi-dancing."

"Julie, honey, you know she wouldn't take any more from us," Emily pointed out. "She wouldn't stay another day at the rest home. She almost balked at letting us take her back in the Rolls."

The Howes' emerald-green Rolls-Royce turned off narrow Kiangse Road, which was palisaded with dark brick tenements, into the more congenial prosperity of Nanking Road on the overcast afternoon in late October. Driver and bodyguard both sat straighter in the front seat, clearly relieved to be finished with the errand that had taken them into raffish Kiangse Road.

The concern Emily and Julia felt for Elizaveta Alexandrovna Yavalenka was not shared by the Howes' servants. On principle, they looked down on all foreigners, except, perhaps, Julia, who was acknowledged as a near-equal because of the Howes' friendship. They particularly despised poor Europeans. Above all, they despised White Russians, those hapless refugees who were now arriving in Shanghai in increasing numbers.

While Elizaveta suppressed her rightful title of countess, a dozen baronesses, five countesses, and even three princesses—all spurious—had appeared among the female refugees who were flocking to the dance halls. Most of those young ladies, Shanghai gossip contended, felt no qualms about providing the sexual services Elizaveta refused. Although they would never say a word to the Howe family, the driver and the bodyguard would complain volubly to their intimates at the indignity of chauffeuring a White Russian who was literally down at the heels of her faded cream silk pumps. Elizaveta had spent almost a month at the nursing home in Jessfield Park convalescing from Spanish influenza. Before taking the train to Peking for the final year of his medical studies, Tommy had told Emily and Julia, "I saw no point in scaring you. It was touch and go for a while there. But she'll be all right now."

Emily glanced at the show window of Sincere's Department Store and observed, "I simply don't know what'll become of Elizaveta now. Do you know that you're now responsible for her? She'd be dead—or still very ill—if it weren't for you."

"I thought that was claptrap, the old China Hands' tale. You said it wasn't true that Chinese wouldn't save a suicidal person because they'd have to look after him the rest of their lives."

"And claptrap it is. Do you think a good Buddhist feels responsible all his life for the caged bird he sets free? . . . Julia, it's much simpler. It's just human to feel an obligation for someone you've helped. The greater the help, the more you'll care. And you practically single-handedly saved—"

"That's not true," Julia interrupted. "If it hadn't been for Tommy, she'd probably be dead. Tommy and you, too. I don't have a red cent to give her. You and Tommy, you've spent so generously."

"For your sake, Julie. Both of us did it for your sake."

"I don't see, Emmy, what you mean by—"

"For heaven's sake, Julie, do you think Tommy gave so much of his time and his money for Liz's sake?"

"Well, why else would he—"

"Now, Julie, don't be foolish. He did it because you care about Liz. Tommy won't say so, of course. He's too darned reserved—gets it from his English schooling. But his Chinese nature would probably have made him walk away from Liz and her problems if he hadn't been doing it for you. Remember the coolie on Avenue Joffre—how we had to goad Tommy into calling the Red Swastika Society."

"You mean you think Tommy—"

"Of course, you goose." Emily hesitated, pretending great interest in the brilliant silks spilling over an outdoor counter. "But . . ."

"But what? I really don't know how I feel about Tommy, but, naturally, I want to hear what you think about—"

"You don't necessarily want to hear what I've got to say." Emily was almost brusque. "Remember your cousin Bobby and me? Remember how disturbed your folks were? Well, Julie, I'd be very careful if I were you. You don't want to get *too* involved. There's no future in it, not with the Howes' pride of race."

"What about Richard?" Julia instinctively rebutted. "What about you and Richard?"

"That's different. Nobody could ever go overboard for Richard, especially not me. He's not the type to take seriously. And I'm not taking anyone seriously just now. Certainly *not* a foreigner, for heaven's sake. . . . But you're different from me. You take things too much to heart. Just don't take Tommy to heart."

"Why are you warning me off—for his sake or for mine?"

"For both your sakes," Emily said. "Tommy is complicated. He has at least two, maybe three, sides: doctor, patriot, and playboy. He's engrossed in medicine, and he's passionately involved in politics. . . . But, after twenty hours of duty in the wards, he can't just turn off and go to sleep. He has to wind down. Tommy relaxes from the long hours and the constant tension with a *very* active social life: the old 'wine, women, and song' routine. In Shanghai, as you know, that's very easy —particularly with a crony like Joshua Haleevie."

"Emmy, Tommy's certainly not a profligate. He's not a rake."

"Of course not. It's just his way of relaxing. Also, he's a Howe—with all that goes with it. Even if he weren't so good-looking, there'd be an endless supply of girls eager to help him. . . . He is my brother, and I love him dearly. But he's also a very, very complicated character. Julie, just enjoy your time in Shanghai—and forget about Tommy."

Christmas of 1921 was to be the first Christmas ever in Shanghai for Julia and the first for Emily in a decade. The flush of postwar prosperity was fading, and Christmas was an alien festival to the Chinese, who were the great majority of the population. Nonetheless, the holiday was becoming increasingly more commercial, which appealed to the commercial metropolis. Shanghai scintillated just before the Christmas of 1921.

Amid the glittering festivities, Rachel Haleevie's Thursday At Home was certain to be the most splendid. She insisted that it was not a Christmas party, since no Orthodox Jewish household would celebrate the Christian festival. Nonetheless, sparkling company and lavish hospitality would assuredly make Rachel's last At Home of the year the crown of the season.

Although Tommy had to spend the holiday working at the Peking Union Medical College Hospital, Julia reveled in the cosmopolitan gaiety. She was following Emily's advice not to take Tommy to heart, and she was by no means bereft of other admirers. She was particularly looking forward to Lady Haleevie's reception at Jade House, which was a microcosm of her beloved Shanghai.

Julia was intensely devoted to the international metropolis. Shanghai was unique. The great port on the Yangtze River, which drained the world's most heavily peopled basin, was not yet eight decades old. A stripling among great cities, it was as vain as a beautiful eighteen-year-old girl—and the most exciting place on earth. This Christmas Julia truly believed that Shanghai was as fascinating as its champions proclaimed it.

The International Settlement, they said, was a perfect example of many nations cooperating for the common welfare. Some 25,000 foreigners lived amid a total population of 800,000, which was constantly expanding because the Settlement welcomed a hundred nationalities, races, and religions. Some champions extolled Shanghai's harmony: the lower orders laboring dutifully, and the aristocrats governing selflessly for the general welfare. Some boasted with perverse pride that Shanghai was the world capital of vice, and that all its vaunted glories were based upon virtual slave labor. Yet even those detractors argued that the new League of Nations should model itself on the Settlement in order to assure worldwide cooperation, peace, and prosperity.

Sir Judah Haleevie's Jade House was the epicenter of that truly international community. No Chinese could epitomize Shanghai because Chinese always belonged first to China. Few foreigners epitomized the city—they owed their first allegiance to their own countries. The Haleevies were, however, Shanghai incarnate. They gave loyalty to no other place on earth, although they paid reverence to Jerusalem.

Since the doors of Jade House were open to all friends of the family and their friends, Joshua Haleevie had casually asked Julia and Emily to the At Home four days before Christmas. They were favorites of his mother, and they would in any event have been invited. It never occurred to Joshua that they would even dream of asking Elizaveta Yavalenka when he as casually added, "Do bring anyone else who'll be fun."

Elizaveta would most definitely not fit in. Joshua's relationship with the complex White Russian was itself complex. He had quickly forgiven her for the desolation—not to speak of the anger and the suspicion—

he had felt when she mysteriously disappeared for two months. He had, however, demanded in exasperation: "Why in the name of God didn't you come to me? Why did you go to Julia, which really meant going to Tommy Howe? I would have been delighted to help. I still am. In the future, just send me the bills."

"It's really quite simple, my darling," she had replied. "I'm already taking a great deal from you. You're giving me great pleasure. Also great affection, which is returned in full, though perhaps I shouldn't admit it. No, Joshua, I couldn't take any more from you. Roses and champagne, even caviar . . . yes, I'm delighted. But I can't accept shoes or potatoes —and definitely not medicines."

Julia and Emily, of course, did not know of that conversation. Nor did they know that Joshua had not asked Elizaveta to his mother's last At Home of 1921. More sensitive to emotional nuances than they had been when they arrived, they did realize that it might be embarrassing for Joshua to invite his mistress to the reception. (They were now also aware that mistresses were not found only in the novels of Alexander Dumas.) But, still naïve, they saw no reason why Elizaveta should not come to Jade House under their sponsorship. Rachel Haleevie need never know what Elizaveta was to her son Joshua; nor need she know about Elizaveta's temporary work as a dance hostess.

Wise, though precisely the same age as the young century, Elizaveta had weighed their invitation against Joshua's failure to mention the reception. She had vacillated for some time. Her reckless streak and her selfish calculation both impelled her to accept. Her aristocratic pride and her common sense both told her to stay away.

She did not wish to embarrass Joshua, although she was annoyed by his silence. She was, however, deeply curious regarding his background. She wondered about the formidable parents who could make a twenty-nine-year-old former captain of infantry sometimes behave as if he feared their disapproval above all else. Moved by impulse as much as curiosity or calculation, Elizaveta had finally decided to accompany Julia and Emily. Her outward self-assurance did not, however, completely conceal her trepidation.

Elizaveta's prejudices were, like herself, complex but flexible. She hated the Bolsheviks for their violent disruption of her life and for the cruel deaths they had inflicted upon so many of her friends and relatives. She knew that there were many Jews among the Bolsheviks. Yet her father, a leader of the liberal nobility, had taught her that it was not only stupid but self-damaging to despise an entire group of human beings. He had counseled her to scorn the contemptible and to esteem the admirable—regardless of their origins. Therefore, she did not hate all Jews.

Elizaveta had learned, however, that most Shanghai Jews hated Russians, particularly the Russian aristocracy. She was glad she did not call herself countess, not only because the title would seem ridiculous in her circumstances, but also because it would further inflame the Haleevies' prejudices. Yet even if they did not object to a White Russian aristocrat, Joshua's parents were unlikely to welcome a young woman of her own curious profession.

Nonetheless she decided to attend Lady Haleevie's At Home, after warning Julia and Emily that her presence might prove embarrassing. Their goodwill dismissed her fears, and she decided that, at worst, she might be uncomfortable. At best, she would enjoy herself—and learn much more about her lover.

Accordingly, she chose from her mother's wardrobe a dress of crimson satin. Although demurely cut, it accentuated her voluptuous figure, set off her porcelain-white skin, and emphasized her black hair.

Azaleas in porcelain jardinieres made the long corridors of Jade House glorious with their bronze, gold, and vermilion flowers. Scarlet poinsettias and winter-flowering cacti fringed with mauve flowerets adorned the dove-gray drawing room, where Rachel Haleevie was receiving her guests.

Elizaveta was shocked by her own response to the mansion. She resented the multiplicity of rooms, and the lavish furnishings struck her as vulgar. A moment later she realized with chagrin that she was envious—and intimidated.

Envy she might reasonably feel, in view of the tawdry surroundings in which she now lived. But why, Elizaveta wondered, should she be intimidated by a bourgeois mansion? She who had danced in the Winter Palace in St. Petersburg, she who had ridden for three days in a straight line without reaching the boundary of her father's estate.

But she would never again know the splendor that was her birthright. She would never again enjoy even bourgeois opulence like Jade House. She had fallen from the stars into the mire.

Her thoughts returned to the present when she saw Joshua among the throng in the drawing room. He barely nodded, but Lady Haleevie received Elizaveta warmly. That welcome was in part a tribute to Emily and Julia, who introduced her as their close friend. Rachel's blond head inclined toward Elizaveta's dark head when they sat side by side on the gold brocade sofa, talking of the glory of St. Petersburg, which the older woman had seen with her banker father decades earlier.

Unshed tears made Elizaveta's eyes glow. She mourned the days now forever lost, and sentimental Rachel Haleevie patted her hand consolingly.

Five years earlier, the adolescent Elizaveta would have resented that patronizing gesture from a bourgeois Jewess. In her troubled twenty-second year, Elizaveta clung for an instant to Rachel's soft white hand. When she rose to free the place beside the hostess for another guest, she marveled at the misgivings that had almost kept her from coming—and she responded eagerly to Lady Haleevie's warm invitation: "Do call again. Any time, not only Thursdays."

"You were right, and I was wrong," Elizaveta confided happily to Emily and Julia. "She's lovely, and she asked me to call again soon. Sometimes it's folly to be too wise."

"I still don't see why you were so worried," Julia observed. "You're not just presentable. You're beautiful. No wonder Lady Haleevie wants you to come again. You'll brighten up her soirées."

"You're both too generous." Elizaveta bestowed a delighted smile upon the crowded room. "But I wonder . . ."

"Wonder what, Liz?" Emily was impatient with Elizaveta's pensive pauses.

"She doesn't know where I'm working," Elizaveta declared lugubriously. "If she finds out . . ."

Impatient with Elizaveta's imaginary fears, Julia was pleased to see her uncle across the Victorian drawing room. Sir Judah Haleevie's conservatism had conspired with the mansion's great number of ballrooms, drawing rooms, libraries, conservatories, and reception halls to frustrate Lady Haleevie's feminine compulsion to redo Jade House completely. Ponderous tables and massive lamps with fringed shades still flanked overstuffed brocade sofas. That nineteenth-century decor was a curious background for sleek, glib, and charming John Pavernen, that quintessentially twentieth-century man. Most of the men and women at whom he smiled were also riding the buoyant tides of the 1920s. That decade, they already knew, was destined to transform not only Shanghai but the entire world, with its inventions and its enterprise.

"Why, Julia, honey," John Pavernen said. "I didn't realize you knew . . ."

Over his left shoulder, Elizaveta scornfully contemplated a plump Italian matron whose beaded dress was the same scarlet as her own. But Emily had noted the fleeting recognition that crossed John Pavernen's features when he saw Elizaveta. Julia, however, was too delighted at seeing her uncle, whom she adored as the archetype of the Shanghai go-getter, the man of the future.

". . . knew the Haleevies so well," John Pavernen improvised smoothly. "Emily, you're as lovely as ever. Won't you introduce me to your friend?"

Elizaveta smiled coolly and extended a hand tipped by crimson nails.

"Elizaveta? Do they call you Liz?" Jack Pavernen twinkled. "But Elizaveta Alex—an—an—dro . . . I can't say it!"

Elizaveta repeated her full name, rolling her *r*'s like a tragedienne of the Moscow Arts Theater, while Julia smiled at her uncle's drollery. Emily marveled that John Pavernen's overacting did not reveal to his niece that the young Russian woman and he had already met.

"Uncle Jack! Just the man I wanted to see!" Julia said. "Liz needs . . . would like to find work. I thought with the new project you might be able to find—"

"I'll see what I can do." He smiled. "Though Miss . . . Miss Yar—vava . . . lenka is mighty quiet. Is she really interested in a dull nine-to-five job?"

"I am interested in work, Mr. Pavernen." Elizaveta did not smile. "May I ring you?"

"Sure thing. Julie knows my number. In fact, she's *really* got my number. Makes me jump through hoops. Now, if you'll excuse me, ladies, I'll . . ."

"Isn't he a scream?" Julia asked proudly.

"A *bolshoi* scream," Elizaveta agreed gravely. "What's that word you taught me. Ah, yes, 'humdinger.' Your uncle is really a humdinger."

"You must be talking American." Joshua Haleevie appeared carrying a salver laden with silver goblets. "Now, I'm *not* offering you ladies eggnog. We *never* serve Christmas eggnog in this house. But the milk punch bears a certain resemblance."

"How lovely, eggnog . . ." Julia began, but yielded to Elizaveta, whose eyes were shining with nostalgia: "We always had eggnog for Christmas. With a nip of rum and a spoonful of brandy. It's five years since I tasted eggnog."

"Eggnog with rum and brandy?" Julia sipped inquisitively. "We never had liquor in our eggnog. It does taste . . ."

Julia's delighted discovery went unremarked, for Emily was staring speculatively at a newcomer. Jade House was an odd setting in which to see the favorite general of President Sun Yat-sen of the Canton Republic of China. But the red-haired American vice-consul Harrison

Parker Smythe III was unquestionably conversing with Chiang Kai-shek.

The general spoke no English, and his heavily accented Mandarin was virtually unintelligible. Emily revised her assessment of brash Harry Smyth and steered Julia toward the pair. Joshua linked his arm through Elizaveta's and led her away, saying, "I want you to meet some interesting people."

Dreading Elizaveta's inevitable humiliation at the hands of his beloved—and stringently conventional—mother, Joshua had originally retreated to the conservatory. Moved by concern for Elizaveta, he had returned, to find the two women taking obvious pleasure in each other's company. He concluded that he had once again underrated his flighty but kindly mother. Repentant and exuberant, he had then decided to introduce Elizaveta to the company.

"Herr Graf von Schweinitz and Madame Lollard. Mr. Chow, the match king, and General Li . . ."

Elizaveta filed every name away in her memory. Any one of them might, in the future, prove vital to her survival. She did not like calculating the potential usefulness of everyone she met, particularly every male. But it was necessary.

Nonetheless, Countess Elizaveta Alexandrovna Yavalenka, for the first time since fleeing Vladivostok fourteen months earlier, considered the possibility that she might be able to lead a normal life. Not the splendid existence of the Russian aristocracy, which had been eclipsed forever by the Bolsheviks. Perhaps, however, a normal bourgeois life, a comfortable and decent life.

The Christmas spirit formally repudiated by the Haleevies was palpable in the overheated room, where a string quartet alternately played arrangements from Bach cantatas and popular tunes such as "Dardanella." The glow of candles and the fragrance of flowers contrasted poignantly with the glare of neon and the reek of cheap perfume, amid which Elizaveta worked.

She had been welcomed warmly to Jade House. Lady Haleevie had offered feminine solidarity, rather than the humiliation Elizaveta had feared. Perhaps, she mused, Shanghai was not entirely a heartless wasteland.

John Pavernen she had snubbed automatically, though she had immediately known his face. She now remembered that she had met him in a sumptuous apartment on Szechwan Road; the cocaine-and-roulette party had been attended by eminently respectable men—and not a single respectable woman. He had obviously recognized her, but

Elizaveta knew that Julia would plead her case with him. Why should she not take from John Pavernen the respectable job she had so long sought in vain—and, at the least, gain time to contemplate her future?

Rachel Haleevie's unaffected welcome had made Elizaveta feel she was not irretrievably lost in the twilight world. When John Pavernen virtually promised to find work for her she envisioned a new life. When she left the party with Emily and Julia she was bubbling with gaiety.

Her friends were going to a pre-Christmas dinner with those devout Methodists the Soongs. Elizaveta decided to ride with them in the emerald-green Rolls-Royce. She chatted brightly, repeatedly reminding the delighted Julia to keep after John Pavernen.

After they parted, Elizaveta's volatile Russian spirits still soared. The job was already a reality in her heated imagination. Her exhilaration was not diminished by the cold rickshaw ride to her dingy home at the wrong end of Kiangse Road.

After climbing five flights of stairs, Elizaveta found the door half open to the small room her landlady optimistically called a studio apartment. His navy blue cashmere overcoat still buttoned, Joshua Haleevie sat in the dilapidated wing chair beside the convertible studio couch. He had lit the gas fire, which was fed by a coin-operated meter, and the dank chill was just yielding to the jagged blue flames.

His eyes gazed an instant longer into those flames, reflecting their somber shadows. When he looked up, Elizaveta saw that his lips were compressed as if guarding a secret. A frown line dividing his dark eyebrows, he stared at her and smiled without joy.

"What a delightful surprise!" Elizaveta was exuberant. "I've got a bottle of vodka somewhere . . . and a smidgin of smoked sturgeon. Do take your coat off, my brave captain."

"This is not really a social visit, Elizaveta." He dutifully hung his coat in the minuscule foyer. "It's more of an antisocial visit."

"And what does that mean, my darling?" She was still joyous and kittenish. "This uneducated Ukrainian peasant girl does not know such an English word."

"Harry Smythe let it slip. Unintentionally, I think. He told my mother where we'd met you. And she—"

"And she?" Elizaveta stood stock-still amid her shattered illusions. "What did she say?"

"She said . . . she said she was very sorry . . . in fact, distressed . . . but she had no choice. She wanted to write you a note. But I said I'd come myself. Well, you can guess . . ."

"I can—assuredly. But since you've come all this way, you might as well tell me. What is Lady Haleevie's message?"

"Mother wants you to know she liked you enormously—and she was looking forward to seeing you again. She had thought of helping you find some congenial position. But . . . it's nothing personal, she stresses. Under other circumstances, she would like nothing better than to have you as a friend. She may still be able to help you find a position. But . . . but she . . ."

"But, Joshua?" she probed. "Be done with your 'buts'!"

"But there can, of course, be no question of your coming to Jade House again. She regrets it, but she must make that clear."

"Why this great hurry to tell me, Joshua?" she flared. "Apparently you couldn't wait to rush over here to give me the news!"

"I didn't want you to be embarrassed further," he said. "I didn't want you to make plans . . . to talk about seeing us. I didn't want you to be shown up for bragging and fantasies."

Her emotions oscillating wildly, she said, "You do have a good heart, my dashing captain, don't you? I'm grateful."

He stared at the threadbare carpet and stammered: "Of course I'll do everything I can to help you. My God, I had no idea you lived so . . . so meanly. I'll push Pavernen about a job for you. Or find you something myself, I promise. Whatever I can do—"

"I really don't think there's any need." Elizaveta neatly tidied up the rubble of her illusions. "I'll make my own way, thank you. Be assured that I can. I'll find myself a protector—some good and rich man. But only one—one at a time. Nothing to do with you and me, though. I still feel about you . . ."

Joshua stood mute as she locked the door of the studio apartment. Reaching behind her, she undid the topmost of the hooks that fastened her scarlet dress. She then turned her back to him.

"Well, then," she said gaily, "be a dear and undo me."

"For God's sake, Elizaveta!" he protested. "Don't be mad. For my sake! I promise I'll try again. I'll definitely find you something. . . . In time, maybe, even we—"

"Maybe nothing," she said, laughing. "Just undo me, please. It's what I want, I assure you."

APRIL 23, 1922

The distant knocking troubled Julia's sleep but did not quite awaken her. She pulled the pillow over her head but could not shut it out. When the din persisted, she resignedly groped for her cotton dressing gown. Her eyelids reluctantly parted to the bright dawn.

An instant later her green eyes opened wide in surprise, and she hurriedly slipped the dressing gown over her lace nightdress. She was not in her familiar bedroom in Harmony Hall, which she had occupied since her arrival in Shanghai. Taking in the sparse furnishings and the sloping ceiling, she remembered. For the first time she was living in a home that was all her own. Like so much else, she owed it to her friendship with Emily Howe.

Tommy had offered Julia his loft-apartment when she felt she could no longer impose on his parents' hospitality. His mother had urged Julia to stay, delighted at having not one but two daughters in the house. Despite her affection for Eurydice Howe, Julia pointed out that she was no longer a lady of leisure. She could not live so far from her place of employment, in John Pavernen's office in unfashionable Hongkew, north of Soochow Creek.

When his mother left the room shaking her head sadly, Tommy had suggested, "Julie, why don't you take on my attic? I won't be living there. I'll be in Peking for another year, and then interning at Shanghai General Hospital. The rent is very low because it belongs to my father. Fortunately, he can hardly remember every property he owns. I fixed it with old Lau, his office manager. Do take it, Julie. I'd hate to see the flat go to waste."

Although the alarm clock on her bedside table read 6:45, the knocking resounded through the loft. Julia's mules glided across the teak floorboards of the cavernous sitting room. She pushed back the folding steel grate and mechanically opened the bolts, deadlocks, and chains that secured the front door.

All those safeguards were not really necessary. Foreigners were virtually sacrosanct in the Settlement—unless they sought out trouble. The ordinances of the Shanghai Municipal Council, enforced by the foreign-officered police, ensured her security. She felt no apprehension about dawn visitors, although the building was far downtown at the junction of Kiukiang and Honan roads, just around the corner from commercial Nanking Road.

"Dieh-wah gong-si . . ." a male voice called. "Telephone company for installation."

Tightening her sash, Julia swung the door open. Three smiling men in the uniform of the Shanghai Telephone Company proffered identification cards bearing their pictures and their descriptions in both Chinese and English.

The United States was efficient, but even Americans did not get such cheerful service early on a Sunday. Some detractors said the Chinese could never master modern inventions but would always require supervision by mechanically minded foreigners. Others said the Chinese were clever as monkeys. Show them how, and they'd do the job perfectly ever after—as long as there was no need to make changes. Julia herself found the Chinese ingenious and adaptable, both willing and hard-working. The old China Hands said she was blinded by a newcomer's enthusiasm—and would learn better. It was only monkey cleverness.

"Not monkeys, but donkeys," Tommy had once mused. "Awkward, intelligent donkeys—not graceful, stupid horses. Like donkeys, Chinese are hellishly independent. We won't work unless we know why—unless we're decently rewarded. That's why it's so hard to govern the Chinese."

Julia smiled at her fond memories of Tommy, whom she had seen only once in the past six months, when he returned to Shanghai for a few days at the Chinese Lunar New Year. She showed the workmen the corner where she wanted the telephone. When she returned to her tiny bedroom to dress, they were pounding again. She had assumed that laying telephone wires was a relatively silent task, but the din sounded as if they were tearing down the walls.

She emerged into clouds of plaster dust, through which wafted the beguiling smells of bacon and coffee. Her new amah had evidently arrived on the heels of the workmen. Lao Zee, who had been introduced by Emily's old nursemaid, Ven Jyeh, was preparing fruit, toast, and scrambled eggs with bacon. A straw suitcase and a cloth-wrapped parcel lay at her feet in the small kitchen, but she was already wearing the amah's uniform of white tunic and black trousers.

"No pay Missy porridge and kippahs. More bettah, Missy not eat so muchee," Lao Zee declared. "Fat Missy nevah catch man. Europ'en mastah very funny. Chinese man very much like fat lady."

The amah had taken command. Julia contentedly watched her bully the telephone men and tell the delivery coolies where to place the furniture. The Shanghai Secondhand Store, which paid no heed to Sunday, boasted in advertisements that it "commanded the resources of over one hundred of the leading pawnshops, thus guaranteeing low prices and high quality."

Emily had, however, declared that the prices were outrageous, only for credulous foreigners. Emily loved shopping expeditions, but Julia hated the endless bargaining. Emily was alternately very Chinese or very emancipated. Predicting her reactions was like picking up quicksilver from a broken thermometer.

Lao Zee eagerly trotted to answer the ringing telephone, but returned to announce, "Only silly testee." For half an hour, the instrument pealed at intervals. Julia was surprised when the gray-haired foreman told her in English, "Mr. John Pavernen has rung through. He would be glad to talk with Miss Julia Pavernen."

Marveling at that formal summons, Julia saw with surprise that the sitting room wall was again intact, the telephone wires completely hidden. The foreman waved her to the extension in the bedroom.

She dubiously lifted the candlestick base with the conical mouthpiece. Although invented forty-five years earlier and developed rapidly to fill the military needs during the Great War, Alexander Graham Bell's telephone was still largely used in offices. It was rarely seen in homes. Ladies and gentlemen would never prefer the telephone to handwritten notes for social communication.

"Julie, is that you?" John Pavernen's baritone crackled metallically. "How are you, honey? Snug in your new little nest?"

"Hello, Uncle Jack. It's lovely. They just put the telephone in. You're the very first caller."

"I just thought I'd give you a ring. Now that you're working for me, you've got to have a phone. See how convenient it is?"

"A little early to tell, I'd say."

"Julie, honey, a message just came to my cable address: 'Happy Easter darling stop when planning come home question mark all our love mother and dad.' You want to answer? The messenger's waiting."

"Not now, Uncle Jack," Julia replied after a pause. "I'll send an answer later, when I've had time to think. I don't want to go home—not for a while, anyway. But I'm not sure how to tell them."

"Whatever you want. Just as long as you don't leave me in the lurch. I'll try to get to your housewarming party, but I've got a big deal cooking."

"On Easter Sunday? Well, I guess that's what it takes. Oh, Uncle Jack, what about Elizaveta? It's been a long time since—"

"I haven't forgotten. I can find something for her in real estate. Even more Russians'll be coming soon—and they can't *all* be broke."

"Thanks a million, Uncle Jack. You're wonderful."

Replacing the earpiece on its wishbone rest, she noticed the clutter of valises and trunks in the bedroom. Lao Zee would make short work of reducing that chaos to order. Julia grinned in self-derision. A year earlier she would have cleared up the mess herself. She could almost hear her mother's voice: "Darling, you can't leave your room like this. Ladies just don't."

Julia felt guilty about her parents. She knew how much they missed her, and she certainly no longer resented their having sent her away to the George School that year when she was ten and her father was so ill. But, whenever she thought of going back to Plattsburg and leaving Shanghai, her heart sank.

Now that she was supporting herself, she would certainly stay another year. After a year or so, some time in the blur of the future, she would definitely go back.

She was eager to learn more about China, which was Tommy's country. Above all, she wanted to know more about him. Exactly how did his mind work? Was he really shy or was he aloof because of his Chinese heritage? It was just as well that he was in Peking. His continued absence was giving her time to sort out her own feelings.

Dissatisfied with the cotton dress she had flung on earlier, Julia dropped to her knees before the big steamer trunk. Her mother would hardly have approved of her blowing her last penny on new clothes after John Pavernen hired her for his new company, JPEnterprises. Tumbling garments out of the drawers, Julia rose clasping a froth of pale green satin. Her new lounging pyjamas, which she had designed herself, were more sophisticated than the green-beaded black silk pyjamas she had worn last summer. The cuffs and the stand-up collar were demurely banded with embroidered asters and butterflies, and the pale green shade contrasted provocatively with her tawny hair.

Julia no longer felt guilty at applying a film of face powder and a touch of lip rouge, although further self-adornment would, at twenty-one, be not only excessive but unattractive. Her forte was simplicity. She closed the silver clasp of a chunky, old ivory bracelet, and, after inserting a Chesterfield cigarette into her six-inch ivory holder, was ready to face the day.

She abruptly dropped the holder, clapped her hand to her mouth, and looked fearfully at her bedside clock. In haste, she pulled a linen duster over her lounging pyjamas, jammed a felt cloche on her head, and raced down the stairs.

Unfortunately, the elevator was again out of order. Fortunately, a public rickshaw was passing outside. She promised the coolie an additional thirty cents to hurry and sat back, hoping she would not be too late for Easter services.

Joshua Haleevie's runabout gleamed before the door when Julia returned home shortly after noon. Behind it, the Haleevies' seven-passenger Marmon stood at the curb like a pearl-gray ocean liner at a wharf. Perhaps Joshua was actually enacting his fantasy; perhaps the limousine carried a footstool for the convenience of female passengers. The enormous Marmon certainly carried his house-warming presents.

Smiling in anticipation, Julia climbed the stairs. She was tired, and her feet hurt. She had failed to find a rickshaw to carry her back from church. She was perspiring because she could not take off the linen duster that concealed her frivolous pyjamas. That display would have offended the pious ladies in their Easter bonnets and new dresses.

Besides, she might have been mistaken on the street for a dance-hall hostess returning from an assignation. Julia had learned much during the nine months since her arrival—not all of it pleasant. She felt quite removed from the naïve girl who had disembarked from the *Empress of Australia.*

When she opened the door, she heard a catchy melody. Joshua was cranking a Victrola, and a black Bakelite disc was pouring Cole Porter's brassy "China Doll" through its curved horn. Elegant in a blue linen Norfolk jacket and wide-legged flannel trousers, Joshua ceremoniously kissed her on both cheeks. Although she would have been shocked by that effusive greeting nine months earlier, Julia now laughed in delight.

Her small head balanced on her swan neck, Elizaveta threw her arms around both her lover and her friend. Before she was enveloped, Julia took in the long white kaftan crossed by mock bandoliers and cut close to Elizaveta's voluptuous figure. Red half-boots and a karakul hat completed the image of a daredevil Cossack.

"I weep that it is not Russian Easter!" Elizaveta parodied the Slavic melancholy that sometimes overcame her. "But I'll try to be jolly. I know you'll be very happy in your new flat, Julie."

"Though I says it as shouldn't, we're gonna make you happy, luv." Joshua was an unconvincing Cockney. "Lookee there!"

Beneath the high north window were stacked ten cases of Pommerey champagne. On the long table a silver tray stood laden with smoked salmon and sturgeon. Julia smelled the two delicacies she liked best. The braised meat aroma was Russian *zakuski,* small horns of pastry. The scent of sweet vinegar and ginger heralded the miniature purses of translucent dough the Shanghainese called "little steamer dumplings." The Haleevies' chauffeur emerged from the minuscule kitchen with a salver of fresh caviar and buckwheat blinis. Behind him, another manservant carried a block of ice that encased a bottle of vodka.

"I didn't expect *this* when you said to leave the arrangements to you," Julia protested. "It's just too much . . ."

"Never too much! Never!" Elizaveta's normally crisp English was today furry with Slavic consonants. "It is men's duty to give—lavishly! It is women's duty to enjoy—delightfully! Never say *too* much. Only drink and eat, laugh, and sing—and *drink*!"

Since it was obvious that both her friends had already done so, Julia lifted a thimble-glass of vodka.

"And also eat!" Elizaveta admonished. "If you take a little bite with every sip, vodka will make you merry. If you don't, you'll become depressed and weepy and—"

"—Russian!" Joshua interjected. "Mad Russian!"

Julia wondered again whether Tommy could possibly be right about the son of the Jewish multimillionaire. He had confided his suspicion that Joshua was "a big gun in the intelligence game in Shanghai." But Joshua's antics made him appear no more than a feckless and overprivileged playboy. Perhaps that was the idea.

She also wondered for the hundredth time why Tommy was so determinedly absenting himself from Shanghai. Perhaps it was, as he had said, because he was so busy preparing for the examination that would qualify him as a doctor. Perhaps he too was, struggling against feelings he feared were, at the least, unwise. Yet what they felt for each other was, of course, not love but just great affection. How could they possibly love each other?

Whatever it might be, it was not Julia's ideal of a grand passion. Yet she felt wonderful when he was there—and she felt a little lost without him.

The footsteps on the stairs were muffled by Boris Chaliapin singing the clock aria from *Boris Gudounov* through the Victrola's scalloped horn. Hearing Harry Smythe shouting greetings from the hall, Julia took Elizaveta's arm.

"Come see my new dress," she invited. "Before too many arrive."

"But while she can still see." Joshua grinned. "I'll hold the fort while you two exchange the secrets of the boudoir"

"We had a couple of bottles of champagne before we came," Elizaveta confessed as the bedroom door closed. "Now where's that new dress? Your taste is really improving, pet. Those pyjamas are fabulous."

"It's not about dresses, Liz. Uncle Jack says he can find a job for you. Also, I thought you might like to move into my spare bedroom." Tactfully, Julia did not stress the contrast between the loft-apartment and Elizaveta's sordid little bed-sitting room. "As a favor. I could use a little help with expenses."

"A job? What kind of job?"

"Something to do with real estate. Selling and renting houses and apartments, mainly to Russians."

"I shall talk with him," Elizaveta said judiciously. "But I think not. I do not know that I shall have time."

"Time? Are you that busy? With what?"

"Many things, Julie, many things. Life is not all champagne and caviar. . . . Also I have the most wonderful plans. Some day I shall tell you, some day soon."

"If you really don't need the job anymore, I'm happy for you. But do think about it. And what about moving in? It would be fun, wouldn't it?"

Elizaveta Alexandrovna Yavalenka gazed at Julia Pavernen. Her full lower lip trembled with suppressed laughter, and her thick lashes veiled her midnight-blue eyes.

"I'm touched by your offer," she finally said. "It could be great fun. But I'm afraid you'd cramp my style."

Believing that reluctance was mere politeness, Julia persisted. Elizaveta rejected her entreaties but would not explain how her style would be cramped.

"Julie, there's no point in going over it again," she finally said. "And I want a drink. Anyway, I like my present way of life. I wouldn't change it for the world."

Hurt by Elizaveta's rejection, Julia nonetheless bit back the obvious retort. The wild Russian would have to change her way of life after Joshua proposed, as he obviously would, and they were married.

The loft was filling up with guests. Julia shook hands with Harry Smythe, who introduced a fluffy Belgian blonde. She offered her cheek to Richard Hollings. The Englishman's dark eyes searched the room, and for an instant his flat-planed face was desolate. Richard's occasional sadness, Julia and Emily firmly believed, arose from the horrors he had seen as a lieutenant on the Italian front. He, however, insisted that he'd had a "cushy job in intelligence." Finding that Emily was not present, he pushed a lock of hair back from his forehead and asked, "Who is that big Chinese chap?"

Following Richard's gaze, Julia saw a large man in a blue cotton tunic sipping champagne under the north window. He must have come in while she was in the bedroom with Elizaveta. His shrewd eyes and heavy cheekbones were tantalizingly familiar, as was his inherent authority. Still trying to remember him, Julia saw that he was cradling a black-and-white puppy in his left arm.

When he bowed in greeting, Julia remembered: he was Chang Kuo-tao, Tommy Howe's mysterious radical friend. She had met him at that Federation of Students meeting where the zealot in homespun, whose name she could not remember, made such a long speech.

"Hsia Tan-ssu Hsien-sheng chiao wo lai kao-su . . ."

The newcomer was clearly perplexed by her obvious incomprehension of the tide of Mandarin. But Julia, who recognized Tommy's name, Hsia Tan-ssu, begged Chang Kuo-tao in her hesitant Shanghainese to continue. He replied in more fluent Shanghainese, and somehow they understood each other.

He had, he said, seen Tommy in Peking on his way back from Moscow. Moscow? Julia wondered what on earth a young Chinese labor leader was doing in the Bolshevik capital.

The puppy, he said, was Tommy's housewarming present. Although a nuisance on the train, it was really a good little dog. Lion dogs were prized as temple guardians in their native Tibet, he said, though they did not grow very big. The puppy's name was Tang Jo-wang. When she took it in her arms, a pink tongue kissed her fingers.

"Take care," Chang Kuo-tao warned. "And before I forget, I've also got a letter for you."

She put the puppy down just in time, for a small puddle appeared on the floorboards. Lifting the dog again as a clucking Lao Zee appeared with a damp cloth, Julia hugged him to her bosom. He was a present from Tommy, the first present Tommy had ever given her. Apologizing to Chang Kuo-tao, she tucked the puppy under one arm. With Tommy's letter clutched firmly in her hand, Julia returned to the privacy of her bedroom.

The letter's mere existence was almost as important as whatever it might say. Tommy had previously written her a few brief, businesslike notes, mostly about the apartment. He had never before sent her a letter that crackled within its brown envelope, thick with many sheets bearing his words in his own hand.

"Julia, my dear," it began, which was a great improvement over his previous prosaic salutation: "Dear Julia." After that promising beginning, she saw as she read rapidly, the letter rather went downhill. She reminded herself that it was the letter itself that really mattered, not necessarily what it said, and she raced through two pages describing his hectic schedule. Was that long description not a roundabout apology for his protracted absence and his meager communication?

Although her obligation as hostess demanded that she return to her guests, Julia had to read the letter through. Yes, that was better. He wrote that he hoped to see her soon and that June was only a little distant from April. He wanted to see her as much, it seemed, as she wanted to see him. And instead of his previous "Sincerely," or just plain "Yours," he closed the letter with "Fondly."

Julia lifted the puppy and looked into his melting brown eyes. She hugged him again before putting him back on the floor, which, she saw with a smile, Lao Zee had already covered with old newspapers. Tommy's gift would obviously be cherished.

Reluctantly tucking the letter back into its envelope, Julia hesitated for an instant. Even more reluctantly parting from the letter, she put it into her top drawer under her stockings, where she would see it every day. Julia knew she would always treasure that letter—although she would certainly not allow herself to become too fond of Tommy. For both their sakes, things could not go much further. Not, of course, that there was the slightest danger.

Eyes shining, Julia returned to the sitting room. Her gaze instinctively sought the big man called Chang Kuo-tao. When she saw him standing alone under the window, she resumed her conversation with Tommy's messenger.

He had, he said, just been to Moscow to attend the First Congress of the Toilers of the East. Replying without hesitation to her direct questions, he pronounced that pretentious name in clumsy English. He was, he added, the delegate of the All-China Secretariat of Labor, though himself no *toiler* (again an English word), but only a *clerk* (once again English). Neither secret nor specifically Bolshevik, since Dr. Sun Yat-sen's National People's Party had also attended, the conference had launched a "campaign to unite the exploited masses of Asia."

They parted with mutual congratulations on having been able to communicate so clearly. Chang Kuo-tao said he hoped to see her again. Perhaps she would have time to teach a few hours at the foreign languages school his group was organizing.

"And what group is that?" she asked.

"Just the Secretariat," he replied promptly. "The All-China Secretariat of Labor. I'm the director."

"Oh," Julia said, "I thought I'd heard of another organization—a political party?"

"Ah-la fu hsiu-deh!" he replied in emphatic Shanghainese. "I don't know anything about that!"

Housewifely instinct drove Julia into the kitchen, but Lao Zee expelled her, declaring, "More bettah Missy go talkee guests. More bettah you catch small piece drink and make merry. But no wantchee drink too much!"

The loft no longer appeared cavernous now that it was filled with chattering guests. After pushing her hair into place, Julia lit the Chesterfield in her ivory holder and rejoined her guests.

Richard Hollings smiled at her fleetingly. His gaze then returned to the front door, where Emily Howe was just entering. She removed her black silk coat, revealing a striking blue crepe *cheongsam.* Richard's eyes glowed, and he pushed through the throng.

Julia knew the Chinese brother and sister who had come with Emily. T. V. Soong wore a businessman's double-breasted blue suit, and tortoise-shell glasses were balanced on his broad nose. Mayling Soong was even more striking than Emily. Her face was heart-shaped, and her complexion justified the cliché "skin like a camellia petal." A red felt pillbox perched saucily on her glossy hair, but her green silk *cheongsam,* although nipped slightly at the waist, was too loose to show off her trim figure.

"Julie, you remember Mayling Soong, don't you?" Emily asked. "And her big brother Tze-ven? Everybody calls him T.V."

Richard Hollings whispered urgently into Emily's ear, and she allowed him to lead her away.

"How are you enjoying Shanghai now, Miss Pavernen?" Mayling Soong asked.

"I adore Shanghai. It's wonderful. I just wish my Shanghainese was better. I'm studying hard, but . . ."

"We prefer to speak English." T. V. Soong's American accent was minutely marred by slurred consonants. "I was at Harvard when May was at Wellesley. My sisters and I always speak English to each other."

Mayling added: "It's just natural. We're all American-educated. Ailing, my oldest sister, we call Nanny. And Chingling—Madam Sun Yat-sen—is Rosamonde. I'm only Mayling, little May, the youngest."

"A friend," Julia began, "has just sent me a puppy . . ."

"Hiya, T.V. How you doing?" Vice-consul Harry Smythe offered a tray of drinks. "Miss Soong . . . Mayling . . . how are you?"

"Yes, Miss Pavernen?" Mayling ignored Harry. "You were saying?"

"The puppy, he's adorable. From Tibet, I'm told. He's called Tang Jo-wang."

"What a funny name for a dog, unless . . ." Mayling almost giggled.

". . . unless he's a religious dog." T.V. completed her thought.

"A religious dog?" Julia repeated blankly. "Well, they do say the lion dogs guard the temples in Tibet."

"Lamaseries," Harry Smythe corrected automatically. "They have lamaseries in Tibet, not temples."

"Also temples, Mr. Smythe," Mayling said with some asperity. "My brother can tell us about the name."

"Tang Jo-wang is the Chinese name of a German Jesuit who came to Peking in the seventeenth century," T.V. explained. "He was a great teacher of science, theology—and gunnery. His original name was very long: Johann Adam Schall von Bell."

"I'll call the puppy Adam," Julia decided. "I could hardly call him Father Schall."

"How come you're so up on this Father Schall, T.V.?" Harry Smythe's carrot hair gleamed brassy in the afternoon sunlight. "Never heard of him myself."

"Then he couldn't be important, Mr. Smythe!" T. V. Soong pointedly turned to address Julia. "An ancestor on our mother's side was Schall's greatest convert. He was Hsü Kwang-chi, baptized Paul Hsü. He became grand chancellor in the Ming Dynasty. Prime minister we'd say today."

"But you're not Catholics, are you?" Harry Smythe apparently did not know that he had been snubbed; insensitivity was a decided advantage for a diplomat. "I know your family's not."

"You *are* well informed, Mr. Smythe." T.V.'s distaste for Harry Smythe was tempered by his respect for the brash American's official position. "We Soongs are all Protestants. So are my brothers-in-law. Rosamonde's husband, Dr. Sun Yat-sen, was converted in Hawaii. Ailing's husband, H. H. Kung, is the seventy-fifth lineal descendant of the Sage Confucius. He doesn't call himself duke, though it's the Kungs' hereditary title. He's prouder of being a Yale Ph.D."

Julia decided some Chinese really did worship their ancestors. T. V. Soong obviously worshipped not only his own ancestors but the ancestors of his brothers-in-law.

"Not very Christian, though, cozying up the Bolsheviks, is it T.V.?" Harry Smythe was unimpressed. "If Sun Yat-sen's such a good Christian, how come he's hobnobbing with the Comintern's agents?"

"You know, Harry," T.V. replied candidly, "Socialism may be necessary for China."

"What do you expect?" Mayling demanded. "England and France aren't interested in helping the president. Even America won't help. Dr. Sun Yat-sen stands for progress, but only the Bolsheviks are willing to help him."

"Don't give up hope," Harry Smythe advised. "Some Americans are certainly trying to help Dr. Sun. Some also have a lot of faith in General Chiang Kai-shek."

"He *is* a remarkable man," Mayling said softly. "I also have much faith in General Chiang."

The party was thinning out. Returning to her bedroom to repair her makeup, Julia recalled Emily's tart observation: "The worst thing about being the hostess is having to wait for the last guest to leave before you can take your shoes off."

Julia was still enjoying the party. Although she felt delightfully uninhibited, even exuberant, she was not even slightly tiddly. What's more, she could prove it. Out of all the bantering conversations, the laughter, and the jokes, she remembered best her serious discussions with Chang Kuo-tao and T. V. Soong.

Before rejoining her guests, she burrowed under her stockings and found Tommy's letter. Yes, as she had thought, he said he was working very hard. Although he could not quite tell her outright that he missed her, he said that he was "greatly looking forward" to seeing her. From the reticent Tommy that was virtually a declaration.

She was exhilarated, but she was also afraid. Telling herself there was no harm in a little flirtation, Julia tucked the angelically drowsy Adam under her arm and returned to the loft.

"Where's Liz?" she asked Emily. "I want to propose a toast—I want to thank Joshua and Liz for the champagne and the food . . . for making this such a wonderful housewarming."

"They asked me to say good-bye for them," Emily replied, and behind her Julia heard an unidentifiable male voice murmur: "Elizaveta Alexandrovna Yavalenka, the tart with the heart *for* gold."

She was, however, too tired and too happy to take that remark as anything but a joke in poor taste.

Coming back to Harmony Hall always cast a faint shadow over Emily's normally blithe spirits. The ceremonial unlocking of the ponderous iron gates was positively medieval, as was the ritual search of the emerald-green Rolls-Royce, although a bodyguard always rode beside the chauffeur. The dark figures among the bright rhododendrons of mid-May were like henchmen guarding the castle of an evil baron in the Dark Ages. Accustomed to the casual freedom of America, Emily felt stifled by her own family home.

That constraint was not only physical. Her father was forward-looking, though canny, in business; he was enlightened in politics, as demonstrated by his strong support of Dr. Sun Yat-sen; and he was intellectually progressive—or he would not have sent his two youngest children abroad for education. Donald Howe was, nonetheless, conservative regarding his family. Like Confucius twenty-five hundred years earlier, he believed that the cornerstone of a moral and harmonious social order must be children's unquestioning obedience to their parents —no matter what their ages. As the gravel of the driveway crunched under the tires of the Rolls, Emily felt that she was returning to a prison with two grim warders.

Yet she truly loved her parents, whom she had so recently rediscovered. Why, she wondered, did she persist in deceiving them? Was it really necessary to pretend that Richard Hollings did not exist? The answer was instantaneous: certainly—if she was to continue seeing the Englishman.

Why, then, was she so determined to continue seeing him? Although he was very attractive, she knew she could let him go any time she chose without feeling any great pangs. She would miss him all right, but as she had assured Julia, theirs was hardly a grand passion.

Moreover, Emily asked herself, why was she attracted to a foreigner? Despite her superficial Westernization, she knew she could never marry a foreigner. Nor was Richard likely to ask her.

Perhaps, she speculated, that was his greatest attraction. He could not constrain her because he, no more than she, would ever even think of marriage. Above all, she was proving her independence by seeing him —precisely *because* her parents would disapprove. Freedom, not Richard, was the true goal of her actions.

Freedom, Emily concluded, for its own sake, as well as freedom to fulfill her personal aspirations: to fight to transform China for the common good and to liberate China's enslaved women. She would no more give up her individual liberty to Richard than she would submit to the silken bonds of tradition.

Despite her grim resentment of the oppression suffered by China's women, Emily's temperament was optimistic. Recovering from her depression while the Rolls traced the winding driveway to the stone tower of the reception hall, she was again cheerful when she alighted with an armful of textbooks. Visiting Julia in the loft-apartment on Kiukiang Road always left her in high spirits. The black-and-white puppy was also comical, although his mistress was perturbed because at three months he was as big as a full-grown spaniel. Adam somehow possessed the same naïve and good-hearted enthusiasm that made Julia a delight.

Dedicated to her new job, Julia was almost ludicrously secretive about her uncle's business. Her dedication would have kept the former roommates from meeting as frequently as they had in the past if John Pavernen had not decreed that Julia must continue her study of Shanghainese for the benefit of JPEnterprises. Eager to regain command of her native tongue, Emily was happy to join those private lessons—and to escape the confinement of Harmony Hall.

The tutor's rudimentary English made her assistance essential, and her advanced lessons did not interfere with Julia's elementary lessons. Moreover, Venerable Master, as they addressed the forty-two-year-old scholar, had opened a door on an exciting prospect for herself. He contributed popular articles on historical and literary themes to a number of the hundred and forty-four newspapers and magazines Greater Shanghai's two and a half million Chinese insatiably consumed. At his suggestion, she had written about her experiences in America for the Chinese-language *Women's Weekly*.

Venerable Master's enthusiasm was only in part inspired by the fees he received for placing the articles and polishing her writing. He truly had great faith in her. With his encouragement, Emily was rediscovering her joy in telling stories.

After starting with fairy tales for children, she was now writing light romances. Not daring to publish under her own name, she was gratified by the growing popularity of her pen name. Je Hsin, literally "Hot-Hearted," really meant "Enthusiastic."

Venerable Master's enthusiasm diminished slightly when the monthly *China Today* asked his protegée to write regularly on the plight of women. Her increasingly strident tone distressed that gentleman-scholar of the old school.

She was not a gentleman, Emily replied reasonably to his objections, and not much of a scholar either. He should therefore not expect from her the literary grace of a gentleman-scholar. Besides, she added, Chinese of the old school required of their women fecundity, subservience, chastity—and no more. Having developed that theme in her latest article for *China Today* earlier that afternoon, Emily had taken mildly malicious pleasure in watching Venerable Master sputter with indignation while he dutifully—and scrupulously—corrected her prose.

Stepping out of the Rolls into the late afternoon sunshine, Emily was a little ashamed of enjoying her tutor's distress. Nevertheless, men like him—well-meaning, decent men—would have to be compelled to change their attitudes radically before China's downtrodden women could lift up their heads. His anger was actually encouraging; it proved that her arguments were hitting home. She was, however, only fighting the opening battles of what would clearly be an arduous and protracted campaign to emancipate the female sex.

In her preoccupation, Emily was startled when the door of the circular reception hall was opened by Old Woo himself. The six-foot-two majordomo was imposing with the green-and-gold seal of the Howe family on the breast of his white long-gown, which was only a shade lighter than his silver hair. Born into the service of the Howes, Old Woo would condescend to welcome an ambassador or a governor—if he approved of them. Even the master of Harmony Hall did not expect his majordomo to greet him in the reception hall every day.

"Yuelin, Yuelin Siu-jyeh . . ." Old Woo's tone was portentous. "Emily, Miss Emily, your parents are waiting in the library. The master wishes you to come immediately."

Emily's heart skipped a beat. Something fearful must have happened in the few hours she had been away. Perhaps Tommy was injured—or worse. Perhaps one of her parents was critically ill. Perhaps the Howe enterprises had encountered a major setback.

Her heels clicked across the marble floor of the hall, drummed on the teak corridor, and were finally muffled by the blue-and-white Tientsin carpet in the library. Donald and Eurydice Howe sat side by side on the purple-flowered cretonne sofa beneath bookcases rather sparsely furnished with silk-bound boxes of classical works. They were essentially modern parents, but they looked terribly old-fashioned. Despite his black-rimmed spectacles, and the lavaliere watch pinned to her imposing bosom, their severe expressions made them resemble a Manchu Dynasty ancestral portrait.

"*Ah-ba! Mng-ma!*" Emily spontaneously spoke in the slurred Shanghainese of her childhood. "Daddy! Mamma! What's wrong? Why're you looking so sad? Has something awful happened?"

Her mother's stern expression did not alter, but her father's eyes blinked behind his thick lenses.

"Nothing is wrong, Yuelin." Her mother's tone belied that reassurance.

"Nothing at all is wrong, Yuelin." Her father's smile was strained. "It's just that—"

"Actually, daughter, this is an occasion for joy." Eurydice Howe casually interrupted her husband—as she never would in public. "We're all very happy. It's a time for rejoicing!"

"Well, you don't look it." Emily was blunt in her relief—and her suspicion. "You've frightened me half to death. What's it all about, Daddy?"

"We wanted you to know immediately," he replied. "So I told Old Woo to send you in the instant you got back."

"Something to do with me, is it?"

"Something wonderful for you," her mother replied. "We are delighted to tell you that you will be married in October just after the Mid-Autumn Festival. Yuelin, we're so happy for you."

Emily stood rooted on the blue-and-white carpet, her lips parted in astonishment. Through the blood pounding in her ears, she half heard her father add: "It's a wonderful match, Yuelin. Nien-lao is a fine young man, and the Lis are a deeply respected family—old scholarship and old money, too. It's a magnificent alliance for both families!"

"Isn't this . . . Don't you think . . . I can't see . . ." Emily stammered in shock. "It's all so . . . so abrupt! I can hardly think . . ."

"You've known him all your life, my dear," Eurydice pointed out. "You were betrothed to Nien-lao when you were four. You've always known that you two would marry. Eighteen years ago is hardly abrupt."

"Mother, that . . . that was only a formality. Daddy told me so over and over again. When I was old enough, he used to say, *perhaps* I'd marry Nien-lao. But only if I wanted to. Daddy always promised. And now this! I can't believe it!"

"Your father has always been too indulgent." Eurydice's lips hardly moved. "He's always allowed you too much freedom . . . pampered you. His only daughter! His thousand ounces of gold!"

"Formality or not, Yuelin, the engagement stands." Donald Howe ignored his wife's outburst. "It was never amended—and it was certainly never canceled. The Lis and the Howes have now decided that the marriage will take place in October. As you know, marriages are always arranged by parents to assure the best for their daughters."

"The best for their daughters?" Enraged by his assumption that she would do exactly as he directed, Emily was appalled by the sudden realization that she probably would. "Why don't you say the best for themselves—and their families? What *they* think is the best. Daughters don't matter! This daughter matters least of all!"

Eurydice Howe's lips clamped shut. Parental authority had declared its decision, and there was no more to be said. The marriage would take place as arranged. Further discussion was not merely unnecessary but could lead to acrimony, perhaps to unfilial protests, unladylike tantrums that Emily would later regret. Children had to be told what to do— particularly female children.

"Now, dear, you know very well we're only thinking of what's best for you." Her father was still trying to placate her. "And we gave it a lot of thought."

"But *you* decided, Daddy. You didn't even *talk* to me! You simply disposed of my life. . . . Disposed of me!"

Father and daughter stared at each other. Both feared a head-on confrontation, and both strove to control their anger. Donald Howe studied his hands, which were crossed on his paunch. Standing frozen on the blue-and-white carpet, her textbooks clutched to her bosom, Emily felt her knees tremble.

"Father and mother. Esteemed parents. Won't you open your hearts?" she pleaded. "Only listen to me! Can't you reconsider? I can't even remember what Nien-lao looks like! It's *so* desperately important to me. Can't you just . . ."

Her father and mother faced Emily like implacable Buddhas—stone-faced, immobile, unreachable. Their ears were deaf to prayers, and their hearts were locked against clemency.

Emily realized in despair that she had no choice, not in their world. Since she *must* submit, it was better to submit with good grace. Bowing to the two remote figures, she began to compose a litany of self-abnegation. The years fell away, and the centuries unwound. Emily prepared to submit to a fate she hated, just as a weeping princess of the Han Dynasty had two millennia earlier submitted to the emperor's command that she marry a chieftain of the Hunnish barbarians.

No, not like that princess! Like a peasant girl called in from feeding the chickens to be told that she was to be sold to a lecherous old landlord. The emperor had explained to the princess the reasons of state that made her distasteful marriage necessary. The grasping peasant father would curtly pronounce the life sentence—as her own urbane banker-father had just done.

She was, Emily realized with horror, on the verge of formally bending to her father's will—as she had already bent in her thoughts. Rage flamed in her heart—rage at her own slave mentality, rage at the age-old docility of the Chinese lady, who would accept humiliation, privation, even death rather than raise her voice in defiance. She had almost betrayed everything in which she believed. After hoisting the banner of women's rights, she had almost given way meekly at the first assault on her position. Even stronger than her righteous anger at her parents, Emily felt white-hot contempt for herself.

Her books dropped from her arms, and her hands rose as if in imprecation. Eurydice Howe stared impassively, but Donald Howe dropped his eyes before his daughter's gaze.

"Why?" Emily demanded. "Why are you doing this to me? Have I injured you? Is that why you want to punish me? What have I done to deserve such treatment?"

Donald Howe did not reply, but sat still as a carved image of the God of Wrath. He flushed scarlet and an instant later grew so pale that his gray eyebrows appeared dark. His hands clutched his chest, and his face turned gray.

"You . . . must . . . be . . . married!" he wheezed. "And *very* soon!"

"Your poor father!" Eurydice interjected sternly. "What you are doing to him! He'll have a heart attack if you're not careful. And all because he loves you and wants the best for you, you foolish girl."

The chief antagonists ignored her interruption, like two gladiators who cannot allow themselves to be distracted for an instant from the mortal threat of the other. His leaden color hardly altered, Donald strove to speak calmly, but his voice rose in fury.

"You force me to tell you the reasons, you ungrateful child. Of course the engagement was a formality, a convention, no more, as I used to tell you. However, I have now made it binding—irrevocable. You cannot . . . absolutely cannot . . . cast it off."

Emily had never before seen this implacable face. Her father continued: "Why have I done so? Because this is your last chance. No other gentleman of good family would marry you, not after the revelations I am in honor bound to make. But the Lis, in their magnaminity, are prepared to overlook your notorious behavior. They will honor the contract of betrothal, despite your . . . your ill fame. You should go down on your knees and thank heaven for the Lis' tolerance."

Stunned by her father's incomprehensible accusations, Emily finally replied, "Father, I don't know what in heaven's name you mean. My notorious behavior? My ill fame? What on earth *are* you talking about? Tell me! Please tell me! I'm afraid you've both gone mad."

"He's talking about your disgusting behavior," Eurydice Howe declared. "Your secret trysts, your assignations with that long-nosed Englishman. He's also talking about—"

"—your shameless articles for the filthy mosquito papers," Donald Howe roared, his color high. "A daughter of mine writing pornography! I can hardly believe it, even now! And you dare . . . you dare say *we* are mad!"

"Father, that was unforgivable." Starting contrite and low, Emily's tone rose with her temper. "But I swear to you I've done nothing to be ashamed of. Nothing! I couldn't tell you about . . . about my seeing Richard. But we've done nothing wrong. *Nothing,* I tell you, that is in any way shameful. And—pornography? Pornography! My God, how could a virgin write pornography? They're only little tales of young women—only romances to amuse. Have you read them? Even one?"

"We would not allow them into the house," Eurydice replied flatly. "But your father *has* read your political articles. Red Bolshevik propaganda! Nothing less!"

"Bolshevik propaganda? My articles only tell women about their rights."

"Next thing," Eurydice continued, "you'll be advocating naked parades to show that women are equal and unashamed. Probably march naked yourself, just like the Bolsheviks. I always told you, husband, this comes of giving girls education. Letting her go abroad was madness. Perhaps your daughter is correct. Perhaps we are mad to try to do the right thing for her."

"Is it right to force a young woman into an arranged marriage she detests?" Emily retorted. "Right to berate her like a clumsy scullery maid for writing a few little stories? My God, I thought you'd be proud of me."

"Well, you didn't rush to show them to us, did you?" Eurydice continued. "But all that is past now. You'll forget about your scribblings after you marry Nien-lao. Think of the lovely ceremony. You'll see how happy you are."

"Mother, I'm neither an infant nor a fool," Emily retorted. "Don't talk to me like one."

"How else should your mother talk to you when you act like a fool?" Donald demanded. "She's right. Six months after your wedding, all this nonsense will be forgotten."

"You're assuming, Father, there will be a wedding. I'm not so sure."

"Don't be foolish, my daughter," he said. "What else can you do, should you dare disobey me? How would you live?"

"I will *not* marry Nien-lao, I tell you!" Dropping her books, she dashed out of the library. "I just can *not*!"

Emily's initial reaction was much what her parents had expected, although her vehemence surprised them. The American influence, naturally. Nonetheless, in time she would obey them.

Stumbling up the stairs to the sanctuary of her bedroom, Emily paused stricken on the landing. She clapped the back of her hand to her lips and demanded aloud of herself: "Good God, what *would* I do? What could I *possibly* do?"

MAY 29, 1922

A new telephone, which ingeniously combined mouthpiece and earphone in one handset, stood on the mahogany desktop beside the brass sign that read: MISS J. PAVERNEN. An Underwood typewriter pushed against the wall on its wheeled stand was concealed under a black cover.

It was John Pavernen's wish that the typewriter be inconspicuous. Julia was a director and second vice-president of JPEnterprises, Inc. Since she was emphatically not a secretary, she was not to display the typewriter, which was the symbol of emancipated women who, he joked, declared: "We will not be dictated to by men!"—and promptly got themselves jobs taking shorthand!

Julia was delighted by her new position in late May of 1922, and she was fascinated by her uncle's business affairs. She had heard him called Quick Jack, and she resented the implication of that nickname. But she felt it was also a tribute to his live-wire ways.

Nor was she fazed because the office was situated in a somewhat rundown tenement in Hongkew. Although the name Hongkew romantically meant "The Beginning of the Rainbow," the district northeast of the juncture of the Hwangpoo River and Soochow Creek, which had once been the American Settlement, was now largely Japanese—and thoroughly unfashionable. John Pavernen maintained he had "gotten in on the ground floor" of a fast-developing neighborhood. Julia sometimes wished the office was on the ground floor, not up four flights of rickety stairs.

She was, however, not disturbed because she was not just the second vice-president but the only visible director, aside from President John Pavernen. A Mr. Chow Kasing was first vice-president and secretary-treasurer, but incessant illnesses kept him from the office. Julia was not only office manager but filing clerk, typist, and telephonist—in fact, the only employee of JPEnterprises aside from Little Pow, who was just ten years old. That wide-eyed waif ran errands and energetically swept out the office, chattering rapidly in Shanghainese so slangy that she initially understood no more than one word in five.

Julia's grasp of Shanghainese had improved greatly. Unfortunately, she could not pretend not to understand the hard-luck story that preceded Little Pow's plea for a raise of a dollar a month. She responded with a colloquial rebuff, and the waif grinned good-naturedly, shrugging his frail shoulders within the cut-down long-gown that enveloped him. That hand-me-down had faded to the palest cerulean blue owing to laundering that, though infrequent, had extended over two decades. Winter and summer, Little Pow wore the tattered cotton garment to show that he was one of the elite employed in offices rather than in manual labor.

Julia fished in her purse and handed him a shiny silver dollar bearing the eagle-and-snake emblem of Mexico. Among the coins of many nations circulating in the International Settlement, the Chinese favored the "dollar Mex" because of its high silver content.

"A present from me," she told him. "Not from the company."

She knew Little Pow would hardly believe that any sane person would freely give that immense sum, equivalent to fifty cents American, out of her own purse, when she could charge it to the company. One dollar Mex was no small sum to her either.

Julia realized that it was conscience money. Shanghai was not only champagne, caviar, and dancing, but also cholera, starvation, and sixteen-hour workdays in squalid factories. The silver coin was her offering to the jealous gods of fortune, who were treating her so well. Julia reveled in her work, but she could not expect a raise for some time. JPEnterprises was a young concern, still growing and still short of cash.

Behind the partition, the president's office was hardly larger than her cramped anteroom. The fragrance of Havana cigars and Scotch whisky was, however, gradually overcoming the reek of new paint and the overripe odor of cheap sisal floor-matting.

John Pavernen had repeatedly impressed upon Julia, and upon those suppliers or customers who climbed to his aerie, that JPEnterprises was concerned not with display but with quality. That meant the finest materials, the best craftmanship, and absolute integrity in endeavors ranging from real estate through rattan furniture to insurance.

The most exciting venture was the most recent one. Riverview Manor was the biggest prize that had yet come John Pavernen's way. An absentee German owner had commissioned JPEnterprises to renovate and sell sixty-five Chinese-type houses on the outskirts of Hongkew. The potential profit was great, but the reputation to be gained was even more valuable.

Julia frowned, and her tawny eyebrows drew together. She would not pluck them into the half circles of astonishment that were fashionable. Before he left for Canton to sell second-hand machine guns to Dr. Sun Yat-sen's Nationalist Army, her uncle had given her a lecture on Shanghai's ways.

"Everybody in this town is a crook. Remember that," he had told her. "Everybody from the chairman of the Municipal Council and the British consul-general right on down the line. Even the judges of the American Court and the Mixed Court. Not criminals, maybe, but definitely crooks. There's only one exception: the U.S. consuls aren't crooks. But they've never been very bright."

The doorbell pealed, diverting her thoughts, but no shadow obscured the gold-leaf lettering on the glass-paneled door. When the bell pealed again, she realized that it was the unfamiliar ring of the new telephone. Gingerly, she lifted the handset.

"Haloo! Haloo!" a guttural voice bellowed. "Iss dot Yut Pay Enterprises? I better like speak Herrn . . . Mr. Pavernen . . . *sofort,* right now."

"Yes, Mr. Vass, this is JPEnterprises," Julie assured the mercurial German building contractor. "But Mr. Pavernen isn't in."

"Pavernen!" Vass shouted. "I must speak Pavernen right now."

"I'm very sorry, Mr. Vass. Mr. Pavernen is in Canton and won't be back for at least a week. Can I help you?"

"Help? Are you architect? Are you sanitary inspector? Are you plumber? How can you help?"

"If you'll tell me what's wrong, Mr. Vass, I could try. Perhaps I could get in touch with Mr. Pavernen if it's absolutely essential."

"Who's there?" he demanded. "Is that nine-one-four-seven? Whom do I speak?"

"This is Julia Pavernen, Mr. Vass."

"Ach, the little niece. So, is your problem too. It gives no baths. I could not get bath anywhere in Shanghai."

"Are you sure?" She stalled, uncomprehending. "Quite sure?"

"Am I sure? Of course! I need bath very bad. But I cannot get bath anywhere. And I need sixty-five."

"Sixty-five? Sixty-five baths?"

Julia envisioned the porcine Vass attempting to wash away the cumulative guilt of his many years of chicanery—by sixty-five successive immersions.

"So, you see, young lady? Where can I find sixty-five baths? There is not one in Shanghai. I even tried Hankow and Ningpo. But nothing —not one imported since three months."

"Oh, bathtubs!" Julia grasped his meaning. "And there's nothing else you can use? No, I see. A bathtub's a bathtub, and nothing else will do. Doesn't anyone *make* bathtubs here?"

"*Make* baths? I think not . . ." Vass paused portentously. "But maybe I have idea. Is all right if a little heavy, no?"

"Why not, Mr. Vass? If a bathtub holds water, what matter if it's heavy?"

"Have idea of genius. I report myself later. Good-bye."

A minute after Julia returned the handset to its cradle, the bell rang again. Removing her right earring for comfort, she lifted the handset again.

"Julie? Julie darling? I'm so glad I found you." Usually cool, Emily sounded distraught. "I must see you! I must talk with you!"

"Of course, Emmy. I can't get away from the office till six. But any time after . . ."

"Thanks, Julie, many thanks. I don't know what I'd do without—"

"What's wrong? Still the deadlock with your folks?"

"It's not a deadlock anymore. When they sprang this marriage on me a couple of weeks ago, I told them I just wouldn't. And they haven't said a word about it since."

"Then, you've won, Emmy."

"It's not that simple," Emily sighed. "They're making preparations, just as if I'd agreed. They're going to steamroller me—no matter what I say."

"Emmy, how can they? Just make it absolutely clear you *won't* go through with it. They can't risk the loss of face . . . the scandal . . . of your refusing at the last minute."

Julia shifted the telephone to her left ear after removing the second antique brass earring embossed with the *shou,* long life, ideogram. She nodded to Little Pow, who poured her a cup of jasmine tea. It threatened to be a long conversation, but she could not tell her unhappy friend that the line had to be kept clear for business calls.

"You don't understand," Emily expoded. "If I make a scandal, I'll be branded a scarlet woman. People will say I'm *afraid* to marry because I'm shopworn. Sure, my parents will suffer, but it'll be ten times worse for me. They're counting on that. Besides, they know I cannot—just cannot—make the family lose face."

"So there's nothing you can do? Absolutely nothing?"

"I can hardly run an ad saying: *The marriage arranged between Miss Emily Yuelin Howe and Mr. Li Nien-lao eighteen years ago will not take place.*"

"Emmy, suppose . . . just suppose you disappeared. One fine morning you're not there. Then what?"

"They'd have to call it off," Emily answered immediately. "Invent a plausible excuse and call it off. Or risk looking like perfect fools."

"Well, why don't you? Why not just disappear?"

"How can I?" Emily sounded irritated. "Julia, you're not taking this seriously. It's not a game."

"I am serious. Not disappear so no one knows where you are. Disappear so everyone knows where you are." Julia's plan crystallized as she spoke. "Why not move into the loft with me? Your folks'll have to act as if they agreed—or lose more face. And they can't steamroller you if you're not under their roof."

"Julie, you know, it just might work. If I'm not under my parents' roof, the Lis are sure to ask questions. And Daddy wouldn't lie outright. Not about something so important."

"What would happen then?"

"I'm not sure," Emily replied, "but it *could* go this way: Daddy decides to get out from under after he sees he can't win. So he regretfully breaks off the engagement. He tells a plausible story. No one believes it, but it saves everyone's face."

"And that could get you off the hook?"

"Could be. I'll try to come to your place about seven, but I can't promise. Not the way things are."

"Oh, Emmy! How's Richard? Do you think—"

"Stop it." Emily laughed. "I'm trying to get out of one match, and you're plotting another—with even more problems."

Julia hung up. Pushing her hair into place, she encountered bare earlobes and scrabbled on her desk for her earrings. Little Pow smiled triumphantly and produced them from his capacious sleeve. The brass hemispheres were mirror-bright after his assiduous polishing. She did not have the heart to tell him that she had valued the antique patina.

Julia pulled out the typewriter and took off the cover. A pile of unanswered letters lay on her desk. Although Riverview Manor was the most ambitious, it was not JPEnterprises' only business. Aligning a sheet of paper, she rolled it into the machine.

Dear Mr. Sylvester. She began a letter to the export manager of United Metal Fasteners, Inc., of St. Louis. *I was happy to have your letter of the 16th of . . .*

The telephone pealed. Grimacing at Little Pow, who was sweeping imaginary cobwebs off the wall, Julia lifted the handset and automatically removed her right earring. No wonder some firms still refused to install telephones, since calls intruded without warning on normal work.

"Here is Smidgelou . . . Smidgelou Tomas," a ripe Middle European accent announced. "My wife is very angry. She says she will kill me."

Never having heard the name before, Julia replied noncommittally, "I wonder how I can help you."

"What are you going to do?" the voice demanded.

"I'm so sorry." Julia said and asked solicitously, "How can I help?"

"It is about my house in this Riverdells . . ."

"Riverview," she corrected automatically.

"Could as well be Riverbottom, all the good it does me. I have paid all installments to datum. Two months ago I was promised, but still no house. Manya fears must soon sleep in streets. She comes out in red bumps—and my life is a weariness."

Cradling the handset in the hollow of her shoulder, Julia leafed through the Riverview Manor receipt file. She found *Smidgelou, T.* and a record of payments.

"Yes, sir, everything is in order. Your house has been allotted . . ."

"When can we move. Two days? Three days? A week?"

"Mr. Smidgelou, we are experiencing minor problems with plumbing. Our suppliers have let us down." She could not tell him they had *no* suppliers of bathtubs. "But I have just talked to our superintendent of construction. He hopes in two weeks . . ."

"In two weeks we shall have our little house?"

"Most likely, sir."

No reason to tell him she had just fished that date from the well of her optimism.

"You'll be hearing from us very soon, sir," she concluded. "By the way, my mother always used vinegar for hives."

She was getting to be as plausible as her Uncle Jack—not exactly lying, just comforting those in distress. The Smidgelous' house in River-view Manor *might* be ready for occupancy in two weeks—if the terrible Gustav Vass solved the bathtub problem.

Grimacing, Julia resumed the letter to United Metal Fasteners.... *We could sell many more thumbtacks if they were colored gold. The Chinese, who are obsessed with that metal, will undoubtedly purchase many thousand gross to imbue their household shrines and their conveyances with the aureate hue of prosperity.* (Uncle Jack had insisted on that last pompous phrase.) *Your brass screws . . .*

"Good afternoon, JPEnterprises . . ." Julia automatically responded to the telephone and automatically removed her left earring. "Oh, hello, Liz. How are you?"

"I'm in trouble, big trouble!" The Russian woman's voice was incongruously blithe. "I must talk with you."

Julia made an understanding noise.

"Joshua wants to reform me," Elizaveta continued. "He wants me to give up my present way of life. He wants me to marry him."

"Oh, Liz, how wonderful! I'm so happy for you! Set the date right now. Don't let him get away."

"I'm not sure I've got him. Rachel Haleevie will hardly let her precious son marry a . . . a woman like me. She won't even have me in the house! Besides, I'm not Jewish."

"Let's take it step by step," Julia said. "First, you're not sure Lady Haleevie will say no. Joshua is only one of seven sons. Surely, she can spare one to a Gentile. Just remember, Joshua loves you very much. And it's his family—his problem to solve."

As she spoke, Julia realized that she had learned a good deal in almost a year in Shanghai. She did not know that Joshua truly loved Elizaveta in the conventional hearts-and-flowers way. Otherwise, he might have been more possessive. But she had learned that there were many different kinds of love—self-sacrificing or self-serving, obsessive or comfortable, overwhelming or casual. Some who thought they were in love might well not be, while others, who thought they were not, might be deeply in love. How could she say Joshua was not in love because he did not act as she expected a lover to act?

". . . and I'm not sure Joshua can stand up to his mother." Elizaveta was still speaking. "Suppose he swore he was going to marry me and she then backed him down. It would be worse than humiliation for him. More like castration."

"Liz, Joshua *will* stand up to his mother. Even a former captain with all those medals can need a little help in breaking away from such domineering parents. But he'll do it. And Sir Judah's a great romantic. In the end, he'll be on your side."

"If Rachel Haleevie works hard enough on Sir Judah, he could cut Joshua off. There could be no money. And money is important, Julie."

"Oh, money! No Haleevie will ever starve."

"Julie, I'm not interested in love in a hovel. And Joshua is incapable of making a living on his own. I may be mercenary, but nothing kills love quicker than poverty."

"If you truly love him . . ."

Julia could hear Elizaveta's sigh: "Love is love—and life is life. I won't risk ruining Joshua's life, not to speak of my own. Anyway, I'm not absolutely sure I *want* to marry him."

"Oh, Liz. What *do* you want?"

"I've been approached by a group of White Russians who want to start a small hotel and nightclub," Elizaveta responded without any perceptible transition. "They want to call it Ikra—which means 'caviar.' A good name, isn't it? But I'd have to match their hundred thousand Mex. Is JPEnterprises looking for a good investment? My Russians will guarantee occupancy of forty percent of the rooms. Would your uncle be interested?"

"Liz, you might as well go to Manchuria for coconuts as to JPEnterprises for nearly fifty thousand U.S. dollars. We're slightly overextended, and we're borrowing, not lending. I'm sure Uncle Jack would like to, but there's no hope here."

"Oh dear, and I thought . . . Then perhaps Emily could help. Her father might—"

"Maybe I shouldn't tell you, but you'll know soon enough. Emily may be asking *you* for a loan soon. She's thinking of moving out of Harmony Hall . . . breaking with her parents."

"That is bad news—for both of us. Pretty soon you'll be the only one with a regular income."

"Why don't you come by the loft for a drink about seven tonight," Julia suggested. "Emily will be there. The three of us can really talk."

As she hung up, Little Pow proudly placed her earrings on her desk. He had polished them again, polished so diligently that they sparkled gold—or as Quick Jack Pavernen would say, glowed with the aureate hue of prosperity.

Julia did not reprimand the boy of all work. She was, rather, happily looking forward to seeing both her friends that evening. Despite their problems, it would be fun to have an old-fashioned hen session.

Elizaveta arrived at a quarter past eight, hardly late by her flexible

Russian standard. She was very cheerful, and they talked for hours. But Julia became more and more worried about Emily's failure to appear.

Finally, she lifted up her courage and called Harmony Hall. Old Woo, the majordomo, told her: "Miss Yuelin left two hours ago. No, I don't know where she was going. Perhaps she'll show up soon."

But Emily did not appear that night.

When John Pavernen returned from Canton a few days later, Julia was deeply worried about Emily. She had heard not a word from her friend. The Howes' majordomo was evasive, and neither Donald nor Eurydice Howe would speak with her on the telephone. She could not appear uninvited at Harmony Hall, and Tommy was out of reach in Peking.

For the moment, however, concern for her uncle displaced her concern for Emily. He was obviously exhausted. His green eyes were dull, and the aura of his charm flickered feebly. Most worrying of all, he was, this once, not at all curious about either business matters or her personal affairs. He had told her when he entered the office that his mission to Canton had failed.

"Couldn't sell them a single cartridge," he had said. "That letter to Sun Yat-sen from T. V. Soong turned out to be a dud. Circumstances, though, not the president snubbing his brother-in-law."

Even allowing for his disappointment, John Pavernen seemed extraordinarily depressed. Julia curled her feet under her in the cracked red-leather chair of the inner office, lit a Chesterfield, and blew out a cloud of smoke. Her uncle carefully selected an Upmann panatela from his crystal humidor, pierced the tip, and lit it with the lighter presented to him by the Colt Armaments Company: a gold-plated fifty-caliber cartridge.

This was no time, Julia decided, to trouble him with her worries about her friends. She was most concerned about Emily, but Elizaveta was getting into dangerously deep waters in her search for capital for the private hotel that was to be called the Ikra. Julia even hesitated before introducing business matters, but she had to speak to her uncle about Tomas Smidgelou's house in Riverview Manor.

"Uncle Jack," she began, "Vass the builder has been after me. He can't find a single bathtub anywhere but—"

"Not another red cent for that old horse thief."

". . . he has a solution," she continued. "Says it'll be cheaper than regular tubs if he makes them out of concrete . . ."

"Concrete? Absurd!" John Pavernen broke in. "Riverview's not the Ritz. That's for sure. But concrete bathtubs? They'd look awful."

"He plans to mix in marble dust for a smooth finish. Like a Roman bath, so beautiful it shall be, he says."

John Pavernen grinned at his niece's mimicry of Gustav Vass and puffed on his Havana cigar.

"Marble bathtubs in Riverview Manor in Hongkew!" he exclaimed. "That'll knock some people's eyes out. . . . Tell him to get started right away. I don't need angry subscribers defaulting on their payments."

"I've had a few angry subscribers. Otherwise, there're just one or two little things. Everything else can wait . . ."

John Pavernen dealt competently but abstractedly with the other problems Julia presented. Then he inquired querulously about the oscillating electric fan they had received as a sample from Cleveland, Ohio. Since her thin shantung dress was clinging damply to her shoulders, Julia happily fetched the fan from the cupboard where Little Pow stowed it each evening. The waif was absent, having pleaded illness. He was generally ill on race days.

When she returned, her uncle had taken off his tan jacket, but his striped tie was still tightly knotted under his heavy starched collar. Yet he was a little less tense with a tumbler of scotch and water clutched in his hand.

"I'm a little shook-up," he said almost shyly. "Are you wondering what's happened to your old Uncle Jack?"

"A little. You don't seem your usual self."

"You can say that again." He sipped his drink. "As you know, they ran President Sun Yat-sen out of Canton."

"I saw a report in the *North China Daily News,* but it was vague. Dr. Sun seems to pop in and out of power just like a warlord."

"I never paid much attention to warlords before. A few dollars' bribe here, a few dollars there—and they let you get on with business. As long as the Volunteer Corps kept them out of the Settlement, I figured they could fight each other all they wanted. Civil war is good for the gun business. . . . But one of these days one of them is going to take over

China. With one fellow running the whole shebang, it could be a different story for you and me, Julie."

"Please tell me what happened in Canton," she interjected. "And
what happened to *you*?"

"Well, after they let me out of jail . . ." He raised his voice over the
buzzing of the fan. "That, mind you, was *after* they put me up against
a wall in front of a firing squad. Maybe I better begin at the beginning . . ."

Proud of his new knowledge, John Pavernen anatomized for Julia the
rival factions of warlords that were fighting for mastery over China. Dr.
Sun Yat-sen, whose National People's Party loosely held Kwangtung
Province in the far south, was, strictly speaking, not a warlord. Dr. Sun
was, however, allied with the dominant warlord of that province, and
he was seeking other warlord allies against the grand coalition of northern warlords.

It was confusing, John Pavernen acknowledged, but there was no
need for Julia to remember the details. The present warlord alliances
would soon shift—as they had been shifting continually since 1915.
The great prize was Peking. Whoever controlled the old imperial capital
appointed the nominal president—and enjoyed the benefits of automatic foreign recognition of whatever regime held Peking. Those benefits included the substantial income from the Chinese Maritime
Customs, which was administered by foreigners.

"Anyway," John Pavernen continued, "Sun Yat-sen's been cozying
up to the warlord of Manchuria way up north, Chang Tso-lin, the one
they call the Old Marshal. Dr. Sun wants the two of them to join up
and squeeze out the others, especially Feng Yü-hsiang, that pious fraud
called the Christian General. You know, old Sun's not all that different
from the warlords . . ."

"Uncle Jack, that's just not true! The Nationalists *are* different!" Julia
had been indoctrinated by those staunch champions of the Nationalists
Emily Howe and Mayling Soong. "Sun Yat-sen was actually *elected*
president by the National Assembly, even if it was ten years ago. The
Nationalists are fighting for an ideal. And they'll win, in the end."

"Nice little speech, Julie. But what the good doctor needs now isn't
ideals but more troops, more guns, and a secure base. He's not looking
too well. Anyway, here's what happened in Canton. It started off
fine . . ."

The Victoria Hotel in the minute British Concession on Shameen
Island had welcomed John Pavernen warmly. The rattan furniture mak-
ers he served as export agent had left him gifts of tropical fruit and

bourbon whiskey. He slept well in the high-ceiling bedroom beneath the ghostly cloud of the mosquito net. He was awakened by an invitation from the Office of the President of the Republic of China. Since the letter was written in idiomatic English with American spelling, Madame Sun Yat-sen, the former Rosamonde Soong, was obviously still acting as her husband's English secretary.

John Pavernen was, however, received by neither the president nor the first lady. Instead, he waited seven hours before he was shown into a small office crammed with files, field telephones, maps, a squat steel safe, and the ruddy corpulence of a middle-aged foreigner in a Nationalist uniform. In fluent though heavily accented English the officer introduced himself as Colonel Bowe, the president's military secretary. John Pavernen could not tell whether that was the man's original name or a pseudonym. He did not much care when he gathered that Colonel Bowe was eager to purchase at least a hundred Vickers machine guns, as well as quantities of grenades, rifles, and pistols.

Payment would pose no problems. T. V. Soong, financial adviser to the president, was collecting substantial funds from forward-looking capitalists, foreign as well as Chinese. Besides, both Colt and Vickers were anxious to get a foot in the door of the man they vaguely understood to be the legitimate president of China. Sales could be enormous if the Nationalists actually mounted their planned Northern Expedition to crush the warlords. The gun-makers were therefore offering exceedingly generous terms.

At that point, John Pavernen still knew little more about the warring factions than that they needed arms. He therefore accepted without reservation Colonel Bowe's assurance that indiscipline among the city's garrison was not serious. Nor did he ask why President Sun had just felt it necessary to leave the fighting front and hasten back to restive Canton to restore order.

Colonel Bowe, however, volunteered that some twenty-five thousand unruly soldiers could be a problem, because they owed allegiance to the local warlord rather than to Dr. Sun. Still, that warlord was a devoted member of the National People's Party who had recently congratulated Dr. Sun on the Nationalist military victories that were preparing the way for the Northern Expedition. And only yesterday he had telegraphed from his field headquarters to reaffirm his loyalty.

"Ugly rumors, no more!" Colonel Bowe exploded. "It's not true that our Cantonese warlord is encouraging his troops to loot and riot in the city in order to undermine Dr. Sun's authority."

"Why are you telling me all this?" John Pavernen asked. "Aren't you worried about scaring me off?"

"Better you should hear the truth from me than falsehoods from others."

John Pavernen returned in his sedan chair to the Victoria Hotel through crowded streets where soldiers in mustard-yellow uniforms strutted. They thrust civilians aside with their rifles, and they lifted goods from those shops whose proprietors had not yet put up padlocked wooden shutters. The chair coolies twice darted into narrow alleys to avoid squads that were searching passers-by for valuables.

At seven in the evening, downtown Canton was normally tumultuous with color, light, and noise. Tonight, that district was rapidly emptying as the last furtive pedestrians hurried home to safety. Even the painted sing-song girls and the swaggering pimps forsook the soldiers, who were their natural prey, to retreat behind barred doors. The miniature pagoda-roofed platforms of the traffic police were deserted, as were theaters, teahouses, and restaurants. The stillness was, however, punctuated by shots, by the laughter of drunken privates, and by the screams of terrified women.

For the first time since he came to China, John Pavernen was fearful for his own safety. Why had Colonel Bowe allowed him to brush aside the offer of a military guard as if it were an empty courtesy? Did the colonel perhaps feel that any escort he provided would be more provocative than protective?

The sedan chair crossed over the humpbacked bridge to Shameen Island, the British Concession on the man-made sandspit in the Pearl River. Among the Victorian bungalows with their tennis courts and English gardens, he was no longer frightened by the frenzy of the native city. When the coolies trotted past Grimaldi's Café to the pillared entrance of the Victoria Hotel, John Pavernen had convinced himself that his fears were groundless.

After dining on *canard à l'orange* and drinking a reasonable claret, he was ashamed of his near-panic. He had, after all, always advised newcomers not to be alarmed by the ferocious-looking warlord troops. Their officers knew that foreign soldiers and foreign gunboats were never more than a few days away and would wreak terrible vengeance if foreigners were molested.

He carried a brandy-snifter to his room and sat smoking a cigar and calculating again the likely profits of the arms deal. Just after ten he climbed into the high brass bedstead and closed the mosquito net.

John Pavernen was surprised but not alarmed when he was shaken awake at half past eleven. He recognized the tan Nationalist uniform of the lieutenant who explained in halting English: Colonel Bowe apologized for the intrusion but wished to see the gentleman immediately. Since he could imagine no other reason for the summons than quick agreement on the deal, Pavernen hurriedly dressed. It was an odd hour, but many Chinese liked to do business in the middle of the night.

Humming to himself, he brushed his hair to its normal patent-leather sheen. He then followed the lieutenant through the moonlit tranquillity of Shameen Island. Nodding to the startled British sentries at the humpbacked bridge, he crossed into Chinese territory.

Six soldiers trotted beside the sedan chairs carrying the lieutenant and himself. The chairs' swaying was hypnotic. His eyes closed, and he dozed off as he was borne through the dark, deserted streets.

When the coolies halted abruptly, Pavernen awoke with a jerk. The wicker-and-bamboo sedan chair dropped to the cobblestones. He heard a shot, then two more. He could see little, for he was virtually seated on the ground, but the Nationalist lieutenant floundered out of his sedan chair, snatching at his holstered pistol. A rifle fired. Incredulity painted on his broad face, the lieutenant was flung backward.

A captain in the mustard yellow of the warlord army stepped out of the shadows, his revolver drawn. He was followed by a sergeant with a bayonet fixed to his rifle. The blade plunged into the lieutenant's throat just above the collar bearing the gold bars of his rank. He squealed and fell, bending from the waist as if in prayer.

Two Nationalist privates already lay unmoving on the cobblestones. The other four had vanished into the night with the chair coolies. Revolver dangling in his hand, the warlord captain looked down at the American.

"I've never been so scared in my life," John Pavernen recalled days later in the safety of his office. "It turned out that both Colonel Bowe and the warlord captain thought they could use me—as an American. The colonel thought my presence would protect Doctor and Madame Sun. The other gang was afraid I could get the U.S. Marines to avenge myself and the Suns. So they locked me up. . . . But I'm getting ahead of my story. While I was cooling my heels in a cell on the morning of June 16th, the warlord made his move against the president. Madame Sun Yat-sen told me about it later in Hong Kong."

Rosamonde Sun knew she was dreaming, John Pavernen recalled. She therefore dismissed the distant shrilling of a telephone. She was again walking happily on the campus of her alma mater, Vanderbilt University, when her husband's hand on her shoulder awakened her.

"They're coming!" he said tersely in English. "I've just had a telephone call. We've got to get out of here."

Her voice still muzzy with sleep, she replied, "Darling, *you* must go. I'd only slow you down. I'll stay. No one will hurt a woman."

The president finally agreed. If he was killed tonight, all the hopes of China would die with him. Sun Yat-sen slipped through the gates accompanied by ten soldiers, while fifty men remained under Colonel Bowe's command to protect Rosamonde. Fortunately, their mansion was several hundred yards from the imposing Presidency Building, which was certain to be the mutineers' chief objective. With luck, the rabble would overlook the mansion and the long bridge that connected it to the Presidency.

Half an hour later, the first volleys raked the mansion. The warlord assailants were firing from the slopes above and below. Through the shuttered windows, Rosamonde Sun and Colonel Bowe heard high-pitched shouts: *"Saat! Saat! Saat Sun Yat-sen!* . . . Kill! Kill! Kill Sun Yat-sen!"

The warlord of Canton had not only ordered the assault but had told his troops they could loot the city if the coup succeeded. He had also promised $200,000 Mex to the man who killed President Sun.

Colonel Bowe ordered his men not to reveal their positions and exhaust their ammunition by returning fire in the darkness. But dawn came at 5:46, and a storm of metal swept the mansion. When the rifles and machine guns of the defending troops briefly squelched the assailants' volleys, warlord field guns began to pound the vulnerable target. Most shells fell wide, although some hit the upper stories. By eight in the morning, the pitiless sun lit the breaches in the walls. The defenders' ammunition was almost exhausted; twenty had been killed, and most of the remainder were wounded.

The only escape route was the bridge to the Presidency. Proud of his idiomatic English, Colonel Bowe warned they might be "leaping from the frying pan into the fire." But there was no alternative.

With two volunteers, Rosamonde Sun and Bowe crept along the bridge, shielded by the railing. Most bullets flew wide, but one lucky shot hit Colonel Bowe in the thigh.

The two soldiers dragged him into the Presidency. Assisted by its relatively unscathed defenders, they carried Colonel Bowe to a bedroom and staunched the bleeding. If they fled the Presidency, they would have to leave him behind.

The warlord troops were not only virtual savages but poor marksmen. They had inflicted no major damage after seven hours, but the commander of the garrison chose to join them because he knew they must win. He offered to speak up for Madame Sun, but he could not guarantee her security. The two privates of the president's bodyguard chose to remain with her.

Rosamonde Sun was close to despair. Giddy with exhaustion, she was seeing the reality of violence for the first time in her sheltered life. She almost broke down when the drawing-room ceiling collapsed under shellfire thirty seconds after she had scurried out of the room. When it became obvious that the Presidency could hold out no longer, she stumbled into the courtyard between her bodyguards.

A stream of soldiers in mustard yellow was pouring through the battered gates. Their bayonets dark with blood, and their faces black with gunpowder burns, they rushed to loot the Treasury and the Customs Office. Amid the turncoats in tan Nationalist uniforms, the victors overlooked the woman staggering out between two Nationalist privates.

The three limped into a narrow lane, appalled by the mass slaughter in the streets. Bayonets, small arms, and artillery had made a bloody shambles of the district surrounding the Presidency. Soldiers and civilians lay together in death, their blood intermingled in the dust of shattered walls. Two men squatted in the ruins of a shelled hut and gazed into each other's eyes like children staring each other down. Both were dead—killed by the freak shock wave that left them unmarked.

"Shoot me! Shoot me now!" Rosamonde pleaded through cracked lips. "I can't possibly escape. Shoot me now! Don't let those savages get me!"

"Now, Madame," the plump senior guard assured her, "it will be all right. Please come along now."

They supported her between them, lifting her over the rubble and swinging her across shell craters. When they heard a column tramping near, they hid her with their bodies.

"Play dead!" the plump guard commanded. "It's our only chance!"

The three fugitives lay still amid the corpses until the column had passed. Rosamonde stumbled and retched as they finally half-carried her into an isolated farmhouse. When the middle-aged farmer demanded that they leave, the guards threatened him with their bayonets.

She then collapsed. When she awoke, the younger guard was sponging her face, and the elder was peering out the door. A shot sounded, and he crumpled to the floor.

"Don't look, Madame!" the younger said. "He's finished."

Totally despairing, Rosamonde Sun heard above the clamor of field-pieces the unmistakable roar of naval guns—and she knew the warlord had no warships. Loyal gunboats were bombarding the traitor's forces. Lulled by the guns, she finally slept.

Their unwilling host was delighted to say good-bye early the next morning. Lest they tarry, he offered patched trousers and a torn shirt to the guard. He gave Rosamonde Sun his wife's cast-off black pyjamas and old conical straw hat. Clutching a basket with a few vegetables and eggs, she looked like a farm woman.

"That was about it," John Pavernen told Julia. "She got a sampan to take her downriver to the president, who had found refuge on a Nationalist gunboat. If she'd gone with him in the first place, Rosamonde would have had a smooth passage. He's still on the gunboat—hoping to rally his forces and retake Canton. Rosamonde left for Hong Kong, still in her old-lady disguise, to look for outside help."

"You left out only one thing, Uncle Jack," Julia observed. "What the rebels did to you."

John Pavernen looked abstracted for a moment before replying: "What they did to me? Oh, yes. They put me up against a wall in front of a firing squad. I think they were just trying to scare me. They certainly succeeded. Then the Cantonese warlord decided to let me go. He apologized for his officer's mistake. Wanted no trouble with the Americans. God bless the Stars and Stripes!"

15

AUGUST 3, 1922

In August, Julia concluded somberly that the Howe family had closed ranks against her. What other explanation for her inability to uncover any news of Emily? Even Tommy was uncommunicative. His letters did not tell her what had become of his sister, although he must have known. Almost two months had passed since Emily's last telephone call —and Julia had no more idea of her friend's whereabouts than she had had on the evening when Emily failed to appear at the loft apartment.

Still deeply worried, Julia was, however, no longer frantic. If Emily was ill or injured, someone would have told her—if not the elder Howes, certainly Tommy. But the Howes' protracted silence, their refusal even to mention Emily, was eerie. It was as if they had banished her to a nunnery and now wished to banish her from their thoughts.

But Tommy would never conspire to spirit Emily away. He was too enlightened to go along with such medieval cruelty. Yet was he enlightened when family pride was at stake? How well, Julia wondered, did she really know him?

She squirmed in the roomy rosewood chair that was her latest find at the Shanghai Secondhand Store. Her skin, she decided, was not a perfect fit. In places as loose as an elephant's hide, it was elsewhere almost painfully tight. The brutal weather of early August was making her both edgy and lethargic. Yet the temperature had finally dropped to eighty-four degrees at nine in the evening, and the humidity was below eighty percent for the first time in weeks.

Richard Hollings had given her those figures when she telephoned him. Although amused by her sudden interest in statistics, he had then asked dolefully, "Not a word about Em? Not the breath of a rumor? Has she dropped off the edge of the world? Damn it, Julie, I miss her."

If only Tommy would come back from Peking! He always knew what to do, and he jauntily cut through problems that baffled her. Even if it were a stranger rather than his own sister who had vanished, his persistence, his intelligence, and his courage would find her. But Tommy was still in Peking.

Although he was to begin his internship at Shanghai General Hospital in mid-September, he had lingered in North China after receiving his M.D. in late June. In her letters, Julia had only hinted at her disappointment at his continuing absence, but she had naturally told him forthrightly how worried she was about Emily. His replies were reassuring but vague. Emily would be all right, he wrote, and he would come back to Shanghai just as soon as he could.

Damn it, Julia echoed Richard Hollings, she did miss Tommy—and not just to share her worries about Emily. She missed his laughing eyes behind the black-rimmed glasses he quite unnecessarily wore to give himself more authority. She missed his stubborn chin with the minute cleft, and she missed his slow, sensitive smile. Harry Smythe was a pleasant escort whose ritual passes were easily blocked. But she missed Tommy Howe more than she had ever thought it possible to miss any man. Yet they had not even kissed.

The mystery of Emily, however, shadowed all Julia's thoughts. Donald Howe had received her courteously when she finally worked up her courage to call on him in his office in the McBain Building on the Bund. He had smiled amiably but had simply shaken his head when she pleaded for news of Emily. Less amiable when she ran into him at a charity ball at the Columbia Country Club, he had said frostily that his family's affairs were not a subject for gossip at a public dance.

Bracing herself, she had marched up the driveway of Harmony Hall and cornered the white-haired majordomo, who appeared fond of her. But Old Woo had shaken his head, saying obdurately, "Miss Emily is not available!"

Julia could therefore only wait and hope, bolstered by Tommy's assurances that all would be well. Moreover, she had her own problem. Her parents had begun pressing her to return at Easter. The emotional pressure was now rising. It had been more than a year, they wrote. It was past time for her to have had her fill of the Orient.

Julia was not ready to go back to Plattsburg. She had put her parents off with vague promises, always hoping her father would not ask his younger brother to end her employment. If she had no money coming in, she would have to go back. But she was determined not to desert the most cosmopolitan city on earth. Also, there was Tommy, although he had said little outright to encourage her. Certainly, she could not leave until Tommy returned and gave her the opportunity to decide exactly how she felt about him.

Emily, too! How could she possibly leave when she did not know what had become of her closest friend? That would be desertion, leaving Emily in the lurch.

So many good reasons for staying, so many new responsibilities. Julia feared that Elizaveta was getting into trouble because of her obsession about owning her own private hotel. But she would think about Elizaveta in a moment. A more immediate problem was Tomas Smidgelou, whom she had months earlier promised that he could move into Riverview Manor in two weeks' time.

Now a familiar voice on the telephone, Mr. Smidgelou was still homeless. Although Gustav Vass had manufactured and installed sixty-five concrete-and-marble bathtubs, the houses were still not ready for occupancy. The electrical wiring and the plumbing were far from completion.

If John Pavernen and Gustav Vass did not solve all those problems very soon, JPEnterprises could collapse. After Little Pow, Julia would be the first casualty. Lack of funds could force her to leave Shanghai.

And what would Uncle Jack himself do? No longer deluding herself, Julia recognized that he was essentially what Shanghai called a small-piece taipan, a small-time businessman. Although the several civil wars raging throughout China created a lively market, even his arms deals were in the doldrums. He had smiled unhappily and confided, "I could sell ten million dollars' worth of guns tomorrow. It's easy to find buyers, but damned hard to find payers!"

With her uncle so depressed, Julia could not bother him again with the hopes of Elizaveta Alexandrovna Yavalenka. He had earlier promised to consider Elizaveta's need to match the capital promised by the syndicate of Russians. But Julia felt it would be graceless—and pointless —to press him.

Elizaveta talked chiefly of her planned hotel. Boasting both a cabaret and a gambling casino, the Ikra, Julia saw with her newly opened eyes, would almost certainly also be a house of assignation. Elizaveta's goal was no longer sheer survival but the wealth that would bring power.

Refusing to take money from Joshua, she now enjoyed the "protection" of a very rich Frenchman. But he was not so foolish as to help her toward independence by lending money to her. Elizaveta had confided with breathtaking candor that she was therefore trolling for cash among the secret societies. She had set her heart on hooking the Supreme Lord of the Floodgate Fraternity, the man called the Green Dragon, who dominated the Shanghai underworld.

She would manage, Elizaveta had replied hotly when Julia warned that the secret-society chieftains would impose unacceptable conditions with their loans. She could manage, Elizaveta had replied equably when Julia declared that her new friends were murderers, drug peddlers, and extortionists. She was managing well, she had replied flatly when asked whether some of her new friends were not rather disgusting.

Elizaveta had only laughed when Julia urged her to give up her perilous way of life and marry Joshua. Ostentatiously unafraid that Joshua might lose patience with her capriciousness, she had only laughed. She had said that she loved danger and excitement—and also loved Joshua truly. Elizaveta did love Joshua, Julia concluded, but not enough.

Julia sipped green tea and wriggled into a more comfortable position. When the doorbell rang, she wondered where Lao Zee was. The amah should already be back from the meeting of her Buddhist sisterhood. Julia laughed aloud at herself. How quickly one became accustomed to being waited upon!

"I'm coming!" she called. She swung the heavy door open and stared in amazement at the slender figure standing in the gloom of the hall.

"Emmy! Emmy darling!" Julia hurled herself at her friend. "Oh, Emmy! I was afraid something terrible had happened to you."

"In a way, it has. Let's sit down and have a drink," Emily said weakly. "Catastrophes make me tired."

Julia busied her hands preparing the gin-and-tonics they had learned to drink in Shanghai. Though bitter, the quinine in the India tonic water was refreshing. Mechanically chipping at the block of ice and cutting the lemon, she studied her old roommate, who was staring dejectedly at the squares of light in the high north window.

"Well, here you are," Julia said with forced cheeriness. "Now tell me everything. What have you been up to?"

"I tried, Julie!" Emily blurted. "I tried so hard to make myself do what they wanted. I knew I shouldn't, but I tried. And all I did was postpone the catastrophe."

"Catastrophe? You're not ill are you? You're looking terribly thin."

"I've broken with my parents—totally. We had a terrible fight, and they threw me out. For me . . . for any Chinese . . . a break with the family is like being half dead. Without a family, I can't feel myself a whole person. My fine Western ideals about individual liberty don't mean much now. I'm like jetsam cast up on the shore."

"Oh, Em, I'm so sorry. I can only imagine how you feel." Julia pressed on, since it would obviously be good for Emily to talk about her ordeal. "Tell me why you disappeared. Where were you? And what have you been doing?"

"I'm sorry, Julie, that I couldn't speak with you. Not you above all. You would have wormed it out of me—and then the whole world would've known. You're sometimes too confiding, you know. They made me swear not to get in touch with you. Tommy had no choice either. The family had to come first."

"I don't understand. What disgraceful secret were you hiding?"

"Not just my unfilial behavior, Julie, though that was bad enough. Above all, my parents could *not* let it be known that they were making concessions to me. They would have looked weak and foolish, flouting all the old morality. People would've lost faith in my father's judgment . . . his business judgment, too."

"Concessions? Your folks seem pretty tough to me."

Emily observed that most Chinese parents, even in the enlightened 1920s in cosmopolitan Shanghai, would either have locked up such a disobedient daughter or have disowned her immediately. Instead, her parents had accepted her promise to think "very seriously about marrying Li Nien-lao." They had even agreed that the prospective bride should, against all precedent, be allowed to get to know her fiancé before the marriage.

Donald Howe had found a way that would not cause scandal. Emily and Nien-lao had both gone to Hong Kong, staying with their respective cousins in the Crown Colony. Eurydice Howe was chaperone to her daughter, who had a year earlier crossed the Pacific Ocean unchaperoned—and unscathed. British Hong Kong was even more old-fashioned than Shanghai.

"I couldn't stand him, Julie!" Emily erupted. "He's ghastly. Far worse than I thought. A brainless playboy. But what could I do? Then Mayling Soong turned up—and advised me to say no. To have nothing more to do with Mr. Li Nien-lao."

Emily sipped her drink and added inconsequentially, "It's funny about May. Under that demure exterior, she's very strong, and she's all for women's rights. No arranged marriage for her! But she's sweet on General Chiang Kai-shek. She's worried because he's staying with President Sun Yat-sen on that gunboat near Canton."

Emily chattered breezily, but her appearance belied her manner. Her slenderness was now almost emaciation, and the big rosewood chair all but swallowed her fragility.

"May swears she'll never marry by arrangement," Emily continued. "She's half in love with Chiang Kai-shek, but he's already got a wife, so there isn't much hope for a good Methodist like May. Women are funny, aren't we?"

"I guess so, Emmy. What happened to you then?"

"Father joined us when I said flatly there was nothing doing. He was so angry, I thought he was going to beat me."

Donald Howe had raged and stormed. He had called upon heaven to punish his unfilial daughter. He had raised his right hand to chastize her, but his arm had fallen back to his side. He felt remiss in his duty, but he loved his disobedient daughter too much to strike her.

Emily was disobedient but not defiant. Aside from her refusal to marry her parents' choice, she was responsive to their wishes. Her father accordingly instructed her to spend the summer away from Shanghai in North China. She was to think about the consequences of her behavior and to consider her decision once again.

She had replied in anguish, "Can't you see that you want to inflict a life sentence on me? Oh, Daddy, *why* can't you see?"

Emily had languished in the unfamiliar north for two months. Bound by his duty to the family, Tommy had stayed with her. But he, too, had urged her to reject the arranged marriage.

Upon returning to Shanghai a few days earlier, Emily had sidestepped a confrontation by telling her father she was still thinking. She *was* thinking—above all, thinking how much she loathed Li Nien-lao. But her father could no more reconsider his decision than he could leap over the Great Wall of China.

The crisis had finally broken just after supper that same evening. It was almost an anticlimax, for passion had already been spent on both sides, leaving only the bare bones of resolution. Eurydice wept quietly, her well of tears almost exhausted. Donald declared hoarsely that he would disown his only daughter if she did not comply. But she could no more surrender than he could relent. Without rancor, he had finally told her to leave Harmony Hall.

"Well, what now?" Julia was briskly practical. "Where do you go from here?"

"I was hoping I could stay here awhile."

"Of course! It's practically your apartment, and it's certainly

Tommy's. Anyway, I was lonely! I'd love to have you as an apartment-mate."

"Thanks, Julie." Emily smiled pallidly. "They'll send my clothes over in the morning. All due courtesies, you see. It's just that I am no longer their daughter."

"What will you do, Emmy?"

"Don't worry. You won't have to support me. . . . You know the Women's Commercial and Savings Bank on Nanking Road, the first in the whole world run by females? Well, I've bought myself some shares —and a job goes with them. Grandpa Howe left a little money just for me. He was unusual. He felt a girl needed some money of her own. So I'm going to be a banker."

"Well, that's not so bad is it? And there's Richard, of course. He's been frantic."

"Yes, Richard, but later. . . . You remember, Julie, how we used to complain about being pushed around by our parents? We swore we'd stand up to them. Well, I've stood up to mine—and I'm devastated! I'm heartbroken!"

"It'll be all right, Emmy. They'll come round. You'll see."

"Julie!" Emily flared. "They *won't* come round. You don't know how pigheaded Chinese can be!"

Richard Hollings would just have to wait until morning to hear that Emily had returned. Her friend, Julia decided, was too exhausted to speak to anyone, even Richard.

16

AUGUST 26, 1922

Julia knew she had no right to be annoyed. After all, what was Tommy Howe to her? Or she to him?

Returning to Shanghai three days earlier, Tommy had lovingly telephoned his sister on the first afternoon. But he had not come to the loft apartment. Instead, he had explained off-handedly to Julia, who answered the telephone, that he had "a great number of things to see to."

He was undoubtedly very busy at the end of August just before starting his internship, and he was entitled to be a little puffed up at finally qualifying as a full-fledged physician. Besides, he had promised to come by just as soon as he could. He was, he had said, anxious to see them both.

Why then did she feel let down? She could hardly have expected Tommy to rush round and take her in his arms the minute he returned from an absence of more than half a year. True, they had written some letters to each other. But that was all there was to their relationship. Strictly speaking, it was hardly a relationship at all. He had never so much as taken her in his arms, much less kissed her.

Her dejection, Julia decided, was just the Saturday-night blues. Strange how American girls were conditioned to feel that something was very wrong if they were not taken out on a Saturday night. It was childish, but there it was.

Worse than childish, her dejection was stupid. She did have someone to take her out. Harrison Parker Smythe III was sitting on the rattan sofa in the big sitting room, impatiently twiddling the knobs on his binoculars while he waited for her to reappear. After the long afternoon they had spent at the Racecourse, she needed to come home to shower and change. Well, his patience would soon be rewarded—if he considered her company a reward.

She slipped the pale green silk dress with the scalloped hemline over her head, tied the belt, and pirouetted before the full-length mirror. She would do, she decided; she would do very well. Harry wanted her to look her best for dinner at the fashionable Sun Ya restaurant with his friends from the consular corps.

Giving her long hair a final stroke of the brush, Julia reflected that Harry had been acting rather proprietorial lately—with no justification. Although they had been out together from time to time during the past half year, she had given him no encouragement aside from chaste good-night kisses. Besides, she suspected that she was only a substitute for Emily, whom Harry had been besieging with invitations since her reappearance.

Emily would have had no time to see more of Harry even if she had wished to. Richard Hollings was leading her on a round of hectic gaiety, determined to dispel her depression over her break with her parents. Engrossed with Richard, Emily insisted she would have nothing to do with Harry beyond conventional politeness. But she had been charming to him before leaving with Richard for the jai alai matches. Emily believed that the American was in love with China, and that she attracted him chiefly because she was Chinese.

Julia passed a powderpuff over her nose and applied lipstick sparingly. Smoothing the silk over her hips, she opened the door to the sitting room. Harry Smythe sprang to his feet, his punctiliousness in sharp contrast to his normal Ivy League casualness. He pulled back the sleeve of his tan poplin jacket, looked at his watch meaningfully, and said, "Just time for a quick one, if you'd like."

"A gimlet would be fine," she agreed.

Very much at home, Harry was pouring the gin over the lime juice and ice when the doorbell rang. Julia opened the door—and saw Tommy Howe, his white sharkskin suit gleaming in the dim hall. Tommy smiled in greeting and stepped uninvited into the sitting room. His nonchalance faltered momentarily when he saw Harry Smythe. He blinked, then smiled again.

"Darling!" He addressed Julia alone. "So glad you're ready."

"Ready?" she asked. "Tommy, what . . ."

"Half your charm, Julie darling, is your vagueness," Tommy said provocatively. "You haven't forgotten, have you? We're booked for dinner tonight at the Soongs. . . . Evening, Smythe."

"The Soongs? But Tommy . . . Oh, yes. Of course. Was it really tonight? This is embarrassing. You see . . ."

It was embarrassing, very embarrassing, Tommy's barging in to the apartment talking about a mythical appointment. It would, however, have been far more embarrassing to deny that appointment and, almost certainly, get into an argument with Tommy while Harry looked on.

She was furious with Tommy, but what else could she do except play along with him? She was furious, Julia decided, though not *only* furious.

Harry Smythe was not, however, prepared to be supplanted so easily. He flushed but continued mixing the gimlets, even setting out a third glass for Tommy.

"There you are." Harry placed the gimlets on the Indian shawl that covered the packing-case coffee table. "Now, what's all this about? Julie and I are off to the Sun Ya in a minute."

"Oh," Tommy replied equably, "I assumed that you were waiting for my sister. Where is Em, by the way?"

"She's gone out," Julia said dully, "with Richard Hollings."

"Oh, yes," Tommy said. "Stupid of me to forget. . . . No need to hurry with your drink, Smythe. There's loads of time. We're not due at the Soongs till eight. . . . A shame I can't ask you along, but it's a sit-down dinner."

Harry gulped his gimlet, his brash self-assurance reduced for a moment to speechlessness by that double affront. He would, in truth, be pleased to dine with the Soongs, who were a prime source of information on Chinese politics, his professional obsession. He also knew, as did all Shanghai, that the Soongs did not serve Western food at home. And there was always room for one more at a Chinese dinner.

"I find it difficult to believe that Julia would make such a mistake," Harry said. "Totally forgetting your appointment and making two dates for the same—"

"But she did, didn't she?" For the first time, Tommy condescended to discuss the imbroglio directly with Harry. "So that's about all there is to it."

"Julie," Harry demanded, "did you really—"

"I'm sorry, Harry, very sorry!" She could not contradict Tommy and make matters even worse. "It's so silly of me. Can you ever forgive me?"

"If you say so," Harry said dubiously.

"Now do tell me what's been going on in Shanghai, Smythe," Tommy invited expansively. "Any new scandals in the consular corps? What about old Haskell Haroonian? Does his will still provide that his body be stuffed and sat down in the drawing room so his wife won't forget him?"

"I never heard that tale." Harry was intrigued despite himself. "Is it really true?"

"I'd swear to it, chum," Tommy replied. "But now, if you'll excuse us."

"I've got to be going myself," Harry said stiffly. "Julie, I'll be seeing you. And you . . . you, too."

When the door closed behind him, Julia turned upon Tommy, who was chuckling aloud. When she looked at him, her emotions were so confused that she could not speak for a moment or two. Against her will, she joined in his laughter. Then she quashed her amusement and looked sternly at him.

"I hope you're pleased with yourself, Tommy Howe," she said hotly. "You've embarrassed me desperately. You've insulted a good friend. Harry must think I'm mad. And all you do is chuckle."

"He was funny, though, wasn't he?" Using the same tactics that had frustrated Harry Smythe, Tommy refused to acknowledge her accusations.

"Now, Tommy, this is—"

"Dear me," he interrupted. "Harry went off so fast, he forgot his binoculars. I won't be a second."

He scooped up the binoculars and darted out the door, giving Julia time to compose herself. When he returned five minutes later, she was delighted to see him—and she was very angry at his high-handedness. She was humiliated by his treating her like a ninny in front of Harry —and she was exultant because he cared enough to be so masterful.

"What did you say to him?" she asked.

"I only told him he'd forgotten his binoculars."

"And that was all? I hope so."

"Actually, not quite all. I . . . ah . . . suggested that he not waste his energy trying to see you. Not for the next week, at least."

"Tommy, that wasn't very nice. What gives you the right to—"

"It's not a question of right, Julie. Actually, it's very simple. We've only got a week before I have to bury myself in the hospital. And we are going to play—just you and me."

He pulled her close and kissed her for the first time. Julia was astonished. This was like no kiss she had ever known. It was more like a tidal wave, she had half-decided when she stopped thinking.

17

OCTOBER 25, 1922

"Keep it light, my girl!" Julia had advised as she left the loft apartment shortly before Richard was expected. "Don't get too intense!"

That well-meant advice was at least a month too late at the end of October 1922. Besides, Julia herself was intensely involved with Tommy Howe—when he could escape from Shanghai General Hospital, where a junior intern worked a hundred hours a week.

"If we'd kept it light," Emily sighed to Richard an hour later. "I would have missed this . . . this pure pleasure."

"Great pleasure, Em." Richard grinned. "And too pure—much *too* pure!"

She plucked an orange cushion from the rosewood chair and flung it at his head. It sailed over the rattan sofa and grazed the standing lamp, which had been improvised from a five-foot-long Tibetan brass horn. Richard rose and scooped Emily out of her chair. He cradled her head in the curve of his neck and buried his face in her musky hair.

"Just don't tease me with talk of *pleasure*," he complained lightly. "It's hard enough already."

Though a retort sprang spontaneously to her lips, Emily chose to ignore the double entendre. Neither stupid nor ignorant, she did not lack the courage of her emotions. She was, she concluded in exasperation, just inhibited—badly inhibited.

It was 1922, not 1822, she reminded herself. Not only manners but morals had altered radically. Intelligent young women now sealed with their bodies the pledges made by their hearts.

Yet she hung back. Although Richard was not always insistent, she felt guilty at thwarting his natural desires—and her own. But the inhibitions passed on by a hundred generations of Chinese ladies were too strong.

Still, she gave herself to his caresses—and tingled with sensual pleasure. She loved his kisses, and her tongue darted in return. The rough touch of his hands against her skin, the prickle of the stubble on his jaw made her feel small, fragile, and protected.

Nonetheless, she froze whenever his hand moved toward the delta between her thighs. In spite of herself, she stiffened—and he felt her involuntary rejection. She could neither feign receptivity nor give herself wholly.

Richard might cajole her, but he never blamed her. His good humor naturally made her feel guilty, as if she were a miser of emotions. Though he seemed resigned, if not content, to wait, she feared that indefinitely postponing physical consummation could destroy their love.

Nonetheless, the exhilaration that flared in her whenever they met— even if they had been apart only an hour or two—made the sky itself bright. His cynicism and his reserve dissolving, Richard had in turn told her that he felt his heart leap against his ribs whenever he saw her.

He was telling the truth: their powerful feeling for each other bound them together despite their differences. He was an Englishman who had come five years earlier to the alien culture of China, while she was a treaty-port Chinese who had spent much of her life in the United States. Yet they had discovered large areas of knowledge and many attitudes in common. For the first time in his extensive—though shallow—experience of women, Richard Hollings loved a woman as much with his mind as with his body. The interplay of their minds offered delights almost as exquisite as the interplay of their emotions. The complete physical intimacy they both desired, he concluded, he must attain through her mind. Not to seduce her intellect, but to seduce her body *through* her intellect—and thus overwhelm her inhibitions.

He set Emily down in the rosewood chair. Though she felt regret, she was inured to his breaking off their embraces when, as he had explained with slight embarrassment, he could no longer bear the physical tension they aroused. She smiled, penitent and silent.

Abruptly, he started an abstract discussion: "You'll never succeed. It's against nature. Men want baubles as much as women do."

"What *are* you talking about Richard? I don't want baubles. I only want you."

"If only that was completely true, darling. But I was just thinking that China would never succeed as a republic. Men—and their wives—want geegaws. The old Confucian dynasties cleverly handed out the bribes: medals, peacock feathers, and titles of nobility. Britain does the same today. Giving titles is the cheapest—and not the worst—way to run an empire."

"What have those baubles got to do with running a country?"

"If a man hopes to become Sir Alfred Smith or Lord Puddleby, he'll work efficiently—even stay reasonably honest."

"I don't believe titles make that much difference," she said. "Shanghai makes Hong Kong look like a sleepy backwater, though men like my father can't expect knighthoods." Emily stalked back and forth as she spoke. "Shanghai is dynamic because there are many nationalities here, not only stodgy British and cheeky Cantonese. And they all compete. They rub against each other—and they generate an electric atmosphere which galvanizes the Chinese of Shanghai, whether they're coolies or capitalists. The Settlement offers freedom for enterprise, not just security. No titles, but profits and good wages."

"Riding your hobbyhorse again? Adam Smith, invisible hand, free enterprise, and all that." Richard mocked gravely. "And how are things at the ladies' bank?"

Emily bridled at the smugness that oiled his voice when he spoke of the Women's Bank. A self-declared Bohemian, Richard despised all commerce and savagely condemned the misdeeds of Shanghai's taipans. He agreed with Jack Pavernen that all of them were crooks. Condescension colored his tone when he discussed the modest premises at 219 Nanking Road where Emily spent her working days. His dark eyes sparkled maliciously; his lips curled scornfully; and his lean body slouched even lower—all to signal his contempt. Only a foolish woman, he had once said unguardedly, would surrender her birthright of femininity to compete in the grubby realm of commerce.

Emily was still puzzled by his attitude. How could he show such contempt for her work when he was insistently wooing her? He could not be jealous of her titles: assistant cashier and chief loan officer. Perhaps he begrudged the time she spent at the bank. Perhaps it was something fundamental. Although his avowed Bohemianism forced him to endorse women's rights, she sometimes sensed that her militant feminism irritated him.

Emily shivered. The damp October chill was creeping into the loft despite the pot-bellied stoves glowing at either end of the cavernous living room. She shivered despite the gray flannel suit with the full skirt she had worn to the office and to a quick supper at Jeffrey's Kitchen. Her eyes unseeing, she stared pensively into the distance.

"I didn't mean to annoy you." Dick was sensitive to her mood. "I'm honestly concerned. You say you like the work, but do you truly?"

"Of course I do!" The weight of her resentment lifted, and she laughed. "I'm also earning a living!"

"You must enjoy it! How many times have I offered to help? And there is your writing."

"My writing couldn't keep that great oaf of a puppy Adam in bones. Anyway, you're not much better off than I am. How could I accept your financial help? I don't even know what you *mean* by help."

"I mean we could marry," he said aggrieved. "Not tomorrow but some day very soon. As soon as I get the deputy editorship and the rise that goes with it."

"If we wait for the paper to give you that raise, we could wait forever. Anyway, I've told you, I don't even want to think about marrying now. There're too many things I want to do. Meanwhile, I enjoy the bank. It's a new world, as exciting as Tibet or Timbuktu."

"Only chap I met who'd been to Timbuktu said it was duller than Swansea on a wet Sunday after chapel." He was relieved by her refusal to discuss marriage, which he did not really want to think about. "Why is the bank so fascinating? Tell me, for example, what you did today."

"It may surprise you. I talked the loan committee into putting up a hundred thousand Mex for a new hotel on Kiangse Road."

"A hundred thousand isn't small change. But why so jubilant?"

"The hotel is to open next month. It's to be called the Ikra, and the proprietress is Elizaveta Alexandrovna Yavalenka. Now what do you think of that?"

"You've torn it now, really torn it. Indignant husbands and fathers will swoop down in moral outrage and carry all you innocent banking ladies back to your homes. Don't you know—"

"We're not *that* innocent!" she flared. "We're all quite aware that Liz hasn't always behaved perfectly. So don't—"

"Hold, enough!" He raised his palm defensively. "You know I was joking. How in the name of God did you get respectable ladies to put up the money for . . . ah . . . a *maison de rendezvous*?"

"A cathouse, they say in South Philadelphia." She smiled grimly.

"Frankly, I had to fight my own instincts. She is exploiting women, but I can't stamp out prostitution in Shanghai single-handed. Better that a woman should . . . Anyway, our business, I told them, is doing business: profits for the Women's Bank first, and promoting female business interests second. No reason to base loan policy on personal morals—unless the applicant's morals affected her credit-worthiness. We'd received a businesslike application from a businesswoman in need of additional capital, and we had to consider it on its merits. If the figures checked out, how could we refuse the loan? Turning Miss Yavalenka down would prove what the men said: Women in business are ruled by their emotions, rather than hardheaded commercial considerations."

"Brava!" He applauded lightly. "A magnificent performance. I take it they granted the loan."

"Of course! What else could they do?"

Although Richard regarded the Women's Bank condescendingly, he was pleased by Emily's growing self-confidence, which sprang from her success in business. Whatever love might be, he knew he loved the deceptively frail-looking Chinese girl. Why, otherwise, would he tolerate his peculiar position? He was her lover, but not wholly, because the emancipated young woman was not wholly emancipated, but was inhibited by traditional restraints.

"What's next?" he asked gravely.

"As a matter of fact . . ."

Darting into the kitchen, Emily returned with two champagne flutes and a frosted bottle of Krug 1912, the last of Joshua Haleevie's housewarming present.

"I'll do that," he offered. "Opening champagne is a man's job."

"Not tonight, darling. To Elizaveta and the Ikra! To success! To the Women's Bank!"

The wine frothed in the crystal flutes, paler than moonlight and fragrant as yellow roses. Bubbles beaded the sides and the rim, constantly forming and dissolving.

Through the flute Richard surveyed Emily's features, which were as pale and patrician as the champagne. It was ironic that he should give her his affection unreservedly after years devoted to ladies who were far more adventurous sexually. Odd, too, that the lady to whom he wished to dedicate his life was Chinese.

Suppose he brought Emily home? His bigoted father would scorn her as "a yellow bint." His genteel mother would sniff bronchially and flutter in fear of the neighbors' disapproval. No, he would never bring

Emily home to them. He would never give them the chance to humiliate his wife . . . if, of course, she finally consented to marry him.

Besides, she could well look down on his parents' manner of life, which was meager beside her family's gilded existence. Now chief clerk to the leading solicitors in Leeds, his father had moved a world away from his grandfather, a shepherd who owned only his crook and his dog. Richard's own ascension, first to public school on a scholarship and subsequently to the University of Cambridge, after attaining a lieutenancy in the Intelligence Corps, created an even greater distance between his parents and himself.

Yet they felt he had thrown all his advantages away. After working briefly as a junior reporter on the *Yorkshire Post*, he had accepted an offer from the *North China Daily News*. Only his connection with *The Times* had saved him from his parents' total condemnation. To them *The Times* was not a newspaper but an institution—less than the Crown, but almost as exalted. But he still lived in that abyss of evil, Shanghai.

He had come to Shanghai to escape his parents' withering respectability—and to conquer a new world. He knew with absolute certainty that he would conquer. He would throw their condemnation back in their teeth by becoming the best-known journalist in the world.

Would marrying Emily help him or hinder him? He did not really know, and at that moment he did not really care.

"You're far too pensive." She brought out a second bottle of champagne. "No thinking allowed tonight. I'll fix you."

She sprang exuberantly to her feet and circled the loft, flapping her arms like wings.

"We're celebrating," she burbled. "Celebrating my victory. I stung them quick as a bee. Now I'll sting you."

Rasping staccato in her throat, Emily hurled herself onto his lap. Her skirt rucked up when she turned and twined her arms around his neck.

Richard touched his lips to hers and tasted the heady fragrance of champagne in her mouth. A few glasses could exhilarate a slender girl who was, despite her bravado, unaccustomed to champagne's insidious sparkle. He regretfully drew back and loosened his embrace. He must not seduce her now, even if she was only a little tight. It would not be honorable. And she might never forgive him.

"What's wrong?" she demanded. "Don't stop. If we're ever to . . ."

When he still hesitated, she declared hotly, "Don't be so damned gentlemanly. I'm not drunk."

She took his hand in both of hers, gravely kissing it, and placed his palm on the long-forbidden silk-covered delta.

"Now show me!" Her breath tingled in his ear. "Show me everything!"

He slipped his arms under her and rose from the sofa. Her liquid eyes gravely studied his face. Silent for fear of breaking the mood, he carried Emily to her bed. She drew him down to her.

"I'm not drunk, you know." She kissed his ear and whispered, "I'm just pretending."

He had seen her drink more wine with less effect—and it was too late for scruples. One way or the other, she might never forgive him. He began undoing her gray flannel jacket, kissing her lips after each button.

"It's just like peeling an orange." She chuckled. "A juicy orange."

Richard gasped in delight when she was naked on the aquamarine coverlet. With the lipstick all but kissed off, her mouth was a faint vermilion; her skin was pale ivory; and her nipples were light pink. He laid his head on her breast, and she held him to her. An instant later, she stiffened and drew away.

Too late, Richard thought, believing himself cool in judgment despite the blood pounding in his ears. If he drew back now, they would never be so close together again. Whatever she thought she felt, he would not falter unless she resisted strongly.

She might afterward be infuriated or disgusted. But he had to risk that.

Although her eyes were closed, Emily was acutely aware of his every movement. When she felt him heavy upon her, her hips moved tentatively of their own and her thighs parted. She screamed in fleeting pain a few moments later.

Much later, Richard kissed her breasts and drew the coverlet up. Her lips in the hollow of his throat and his lips against her temple, they lay quietly for a time. Her tears were damp on his shoulder.

She finally whispered, kissing his shoulder, "That was nice, Richard, very nice. But why do people make such a fuss? Is that all there is to it?"

He smoothed the damp tendrils of hair off her forehead and kissed her eyelids before he replied, "No, that's not all, not by a long shot. Especially for a woman. I've been told that women can feel so intensely that—"

"Who told you?" she interrupted. "No, never mind. I don't want to know. You're sure?"

"Quite sure. Exquisite feelings . . . sensations so intense they almost consume—"

"Well, that won't be necessary!" she declared judiciously. "Though it could . . ."

As he leaned over to kiss her, she said, "It could be true. We must try again—very soon. I suspect I could get to like it!"

18

DECEMBER 22, 1922

The house was unpretentious, just another six-story tenement on Kiangse Road. The drab red-brick façade belied the Edwardian opulence within, and the old-fashioned brass bellpull had been burnished by many palms over the years. Beneath it, IKRA was engraved on a brass plaque that, after only four weeks, was minutely worn by assiduous polishing. Discreetly lowered shades asserted the house's respectability.

The raffish Delage coupé, which gleamed sapphire when the streetlamps came on at five in the afternoon, marred the impression of stolid bourgeois virtue. Behind it, a Marmon limousine was discharging champagne, brandy, and claret. The chauffeur chivied the porters who were carrying the cases into a bijou elevator with heliotrope velvet curtains.

The owner of the Delage was fretting in the red plush parlor. Joshua Haleevie felt that his Christmas presents were more welcome than himself. The bottles were being sent directly to the private apartment on the top floor, but he still awaited a summons. The concierge had passed on Elizaveta's regret that she could not at that moment even say a word on the internal telephone system, whose installation Joshua had supervised. Smiling in strained resignation, he flung himself down on the red-striped settee to sip his brandy and soda.

All males were temporarily excluded from the private sitting room, where Elizaveta Alexandrovna Yavalenka was entertaining Julia Pavernen and Emily Howe. After the Edwardian pomposities of the public rooms, Elizaveta's apartment was refreshingly simple: white rattan furniture and mint-green cushions. With her only female friends, Elizaveta could relax. She could even show her true face beneath her professional hauteur, which was modeled on her godmother, Grand Duchess Olga, who had been murdered by the Bolsheviks with her parents, the czar and the czarina, in 1918.

Elizaveta dramatically drew on a dark Egyptian cigarette through a lapis lazuli holder. When she glided toward the window, her sable-edged train swirled. Her guests' afternoon dresses seemed drab beside her chartreuse evening gown with the diamanté embroidery.

"It's all theater, of course." Even in her professional regalia, Elizaveta was not above self-satire. "I'm selling illusion, you know. How do you like this little number? Mummy's favorite court dress. Properly worn with a tiara, but I thought that would be going too far."

She poured Lapsang souchong from a silver teapot into bone china cups and served lemon slices with silver tongs heavy with embossed silver grapes. No prop had been omitted that would complete the illusion of an opulent private mansion during the reign of King Edward VII.

"Smashing, isn't it?" Elizaveta almost dissolved into giggles. "My dears, it's great fun. Such a lark!"

Julia's newly acquired tact sugared her comment: "It's brilliant, Liz. The Ikra even smells just right. Those musky perfumes, and the armoa of cigars and Napoleon cognac."

Julia had assured herself that she was not shocked by the Ikra's obvious purpose. Emily had noted primly in her office diary: "Inspecting premises on Kiangse Road on which a mortgage is held." Elizaveta had already led them on a tour of inspection.

The suites on the fifth floor were sealed by formidable padlocks and reserved for permanent guests. The salons and dining rooms on the first two floors were public, as were the casino and the ballroom in the big circular extension in the rear. The bizarre splendors of the suites on the third and fourth floors were, however, designed for the most private of activities.

The Caligula Suite was built around a nine-foot-square marble sunken bath, which was flanked by a marble slab for massage and a marble dais with a marble bench "for a lute player." The bath chamber was paneled with creamy travertine marble and heated by gilded radiators to seventy-eight degrees.

Behind other doors lay a Japanese pavilion, as well as apartments in the styles of the Egypt of Amenhotep and the France of Louis XIV. A cubular chamber with red strip-lighting featured a chain-festooned post hung with knouts, quirts, and whips. Julia had not dared ask about the enigmatic black-and-silver machines in the bathroom, and Emily had turned her eyes away.

"It's nearly six," Elizaveta announced when they left those dark male-oriented fantasies for the immaculate feminity of her sitting room. "The sun's just over the yardarm. And I've just time for a drink and a gossip."

"Only one ship in the Hwangpoo today with a yardarm, an old four-masted grain-carrier from Southampton." Emily was tart. "And the sun's been over that yardarm for an hour. It's dark outside."

"Yardarm or hard arm," Elizaveta laughed, "I want some of Joshua's champagne. It's fit for a board room, he says, or a bawd's room."

Emily smiled thinly at that defensive ribaldry, and Elizaveta looked at her speculatively. She was markedly more attractive, her bosom fuller and her skin glowing. There was one obvious explanation for that radiance—and for Emily's casual understanding of Elizaveta's double entendres. The Englishman who looked like a Frenchman must have finally succeeded in getting her into bed. Why did the Chinese make such a fuss about sex?

Seeing Julia blush, Elizaveta asked slyly, "Still a virgin, Julie? What's the matter with Tommy? Does he need guidance from his sister?"

Having reduced both her guests to appalled silence, Elizaveta sipped her champagne. Her friends expected her to be outrageous.

"Liz, time will cure most things, including my virginity," Julia responded resiliently. "I won't tell you how to run your business—so don't tell me how to run my life. . . . Those padlocked rooms on the fifth floor, who uses them? And what do they do there?"

"Not what you think. Very respectable Russian gentlemen stay there. As Emily knows, they put up half the capital for the Ikra. Though the Whites have been forced out of Siberia, they still hope—and plot. Also, they buy arms. Your Uncle Jack's often here to see them."

"Aren't you giving away secrets, Liz?" Emily's tone was barbed. "I thought ladies like . . . like you . . . never told who their . . . ah . . . clients were."

"I didn't say he was a client. Only that he visited my fifth-floor lodgers. And I do not require instruction from—"

"Poor old Uncle Jack could use some new business," Julia interjected to head off an open quarrel. "He's got a new Korean girl friend, and she's expensive. Anyway, the armament business is so slow he probably couldn't afford your—"

"What about Riverview Manor? Have you solved your problems there?" Elizaveta's insatiable appetite for gossip was a professional asset. "I warned you that builder fellow, Vass, wasn't to be trusted."

"Vass finished everything two months ago, even the concrete bathtubs. Marbleized, he calls them. Everyone's moved in. But the banks have taken all the money."

A telephone rang, and Elizaveta lifted the brass-and-malachite instrument from behind a cushion.

"Yes, my love, do come up now," she said throatily. "I'm afraid I forgot about you. We were having such a good time. . . . No, I won't. Never again, I promise. . . . He is? When? Oh, now. That *is* interesting. Good-bye, darling. Hurry!"

Julia was disturbed by Elizaveta's casual treatment of Joshua. Elizaveta was amused by Julia's obvious distaste for the business of the Ikra, despite her forthright acceptance of the trade in guns. Yet the commerce in flesh was, at worst, a simulacrum of love, while the commerce in armaments was, ultimately, death.

Elizaveta considered her own trade moral, indeed benevolent, compared with John Pavernen's trafficking in guns. A good house gave much pleasure—and no pain to either patrons or practitioners, unless they wanted pain. A good war was impossible, since all war inflicted pain and death—even the mock wars of the warlords.

The countess who rarely used her title felt aristocratic disdain for bourgeois sexual morality. She did not, however, believe in "free love," which was as bad for the heart as it was for her business. She did believe in love and was, therefore, amused by the middle-class inhibitions that disturbed her friends. But she did not speak of her reflections on love and war. Her lover was on the point of arriving, and it was her rule not to discuss serious matters with men.

"Joshua's on his way up," she remarked instead. "He says General Chiang Kai-shek is also honoring my humble establishment. Natty as an organ grinder in a velvet-collared chesterfield and a checked suit."

"Poor May Soong. She mustn't ever know he comes here," Emily said. "How she can moon after a man with a wife and two half-grown sons! And now this!"

"You've done it now, Liz," Julia taunted. "You've told us the name of a client."

"Hardly, my dear. General Chiang Kai-shek visits a gentleman on the fifth floor. Though he does patronize other houses, I hear. When he comes to the Ikra on *my* business, my lips will be sealed. But in Shanghai *everyone* talks about business and politics."

". . . and love!" Emily retorted, while Julia insisted, ". . . and sex!"

"If I'm not mistaken," Joshua Haleevie interjected, stepping out of the elevator, "you're talking about my favorite subject."

"What's that, my darling?" Elizabeta lifted her face for his kiss. "Business or politics?"

"Neither," he replied. "Only love."

"And sex?" she teased. "They don't always go together."

"With me, they always do," Joshua declared. "But we're embarrassing your guests. Good evening, ladies."

Joshua had acquired his upper-class English accent at Harrow, and to American eyes, his manner was typically English. Restrained, almost inhibited, he never wore his Distinguished Service Cross, not even when in uniform as a major of the Shanghai Volunteer Corps. Yet his bow was continental, almost Levantine, and his manners were by a hairbreadth too good to be quite English.

Although his pale blue eyes were sometimes clouded by introspection, the thirty-year-old son of the immensely wealthy Sir Judah Haleevie was considered a playboy by fashionable Shanghai. He was, nonetheless, devoted to his Russian mistress, who treated him so casually. Although his words were light and sometimes cynical, he was always kind and, Emily sensed, vulnerable.

General Chiang Kai-shek would have been appalled to learn that Joshua Haleevie had recognized him. His fedora had been pulled down and his collar raised to conceal his features. Later all would come out, but not just yet.

There was, fortunately, little danger of premature disclosure. The White Russian proprietress, who was young and naïve, believed her sponsors were White Russian loyalists drawing on the gold hoard of the czars. Should she learn of his presence, she would assume that he was involved in their childish schemes.

Chiang Kai-shek was repelled by the Ikra's overwhelmingly foreign character, which was displayed by the wreaths, the mistletoe, and the colored ribbons celebrating the Christmas season. His mood was, nonetheless, buoyant, as became the chief representative of the National People's Party. President Sun Yat-sen had entrusted these life-or-death negotiations to him alone. They had learned to depend on each other during their fifty-three days together on the gunboat off Canton before the Old Man finally agreed to retreat to Shanghai.

Dr. Sun's house at 29 Rue Molière in Frenchtown was not only a more comfortable but a better base than the gunboat. The Nationalist leader was in close touch with both Feng Yü-hsiang, who was called the Christian General, and Chang Tso-lin, the Old Marshal of Manchuria. Dr. Sun was, nonetheless, fed up with warlords, having concluded that only when all warlords were crushed could China attain his three goals: national power, general prosperity, and universal democracy.

Undeterred by repeated failures, even the gory Canton Mutiny, President Sun was now seeking allies abroad to support the Northern Expedition that would destroy the warlords. Sun Yat-sen was a Christian, but Christian powers like Britain and America would not help him, largely because the present disorder was too much to their liking. He therefore believed his best hope was an alliance with the Communist International in Moscow—and with its protégé, the Chinese Communist Party.

The Comintern offered not only gold and guns to Dr. Sun's National People's Party but, almost as important, agitators skilled in fomenting revolution and generals skilled in waging civil war. Moreover, the new Communist Party of China was mobilizing a new political force by fostering a militant labor movement. Rapidly becoming more powerful, the Communist Party had in the year and a half since its First National Congress in Shanghai brilliantly instigated politically aimed strikes by miners, railway workers, and seamen. Working closely with the Communists would greatly strengthen the National People's Party—and Chiang Kai-shek was now entrusted with the responsibility for arranging that cooperation on the best possible terms.

When, on December 22, 1922, General Chiang ascended to the fifth floor of the Ikra amid the Christmas decorations that so irritated him, most members of the Chinese Communist Party had already become members of the National People's Party. There was no alternative, even for such independent men as Chang Kuo-tao, the labor leader, and Mao Tse-tung, the firebrand from Hunan Province. Regardless of their personal inclinations, the Comintern had ordered them to join the Nationalists. They had obeyed, rather than breach the Communist Party's discipline by individualistic disobedience. If the Nationalists and the Communists could today agree on outstanding issues, the two militant political parties would announce their new alliance—and soon sweep to power over all China.

Chiang Kai-shek knew that alliance would be the most significant development since the Revolution of 1911 overthrew the Manchu Dynasty. No more than the Communists, however, did he believe the alliance would endure indefinitely. Each side planned to use the other and then throw it aside "like a squeezed lemon," as Chiang himself said in private.

"Come in, General." The small, bearded European who responded to

Chiang's knock spoke excellent Mandarin. "I believe you know Mr. Chang Kuo-tao, the labor organizer."

The heavily padded door bearing the number 555 ensured against eavesdropping. But when the door closed, microphones hidden in the room relayed the conversation to the basement, where two plainclothesmen listened through bulky earphones and jotted Chinese shorthand.

Joshua Haleevie had planted those microphones when he installed the Ikra's internal telephone system. Although Joshua's role was not precisely defined, Tommy had been right when he told Julia of his suspicion that their friend played a major part in the Settlement's intelligence operations.

Because he was a volunteer with excellent connections in London, Joshua was extremely powerful. He was to report to London that Nationalists and Communists had finally reached a firm agreement. By its terms, all members of the Communist Party were also to become members of the National People's Party, and the Communist leaders were to hold high office in the Nationalist hierarchy.

Joshua was then to relay his own interpretation: First, the Soviet Union, working through the Communist International, had won a decisive political victory. Second, the Communists would increase their influence enormously by joining Dr. Sun Yat-sen, who possessed great personal prestige and a standing army. Third, the critical new phase in the struggle for China that had just begun was likely to be crowned by a sweeping victory for the new alliance.

A sealed envelope was passed from the Comintern agent to General Chiang Kai-shek to seal the pact. Joshua therefore could not tell London the exact amount of the first installment of the subsidy Moscow was to pay the Nationalists. He could, however, report: "The sum is very substantial—a heavy weight of gold, which will tip the balance of power."

JANUARY 23, 1923

"Tommy, please mind your own business." Julia's tone was light, but her green eyes were chilly. "It's got nothing to do with you!"

"You're almost living at that brothel. And you've got my sister involved up to her neck." Tommy flushed. "Then you have the gall, the infernal gall, to say it's nothing to do with me. Is Emily nothing to do with me? Are *you*, may I ask, nothing to do with me? Bloody hell, woman!"

Despite her half-defensive irritation, Julia smiled. The English public school rhetoric Tommy fell into when he was indignant always made her laugh, and she could not stay angry at him when she was laughing at him. Like his upper-class English drawl, his words contrasted with his features, which might have belonged to a Confucian philosopher-official. Except for his sensitive mouth, he looked detached and aristocratic. Schoolboy epithets fell incongruously from the lips that might have graced a Tang Dynasty poet.

"Bloody hell yourself!" she retorted, still laughing. "Sometimes you're so narrow-minded you make your famous great-great-grandfather look easy-going."

Between amusement and pride, Tommy had once told her about the ancestor who refused to recognize the Manchu usurpers as the legitimate rulers of China. As stubborn as he was long-lived, that mandarin had fled to remote Szechwan Province, where he always wore the official robes of the overthrown Ming Dynasty. When he died at eighty-six, his last will had directed that he be buried in those robes.

That streak of puritanical stubbornness had evidently passed to

Tommy, the descendant in the tenth generation of that unswerving loyalist. Tommy should have been relaxing during these rare hours of freedom from Shanghai General Hospital, where his protracted working days were further prolonged by ward duty every second night and every second weekend. Instead, he was hotly—and proprietorially—questioning Julia's relations with Elizaveta Yavalenka and the Hotel Ikra.

Julia had peremptorily cleared the loft apartment to receive its former tenant. She had pushed out not only the amah Lao Zee, who left a cold supper, but Emily and Richard, who wanted to make it a convivial evening. They had gone docilely when she asked, even Tommy's sister recognizing that Julia had the right to insist upon seeing him alone.

Aside from Julia and Tommy, only the devoted dog called Adam remained, staring with adoring eyes at the two humans. But Tommy was not relaxing. Instead of basking in Julia's affection, the young doctor was restive. He had just reprimanded her almost intemperately for "frequenting the sordid brothel that Russian tart runs—and also tempting my innocent sister to frequent it."

Refraining with an effort from commenting on his sister's innocence or lack of innocence, Julia patiently pointed out that neither Emily nor she *frequented* the Ikra. Three visits to their friend Elizaveta in a month hardly made them habitués. Besides, she said, the Ikra was certainly not sordid—anything but. Nor was it a brothel. Obviously the Ikra, like any hotel, rented out rooms, but no woman other than Elizaveta and the maidservants lived on the premises.

"A knocking shop is still a knocking shop," Tommy snorted. "Even if it sends out for its tarts."

Julia was irritated by Tommy's old-fashioned morality, although she was herself troubled when she thought about the Ikra's real purpose, which she of course knew full well. But she was living in the third decade of the innovating twentieth century. The rigid rules of the past no longer applied.

Still, it was good to know that Tommy's standards for men differed only slightly from his standards for women. And he kept to those standards. A modern man, he would now hug her and kiss her, but he would not cross certain lines. Julia often wondered about the delights at which Emily's reticence hinted, delights that Elizaveta's earthiness extolled. Sometimes she ached for those unknown—and still forbidden—pleasures. Yet she would not know how to seduce Tommy, even if she were certain that she wanted to. Despite his puritanical streak, an assertive male like Tommy had certainly had experience of women. But he would not dream of seducing a woman like her.

The emotional aspect was, Julia reminded herself, far more important than the physical. By the early winter of 1922, she felt certain that Tommy's affection for her was neither passing nor shallow. He was, she sensed, kept from expressing his deeper feelings largely by his innate reserve, which derived equally from his Chinese heritage and his British schooling.

Unless his affection for her was strong, he would not take her to Harmony Hall to dine with his parents, to whom she had, of course, first been introduced as Emily's friend. Ironically, the daughter of the house had been driven out because of her affection for a foreigner, whom she might well marry, whereas the son of the house freely entertained a foreigner, whom, his parents were obviously confident, he had no thought of ever marrying.

Chinese society treated women far more unfairly than did the West. It was the double standard enshrined: wholly different rules for men and women were integral to Confucian society. The ultrarespectable upper class, to which the Howes belonged, held as inviolable the prohibition against marrying outsiders.

Julia really had no idea what future, if any, lay before Tommy and her, though no young woman of almost twenty-two could avoid speculating on marriage. She did, however, know her own mind: Someday she might wish to marry Tommy Howe, but she definitely did not wish to marry him today or tomorrow. Nor even a year from today, which was as far into the uncertain future as she could project her thoughts.

She was fond of Tommy, very fond. But, Julia assured herself, she was not in love with him. The great exhilaration she felt whenever she saw him was illusory. She must not mistake infatuation, however exhilarating, for love. Besides, she would not wish to live in Shanghai all her life. Actually, she wondered how to tell her parents that she would be staying just a few months longer.

Tommy, for his part, never alluded to any hope that they would be together tomorrow or the day after, not to speak of next year. Perhaps he simply assumed that they would, though the permanence of marriage evidently never entered his mind. Given his background, he undoubtedly considered marriage to a foreigner impossible—if he ever thought about it. Perhaps she was to him no more than a passing entertainment, piquant because she was American. In that case, why in God's name did he not at least *attempt* to seduce her.

"Unlike my stubborn old ancestor, I'm open to conviction," Tommy was saying. "Why don't we drop over to the Ikra and have a look at Elizaveta's innocent little establishment?"

"Drop over to the Ikra?" Julia stalled for time. "I'm not really sure that's a good idea. Emmy and I only visit in the afternoon, when Liz has some spare time."

"Which proves what I said!" Tommy snorted. "She's far too busy in the evenings with her flock of tarts. Now will you please stay away from that ruddy brothel?"

"I will not!" Julia shook her head decisively. "And I won't ask Emily to stay away either. And as far as I'm concerned, you can go there any time you want. I won't mind . . . I guess."

"You only guess, do you?"

"Oh Tommy, don't be tiresome. Of course I wouldn't like it, even if we're not . . . Anyway, I assure you Liz isn't luring Emmy and me into a life of sin. What's more, you started the whole thing. You took us to St. Andrew's Café. You practically introduced us to Liz. So how can you talk?"

"It was different then," he said. "It was just a lark—and there were four of us to guard your innocence. How was I to know that you and Elizaveta would become such close friends? How was I to know that she would become . . . ah . . . what she's become? Everything was totally different then."

"What do you mean by *everything*? What has changed so totally since that night?"

"Julie, you must know what I mean. You certainly should know. I didn't feel then . . . I didn't feel about you the way I do now. You see, don't you? Everything was different!"

The telephone shrilled—and kept Julia from coaxing Tommy into expanding the strongest declaration of affection he had ever given her. But she could not ignore the summons of the upright instrument. She sighed and lifted the earpiece from its wishbone rest.

She heard a high-pitched static rather than the crackling that normally preceded Central's cheery greeting: "Is that nine-oh-six-five-four?" After almost half a minute, Central did say, "Nine-oh-six-five-four? I'm sorry. Interference on the line. Your caller has disconnected."

Their promising conversation had also been disconnected by the telephone's interference. Julia nonetheless hopefully seated herself beside Tommy on the rattan sofa. He took her hand, and she felt he would again talk of his feeling for her. The gesture was, however, intended to soften his next words.

"I'm not desperately worried about your being corrupted," he said.

"Not in *that* sense. Not . . . ah . . . physically. The false values of a place like the Ikra are dangerous. Still—"

"Tommy, *all* Shanghai is false values," she broke in. "It's all tinsel and champagne and bright lights and caviar. And I love it. I love it, but I don't kid myself that it's real—certainly not for a lifetime."

Tommy was not drawn by her provocative disclaimer about not spending a lifetime in Shanghai. Instead, he said abruptly, "Shanghai is also hunger and misery. . . . Any rate, I was on the point of remarking that something else is worrying me. I don't like the closed little world you and Emily and Elizaveta are creating. You're like spies . . . enemy spies . . . in my world, the male world. But you always go back to your secret female world, as if it were another planet. I don't like your keeping apart from me . . . having a secret life I can't share. I don't like not knowing what you're up to. I care too much for you. Sometimes I think I care far too much for you."

Julia caught her breath. He was coming close—very close. He had not yet said he loved her. But he had said that he cared for her greatly.

"Poor Tommy!" she said provocatively. "There is *no* secret female world full of mystery and black magic. There's only silliness and gossip. . . . Oh, I'm so glad you're jealous."

She hugged his arm exuberantly, intensely aware of his shoulder pressing against her breasts. Exactly how did it feel to him, she wondered, raising her face. His mouth was hard against hers, and his lips parted. A heavy yet delightful languor crept over Julia, and she waited expectantly. Even if he did not tell her more ardently how much he cared, he would certainly tell her again. She was waiting and wondering how she would answer when the telephone shrilled again.

"Drat it!" Julia exploded. "Damn it to hell!"

She rose to placate the squalling instrument. Tommy smiled at her vehemence, but he looked for an instant as if he had lost something vital.

"Yes, I'll wait. Connect them as soon as you can." Julia irritably bit off her words. "Yes, it is. Who's that calling?"

"Smidgelou Tomas here!" In spite of herself, Julia smiled at the Middle European voice. "I am warning you."

Inured to his bizarre English, she only responded, "Hello, Mr. Smidgelou. What's the trouble?"

"We are having fires, two fires in one day."

"Then the stove draws well, and your house is warm? I'm glad."

"Is not fires in stove, Missy. Is fires in walls."

"Fires in the wall, Mr. Smidgelou? How can that be?"

"I do not know, Missy. Manya and me are sitting happily in new home. And then, boom, fire is coming out of wall."

"Anyone hurt? Any damage? I am sorry, Mr. Smidgelou."

His chin propped on his palms, Tommy leaned over the back of the sofa and entoned funereally, "Never admit liability. Never acknowledge fault. Golden rules for young doctors, also applicable to embryo real-estate taipans."

She waved him to silence and continued: "Of course we'll take care of it. Probably some minor fault. And everything's all right now?"

"After throwing water on fire, all is right. Only underneath, where paint is washed off, wall is a little green."

Since there was no injury and only negligible damage, Julia dismissed the incident as a freak. She would of course have the contractor Gustav Vass check, but she laughed as she told Tommy. To her surprise, he frowned. Still, men loved to make a fuss about anything mechanical. Automobiles, plumbing, and electricity were the sacred mysteries they cherished, as women cherished the mystical travail of childbirth.

"Spontaneous combustion?" he muttered. "Don't see how, unless there's sulphur in the plaster. But that's ridiculous."

Julia smiled fondly as he pondered aloud: "Jack Pavernen's proud of having electric lighting and sockets throughout. Julie, your man better take a close look at the wiring. Faulty insulation, maybe."

"And the green on the walls, Tommy?" She was minutely alarmed. "What could that be?"

"I'll be bug—I really couldn't say. Mold perhaps. But why *underneath* the paint. Sorry, Julie, I really couldn't say. But it sounds like trouble!"

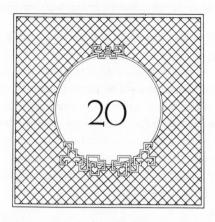

Staring through the grimy window of the train, Tommy Howe wondered whether it had been wise to accept the invitation from Chang Kuo-tao, the Communist leader Julia fondly recalled as "the big man who brought me Adam." His friend was to preside over the Inaugural Congress of China's first major labor union on February 2, 1923—with the blessings of the warlord who controlled Peking. The Peking-Hankow Railway Workers' General Union was the leader of the rapidly expanding labor movement dominated by the Chinese Communist Party. And Chang Kuo-tao was the prime mover.

His destination was Hankow, which bestrode the Yangtze River some 500 miles southwest of Shanghai. He would, however, travel by a roundabout route that took him 1,200 miles by train, ferry, and train again. The alternative was a slow voyage aboard a Yangtze River steamer. The railways were rudimentary, and neither buses nor cars dared venture onto the dirt tracks of the interior. Medieval China began just outside modern Shanghai.

By the time he reached Hankow, Tommy almost wished he had come by steamer. Having deliberately taken the long journey through the interior of China, which was hardly more familiar to him than the Valley of the Nile, he had in four days seen so much hunger, squalor, and disease that he almost despaired. The wretched peasants doggedly ploughed the meager soil and kept death at bay for another year or two. Their lives were not even medieval but primitive.

Hankow was more advanced. Its people lived in relative comfort—largely because it was a treaty port, like Shanghai, developed by foreigners. Imperialist stronghold or not, he was delighted to alight from the bone-shaking railway carriage at Hankow.

Self-important in a red-peaked cap, the stationmaster strode across the windswept platform, his eyes swiveling beneath the patent-leather visor. Tommy was just stepping down to the platform. He waited while Tommy read the curt note: *In haste: Plans changed. Return immediately to Chengchow where Congress will convene. Kuo-tao.*

"Same compartment, Doctor," the stationmaster said. "The train turns around here. Only twelve to fifteen hours back to Chengchow. It's not even four hundred miles."

During the long journey to Hankow, Tommy's mind had been crowded with new impressions of his native land. During the monotonous return to Chengchow, his thoughts focused on Julia and their last evening together.

It had been a close call, a damned close call. He had almost asked her to marry him.

He was fond of Julia, very fond. Actually, he thought he loved her. He knew he was completely happy only when they were together.

But marriage was another thing. His parents would come down on him like ten tons of bricks if he even breathed the notion of marrying as he pleased. It would be infinitely worse if he wanted to marry a foreigner.

Anyway, he wasn't ready for marriage yet. He wasn't even ready to think about marrying. He had too much before him—too many professional challenges and too many patriotic responsibilities.

If he could only take it as lightly as most fellows did! But he couldn't treat Julia like a superior call girl. He could not just use her, but he could not possibly marry her.

He would have to give her up, he decided. Immediately, fear of never seeing her again made him feel hollow and cold. What would become of them?

His journey finally ended at six on the evening of January 31, 1923, in Chengchow. Once an ugly market town, Chengchow had swollen into a hideous semi-industrial city; it was the one place in all China where north-south and east-west railway tracks crossed.

Coughing in the soot swirling over the snow-banked platform, he found the stationmaster's office, where Chang Kuo-tao was ensconced like a feudal potentate among white canvas sacks crammed with propaganda pamphlets. Flicking coal dust off the splintered bench, the labor leader asked without preamble, "Do you remember Mao Tse-tung? The thin fellow with the mole on his chin? Always wears an old-fashioned long-gown of homespun. A country bumpkin, a real yokel!"

"Why so hot under the collar about old Mao?"

"The damned fool thinks he can make a revolution and seize power by organizing the countryside. But the peasants have got no more coherence than a sheet of sand, as Sun Yat-sen says. Helluva foundation for a revolution. Well, let Mao pick hayseed out of his hair. We're on the right track to power here, the railway track. I'm organizing the proletariat: industrial, transport, and mining workers. I've got the revolution in my palm."

When Chang Kuo-tao cupped his hands, Tommy saw that they were not calloused like a worker's but soft like a scholar's. But the big man wore the quilted cotton jacket of a manual worker. His broad face was grimy, and stubble sprouted beneath his heavy cheekbones.

"Protective coloration." He grinned at Tommy's scrutiny. "The big warlord in Peking is friendly: Wu Pei-fu, who's called the Scholar General. But his police aren't friendly."

Tommy saw by Chang Kuo-tao's flushed cheeks that he had fortified himself against the cold with *baigarh*, the foul-smelling Chinese vodka. Normally expansive, he was now ebullient. He asked after Tang Jo-wang, the Tibetan dog, and after Joo-li, the foreign woman. He grinned when Tommy spoke of Julia's dismay over the dog's bounding growth. He laughed when Tommy said the amah Lao Zee predicted direly that the dog would be bigger than a water buffalo when fully grown. The acting secretary general of the Communist Party of China was in roaring good humor.

Though no moonlight penetrated the alleys, kerosene lamps glimmering through oiled-paper windows occasionally lit the slimy cobblestones. Ignoring the squalor, the Communist did not pause in his spirited analysis of Chinese society when a mangy dog chased a sleek rat, into a wicker basket. When the lid dropped, a lean arm reached out a window for the trap.

"To feed his pet snake!" Chang Kuo-tao smiled. "When it gets fat enough, he'll eat the snake."

Except for that aside, the revolutionary spoke like a proud father of the forthcoming Railway Workers' Congress. He talked compulsively about politics. "Did you know that the Communist-Nationalist alliance was sealed at the Ikra Hotel? What's more, the chairman of the committee to reorganize the National People's Party is no one else than the secretary-general of the Chinese Communist Party. Not bad, huh?"

Tommy bit hard on his pipe when his friend continued: "I don't trust this new alliance. Moscow tightened the screws . . . insisted we all join the National People's Party. But Moscow's paying, so Moscow's calling the shots—for the time being."

"Hard luck for your lot, wasn't it?" Tommy probed. "The Communist International joining Sun Yat-sen in a declaration that China isn't ready for communism."

"Although Moscow is also supporting the Nationalists," Chang Kuo-tao insisted, "Moscow's still behind us. Tomorrow, we Communists will show just where power really comes from in China."

"With, say, four hundred party members," Tommy asked quietly, "among four hundred million people?"

"A single spark can start a forest fire!" The Communist quoted the traditional saying with relish. "Just watch the sparks fly tomorrow."

The delegates to the Inaugural Congress of the Railway Workers' General Union began entering the Pulo Theater early on the morning of February 1, 1923, confident of the tolerance of the warlord who controlled Peking and North China. Because of his reverence for the teachings of the Master Confucius, Wu Pei-fu was called the Scholar General—admiringly by his friends, derisively by his enemies. Professing the same deep concern for the common people as Confucius, he encouraged the labor movement. He also used Communist inspectors to purge his enemies on the railways and impose his absolute control. In return, the Communists were permitted to organize the Railway Workers' Union, which was the biggest in China's history.

When the union leadership published announcements of the forthcoming Inaugural Congress in all major newspapers, the conservatives had put pressure on the Scholar General, who immediately reversed himself and banned the congress. Yet he had only yesterday told a union delegation that the decision was qualified: He could permit no full-dress, *formal* congress, but he would not object to a simple celebration. The Communists had decided to go ahead with the celebration, believing it would have the same effect as the congress.

Dressed like his friend in a blue jacket with a choker collar, Tommy was borne into the Pulo Theater on a wave of hope. Nonetheless, clutching his brown Gladstone medical bag, he was enveloped by the nostalgic smells of the auditorium. The rank odor of performing bears mingled with the chalk dust from acrobats' shoes and the cloying scent of the cheap perfume on the hot handtowels that vendors flung to the audience.

By nine that morning the tiers of benches were filled with delegates in their holiday clothes. Although their faces were scrubbed, the workingmen's hands were ingrained with grime. On the stage, a trestle table stood before the folding wooden chairs that awaited the leaders. Men in the dark blue uniforms of the theater staff were putting the last touches on the preparations.

Chang Kuo-tao strode toward the stage, where a few labor leaders were speaking to the blue-uniformed attendants. At their center stood a small man with a hooked nose, a heavy mustache, and a sickly complexion. His uniform glittered with brass insignia, and a revolver was holstered on his hip.

Tommy saw that all the men in blue uniforms had revolvers. They were not attendants, but policemen. And police reinforcements were streaming down the aisle. Through the open doors, Tommy heard marching feet and a blaring bugle.

"What's all this?" Chang Kuo-tao scrambled onto the stage. "What the devil's going on?"

"You can all just get the hell on out of here," the police chief was repeating. "There will be *no* meeting and *no* inaugural ceremony."

"The general himself assured us we could hold the celebration," the union's heavy-bodied first secretary persisted. "No congress, just a simple ceremony."

"What's the difference?" the police chief demanded. "I'll give you five minutes to disband. After that, somebody's going to get hurt!"

Stepping between the first secretary and the police chief, Chang Kuo-tao directed his colleagues not to argue—not with police inside and soldiers outside. The Inaugural Congress would, he said, meet elsewhere under more favorable conditions. The leaders obediently shouted to the delegates in the auditorium that the meeting was postponed and told all to leave peacefully.

A few rose but most remained seated. The diehards stamped their feet, shouted, and hissed. Emboldened by that outcry, the first secretary made a megaphone of his hands and screamed, *"Kung-hui wan sui! . . .* Long live the union!"

The crowd responded: "Long live the Peking-Hankow Railway Workers' Union! All hail the Inaugural Congress!"

Pale with rage, the little police chief clapped his hand over the secretary's mouth. He declared furiously that the outcry had violated the ban on a meeting, and he clung to the stout secretary like a terrier attacking a bear. Still shouting slogans, the delegates marched out of the Pulo Theater into the rainy morning.

Still raging, the police chief ordered his men to seize the workers' banners and placards. The police were not gentle. They tore apart the big floral tributes and ripped up the good-luck banners.

Tommy sauntered glumly through the sour drizzle. He had come a thousand dreary miles from Shanghai for this fiasco. The Communists' trade union movement had been humiliatingly defeated in its first confrontation. The Communist leaders, especially the self-assured Chang Kuo-tao, had been criminally naïve. How could they believe that a reactionary warlord would tolerate—much less encourage—the labor movement?

Swinging the Gladstone bag dejectedly against his knee, Tommy returned to the hotel. He found the labor leaders, young Communists and older working men, crammed into the big room on the second floor he shared with Chang Kuo-tao. They were not talking of retreat, but of retaliation. Restored to his normal ebullience, Kuo-tao was no longer restraining them but was encouraging a total strike.

The union demanded that the police chief and senior railway officials be formally reprimanded; the police were to withdraw from the union's offices; and, finally, all workers were to be granted one full day off a week and one week of paid vacation a year.

When Wu Pei-fu, the Scholar General, refused to consider those demands, the strike became inevitable. Chang Kuo-tao was convinced that the rising wind of workers' power would frighten the Scholar General. Hankow was to be the storm center.

With remarkable solidarity, every last worker walked out, closing down the Peking-Hankow Railway. By February 6, 1922, quick victory seemed inevitable. For the first time facing the power of organized labor, the demoralized authorities were yielding.

The army had failed to get the trains rolling after arresting and beating scores of engineers. The Provincial Council of Trade Unions had staged a mass demonstration in Hankow to demonstrate its total support for the railway workers. More than ten thousand militants had marched to the industrial suburb of Kiangan, where the railway workers lived near the repair shops for carriages and locomotives—and pledged a mass walkout. Hankow and its sister cities, which were collectively called Wuhan and were second only to Shanghai industrially, would be paralyzed.

That evening, the provincial governor proposed that serious negotiations should begin the next day. The authorities, who had initially refused to talk, were now begging for talks.

Tommy Howe watched the railway union's resurgence with wonder from the window of his improvised clinic for workers' families in the schoolhouse that was the strike's headquarters. He looked out at the gaudily decorated town square of Kiangan, and his heart lifted.

As the dusk of February 7th descended, children swarmed around hawkers of chestnuts, toys, and candy apples. The leather shadow-puppets captivated their audience with the adventures of the grand master of deception, General Tsao Tsao. Two dumpling vendors, their stocks exhausted, banked their cooking fires and retired.

Four scrawny dogs chased a phantom cat through the half light, and a two-string violin shrilled plaintively. Workers in their holiday clothes squatted to watch single-stick fencing, and their wives gossiped near the bamboo stage in the center of the square. The news blew like a breeze across the square: "They're coming. . . . They're coming to talk. It's all over except the talking! Time for a victory party!"

Yet Chang Kuo-tao was again cautious. He told the men chosen to negotiate with the governor's delegation not to reveal their identity until the talks actually began. That was just prudence.

Thunder rumbled in the north, and Tommy instinctively glanced at the sky. The pallid winter sun was setting at five o'clock, but no dark thunderheads thrust through the tufts of white cloud. Thunder rumbled again: a prolonged peal followed by staccato cracks.

In the succeeding silence, two youths wearing red armbands loped across the square to strike headquarters. Although flushed and panting, they radiated self-importance, obviously bearing portentous news. As one dashed past, the second addressed Tommy.

"Daifoo, ta-men . . ." He used the respectful title for a doctor. "Master Physician, they're attacking the union office at the station. Police and troops with big guns. It's all over. You've got to get away."

Within two minutes, the strike leaders were pelting out of their headquarters into the alleys. The news raced through the square, and the revelers dispersed. Less than ten minutes after the messengers' arrival, Chang Kuo-tao and the first secretary of the railway union left the empty schoolhouse. In the square, the puppet-master and his apprentice were still packing up their little leather actors.

"Come on, Tommy!" Chang Kuo-tao urged. "We're all getting out."

"I'm not coming." Tommy made his decision as he spoke. "I've been deadweight for a week, a passenger on the railway strike. If there is going to be shooting, I'll be needed here to look after the injured."

"If that's what you want." Chang Kuo-tao shrugged. "Just don't kid yourself that your profession will protect you. *My* business is to survive."

"*I-lu ping-an!*" Tommy replied. "A peaceful journey then!"

Assisted by women whose children he had treated, Tommy laid out bandages and the few drugs remaining in his Gladstone bag. Also bottles of *baigarh,* which would serve as anaesthetic as well as antiseptic.

A ruffle of rifle fire heralded the arrival of the Scholar General's troops. Tommy dropped to his knees behind the schoolhouse's stone wall and peered over the windowsill as hobnailed boots crashed in the square. Smart in dark green woolen blouses, their matching breeches tucked into rolled puttees, the troops halted with the finicky precision of carriage horses. Under the command of sergeants, small units began searching the lanes and the houses.

Tommy rose, his fear seeping away in relief. His meager medicines would, after all, not be needed.

The door crashed open behind him, and he heard the clatter of rifle bolts. He turned to see a weedy officer pointing an enormous pistol at him. The muzzle wavered erratically.

"I'm a doctor." He improvised a story. "A doctor from Shanghai. Nothing to do with this . . . this strike."

"A doctor?" the officer retorted. "Also a Communist, no doubt. All you Shanghai scum are Communists."

"A Communist? Never! Just a doctor visiting friends in Hankow. The Reds forced me to treat their people."

"Come along!" the weedy officer snapped. "I've got my orders. Round up all suspicious types."

As he turned toward the door, Tommy heard glass breaking. He glanced back to see soldiers snatching up the bottles of *baigarh.* The darkness outside was lit by the flare of torches and by occasional muzzle flashes. Hands tied behind his back, Tommy was turned over to a stout sergeant who wore a benevolent smile. He was forced to squat on the rock-hard ground—but realized he would not be shot immediately.

The dark mouths of alleys spewed the search parties into the light of windblown torches. The soldiers' bayonets jabbed the strikers they had found in hiding. Blood shone on the strikers' holiday clothes.

Tommy rose to ask permission to treat the wounded. The sergeant slammed him across the face. Toppled by shock as much as by the blow, Tommy sprawled on the ground. For the first time in his life an inferior had struck him.

He squatted again, waiting for an officer and watching the search parties returning with their prey. Not all the captured workers, he consoled himself, were wounded, not even most. Smiling wryly, he reminded himself that even one injured man denied treatment was a tragedy.

"They killed Lee and Wang. Chopped off their hands." Captives' voices murmured behind him. "Got old Liu, too. There was one union leader who didn't run away."

Eighty or so captives were finally assembled in the square, their faces shadowed in the torches' wavering light. The colonel in command shivered in his fur-lined trenchcoat and instructed the guards: "Bring them inside in batches of five."

Shouldering his way into the first group, Tommy was determined to plead for permission to treat the wounded. To his surprise, the colonel immediately agreed.

Tommy cut and stitched mechanically. Although his eyes were on his work, his ears were cocked to the colonel's sharp questions and the workers' stumbling replies. He glanced up to see officers examining the men's hands for the soft palms that would reveal a professional agitator rather than a working man.

Prodded by rifle butts, most of the captives were turned out of the schoolhouse almost as rapidly as they were led in. After two hours, only four remained. Tommy recognized three as labor leaders. The man called Lin was chairman of the Kiangan branch of the railway union. Concentrating on a suture, Tommy missed the next few questions and answers. When he looked up again, the thin colonel was motioning the four men toward the door.

"After you, gentlemen!" He was elaborately ironic. "We'll soon see whether you don't change your minds. You *will* damned well tell the men to go back to work. And they *will* obey you. A few words or your lives!"

Tommy watched the labor leaders in their holiday best walk between lines of bright bayonets now lit by the moon as well as the torches. The drama he saw through the murky window glass was mute.

The colonel harangued branch chairman Lin, obviously pressing him to declare the strike over. A word from their leader would presumably send the workers back to their trains and their workshops. When the colonel paused, Lin shook his head.

The sinister drama played itself out in silence. The colonel made a final appeal, and Chairman Lin shook his head for the twentieth time.

The colonel nodded sadly, and a squat sergeant trotted into the circle of torchlight. Almost negligently, he reached over his shoulder to extract a two-foot-long half-moon blade from the sling on his back. When he twirled the great scimitar, the blade caught the moonlight. Graceful as a ballet dancer, he lifted the scimitar with both hands.

Chairman Lin's eyes blinked rapidly and followed that movement. When the sergeant swept the scimitar down, an arc of fire flared in the torchlight. The half-moon blade chipped the frozen ground three inches before the labor leader's toes.

The colonel reiterated his demand. He received the same reply—an obdurate shake of the head.

Resignedly, he turned away. While Chairman Lin's eyes still watched the colonel, the half-moon blade descended. His head tumbled to the ground, and blood spurted from his neck as he fell.

The remaining labor leaders were not accorded the same kindness. The sergeant did not kill them unaware. A half hour passed while threats and demands evoked the same blank refusal before the last man was beheaded.

Spitting in disgust, the colonel returned to the schoolhouse. Despite his fur-lined coat, he was suffering from the intense cold. He flailed his chest with his palms and asked for *baigarh.*

"Cretins! Idiots! What makes them do it?" he demanded. "All the rabble will be back at work in a day or two anyway. Why didn't they buy their lives? Only a word! I can't understand it."

A deferential junior officer spoke to him in a low murmur.

"The heads?" The colonel negligently pronounced the labor leaders' epitaph. "Why, the dogs'll be glad . . . No! Hang their heads on the telegraph poles in front of the station. A lesson for all concerned!"

21

MARCH 3, 1923

"By Shanghai standards she's just a good plain cook," Tommy said appreciatively. "But by English standards she's a genius, your Lao Zee."

On a damp evening in early March, Tommy was visiting the loft apartment for the first time since his return. Only in the last week of February had he been released by the warlord colonel, who was convinced that all Shanghailanders were Communists, particularly such intellectuals as lawyers, teachers, and doctors. He had been instructed to release Tommy by Wu Pei-fu, the Scholar General, who wished to please the multimillionaire Donald Howe. The colonel had not been blind to the advantages of holding captive a competent physician. Tommy had treated complaints ranging from syphilis through tuberculosis to shrapnel wounds. Professionally, he was almost sorry to board the Yangtze River steamer for Shanghai.

Tommy had flouted his mother's advice to rest before returning to Shanghai General Hospital. After two days he had finally found time to dine with Emily and Julie.

The other guest, Richard Hollings, was also eager to hear firsthand about the strike, whose details had been obscured by rumor, censorship, and bad communications. Although a flood on the Yellow River that killed tens of thousands was hardly worth a paragraph in *The Times*, great interest had been aroused by the "firm suppression of the Anarchist-Communist plot to paralyze China's railways." Nowadays London was very much aware of the Red menace.

Yet no other reporter had the details, Richard smugly told himself, stroking Adam, now almost eighteen months old and as big as a calf.

Though Adam's bushy tail knocked ashtrays off the coffee table, his great brown eyes looked at the world with melting tenderness. Julia had even forgiven Tommy for giving her a puppy who became an enormous mastiff instead of a small lion-dog.

"Plain cooking or not," Julia answered Tommy's left-handed compliment, "everything is *so* good."

"I do like a hostess who isn't afraid to blow her own horn," Hollings said. "This is delicious. What is it, Julie?"

Julia had no idea of the name of the dish in the earthenware casserole. She only knew the big meat balls were enticing in their nest of braised Chinese cabbage.

"Do stop teasing, Dick," Emily directed. "It's *shih-tzu tou*, lion's heads."

Emily had planned the meal. Having been indoctrinated in the rituals of the table by her old-fashioned mother, that emancipated young woman firmly believed that a whole fish must precede the soup that ended a meal. But Lao Zee had been unable to find a suitable fish in the market on a stormy day. Fretting because the welcome dinner for her brother was ending with tiny shrimps and *mao tou*, miniature lima beans, Emily was irritated by Julia's chuckle when the amah presented the eight-treasures soup.

"The beans reminded me," Julia said contritely. "I can't help laughing every time I think of Gustav Vass and the hanging gardens . . ."

The men looked up inquiringly. But Emily cut off their questions with a wave of her hand while Lao Zee ladled the broth and the delicacies out of the big green squash, which was called winter melon. The eight treasures were dried scallops, black mushrooms, smoked ham, duck breasts, straw mushrooms, deer tendons, duck gizzards, and lotus seeds. Although Cantonese in origin, the soup was a favorite of Tommy's.

"That's Chinese genius." Tommy repeated the same words every time winter-melon soup appeared. "You eat the tureen, too. Nothing wasted and no washing up."

After they had raised their cups of yellow rice-wine to salute the soup, Emily's nod gave Richard permission to ask, "What's all this about Gustav Vass and hanging gardens?"

"Dick, you mustn't write about it," Julia cautioned. "Tommy, do you remember when my phone pal Smidgelou Tomas complained of fires in Riverview Manor and the walls turning green?"

"What," he asked, "did it turn out to be?"

"The fires were serious—or could've been." Julia no longer smiled. "Vass had twisted bits of old electric wire together to save money.

Hardly any insulation at all. The joins rubbed as the new walls settled
—and sparks flew. Presto, mysterious wall fires."

"The hanging gardens, Julie?" Richard reminded her.

"It was very strange. Grass and wild flowers were growing out of
walls. Gustav Vass said deadpan, 'Miss Julie, such beautiful gardens
indoors in winter! Like the wonderful hanging gardens of Babylon.' "

"How did the plants get there?" Richard persisted.

"Mr. Vass didn't waste money on plaster. He just scooped up mud
from Soochow Creek. No wonder the walls are sprouting plants."

"I'm glad you think it's funny," Tommy said. "Quick Jack Pavernen
could be in more trouble than he knows."

"Uncle Jack'll find a way out," Julia replied. "He always does."

"Let's move and let Lao Zee clear up," Emily interjected. "Then,
brother dear, you can tell us about your adventures."

"Nobody wants to hear my boring story."

"Let us judge that, old boy," Richard urged.

"If you insist. It all began, you know, when Julie and Em dropped me
off at the North Station . . ."

Adam thumped his plumed tail on the floor. The light was subdued,
and they were seated around the glowing potbellied stove. Intently
watching Tommy's shadowed face, Julia confessed to herself that she
was already half in love.

Tommy described the enforced end of the Inaugural Congress and the
decision to call a total strike. He told of the high hopes that ended with
the slaughter of the strike leaders, and how he himself was spared by
the warlord colonel. He was talking about his friend Chang Kuo-tao's
escape to Hankow disguised as an illiterate peanut vendor when the
telephone shrilled.

"Hello. Is Smidgelou Tomas here."

Julia was slightly apprehensive. Tomas Smidgelou loved the telephone, but he would call her at home only in an emergency.

"Everything all very fine. Donkey-dorey, since no one is killed."

"Killed, Mr. Smidgelou?"

"Is the bathtub, Missy. The marbleized bathtub still beautiful and
shining."

"I'm delighted, Mr. Smidgelou."

"Very strong bathtub. Is making wonderful centerpiece. But not good
for eating off."

"Why in the world would anyone want to eat off the bathtub?"

"Because it gives no more a table in dining room. Is thus necessary
to eat off bathtub."

"Do you need a dining-room table?" Julia knew he would shortly get to the point. "Can't you find one?"

"Must be very special table to fit over bathtub."

"To fit over the bathtub?"

"Bathtub is now where table once was. Hole in ceiling makes house airy, though not so nice in cold March weather. Lucky no one is hurt when bathtub falls down."

"Oh, my Lord! You mean the bathtub fell through the ceiling into the dining room?"

"Because marble is heavy, and cement is heavy. Together twice as heavy. Also, Mr. Kratcher next door asks me tell you no one is hurt by him either."

"You're not the only one? Those blasted bathtubs. We'll set that right just as soon as—"

"Missy Pavernen, no one is paying more money for Riverview. No money till all bathtubs replaced. Sorry, Missy, but all tenants ask me to tell you: *No more money!*"

22

JUNE 23–AUGUST 15, 1923

"If only you could write," Emily exclaimed, "you could join my one-woman syndicate."

"Well, I can't," Julia replied. "So I've got to find some other way to make money. Or else, I guess, go home. It's terrible being unemployed."

Emily sighed in exasperation. She could once have taken the sums her friend needed from her allowance and hardly felt the pinch. Nowadays, she was hard pressed to pay her own share of the housekeeping.

Otherwise, Emily was gloriously alive, both emotionally and intellectually. She had never been happier, and she had never faced so many practical problems. Accustomed to spending without consideration from a purse constantly replenished by her father, she was now astonished at the speed with which money vanished.

Since Julia and she were often taken out to dinner, they could just manage to pay for necessities like food, the amah, and electricity. Although their friends rarely appeared without gifts, the essential luxuries were almost beyond reach: telephone, clothing, Victrola records, and books. If Tommy had not secretly paid the small rent from his allowance, they might have had to move out. As it was, Emily's articles for Chinese-language periodicals almost covered the necessities, while their occasional luxuries were provided by the occasional pieces she wrote for the Philadelphia *Public Ledger,* a connection Harry Smythe had arranged. The vice-consul bore her no grudge for rejecting him.

Although those pieces had evoked inquiries from *Liberty* and *The Ladies Home Journal,* Emily would not be diverted from her work for Shanghai publications, which provided their daily food. The American magazines paid far better, but they reserved the right to reject her articles.

Emily was drawing no salary from the Women's Bank, although she had sunk her grandfather's legacy in that idealistic venture. Still, she endorsed the board's decision to function as a cooperative. Since all the shareholder-employees could obviously afford the deprivation, they would each receive a token five dollars Mex a week until the Women's Bank began making a profit.

However, Emily could not really afford that gesture when her apartment-mate, Julia, was out of work. John Pavernen had been overwhelmed by the tide of disasters raised by Gustav Vass's ingenuity. Quick Jack could talk his way out of spontaneous fires and "hanging gardens," but even he could not explain away ceilings that collapsed beneath ponderous concrete bathtubs.

Tomas Smidgelou's threat had proved lethal. When installment payments ceased and an impromptu residents' association sued JPEnterprises for fraud, John Pavernen had simply dissolved the company. Since a nonexistent company could not employ an office manager, Julia was penniless. Retiring to his flat and his Korean mistress to recoup, her uncle had, fortunately, remembered that the Underwood typewriter did not belong to JPEnterprises but was his personal property. Not Julia but Emily fell on the typewriter with delight. Within a week, she had taught herself to type.

Emily was less enthusiastic about another remnant of JPEnterprises. Little Pow, the office devil, had followed Julia home like a lost dog after she locked the office door for the last time. He was sleeping beneath the kitchen table beside Adam, the Tibetan mastiff. He was also trying with inexhaustible energy and good humor to make himself agreeable—and indispensable.

"Little Pow makes five, you know," Emily observed pointedly. "The two of us, the amah, Adam, and Pow. Five mouths to feed on a guaranteed five dollars Mex a week."

"At least Adam earns his keep." Julia laughed. "We'll never have burglars with dog-same-size-pony on guard."

"Julie, why can't you be serious? It's no laughing matter."

"Em, why not let Lao Zee go? I'd hate to see her leave, but—"

"Are you mad?" Emily demanded. "You know it's impossible to keep house in Shanghai without an amah."

"Lots of poor folk manage. Anybody'd think you never left Shanghai —much less spent years in the U.S. learning the pleasure of doing for yourself."

"Some pleasure!" Emily snorted. "I haven't noticed you doing that much around the house."

They were chatting in Emily's minute bedroom, while she dressed to attend the Shanghai Amateur Theatrical Society's presentation of *H.M.S. Pinafore* at the Grand Theatre. *The Mikado* had been ruled out as possibly offensive to the Japanese. Julia picked up a cut-glass bottle and sniffed while Emily twisted her head to glare at the crooked seams of her smoky silk stockings in the mirror on the back of the door.

"Put that down!" she said. "Richard swore I'd never get another present if I let you touch the Shalimar. Anyway, we can't both wear the same perfume."

"We won't!" Julia grinned. "Different skins give different scents to the same perfume. You were saying?"

"Oh, yes. We can't possibly let Lao Zee go. She eats very little and her wages are laughable. Besides, what would become of her?"

"Noblesse oblige, eh? Anyway, Lady Emily could never get her own breakfast." Despite her bravado, Julia suddenly felt lost. "Oh, Em, what *are* we going to do? And it's all my fault! . . . If you could put us in the way of selling a few guns, it would help a lot. Uncle Jack could open a new office, and I—"

"I'm not getting very far. T. V. Soong promised to speak to Dr. Sun Yat-sen, and Mayling will talk to Chiang Kai-shek. But the Nationalists are a faint hope. Moscow is financing them, and Moscow tells them what they can buy."

"If you could only get me in to see Dr. Sun. . . . I'm not a bad salesman."

"You're not serious, are you? The gamble's not worth the journey to Canton."

"I forgot he'd gone back. Of course! That's why Tommy's Communist friend was on his way to Canton. Do you remember Chang Kuo-tao, Emily? He's offered me work."

"Unlike you, I don't forget Chinese names, Joo-li." Emily laughed. "What kind of work?"

Even the thought of burly Chang Kuo-tao was incongruous in Emily's bower of carefree femininity. Her negligence about her room contrasted with her orderly mind and with the primness that sometimes frosted her manner. Face powder swirled around half-used lipsticks and cut-glass vials on her tiny dressing table. Three odd stockings were flung across a gilt chair; a lacy crepe de chine slip lay on the pink coverlet; and two dresses cascaded out of her wardrobe, emerald green and old rose.

Chang Kuo-tao, Julia recalled, was very earnest at twenty-six, which was, after all, a ridiculous age for a major political figure in a society that still believed men reached the years of discretion only at sixty. But the big man's colleagues were hardly older; only the secretary general of the Communist Party was over forty. In mid-June 1923, powerful young men were striving for a new China.

Coming by for tea, Chang Kuo-tao had recalled suggesting earlier that Julia might teach at the Communists' foreign languages school. With touching formality he had invited her to teach English at Shanghai Labor University, a new institution that boasted a veteran Nationalist author as president and a brilliant young Communist journalist as dean of studies. Labor University would not make excessive demands on her precious time, Chang Kuo-tao promised. Besides, it would pay her traveling expenses and provide some meals.

Julia was almost as much attracted by the revolutionary cause as by the prospect of meeting interesting people. She could not, however, tell Chang Kuo-tao that she suffered from lack of money rather than lack of time. The radical leader had obviously judged her, like all foreigners, to be so wealthy that offering her a wage would be insulting.

"Well, if I do teach at Labor University, Harry Smythe should be happy," Julia reflected aloud. "He's always asking me about the Nationalists—chiefly because he thinks you know all about them. And he's always urging me to get closer to the Communists."

"Be careful if you're planning to spy on the Communists." Emily laughed. "Just look what happened to Mata Hari!"

Tommy Howe watched the waiter descend the spindly wrought-iron staircase of St. Andrew's Café bearing precise directions to the bartender for making the Brandy Alexander that was Julia's latest passion. Carefully not looking at her, he broke off his abstracted humming of "Poor Little Buttercup" from *H.M.S. Pinafore* and declared, "You know that's not the real reason. . . ."

"What's not the real reason for what?" Julia asked. "Did I miss something you said?"

"I didn't say it. I was just thinking aloud," he replied. "I was thinking of Hollings. He's *not* the real reason my parents threw Emily out. It was basically because she wouldn't marry Li Nien-lao. Because she humiliated them by refusing the man they'd chosen."

"And if Richard weren't European? Suppose he'd been Chinese?"

"Wouldn't have made any difference." Tommy sounded very certain. "They wanted her to marry Li Nien-lao—and nobody else."

"Suppose she hadn't been going around with Richard?"

"I take your point. Then they might not have insisted on her marrying Nien-lao *immediately*. But that's not the issue." He paused, feeling himself on shaky ground. "What I'm trying to get over, what I want you to understand, is this. It was *not* because Dick's a foreigner that the parents disowned Emily. You do see?"

"I suppose so," she responded dubiously. "If you say so, Tommy. But what's that to do with the price of baked beans in Boston? What're you getting at?"

"I'm not absolutely sure, but please bear with me." He took off his prop glasses and laid them on the marble tabletop. "Yes, of course. Since it wasn't because he's a foreigner, it's nothing to do with you and me. You do see?"

"Through a glass darkly."

For the twenty-fifth time that hot and humid evening, the waiter in the outsize white jacket trotted up the wrought-iron staircase; Julia's Brandy Alexander foamed in a narrow glass on his tin tray. Welcoming the interruption, Tommy took a long pull on his tankard of vodka and lime juice.

"What I mean," he persisted, "is that the break between Emmy and the parents was not *primarily* because Richard is a foreigner. I've certainly proved that to you, haven't I?"

Julia was elated, expectant—and uneasy. Tommy was evidently moving toward a proposal, although his rationalization of his parents' attitude was hardly convincing. But that was not the crux of the matter. Even if she were inclined to think seriously about marriage to him—or anyone else—now, the way he dwelt on his parents' opinions would put her off. How could she even consider marrying a man who was more concerned with his parents' feelings than her own?

"And the parents haven't objected to you," he summed up. "Not at all!"

"That's fine, Tommy." Julia forced a smile. "Did you ever think that *my* parents might object?"

"How could they?" He was genuinely puzzled. "We haven't done anything anyone could object to. Not that it's been easy for me to . . . You *are* quite a girl, Julie."

Julia flushed with pleasure at that gallantry. She had no intention of marrying Tommy, now or ever. Indeed, she was trying to spare him a flat rejection by diverting the conversation. Yet despite herself, she laid her hand palm up on the table in invitation.

Her present life was too full, far too exciting, for her even to consider marriage. Besides, she could not marry any man whose fundamental values were so different from her own. Nonetheless, she closed her fingers tightly on Tommy's when he placed his hand in hers, and she clung for an instant.

Despite her spontaneous pleasure, Julia was appalled. Tommy's blindness to certain matters epitomized the reasons she could never marry him. Although educated abroad, he could not immediately comprehend that Caucasian American parents would probably object to their daughter's association with a Chinese man. He was blinded by the ancient Chinese conviction of absolute Chinese superiority.

"Oh, I see," he said an instant later. "Yes, of course, they could object. Do they?"

"I don't confide my every movement to them," she replied. "But they probably would—if I told them."

"Well, that makes us even, I'm afraid." He grinned ruefully. "You know I wasn't telling the whole truth about my parents' feelings either. Of course, they don't know all about us. Not that I—"

"Somehow, Tommy, I'd suspected that."

Fending off the imminent proposal, Julia sipped her Brandy Alexander—and was suddenly revolted. The cocktail was sweet and sticky, not creamy and smooth as she had believed a moment earlier. She pushed aside her glass and lit a Chesterfield.

"But, regardless, there's something I want to say . . . must tell you." He paused and looked into his tankard. "Julie, I . . ."

Like most young women, Julia had dreamed of this magical moment. In her fantasies, she had sometimes sacrificed Tommy's love because it was not right to bring children of mixed blood into a world bristling with racial prejudice. Sometimes she had blissfully agreed, careless of all practical considerations, including her own parents' shock. At this real moment, however, she was totally preoccupied with sparing him a rebuff. She must refuse him, but she shrank from hurting him.

But was she only concerned not to hurt him? Did her fingertips tingle solely because she was keyed up to avoid embarrassing him? Did she see his face with extraordinary clarity against the green leaves of the giant pot-plants only because she was worried about his being humiliated when she told him she could never marry him?

"You're not with me." He broke into her reverie. "You didn't hear half of what I said, did you?"

Julia looked at him candidly, smiled in apology, and confessed, "I guess I was somewhere else, Tommy. You needn't say anything more, you know."

"But I will. I don't *need* to. I *want* to, even if you . . . Oh, Julie, we go so well together!"

"Tommy, I'd love to . . ." Trying to soften her rebuff, Julia realized, she was almost saying the wrong thing. She hastily amended her words: "But, I'm afraid that—"

Her hesitation hardly penetrated Tommy's concentration, and he continued: "If only I could ask you to marry me. That's what I want, regardless of the parents' feelings . . . regardless of everything."

"I see, Tommy." She was, for a moment, desolate with disappointment, and, for a moment, she wondered what she really wanted. "I do see. . . . But it's not your parents' feelings that . . . that concern me. It's—"

"Julie, I'm so sorry!" He was again sensitive to her emotions. "I only thought that you were troubled by the way they treated Emmy. No, Julie, it's nothing to do with them. Not fundamentally. Only that I . . . I love you. Julie, I do love you so much."

Julia melted. He had never before that moment said those words. Tears started in her eyes, and her voice was husky when she finally said, "Tommy, darling, I think you're wonderful. And . . . and I love you, too. Truly I do."

He sat stock-still for a moment, as if astonished by her declaration. Automatically, he lifted his tankard to his lips. As her words struck home he stiffened and carefully set the gleaming tankard down on the white marble table. He gripped her wrists and pulled her toward him, forgetting that they were in a public place.

"You really mean it, don't you. You really do!" he marveled. "Then everything's all right! I'm very happy!"

Julia leaned across the table and kissed him. After a time, she said slowly, "Tommy, darling, I'm so happy I'm almost delirious."

"When did you first—" Beginning the same question at the same instant, they both laughed in delight and spontaneously raised their glasses in a toast to each other. Julia was surprised: the Brandy Alexander was once again delicious.

"But, you know—" Once more speaking the same words, they both stopped. Then Julia said, "You first, Tommy. What were you going to say?"

He looked down at their clasped hands before resuming hesitantly. "It's a little hard to get out, Julie. Especially now! But it has to be said. You do know, we can't possibly get married right now, and I—"

"Tommy, who said anything about marriage?" she demanded. "Let's take what we have . . . what we've been given . . . and not worry about marriage. . . . I do love you! . . . But that doesn't mean I want to marry you—or feel I must. Certainly not now, perhaps not ever. Don't say any more about marriage, please."

"I'm afraid I must, Julie." He released her hand and sat back stiffly. "It's only fair. My parents' attitude. It's an obstacle, a major obstacle, perhaps decisive someday. But right now it boils down to something much simpler: I've got no idea when I'll be able to marry. There's my internship and, after that, residence. Years of hard work before I specialize. . . ."

"I don't want you to worry about such things," Julia said firmly. "I love you, Tommy, but I don't necessarily want to own you. . . . Not yet, at least." She smiled to soften her words and added, "For me, too, there are problems. Do I really want to spend the rest of my life in China . . . even with you, darling? Also, I suspect that you're talking about marriage because you know I'm down on my luck. But this damsel in distress doesn't need rescuing. . . . Forget about being a knight errant. Let's take what we've been given and enjoy it to the hilt and make it last as long as possible. And let's not worry about the future."

Julia gripped his hand and, marveling at her own words, declared, "I do love you . . . very much. I didn't really know it until this moment. Tommy, just tell me again."

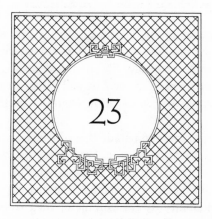

23

AUGUST 24–SEPTEMBER 16, 1923

Having looked forward to the dinner-dance at the Columbia Country Club, Emily Howe uncharacteristically yielded without protest when Richard Hollings demurred at taking her.

"The annual bunfest of the American Universities Association will just have to manage without me," he said. "Of course, if you want to go alone . . ."

"That wouldn't be much fun, Dick."

Emily kissed his cheek. She was still contrite at having involved him in a very formal—and very tedious—Chinese-style banquet given by T. V. Soong, the brother-in-law of President Sun Yat-sen. Seeking information, Richard had found boredom. She could not, the following week, impose a peculiarly American social ordeal upon him.

She had, Emily acknowledged to herself, met her match. Richard could be almost as imperious as she—and perhaps more capricious. Still, it was worth putting up with his moodiness for the joy he also brought her. She no longer bragged that no man could touch her heart.

When Emily reneged, Julia Pavernen felt she had to go to the dance with Harry Smythe and his friends from the consular corps, who were among their original party. Tommy, as usual, was working. Elizaveta and Joshua would have been more fun, but Elizaveta was barred. All Shanghai knew that her private hotel was a great success; all Shanghai also knew that the Ikra was a house of assignation. Ostentatiously tolerant of all races and religions, the Columbia Country Club vigilantly excluded any female who might besmirch the purity of American womanhood—or, in this case, American manhood.

As she had expected, Julia felt out of place with the lacquered ladies and the hearty men in white dinner jackets among the cretonne drapes and the blond maple furniture. She had said she'd go only to please Emily, who had now deserted her. She had feared that the members of the American Universities Association would be stuffy. Actually they were bumptious.

The Chinese, who came to parade their distinction in having studied abroad, were initially very genteel. The Americans, who came to troll for business among the well-to-do Chinese, were initially very affable. After two highballs, genuine camaraderie sprang up, and they all vied to prove their amiability by the volume of their conversation.

The young diplomats at Julia's table, nonetheless, chattered in soft-voiced preoccupation about home leave, cost-of-living allowances, and their next postings—as diplomats always did. Harry Smythe, however, proved himself a remarkably light-footed dance partner. He talked, as always, primarily about Chinese politics. Finding that subject ever more compelling, Julia listened eagerly and made occasional contributions.

"Sun Yat-sen's going sour on us," Harry confided, expertly reversing to the beat of "Dardanella." "Since he got back to Canton, he's been denouncing the free enterprise system. He's getting more and more socialistic. Free enterprise *only* gave him an education, a profession, and a career. He's also denouncing all the foreign powers as imperialist leeches—except the Soviet Union, of course. Trouble's brewing."

"Why the abrupt turnaround?"

"It's mostly sour grapes, I guess," he said. "But why don't we go to the horse's mouth—or at least the mare's?"

Harry pointed his chin toward an alcove. When he spun her around, Julia recognized T. V. Soong, who was resplendent in black dinner jacket and wing collar. Although she had never met T.V.'s elder sister, who was the young third wife of Dr. Sun Yat-sen, Julia knew immediately that the small woman in the silver *cheongsam* adorned with diamanté lotus flowers must be the first lady of the resurgent Republic of China. She was enthroned like a queen in a rattan easy chair while young Chinese and young foreigners swarmed around her like courtiers. Some actually sat at her feet, which were small and neat in silver pumps.

With resigned courtesy, T.V. presented Harry to his sister. He was more animated when he introduced Julia. The first lady greeted them both with the same warmly.

"I hope you'll soon call me Rosamonde," she drawled in her soft southern accent. "Most of the young people do. After all, I'm not so much older."

Some ten years seemed a gulf to Julia at twenty-two, although Rosamonde Sun certainly did not look old. Even when a smile lit her symmetrical face in response to Julia's praise of her dress, almost miraculously, not a single crinkle marred the perfection of her features. She still looked like a painted Chinese doll.

"This dress? It's not so new," Rosamonde Sun said. "Actually, it belongs to my older sister, Ailing"

"Madame H. H. Kung," T. V. Soong supplied. "We call her Nanny in the family. Her husband is the seventy-fifth lineal descendant of Confucius. And a very canny banker, too!"

"T.V., sometimes I think you're not interested in anything but family pedigrees and money," Rosamonde chided. "Though you are doing an excellent job raising money for my husband's cause."

Julia knew that T. V. Soong was the financial wizard of Dr. Sun Yat-sen's National People's Party, although his personal contributions did not equal those made by Tommy's father. She also knew that Tommy's father was worried by Dr. Sun's swing to the left. But where else could Donald Howe take his money and his hopes for China? Certainly not to the warlords who entwined or fanged each other as capriciously and venomously as a basketful of vipers.

"So, Mr. Smythe, you work for the State Department," Rosamonde remarked. "A pity Washington is becoming so . . . so uncooperative that my husband has to turn to Moscow."

"Uncooperative, Madame Sun?"

Even Harry Smythe's brashness was muted by Rosamonde's formidable combination of sweetness and forthrightness. Even he looked surprised when she replied, "Didn't they tell you my husband offered your country a chance to run China? Only recently, President Sun pleaded with the American minister to get the U.S. to lead Britain and France in a military occupation of all China's major cities. And also to send engineers, judges, and professors to administer the country. After five years, the foreign powers would withdraw, leaving behind a unified, prosperous, and democratic Republic of China."

"Was he really serious?" Julia asked. "It sounds like a desperate measure."

"He was deadly serious!" the first lady replied. "But the American minister thought he was joking—or mad. So that was that."

"And so he's going over to the Bolsheviks?" Harry Smythe asked brashly. "A little dangerous, isn't it?"

"We've tried over and over again to get help from the capitalist powers," Rosamonde Sun replied. "Now we're getting the support we need from the Soviet Union."

The National People's Party, she added, had to become centralized and rigidly disciplined like the Communist Party of the Soviet Union. Otherwise, the Nationalists would never be able to destroy the warlords and drive out the imperialists.

Harry ostentatiously shrugged his shoulders, conveying, in part, incredulity and, in part, resignation. T.V. ignored the broad gesture, and Rosamonde was immersed in her own discourse.

"Did you know," she asked, "that General Chiang Kai-shek was going to the Soviet Union for my husband? He'll spend several months studying the Soviets' Red Army and the organization of their Communist Party. Good models for us."

Harry, who had not known, whistled softly at that news and said again, "It's a very dangerous game. Given half a chance, the Bolsheviks will destroy the Nationalists. Have you forgotten that the Chinese Communist party is Moscow's creature?"

"*Was*, Mr. Smythe." Rosamonde spared him a sliver of her attention. "The Chinese Communists *were* the creatures of the Bolsheviks. But the Chinese Communists are now no more than left-wing Nationalists."

"If you can believe Moscow won't favor the Communists, you'll believe anything."

"Why, Mr. Smythe? Why, when Moscow can work directly with the Nationalists, who already have an army, a following, and a program?" Rosamonde turned to Julia and abruptly changed the conversation. "Unfortunately, General Chiang Kai-shek doesn't stand a chance of marrying my sister Mayling. Not as long as he's a pagan. My mother, Mammie, will never stand for it!"

Julia was intensely curious about the general's strange courtship of Mayling Soong. It was not every day one saw a married man wooing a potential bride as if he were totally unencumbered. But she could not pursue that intriguing subject. Perhaps regretting her minor indiscretion, Rosamonde again switched the conversation.

"My husband has given me responsibility for mobilizing China's women," she told Julia. "I have great plans."

"My friend Emily Howe would be very interested. She feels strongly about the oppression of women."

"Oh, Emily." The first lady offhandedly dismissed Julia's friend. "A bit too rightist, I'm afraid." Enthusiasm suffused her voice when she resumed: "I'm forming women's unions and starting schools for women propagandists. After fighting alongside the men, women will be entitled to demand their full rights when the Nationalist revolution triumphs."

"Emily would love to help," Julia said. "And I would, too."

"Don't worry about Emily," Rosamonde counseled. "But you can help a lot. I hear you've been asked to teach English at Shanghai Labor University. You must do so. You'll help us build a glorious future for China. And you'll hasten the liberation of women everywhere."

Julia, who had been undecided about teaching, warmed to Rosamonde's words. Tomorrow she would tell Tommy's friend Chang Kuo-tao that she accepted his offer.

Harry, who was incapable of remaining silent for five minutes, broke in hotly, "Madame Sun, I sympathize with your objectives. But let me tell you, your tieup with the Bolsheviks is the biggest mistake you could make. They'll chew you up and spit you out—"

"Attaboy, Harry! You tell her!" a slurred male voice interrupted. "Old Doc Sun's just a Commie stooge now. He's sold out to the Bolsheviks like a whore—for money. And what does that make mealymouthed Madame Sun? Maybe the stepmother of the goddamned country. Maybe worse!"

Shocked, Julia turned on the intruder. He was short and quite thin, except for the potbelly that bulged beneath his black cummerbund. A synthetic social smile still lingered on his lips, although his light blue eyes blazed. She recognized the manager of the biggest American shipping line—and she saw from the flush on his cheeks that he had been drinking heavily.

"You're disgusting!" Julia said coldly. "Drunk, for one thing. You're a guest in China. Yet you dare to insult the first lady. How you can—"

"Listen to the little bitch." The American lifted his hand. "Know everything, do you? Chink-lover, are you? What you need is a good spanking!"

He clutched her shoulder as if determined to carry out his threat. Without saying a word, Harry slapped the man's arm aside, spun him around, and marched him away.

Rosamonde Sun hardly took note of the rough byplay, and Julia's anger was overcome by her admiration for the first lady. She had never met a woman she admired so much. She knew that Madame Sun would be an inspiration to her as long as she remained in China. And afterward, too!

. . .

Julia had never seen Emily and Richard bicker, but she always knew when they had quarreled. Afterward, Emily was always excessively sweet, while his humor, always cutting, became savage. Their intense relationship, Julia gathered from Emily's hints, sometimes soared to heights Tommy and she never experienced—but as often plunged into savage dissension. Emily had confided after one tumultuous quarrel that Richard was jealous of her professional life. When his inhibitions were short-circuited by whisky, he belittled both her journalism and her fiction. He also spoke sourly about the Women's Bank, deriding not only Madame Wang, the earnest manager, but Emily's own work. Asserting that Emily had set Elizaveta up in a gilded brothel with the bank's funds, he asked, "What is actually the oldest profession for women—whoring or usury?"

"Emmy, why do you put up with it?" Julia asked one evening. "No man is worth so much grief!"

"Don't say that, Julia Pavernen!" Emily retorted. "Don't *ever* say that! Richard is well worth it. . . . And it's not all one way. He was furious when I scooped him."

"You scooped him?"

"The Philadelphia *Public Ledger* had the story before *The Times* of London when T. V. Soong became finance minister in the Canton government. Hardly an earth-shaking development, but interesting."

"Just the sort of thing that fascinates poor Harry Smythe," Julia remarked. "Did you hear they're sending him to Rome?"

"Rome! Harry's Mandarin'll be a great help there!" Emily observed. "Dick and I made peace, even though he still feels I was obliged to tell him *before* I filed my story. Lately, though, we've been arguing about marriage."

"You mean he doesn't want to get married?"

"That was a couple of months ago. Lately he's been badgering me to agree, in principle at least, to marry him—even if we don't set a date."

"Emmy, that's exciting. What did you say?"

"Julie, I'm not ready to marry Dick—or anyone else—right now. And he is a foreigner."

"You mean that still bothers you? I thought—"

"I guess I'm more old-fashioned than I thought. It's funny. I do love him, I think, and . . . and everything else. But the thought of marrying him . . . of having children with blue eyes! . . . No, never!"

"That's impossible, Emmy. Don't you remember your genetics? You both have brown eyes. Because brown dominates, you can't have blue-eyed children. Not unless some remote ancestor left you a blue-eyed gene—some Chinese lady who didn't mind foreigners!"

"Now don't get huffy, Julie. You know what I mean. . . . Anyway, Dick and I are even. Sometimes he doesn't want marriage, and sometimes I don't."

"That's a fine basis for a lasting relationship." Julie laughed away her irritation at Emily's racism. "You can go on forever that way—if you don't kill each other first."

After much cajoling, Tommy agreed to take Julia to the exhibition of jujitsu and sumo wrestling at the Olympia Theater. He was reluctant because it was a Japanese performance, sponsored, as the advertisements declared, "to strengthen the friendship between the Chinese and Japanese nations." Behind such hypocritical avowals, he believed, Japan was trying to conquer China. Julia was eager precisely because it was a Japanese performance. Pan-Asianism, all the nations of Asia uniting against imperialism, was a major article of the new creed she was acquiring from Rosamonde Sun.

Only three weeks had passed since their meeting at the Columbia Country Club, but Julia's outlook had already altered radically. Rosamonde could always spare a half hour from her hectic schedule to instruct her new American friend about the real China that lay beyond Shanghai—and beneath Shanghai's surface glitter. At the Labor University, where Julia had begun teaching evening classes in English, she was dazzled by the brilliant dean. Like most of the faculty, he was an avowed Communist.

Tommy was not as happy about her intellectual growth as she might have expected. He virtually ignored her new enthusiasm for both China and the revolutionary struggle, pleading that he was too tired for such elevated topics. Still, she tried again when they were seated in the Olympia Theater, awaiting the performance. Inspired by her new visions, Julia was uncharacteristically insensitive to his feelings. Irritated by her mock profundity, Tommy was, for once, brusque with her.

"Now I really understand how you feel about China," she said. "Desperate cases require desperate measures—even bloodshed. You can't make an omelet without breaking eggs."

"Please spare me the clichés," he replied. "It's broken heads you're talking about, not broken eggs. I saw too many split skulls during the railway strike. Violence may be necessary, but we don't need to cheer it."

"I wasn't thinking," she apologized, but added, "Anyway, it's going to happen."

When he did not reply, Julia subsided into silence. She wanted to tell Tommy more, and she wanted to hear his thoughts. But she would get nothing out of him except irritable retorts while he was in his present mood. She took his hand and, instead of speaking, looked around the theater.

The Howe name had performed its usual magic. They were seated in easy chairs on the stage, close to the platform with the straw matting. Hoping to win them over, the Japanese impresario had himself met them at the door and bowed them to their seats. Green tea, *sake,* pumpkin seeds, and *sembei* were arrayed on the low table between them in exquisitely simple Japanese pottery. Tommy tucked his Gladstone bag under his chair and sipped tea, stubbornly refusing the *sake* because it was the enemy's drink.

The audience was largely male, although pastel kimonos and bright evening gowns shone in the first rows. Despite Julia's enthusiasm for pan-Asianism, the festoons of bunting bearing the red sun of Japan made her uneasy. The blood-red discs dominated the occasional five-barred flags of the Peking regime, which the foreigners recognized as the legal government of the Republic of China. The white sun of the Nationalists' flag was not seen, although President Sun Yat-sen was at that moment talking with Japanese emissaries in Canton.

After the impresario had spoken at length in Japanese, the Japanese consul general addressed the audience in almost unintelligible English. He was followed by a Japanese vice-consul who spoke fluent, idiomatic Shanghainese.

Tommy leaned over and said to Julia behind his hand, "All sweetness and light, isn't it? Traditional Sino-Japanese friendship and cooperation against the plunderers from the West . . . coprosperity for all Asians. . . . But, Julie, it's all rubbish."

"Tommy," she objected, "the Asiatic peoples have got to work together."

"The Japs' object isn't to work together. They're aiming to make China a Japanese colony, the better to exploit Chinese raw materials and Chinese labor. It's only four years since May 4, 1919, when Peking students, led by my friend Chang Kuo-tao, rioted against Japanese demands on China. Japan is a threat, not a friend."

"All right, Tommy. Let's discuss it later. The bouts are about to begin."

Although she leaned forward, feigning rapt attention, Julia was disappointed by the jujitsu, which consisted largely of young men in white pyjamalike costumes jumping around on the straw matting. Occasionally they closed with each other, but only for a few seconds. Less frequently, they grappled on the floor like American college wrestlers. But those encounters, too, were soon over.

Julia swallowed a yawn. She could not let Tommy see she was bored after dragging him to his enemy's performance. Out of the corner of her eye, she saw with surprise that he was leaning forward intently.

Concealing a smile behind her palm, she leaned back. She no longer felt guilty, for he was obviously enjoying himself.

The last bout was more interesting. The first competitor was quite tall for a Japanese, almost six feet. But his opponent dwarfed him. The Russian called Vorobyof, the announcer declared, had perfected his skill in the academies of Kobe after fleeing the Communists in Siberia.

The word "Communists" was pronounced with ostentatious detestation, and Tommy whispered, "So Rosamonde Sun wants to work with both the Communists and the Japs. Tommyrot! . . . She's not really interested in politics at all. Only in herself. It's just being married to old Sun Yat-sen, politics *is* herself now."

"Shush, Tommy," Julia said. "I want to see this."

Enormous in his loose white garments, Vorobyof let his opponent come to him. Although he looked like a stripling beside the Russian giant, the Japanese advanced confidently. From a distance of four feet, he launched himself at Vorobyof's solar plexus, his fists clenched together. The Russian moved with extraordinary speed for his size, but not quite fast enough. The double fist struck him in the side.

Vorobyof stepped back. The Japanese advanced confidently, his arms hanging at his sides. The Russian now retreated openly.

The audience's sigh of expectation was followed by a full-throated cry. Julia shivered involuntarily. She had read about mobs crying for blood but had never before heard that cry. Despite her revulsion, she, too, leaned forward.

Cigarette smoke swirled in the shafts of the spotlights. A feral smell swept the theater: sweat and dust, stale tobacco and hair oil, a whiff of decay and a pungent male odor. Julia shivered again.

Vorobyof moved forward, and the Japanese sprang to meet him. Their flashing arms moved too fast to see, but the Russian again shuffled backward, apparently hurt.

The Japanese leaped, both his arms extended before him. The Russian stepped forward, and the rigid fingers of his left hand probed the soft spot beneath his opponent's chin. His right hand grasping his opponent's left arm, he lifted abruptly. The Japanese was hurled by his own momentum onto the matting.

The Russian did not release his grip as his opponent fell. Instead, he exerted a twisting motion, one hand grasping the man's shoulder, the other at the wrist. The Japanese appeared to diminish in that grip, his muscles going slack and his face turning pallid.

"Good big man beats good small man," Tommy joked to relieve the tension. "So much for the magic of jujitsu."

"Something looks very wrong . . ." Julia began, but Tommy was already reaching under the chair for his medical bag. He stepped into the ring as the Russian released his opponent.

The Japanese had bitten his lip so hard that blood was streaming down his chin. Despite his Spartan self-discipline, he began thrashing back and forth on the straw matting. His feet drumming on the soft surface, he screamed shrilly.

As Tommy leaned over the man, Julia saw with horror that the Japanese had been deformed by that last brutal hold. Behind his right shoulder a mishaped wedge protruded, stretching the skin monstrously. As he rolled on the matting, his right arm flopped limply like a boneless tentacle.

She gasped in surprise. Tommy had thrust his foot into the man's armpit with some force and was now grasping his right elbow, which offered no resistance. So rapidly that Julia could hardly follow the motion, Tommy forcefully brought the arm up and across the chest. The instant he completed that apparently brutal movement, the Japanese stopped screaming.

The defeated man sat up, gingerly felt his shoulder, and smiled incredulously. Still unspeaking, Tommy took a length of black cloth from his Gladstone bag and tied a sling that brought the man's hand up touching his left shoulder.

No more than a minute after he had left, it seemed, Tommy was again sitting beside Julia, murmuring, "Dislocated shoulder." He sipped green tea while the Russian helped the Japanese leave the stage. Vorobyof's blunt Slavic features expressed neither satisfaction nor remorse.

Julia took Tommy's hand and laid it on her thigh. Gripping his fingers, she whispered, "Well done, Doctor."

He smiled, shrugged minutely, and replied: "It looked rather flashy, didn't it? Dead easy, actually."

"Brilliant nonetheless! I've never seen you in action before. Pretty spectacular!"

"Nonsense! Anyone could . . ." Tommy looked away in embarrassment and suggested: "Look here, Julie. I can see this isn't your cup of tea. Shall we go?"

"Let's stay a little longer. I've never seen sumo wrestling. One bout —and we'll go."

Two enormous Japanese waddled from the wings while the impresario introduced them. Their voluminous robes enveloped them like tarpaulins draped over monumental statues. The stagehands were laying out a white rope in a large circle. They scurried away as the wrestlers ponderously mounted the platform.

When they shed their robes, Julia stared in astonishment, almost awed by their bulk, which glistened with oil. Well over six feet, each easily weighed more than three hundred pounds.

The wrestlers stalked around the rope circle, displaying themselves as arrogantly as prize bulls. They flexed their slablike arm muscles; they planted their incongruously delicate feet heavily; and they swung their bulging shoulders menacingly.

In addition to the black silk cord securing his archaic topknot, each wore only one garment. Broad black belts girdled, but did not contain, their great bellies. As they postured, Julia saw that black strips stretched between their powerful haunches and that their genitals were confined in black pouches. Dwarfed by ponderous bellies, those pouches nonetheless bulged suggestively.

"Just one bout." She gripped Tommy's fingers and whispered, "I promise. Then we'll go."

At the referee's command, the wrestlers crouched facing each other. Supported on their hands, they were two immense golden bullfrogs in mortal confrontation.

Hands moved with great speed, snaking toward each other's belt. Clutching those belts, the two rose. When their shoulders smacked together, they scrabbled with their feet for purchase. Heaving against each other, they grunted and snorted like fighting bulls locked horn to horn.

One stepped forward, throwing his opponent off balance. Turning slightly, he threw his arms around the other's shoulder and heaved prodigiously. His opponent grunted and stepped into the embrace, almost as if they were not fighting but caressing each other in some monstrous fashion. Seeking more leverage, the first fleetingly planted one foot on the white rope that defined the ring. The crowd groaned, and the bout ended.

While the sweat-dripping wrestlers resumed their robes, Tommy asked in disgust, "Is that all there is to it? Let's go."

"I'm ready now," Julia replied. "You know, Tommy, it's got something—even if it is so quick. Another day, I'd like to see a few bouts again."

"We can always hang about if you really want—"

"No, darling. I'm ready. All ready."

Julia turned the key in the front door of the loft apartment with a conviction of inevitability. She had opened that door hundreds of times, as had Tommy before her. They had opened it together dozens of times. But this time was utterly different. Her heightened sensibility told her that he, too, felt the inevitability.

They had all but spelled it out for each other. Without discussion or even conscious thought, they had sealed their new commitment while they were leaving the Olympia Theatre.

"It's still early," Tommy had said, glancing at his watch. "Why don't we drop into St. Andrew's Café for a drink?"

"Let's not," she had replied. "We can relax at the apartment."

"What about Emmy and Dick? I don't feel up to my energetic sister tonight. Nor Hollings either."

"No worry there. They've both gone to church. . . . Won't be back for hours."

"Church! Dick Hollings? That's a new one."

"Not to pray." Julia laughed. "Elizaveta asked them to some meeting about White Russians at the Orthodox Church. She's worried about all the Russian refugees flooding in. Emmy and Dick thought there might be a story there."

"Good! I do love my sister, but I can do without her company tonight."

"We won't be bothered. I promise you we won't. We'll be all alone."

That conversation echoed in Julia's mind as Tommy swung the door open. She knew she had promised him much more than seclusion.

Her nerves were strung taut, although not unpleasantly. She felt not tension but anticipation, and her perception was preternaturally acute. She saw Tommy with extraordinary clarity, as if he were lit by arclights.

They had, she realized, been standing just inside the door staring wordless at each other for almost a minute. She knew again that Tommy felt just as she did. The spell that bound them kept them from speaking, and their silence sealed their understanding.

His hands resting lightly on her shoulders, he still gazed at her. Very slowly and very gently, he drew her close and kissed her lips lightly. The spell grew stronger, and she pressed against him. Stepping back, she took his hand, thinking to lead him to her bedroom. But she stopped in midstride. She knew what she wanted above all else, but she did not know beyond all doubt that that was his wish as well.

Tommy held her hand an instant longer before pulling her close again. He kissed her very hard, and she no longer had any doubts. Julia kissed his cheek gently, her lips fluttering across his cheekbone.

Her arms went around his neck, and she kissed him hungrily. When she felt the arms that held her tremble, she whispered against his throat, "We've waited long enough, darling! Too long!"

The dusk of September 16, 1923, fell like a benediction on the city, indigo in the east and violet in the west. The streetlamps on the Bund were luminescent pearls, and even the seagulls circling over the Hwang-poo momentarily stopped their caterwauling. Tommy Howe walked briskly through the incipient chill of autumn, hoping to clear his head of the ether fumes and the antiseptic stenches of the hospital. His imagination caught by the fairyland atmosphere, he remembered the magical summer that was now closing.

The familiar streets still glowed with otherworldly radiance, and enchantment still gilded the commonplace housefronts. Poets obviously knew better than neurologists: Love *could* alter one's perceptions. There was no physical reason—within himself or outside—for the unearthly radiance that transfigured Shanghai. Only love!

He was content in his love for Julia. For her part, Julia was blithe, although her finances remained precarious. They knew they would not marry soon, if ever. But they knew, too, that they loved each other.

The physical act of love sealed their unity. Sleeping together now seemed only natural, in fact inevitable. Julia confided that at first she felt it pleasant enough, but soon discovered that it was ecstasy. Yet above all, they saw each other in an entirely new light. The familiar companion was transformed into a new being. They might already have been married—without the lifelong obligation that stifles spontaneity.

The only trouble was that, however irrationally, Julia now refused to allow Tommy to pay the rent on the loft-apartment. Curiously, her only gainful employment, which had been arranged by Joshua Haleevie, was diametrically opposite in political character to her voluntary teaching at the Labor University. Julia was earning fifty dollars Mex a month by teaching English at the Maritime Customs College, where Chinese youths were trained to serve the status quo, which meant the corrupt Peking regime and foreign imperialism.

Tommy sidestepped a rickshaw, moving somewhat slowly because he was caught up in his own thoughts. The shaft struck him a glancing blow, and the spell was broken.

Rubbing his bruised hip, he realized that the enchanted summer of 1923 was coming to its end too soon. Although he hated superstition, he feared that retribution would follow such great joy. Who, he wondered, would pay the inevitable reckoning?

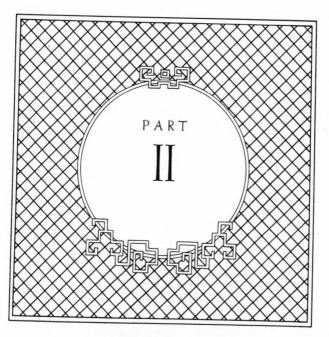

PART

II

MEETINGS

1926-1927

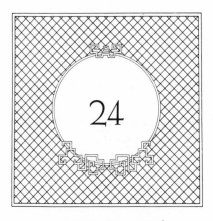

MARCH 8, 1926

The orderly pulled his tunic taut so that not a single crease marred the tan cotton. He rebuckled the brown leather belt from which his scabbarded bayonet hung, wiped his sweaty palms on his breeches, adjusted the puttees that spiraled up his calves—and knew he could delay no longer. Stifling his fears, he knocked on the door of the anteroom.

If he could get past the gimlet-eyed aide de camp, he would be all right. He had been assured that the general was too preoccupied with grand strategy to be alert to any danger.

Fortunately, the aide de camp, who wore the gold chrysanthemum of a major on his shoulder straps, was chatting with a tall officer who wore the two chrysanthemums of a lieutenant colonel. Otherwise, that colonel looked distinctly unmilitary with his black-rimmed glasses and his long hair that almost brushed his choker collar at the back. The aide de camp glanced up and saw, as he did every morning, the orderly carrying the general's leather briefcase, its bulging pockets secured by brass clasps. He nodded toward the inner office, and without knocking, the orderly opened the door bearing the signs COMMANDER IN CHIEF, NATIONAL PEOPLE'S REVOLUTIONARY ARMY and COMMANDANT, WHAMPOA MILITARY ACADEMY.

General Chiang Kai-shek looked up in momentary irritation at the intrusion. His eyes returned to the intelligence report he was annotating when he saw the orderly, but he looked up again and demanded, "You're new, aren't you? Where's Wang?"

"Wang's a little under the weather, sir. He asked me to bring your papers."

"Very well, then," the general said. "No, not on the table."

"Wang told me the briefcase always goes on the table behind you, sir."

"Just lean it against the leg of the desk, easier to hand," Chiang Kai-shek directed. "And then get out. You're wasting my time."

The orderly propped the briefcase against the heavy leg, smoothed down the flap, and plucked a hair-thin wire from the brass lock. When the door closed, the general had almost forgotten the intrusion. He was absorbed in his grand strategy for uniting the nation under the guidance of the National People's Party.

The National Revolutionary Army was soon to march out of its base at Canton in the far south on the first stage of the Northern Expedition. Its goal was Peking, the northern capital, but it would first have to crush the warlords who still ruled most of China. Chiang Kai-shek was, however, confident of final victory.

Under officers trained at the Whampoa Military Academy, the Revolutionary Army included Communists as well as Nationalists. The campaign was actively supported by the Soviet Union, which provided munitions and money. Operating conspiratorially behind the façade of the Communist International, the Soviets had also sent a first-generation American called Michael Borodin to Canton as senior adviser to the Nationalists. Greatly outnumbered by the warlords' forces, the Revolutionary Army was the only modern army in China. It was intelligently led, tautly disciplined, and well armed. All the omens were auspicious.

However, Canton itself posed problems, as Canton had since the mutiny of 1922 forced Sun Yat-sen to seek refuge on a gunboat. The Communists were the major problem, Chiang Kai-shek believed, just as he had foreseen since negotiating the first agreement with them at the Ikra years earlier.

Only a week ago, Communist triggermen had been gunned down by his bodyguards as they were lifting their pistols. In that latest attempt to murder him Chiang Kai-shek saw another tribute to his constantly growing power. The Communists obviously considered him the chief obstacle to their plan to hijack the Nationalist revolution and ride to power over China.

He had lived with the threat of assassination ever since Feng Yü-hsiang, the so-called Christian General, sent secret-society gunmen to ambush him as he left the reception for Donald and Eurydice Howe's thirtieth wedding anniversary. Recalling that incident, Chiang Kai-shek remembered that the Howes' son Thomas was waiting to see him, undoubtedly ill-at-ease in his new uniform of a lieutenant colonel in the medical corps. The young doctor would just have to wait until his commanding general was ready to see him. Chiang Kai-shek was reviewing his strategy, assessing the role of powerful men like the warlord General Feng Yü-hsiang in the complex political and military drama being played out in China.

Chiang's wide mouth twisted in distaste. The Christian General was as constant in his religion as in his alliances—that was, *not at all.* Now besieged by the warlord allies he had betrayed, he was deserting his troops and slipped away to Moscow to plead for help. As usual, the Russians were playing all sides against the middle.

The treacherous Christian General was no immediate threat. Chiang Kai-shek was, however, disturbed because that arch conspirator, the Comintern's senior agent, had also slipped away, perhaps to Moscow, to further some new plot. Michael Borodin now directed all Communist activities in China. A member of neither the National People's Party nor the Chinese Communist Party, he was not even Chinese. Yet the Comintern's agent exercised greater power over the National Revolution than any other man except Chiang Kai-shek himself.

The commanding general shook his head and reproached himself for allowing his mind to wander. He selected a new bamboo writing-brush from the ten bristling in his burnished brass brush-holder and jotted further notes on the intelligence report before him.

Canton, the metropolis of the south, was as intractable as the ram that was its symbol. He recalled the word he had first heard in his cadet days in Tokyo. Canton was *schizophrenic.* The city had a split personality.

On the waterfront Western structures like the colonnaded Post Office looked over the white steam-ferries that plied to Hong Kong—through thousands of moored sampans on which entire families lived the same lives their ancestors had ten centuries earlier. The metropolis reeked of decaying vegetation, yet its cuisine was emulated throughout the world. Behind modern department stores flourished opium divans run by secret societies and local warlords.

The revolution had cast a red hue over Canton. Crimson propaganda banners spanned medieval lanes, and scarlet pennants bearing fiery slogans hung from ancient temples. The few motorcars were monopolized by "revolutionary personages" wearing red neckties over their tunics' choker collars and by warlord generals, whose bodyguards sprawled on the cars' fenders. Canton was the only metropolis in all China where the Communists could operate in the open. The offices of the provincial committee of the Chinese Communist Party on Wen Te Road were hung with red bunting, as were the windows of the many trade unions and "mass organizations" the Communists controlled. In the scarlet-painted doorways, young women with bobbed hair and fanatical eyes were jostled by officers with gleaming Sam Browne belts, by grimy workers, and by barefoot peasants.

Like Napoleon, whose campaigns he had studied at the Tokyo Military Academy, Chiang Kai-shek could do several things at once. Looking down, he saw that his mind had been operating simultaneously on three distinct levels. While reading the intelligence summary and at the same time considering the problem of Canton, he had defined his overall strategy. The general read his succinct summation with pleasure:

> The Russians are essential. They provide arms, gold, and advice. Only the last can we dispense with.
> Borodin I must therefore tolerate. The Chinese Communist Party I can do without.
> The weasels of that party are trying to split us Nationalists by dividing the military arm from the political arm. They are smearing my reputation and wooing the civilian officials of the National Government.
> Ultimately, I must assume civil power as well as military power. Immediately, I must crush the Communist menace. I cannot drive the Communists out of the National People's Party just now. Doing so could alienate Moscow, which provides our funds. But I must strike at the Chinese Red conspirators just as soon as I can find—or create—a plausible pretext.

Satisfied that he had defined his immediate problem, Chiang Kai-shek laid down his writing-brush. But he could not waste time on self-congratulation. His index finger moved toward the bell push under his desk to summon Dr. Howe, who had requested an interview. Almost touching the button, his finger was halted by an alarming thought.

It was unusual but not extraordinary for his regular orderly to talk a friend into performing his duties. It was, indeed, usual when the orderly was "under the weather," which meant recovering from a drinking bout. But there was something peculiar about today's substitute.

The general singled out that peculiarity. The orderly who brought the briefcase had been sweating heavily, although the March morning was brisk. Yet it was obvious from his accent that he was a southerner.

The general allowed himself a chuckle rather like a watchdog's bark. He was getting skittish—and imagining dangers. The substitute orderly might be bothered by the heat because he had recently returned from the north. The man might be suffering from a cold or a hangover. A dozen innocent explanations were possible.

He would look a fool if he made a fuss about a blameless enlisted man. Above all, he could not appear anything less than a fearless, death-defying leader to his men. His index finger stabbed the bell push decisively.

While waiting, Chiang Kai-shek recalled his information on the young doctor. From agents' reports, from the letters of Mayling Soong, and from his blood brother, the Supreme Lord of the Floodgate Fraternity, he knew that Dr. Thomas Tan-ssu Howe was a close friend of the Communist leader Chang Kuo-tao. However, the doctor's father was a major financial supporter of the Nationalists, and his sister Emily served the Nationalist cause by her writing. Dr. Howe was therefore to be spared. Had he not been his father's son, he would have been declared suspect by the Nationalist secret police and quietly "cleared away."

Volunteering to serve with the Northern Expedition, Tommy had reported to headquarters Canton in January 1926. He was astonished at being appointed a deputy surgeon general with the rank of colonel. Chiang Kai-shek had laughed at Tommy's misgivings and had dismissed his wish to serve as a field surgeon with an infantry battalion. He had finally offered: "If you insist, I'll demote you to divisional surgeon with the rank of lieutenant colonel. But no lower. We don't have enough doctors."

When Tommy thanked him, General Chiang had made a mental note: Whatever his political errors, young Howe is a man of personal honor. By rejecting higher rank for a more dangerous post, he has displayed true Confucian virtue.

When Tommy again entered the commander in chief's office, he was again struck by the force of the general's personality. Chiang Kai-shek was decisive, and his deep-set eyes were bright with intelligence. As became a professional officer, his hair was cropped short and his uniform was plain. His new mustache could wholly conceal neither his sensitive lower lip nor the lines his dedication to duty had engraved around his mouth. The general, Tommy recalled, was just thirty-nine years old.

Chiang Kai-shek saw in Tommy Howe, who was ten years younger, the prototypical Chinese intellectual: intelligent, passionate, and naïve. The eyes in Tommy's narrow face seemed vulnerable, and he was pallid after two years in the wards of Shanghai General Hospital. Chiang noted with approval the pains his visitor took to look older and more responsible: the curved meerschaum pipe, the spectacles, and the worn Gladstone bag.

Peaked cap tucked under his arm, Tommy saluted briskly. But the lieutenant colonel was clearly a civilian in uniform, lacking the robotlike rigidity drilled into professional officers.

Although still lean, Tommy had filled out since Chiang Kai-shek had known him casually as Donald Howe's youngest son. He had also matured perceptibly during the two months since his arrival in Canton. The faint lines of strain at the corners of his eyes showed how hard he had been working to build the medical service of the National Revolutionary Army.

"Sit down, Howe," the general directed. "Sit down and tell me why you needed to see me."

Tommy opened his Gladstone bag, withdrew a large envelope bearing Donald Howe's vermilion seal, and handed it to the commander in chief. He said, "Sir, my father sent this letter with . . . ah . . . a trusted friend. He instructed me to give it you immediately."

"I'll just open it, since Mr. Howe says it's urgent."

The general poured tea for Tommy and refilled his own cup before slitting the envelope with the bayonet that lay on his desk. Despite his stringent self-control, a smile flickered when he withdrew the smaller envelope tucked into the folds of Donald Howe's lengthy message. As duty demanded, he put aside the letter from Mayling Soong to scan Donald Howe's.

"Your esteemed father commends you to my care," Chiang Kai-shek at length said. "He expects you to return unscathed as soon as the Northern Expedition ends. He will be pleased if I can dispense with your services earlier."

"A parent's natural concern, sir," Tommy responded to the oblique censure. "But I know that a soldier serves where he's sent—until he's relieved."

"Don't feel bad about being assigned as a divisional surgeon. Yes, that posting will please your father. But even division headquarters can be shelled or overrun."

"Yes, sir." Tommy took in the unspoken message: the general would not offend an influential backer, but he would not be dictated to. "Though I'd still prefer regiment or battalion."

"I've already told you I don't have so many doctors I can assign them to battalions. Now tell me, Howe, what's the latest news from Shanghai? What did you hear from this trusted friend who brought your father's letter?"

Tommy hesitated for only an instant. He had learned that complete candor was often a mistake. But he could certainly speak candidly to his commanding general.

"Everything's going well," he replied. "My friend says there is now smooth cooperation between Nationalists and Communists in Shanghai. Lately, the leaders of both groups have been meeting regularly in the Soviet consulate."

"Not at that plush brothel, the Ikra, anymore?" Chiang Kai-shek commented. "Tell me more about those meetings."

"Not much to tell, sir," Tommy responded. "Though it is odd that Chinese need to meet for safety in a foreign consulate. But that's Shanghai, isn't it? At first, the moderate Nationalists were suspicious of the Communists. Through their meetings, however, the two are becoming a united force . . ."

Chiang Kai-shek tamped down his anger. He was himself wooing the moderate group within his National People's Party. Preoccupied with Canton, he had overlooked the moderates' flirtation with the Communists in Shanghai. The tendons of his neck stood out, but his benevolent smile did not alter.

Although Tommy was not intimidated by that grimace, he said tentatively, "Sir, there is one other thing. My friend . . . the one who brought the letter . . . would like to greet you. If you have a moment to spare . . ."

"My schedule is full, Howe," Chiang Kai-shek replied acerbically. "This friend of yours, who is he?"

"It's not a he, sir. My friend is a lady. She's waiting in my car. If you could spare a few minutes . . ."

"I see." The general smiled broadly. "Sorry, but I can't help you impress your little friend today."

"With respect, sir, she's not a little friend!" Tommy persisted. "She's a foreign lady and—"

"Certainly not! I've got no time to waste with foreigners—particularly female foreigners."

"Sir, she's a friend of my sister, Emily." Tommy was undaunted. "And also a friend of Miss Mayling Soong."

The cloud of anger passed from the general's face, and he said, "In that case, bring her in! Just a short visit. But by all means bring her in."

When the door closed behind Tommy, General Chiang's hand strayed toward the unopened envelope from Mayling Soong. He snatched his hand back as if it were red hot. Duty first, he reminded himself, always duty first. The situation reports awaited his attention. Swiveling in his chair, he reached for the briefcase propped against the heavy leg of his ebony desk. His fingertips just brushing the handle, the decisive general uncharacteristically changed his mind again.

He would not immerse himself in situation reports until he had digested the information from Shanghai in Donald Howe's letter. He might even allow himself to glance at Mayling's letter before opening the briefcase. The jasmine scent was tantalizing—and her letters were always informative. But first he read again the vital closing paragraph of Donald Howe's letter.

> We look to you, General, as commander in chief of the armed forces. The civilian officials of the Nationalist Government are weak and wavering. Here in Shanghai matters are not good. The university students and the workers, both led by the Communists, are uniting against the capitalists. The business community fears new attacks led by Communists upon its rights and its property. We depend upon you to prevent such attacks. Additional funds are, of course, available.

Chiang Kai-shek grimaced and rubbed the back of his neck. He was depleted emotionally and worn physically by constantly defending the National Revolution against the Communists' ceaseless attacks. It was now time to counterattack.

The self-disciplined soldier allowed himself a diversion. Opening the jasmine-scented envelope with an impatient thumbnail, he read Mayling Soong's ideograms. Her letter ended:

> Esteemed General, you must strike very soon. We cannot permit events to pass us by. Your destiny is at stake. Our future is also at stake, yours and mine. My mother will never permit me to marry a nonentity. We must be worthy of each other!

Those words galvanized the general. All his information pointed to the same conclusion: he must *immediately* crush the conspiracies of the Chinese Communist Party. The problem was no longer what to do but how to do it. Precisely what pretext to use to justify his counterattack? Precisely when and where to strike at the Communists?

Chiang Kai-shek permitted himself to reread Mayling's letter before turning to the accumulation of reports on his troops' health, supplies, and training. He was bending in resignation to pick up his crammed briefcase when a thought struck him: regardless of war and revolution, a Chinese gentleman must receive his guests with due hospitality. He sent the mess servants scurrying to bring fresh tea and sweet cakes for the foreign woman who was a friend of Mayling.

When Tommy knocked, Chiang rose from his massive ebony desk. His dignity would not permit him to open the door himself, but he would meet his guests halfway. He called out "Come in!" and waited beside a low ebony table inlaid with mother-of-pearl and surrounded by easy chairs covered in white linen.

The foreign woman surprised Chiang Kai-shek. He had somehow expected her to be tall and gawky, but she was small and voluptuously curved. She was roughly Mayling's age, though it was hard to tell how old foreigners were. Her hair, which just brushed her shoulders, was a rich tawny hue. Her yellow pongee dress clung so closely that he wondered if she was wearing anything under it. But all foreign women were bold.

Clutching her straw handbag like a life-preserver, Julia felt anything but bold. She had not wanted to see Chiang Kai-shek just yet, but Tommy had insisted that she could not miss the opportunity. It might be her only chance to carry out her mission for her uncle John Pavernen. She had expected the general to be stern, but he smiled warmly and solicitously seated her in an easy chair at the coffee table.

"I hope you'll like the tea," he said. "It's picked on the slopes above my native village."

"It's delicious," she said, "and, somehow, familiar. How could I have tasted—"

"At the Soongs', perhaps? I always send the Soongs a few pounds from the pick of the crop. . . . You brought the letter from . . . ah . . . Mr. Howe, did you?"

"And the letter from Mayling." Julia knew that he would not ask directly about the woman he hoped to marry. "She is very well . . . blooming. But I can tell she misses you."

"Ho! Ho! . . ." Chiang Kai-shek responded. "Very good! I'm grateful to you."

Although determined to charm the general, Julia smiled at the irony of her helping the romance between two people she did not particularly like. She could not warm to Mayling Soong, whom she found cool and narcissistic—in short, emotionally flat. The general represented almost everything she had learned to hate at Shanghai Labor University. Beneath his revolutionary mask, she saw the ambitious reactionary who opposed the progressive movement.

Julia had been happy to run errands for the secret Communist Apparatus. She had passed on information acquired in foreign circles, such as police tactics against the strikes that had been roiling Shanghai and China for two years. The Communists had welcomed her assistance—and improved her political consciousness. With Tommy away for some time, she was glad of her new circle of friends.

Like her, Tommy apparently assumed that they would marry one day. But she was not worried about marriage even at twenty-six, although she knew that time would *not* automatically sweep aside the obstacles. She was still disturbed by his antiforeign feeling. Besides, he had not confronted his parents with the possibility of marrying a foreign woman. Julia believed that both Donald and Eurydice Howe liked her. But she would not deceive herself. They tolerated her relationship with Tommy, whatever they thought it was, because he was entitled to sow his wild oats—and because they *knew* he would never marry her.

Anyway, Tommy and she had been enjoying themselves too much in the heady atmosphere of mid-1920s Shanghai to worry about marriage. Besides, he had to complete his medical training first. He should now have been completing the first year of his residency, which would have meant only two more years at Shanghai General Hospital before specializing. His progress had been stalled when he joined the Revolutionary Army—for how long no one could tell.

Julia loved Tommy even more for his patriotism, but it was hard to say when they could eventually marry. Meanwhile, they had made no formal commitment. Nonetheless, Julia felt, they were pledged to each other. Still, marriage was not that important!

Lost in her own thoughts, Julia just heard Chiang Kai-shek ask in his crabbed Shanghainese, "And what brings you to Canton, Miss Pavernen?"

"Aside from Tommy," she replied, "I wanted to see the capital of the revolution. So, since my uncle was coming on business . . ."

"And what is your uncle's business, Miss Pavernen?"

"He can provide armaments, Commandant."

"I like your calling me Commandant." Chiang was disarmingly ingenuous. "I treasure that title even more than the title of commander in chief. As commandant of the Whampoa Military Academy, it is my proud responsibility to train China's next generation of officers. My students will shape the future of our country. . . . Armaments, you said?"

"Machine guns, trench mortars, and rifles, Commandant."

"That *is* interesting," Chiang mused. "I need another source of supply, not only the Russians. How soon could your uncle deliver—"

The buzzing of the internal telephone interrupted him, and he pondered for a moment after his aide reported, "Commissar Chou En-lai will be here in two minutes, General. You have a meeting scheduled."

Chiang Kai-shek decided not to risk arousing suspicion by making his Communist associate wait. He was, unfortunately, noted for punctuality in an unpunctual nation. Chou En-lai might wonder if he postponed their appointment. The political commissar was only twenty-eight, but he was very acute. Working together for almost three years, they had also learned each other's quirks.

"Send him in," Chiang said into the telephone, and then to his guests: "You're in luck. My director for political training is coming by. A Communist comrade called Chou En-lai."

Chiang Kai-shek smiled but spat out that name like a bad oyster. Julia was nonetheless smitten when the man himself entered the office. She knew him by reputation as a brilliant negotiator and propagandist, but she had not expected such compelling, mobile features or such liquid, expressive eyes. When he acknowledged Chiang Kai-shek's introduction in slightly accented Shanghainese, she gave part of her heart to Chou En-lai.

"I've heard your name, Miss Pavernen," he said. "Spoken most favorably. A pity the imperialists closed down Shanghai Labor University. Your work was much appreciated."

"Nothing to your work, Commissar," she replied. "Nothing to directing political training for the Revolutionary Army."

"To the contrary. My work has the same purpose as your teaching. At the Whampoa Academy, we raise our cadets' political consciousness. We also train activists to undermine the enemy's morale. We are mobilizing actors and poets, journalists and musicians, even bill-posters and song-writers, all to—"

"Some people can't talk about anything but politics." Annoyed by the mutual congratulations, Chiang Kai-shek broke in brusquely. "On more practical matters, tell me, Miss Pavernen, exactly what weapons your uncle can supply."

"The rifles are U.S. Model 1917's, Commandant." Julia rallied, although taken aback by his abruptness. "Also Browning machine guns, watercooled."

"I'll take two hundred Brownings." The general made up his mind.

"The price must be right, but it's not the vital factor. You *can* guarantee prompt delivery?"

Julia was wondering how early she dared promise delivery when Chou En-lai interjected: "Commandant, I believe that all arms purchases must be approved by the—"

"Now, Commissar, we mustn't trouble our visitor with our administrative arrangements." Chiang Kai-shek's reprimand was silky. "Miss Pavernen, I'll also take ten thousand Model 1917's, again assuming prompt delivery."

"Prices naturally depend on quantity and delivery dates," Julia ventured. "Also how much ammunition and—"

"I'm not a merchant! I never haggle!" Chiang Kai-shek's disdain for commerce perhaps explained his failure as both merchant and stockbroker. "Just give my chief clerk the details."

Julia almost pitied Commissar Chou En-lai, although he could obviously look after himself. He had been subjected to a cruel loss of face by General Chiang Kai-shek, who was a baffling mixture of incompatible elements: courtesy and arrogance, diplomacy and ineptitude, generosity and callousness. General Chiang had obviously intended to make her think less of Commissar Chou by humiliating him. Instead, Julia felt a bond with the vital young Communist leader, who had looked intently into her eyes when he praised her work at Labor University.

Apparently unmoved, Chou En-lai rose and said, "General, I must be on my way. I don't want to drive your guests out with dull administrative matters. Perhaps later . . . Miss Pavernen, Colonel Howe, if you'll excuse me, there's work to do. Delighted at meeting you."

Chiang Kai-shek remarked after the door closed, "Charming, isn't he? But a soldier, no! Can you believe that young fellow is chairman of the Military Committee of the Chinese Communist Party? At least, he's a gentleman, unlike that bumpkin Mao Tse-tung. Mao is obsessed with the peasants, but the peasants don't matter."

The general's expression altered when he said to Julia, "Brownings, watercooled, you said? Any modifications? Will they take seven-point-nine ammunition?"

"I really don't understand the technical details, Commandant," Julia replied. "I'd have to ask my uncle. He did say they were basic watercooled machine guns. I can let you know this afternoon whether—"

"No matter. I've got the answer right here." Rising and striding across the room, Chiang Kai-shek stood before his desk and shuffled the papers in his hold basket.

"I know it was here," he said. "If they'd just stop fiddling with my papers . . ."

His mood again altered abruptly. He slammed his fist down on the desk in exasperation and said, "If only . . . But here it is. Just a second and I'll . . ."

His words stopping abruptly, the general cocked his head. He could not see the briefcase that had been dislodged when he struck the desk, but he could hear a peculiar hissing. He flung himself face down on the carpet, clasping his hands behind his neck. Julia wondered if his lightning changes of mood indicated some kind of mental illness.

"Detonator!" the general exclaimed. "Get down!"

Tommy seized Julia by the shoulders before she was aware that he had moved. He flung her down on the carpet and fell on top of her. In the silence, she heard the faint hissing that had alarmed Chiang Kai-shek.

An instant later, the big office seemed to rise into the air. A wave of brilliant light blinded them, and the explosion battered them.

"A strange mission for a young lady!" Richard exclaimed. "You mean *you* actually talked Chiang Kai-shek into buying all those guns? Just you alone?"

Emily raised her eyebrows at her lover's male condescension. But she did not speak for fear of interrupting the story.

"Uncle Jack asked me to help and I did," Julia said. "Tommy calls him a flea in the golden shirt of capitalism. I also know what he's like. But he is my uncle, and he's been very good to me, and I do love him—despite his faults. So I helped. And the commission he's paying will help keep me going."

"As simple as that, was it?" Emily asked. "You just waltzed into General Chiang Kai-shek's office, showed a little leg, and got him to sign the contract?"

"Well, not quite," Julia conceded. "You see, Tommy got me in to see the general and . . ."

Having just arrived in Shanghai after a long train journey, Julia was eager to tell them about her eight days in turbulent Canton. When she entered the loft apartment on Kiukiang Road at six in the evening, she had been surprised to find Richard Hollings lounging on the rattan settee with a whisky and soda in his hand. He was usually at the offices of the *North China Daily News* at that time. But newspapermen worked odd hours.

"So that's what happened." Julia summed up after telling them about the explosion that just missed killing Chiang Kai-shek. "Tommy was wonderful. He had a gash in his arm, but he patched up the general first.

Poor man was streaming blood from a wound in his forehead. The splinter almost took out his eye. I was almost ashamed of being unhurt. Tommy shielded me, as I said."

"And this explosion?" Richard asked. "A bomb obviously, but where did it come from?"

"Later they worked out what happened," Julia replied. "The bomb was put into the general's briefcase by a man pretending to be filling in for his orderly. They found the real orderly in a latrine with his throat cut. It was a time bomb, they decided."

"But what set it off just then?" Richard persisted. "And what about that hissing sound?"

"I'm not sure about the technical details," replied Julia, who was actually quite sure. "But the hissing was acid at work. As I understand it, the bomb was supposed to explode when the acid ate through some kind of barrier—maybe a wooden plug—and set off the detonator. It was also sensitive to vibration, so that it couldn't be defused easily. When Chiang Kai-shek pounded the desk, it went off."

"And if he'd been sitting behind his desk . . ." Richard suggested.

"He would have been finished," Julia agreed. "I thought it would make a good story for you newshawks. General Chiang's miraculous survival, I mean."

Emily did not reply, but Richard declared, "Not for me, unfortunately. It's too old and stale for *The Times*. The *Boston Globe* might be interested, but . . ."

"What about the *North China Daily News*?" Julia asked. "Surely the *News* would be interested."

"It's a marvelous story for the Chinese-language press," Emily interjected. "But Dick can't write it for the *News*. You see—"

"I've been sacked," Richard exploded. "Thrown out like a junior clerk caught pinching the petty cash."

"Dick, that can't be true," Julia said. "Why, you were doing so brilliantly. I thought . . . we all thought . . . you'd be made deputy editor. And now this. After everything you've done for the *News*!"

"*Because* of what I'd done for the *News*, Julie," he replied. "The editor called and told me I was being sacked because my coverage was too evocative . . . and because I was too pro-Chinese."

"I can hardly believe that," Julia said. "Of course, the *News* is a bulwark of imperialism and capitalism. But even so . . ."

"I should have seen it coming," Richard declared. "My troubles really began a couple of years ago, the autumn of 1923, when I went up to cover the northern warlord war. Do you remember, Julie? *The Times* sent me because the permanent correspondent was on home leave. Unfortunately, it wasn't much of a war, though it should've been . . ."

The anticipated battles between the largest military forces ever assembled in China, Richard recalled, had fizzled out disappointingly. On one side stood Wu Pei-fu, the Scholar General, who had crushed the Railway Workers' Union and who was now defending Peking with a modern naval squadron and almost 200,000 troops. His chief ally was Feng Yü-hsiang, the Christian General, whose loyalty was always for sale. On the other side, Chang Tso-lin, the Old Marshal, who ruled Manchuria, possessed an air force of canvas-and-wood warplanes flown by foreign pilots but commanded by his son, Chang Hsueh-liang, who was inevitably known as the Young Marshal. The Manchurian forces were supported by artillery units provided, trained, and supplied with ammunition by the Japanese.

"We were all expecting a battle," Richard said. "No arranged truce this time, we thought. No silver bullets paid to one side to back off. The Japanese were egging the Old Marshal on. At worst, they obviously reckoned, they'd pick up the pieces after the battle. They did pick up a lot of pieces, but not the way we'd thought."

The Christian General, also in cahoots with the Japanese, had seized Peking behind the backs of the chief contenders. Whoever held Peking was tendered formal recognition by the foreign powers—and was paid the revenues of the Chinese Maritime Customs.

"It was extraordinary," Richard remembered. "I watched Wu Pei-fu —the Scholar General, you know—leave the stage of history. Same plain uniform, not like the Old Marshal's gold epaulettes and stars and orders. Wu Pei-fu just threw in his hand. He boarded his special train, changed at Tientsin to a steamer for Shanghai—and vanished. . . . Even more extraordinary in Peking. All those half-starved country boys of Feng Yü-hsiang's army in their filthy quilted uniforms like the hordes of Genghis Khan. And all of them singing "Onward Christian Soldiers" in Chinese . . ."

The Christian General himself was no crude countryman but an ambitious plotter. He invited the Old Marshal of Manchuria and President Sun Yat-sen of the Canton Republic to confer with him in Peking. The Japanese, who had instigated the Christian General's coup d'etat and armed the Old Marshal, encouraged Sun Yat-sen to believe that he could bring all the warring factions together under his leadership.

Leaving for Peking, Sun Yat-sen confided to his wife, Rosamonde, that the forthcoming negotiations could make the Northern Expedition unnecessary. Although he would naturally use the threat of the National Revolutionary Army, he could by peaceful means again become the president of a unified China.

"No one but old Dr. Sun could command such loyalty," Richard mused. "Except for extreme reactionaries, everyone could unite under his leadership."

"So tragic!" Emily said. "His death on the verge of triumph."

"Just like Moses," Julia added, "Moses seeing the promised land but never setting foot in it."

"I don't know what the *North China Daily News* would've made of Moses." Richard laughed. "But my editor wasn't happy with my coverage of Sun Yat-sen. I've thought about it many times. For the life of me, I can't see how else I could've reported it. As soon as Dr. Sun checked into the Hotel de Pekin on the last day of nineteen twenty-four, the doctors began pouring into his suite—and the rumors began trickling out."

In late January of 1925, Sun Yat-sen underwent an operation at Peking Union Medical College, Tommy Howe's *alma mater*. The American surgeon saw the cancer that was devouring his patient's liver and sadly closed the incision.

There was no hope, Richard continued, but Dr. Sun was a long time dying. His followers—and hopeful successors—gathered in Peking. Only General Chiang Kai-shek remained at his post in Canton. Two men dominated the deathbed vigil: the Comintern's representative, Michael Borodin, and Wang Ching-wei, whom Richard called Lucifer because he was so handsome, so talented—and so corrupt.

Each man got what he wanted from the dying president. Wang Ching-wei, who was Chiang Kai-shek's only rival for supreme leadership in Canton, wrote the president's farewell message. It exhorted the Nationalists to complete their revolution, presumably under the leadership of the man Hollings called Lucifer. Michael Borodin drafted an open letter to Moscow that promised China would cooperate with the Soviet Union in inciting revolution throughout the world. After Sun Yat-sen signed those documents, they let him die.

The opening of the protracted funeral ceremonies displeased fervent revolutionaries. Rosamonde Sun insisted upon a Christian service in the chapel of Peking Union Medical College. Since PUMC was a missionary institution and, therefore, imperialist, most of Dr. Sun's Chinese followers stayed away. To even the balance, the eulogy reminded the predominantly foreign audience between hymns that the dead hero had declared, "I do not belong to the Christianity of the churches, but to the Christianity of Jesus Christ, the great revolutionary."

Then Dr. Sun Yat-sen finally conquered Peking, which had been his objective all his life. He lay in state in the walled Imperial City, while hundreds of thousands shuffled past to gaze reverently at the sallow face with the iron-gray mustache. The white-sunburst flag of the Nationalists draped the coffin and flew in Peking for the first time. Recordings of his speeches hissed incessantly from loudspeakers hung in the trees.

After three weeks of adulation, the body was borne to the Temple of Azure Clouds in the Fragrant Hills northwest of Peking. Nationalists and Communists, students and shopkeepers, artisans and laborers marched in their thousands behind the cortege. They were muffled against the chill April wind, but the white mourning bands on their clothing were bright in the afternoon sun. Above their heads, banners flaunted anti-imperialist and anti-warlord slogans. Bulky in black leather coats, the warlord police watched, for once unable to suppress a demonstration.

"How could I write it any other way?" Richard Hollings demanded of his sympathetic audience. "It was deeply moving. For a few hours, China was united behind Dr. Sun, just as he'd dreamed all his life. . . . I wrote an objective story. But when I got back to Shanghai, the *News* made it plain that it did not like such pro-Chinese sentiments. Pro-Bolshevik, the editor even called me—which is ridiculous. He let me off with a warning. . . . And one good thing did come of it: T. V. Soong was very impressed. He's a Harvard man, and he knows everybody in Boston. T.V. introduced me to the *Boston Globe.* They pay well for the stories they take."

"But why wait so long to get rid of you?" Julia asked. "I still don't understand why the *News* fired you only now. That was all two years ago."

"They warned me," Richard answered. "Perhaps I should have listened. The May Thirtieth Incident last year really did me in. I suppose my masters were tolerant, by their lights. Didn't give me the sack for months afterward. They were most exercised about my reporting for *The Times* and the *Boston Globe.* My cardinal sin was my failure to put Shanghai's best foot forward overseas."

While Richard examined his memories, Julia recalled her own role in the protracted conflict between Shanghai's foreign rulers and Shanghai's Chinese populace that provoked the May Thirtieth Massacre. When the Communists hoisted red flags over the Chinese-ruled district of Chapei to taunt the foreigners in spring 1925, Tommy had not shared her joy. He admired the Communists, particularly Chang Kuo-tao, but he feared their ruthless manipulation of the labor movement. Julia, however, was being drawn ever deeper into the twilight realm of espionage and subversion—to her delight and Tommy's consternation.

"This isn't a Girl Guides frolic," he warned. "The Municipal Council isn't shooting Red agitators—not yet. But that time could come."

"I'm only running a few errands," she replied. "Anyway, I'm, too small a fish for anyone to bother with."

Unabashed, Julia continued to serve as a courier and an informer for the militant Communists, who were inciting strikes in Japanese-owned factories. She often carried messages, sometimes melodramatically tucked into a stocking-top. Her chief value to the conspirators, however, was her access to foreign circles they could not penetrate. Rachel Haleevie's At Homes at Jade House were, as ever, well attended, and influential men talked freely to the impressionable young American woman.

During the last week of May, strikes against Japanese-owned factories mobilized workers and intellectuals. Glad they were not themselves the target, other foreigners tolerantly watched strikers and students parade shouting anti-Japanese slogans and carrying anti-Japanese banners through the Settlement and Frenchtown to the music of hired funeral bands. Chinese policemen happily waved those processions on. They too hated the arrogant Japanese.

The police also stood by when locked-out workmen smashed the gates of a Japanese-owned cotton mill closed because it lacked the raw materials produced by the struck factories. Raging against the idle machinery, the workmen smashed spindles and looms with crowbars and hammers. When Japanese foremen ordered them to get out and drew revolvers, the terrified workmen flourished their iron weapons. The foremen fired, and seven workers were hit. One died amid the broken machinery.

In Canton, Tommy's friend Chang Kuo-tao received an urgent telegram from the Central Committee of the Communist Party: RETURN IMMEDIATELY TO TAKE CHARGE OF NEW WAVE OF AGITATION. WE HAVE MARTYRS TO EXPLOIT. On May 27th, before he arrived, Shanghai Labor University staged a mass rally against the Japanese murderers—and resolved formally to expel *all* foreigners from Shanghai by force.

No longer complacent, the Settlement authorities arrested several student leaders and called up the Volunteers—to Richard Hollings's disgust. He could not report the worst crisis Shanghai had known for decades because he had neglected to resign his commission. He was, moreover, bored because the Volunteers were ordered to remain in their barracks until they were needed.

On Saturday, May 30, 1925, a day of alternating sunshine and showers, Julia and Emily watched the processions on Nanking Road marching to demand the release of the arrested student leaders. Throngs of men waited near Kweichow Road, which led to the Laoza police station. Amid the mushroom field of oiled-paper umbrellas, the corrugated-iron roof of the trolley shelter gleamed slick green when the sun emerged briefly.

Although the demonstrators were carefree, almost jovial, the policemen guarding narrow Kweichow Road were fearful. Chanting antiforeign slogans, several students waved gaily when they recognized Julia. Then they flourished the banners provided by the protest committee: TOPPLE THE IMPERIALISTS! DRIVE OUT THE FOREIGNERS!

Inspector John Everson was remembering the dismissal of the officer who had allowed a Chinese mob to burn the Laoza police station twenty years earlier. His broad head and blunt features sheeplike, he was deeply worried about his career, his plump Chinese wife, and their six-year-old son.

The tide of demonstrators lapped at the khaki rank spanning Kweichow Road. Standing straddle-legged, Inspector Everson replaced his sola topee and roared instructions through a megaphone. After repeatedly—and vainly—directing the mob to disperse, he ordered the ringleaders arrested. Three students were frogmarched into the red brick police station. The tide of demonstrators followed them into the courtyard and the charge room.

Through the open windows, Everson heard the agitators railing against foreign imperialism. Inside his own charge room, other agitators were demanding that he release his prisoners. When his constables drove the intruders out, his prisoners also vanished.

Jubilant at outwitting the foreigners, the good-natured crowd flowed back toward Nanking Road. Two youths paused to chat with Julia and Emily and laughed as they described the melee inside the station house.

A formation of thirty foreign policemen appeared on Nanking Road, pushing through the throng to reinforce the police station. Shouting gleefully, the demonstrators taunted the constables. Almost playfully, students snatched at their holstered revolvers. With grim pleasure, the policemen drew their truncheons to beat back their assailants.

In that instant, the mood of the crowd altered violently. It surged again toward the Laoza station, screaming, "*Sha yang kuei! Sha!* . . . Kill the foreign devils. Kill!"

When the khaki line across the side road buckled under that pressure, John Everson ordered his men to cock their carbines. His final warning was drowned by the mob's screams. He was determined that the Laoza police station would not be sacked again—not with him in command.

"Ready!" he cried. "Aim!"

Those orders were inaudible to the mob.

"Fire!" he screamed. "Fire!"

Twenty-two carbines crashed. Before Everson could halt it, a second volley ripped into the throng.

Nanking Road had never been so still. The appalled silence endured for interminable moments before it was trampled under foot. The demonstrators fled, screaming and swearing over the scuffling of sandals, the clacking of wooden clogs, and the pounding of leather soles.

Twelve did not flee, but lay still on the damp black roadway. Blood seeping into rain puddles swirled iridescent as Julia and Emily took refuge in the deep doorway of a haberdasher's shop.

Within five minutes, Nanking Road was deserted—and John Everson stared half-dazed at the corpses. A few minutes later, the Volunteers arrived on the double. Their Sam Browne belts gleamed; their khaki shorts flapped; and their bayonets glittered. Amid the uncanny peace they set up their machine guns.

Julia released Emily's hand, which she had been squeezing very hard. Turning, she saw that Emily's shoulders were shaking and her eyes were liquid with tears. Deeply moved, Julia started to embrace her friend.

"Don't touch me!" Emily exploded, her eyes fixed on the dead lying in the road. "Not a foreigner! . . . Just look, Julia, just look what you foreigners have done!"

"Did you know?" Richard's voice recalled Julia to the present. "It took me a long time to forgive Emily for her luck in seeing the May Thirtieth Incident."

"Some luck!" Emily said. "Seeing a massacre. . . . Dick, you also found it very hard, to forgive me for something else. Do you remember how angry you were when I filed my eyewitness story to the Philadelphia *Ledger*—and only afterward sent reports in your name to *The Times* and the *Boston Globe*?"

"I know it was irrational." Richard repeated the explanation, as he had in the past. "But *The Times* and the *Globe* are my bread and butter —what little there is of it. The *Ledger's* only play for you.

"Don't be so disgustingly condescending," Emily retorted. "It's hardly play for me. I've just got a more balanced perspective than you.

Dick, you're so tied up with your work . . . so ambitious . . . you're impossible. China's sorrows are *not* staged for your personal benefit. Why—"

Hoping to forestall a quarrel, Julia said, "The pot's still boiling—and anti-imperialist feeling is rising."

The pot was boiling furiously, as she had just seen in Canton. Since students in China enjoyed almost the same reverence elsewhere tendered royalty, boxing champions, and successful confidence men, the May Thirtieth Incident was not merely an atrocity but a desecration. All foreigners, but particularly the British, were the butt of universal anger. A seaman's strike in Canton cut off British imports, and a general strike paralyzed the British Crown Colony of Hong Kong. New adherents swelled both the Chinese Communist Party and the National People's Party, while liberals abroad began to talk of pulling out of Shanghai. The campaign to exploit the martyrs, which was managed by Tommy's friend Chang Kuo-tao, was initially a spectacular success, as was the general strike in Shanghai.

Julia had felt a profound loss when the Municipal Council closed down Shanghai Labor University lest it breed more patriotic agitators. The strike then forced all foreign-owned mills and factories to suspend operations, closing even foreign-language newspapers. Julia was again unemployed when the Maritime Customs College suspended classes. Even man-cart, rickshaw, and wharf coolies stopped work, halting all trade.

The street demonstrations never flagged; plays, skits, and cabarets bitingly attacked the foreign imperialists. The patriotic actors and the patriotic press were supported by patriotic capitalists like Donald Howe.

At the beginning of September, the British-run Shanghai Power Company cut off electricity to such patriotic capitalists. By the end of September, the general strike was over.

A week later, Shanghai was booming again. Millionaires became wealthier, and the poor toiled harder for their pittance. But neither Nationalists nor Communists abandoned their struggle against foreign imperialism.

"The pot is boiling very hard," Emily repeated, and Julia realized that it was now mid-March 1926. "It could boil over again any time."

"That's what the editor said when he gave me the sack," Richard said. "Anything could happen. Ruining trade was just the beginning. Bomb-throwing was only a start. The old fool actually believes the Nationalists plan to massacre all foreigners."

"Not all, Dick," Emily said. "We'll keep a few to amuse us."

Richard smiled but continued: "Then he sacked me. Said my coverage was too well-informed, which meant I was probably an agent of the Chinese Bolsheviks. And he wouldn't keep a Red on his payroll."

"Dick, what can you do?" Julia asked. "What about your career? You're not going to have to leave, are you?"

"I'll manage," he replied. "With the little I saved and my occasional pieces for *The Times* and the *Globe*. No fun trying to live on a pittance, but I'll get by. For a while, at least!"

26

MARCH 15–APRIL 16, 1926

On March 15, 1926, a brisk sunlit day, Elizaveta Alexandrovna Yavalenka was close to despair. She had discovered that she was the victim of a conspiracy—and the Ikra was threatened.

Sometimes she felt far older than twenty-seven, for she had endured too many hardships too young. The private hotel was her consolation and her pride. It was also her family, for she employed her fellow Russian refugees as cooks, guards, handymen, and, inevitably, courtesans. She believed she loved Joshua Haleevie—in her own way. But she would not perish without him. Without the Ikra, she would be inconsolable—and the Ikra was threatened.

The opulent hotel was extremely expensive to run, and receipts were dwindling. Despite the building boom, her clientele was falling off. Worse, the original Russian sponsors had abruptly cut off their subsidy because discreet access to the Ikra's private rooms was no longer necessary. After Peking recognized the Soviet Union and the Russian consulate in Hongkew was turned over to the Bolsheviks, Chinese Communists and Nationalists met the agents of the Communist International at the consulate in secret—and in perfect safety.

Elizaveta had finally realized that she was a dupe. She had for years been deceiving herself. The Ikra had been subsidized not by White Russians but by the Bolsheviks, who were now demanding immediate repayment. The sum was immense: $100,000 Mex, about $50,000 in U.S. currency. On Joshua's advice, she told the Bolshevik lackey who passed as a diamond merchant that she would not give him a single copper cash. He had threatened violence, his habitual smile still curling his lips.

The $75,000 Mex she still owed the Women's Bank must, however, be repaid on schedule. An aristocrat turned hotel keeper could not indulge herself in aristocratic disdain for debts.

Joshua was her prop in those terrible days. He would do anything for her—and therefore for the Ikra. But she would not take money from him. When her name was clouded by rumors of extraordinary vices, he traced the slanders to the ever-smiling diamond merchant. Mobilizing his own mysterious resources, he dammed the malicious gossip.

Elizaveta's volatile spirits were rising, but she suffered a new blow when Joshua reported his conversation at lunch. Sterling Fessenden, the powerful American secretary general of the Municipal Council, had told him that the International Settlement was being pressed by both England and the United States to ban prostitution. Puritanical church groups in both countries were horrified by missionaries' reports of debauchery and vice in the foreign enclave.

"You might as well ban chopsticks," Elizaveta scoffed. "Either way, Shanghai would collapse."

"Sterling's got to put up a good show," Joshua said. "The pressure's coming directly from the White House and Number Ten Downing Street."

"What can they do, my darling? Pass an ordinance against sin? Issue a decree making virtue obligatory?"

"Actually, Sterling's hit on a rather novel scheme. It'll pacify the killjoys—and do the least possible harm."

"And this miraculous scheme is?"

"A lottery's to decide which houses are to close, which go first. The missionaries claim there are more than six hundred in the Settlement."

"A little low, that figure." She smiled, but shivered. She knew that she had made some good friends—and some bad enemies.

Elizaveta drew some reassurance from the Ikra itself. Her mint-and-cream sitting room was a sanctuary. Cool in summer, it was bright during the winter, when rain and fog were broken only by snow flurries. Nonetheless, she nervously pleated her orange skirt between her thumb and forefinger.

"There's no need to be afraid, Bess." Joshua used that nickname only in private.

"I am afraid," she confessed. "Can you find out exactly how Sterling Fessenden plans to run his lottery?"

"He's leaving the mechanics to the Revenue Department. Old Sampson there has run dozens of lotteries."

Although Elizaveta liked the brisk Englishman, she asked doubtfully, "But will he fix it for me?"

"Probably not. But the Council's in no hurry. It's got to placate the puritans, but the process will be dragged out for years."

Despite his optimistic words, Joshua knew the Ikra was in danger. Closing a foreign-owned bordello would particularly please the missionaries. Joshua did not really want to save the Ikra, which was his only rival for his mistress's affections. If the hotel was closed, she might finally agree to marry him. Yet he could not inflict on Elizaveta the sorrow she would suffer if the Ikra went under.

Besides, he had to break down his parents' opposition to such a blatantly unsuitable marriage. Elizaveta would not agree to defy the Haleevies; she said candidly that she had no desire to have a pauper for a husband. Fearful of losing her, Joshua would take her on any terms —as he now did.

If she would not marry him, he wondered uneasily, how would she react to the eminently suitable marriage his mother was pressing upon him? Would it destroy their relationship? He was thirty-four, and it was past time for him to marry. Yet, even if he did, he would never give up the mercurial Elizaveta, who alone could dispel the spells of melancholia that still oppressed him eight years after the Great War..

The month of March was very kind to Elizaveta. At the month's end the Ikra was taking more than enough to cover its substantial outgoings —and her large personal expenditures. The day the first luxury tour group checked in, she resumed her practice of giving a tenth of her income to the Russian Orthodox Church, which served the White Russian community's material needs as well as its spiritual needs.

When Quick Jack Pavernen proposed that passengers of cruise liners stay at the Ikra, he had advised: "You've got to give the place more flavor! It's stuffy now, too tame for rich round-the-world trippers trying to fight boredom."

Accordingly, Elizaveta had for the first time admitted her professional ladies to the casino and other public rooms. Most knew better than to behave raffishly in public; some were even finicky. Two of her ladies, a Javanese and a Greek, rejected the raddled French countess with the orange hair who had proposed they make a foursome in the Caligula Suite with her lightly mustached traveling companion, who claimed to be a Rumanian baroness.

Although she regretted parting with the respectability that had cloaked the Ikra when it was a discreet brothel, Elizaveta was reasonably happy. Nonetheless, her Slavic temperament lit upon new worries: the absence of any further news, or even gossip, about the lottery to close the brothels; and Joshua's excessively good humor, marred for some months by neither depression nor anger. Fearing unpleasant surprises, she was not surprised when the first unpleasantness duly occurred.

The *North China Daily News* headline read RAFFLE SCHEME ENSURES EQUITY.

The Municipal Council has arrived at a way to ensure perfect justice in the lottery to determine which houses of pleasure are to close to elevate the Settlement's moral tone.

Establishments in the French Concession will not be affected. The French Consul observed, "To be French is moral tone enough."

During the next ten years, all brothels in the Settlement will be shut—at the rate of twenty percent every two years. About twenty-five percent of those in the first drawing will be foreign-owned.

"The Settlement has a responsibility to entrepreneurs," a spokesman of the Municipal Council declared. "We cannot wantonly close brothels any more than we can arbitarily close other businesses. Shanghai lives by trade."

Elizaveta threw down the newspaper and lifted the telephone. Her fingers trembling, she thrust a Murad into her lapis lazuli holder. When she reached him, Joshua could almost see the angry flush mantling her cheekbones.

"Yes, I've read it," he said. "I was on the point of ringing you. Don't fret, Bess. It's still a long way off. Somehow, we'll—"

"How can I fight it?" she demanded. "What more have you heard?"

"Nothing. But I'll make it my business. Don't worry about that twenty-five percent foreign business. There's always a way."

Elizaveta was somewhat happier when she replaced the telephone's malachite-and-brass handset. Was the Ikra, she nonetheless asked, really worth such anguish? Perhaps she should simply get rid of her professional ladies. But could the Ikra support itself as a normal hotel? Besides, life would be intolerably dull!

What, she wondered, would life be like as Joshua's wife? Other Russians had left the profession to become respectable wives and mothers. But none of them had married into families even remotely as powerful—or as pious—as the Haleevies. Nor had any of those women made themselves as conspicuous as she had.

If they married, perhaps the Haleevies would give Joshua a handsome allowance to leave Shanghai. There were worse things than living comfortably in London, Paris, or Rome—even New York, at a pinch. But how could any nation prohibit wines and spirits as the Americans had?

Actually, marriage might not be such a bad idea. The prospect was for a moment rather tempting. How nice to be cosseted, instead of contending with paranoid bartenders, temperamental cooks, and mercurial ladies of pleasure—not to speak of mothering the entire White Russian community.

She did love Joshua, Elizaveta told herself, indulging in the self-denigration he disliked, insofar as she was capable of an unselfish emotion. And Joshua undoubtedly loved her. Still, it was some time since he last pressed her to marry him. Although he said his proposal was always open, he must be induced to press her again—of his own volition, of course. Perhaps he felt discouraged. She could soon fix that, if she really wanted him—or any one man—for life.

Shortly after Julia and Tommy had called on him, General Chiang Kai-shek launched his counterattack against the Communists. It was imperative that he assert himself. China required a strong leader to deal not only with the Communists but also with the Japanese, who were growing more aggressive every day. Saving him the labor of manufacturing a pretext, his enemies provided a plausible reason for his counterattack.

On March 18th, the general received a puzzling telephone call. The gunboat *Chung Shan,* a junior officer reported, had just arrived at the Whampoa Military Academy south of Canton. What were the commander in chief's orders?

"On whose instructions," Chiang Kai-shek demanded, "did the *Chung Shan* leave Canton?"

"The commandant gave the order, they say," the officer replied. "The commandant of the Whampoa Academy."

Chiang Kai-shek stared in speculation at the wall map. He was himself commandant of the Whampoa Academy, and he had given no orders to move the *Chung Shan*! His instinct, which never erred, told him that the unauthorized voyage was connected with the repeated attempts on his life. How better kidnap—or kill—him than by luring him aboard the *Chung Shan*?

On March 20, 1926, Chiang Kai-shek proclaimed martial law in Canton. More than twenty Communist leaders were summarily detained, Commissar Chou En-lai among them. Soldiers boarded the *Chung*

Shan, which had dutifully returned to Canton. An infantry regiment officered largely by Communists was disarmed, and the rifle-carrying militia of the Communists' Hong Kong Strike Committee was ordered disbanded.

The provisional capital of Canton lay in Chiang Kai-shek's palm. Although he had become the most powerful figure among the Nationalists, he did not immediately assume the rank of generalissimo.

He still had to deal with the chief of the civilian government, the man Richard Hollings called Lucifer. Nonetheless, the labor leader Chang Kuo-tao told Tommy Howe of the new political reality: "Chiang Kai-shek is supreme—for the moment. We Communists will go on talking with him. But we'll soon be fighting him."

"It's a matter of principle, you see!"

Joshua Haleevie threw out that cryptic remark as his blue Delage bowled south toward Avenue Edward VII, where the French Concession began. Beside him in the open cockpit, Elizaveta Alexandrovna Yavalenka clutched at her wind-whipped headscarf, only half-hearing Joshua's observation.

"I said it was a matter of principle." He raised his voice over the rush of air. "Whether you're for it or against it."

"Against what?"

His clear eyes, Elizaveta saw, were the same light blue as his linen blazer when he explained: "Today, April 14, 1926, the Shanghai Municipal Council seated three Chinese members—for the very first time."

"Why only now? It is a Chinese city."

"Is it *really* a Chinese city, my love? Europeans built most of Shanghai. You remember, the Council's Chinese Advisory Committee resigned *en bloc* a year ago to protest the May thirtieth massacre. Some people argue that no Chinese—not even rich, tame Chinese—should be allowed on the Council, now or ever."

"And what do you say?"

"I say all Shanghai must ultimately belong to the Chinese—and it will. But not just yet, may it please the Lord. Meanwhile, I'd favor a few gestures toward Chinese self-esteem. And, meanwhile, I'd get away with everything I can—for just as long as I can."

As the Delage turned into Avenue Edward VII, Elizaveta marveled at Joshua's typically British blending of lofty principle with unabashed practicality. She also wondered why he had been silent about the sex lottery, as the Chinese called it, that could decide the Ikra's fate. A month after the article in the *North China Daily News,* Joshua still said he knew nothing more. When she had pressed him for news earlier that afternoon, he had patted her shoulder reassuringly—and had advised infuriatingly: "Not to worry, old girl. It'll all come right. I'll explain later."

The Delage, so dashing when new five years earlier, now appeared quaint. Nonetheless, pedestrians stared at its elegant lines.

The streets of Frenchtown exuded the same faded Gallic elegance as the Delage. As in France, fat curbside pillars displayed advertisements, while Chinese as well as foreigners strolled homeward with long loaves of bread under their arms. Even the smells were subtly different in Frenchtown. Beneath the usual Shanghai bouquet of vinegar, incense, and mildew floated heavy floral scents and the acrid odor of dark Galloise cigarettes. Paris on the Hwangpoo, Elizaveta thought.

The runabout entered the drive of the Cercle Sportif Français, which everyone, including the French, called simply the French Club. In the semicircular white building, monumental beneath its roof garden, fashionable Shanghai relaxed and played under the jaunty *tricolore*.

Shanghai was a city of clubs, but the Cercle Sportif was the only club to which Joshua could take Elizaveta without fear of rebuff or insult. Like the Americans' self-consciously virtuous Columbia Country Club, the self-consciously tolerant Cercle Sportif imposed no racial restrictions. But the French did not ask about a woman's professional or marital status. Elizaveta had declared that she no more regretted her exclusion from the other, stuffy clubs than she did her exclusion from Jade House. But Joshua knew she bitterly regretted his mother's refusal to receive her.

Women in bright summer dresses and men in white linen jackets sat on the verandah. Two vivacious Frenchwomen in tennis dresses that barely came to their knees were chatting and sipping green drinks. Elizaveta suddenly felt out of place in her beige lace cocktail dress with the demure neckline that framed a strand of pearls. Then she saw the wife of the managing director of the Banque de l'Indochine, who wore an evening gown with a plunging neckline and a scalloped hem outlined by gold sequins.

Elizaveta was beset by regrets. How lovely it would be to attend a gala ball again! Once again to be a welcome guest who stirred the other ladies to envy, rather than a professional hostess to men escaping from their own women!

The waiter wore the invariable black trousers and white tunic. Joshua normally ordered in French. Pidgin was condescending, and the colloquial Shanghainese of his boyhood provoked too much praise. But he hailed the waiter as "*Woo Doo-kuh-tow!* . . . Fatty Woo!"

The two men had chatted like the old friends they obviously were, and afterward Joshua remarked to Elizaveta: "Good chap, old Fatty! His father worked for us for years. But he wanted to better himself. He's a captain here, which isn't bad."

"Joshua, isn't it time to tell me?" Elizaveta sipped *citron presse*, which was only fresh lemon juice and Vichy water. "Have you heard something new about the lottery?"

"Sorry it took so long. My mother shut up the chaps who usually keep me posted."

"And why should your mother get involved?"

"You won't like this!" Joshua warned. "She wanted the Ikra to close, so you'd quietly vanish into—"

"Find my own level, you mean?"

"Perhaps that's what she meant. But I got the impression she hoped you'd marry someone else if the Ikra closed."

Joshua had to draw Elizaveta off the scent. Still hoping she would marry him, he could not admit that her guess was right. Her prospective mother-in-law had declared that Elizaveta's place was in the gutter.

"I see. And is she still pressing you to marry a good Jewish virgin?"

"She's got three or four candidates, all nubile maidens with wealthy fathers. But there's safety in numbers. I'll begin to worry when she narrows it down to one."

"And your father? How does he feel?"

"Marrying is women's business, he says, though he doesn't believe it. But he's getting annoyed at her machinations."

"Machinations? How fascinating! Tell me more."

"I suppose I must. She tried to rig the lottery—to make sure the Ikra would be padlocked."

"That wasn't too clever. From her point of view, I mean."

"So my father said." Joshua chuckled. "He told her I'd be more likely to marry you then, in order to look after you. Believe me, I had no idea all this was going on. . . . Look here, Bess. Let's get married tomorrow. You know old Captain Hyde, my step-grandfather, left me something. It's no fortune, but—"

"Later, darling, please. I'd love to talk about it—later. First, I want to hear about her plots. They're a real threat. . . . They could alter my life."

Joshua's heart sank, but he bit back the obvious retort: So could marriage alter your life! Instead, he replied lightly, "Father pointed out to her that closing the Ikra could well drive you into my arms. When I told him I'd asked you to marry me, he only smiled and said, 'Every man goes to the devil in his own way—or to heaven.' "

"Charming, I'm sure! At least, he didn't condemn me outright."

"The opposite, perhaps. Any rate, he's now vetoed all plots. There'll be no pressure to close the Ikra—and no pressure to keep it open either."

"How noble! And when do I learn my fate?"

"I'm available any time, Bess, but you'd be well advised to move fast!" He laughed without mirth. "But I gather it's the lottery that interests you—not me. It'll be some months before the drawing. Of course, everyone's hoping it will all be forgotten."

"That's a great relief, darling. I'm so relieved!"

"Then let's have a word about you and me, shall we? I do—"

"A moment, darling, just a moment or two," she cajoled. "First, I'd like a very cold bottle of champagne. To celebrate!"

For several months after being dismissed from the *North China Daily News* as a traitor to his countrymen and his race, Richard Hollings had lived on his meager savings and his irregular contributions to *The Times* of London and the *Boston Globe*. Except for simple, dramatic events, developments in China were complex, indeed convoluted—and very confusing to outsiders. But the *Globe* was a serious newspaper. It believed in educating its readers as well as entertaining them.

Late one evening in mid-April, Richard appeared at the loft apartment waving a small white envelope scrolled in blue: *Mackay Radio and Telegraph Company*. Gesturing expansively, he demanded: "Just listen to this cable from the *Globe:* 'Hollings: Any interest in staff job covering China and Far East? Salary three thousand five hundred dollars yearly plus reasonable expenses, adjustable upward depending success NANA syndication. Regards, Smithers.' "

Emily was momentarily speechless in delight, but Julia asked, "What is NANA?"

"The North American Newspaper Alliance—which serves hundreds of papers," Emily replied from the summit of her superior knowledge. "Oh, Dick, it's wonderful!"

Hollings exuberantly threw his arms around both of them. Disentangling himself, he waved the telegram again and asked, "Do you know what this means?"

"You're on your way up, Dick!" Emily fully regained her power of speech. "On the way to great success. I said your pieces for the *Globe* were brilliant. I'm so happy for you."

"For us, Em, for *us*! With thirty-five hundred dollars from the *Globe* and, say, four hundred pounds, two thousand dollars, from *The Times* a year, I'm independent. *We're* independent! We can go anywhere we want to in Asia."

"China and Far East, they say," Emily mused. "But I can't get away from the bank just any time I please. Does this mean you'll be away a lot?"

"Of course not," he reassured her. "It only means I have carte blanche to travel when I want to. It's wonderful!"

Chuckling at the exhilaration displayed by the normally cool Englishman, Julia slipped into the kitchen. She wished to leave the lovers alone while she got the bottle of champagne kept in the icebox for emergencies. She waited for some time before returning to hear Emily say glumly: ". . . that case, we'd better leave it for a while. No point in marrying now."

Richard nodded in equally glum agreement. Both appeared distracted when they lifted their glasses in response to Julia's toast: "To the great foreign correspondent! The new Richard Harding Davis."

JULY 9, 1926

Although heavily occupied by his duties, Tommy Howe watched Chiang Kai-shek's skyrocket rise with fascination. By July 1926, Mayling Soong's admirer had been confirmed as commander in chief of the National Revolutionary Army with the rank of generalissimo—and was garlanded with other offices in the National Government and the National People's Party. His personal authority was now supreme in Canton, primarily because he had moved so decisively against the Communists. The Communists nonetheless remained partners in the revolutionary alliance.

Tommy was himself creating a medical corps for the Northern Expeditionary Force of a hundred thousand soldiers, which was to challenge warlord armies a million strong. The surgeon general of the National Revolutionary Army was an elderly pediatrician who was more concerned with politics than with medicine. He had accordingly appointed Tommy acting deputy surgeon general and had given his enthusiastic subordinate "responsibility for organizational details." While struggling with shortages of medicines and instruments, Tommy was trying to relieve the dearth of doctors by appealing to his classmates at the Peking Union Medical College.

Exhausted by fighting the obstructive bureaucracy of the fledgling Nationalist movement, he longed for the loft apartment in Shanghai— above all, for Julia. Since he was now compulsively virtuous, he found diversion in Canton's improvised motion picture theaters. Though he often fell asleep, he also picked up the jargon of the movies. In Chinese, leading players like Charlie Chaplin and Mary Pickford were called *ming-hsing*, bright stars.

Most of the bright stars of the National Revolution had already been eclipsed by the brightest star, Generalissimo Chiang Kai-shek. His chief rival, Wang Ching-wei, the head of the civilian government, whom Richard Hollings called Lucifer, had fled to France, ostensibly to be treated for chronic diabetes. Reinstated as deputy chief political commissar of the Expeditionary Force after brief detention, Chou En-lai had gone north with the first regiments. Deprived of his position in the hierarchy of the National People's Party, that other zealous revolutionary, Mao Tse-tung, had gone to Shanghai to direct peasant affairs for the Central Executive Committee of the Chinese Communist Party.

One star had, however, reappeared. Michael Borodin had returned to Canton to play a supporting role where he had once been the costar. His orders from Moscow were to patch up a compromise peace between the Nationalists and the Communists at any cost. The Comintern accordingly forbade the Chinese Communists to leave the National People's Party, and the Communists reluctantly obeyed.

Tommy's friend Chang Kuo-tao roundly denounced Moscow's obduracy. Although the second man in the Communist Party, he was powerless to fight that decision in Canton. Accordingly, he was leaving for Shanghai the next morning.

Canton was being deserted, but the acting deputy surgeon general awaited the pleasure of his commander in chief. The Generalissimo would not take the field until he had extracted the pledged $500,000 from the chamber of commerce and had been given the four thousand coolies promised by the trade unions. Nor would Comintern agent Michael Borodin leave Canton until the Generalissimo did.

On the evening of July 9, Tommy Howe stood between Chang Kuo-tao and Michael Borodin in a small square in Canton. They were watching the cadets of the last graduating class of the Whampoa Military Academy swear the oath of allegiance and receive their commissions. The towsled palm trees were black against the violet twilight. As the dusk deepened, the candles on the altar cast an otherworldly glow over the khaki ranks drawn up before the shrine at the front of the square.

"Like young crusaders," Borodin commented. "Medieval squires on the eve of being knighted."

Duly translating for Chang Kuo-tao, Tommy was amused, for he knew that his practical friend was uneasy with the Comintern agent's romantic streak. Chang Kuo-tao, who knew as much about medieval

European history as he did about the reproductive cycle of the trout, replied, "Let's hope they have the same success."

Their smooth faces taut with emotion, the new lieutenants bowed to the portrait of Dr. Sun Yat-sen enshrined on an altar before crossed Nationalist flags bearing the jagged white sun. The pale smoke of incense sticks drifted over the stubbled heads revealed when they reverently removed their caps. When they bowed in unison, their stiff new Sam Browne belts creaked.

Hobnails clashed on the pavement as they marched off. The National Revolutionary Army boasted that even privates now wore leather campaign boots. It was the first Chinese army ever to make that modest claim. Its enemies, the warlords' soldiers, still campaigned in cloth shoes or straw sandals.

The ghostly files vanished into the dusk. Tommy and his companions turned toward an alley half-lit by the moonlight that spilled over scalloped gray tile roofs.

"Well, comrades, we'll all be moving north tomorrow." American nasality overlaid Borodin's Middle European vowels. "A pity you're going to Shanghai, Kuo-tao. Dr. Thomas and I will miss your—"

A rifle shot nearby interrupted him. A moment later, two more shots sounded at a distance. After waiting a moment, Borodin shrugged and picked up his remark: "We'll miss your company and your counsel."

Tommy was not so casual. He had not learned to ignore the frequent exchanges of fire between the police and the Communists' armed militia. But, hearing no further shots, he began his translation of Chang Kuo-tao's reply: *"Tung-chih, ming-tien wo-men tou . . .* Comrade, tomorrow we'll all—"

The emphatic rattle of a submachine gun halted him. A heavy machine gun began firing, and bursts of red tracers sprayed across the moonlit sky. Men shouted in the distance, and a woman screamed in terror.

"Bo-lo-ting, che chiu shih . . ." Chang Kuo-tao shook his clenched fists at the sky. "Borodin, is *this* what you want? Police crushing the workers in the name of the National Government—the government the Comintern supports! By heaven, it's past time for us to break with the murdering Nationalists!"

"My friend, you're too impatient," Borodin replied equably. "We Communists can only work with the tools to hand. The revolution hasn't yet reached the stage where a break is—"

"There's no excuse for this!" Chang Kuo-tao was impassioned. "How can you justify Communists' continuing to ally ourselves with the rightists? How can you justify Communists' supporting the Generalissimo, the man who is crushing the workers, the man who has attacked us Communists? That's madness! It's strategy run wild."

"My friend, I share your indignation. But we must ensure a firm rear base for the Northern Expedition."

"Is that all-important, Borodin? How can the Comintern still urge the Chinese Communist Party to become just another part of the National People's Party? Are they *all* mad in Moscow?"

Neither man looked up at the red glare of flames on the tile roofs a few streets away. Though himself distracted, Tommy duly translated the Comintern agent's reply: "Moscow is not mad, just obsessed with its own problems. But what would *you* do, my friend?"

"It's too late!" Chang Kuo-tao exploded. "Far too late. I would have moved earlier. I would have seized Canton. I *urged* it then. We were certainly strong enough."

"Many believed so. Perhaps we actually were strong enough. Yes, I suppose we were."

The Comintern agent fell into meditative silence. Chang Kuo-tao's big face was pallid in the moonlight, and he stared at Borodin, astonished by that admission. The flames balefully reflected from the low-lying clouds painted both men's faces red.

"Then why didn't we act?" Chang Kuo-tao demanded. "Why did you —on behalf of the Comintern—forbid us to seize Canton?"

"Because, my dear comrade-in-arms"—Borodin spoke very slowly— "because we could not have *held* Canton. If there had been one chance in four that we could maintain control of this city for even a year, *I* would have been the *first* to attack the Nationalists. I would have ignored the Comintern's instructions and led the assault myself."

After pausing to let Tommy finish translating, Borodin declared passionately: "Since there was *no* chance whatsoever, I blocked any foolhardy action. Yes, I went along with Chiang Kai-shek. And I would do it again. We Communists can always break with the Nationalists. We can always attack Chiang Kai-shek. If we do so prematurely, before we possess a secure power base, far greater disasters will follow. It would be a catastrophe!"

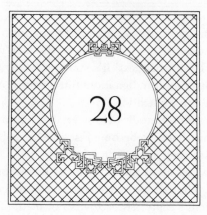

28

JANUARY 27–FEBRUARY 28, 1927

The grubby index finger nudged aside Julia's crimson-varnished nail and stabbed decisively at the point on the big wall map where the three cities huddled in the bend of the Yangtze River. Little Pow, the boy of all work who had attached himself to Julia after JPEnterprises' failure, beamed in triumph. Wuchang, Hankow, and Hanyang, collectively called Wuhan, were at the beginning of 1927 the provincial capital of the Nationalist Republic of China.

"All b'long Chinee now. Never b'long British again!" He abandoned his rough English for Shanghainese: "Never again a British Concession in Wuhan. The National Revolution has reclaimed our territory. We will never surrender Wuhan. We will die, but we will not surrender!"

"Shall we get back to the lesson, Little Pow?" Julia, who shared his sentiments, was amused by his oratorical flourishes. "You won't agree with the editorial, but you must understand it."

Little Pow resumed his seat at the rosewood desk under the north window of the loft apartment. Despite the smoky kerosene heaters that supplemented the potbellied stoves, the cavernous living room was chilly that late January evening. Julia was, however, reasonably warm in a blue silk *cheongsam* quilted with raw silk. Little Pow's padded long-gown had been cut down after being cast off by Tommy Howe, who was almost a foot taller.

"By all means, venerable teacher." The waif grinned and switched back to English: "Almost half my country already Generalissimo Chiang Kai-shek freed from warlords. Only half year since Rev'l'tionary Army marches out of Canton. Pretty soon Generalissimo also take back Settlement and Frenchytown."

"We must get back to the lesson." Julia saw no point in correcting his mangled syntax when he was so exuberant. "You remember the editorial said Generalissimo Chiang was wrong to occupy the British Concession at Hankow."

Little Pow picked his way through the *North China Daily News*, finally exclaiming, "Ai-yah, here it is! I speak first like always?"

Julie nodded, and he self-importantly cleared his throat before reading aloud: "When Chinese whom Comrade Borodin has bought declare war on us, we should have the courage to admit to ourselves that we are facing war."

Enthusiasm glowed on Little Pow's bony face, and his small, scarred hands clutched the newspaper. The hysterical editorial from the newspaper Richard Hollings called "the mouthpiece of the plutocracy" was not a happy choice for their semiweekly lesson. But it was too late to correct that mistake.

"It is already war." Little Pow reverted to Shanghainese. "The teachers at the Workers' Night School say the Settlement police could close us down any minute. But we are vigilant. And we are well organized now."

Although Julie protested feebly that they must get back to the lesson, Little Pow reached inside his enveloping long-gown to produce a white armband bearing two red ideograms: *Min Ping*, People's Militia, and confided, "I carry messages for the leaders."

Julia was thrilled. Generalissimo Chiang Kai-shek's army of Nationalists and Communists, fighting as one, was presently moving eastward from Wuhan toward Shanghai. Before the National Revolutionary Army arrived, the aroused masses, led by the Communists, would have taken much of the city. The former dean of Shanghai Labor University had drawn up a brilliant "Plan for the Shanghai Uprising," and Commissar Chou En-lai commanded the underground army that would seize Chinese-ruled Greater Shanghai, the populous districts surrounding the foreign concessions. Little Pow was a courier for that force.

Julia knew of no plan to seize the enclaves ruled by foreigners, the International Settlement and the French Concession. Of course, she did not know everything, but the Municipal Council knew rather less than she did. While the National Revolutionary Army was rolling from South China to central China, the foreigners had swung from disdain to near-panic. As a quarter of a million fearful Chinese crammed into the concessions, the foreigners had sworn to defend their property to the death. Although some foreigners soon discovered urgent business elsewhere, Julia was eager to see the triumph of the revolution. She would have remained in Shanghai even if she had not loved Tommy—and China.

The taipans had sent cablegrams pleading for reinforcements against the Red hordes of Chiang Kai-shek, since neither the Volunteers nor the Yangtze gunboats could defend the concessions from mass attacks. The foreign powers were sending regular ground forces and naval flotillas. But the buildup could take months, and the Revolutionary Army was already marching on China's old capital of Nanking, 250 miles upriver.

And what was she, Julia Pavernen, still formally unattached at twenty-six, doing while, as the Chinese said, "the earth reeled and the heavens shook"? A new era was emerging from the womb of history, and she was earning a bare living by teaching the future servants of imperialism in the Maritime Customs College. She was also reading news bulletins for XMHA, the most aggressive of Shanghai's new radio stations. She was, in addition, tutoring Little Pow in the unwelcome leisure left by Tommy's long absence.

Tutoring a fifteen-year-old when China was in flames! While not as callous, it seemed almost as futile as Nero's fiddling while Rome burned.

But not quite! Little Pow's talents were well worth developing. He was dedicated to the Communist revolution. Moreover, he embodied the revolution. He was a son of the exploited masses, who were rising in wrath after centuries of oppression.

Little Pow, who had never really known his parents, cherished dreamlike memories of a thatched hut beside a pigpen among silver paddy fields. He also remembered a father with strong hands helping a sweet-faced mother feed her chickens. Julia discounted that idealized vision as the fond fabrication of his Auntie Zee, who had taken refuge with him in the industrial slum called Pootung when he was no more than two years old.

"The revolution against the Manchus uprooted me," he had learned to declaim at the Workers' School. "But the National Revolution will restore my ancestral acres."

Of course, Little Pow had no desire to return to the countryside. He did not even know where his ancestral acres lay, since Auntie Zee had died when he was just five. Bereft of family in a family-centered society, Pow became a creature of Shanghai's alleys.

He had somehow survived the next six years, drifting friendless through the city. Although Pow was reticent about that period, certain allusions had led Tommy to suspect that he had spent several years in a "small-boy house," a homosexual brothel in Frenchtown. Because the Workers' Night School encouraged its students to "spill out the bitterness of oppression" Pow had recently talked more freely about his life before John Pavernen found him begging on a corner.

The bright, undefeated eyes in the haggard child's face had attracted the attention of the man the waif reverently called Mastah Jon. Pow's hands had then attracted John Pavernen's interest. Scalded scabrous pink, they were so raw he could hardly pick up the occasional perforated copper passersby flung him.

The waif had later grown sturdy on the casual bounty of the Pavernens, a diet far richer than half China's four hundred millions ate. But he was stunted by his early deprivation. Perhaps five foot five in high heels, Julia looked down on his five foot one. If he lived to be ninety, he would always be called Little Pow.

His reserve and his dignity were formidable, whenever he could talk about the misery of his early childhood. Drawn out by Tommy, he had earlier revealed why his hands, now seamed with scars, had been so hideously scalded when John Pavernen found him. Pow had instinctively reverted to Shanghai colloquial so thick that Tommy had to explain many expressions to Julia—and had to suppress some searing obscenities.

"For maybe two years or so after Auntie Zee passed from the world, I do not remember anything at all." Tommy believed Pow had erased from his memory the time spent in the small-boy brothel. "After . . . after I ran away, I knew I would die. I did not die because the foreigners' cigarette factory gave me work. Then I almost died *because* of the factory. The work . . . so hard and so dangerous. Sometimes only fourteen hours a day, but mostly sixteen. And so little food, scraps not good for pigs —rotten cabbage with maggots crawling. Sleeping on cold, wet stones."

"Your hands?" Tommy had probed gently. "Did they get burnt and broken in the cigarette factory?"

"No, Dr. Tom, not in the cigarette factory. In the silk mill after I became foreman . . ."

"Foreman?" Julia had exclaimed. "How could you be a foreman when you weren't even ten?"

"Most workers are much younger, Missy Joo-li. Small girls of six or seven. Maybe eight, but no more. Little fingers can better unreel threads from silkworms' cocoons. And girls get no pay. They must work off the buying-in price the bosses pay their fathers. It can take four, maybe five, years. All the time they are fined if the work isn't perfect. But the bosses usually let the girls go after four years. Their fingers get too big and clumsy. Also, their eyes are spoiled by always looking for tiny threads in dark rooms."

"It must have been horrible, Little Pow!"

"Like pictures of Buddhist hell, Miss Joo-li. Only one tiny window high up, so no air at all. No breeze, because even the tiniest breeze can snap the very fine threads. Small girls stand all day and long into night at childsize machines unreeling threads over basins of boiling water that make cocoons soft. They must all the time dip hands into water. So all are scalded, all red and bleeding and puffy with boils full of pus."

"And *your* hands, Pow?" Tommy asked. "Did you have to unreel cocoons in boiling water, too?"

"How could I, Dr. Tom? My fingers were already too big, too clumsy. My hands were my own fault. I did not so quickly learn I must look out for myself—only myself always. You see, bosses always beat small girls for working too slowly. One day a man and a woman came into our room very angry. All are useless little mouths, the woman says. Mouths always eating . . . hands not working. Small girls, she says, are only fit to be whores."

Julie had taken Little Pow's scarred hand when he closed his eyes as if to shut out the memory.

"The woman is worse than the man," he had resumed without prompting. "She says they will make example of smallest girl. So they tear off her little trousers and the man beats her with bamboo cane till blood runs. To show everyone the punishment for laziness. The woman is crazy mad. She holds the smallest girl over the boiling water and starts to throw her in.

"I do not think, but jump at the woman—and the smallest girl runs away. The man swears he will make example of me. But I wriggle too much for them to lift. So they grab my hands and hold in boiling water. Then the woman beats my hands with the bamboo cane till blood runs and bones crack. Afterwards I run away—and Mastah Jon finds me. Otherwise, I will surely die."

Recalling that terrifying account, Julia looked at Little Pow, who was still frowning at the newspaper. He was now self-reliant, though he still slept under the kitchen table, companionably nestled against the Tibetan mastiff called Adam. He more than repaid the small expenditure for his keep by running errands, helping the amahs with heavy work, and gathering information for Emily's articles. Julia believed he would render great service to the Chinese people. The myriad street children of Shanghai could go anywhere almost unnoticed—as couriers and spies.

Little of importance escaped the big black eyes in his triangular face.

The telephone's bell broke into Julia's revery, and she reluctantly rose. Fear for Tommy, who was campaigning somewhere, tightened her throat every time the telephone rang.

The kitchen door crashed open, and Adam bounded into the living room in response to the telephone's summons. He was three feet high, and his plumed tail wagged violently. Fortunately, the ashtrays and ornaments on the coffee table were now beneath its arc, but Julia reached for the lamp.

Adam clamped his great jaws on Little Pow's arm. The laughing youth and the dog sprawled together on the floor. Adam's bellowing almost drowned out the telephone.

Julia shouted into the mouthpiece, "Just a minute!"

With Little Pow, who was still laughing, helping her pull Adam's iron-spiked collar, the mastiff finally allowed himself to be dragged into the kitchen.

"Sorry," Julia told the instrument. "A slight disturbance here."

"That cussed dog again?" John Pavernen asked. "Why don't you get rid of him? He's a confounded nuisance."

"No, Uncle Jack, I certainly won't. Adam is the world's best burglar insurance. Anyway, I'm very fond of him—and Tommy gave him to me."

"You are edgy today."

"Every time the phone rings I just *know* something terrible has happened to Tommy. Now, how are you?"

"Fine, just fine!" His tone was elaborately casual. "As a matter of fact, I'm tickled pink. They've made me an ambassador!"

"That's just wonder—" She broke off in mid-word. "You're teasing. Who's made you an ambassador?""

"Why the Municipal Council. An ambassador for the Settlement."

"Now I know you're teasing. How can the Settlement appoint an ambassador? It's not a country."

"For present purposes it is. A semiautonomous entity which stands in peril. So the Municipal Council needs an ambassador."

"Ambassador to who? To where? Are you going to Peking to the old warlord regime? Or to Wuhan to the new Nationalist regime?"

"You'll see, Julie. Naturally, I can't say any more on the phone. Let's just say I'm the ambassador to a powerful neighbor."

On the last rainy day of the rainy February of 1927, John Pavernen had already made six trips through the barbed wire that ringed the

International Settlement. Behind him lay a community guarded by the greatest concentration of foreign troops and warships ever assembled in China. Before him in Chapei, the Chinese-ruled district just north of Soochow Creek, lay the headquarters of the nearest of those military potentates who were called warlords.

Quick Jack's mission had been conceived in desperation. Although the National Revolutionary Army of Chiang Kai-shek was still hundreds of miles away, the foreign taipans at the Long Bar of the Shanghai Club felt the foreign community was already beleaguered. The siege atmosphere was intensified by the troopships and warships of nine nations steaming up the Yangtze. Some forty thousand foreigners were already protected by more than twenty thousand soldiers, including two thousand men of the Volunteers, all under the command of a British general. Their additional shield was forty-four warships, including an aircraft carrier, all under the command of an American admiral. Yet the more protectors the concessions acquired, the more frightened they became.

The foreign powers' resolution was largely illusory. Despite reinforcements, the British had already yielded to the Nationalists control of their British Concession at Wuhan. With that concession gone, Shanghai's concessions might be the next to go. Despite barbed wire, pillboxes, airplanes, and cruisers, foreigners were terrified by visions of Chinese Bolshevik hordes trampling down their defenses to pillage, rape, and slaughter.

The specter of betrayal haunted the more sophisticated. Chinese pretensions had in the past always been firmly quashed by foreign military power. Ominously, however, the previous year British gunboats had broken off a confrontation with a Yangtze River warlord, content with a standoff. Yet only overwhelming victories could keep the insolent natives convinced that foreign power was unchallengeable, making foreigners and their property therefore inviolable.

Private messages from Europe and America candidly underlined the moral: *The intrusive press, the hypocritical League of Nations, and moralizing do-gooders have made aggressive tactics outmoded in China—if not impossible. Foreign Shanghai will, perhaps, be defended—depending upon circumstances. But there is no possibility of carrying the battle to the enemy.*

That unpleasant reality so dominated John Pavernen's thoughts that he was virtually unaware of the raw weather as his black Studebaker touring car crossed the Garden Bridge from the waterside Bund toward Chapei. Despite the Manchurian fox coat that was Tommy's birthday present, Julia shivered in the gusts that rattled the leather-and-isinglass side-curtains. Coopted as her uncle's interpreter, she had brought her own aide along. Respectably dressed by his Mastah Jon's generosity, Little Pow was perched on the jumpseat. The larger an ambassador's suite, the greater his face.

The burly figure beside John Pavernen was as impressive as a half dozen ordinary attachés. The forty-two-year-old soldier, who had been invalided out of the British Army as a major, called himself Brigadier General Sutton. That rank had been bestowed by his patron, the Old Marshal of Manchuria, who was for the moment also master of Peking and North China. Foreigners, however, called him One-Arm Sutton because he had lost his other arm at Gallipoli.

Sutton's six-foot-two-inch frame awed the short-statured Chinese and his Old Etonian hauteur intimidated even that arrogant nation. He was hawking the trench mortar he had perfected in a Manchurian arsenal. Only eighteen inches long, the miniature weapon flung a finned shell high into the air to fall almost vertically on enemy positions. One-Arm Sutton said he could supply a hundred and fifty patent mortars, each with a thousand mortar bombs—and John Pavernen's lust for a good deal had not been banked by his new semi-ambassadorial dignity.

The Studebaker swept past the North Railway Station, where an armored train waited with steam up. The Stars and Stripes fluttered on one fender of the touring car and the Union Jack on the other, although neither Pavernen nor Sutton was entitled to display his country's flag. The local warlord, General Soo, was not likely to jib at technicalities. Himself technically subordinate to One-Arm Sutton's patron, the Old Marshal, General Soo was ferociously independent in pursuit of his own interests.

Barbed wire was woven through the formidable spikes that topped the brick walls surrounding the warlord's commandeered mansion. Despite its flags, the Studebaker waited almost five minutes at the chained and padlocked wrought-iron gates, which were backed by sheets of corrugated steel.

A pair of guards carrying Lee-Enfield rifles with fixed bayonets sauntered to and fro. Their lax discipline was just strong enough to keep them from retreating from the rain into the candy-striped sentry boxes beside the gates.

From the wooden towers above the brick wall, guards in mustard-yellow tunics pointed their tommy guns at the Studebaker. Their broad peasant faces were self-consciously ferocious, but they were sheltered by unmilitary oiled-paper umbrellas.

"Looks after himself, don't he?" Little Pow stage-whispered in Shanghai argot. "Damned semifeudal rotten egg!"

"Shush, Pow!" Julia cautioned. "Your loose tongue will get us all into trouble."

Julia reassured herself: Of course she was not soiled by the presumably dirty work of espionage. It was her duty as a decent human being to report the foreigners' plans to the Communists, as she had done since the May Thirtieth Incident. She had therefore accepted her uncle's invitation to be his interpreter, although she was a little weary of his devious commercial plots. She would report this day's intelligence not only to the dean, who was the strategist, but directly to Chou En-lai. The handsome political commissar had been detached from the dissension-ridden National Revolutionary Army and assigned by the Communists as the effective commander in chief of the militant Shanghai underground: the trade unions, the craft guilds, the People's Militia, and the left-leaning secret society lodges that would seize Greater Shanghai.

The wrought-iron gates creaked open for a tall Cossack officer with bandoliers crossing his white tunic and a gray caracul shako cocked on his blond head. Flicking his silver-handled riding crop against his thigh, he leisurely examined the touring car with ice-blue eyes. Without speaking, he rapped the fender and pointed his riding crop at the open gates. The Studebaker rolled between the green-black pines that lined the driveway and half hid Cossacks cradling tommy guns.

"The Old Marshal's got his Russian bodyguard, too." One-Arm Sutton's Etonian vowels were languid. "Big face for him: the white man serving the yellow man. These Russkies will do anything for a few dollars."

"They don't have much choice, do they, General?" Julia was irritated by the Englishman's condescension. "And I've heard that they're brave and loyal."

"They've *got* to be brave, my dear. They can't desert and merge into the populace—not in China. Loyal? At least, the warlords think so. Because the Russkies can't talk to the enemy, they're meant to be unreachable—unbribable. Tommyrot! Silver and gold are the same color in any language."

When the sun emerged momentarily, iridescent tiles gleamed on the cupolas and domes at the end of the driveway. The inspiration of the Taj Mahal was further apparent in the long pool that reflected the mansion's arabesque splendor. Julia was equally impressed when she saw the warlord waiting in the foyer, having come to the door to receive his honored visitors.

General Soo was stooped and frail, hardly the burly bandit she had imagined. His slate-dull eyes revealed pinpoint pupils, and she understood his emaciation. The most brilliant chef could not tempt a man who preferred the oblivion of opium. The general's snow-white mustache accentuated his fragility, making him appear cadaverous. Had this elderly gentleman actually beheaded fifty-eight farmers for concealing the nonexistent hoard of gold bars he had believed buried in their fields?

Yet few field marshals had ever been so gloriously uniformed. The metallic gold fringes of the diamanté-starred epaulettes on his narrow shoulders almost met the gold braid twining on his sleeves. His broad ribbons, enameled stars, shining medals, and cascading aiguilettes were so heavy that he leaned on the arm of his Cossack aide.

"My dear General!" John Pavernen gushed. "We are profoundly honored. That you should receive us yourself . . ."

Though almost gagging on that florid greeting, Julia dutifully translated. She was equally revolted by the warlord's oleaginous reply: "Not at all. I am unworthy. I fail to honor Your Excellency sufficiently. Yet how could I be ceremonious with my elder brother?"

Strewing "unworthy"s, "esteemed"s, and "honored"s like Roman victors throwing coins to the crowd, they paraded down a long corridor with a checkered marble floor. The sitting room was so magnificently vulgar that Julia could not take in all its crass splendors. Through half-open double doors she glimpsed a dining room where a round table was set with a gold Chinese-style service for eight. Semiprecious stones inlaid on the pink marble walls depicted a pair of unicorns and a pair of phoenixes. Since the mythical beasts had been drawn by sensible Chinese, there was none of the hypocritical Occident's nonsense about their being asexual. The larger unicorn possessed unmistakable—indeed gigantic—male attributes, while the larger phoenix was gaudily male.

"Can take off and take with! Easy to load on train."

Noting Julia's fascinated gaze, the general was addressing her in pidgin Shanghainese. He apparently wished to impress her not only with his great wealth but with his prudent provision for its preservation.

Did he believe he could pile all his loot into the armored train waiting at the North Station? Impossible! The National Revolutionary Army, now more than 300,000 strong, already held most of South and Central China. Moreover, its pincers were closing on the only gateway to North China, Nanking, where passengers crossed the Yangtze by ferry to board the Peking train.

Weary of small talk, the warlord turned to One-Arm Sutton's patent mortar, thus obliquely denying the readiness for flight he had earlier implied. Since he talked about buying those new weapons, he was evidently not on the point of packing up his hoard and running away.

Chinese etiquette frowned upon discussion of business until the overfed company was soothing its overburdened digestion with nicotine. Yet they were still picking at the smoked duck's tongues that had begun the gluttonous repast when the warlord asked, "General Sutton, how many rounds a minute does your mortar fire?"

Julia talked her way around the military terms she did not know. Technical Chinese used new combinations of old ideograms for new objects. A trench mortar was *po-chi pao*, literally, "intense-attack cannon." Startled by the warlord's technical knowledge, Julia was surprised when he declared, as the shark's-fins-and-oyster soup arrived, "All right, my friends, I'll take a hundred."

"And, shall we say, a thousand bombs for each, my esteemed friend?" One-Arm Sutton purred over his first firm order in seven years of hawking his mortar around China. "Ambassador Pavernen will discuss terms."

"If they're to be any use," General Soo stipulated, "delivery no later than a week from today."

Orderlies presented a platter under a silver dome on which a scaly dragon coiled. That Cantonese delicacy, called Dragon in Spring, offered thumbnail slivers of white cobra meat sprinkled with yellow chrysanthemum petals.

Gulping manfully, Quick Jack Pavernen forced down the snake meat. The orderlies' silver-gilt ladles and gold-chased chopsticks immediately provided generous second helpings. Fearful of offending his host, Quick Jack lifted sauteed cobra to his mouth with his ivory chopsticks—and smiled. His sallow cheeks were greenish, and greasy perspiration speckled his forehead.

Unable to force himself further, he laid his chopsticks down and asked, "Can we talk about the big deal now? Ask him softly, Julie. Don't shout it out to the whole world."

The warlord waved the orderlies out. After the latch clicked, he waited until the commander of his Cossack bodyguard returned and nodded confirmation that there were no eavesdroppers. The benevolent smile on the warlord's bluish lips then invited the unofficial ambassador to speak.

"I am happy to report that we have an agreement: an honorarium to you in appreciation of your defending Shanghai," John Pavernen said. "The mortars will be a gift, a contribution to the common welfare. The crates of personal belongings Your Excellency confides to our trust will be stored in guarded warehouses."

General Soo's wrinkled features beamed goodwill, and he asked, "What of the checks for my honorarium? Remember, certified checks —not gold!"

"Certified checks will be drawn on the Hong Kong and Shanghai Banking Corporation. The total sum is"—John Pavernen paused dramatically—"exactly one million silver dollars."

"Good! Good!" The general raised his porcelain wine-cup. "And your fifty thousand commission will be paid in gold, Excellency."

He tapped his cup with a chopstick to summon the orderlies. Just before the door opened, John Pavernen insisted: "In return, General? Just for the record."

The warlord flicked a long-nailed index finger; the door closed; and he pledged: "I shall defend Greater Shanghai and the foreign concessions to the death against the Red bandits. At any cost, my hundred thousand brave soldiers will defend Shanghai."

John Pavernen knew that General Soo could muster no more than 65,000 men. He also knew that One-Arm Sutton could not possibly produce a hundred mortars in a week's time. Such transparent deceptions merely demonstrated mutual goodwill. In reality, the warlord's treasure stored inside the Settlement would ensure his keeping his word, while the certified check would be his surety from the foreigners. However, both Soo and Sutton would be paid as if for full performance —and John Pavernen would receive commissions on both transactions from both sides.

Two orderlies carried in a red suckling pig on a gold platter, and two others carried silver wine-coolers holding magnums of Veuve Cliquot. Though General Soo thought bubbly wine fit only for women, his Cossack officer had told him that foreigners always drank champagne to celebrate.

While the orderlies were distributing morsels of honey-roasted pork and filling crystal goblets with champagne, General Soo reached into his pocket for a small packet. On his urging, Julia undid the silk cord. She gasped at the double strand of pearls glowing like miniature moons against their scarlet silk wrapping.

Had she been less preoccupied, she still would not have understood the orderly who whispered into the warlord's ear in rough Shantung dialect, "Colonel Chang has decoded the telegram. The ship will be at Woosung for loading ten days from now."

29

MARCH 7, 1927

"You and Dick go with them," Julia told Emily. "I'd feel like a fifth wheel."

"That's nonsense, and you know it," Emily replied. "We all want you to come along. For one thing, you make Joshua laugh."

"Em, I don't feel like a court jester today."

"Just a drive around town and a drink, Julie. It can't hurt you. Liz is definitely coming, and she'll miss you. You've always been closer to her than I have."

"Emily, I said *no!*"

"All right, Julie. Don't bite my head off. But there must be more to it than that to make you so grumpy."

"I suppose there is. More to it, I mean." Julia abruptly lit a Chesterfield. "Em, it's almost six years now since we came to Shanghai together. Maybe it's time for me to go home to Plattsburg. Before it's too late."

"But I thought you were so happy here. And Tommy . . ."

"I was . . . I guess I still am. It's not just Tommy. Who knows what'll become of Tommy and me if I stay? But that's not the reason."

Emily turned from her dressing table, where she was experimenting with a new eyeshadow, and looked gravely at her friend. She faced the mirror again, wiped off the pale blue cosmetic with a muffled exclamation of annoyance, and picked up her tortoiseshell hairbrush before demanding, "You're not serious are you? Tommy would be crushed."

"I'm not so sure of that. Anyway, if it weren't for Tommy, I'd be on the next Dollar liner across to San Francisco."

"Julie, we'd all miss you terribly. Shanghai wouldn't be the same . . ."

Emily restrained her impatience with some difficulty. "What is all this about? You know you'll tell me in the long run. So why not tell me now?"

"Em, you're not going to like this. Not a bit." Julia stubbed out her cigarette. "I guess I'm just fed up . . . fed up with China. Having to be nice to that disgusting General Soo just about finished me. Em, I sometimes wonder what I'm doing here. There's just too much brutality and too much suffering. And I know I can't do anything about it, even though I sometimes kid myself."

"You've just got the blues. Tommy's been away more than a year now. Would that have something to do with it?"

"Of course, Em. But even if he were here all the time . . . My folks are pressing me to come back, if only for a visit. And I'm beginning to think they're right."

"I don't want to be crass, sweetie," Emily said. "But where would you get the cash? They don't give away cabins on the Dollar Line. Somehow, I can't see you taking a deck passage."

"Uncle Jack's got some deal on with the Dollar Line. They owe him a favor. And he says he could take it out in trade, a passage for me."

"You've got that far have you? I'd really hate to see you go, Julie."

"Well, Em, it's not going to happen tomorrow—or even the next day. I can't go till I've seen Tommy again. And God knows when that'll be. And, if after six months or so he still hasn't come . . ."

Elizaveta Alexandrovna Yavalenka glanced unhappily at the touring car waiting beside the Haleevies' new canary-yellow Hupmobile for the traffic light to change. Her carmined mouth curled in distaste, and she plucked at the tassels of the cashmere shawl she had prudently thrown over her light shantung dress. The evening was unseasonably warm, but it was only early March.

An enormously corpulent Chinese occupied the entire rear seat of the open automobile, his soft bulk oozing across the kidskin upholstery. His sparse ash-gray hair sat like a cheap toupee above his bloated face, and rolls of fat encircled his neck like a ruff. His small features were almost infantile, as characterless as a face stamped on a child's balloon.

The faces of the two young women sitting opposite him on the jumpseats were covered with white powder so thick it would crack if their rosebud mouths ever smiled. Almost obscured by eyeshadow and mascara, their eyes glinted occasionally, rather like cats' eyes in a cave. Sing-song girls, Elizaveta noted with professional disdain, unable to take her own eyes off the touring car.

A footman sat beside the driver, and two guards perched on the running boards. All four were Russian. All were dressed in white riding breeches with matching brass-buttoned tunics. And all were armed. The footman, she saw with horror, was a count, a former brigadier general who had once been colonel of her brother's regiment. The flower of the Russian aristocracy were now bodyguards for Chinese plutocrats and Chinese tarts!

"Who's that fat fellow?" she asked. "He looks as if he should be rendered down for lard."

Emily Howe glanced incuriously at the touring car as the light turned green and said, "Never saw him before. But he's certainly greasy with prosperity."

Hoping to relieve her depression, Emily had worn a fire-engine-red blouse and a striped blue skirt that swirled gaily around her knees. She did not quite know why she was glum. She was riding a wave of triumphs at the Women's Bank; her physical relationship with Richard Hollings had been particularly satisfying lately; and they had not quarreled seriously for several weeks.

"He ought to be prosperous, Em," Joshua Haleevie observed from the jumpseat. "That's old Zee Veeon. Cutpurse Zee, they call him. He's king of the pickpockets—among other things."

"You know him—and Emily doesn't?" Richard asked. "How's that?"

"He's a big investor in real estate," Joshua replied. "We had the devil's own time turning him down. But he's into too many rackets."

"Rackets?" Richard asked aggressively. "Can a single rich man in Shanghai honestly say he's *not* a racketeer?"

"Steady, old boy."

"Don't patronize me, Haleevie!" Richard retorted. "You know I'm right."

"Not really," Joshua said negligently. "When you've learned a little more about Shanghai, do come back. We'll discuss it then."

"Gentlemen, please!" Elizaveta was depressed by the degradation of her fellow Russians—and a little, also, by her own position. She therefore snatched at a diversion, having sensed that Emily's mood matched her own.

"I want to know my future," she said. "Does anyone know a really good fortune-teller?"

"The one at the Great World, the amahs say," Emily replied. "Called Gold Mountain."

"We're not far away." Joshua's good temper appeared restored. "What about it?"

The chauffeur steered the big yellow Hupmobile toward Avenue

Edward VII, and Elizaveta threw Joshua a grateful glance. Her spirits were already rising, for she was always amused—and slightly awed—by fortune-tellers.

The Hupmobile skirted the blockhouse that projected into the intersection. The four-square concrete structure, which looked like a sandbagged mausoleum, was intended for a last stand against invaders and street mobs. Optimists derided such fortifications—as well as the barbed-wire perimeters around both the Settlement and Frenchtown. But even optimists acknowledged that the worst peril of the twentieth century now menaced those two foreign enclaves on Chinese soil.

Elizaveta shuddered. Her world had been destroyed by Russian Bolsheviks, and now Chinese Bolsheviks were marching on Shanghai. She could not read the propaganda posters that had mysteriously appeared everywhere, but the stark drawings were like those she had seen in Siberia. A peasant fled a tiger with blood-dripping jaws that, Emily told her, was labeled *Northern Warlords*. A clean-cut Whampoa officer broke the chains that bound an emaciated coolie to a whipping post. Even poor Chinese, Elizaveta knew, would find the reality of Bolshevism utterly different from those idealized pictures.

A rasping like a hundred buzzsaws drowned out the normal din of the streets. A wood-and-canvas biplane swooped low, the Lewis gun behind the rear cockpit swinging menacingly. Six scout-bombers flew daily patrols from the improvised airstrip on the Racecourse to intimidate Generalissimo Chiang Kai-shek's National Revolutionary Army, whose air force was a single aged Fokker.

However the enemy might feel, that show of force frightened Elizaveta. She could not endure another major dislocation.

She glanced at Joshua, who was watching the warplane, and she wondered if he might not be tiring of her obsession with the Ikra. Although he had said nothing, she knew from Julia that his parents were now pressing him very hard to take a suitable wife. Not just Rachel but Sir Judah now sang the praises of a young lady called Charlotte Gubbai, whose family was just as orthodox—and almost as wealthy—as the Haleevies.

Elizaveta's eyes met Emily's, and they exchanged conspiratorial smiles. They were allied against the jagged, dangerous male world of warplanes, sandbags, barbed wire, and guns. Perhaps big boys had to have their toys, but why must they involve grown-up women in their gory games?

Emily, too, was restive. Yet, she reflected, she probably should be grateful as a woman for the crisis, just as she was grateful as a patriot for the revolutionary turmoil that was reuniting China. Otherwise, Richard Hollings would assuredly have been away exploring his new journalistic empire, which stretched from Japan to India.

Glancing proprietorially at Richard, Emily realized she must take the initiative if she wished to marry him. Her depression began to dissipate. Normally undemonstrative in public, she reached across to take his hand. A flush mantled his olive cheeks, which were actually darker than her own, and he squeezed her fingers hard.

Elizaveta momentarily envied the young Chinese woman. If only she could reach across the gulf of social and religious prejudice to Joshua as easily as Emily had just reached across the gulf of racial prejudice. But did she really want to?

Untouched by the women's unspoken tension, Joshua said genially. "And there are our brave defenders."

A hexagonal building of brown brick occupied the entire block at the intersection of Avenue Edward VII and Tibet Road. Beneath its six-tiered white tower, red neon ideograms read: TA SHIH-CHIEH. Before that signboard, which meant "Great World," lounged Annamese soldiers wearing dark blue serge uniforms and steel helmets with metallic crests like scalp locks.

Overtopping the slight Annamese by several feet stood a curious fortification on solid-rubber tires made of riveted armor plate. It looked like a destroyer's turret pierced with rifle slits and capped by a rotating machine gun.

The Hupmobile swung across the boulevard to draw up under the white tower. The chauffeur looked respectfully dubious as he opened the door of the passenger compartment. He advised in emphatic pidgin, "Great World b'long only Chinee men. Foreign peoples more bettah no go visit."

Emily laughed, but Joshua wondered whether he had been wise in yielding to Elizaveta's whim. Foreigners shunned the amusement complex, as Chinese shunned the park opposite the British consulate on the Bund. He did not, however, feel unwelcome or threatened in the vast circular interior, where dumpling hawkers competed with teashops and strolling jugglers vied with traditional operas. But he was repelled by the tumult and the miasma of stale cooking oil, ancient sweat, and rancid pomade. When Richard shrugged in exasperation, Joshua turned his palms up in mute sympathy. Transfixed by hostile stares because of her foreign clothing and her foreign companions, Emily instinctively turned toward the entrance. But Elizaveta clutched her arm.

"Come along, Emily!" she directed. "Help me find the fortune-teller."

Emily scanned the signboards for the one that proclaimed: GOLD MOUN-
TAIN READS FACES. She was jostled repeatedly as she led Elizaveta through
the throng to the booth. Waiting for the faded red curtains to open, she
heard loud stage whispers behind her: "Foreigners' whore! . . . A disgrace to the race! . . . The uprising'll fix her!"

Uncomfortable and apprehensive, Emily followed Elizaveta into
gloom that reeked of cheap incense and cheaper perfume. A hollow
voice spoke from behind the red veil hanging over a small black wood
table: "Please be seated and allow me to gaze upon you, esteemed
ladies."

"For my friend, not me," Emily hastily interposed. "Read her fortune.
Not mine!"

The red veil parted, and a bony hand with long, pale fingernails
placed a tortoiseshell on the table. The shell rocked restlessly, halting
when Elizaveta laid down a second silver dollar. A Chinese working girl
would pay no more than twenty coppers, knowing the predictions to be
spurious, yet believing them implicitly.

"Foreigners cost more." The voice answered Emily's thoughts. "Their
features are craggy and unrefined, and their faces display no proper
pattern. So I must charge more."

The voice trailed off into low keening, which became a low mutter,
and the seer resumed: "I can now tell the foreign lady several things.
She will live a long time, but never where she chooses! She will be
admired by many men, but she will never possess the one she wants.
She will have many children, but none will be her own. Her enemies
will be her friends, and her friends will be her enemies. And she will
be very happy."

Emily duly translated. To Elizaveta's puzzled questions, the voice
only replied, "I am very tired. I can tell you no more!"

"It makes no sense at all," Elizaveta muttered. "Do you think he has
any idea what he's talking about?"

"Yes, Liz, I do. Of course, fortune-tellers can't talk perfect sense—not
and stay in business. But they've got an uncanny instinct. I'm not
saying, of course, that . . ."

Emily parted the curtains to find to her relief that the crowd around
the booth had dispersed. The young women were ignored as they rejoined their men. Richard was smiling sardonically, but Joshua was
flushed and angry. He pointed to a crudely colored poster stuck on the
wall.

"After all we've done for them!" he exclaimed. "After the schools
. . . and the hospitals . . . and all the donations."

Emily read the scarlet ideograms: DEATH TO ALL ALIEN BLOODSUCKERS AND TO CHINESE RUNNING DOGS. The drawing showed a coolie cutting the heads off three writhing serpents with a hoe. Looking close, Emily saw that each head was a photograph of a man's face. She recognized the chairman of the Hong Kong and Shanghai Banking Corporation, who was the standard-bearer of foreign exploitation, and the Old Marshal of Manchuria, Chang Tso-lin, who was the paramount warlord. Although the third photograph was smudged, she finally made out the features of Sir Judah Haleevie. Still, that insult could not wholly account for Joshua's almost incoherent rage.

"Young chap came over," Richard explained. "He looked like a student. Joshua asked him what the poster said, and he translated. In addition to warlord and imperialist plots against China, the poster charges another virulent conspiracy: Jewish capitalists throughout the world have united to plunder China—and their leader is Sir Judah Haleevie. It's grotesque . . . so grotesque it's funny. But Joshua is not amused."

Reading the smaller ideograms, Emily could feel how deeply Joshua was wounded. The Haleevies considered themselves as much a Shanghai clan as the Howes. Turning to reassure Joshua, she saw that Elizaveta, her own perturbation forgotten, was embracing him.

A shriek sawed through the tumult, piercing every ear. The four visitors turned together like clockwork figures. The shriek was repeated, drawing every eye in the Great World.

A group of female coolies in rusty black tunics was trotting toward them. Several were flourishing heavy cleavers, and all were shouting.

"Drive out the foreign whores!" they screamed. "Kill the harlots!"

Joshua stepped in front of Emily and Elizaveta, but Richard exclaimed, "Don't be a damned fool! No time for chivalry . . . defending the ladies. We've got to get out."

Bare feet slapping the flagstones easily overtook high heels, and the furies swirled around their prey. They ignored the men to attack the women.

Grimy hands clutched Emily's clothing. She smelled rotting teeth when an assailant screamed into her face, "Whore for the hairy devils! I'll kill you!"

Elizaveta turned to face the cleavers and the imprecations she could not understand. Her dress tore and her left heel gave way. Feeling herself falling, she instinctively clutched at Emily.

When both fell to the gritty flagstones, Joshua stood over them. Surprised by their triumph, the coolie women circled menacingly. A cleaver flashed in a circle, slicing the air and mocking their vulnerability. Three cleavers then rose, their blades glittering in the gloom. Their downward strokes seemed to fall forever.

A file of Annamese appeared, cutting off the assailants from Emily and Elizaveta. When the soldiers lifted their rifles, the coolie women fled.

The French sublieutenant in command sputtered: "Mesdames . . . you should know the Great World is for *Chinese.*"

Emily and Elizaveta clutched their torn clothing, and Joshua ruefully examined the long rip in his blue blazer. Between relief and indignation, Emily saw that Richard was unscathed. He had prudently—and intelligently—raced ahead to summon their rescuers.

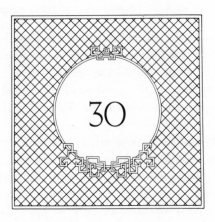

30

MARCH 21, 1927

Always yearning for more sleep, like all fifteen-year-olds, Little Pow awoke slowly and unwillingly. He hated the chill dawn of Monday, March 21, 1927. Mondays were always worst because long association with foreigners had accustomed him to the Sunday holiday, unknown to most Chinese. The boy of all work knuckled his eyes and reached out to pull the long ears of his bedmate, the Tibetan mastiff called Johann Adam Schall von Bell.

He was not alarmed when he touched the cold floor. Always an earlier riser, Adam sometimes strayed. Forcing his eyelids open, Little Pow turned over and almost fell off the bench on which he lay. He then remembered that he was far from the loft apartment on Kiukiang Road, having spent the night in the offices of the Shanghai General Labor Union in Chinese-ruled Chapei north of Soochow Creek. Before leaving the apartment the previous evening, he had urgently advised Miss Joo-li and Miss Yuelin to stay at home until he returned—and to keep Adam locked in the apartment.

Little Pow slipped his bare feet into the old golf brogues Julia had given him when she learned that they wore the same size. He felt his way down the steep staircase to the communal sinks off the rear court-yard. Still half-asleep, he barely heard the clatter of wooded soles or the swishing of cloth soles all around him. Dutifully plying a worn tooth-brush and then energetically scraping his tongue with the handle, he was almost deaf to the guttural gargling and the phlegmy hawking of his neighbors at the long stone trough.

When his eyes at last opened fully, he whistled "The Internationale" through his teeth. Breakfast would be nothing like the delicacies the amah Lao Zee gave him, but only a bowl of rice gruel sprinkled with salted cabbage and, with luck, a sliver of gristly pork. He was, nonetheless, in high spirits. His big eyes sparkled in his triangular face when he slipped his new armband out of his pocket.

Admiring it, he did not hear the grumbling of the hungry men whose path to the kitchen he was blocking. He stood still, tracing the big red ideograms that read: *Chuan Shih:* . . . Special Messenger. When a hard thumb dug into his ribs, Little Pow picked up a rice bowl.

His work would be vital today. Even before the general strike and the mass uprising began at noon, he would carry the orders of Commissar Chou En-lai to the Workers' Militia. Still, there would be glory enough for all, not only for the armed militia, but for the half million workers who were to march through the streets. Glory enough, too, for the guerrillas from the countryside and for the black-shirted musclemen of the secret societies.

Little Pow put his bowl down. Although he had not finished the rice gruel, he was no longer hungry. His mouth was dry, and even thinking of food made his stomach turn over.

Yet today's offensive would undoubtedly be a total triumph. He smiled confidently while cold crab-claws nipped his throat. The tragedy of the Communists' abortive Shanghai uprising in mid-February would certainly not be repeated. He could still see the warlord soldiers from the north slipping their broadswords from the slings on their backs and scything a path through the workers. Blood-spattered and quaking, Pow had escaped only because he was so small and so agile.

Today, however, the Generalissimo's National Revolutionary Army was almost at the gates, its Communist and Nationalist units still campaigning together, despite their differences. Besides, the Workers' Militia had been trained to a high pitch by Whampoa Academy officers in plain clothes. Moreover, the warlords' defenses were crumbling throughout South China after many defeats, and crack warlord units were defecting. Although the warlord General Soo apparently stood firm in Shanghai, his position had been eroded. Neither police nor soldiers had seriously impeded the Communist buildup in Greater Shanghai—perhaps because their information was faulty, perhaps because they were afraid.

Taut discipline, modern arms, and strenuous training had made the National Revolutionary Army far superior to its warlord foes. Yet armed force only appeared decisive. The vital factor was not guns, as Commissar Chou En-lai had repeatedly explained, but spirit.

Though guns were essential at this stage of the revolution, power did not ultimately grow from the barrel of the gun. Decisive political power, which controlled the guns, sprang from mastery over the hearts of men and women. Commissar Chou had summed up: "Propaganda is our chief weapon. We are fighting a psychological war."

Parades and mass meetings, posters and leaflets, traveling singers and theatrical troupes—all fought to win the hearts of the people. Newspapers and magazines, radio broadcasts and towncriers, planted rumors and glowing promises—all undermined the enemy's resolution. Behind the barrages of its psychological warfare, the National Revolutionary Army was relentlessly overcoming the retreating warlord forces, which were still three times its size.

All fear vanquished, Little Pow forced down his rice gruel and returned his bowl to the female comrades in the kitchen. He knew that the commander was briefing his subcommanders in the big office on the second floor.

"Victory is certain!" Chou En-lai was reiterating when Little Pow slipped into the crammed room. "Then why do I go over the plan for the twentieth time? Victory is certain *because* we plan meticulously, *because* we drill hard, and *because* we adhere strictly to our plans. . . . Now the details again: At Chapei West Police Station, two detachments will advance separately wearing ordinary working clothes. Their weapons will be concealed in carrying-poles, valises, and parcels. At precisely eleven thirty-five, the converging columns will . . ."

Little Pow yawned prodigiously, revealing his dingy molars to the female propaganda cadre who was writing down every word the commissar uttered.

"No manners, these street urchins!" She shot him a scandalized look through thick-lensed spectacles; Little Pow grinned derisively and replied in broad Shanghainese, "We are all comrades, Missy, all equal, ain't we? Even spoiled and frustrated daughters of the blood-sucking bourgeoisie are now equal to street urchins!"

The female cadre blushed crimson and looked down at her note pad while Chou En-lai declared, "More than three million people live in Shanghai. Half in Greater Shanghai under the warlord rule, half in the imperialists' enclaves. Forty thousand foreigners . . . and the rest all our brothers by blood.

"We muster half a million workers—some five thousand in the armed workers' militia. Not so many to take over a city of three million, eh? Against us the warlord troops and their police number, say, ninety thousand. The imperialists have about twenty thousand ground troops and twenty thousand more aboard their warships. Formidable odds, eh?"

Little Pow had heard lesser orators inflame men's courage by promising assured victory because they moved with the tide of history. Whatever that was! He had never heard an orator inspire troops to battle by reciting the odds against them.

"Nonetheless, our victory is inevitable because our correct strategy is invincible!" Chou En-lai declared, and Little Pow breathed deep again. "We shall break one stick at a time: first, Greater Shanghai, then the foreign-occupied territories. The imperialists will disgorge their concessions when the pressure hurts them—just as the British did at Wuhan. All but a handful of almost three million Chinese are on our side. And the National Revolutionary Army is hardly a day's march away. The odds are actually with us—overwhelmingly. Our victory is inevitable!"

After that spirited re-dedication at dawn, the exhilaration slowly leaked out of the day. Little Pow was disappointed at not accompanying Chou En-lai on his repeated sallies into the city that was to be the battlefield. Instead, he was instructed to stand by to carry messages to the fighting units. But there were no messages to carry, since shrill telephones executed his mission. Quite extraordinarily, the temperamental Shanghai telephone system was operating faultlessly.

Little Pow had offered his life to the revolution—and all the revolution asked was that he answer the telephone! Occasional rifle shots and bursts of machine-gun fire made him feel even more useless. He was reproached by the roar of mass political rallies and the choruses chanting the songs of the revolution.

When Miss Joo-li asked how he had served the glorious Shanghai Uprising, he would have to confess that he had only talked on the telephone—as any fearful girl could. Simmering with indignation, Little Pow, nonetheless, logged all the messages precisely:

Monday, 21 March 1927
    11:41: Friendly units converge on West Chapei Police Station.
    11:59: Our forces drawing heavy fire, request reinforcements.
    12:18: Additional units attack.
    12:36: Police evacuate West Chapei Station. Most escape owing to our lack of sufficient men to surround them.
    12:59: Fifty rifles and six submachine guns found in West Chapei Station.
    1:16: Policemen seen throwing discarded uniforms into Soochow Creek and donning workers' clothing.

1:31: Enemy resistance weakening. Our units taking control of all police stations.

1:58: Little resistance by warlord troops. General Soo has vanished from his headquarters. Most warlord troops flee, though some join the revolutionary forces.

2:15: Resistance stiffening around armored train at North Station.

2:36: Units at North Station request reinforcement. They report: No Chinese warlord troops involved. Enemy are Russian soldiers commanded by tall, yellow-haired man with short whip. He ignores bullets and never unholsters his pistol.

3:06: Our forces at station urgently require assistance in repelling counterattack of . . .

(Line went dead)

That was Little Pow's last log entry on the day of the great Shanghai Uprising. All telephone communication had broken down, perhaps because shells had hit the exchange. A few minutes later, Commissar Chou En-lai dashed up the stairs to demand reports. Concluding that the general situation was favorable, he concentrated upon the battle at the North Railway Station.

"I need a runner to the units at the station," he declared. "They are to draw back until reinforced. I would rather General Soo escaped with all his loot than lose a single life unnecessarily . . ."

"Commissar, we've just had information regarding General Soo's whereabouts," a staff officer interrupted. "The Wharf Workers' Union reports he boarded a ship at Woosung at dawn. They had no orders to intercept and—"

"Then the White Russians are fighting on their own?" Chou En-lai pondered before directing: "We must give them a way out. Not sacrifice our own men to kill them. They are White bandits, but they're politically insignificant. Now, Little Pow, you're the one I want."

Quivering with pride, the special messenger straightened his red armband. He pulled down his oversize blue cotton tunic and stood at stiff attention, just as the foreign soldiers did before their officers. But Chou En-lai draped an arm around his shoulders and led him to the big wall map. The commissar's tapered index finger traced patterns on the streets of Shanghai.

"Now, Pow, take this route," he directed. "You want the commander at the North Station. He is to pull out any men he has in blocking positions. When the White Russians retreat toward the Foreign Settlement, he is not to interfere. They're not worth a single drop of Chinese blood. Besides, if we treat them leniently, the other foreigners won't fight quite so hard when their turn comes. Now move!"

The fortified boundary between Chinese-ruled Chapei and the International Settlement ran just north of the municipal school and the public market on Elgin Road. A maze of narrow alleys intersected by occasional wider streets, hectic Chapei was home for hundreds of thousands of poor Chinese. They lodged in jerrybuilt tenements and worked in clangorous factories.

As he trotted toward the North Station, Little Pow was astonished by the silence. All the workaday noises were hushed, for all workaday activity had ceased. Spindles no longer sighed in cotton mills, and looms no longer clattered. The tinsmiths' pounding had stopped, and the axles of man-drawn carts no longer squealed. The purveyors to the dead had put up their shutters, imprisoning the sandalwood fragrance of their coffins. Food stores were closed, even teahouses and restaurants. The general strike had hushed clamorous Chapei.

Yet a bass throbbing like a thousand muted kettledrums underlay the silence. At mass meetings the voices of a resurgent people shouted the slogans of revolution. Red banners hung from every building, and demonstrators marched under triumphal arches of bamboo poles decked with rosettes and slogans. The five-barred flag of the warlord government in Peking had everywhere been supplanted by the flag of the National Revolution: a white sun shooting out short triangular rays against a blue field.

Little Pow's splayed feet in their incongruously feminine brogues leaped across potholes and flew over ruts. He pounded through the exultant crowds, gesturing imperiously with his scarred hands and shouting "Special messenger!"

Greater Shanghai was *en fête*. Dandling infants with pink ribbons in their jet-black hair, gulping yellow rice-wine from earthenware jugs, and chanting brave slogans, the citizens of the largest proletarian city in Asia had transformed a *coup d'état* against the enfeebled warlords into a holiday. Jubilant spectators hailed street-corner orators, drowning out their words. The young propagandists of Rosamonde Sun's women's movement were no longer taunted for their boldness, but cheered. Some older women, however, pointed disdainfully at their bobbed hair. Mass rallies boomed exhortations through tinny loudspeakers. Youth groups, trade unions, and Workers' Militia marched to blaring funeral bands before the barricades protecting the International Settlement.

On the edge of Chapei, the pocket handkerchief of open space in front of the North Station was today bereft of its usual pleasure-seekers, coolies, and petty criminals. Little Pow crouched behind the brick parapet above the tracks. Peeping cautiously over the top, he saw thirty or so men in workers' blue clothing lying quite still. The dead were strewn haphazardly across the rails around General Soo's armored train, their red armbands glowing like drops of blood.

The train's funereal-black armor plates were scarred by the bullets' silver tracks, as was the big steam locomotive whose bulbous nose pointed toward Nanking. Four Cossacks lay still at the foot of the ladder leading to the locomotive's cab, but the rifles protruding from the loopholes in the armored carriages spat smoke.

Just out of range, armed militiamen in railway uniforms and visored caps stood in a semicircle. All were grinning proudly, but a grim conductor squatted behind a heavy Browning machine gun on a metal tripod. As Little Pow watched, a young fireman slumped onto the gravel roadbed. His mouth gaping, the wounded man stared in amazement at the blood welling from his thigh.

The machine gun's muzzle moved lazily, and puffs of gray smoke drifted prettily in the sunlight. Little Pow heard the bullets ricochet off the armored train. But some struck home. A rifle slipped through a firing slit in the train's armor and crashed onto the gravel roadbed.

When the train's machine-gun turrets rotated, the idlers around the Browning scurried for shelter. Two Communist militiamen fell to the Russian fire and were soaked by the jets of water from the Browning's punctured cooling-jacket.

Little Pow scuttled away behind the shelter of the parapet. At the entrance to the terminal, he had to spend several minutes convincing the guards that he carried an urgent message for their commander. Still crouching, Little Pow finally reached the improvised command post behind the ticket windows.

The young commander, who wore the uniform of the National Revolutionary Army, was a southerner with the look of an alert squirrel, evidently a Whampoa Academy graduate. When Pow's Shanghainese was translated for him, he immediately declared: "Commissar Chou En-lai gives the order! Pull back all our units and let the Russkies go!"

Little Pow waited two hours for the suspicious Cossacks to leave their armored train. Dusk obscured the widely dispersed figures marching toward the perimeter fence of the International Settlement half a mile away. Sporadic rifle fire harried them, felling two Russians, despite the commander's orders. The gates in the barbed wire surrounding the

Settlement opened when the Sikh sentries saw that white men were seeking asylum.

Swept along by a rush of curious militiamen, Little Pow tumbled into the armored train. To his astonishment, it was empty. The crates of loot he expected to find had either been removed or had never been loaded onto the train. His short legs fully extended, Pow climbed the metal ladder to the cab of the locomotive. He sat on the engineer's perforated-iron seat and tugged tentatively at the control levers.

"Whee-whee! Chuff-chuff!" Little Pow imitated the howl of the whistle and the puffing of the engine. "Chuff-chuff! Wheee . . ."

No longer a soldier of the revolution but a happy child, he swung around to shout orders at an imaginary fireman: "Faster, you addled egg! More coal, son of a turtle-bitch! Before night falls, we must reach Nanking or . . ."

The clear light that flares in the instant between dusk and darkness flooded the cab and lit the figure seated against the heaped coal at its back. A gray caracul shako perched rakishly on the blond head, and bandoliers crossed the white tunic. The Cossack officer's left hand rested casually on the silver head of the riding crop tucked into his boot top. The steel-blue revolver in his right hand, which was propped on his thigh, pointed directly at Little Pow. The enormous muzzle wavered no more than did the fixed, ice-blue eyes.

For thirty seconds, the youth sat frozen in terror. The revolver did not move, and the blue eyes did not blink. Nor did the commander of General Soo's bodyguard speak. Not even the trail of blood moved, the red trail that reached from the dead man's temple to his jaw.

Little Pow hurled himself out of the cab in mortal haste, skinning his hands on the gravel roadbed. The corpse was even more terrifying than the apparition he had thought alive. The malevolent ghost of a foreign devil could haunt him all his days. Through streets vibrant with rejoicing workers he trotted back to the offices of the Shanghai General Labor Union.

John Pavernen and One-Arm Sutton later worked out exactly what had happened before the warlord General Soo left at dawn on the day of the general uprising. They concluded that he had never had any intention of defending the city. He had stayed just long enough to preserve a scrap of face—and to collect the money that credulous foreigners had been eager to pay him to defend Shanghai. He had then loaded his concubines and his choicest treasures on a coastal steamer to Hong Kong, with a fifty-man bodyguard to protect them.

Fortunately, General Soo did not receive the entire bribe promised him to do his duty. The taipans had cannily decided to pay the warlord in installments. A certified check had been drawn on the Hong Kong and Shanghai Banking Corporation for $300,000. That was a third of a million, less a preliminary payment of $18,000 to One-Arm Sutton for the mortars and $15,000 to John Pavernen as broker. The mortars had, of course, not been delivered. In fact, they did not exist.

John Pavernen was righteously indignant at having been cheated of his second commission, which was due from General Soo. But eighty-five large wooden crates were held for the warlord in the godown of the Hong Kong and Shanghai Bank. Those valuables would be delivered only to their rightful owner, for the bank's commercial morality was impeccable. Yet even General Soo might well claim them in vain, for he had failed to live up to his promise—and the bank's commercial realism was renowned.

Somewhere in that impasse, John Pavernen concluded, lay a sterling opportunity for an honest broker like himself. He was entitled to his commission. Moreover the taipans who had sent him on his vain mission would wish to recompense him for not revealing how the warlord had outsmarted them—they would pay him gladly if they could pay him out of the warlord's treasure.

Before opening negotiations with the taipans, he arranged with discreet bribes to have the crates opened. Assessing their contents, he exploded with rage—and then with laughter. Most were packed with paving stones well protected by thick wrappings. Some, however, contained used artillery cartridges. Since the market for brass was moribund, they, too, were worthless.

31

MARCH 24–28, 1927

Colonel Thomas Tan-ssu Howe, surgeon general of the Sixth Corps of the National Revolutionary Army, was ill at ease while he waited for Commander Hugh England, captain of HMS *Emerald*. Commander England's frigid nod had been as disconcerting as his ship's presence in the Yangtze River off Nanking. *Emerald* was 9,000 tons and 570 feet of brand-new heavy cruiser. She could hurl explosives from six-inch surface guns, four-inch antiaircraft guns, and sixteen torpedo tubes. If any other warship anywhere was as powerful for her size, the omniscient Royal Navy was not aware of her existence.

Tommy Howe had been regaled with those details by *Emerald*'s gunnery lieutenant, who recalled being two forms behind him at public school. That enthusiasm had breached the wall of taciturn courtesy behind which the captain wished to isolate his unwelcome visitor. To the gunnery lieutenant, however, it was inconceivable that an Old Radleyan could be anything but a gentleman, whatever flag he sailed under. Manifestly, a gentleman visiting the *Emerald*'s wardroom must not find her hospitality grudging.

The unexpected welcome had somewhat alleviated Tommy's discomfiture over his grim mission. In the company of the young naval officers he had briefly reverted to the casual good fellowship of his school days. He had also concluded wryly that he had more in common with English gentlemen like these, with whom he had grown up, than he did with the half-savage soldiers of the revolution who had killed, raped, and pillaged in Nanking. The Chinese officers were hardly better than the common soldiers. Most officers were incapable of disciplining their men, and some had joined in the looting.

Tommy now had to make amends. He was required to apologize for the unforgivable and to offer implausible assurances that the outrages against foreigners would not be repeated.

Tommy shivered in the wind that wailed across the ship's bridge. He tightened the belt of his camel's hair greatcoat and wondered when the godlike Commander Hugh England would deign to take further notice of his presence. He was anxious to discharge his business and rejoin his fellow Chinese officers, who distrusted his cosmopolitan knowledge as much as he deplored their provincial ignorance.

Upstream, closer to Nanking, the setting sun silhouetted two identical destroyers with gigantic American flags painted on their hulls. The destroyers' guns, like the guns of HMS *Emerald,* were now silent. Even the Nationalist gunboats that had earlier shelled the railway terminus at Putow on the Yangtze's warlord-held northern bank were gone.

Dusk on the great river was still except for the lowing of water buffaloes and the barking of dogs. Nanking, too, was still, though smoke drifted over the walls. The black plumes were thickest above the hillock outside the city walls that was crowned by the compound of the Standard Oil Company of New York where the big petroleum tanks were burning.

By God, Tommy reflected, the newspapers'll make a bloody great meal of this day's work. It won't help the cause one little bit. Shanghai's foreigners will be frightened out of their wits. Good thing Julie doesn't know I'm here.

He could envision headlines throughout the world: THOUSANDS EVACU-ATED FROM NANKING AS BOLSHEVIKS RAMPAGE / U.S. AND BRITISH WARSHIPS SHELL CITY TO SAVE FOREIGNERS / SCORES KILLED AND RAPED / CITY BURNS AS WARLORD TROOPS FLEE / "NATIONALIST" REDS TRIUMPHANT.

It was just about over now, but foreigners had been harassed for several days in Nanking—and a few had been killed. Tommy, who had seen the incident develop, was himself not sure who was primarily responsible. But he had no doubt as to who would be blamed.

Generalissimo Chiang Kai-shek's National Revolutionary Army was already excoriated abroad as "no more than Chinese Bolsheviks" because the Nationalists were allied with the Chinese Communist Party and the Communist International. The outrage had certainly been initiated by the warlord troops, who were now retreating northward. But the Nationalist forces would be blamed, above all their commander in chief, Chiang Kai-shek, whom the foreigners called a Red bandit, although he was striving to eradicate Communist influence in the Nationalist army and government.

Tommy had watched appalled as the retreating warlord troops killed Chinese civilians before escaping across the Yangtze. Peering through his binoculars from the southern district, which the Nationalists had already taken, he saw the soldiers in mustard-yellow uniforms loot buildings and set them on fire. A few hundred Russians were conspicuous in their distinctive blouses. Tommy had seen those hard-bitten mercenaries weep when they were forced to abandon their two armored trains. He had not seen the Russians killing civilians, as had Chinese troops on both sides.

Nanking was a scandal, an atrocity, but it was also a great victory. The National Revolutionary Army had fought few pitched battles, since its reputation and its propagandists terrified the enemy troops. Temporarily unified by fear, however, the warlords had made a stand behind the massive fourteenth-century walls of their last stronghold south of the unbridged Yangtze, which bisected China. They had been fighting with their backs to the river to prevent the Nationalists from sweeping unopposed to Peking, bearing Generalissimo Chiang Kai-shek to power over all China.

Nationalist resolution and Nationalist political warfare were, however, again irresistible. After weeks of skirmishing, the warlords had been driven out of Nanking on March 23, 1927. The Generalissimo had then boarded a gunboat for Shanghai, and his Sixth Corps had occupied the city that was once the capital of the Ming Dynasty.

That night, marauding warlord troops were the chief fear of the seven hundred foreigners in Nanking, four hundred of whom were Americans. In the morning, Nationalist soldiers seeking loot invaded the British consulate and reportedly killed the consul himself. Coming after other outrages against Americans, that attack frightened all foreigners out of Nanking. Some seventy men, women, and children had belatedly fled from the American consulate inside the city to the hilltop redoubt of the Standard Oil Company of New York outside the city walls. Their flight through the smoke of burning buildings was hastened by machine-gun fire, although they were protected by the Stars and Stripes carried high on a bamboo pole. They had also been assured by Nationalist officers like Colonel Thomas Howe that foreigners would not be molested.

Tommy watched their slow progress through his binoculars—and saw them come under sniper fire. He was angry and ashamed when he picked out the Nationalist soldiers gleefully shooting at the hated imperialists. An American sailor in blue dungarees stumbled and clutched his side. After the landing party from the destroyers fired three volleys, the Nationalists retired to look elsewhere for loot and revenge.

Despite his passionate commitment to the revolution, Tommy at that moment felt far greater kinship with the bedraggled foreigners than he did with his brutal countrymen. He also felt personally humiliated when he saw soldiers in Nationalist khaki pounding on the door of the big white house on Socony Hill. They were obviously demanding protection money from the beleaguered foreigners, who he had pledged would not be molested.

Returning to Sixth Corps headquarters, Tommy protested strongly to his general, only confirming his reputation as a foreign-devil-lover. He got the response he had expected: indifference.

Yet the afternoon was extraordinarily quiet. For the first time in weeks the field artillery was still. Only sporadic small-arms fire and occasional shouts broke the silence of the conquered city.

At half past three, the afternoon erupted. For a quarter of an hour an artillery barrage rocked Nanking. From the roof, Tommy saw the British and American warships shelling the approaches to the Standard Oil compound on the hill. He was not surprised when his general summoned him.

"Get yourself aboard that big ship, the English one," the general commanded. "And stop them! They'll tell you they fired only to cover their people's withdrawal to the ships—and no more than a hundred rounds. But the foreign devils have tasted blood. Promise anything, but get them to stop."

Tommy had then set out for the HMS *Emerald* to make more empty promises. After commandeering a sampan, he had boarded the cruiser only after a prolonged confrontation with the officer of the deck. Somewhat soothed by his fellow Radleyan's welcome, he now waited on the wing of the bridge for the captain to deign to talk with him.

Bulky in a bridge coat with gold-striped epaulettes, Commander Hugh England offered a perfunctory salute before speaking: "Colonel Howe is it? If I talk slowly . . . very slowly . . . can you . . . understand?"

The commander bared his stained teeth in a patronizing smile when Tommy nodded and continued: "All right, then. I shall spell it out to you. We will not fire again unless we are fired upon. We will soon have brought all our people safely aboard. But there will be merry hell to pay. Your troops have killed more than fifteen foreigners. You Chinese will regret this day's work. Are you the Johnny who made all those promises to the Yanks?"

"I'm afraid so, Captain. The troops got out of hand." Tommy remembered the officers he had seen looting. "However, I can assure you there will be no repetition. I should also like to offer my personal apology for that misbehavior."

Startled by Tommy's public school accent, Commander England studied him in the glow of the bridge lights before replying, "Your personal apology. Not an official apology, eh?"

"I regret that I cannot unless instructed . . ."

"Well that's that, then." The commander was finished with him. "Just as long as you understand. Any more nonsense and we'll really let go —make the last barrage look like a few firecrackers. You'll be going ashore now."

Tommy was further humiliated by that abrupt dismissal after the Englishman's contemptuous rejection of his apology. Infuriated, he squatted on the scale-speckled deck of the sampan amid the reek of fish. To be scorned like a night-soil coolie by an arrogant foreigner in his own country! He had never been treated so badly in his entire life. For a moment, he felt joy at the foreigners' humiliation—and sympathy with the soldiers who had looted and killed.

The moon had not yet scattered the darkness, and the jagged silhouettes of the foreign warships dominated the Yangtze River. The cruiser and the destroyers were starkly outlined by the orange-and-blue oil-fires leaping on Socony Hill. Greasy black smoke billowed over newly liberated Nanking.

"Since the Nanking Incident your coverage has changed, Dick. You're becoming biased, almost anti-Chinese . . . white supremacist. You're getting to be an old-fashioned damn-the-natives British imperialist like the taipans at the Shanghai Club. I just don't see how . . ."

Emily stopped in mid-sentence. Although she knew she was on dangerous ground, she could not drop the matter. Their bitter disagreements on journalistic ethics could well be projection, as defined in her psychology classes at Bryn Mawr. Perhaps they were arguing an abstract issue because the essential personal issue between them was so explosive. Nonetheless, the question of fair reporting of the National Revolution was too important to gloss over—even if she was courting disaster by this heated discussion in Richard's office in the *North China Daily News* building.

"For God's sake, Emily, don't talk such rubbish!" he erupted. "You're getting too emotional about local politics."

"Local politics to you, but not to me!" she retorted. "It's my future —and my people. China needs . . . deserves . . . sympathetic reporting, not bias and sensationalism. Your exaggeration could just draw the foreigners into the civil war. And where would your precious Shanghai, your Model Settlement, be then?"

"My dear Emily, it's *your* Shanghai. Even *your* Foreign Settlement. *My* family didn't get rich hiding behind foreigners' skirts and squeezing their countrymen. *My* family hasn't . . . Damn it, I'm sorry. I . . ."

Emily appeared even more fragile because she was pale with fury. Yet she half agreed—as her brother Tommy would largely agree—with Richard's description of the Howes. But she wondered again: Was he attacking her family as a substitute for attacking her directly?

"Look here, Em, I'm truly sorry!" he repeated. "But I'm just reporting the way it is. I wish China weren't a bear pit—a dirty great arena for dirty fights. But I can't change that. I'm not God. I'm only a humble reporter."

"You're about as humble as Caligula, Richard Hollings. I don't like your air of superiority to me—superiority to China. All you foreigners are the same. Julie is still carrying on about going back to the States. She's far worse since Nanking. Can't stand China anymore, she says. . . . We Howes were here long before you foreigners appeared. We'll still be here when you're all long gone."

"I have no travel plans, my dear. Except to worm my way back into your good graces."

Emily smiled despite her anger. Yet she wondered again how he could possibly be jealous of her modest success in journalism, as well as resenting her substantial success at the Women's Bank. He called himself a Bohemian, and he asserted that he was not shackled by convention. Yet, like his Victorian father and her Confucian father, he wanted his woman to be modest, retiring, and, above all, devoted to no occupation outside himself.

At least Richard was consistent in his prejudices. Taking her consent for granted, he was again urging her to set a date for their wedding. He really did want to marry her and to protect her. But she sensed that he also wanted to confine her. Her pieces for the Chinese-language press did not affect him. However, once they were married, he would assuredly want to curtail her filing to the Philadelphia *Public Ledger* stories that implicitly competed with his stories for the *Boston Globe*. She feared that his outmoded idea of marriage would stifle her.

It was ironic. She had been disowned by her parents because she would not give Richard up for a conventional arranged marriage. But she could not bring herself to set a date for their wedding.

Nonetheless, she did love Richard, and she wanted to live with him. Even in the enlightened 1920s, however, respectable Shanghai was too straitlaced for that. In Montmartre, Bloomsbury, or Greenwich Village, cohabitation without a wedding was not merely tolerated but was now almost the norm. Yet she could not fulfill her parents' worst expectations by becoming the "little wife" of a foreigner!

Marriage would allow them to live together openly, which would be a great relief. But she would not take the nuptial vows like aspirin.

Emily avoided Richard's gaze, for she did not want him to see that her anger was cooling. She glanced down at the Bund from the window. He had explained his renting an office in the *Daily News* building by saying he wanted to be near the cable office and to read the *News*'s wire-service reports. She knew that he also needed the tension, the sense of being at the center of events that a newspaper office provided.

The office was large, and he had invited her to set her new Royal Number Ten typewriter on a vacant desk. The Royal had been his Chinese New Year's gift, when the ancient Underwood salvaged from the wreckage of JPEnterprises finally proved unrepairable. Emily's eyes misted, and her unshed tears blurred the small pagoda that glowed in the afternoon sunlight amid the industrial slum called Pootung across the Hwangpoo River.

Although he could be scathing about her deficiencies as a correspondent, Richard had given her the typewriter. He had also given her office space. Was it primarily because he wanted to keep an eye on her in the evening, which was when they wrote most of their dispatches, owing to the thirteen-hour time difference to Boston and Philadelphia? Perhaps, however, he was trying to woo her away from her work.

Emily laughed aloud, and Richard glanced at her quizzically. If he gave her an ivory abacus to facilitate her work at the Women's Bank, she should by that same twisted reasoning be doubly suspicious. Anyway, she was a little tired of the bank—tired of the female lusting after money, the fluting female voices, and the female preoccupation with trifles.

"I promised I'd worm my way back into your good graces," Richard said mildly. "Since then, you've gazed out the window, blotted your eyes, and laughed out loud."

"I was thinking of something else."

"What's so laughable? Still my reporting?"

"No, not that. But since you've raised the subject again, what do you think now of your story on Chiang Kai-shek's press conference?"

"A pretty good piece." Richard was defensive. "Not anti-Chinese at all, although you may think it pro-imperialist. But even you don't want the foreign concessions overrun by that Red rabble of Chiang Kai-shek's, do you?"

"Not just now, Dick. China *must* take both the Settlement and Frenchtown back. It's inevitable—in time. But it's impossible just now. Look out this window, and you'll see why."

Richard came to stand beside her. His arm clasped her shoulders, and she felt his warmth through her pink crepe de chine blouse. He proprietorially stroked her hip through her light heather tweed skirt as he counted the ships moored at the men-of-war buoys off the Bund: two American cruisers, one flying the flag of a full admiral; two British cruisers, one flying the flag of a vice admiral; a Portuguese sloop; two Japanese destroyers; and a Dutch cruiser. He knew that most of the international fleet of forty-seven warships assembled to defend Shanghai was lying off Woosung on the Yangtze.

"Nobody's going to trifle with that little lot," Richard agreed. "Certainly not Generalissimo Chiang Kai-shek with his one gunboat."

While he gazed speculatively at the flotilla, Emily gazed at his profile. His usually mobile features were pensive, and his untamed lock of hair fell dark brown over his forehead. His somber eyes moved Emily, and she lifted her hand to touch the vulnerable patch above his cheekbones where a few bristles had escaped the razor. When he turned, her hand dropped.

"Just exactly what is wrong with my piece?" he demanded. "You haven't shown me yours, so I can't compare them."

"Here it is."

032727 CHIANGKAISHEK CCINCC VICTORYWARDING CHINATS ADUNISTATES PRESS GUARANTEED SAFETY FORNPERSONS ETPROPERTY . . .

Richard read the smudged carbon copy and automatically translated into plain English the terse cablese essential because press messages to the United States cost thirty-five cents a word: "Shanghai, March 27, 1927: Generalissimo Chiang Kai-shek, commander in chief of the Nationalist armies sweeping to victory in China, today told American correspondents that he personally guaranteed the safety of foreign nationals in Shanghai, and the security of their property.

"He requested that the foreign powers withdraw their troops and warships, promising the Nationalists would safeguard the International Settlement and the French Concession. He further indicated that the

Nationalists had no designs on the foreign concessions and would make no incursions into them."

"I suppose that's what he said—literally," Richard conceded. "Still, I don't see much difference to my lead. Except that mine's livelier."

"Yours certainly is lively. Practically jumps off the page. Let me see it again." She read aloud: "Shanghai's more than forty thousand foreign residents today awaited invasion by the Nationalist and Communist troops surrounding the foreign enclaves. Despite a last-minute—and hardly unequivocal—promise of noninterference by General Chiang Kai-shek, who commands the revolutionary forces, the foreign community was not reassured. Ears still rang with the vehement demands for immediate military conquest of the Foreign Settlement and the French Concession shrieked at the gigantic Bolshevik rally held earlier this afternoon."

Emily broke off to observe: "It's all how you look at it, Dick, isn't it? Where you place the emphasis."

"Of course it is, my darling Emily. Your copy is written from a Chinese point of view, even though your audience is American. They can't identify with Chinese. They want to know about foreigners, particularly Americans."

"So, I can't see the facts because I'm Chinese?" Emily flared. "These wretched slant eyes of mine, they can't see straight."

"Don't be so touchy, Em. You know exactly what I mean."

"Well, if writing for a specific audience means twisting the facts, I'm glad I'm not so professional—not so quick with a lie."

"Now look here!" Anger mottled Richard's olive skin. "I've never lied! Not to you or in print! Can you show me a single untruth in that story? It's only that your viewpoint and mine are different."

"And not only on politics. Why—"

"Em, let's not blow this up into something between us," he interrupted. "Just consider the facts. The foreign community *is* racked with anxiety. The Communists *are* getting stronger every minute. Who knows whether Chiang Kai-shek can control them? Has he really turned against the Communists, as you imply? I ask you again: just point out a single lie in my story."

"Not outright lies. But what you left out is very significant."

"What did I leave out?"

"You didn't report the Generalissimo's request that the barbed-wire barricades around the concessions be removed because they insult the Chinese people—make the Chinese look like savages. He also promised that no mob would sweep into the concessions as it did in Wuhan. You didn't write a word about that!"

"My Lord, Em! I reported his calling in American correspondents to reassure the Americans. Besides, there's nothing in *your* piece about the word from London. The weak policy followed at Wuhan and, until recently, at Shanghai is now reversed. If the Nationalists want a fight, we'll carry the battle to them. Everything's changed since the Nanking outrages!"

Emily turned abruptly to stare at the map of China hanging above the mahogany bookcase. She clasped her hands before her so that Richard could not see them tremble. She spaced her words deliberately, but her voice quavered when she finally replied, "You know very well your stories on Nanking in *The Times* fanned anger in England. Rapine, and pillage, indeed! . . . There was wanton slaughter. But it was *Chinese* who died by the hundreds under foreign shells! As for rape—"

"Steady, Em. Don't go wild."

"As for rape," she continued, "no single case has been proved. You should know by now that foreign women are abhorrent . . . disgusting . . . to ignorant Chinese soldiers. Such men are deathly afraid. They think white women are witches or evil female spirits who destroy men. Sometimes I wish *this* pagan Chinese woman felt the same way about white men—at least a certain white man!"

"All right, Emily." He ignored her last sentence. "I've already corrected that misapprehension. I've now reported that there were no provable cases of rape."

She turned again to the wall map and gazed as if entranced at the expanse of Manchuria. Realizing that she would not reply, Richard spoke conciliatingly. "About that certain white man, Em. I'm sometimes afraid you feel—"

"It's anti-Chinese prejudice! Bare-faced racism!" She slashed across his words. "Anyway, who'll notice a half retraction?"

"Emily, how could I possibly want to marry you if I was anti-Chinese?" Richard was no longer feigning indignation. "How can you talk so?"

"That's how you feel deep down, even if you don't realize it. Don't you know *anything* about elementary psychology?"

"Forget your psychological mumbo jumbo. Just tell me this: Why would I be begging you to marry me if I was really anti-Chinese?"

"Who knows? Perhaps to debase me." Emily smiled narrowly at her own absurdity. "Maybe to humble all Chinese by making me your slave."

"You'll never be anyone's slave, my dear. And don't try to sidle away from the issue with a joke. If I'm anti-Chinese, how is it I look forward to half-Chinese children? Not because they'll be half-Chinese, but because they'll be half-you."

"Oh, Dick, you know as well as I do that's a smoke screen. Men just don't feel the same way about children that women do. Men don't really think about children until they arrive—if then. But women—"

"So that's why you won't marry me." He laughed. "It's your anti-white prejudice. Your racism! Now I know."

She, too, laughed, but the embers of her anger flared once again. *"If you really want to marry me. Do you?"*

"Of course I do. I've told you a hundred times."

"All right then! If you really want marriage, I *will* marry you." She turned from the wall map to face him. "Before the end of this year. Any day in December! *If* you truly want it then!"

Julia and Emily piled eagerly into the fire-engine-red Plymouth convertible coupé with the folding rumbleseat that Richard called a dickey. Emily had paid $754 U.S. for the car, almost the entire initial dividend on her invested capital just received from the Women's Commercial Bank. Cut off from the great wealth of the Howes, she was nonetheless lavish when she had a little money in her hand.

Sunday, April 10th, was the first chance they had to take the convertible out for a run. With the canvas top down, it was exhilarating to race at thirty miles an hour through the International Settlement. But the streets were far too quiet at seven in the evening. The nervous Municipal Council had closed the gates in the barbed wire that encircled the Settlement, cutting off not only Chinese-ruled Greater Shanghai, but even the French Concession. The Chinese workers and pleasure-seekers who normally swarmed into the concessions were effectively excluded. The empty streets were not only depressing but frightening.

Far more frightening was desperate uncertainty as to what Generalissimo Chiang Kai-shek would do next. He might choose to attack the foreign concessions despite their formidable garrisons. He might have no intention of attacking despite his pledge to drive imperialism out of China. In any event, the initiative lay in his hands.

Chiang Kai-shek's National Revolutionary Army was camped outside the city, while the Communists exercised power over Greater Shanghai through the workers' councils they stagemanaged. The Shanghai Uprising led by Commissar Chou En-lai three weeks earlier had been a spectacular success. All territory surrounding the foreign enclaves had passed from warlord control to revolutionary control—and the foreigners were appalled.

The foreigners were also confused by the splits in the Nationalist ranks. The right wing of the National People's Party, which gave its allegiance to Generalissimo Chiang, had just moved its headquarters to newly taken Nanking. The left wing of the National People's Party, still closely allied with the Communists, claimed to govern all China from the triplet cities on the Yangtze called Wuhan. No foreigner now expected moderation from the Nationalists.

The Settlement's fear was visible in the empty streets. Distracted by her constant worry about Tommy, Julia decided that it was not much fun showing off the new convertible when there was no one to see it. Cast down by the deserted city, Emily agreed that they might as well return to Kiukiang Road and devote the evening to what Richard Hollings called "liturgical feminine tasks."

Those tasks were hardly onerous in Shanghai. Washing out stockings and underclothes; mending and pressing dresses; shampooing hair—such chores were inescapable in America. But not in China, where the amahs looked after clothing and hairdressers came to the apartment for so little it would be sinful not to employ them.

After giving Emily first chance at the luxurious bathroom Tommy had put in, Julia filled the big tub and poured in bath salts. A good soaking in the foaming water should relieve the tension that made her neck ache. Not only the general uncertainty—indeed precariousness—of life amid the crisis disturbed her, but also her constant fear of discovery that she was working for the secret Communist Apparatus.

No one knew, not even Tommy, who had remarked quizzically when he saw her off at the Canton railway station a year earlier: "It's all terribly muddled, isn't it? When it was the Nationalists against the warlords, one could tell the good chaps from the villains. With splits and factions, that's now almost impossible. I'd bet on the Generalissimo's coming up trumps. But despite everything, I can't help liking the Communists' dash and vigor."

Tommy, Julia reflected, was really three separate men: the playboy, the scientist, and the patriot.

Most people saw the playboy Tommy, who joked in Shanghainese or drawled ironically in English, hiding his true nature beneath a cloak of banter. That public Tommy was endearing and amusing.

Quite different was Tommy the scientist, who believed himself removed from both compassion and anger. Such emotion, Tommy maintained, would interfere with his purpose, which was to heal his patients, not to humor them. His actual concern for his patients sometimes drained him so that he was hardly able to speak.

Tommy the patriot was an incongruous blend of fiery passion and ice-cold dedication. He put China above all else, but he could not say exactly what was best for his country. Democratic government or industrial development? National dignity or popular well-being? He only knew China could not have everything at once.

Prolonged separation had clarified Julia's feelings toward Tommy. Above all else in the world, she yearned for his safe return to Shanghai for good. As long as he was with the army she would be riven by fear, the same ceaseless fear that had made her realize how deeply she loved him. She consciously put aside her longing to return to America. When he did return, she would marry him the instant he asked her. If he did not ask, she would be almost as happy—just as long as she could be with him.

He was surgeon general of the Sixth Corps, which had been blamed for the Nanking Incident. Disquietingly, she had not heard from him for several weeks. Yet, she consoled herself, she would have heard if anything had happened to him.

Julia was pleasantly drowsy when she slipped on her scarlet silk kimono and joined Emily in the sitting room. Companionably silent, they listened to Station XMHA's concert on the Atterbury Kent console radio. Lying between them on the red-and-yellow Turkestan carpet, Adam contentedly twitched his plumed tail from time to time. But the telephone's jingling intruded into that domestic serenity.

"I hope I haven't woken you, Em," Joshua Haleevie apologized. "May I drop over? This barn is getting on my nerves."

"I can't think of anyone I'd rather see, Joshua."

"About twenty minutes then."

Hanging up, Emily realized that she had told the literal truth. Aside from Tommy, for whom she longed, both she and Emily were happiest with Joshua. Despite her latest passionate reconciliation with Richard, Emily needed respite from Richard's—and her own—emotional storms. Although Joshua might demand a more stimulating drink, Emily drifted into the kitchen to make tea and sandwiches.

Julia was alone in the sitting room when the telephone rang again rather feebly. Picking up the handset, she heard only static and Central's interrogative "Number please?"

When the telephone rang again, this time demandingly, she realized that she was hearing the front-door bell. That would be Joshua. Releasing bolts, locks, and chains, Julia flung the iron-grilled door open—

though she had been repeatedly warned to find out first who was outside.

She belatedly recalled those warnings when she saw a tall man in a nondescript uniform looming menacingly in the half-lit hallway. He could be a White Russian mercenary seeking refuge or money—and not too particular about how he got them. He could also be one of the reinforcements sent to defend the Settlement. Rogues in the uniforms of eight nations had made the foreign community wary. Tales of rape were not told only of Nanking.

"What is it?" she demanded. "I warn you, I'm not alone!"

"Not another man?" The man stepped forward, and she saw Tommy's face lit by the light through the open door. "I'd hate that."

Julia flung herself into his arms. Her face pressed against his chest, she smelled tobacco, soot, sweat—and a whiff of antiseptics.

"Tommy! Tommy!" she repeated. "Oh, Tommy, I'm so happy! You scared me half to death!"

"Darling! Darling!" he murmured. "Darling Julie!"

She stepped back to study his worn features and said, "You look exhausted. Come in immediately."

Emily embraced him fiercely when Julia shepherded him into the apartment. Amid a flurry of questions, he was finally seated on the rattan settee and handed a strong whisky and soda.

"They thought I'd better come down." He did not say who *they* were. "The army's medical services are a mess in Shanghai."

"How did you get through the Settlement's gates in uniform?" Julia asked. "They're especially barred to Nationalist officers."

"Silver—not love—still conquers all in Shanghai. I simply flung a few dollars about. With my cap in my bag and my trenchcoat over my tunic, I was no longer in uniform." He paused before asking Emily, "Have you seen the parents? Anything new on that front?"

Emily shook her head, almost ashamed that her rift with her parents had not miraculously healed. Her guilt over that rift was no longer acute, but it was always with her—an integral part of her being, like her arms and her legs.

Emily was wistful when she saw her friend's unreserved joy in her brother's return. Perhaps too intellectual, perhaps too cold, she could not give herself so trustingly to Richard—nor, perhaps, to any man. Perhaps she was simply too proud.

Even Julia's posture declared her delight in surrendering herself to Tommy. Careless of her nakedness under her scarlet kimono, she poured herself around his shoulder as if her bones had been liquefied.

Her small, competent hands fluttered around him like restless doves. She stroked his cheek and clasped his hand; she touched his thigh and grasped his arm.

Her unfashionably long mahogany hair tumbled across her forehead, and her eyes glowed green. Her open features seemed to soften, lines and angles melting into curves.

Tommy was grimy after the railway journey from Nanking, and his face was blanched by exhaustion. Despite his stained khaki tunic and his scuffed Sam Browne belt, he appeared very young. Although exhaustion blurred the outlines of his long scholar's face, his eyes shone when he looked at Julia.

Emily was rising, ready to plead weariness and retire, when the doorbell tinkled twice, then twice again. It was Joshua Haleevie's special ring. Emily and Julia looked down at their kimonos in dismay and scurried for their bedrooms.

"By God, Tommy, it's good to see you!" Joshua exploded with delight. "Just the man! Such luck!"

Joshua and Tommy had always gotten along well; they were close but not intimate. Tommy looked hard at his friend after that uncharacteristically exuberant greeting. At thirty-four, Joshua was lean and elegant, his authority enhanced by the touch of gray in his black sideburns and the faint crinkles around his light blue eyes. In his cream silk dinner jacket he looked like a dashing cavalry officer or a brilliant young ambassador. Normally either reserved or breezily nonchalant, he was now agitated and talkative.

"Missed the sinks of iniquity, did you?" he asked. "Revisiting the scenes of your sins?"

"Do forget about the past," Tommy replied. "Lurid, it may've been, but not *that* lurid. . . . The ladies are just slipping into something less comfortable."

"I reckoned Em and Julie could carry the word, but you're just the lad I need." Joshua pulled his earlobe in thought. "You see, I've a bit of a problem. . . ."

"Help if I can."

"Tommy, what do you think of the Supreme Lord of the Floodgate Fraternity and his secret societies?"

"Vermin!" Tommy declared. "Aside from his other crimes, he's ruined more lives with opium than even the Japanese have. You know, of course, that he's also called the Green Dragon—and he's Chiang Kai-shek's blood brother."

Tommy's indignation was briefly diverted when Emily and Julia reappeared more suitably dressed to receive gentlemen callers. They had changed into less revealing dressing gowns and applied the lipstick, mascara, and rouge respectable young ladies used without pretense in the enlightened year 1927.

After bestowing compliments on them, Joshua returned to his purpose: "I pleaded against it, but our American lord mayor Sterling Fessenden has made a deal to save the concessions. The Green Dragon is to save the concessions. In return for five thousand rifles and a free hand, his secret societies will move against the Communists on Tuesday morning. The night before, the Green Dragon will assassinate the Communist leaders."

"Not Chou En-lai?" Julia had a weakness for the dashing Communist leader. "We've got to warn him!"

"I imagine," Tommy said dryly, "that warning Chou En-lai is Joshua's general idea."

"Fessenden and the Green Dragon want to present Generalissimo Chiang with a *fait accompli*," Joshua said. "They reckon the Nationalists will be grateful—and leave the concessions alone."

"The Green Dragon would never make such a vital move without the Generalissimo's knowledge," Tommy pointed out. "His blood brother would have to know. He's pulling the wool over Fessenden's eyes."

"That's interesting, Tommy, but it's not quite enough. What else have you got for me?"

"Honestly, Joshua, I can only offer you an informed view. No top-secret information."

"You know, it stupidly hadn't occurred to me that the Green Dragon was misleading Fessenden about the Generalissimo's ignorance of the plot. I need your other insights."

"Of course you know that the left-wing Nationalists and the Communists are now marching against the Generalissimo. The man Dick Hollings calls Lucifer is back from Europe. He's taken over the government at Wuhan and dismissed the Generalissimo from all his offices. So the Generalissimo is setting up his own government in Nanking."

"He's setting up shop in Nanking? Not Shanghai?"

"Any Chinese government must depend on Shanghai for revenue. But the Generalissimo can't make Shanghai his capital unless he takes over the Settlement and Frenchtown. The last thing he wants is war with the foreign powers!"

"Do you mean there's no real threat to the life of the concessions?" Julia asked. "It doesn't look that way here."

"There is a threat," Tommy replied. "It comes from hotheads on both sides. But not from the Generalissimo."

Emily nodded and said: "That's what May Soong insists. She says her Gimo—she calls him Gimo now—she says he knows he can't rule China without money. He needs dollars right now, and he can only find dollars in Shanghai."

"This is all *very* useful," Joshua purred.

"Now enlighten me, old chum," Tommy demanded. "What's your game? Why're you spilling the beans?"

"Tommy, I'm a Shanghailander like yourself. Above all, I want to avoid killing. I don't want the battle for China to be fought in Greater Shanghai—and inevitably spill over into the concessions. I want you to warn Chou En-lai."

Arms extended over his head, Tommy stretched until he could almost hear his bones creak. After bending for more than twelve hours over the improvised operating table, the muscles of his back were painfully cramped. Peeling off his blood-caked rubber gloves, Tommy rubbed his smarting eyes. Flickering kerosene lanterns, which gave off noxious fumes, had provided the only light after the electricity was cut off.

He had never wished to practice the butcher's trade called surgery. Yet he had been awash in blood since joining the National Revolutionary Army—and the two days just past had been the worst.

He searched for his meerschaum pipe in the pocket of his white coat, which was now red. While his long fingers tamped down the yellow latakia tobacco, his eyes surveyed the rough dressing station. The concrete-floored communal washroom of the tenement near the Shanghai General Labor Union was an extraordinary setting for the emergency operations on wounded civilians he had been performing almost without stopping. But it had been an extraordinary thirty-six hours—even for one inured to both bloodshed and bizarre events by a year's service in the Nationalist army.

It had begun when Little Pow led him to the offices of the General Labor Union in Chapei on Monday morning, three days earlier. At least, Tommy recalled with melancholy satisfaction, he had tried to alert the Communist leadership to its peril, although Commissar Chou En-lai had obviously refused to believe him. He had almost seen suspicion flare in the commissar's expressive eyes.

"Thank you, Dr. Howe," Chou En-lai had said with excessive courtesy. "Of course I know the rumors about the so-called counterattack. But I wonder one thing: Why should our enemies be so anxious to tell me? Do they want me to go on the defensive?"

Chou En-lai was, of course, only twenty-nine, and he was flushed with the vanity of his first independent command. He had naturally said he knew all about the plot to destroy Communist power that had been hatched by the foreigners, the secret societies, and Generalissimo Chiang Kai-shek. No politician, even one so inexperienced, would admit to such a vital deficiency in his information.

Chou En-lai was inordinately proud of his intelligence service. He boasted that his agents were virtually invisible because they were so commonplace: coolies, servants, midwives, and street urchins like Little Pow. He could not believe that those agents had missed all indications of the planned counterattack.

Since the commissar was so aggressively confident, Tommy had delivered his warning and left without further discussion. He had then returned to the apartment on Kiukiang Road to resume with reluctance the discussion with Julia that was ruffling their reunion. Discussion was perhaps too mild a word, although they were not quarreling. After their first delight at seeing each other again, she had confessed, "I've been having some thoughts that may disturb you, Tommy."

She had first told him that she was thinking of returning briefly to Plattsburg to see her parents. She said they were pressing her very hard to come back—even if only for a short visit. She had then acknowledged that there was a slight danger of her not returning to Shanghai once she was settled at home. It was not only the money for the fare, she half-heartedly agreed, but she might well feel that Shanghai had been no more than a waking dream. And how could she return to a dream?

There was little enough to say in reply. He could not in conscience argue strongly that she must remain, for he was too Confucian to stand between a daughter and her parents. Neither could he urge her to go, since that would suggest he was eager to see her leave. Nor could he offer to pay her return fare, since that would offend her.

Fortunately, they had not quarreled but had still been discussing the matter when Little Pow came for him the second time. He could not, of course, reject Pow's plea that he man the emergency dressing station near the General Labor Union. He had now been working, with only amateur assistance, for thirty-six hours. Yet he could not recall a single individual among the more than one hundred gravely injured men and women, as well as five or six children, whom he had treated.

Wearily, Tommy corrected himself. He could recall *only* Little Pow, both legs broken by a hand grenade, and, near the thigh bone, metal fragments that threatened to pierce an artery. Without a doctor, the waif would have bled to death. Though his present condition would cause no concern in a hospital, it would deteriorate without constant care. Yet there was little hope of getting him to a hospital.

The improvised dressing station offered only concrete washbasins, and charcoal braziers from the canteen's kitchen had boiled water to sterilize instruments. In the dank atmosphere the stench of blood and excrement overwhelmed the fading whiffs of antiseptics and anaesthetics. The grimy brick walls and the gritty floor littered with blood-stained dressings made Tommy fear he would never feel clean again.

With a blood-rimmed thumbnail he tamped tobacco into his meerschaum pipe. When he pushed aside the burlap curtain that cut off his makeshift operating theater, the rough fabric prickled his hand unpleasantly.

His remaining patients lay on straw mats on the concrete floor. Some were still. Some muttered and tossed. An old man with a bandage over his eyes keened a monotonous Buddhist prayer.

Little Pow lay under a hanging kerosene lantern in the far corner. A book of crudely colored revolutionary cartoons lay open on the tattered coat covering him. One small hand guarded that treasure, though his eyes were closed.

When Tommy's soles grated on the concrete, the urchin's bruised eyelids lifted. The lantern above him jumped each time a door slammed. In the swaying yellow beam, the inverted triangle of his face was haggard. But his fever-bright eyes welcomed Tommy, and his bloodless lips smiled.

Little Pow ignored the index finger raised to enjoin silence and spoke slowly: *"Tan Yee-sheng . . .* Dr. Tom, I can't sleep any more. Please come talk to me."

"All right, Pow. Talking can't do you any harm." As he squatted Tommy realized that he, too, needed human warmth when the world seemed only wounds and incisions, pain and death. "Well, Pow, it's been quite a time, hasn't it? After your performance, we'll have to change your name. Not Little Pow anymore but Big Pow."

By changing the intonation of the word *pow,* Tommy changed its import so that it meant not "bubble," but "gun." The youth's grin revealed his delight at that accolade from the man he loved almost as much as he did his savior, John Pavernen. Tommy's throat tightened. This battle-scarred veteran, who had survived three campaigns in just three months, was still a child.

"What's happening?" Little Pow demanded weakly. "I can't remember much . . ."

"What do you remember, Big Shot?" Better for the lad to talk, rather than brood in silence on the catastrophe that had overwhelmed his small world. "Tell me and I'll fill the rest in for you."

"I'm trying, but you keep interrupting!" Little Pow said in exasperation. "How much do you know?"

"Let me see. You came for me about six yesterday morning, didn't you? We'd already heard from Richard Hollings"—Tommy ignored Little Pow's grimace of distaste—"that it had started. Hundreds of secret-society thugs had moved out of Frenchtown, wearing blue workclothes and armbands reading 'Worker!' They all carried pistols or rifles. About the same time, the Generalissimo's regular Nationalist troops in the same disguise crossed the Settlement in trucks. They were heading for Chapei, the workers' stronghold. At least a thousand, maybe more."

"No need to guard the Settlement perimeter, our Communist leaders said," Little Pow observed bitterly. "The gates were all barred."

"To stop your people getting into the Settlement, *not* to keep the murderers in."

"The first we knew at headquarters, Dr. Tom, was shooting in the distance," Little Pow began his tale. "Then we received reports that the enemy knew exactly where our posts were—and was attacking without warning. There were some Nationalist troops in uniform, the Generalissimo's troops. But most were phony workers, the Green Dragon's musclemen. Headquarters was a terrible mess. Even Commissar Chou En-lai was dumbfounded for a few minutes. Then they hit headquarters and I . . ."

Listening to Little Pow's account, Tommy envisioned the scene: Chou En-lai's self-confidence momentarily turned to confusion when the windows were smashed by the enemy's opening shots. The commissar dropping to the floor, immobilized by the volleys, and looking in vain for an escape route. He could not counterattack, because the surprise was overwhelming. Outside, all his strong points were being crushed.

"Little Pow!" he had shouted, after issuing emergency orders to his aides. "Little Pow, come here."

"Commissar Chou!"

"Throw away your armband and wriggle out the back way! Save yourself! But, first, get to as many posts as you can—and tell *them* to save themselves. . . . Also, your friend, Dr. Howe. Take him to the emergency dressing station."

Disobeying orders, Little Pow had crept round to the rear of the attacking force. Crouched behind a garbage can in the ashen dawn, he watched the men in workers' blue firing at the union's headquarters. A return volley crashed. The defenders were firing through improvised loopholes where ventilating grates had been pushed out of the walls.

Little Pow's hopes flared, but the union could not hold out against an enemy now being reinforced by Nationalist soldiers in uniform. Their pretense of neutrality abandoned, two regular squads were setting up tubes that looked like bigger versions of One-Arm Sutton's trench mortar. On the point of firing, they were stopped by a colonel who wore a sunburst of medal ribbons and an anachronistic saber. He pointed at the neighboring buildings, evidently warning they could be damaged by misaimed mortar bombs.

Little Pow then knew the enemy had won. He had learned at the Workers' Night School that the enemy cared far more for property than for human beings. Even so, the Nationalists must be sure of victory if they did not use their mortars for fear of damaging buildings. He knew he would never see his comrades again—certainly not Commissar Chou En-lai, who had joked grimly that his name stood first on the enemy's death list.

Little Pow rooted beneath the bamboo scaffolding that clothed a half-built tenement. The construction site was deserted, for all Chapei's workers had gone to ground when they heard the first shots. He found a bamboo carrying-pole, an empty kerosene tin, and a sack of plaster. After filling the tin with water, he slung the tin from one end of the pole and the sack from the other end.

Settling the pole across his right shoulder, he trotted past the North Railway Station toward the gate on Elgin Road that gave passage through the barbed wire, the sandbags, and the pillboxes sealing off the International Settlement. Any reactionary thugs he met would dismiss him as a young coolie too stupid to stay under shelter.

When the ferociously bearded Sikh sentries guarding the Settlement refused to open the gate, Little Pow shrugged. Water slopped from the tin onto the road when he turned away. He trotted eastward toward the vacant lot between the Public Works Depot, which lay inside the barbed wire, and the Municipal School, which lay outside. Seeing no sentries, he loped boldly toward the weed-grown fence.

His small figure dropped into the nullah, the ditch that carried off flash floods. Crawling through mud and debris, Little Pow squeezed under the chain-link fence. He drew his carrying-pole after him and set out for Kiukiang Road.

·　·　·

"I couldn't stay away from Commissar Chou's headquarters, Dr. Tom," Little Pow whispered. "I went back after I brought you here to the emergency station."

Tommy again saw the half-lit dressing station, rather than the scenes the fifteen-year-old had been describing. He poured tea from a thermos, and Little Pow continued compulsively: "After I left you here, Dr. Tom, I went back to headquarters to see what . . ."

Little Pow had joined the crowd gawking at the pockmarked headquarters of the Shanghai General Labor Union after the shooting stopped. He was still playing the ragged young coolie, the bamboo carrying-pole still cocked over his shoulder. That camouflage was probably unnecessary, since a careless festive spirit ruled the victors. Phony workers and uniformed regulars were gleefully toasting each other in looted beer and rice wine.

Disheveled and grimy, Chou En-lai still stood out among the captives, who were herded by soldiers under the orders of a sergeant major. His well-cut gray tunic was torn, and one sleeve was ripped away. But his innate authority still commanded his subordinates—and invited the blows of his captors.

Chou En-lai smoothed his hair and smiled easily. His expression did not alter when a Nationalist captain wearing the aiguillette of a general's aide told the sergeant major, "I'll take charge of this prisoner. They want him at garrison headquarters immediately."

"So you're my jailer now?" Chou En-lai asked lightly. "You were a good student, Shih. And who would have thought when we were at the Whampoa Academy—"

"I'm afraid so!" The officer glared at the sergeant major, who was patently unhappy at being deprived of his chief prisoner. "Fate makes its own rules."

Six enlisted men with bayonet-tipped rifles formed a box around the Communist leader, and the detachment moved off briskly. When the colonel commanding the Nationalists emerged from the captured building, guards and prisoner had vanished around the corner. After questioning his sergeant major, the colonel shrugged elaborately at the vagaries of the high command.

Observing that gesture from the corner of his eye, Little Pow scurried down a lane he knew was a shortcut to the road to garrison headquarters. A half dozen gunmen wearing the brassards of counterfeit workers were lounging in rattan chairs in front of a wine shop whose shutters had been pried open. Otherwise the road was empty.

"Come 'ere, boy!" A gunman with a scarlet face waved an earthenware flask. "Come'n 'ave a drink."

"Did you see a file of soldiers?" Little Pow asked. "Not a minute ago?"

The gunmen shook their heads, and Pow darted toward the junction. That street, too, was deserted. Twenty seconds later, the missing detachment emerged from an alley—without the tattered prisoner.

The bewildered urchin counted six enlisted men and two officers. Curiosity driving out fear, he slipped behind a wall plastered with cigarette advertisements. The detachment marched briskly past his hiding place, hobnailed boots striking sparks from the cobblestones and arms swinging in unison. Both officers were rigidly erect.

Little Pow muffled a gasp. Low on their foreheads, the officers' peaked caps shadowed their features. Yet Commissar Chou En-lai's strong jaw was unmistakable between choker collar and black visor.

Despite the torments of curiosity, Little Pow did not follow the detachment. He did not want to know where his commander was hiding. If he were captured, he would not be able to tell anyone where Chou En-lai had taken refuge—no matter how he was tortured.

"Now, Big Shot," Tommy broke in, "it's time for you to sleep."

"Only a little more to tell, Dr. Tom." Little Pow stubbornly resumed: "That night I couldn't come near you. I was carrying danger on my shoulders. So I went to earth. You can always find a place to sleep behind a billboard or on a construction site. The sidewalk's not so restful. The cops kick you awake all the time.

"Next morning, rumors were flying, mostly launched by the servants at garrison headquarters. Commissar Chou En-lai had disappeared. Nobody knew who the captain was, the one who took him away. Also, the rightists were shooting their prisoners in batches of five. Maybe a hundred already dead, maybe a lot more. And maybe thousands lay dead on the streets.

"Some little union leaders were still alive and free. But they didn't have the foggiest idea what to do. Somebody—heaven knows who—decided to call a general strike. And somebody else got the bright idea of a protest march on garrison headquarters. Some bright idea!"

After the May Thirtieth Incident in 1925, a general strike had briefly paralyzed the International Settlement and the French Concession. The foreign rulers were restrained from total brutality by conscience—and by fear of opinion in their home countries. But a general strike could not possibly intimidate the new Chinese overlords, who never dreamed they might someday stand before the bar of public opinion.

The Nationalists would crush any strike with new massacres. They did not care what others felt, and they felt no compunction themselves. How could anyone shame the unashamed rightists? How could anything touch the conscience of secret-society thugs who had no consciences?

In any event, Little Pow recalled, the new general strike was already faltering when several thousand men and women assembled for the protest march at noon. But the militants were still confident.

The youth slipped on the armband with the red ideograms that read "Special Messenger." He straightened his threadbare jacket, clasped its choker collar around his skinny neck, and ran his fingers through his coarse hair. Although he tried to be nonchalant, his large eyes opened even wider in astonishment when he saw that his neighbors on either side carried old Mannlicher rifles with long barrels. He knew those rifles had been covertly distributed by the Soviet consulate.

"What are *those* things for?" he asked. "Why rifles? The whole idea is a peaceful march, isn't it?"

"Little Comrade, we're not planning to shoot," the man on his right replied. "Not that we wouldn't if it came to it. But for now we're just out to show that the people possess their own powerful armed force. Fearless soldiers of the revolution cannot be intimidated! Got it?"

Dismayed, Little Pow nodded. The slogans his neighbor parroted could inspire revolutionaries to defy danger. But mindless derring-do was precisely what the present situation did *not* require.

The man on his left, who spoke with a northern accent, was evidently a former warlord soldier. A number of deserters had been recruited into the Workers' Militia by large bounties. Little Pow was marching into grave peril between a fool and a mercenary.

Yet his blood was stirred by the sighing of many feet across the pavements. That immense shuffling of straw sandals and cloth shoes was the true anthem of the revolution. Little Pow straightened his back and proudly surveyed the moving ranks. Although too many rifle barrels bristled above blue-clad shoulders, all the rifles were slung. None was grasped ready for immediate action. The presence of women and children further demonstrated the peaceful intent of the march.

"Freedom or death!" Little Pow shouted. "Victory to the revolution!"

A parade marshal glared at that violation of collective discipline, and Pow shifted his eyes to a billboard. At its top, tattered posters proclaimed the virtues of Seven Star, Martyr, and Triple Longevity cigarettes. At the bottom, other posters recommended the healing magic of Special Number-One Cough Syrup. White paint had, however, obliterated the Communist slogans painted in between only two weeks earlier.

A new scene covered the billboard. A two-story-tall hero flourished the Nationalists' white-sun flag over figures representing the evils he had felled: militarism, capitalism, and landlordism. Unappeased, he was trampling a supine Communist under one foot and kicking a bloated imperialist with the other.

The enemy was even stealing the propaganda of the Communist revolution! Little Pow looked down in dejection at his grimy feet in their straw sandals. He responded feebly when the parade marshal called out the next slogan: "Free our innocent brothers!"

What possible impression, he wondered, could words make upon the oppressers' stony hearts. Nonetheless, he shouted loudly when the procession approached the garrison headquarters. He shouted even louder when he thought of the atrocities perpetrated behind those yellow-brick walls, which were topped with broken glass and wicked spirals of barbed wire. He undid his choker collar and shouted even stridently: "Free our innocent brothers!"

Because he was so short, Pow could see only the back of the man in front of him. He was surprised when he heard a volley of rifle shots. An instant later the man in front was hurled to the cobblestones.

Little Pow then saw soldiers in Nationalist khaki working their rifle bolts and firing on their officers' command. The former warlord soldier beside him dropped silently. Pow turned to flee when the man on his right unlimbered the clumsy Mannlicher. That would-be hero was spun around by a bullet before he could level his rifle.

Little Pow dropped to the cobblestones amid slimy straw and yellow hillocks of horse manure. Lifting his head warily, he saw that the volleys had scythed the revolutionary ranks. More than a third of the marchers lay on the cobblestones—wounded, dying, or dead.

To be captured was also a sentence of death. When he rose and bolted, a rattle of shots pursued him. He hurled himself onto the cobblestones, unintentionally somersaulting.

The heavy military bullet took Little Pow in the left calf. Anaesthetized by shock, he ran on for several seconds. A hand grenade explosion flung him down.

When the pain struck, he screamed. Then darkness claimed him.

·　·　·

"So they brought you to me, Big Shot. That's all there is to tell." Tommy Howe wanted to end the tale that was agitating his patient. "Now you *must* rest!"

"All right, Dr. Tom."

"The slug and the fragments will have to come out. But there's no rush."

There was actually every reason for haste. Infection threatened. Besides, the metal splinters could rupture an artery. An X ray was essential. But tomorrow was only ten hours away. By morning the fighting would certainly have ended, and Tommy could then shift Pow to Shanghai General Hospital.

"I'm not even your servant," Little Pow whispered. "I have no claim. But you look after me!"

"You *are* a servant—a friend, too—of my sister and my . . . ah . . . Miss Joo-li. The Howe family will look after you, Big Shot."

Embarrassed by his emotion, Tommy laid the drowsy youth's hand on the quilted cotton overcoat that was his coverlet. He rose to look at his other patients. When a groaning door announced a late arrival, he shook his head wearily. Another patient at this time of night was almost too much to bear. Resignedly, he pushed aside the burlap curtain.

The kerosene lamps were flickering low, but Tommy saw khaki uniforms. The Nationalists were also bringing their wounded to him.

"Yes, sergeant!" he said peremptorily. "What is it?"

"Ha Yee-sahng? . . ." the sergeant asked in Cantonese. "Dr. Howe, are you?"

"Yes. What is it?"

"You're to come with us, Dr. Howe. Under arrest. Garrison commander's orders."

"Do you know who I am?" Tommy demanded. "You couldn't—not if you've come to arrest me."

"Son of Howe Dan-erh. Colonel in Medical Corps. Surgeon general of Sixth Corps now on detached service. That right?"

"Yes, of course. So you see, don't you . . ."

"That's the man I'm ordered to arrest. Come along, prisoner."

"And my patients? Who will look after them? Many are in critical condition."

"And *all* are Communist pigs. Let them learn to pray. Maybe Buddha will look after them."

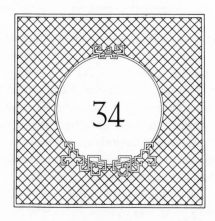

"I don't trust her," Emily declared. "Nobody can be that perfect."

"Em, you're too cynical," Julia replied. "Rosamonde Sun wants just what you want: a better China and a better deal for China's women."

"I guess that's so, Julie. But I can't warm up to her. Anyway, she's too close to the Communists. Now that the Generalissimo has seen the light, there's no excuse for Rosamonde to—"

"Em, it's not quite that clear-cut."

Julia chose her words with great care. Although she hated to mislead her friend, she had often been warned by the clandestine Apparatus against telling anyone, even Tommy, about her work for the Communist underground. She had also been warned not to let herself be identified as a Communist sympathizer. Markedly more mature than the impulsive young woman who had come ashore from the *Empress of Australia* six years earlier, Julia could now curb her normal candor. Still, she disliked dissembling.

"Look here," Emily interjected, "when the Generalissimo himself turns on the Communists and joins up with patriotic capitalists like my father, there's got to be a good reason. But Rosamonde can't see it. She's been spiteful since Dr. Sun died. She won't see that the Communists— and their Russian friends—are bad for China. Also, she's very jealous. If Mayling does marry the Generalissimo, it'll be like poison to her loving older sister Rosamonde."

"Now, Em, that marriage is still a long way off—if it ever comes off. . . . And don't forget what Rosamonde's done for the women of China."

As she spoke, Julia felt that Emily and she were like actresses reciting again the well-rehearsed lines of their well-worn argument about Rosamonde Sun while their minds dwelt on another matter. They were both intrigued by Rosamonde's public attacks on the man who might soon be her brother-in-law—and the master of China. But Emily, almost as much as herself, was obsessed by Tommy's disappearance.

On Thursday, April 28th, more than two weeks had passed since a breathless Little Pow came to the loft-apartment to beg Tommy to treat wounded workers. Like Tommy, Little Pow had vanished into the turmoil unloosed when Chiang Kai-shek and his blood brother, the Green Dragon, who was the Supreme Lord of the secret societies, attacked the Communists. The fighting was now over, and the Nationalists' grip on Greater Shanghai was unassailable. But not a word from Tommy.

"The women propagandists and agitators Rosamonde trained are fighting alongside the men," Julia continued automatically. "Now women can *demand* their rights."

"I'm not so sure of that, Julie. Cutting off long hair and making speeches is one thing. We're talking about practical politics now. If Rosamonde keeps on fighting the Gimo, she won't be able to demand anything. The Communists can't win. If she sticks with them, she won't be able to help the women's cause at all. . . ."

"I wish I were as certain as you are, Em. Don't you see . . ."

Having once thought politics boring, Julia was now fascinated by the complex struggle for China. Tommy's disappearance was a minor event amid the political upheaval from which the new China was emerging. Yet, for a moment, she did not care about politics or even about China. She only cared about Tommy. He was flesh and blood, not an abstraction like freedom or democracy. He was also a vital part of her own life, perhaps a mortal part.

During the first week after his departure with Little Pow, Julia had, of course, worried, but no more than she had worried every day since he joined the National Revolutionary Army. As Emily had stressed, Tommy could have been caught by new orders, perhaps assigned elsewhere. In any event, they would soon hear from him.

It was now more than half a month since Tommy had kissed her good-bye in the pearly dawn—and hundreds, perhaps thousands, had been killed in the massacres that followed Chiang Kai-shek's victory. Julia could not help imagining that Tommy, too, had been killed or wounded.

All efforts to find him had drawn a blank. At some risk to themselves, Emily and she had searched the warrens of Chapei and the mazes of

Hongkew. Emily had called upon her Nationalist friends and contacts. Julia had, more circumspectly, asked the Apparatus to trace him.

Nationalists and Communists had given them much the same reply: *Dr. Howe was last seen at the emergency dressing station near the General Labor Union, where the most intense fighting occurred, on the evening of April 13. Nothing is known of his whereabouts thereafter.*

Julia was harshly made to realize that she had never known either pain or sorrow before this ordeal. Beyond control, her imagination conjured terrible visions. The best she could hope was that Tommy was a captive somewhere. But she could see him lying dead among dozens of unidentified corpses. Even worse, she could see him dying in slow agony somewhere in heartless Shanghai.

"At least Tommy's disappearing has put an end to your nonsense about leaving." Emily's voice penetrated Julia's thoughts. "You haven't said another word about it. I'd say you've changed your mind."

"By no means, Em. It's made me feel even more strongly that I've got to get away. Get back to clean air and simple decency instead of all this corruption. . . . Oh, Em, do you think we'll ever see Tommy again? Sometimes I think I simply can't bear another minute of—"

"Julie, stop it!" Emily commanded sharply. "You can't sit around brooding. Come with me to the lottery. It'll take you out of yourself, and, who knows, maybe we'll learn something. . . . Anyway, we've got to show the flag."

"They could always come to us, *mon cher*," the rotund French colonel twinkled. "No Frenchman would ever disappoint a lady in distress."

Joshua Haleevie grinned down at him and replied, "My dear chap, there's no room. You've already got all the brothels in Frenchtown that'll fit. Besides, they'd soon go bust. Couldn't manage the squeeze."

The forthcoming lottery, they had already agreed, was farcical. Where else on earth would the authorities yield with immense reluctance to pressure to padlock houses of prostitution—and then arrange that only one fifth need close initially? Only Shanghai would strike such a fine balance between civic virtue and commercial enterprise. Only the International Settlement would select the first victims by drawing lots from a globe made of brass wires.

"Squeeze?" The colonel's round cheeks flushed pink like an angry baby's. "Corruption is no worse than in the Settlement, *mon cher.*"

"Far worse, as you well know." Joshua's smile dismissed the French-governed enclave, which was as corrupt as any warlord province. "A little opium is fine. But an administration crammed with addicts! Of course, the Green Dragon, the Supreme Lord of the opium traffic, *is* your honored resident."

"Not a word against Monsieur the Green Dragon!" The colonel's protest was superficially jocular. "Without him where would we be? The Bolsheviks would have overrun us all."

Joshua wondered again whether Tommy Howe had relayed his warning to Chou En-lai. He did not know, for both the commissar and the doctor had vanished into the political maelstrom. The reasonably efficient Special Branch of the Settlement Police could report only ignorance regarding their fate when he had inquired again only today. It was June 4, more than three weeks since the rightists' countercoup.

Shanghai was resilient—and callous. Less than a month after the massacres, this ribald lottery.

It should have been at the Race Club. But the committee had decided that no gambling involving houses of ill fame would sully premises hallowed by the presence of virtuous wives and daughters. The lottery had therefore been shifted to the apricot-plush Art Deco lobby of the new Empire Theater overlooking Soochow Creek.

Despite their official disapproval, several stewards of the Race Club were in attendance. At the chrome-and-crystal bar, a half dozen ruddy taipans were drinking Veuve Cliquot with two young matrons. The Emmenberg sisters were reputed to entertain their intimate friends by bathing in champagne in silver hipbaths placed on their dining-room tables. A score of prowling madams were alert for fresh custom in the predominantly masculine throng. Sleek compradors in silk long-gowns, furtive secret-society chieftains, and flashy modern businessmen dominated the Chinese contingent, which was already making complicated side bets.

Elizaveta Alexandrovna Yavalenka had wanted to attend, declaring, "I must see my fate determined!" She had chuckled a little at her own melodrama, and Joshua had persuaded her that she must not display her fears that the Ikra would be closed. That public appearance, he had stressed, might make it impossible for them to marry when, inevitably, she changed her mind, because her profession would then be a matter of public record. She had finally yielded, and Joshua had promised to telephone the instant the drawing concluded.

Neither Emily Howe nor Julia Pavernen felt any particular inhibition about attending. They were free spirits now. To Emily the great brothel lottery was a choice tidbit for the readers of the Philadelphia *Public Ledger* —to be written in the nicest possible way, of course—and a prime slice of life for her Chinese readers. Julia was candidly fascinated by this latest aberration of her beloved Shanghai; and she even forgot Tommy for a minute or two. They drifted through the throng, nodding to acquaintances and smiling at friends.

Emily's green *cheongsam*, which was daringly slit to the thigh, accentuated her high bosom and her rounded hips. The miniature white jade scepter pinned at her shoulder was set with rubies as brilliant as her fixed smile.

She was deliberately flamboyant because she wanted to quash any rumors about her brother's fate. If he was held for ransom, as she believed, public awareness of his disappearance would make it more difficult to deal with his unknown captors.

Fortunately, not ten persons knew that Tommy had returned to Shanghai at all. Richard Hollings had agreed after a brief struggle not to speculate about Tommy's whereabouts, either in print or in conversation. Moreover, Richard refused to concern himself with trivia like the brothel lottery, however racy. In his absence Emily was free to make a show of gaiety that would mask her fear for her brother.

Although Julia was neither wife nor fiancée, she too could bolster that carefree façade. She was, however, somewhat uncomfortable in the outfit on which Emily had insisted. The height of current style, it nonetheless went a little too far in every respect. Misleadingly, her flame-red sheath, flaring into pleats at her knees, was a declaration of joy, as was her string of pearls and the peacock feather in her mahogany hair. Makeup much heavier than usual camouflaged the ravages of two weeks of near-terror, relieved by sodden slumber only when Lao Zee pressed tiny black opium pills on her.

Emily drifted away to talk with a middle-aged lawyer called Mouthpiece Woo. He had good secret-society connections, and he might know something about Tommy. Standing beside Joshua, Julia smiled and smiled and smiled like a demented chorus girl and watched the gaudy spectacle.

Under iridescent chandeliers of Czechoslovak crystal, slabs of pink sandstone ridged the apricot-silk walls. Deserting the buffet of caviar, smoked salmon, oysters, and lobsters when a gong sounded, the company gathered around the brass-wire globe containing the lots: taipans and their Chinese compradors; pimps, gunmen, and ganglords; commanders, captains, and colonels. Tense with apprehension, twenty or so proprietresses of the more notable houses of pleasure were already standing before the shining globe. Inside each of the 683 brass capsules within that globe was a slip of paper bearing the name of a house.

A corpulent croupier from the Golden Wheel Club rose and bowed to half-mocking applause. He was the only one all trusted, albeit grudgingly, to draw the names. No taipan could draw because every firm had connections with the houses as landlords, creditors, insurers, or sponsors. Municipal employees were excluded because their notoriously low salaries made them eminently bribable. For various good reasons other categories were also excluded: compradors, military officers, lawyers, bankers, even physicians.

The lamps dimmed, and spotlights lanced the smoke-laden air. Their beams splashed red, blue, and yellow on the brass globe, which was spinning so fast the wires seemed to melt together.

"Little Orphan Annie's!" The croupier had drawn the first capsule. "Little Orphan Annie's is to fold!"

"Pipped at the post." A disgusted British vice-consul tore up the slip recording his bet on the survival of Orphan Annie's, which boasted: *A friendly welcome, a reasonable price, and a warm embrace!*

"Eskimo Nell's! Eskimo Nell's is for the deep six!"

A Swedish procuress shepherding two seventeen-year-old platinum-blondes grinned with delight. She not only hated the buxom Berliner who owned Eskimo Nell's, but considered the name an infringement upon her monopoly of the frozen north.

"Venus!" the croupier called out. "Venus of Lappland is going to shut up shop."

The Swede started in shock. Recovering rapidly, she began calculating how soon to put to her friend from Berlin the proposal that they club together to set up a gentlemen's boarding house.

"Hop In Woe!" The croupier entoned the name of the Chinese-owned house, but only the blank-eyed ganglords cared. He selected the next capsule, opened it, and paused almost imperceptibly before calling out, "Starlight! Starlight is wiped out!"

Accepting a goblet of champagne from Joshua, Julia was surprised to see his hand tremble and a froth of bubbles spill down his sleeve. A moment later he was smiling gaily, and she wondered if she had imagined his momentary discomfiture.

After the globe spun again, the croupier extracted another capsule. Deftly unscrewing its cover, he smoothed the rice-paper slip with his thumb before reading, "Little Redwing! Little Redwing's grounded!"

A Japanese major in dress uniform flourished his winning slip and demanded champagne for his party of seven. Though a petite geisha in a pink satin kimono put her finger to her lips, her countrymen's whoops of joy drowned out the name of the next unfortunate.

"Star . . ." The croupier appeared nonplussed, but recovered to read firmly, "Sturgeon! Virgin Sturgeon's for the high jump!"

Joshua turned abruptly to Julia and declared, "No point in hanging about all night, is there? When you've seen one drawn, you've seen them all. I'm off."

Julia waved to Emily, who was standing frozen-faced beside the lawyer called Mouthpiece Woo. She had learned nothing regarding Tommy.

"Whew, I'm glad that's over!" Joshua patted his forehead with his handkerchief when they emerged into the empty lobby. "Never again!"

Emily lifted her eyebrows, and Julia asked, "What's over, Joshua? They're still at it in there."

"And will be half the night," he acknowledged. "I suppose I can tell you two. Mum's the word, though. When he called Starlight the first time, it was bad. But when it came up again! Whew! Lucky he's such a quick-witted little chap."

Emily was still preoccupied, but Julia exclaimed, "You mean the first Starlight was really the Ikra?"

"Go to the head of the class. When the Ikra came up, he palmed the slip and substituted the one he had already written out—the Starlight Club. Then he almost called it again when Starlight really came up. Ladies, the strain has hurt me more than the payoff to my friend the croupier. However, he can now set up his own house if so inclined."

"*You,* Joshua?" Emily emerged from her revery. "You bribed the croupier not to call out the Ikra? How underhanded! How gallant!"

"Never again! I'd be better off if the Ikra was padlocked."

"Joshua, do you really believe Liz would . . ."

Emboldened by these confidences from the normally reserved Joshua, Julia almost told him she was convinced that Elizaveta would never marry him. She was saved from that indiscretion by glimpsing Donald Howe's emerald-green Rolls-Royce parked before the theater. Beside the uniformed chauffeur she saw the silver mane of Old Woo, the majordomo of Harmony Hall.

Emily dashed forward, her hands outstretched. Old Woo stepped out, majestic in his white long-gown with the green seal of the House of Howe on his breast. He took Emily into his arms for an instant. The next instant, he was again the impassive upper servant.

"*Yuelin Hsiu-jyeh, ho-jyeow . . .*" He spoke softly. "Miss Emily, it's been so long. It seems even longer than when you were in America."

"You've come to take me back?" Emily asked eagerly. "They want to see me? My parents want to see me?"

The crusading feminist had given way to the loving daughter, who was agonizing because she was not also dutiful. Nowadays Emily infrequently talked about the guilt—and deprivation—she felt because her stubborn clinging to Richard Hollings had forced her parents to disown her. But her anguish was now written on her face.

"Miss Emily, I have *not* come for you." Old Woo dropped his voice so that the Small Mistress's barbarian friends would not overhear him. "Whatever they wish, your esteemed parents *cannot* send for you. Not until you give up your foolish defiance. But they miss you—terribly."

"Then what have you come for?" Emily was almost brusque in her disappointment. "Is it something about Tommy? Is there news of Tommy?"

"I'm sorry, Miss Emily." Old Woo reluctantly crushed that new hope. "I have only been told to bring your foreign friend to see the master and the mistress. She will come, won't she?"

"Oh, she'll come all right. But why, Old Woo? You must know. You know everything."

"I really couldn't say . . . not even for you. I just don't know."

When Julia entered the circular reception room of Harmony Hall, she regretted having humored Emily by wearing the frivolous red dress to the lottery. Although the *cheongsams* of emancipated Chinese ladies showed their beautiful legs, Emily's mother would undoubtedly be shocked by the expanse of thigh her short skirt displayed no matter how carefully she sat. She was even more conscious of the valley between her breasts bared by the V-neckline. Not even the most daring Chinese women showed their bosoms.

Taboos, like fashion itself, were a matter of taste. She feared, however, that Eurydice and Donald Howe would believe her brief scarlet dress demonstrated that she was untouched by Tommy's disappearance —and perhaps unworthy of him. Yet why should she care what the Howes thought? They would never sanction Tommy's marrying any woman who was foreign and, therefore, odious.

If she herself should eventually wish to marry him! Emily and Dick's stormy relationship was no testimonial for life with a Chinese spouse. Tommy was, of course, totally different. Still, it was not just because Emmy was high-strung. Chronic guilt over her love affair with a foreigner also made her irritable. Would Tommy, too, feel guilty? For that matter would he still want to marry her when he returned?

Donald Howe was rotund in a gray cotton long-gown when he rose from the purple-flowered cretonne sofa. His expression was bland, but he repeatedly wiped his black-rimmed spectacles. Eurydice's smile was tentative, much outshone by the diamond-rimmed lavaliere watch on her blue satin bosom, and she blotted her forehead with a scrap of lace. Her hesitant greeting conveyed the same message as her husband's excessively firm handshake: the Howes were almost as ill at ease as Julia.

Traditional Chinese etiquette, however, ruled. Eurydice poured straw-pale tea and offered pastries filled with crystallized dates. Donald punctilliously inquired after not only Julia's health and her Uncle John's, but the health of her parents, whom he had never seen. After summoning her urgently, the Howes appeared unhurried.

Eurydice finally asked, "My miserable daughter? She is well?"

Touched by that breach of etiquette, Julia told the anxious mother how Emily spent her days. Somehow she managed to omit any reference to Richard Hollings, who took up a good part of Emily's days and a greater part of her nights.

"Emily loves you deeply," she concluded. "I know she misses you terribly!"

"Tell her—" Eurydice began, but Donald broke in: "You need not tell our disobedient daughter that she has broken our hearts. But you *must* tell her something else."

Although she resented his autocratic tone, Julia nodded.

"We must have Yuelin's assistance," he continued. "She is our only remaining hope of finding Thomas. Otherwise . . ."

Hearing Eurydice's muffled sob, Julia silently choked back her own tears. Clawing in her clutch bag for a handkerchief, her fingers encountered her ivory cigarette holder. She jammed a Chesterfield into the mouthpiece, and gratefully accepted the lit match Donald offered with obvious disapproval. Though the smoke stung her eyes and throat, she then listened with apparent calm.

". . . just intimations, but it is our only information," Donald said. "It is possible that Generalissimo Chiang Kai-shek is holding Thomas. Our last report came from a wounded coolie who says he saw them take Thomas away. The men were Nationalist soldiers."

"Why can't you ask the Generalissimo?" Julia was still puzzled by Chinese indirection. "Or T. V. Soong. He *is* minister of finance, after all!"

"T.V.?" Donald expelled a frustrated breath, and Eurydice interjected, "He's only interested in one thing: extorting money from every Chinese capitalist. It takes a lot to keep his precious Generalissimo going. You know—"

"Fifty million from Shanghai already—and no end in sight." Donald was only momentarily diverted from his son's fate by the threat to his pocketbook. "But that doesn't matter. Only Thomas is important. The *only* way is through Mayling Soong. Chiang Kai-shek cannot deny the pleas of the lady he wants to make his wife. Now Yuelin must go to May and—"

"You really think May Soong will do it for Emmy? May's a pretty tough cookie."

Donald continued as if she had not spoken. ". . . go to May and beg her to intercede. Also, she may tell May that a million dollars is available to—"

"Bribe May Soong?" Julia interjected. "Is that a good idea?"

"A contribution, not a bribe. Generalissimo Chiang Kai-shek needs money to pay his armies and finance his new government. A contribution is my patriotic duty. But I cannot embarrass the Generalissimo by approaching him directly. That would appear to be unseemly pressure, you see."

Emily's heart hesitated, skipped, and then raced as she entered the office in the *Daily News* building with Adam, the mastiff, on her heels. Richard was worth it, she told herself, worth even the break with her parents. A lean figure with a smudge on his forehead where his ink-stained fingers had pushed back his rebellious forelock, he looked like a cavalier on a disputed battlefield. He was not often comforting, and he was certainly not dependable. But he was always exciting.

"Bloody animal!" he intoned, and Adam rolled on his back in ecstasy, yipping in a falsetto ridiculous for his great size. "Bloody, bloody animal!"

Emily felt her pulse quicken when he turned and kissed her lightly.

"Hullo, darling!" Richard said. "Back from the knocking-shop auction already? How'd it go?"

"Amusing, but I left early." His insouciance jarred upon her. "What are you writing tonight?"

"The Generalissimo's mopping up the Reds everywhere. Hundreds, maybe thousands, already dead. And he's cobbling together his new regime in Nanking."

"Considering your gift for sensationalism"—she laughed to show she was teasing—"you really should have covered the lottery."

"Are you writing it?"

"I guess not. Too hard to explain to the sober citizens of Philadelphia —and too risqué. Definitely not!"

"Definitely yes! My dear girl, write it as farce or a moral homily, but write it. Titilate your staid Philadelphians. Sex and gambling, courtesans and champagne for the Benighted States of America, a country so hypocritical it outlaws both." Richard grinned at his own eloquence. "Anyway, the political story here is getting too complicated. I'm sure I'm losing thousands of readers."

Emily was shocked. She could not imagine her country's epic struggle toward unity being anything less than compelling reading to Americans and Europeans. Nonetheless, she countered: "Then why don't you write about the lottery? You love poking fun at the stupid heathen."

"Em, the big story's running down here. I'll have to start traveling quite soon."

"What's happening in Japan that's so fascinating?" she demanded. "Or in Southeast Asia or the East Indies? No big stories there!"

"They're fresh, Em—and different. Something new is essential if I'm to—"

"I know what it is, Richard." Her anger flared. "You're fed up with the rambunctious Chinese—*all* of us. The revolution is too untidy for your imperialist taste. The natives are getting uppity."

"Em, please don't whip yourself into a rage. It's just that my reporting badly needs some variety. Not just Communists and Nationalists, commissars and warlords, battles and massacres. China's not the center of the world, you know."

Although touched by his smile, which was at once defiant and wistful, she hardened her heart against his charm and continued: "Center of the world or not, I know you're afraid of the next stage in China. You've begun thinking like the taipans. You won't admit that Chinese brains and Chinese industry make the Settlement prosper. And you'd hate to see a strong central government leading China to prosperity. You're afraid of the power of a united China. . . ."

Richard was daunted by her outburst. He was also marginally amused. He knew his Emily, and he loved her—on his own terms. The sophisticated career woman could sometimes become a gawky American college girl or a shy Confucian lady. But the crusading patriot was the hardest to deal with.

"That's nonsense, Em!" He played to her sense of humor. "Nor do I believe the earth's flat—and I've never smuggled an ounce of opium."

"You would have, Dick, if you could." She smiled despite herself. "All right, you're not that bad. But the birth of a strong and democratic China is inevitable."

"Inevitable, woman? Not in my time. One day, perhaps, but not this decade or the next. Not when your civil wars have five or six sides all fighting each other. Not when China is so inefficient—"

"Inefficient! Why China was—"

"Was efficient in the past, but is not remotely efficient today. Your Yank friends call total disorganization *a Chinese fire drill.* The U.S. Navy goes one better: *a fire drill in a Chinese whorehouse.* So please spare me your . . ."

Richard broke off appalled. He felt as if he were falling through the air. He might have stepped confidently onto solid pavement and had it disintegrate under his feet. He had in the past used stronger language to Emily—and she to him. But he knew that his heavy-handed irony regarding her people was this time disastrous.

"I never knew you were a racist!" She spoke before he could frame a convincing apology. "I should have seen it earlier. Just an old-fashioned bigot. How odd!"

"That was a bit strong, wasn't it?" He tried hard. "But it was only a joke that got out of hand, no more. A joke in very bad taste. Em, you know—"

"Tell me, Richard, suppose I said *yes* right this minute." Her tone was still excessively reasonable. "Would you marry me tomorrow?"

"I'd want to, but I couldn't, Em," he rejoined. "We need time to post the banns. That sort of thing, you know."

"I'm not joking, Richard." She turned to stare through the window at the Bund. "Would you? I *am* asking now. After all your protestations, will you?"

"Tomorrow?" He smiled sheepishly. "You know that's impossible."

"There's my answer, isn't it?" She was soft-spoken—and implacable. "Are you tired of me, too? Not just China, but me, too?"

"Darling, I assure you I love you deeply. And I'm *not* tired of China, though what that has to do with. . . . I haven't had a chance to tell you, but I must take that trip very soon. However, just as soon as I get back from—"

"You needn't look for me when you get back."

"Emily, darling, nothing's changed. This quarrel's only a fantasy. It's all in your mind."

"Take your damned trip!" she exploded. "Leave tomorrow! Tonight, for all I care!"

"I shall!" With some relief Richard gave way to his anger at her carping. "I'll do that . . . and I'll start off right now!"

He snatched up his briefcase, yanked his jacket from the clothes-tree, and slammed the door so hard the glass panel trembled. Emily stared stolidly at the strings of lights that outlined the ships at the man-of-war buoys. Beside her, Adam Schall made a curiously uncanine noise in his throat, half warble and half purr. When she did not respond, he nudged her with his shoulder.

Emily laid her hand on his big head and felt the hard bone beneath the silken coat. When she finally spoke, her voice was preternaturally calm. "Thank you, Adam. I know you're here and you'll always be here when—"

The telephone shrilled, and she lifted the handset to hear Julia sounding as disturbed as herself. "Emily, it is you? When will you be back? I've got to talk to you."

35

JULY 17, 1927

"If there were any word of Tommy, I would have told you," Joshua said. "He might just as well have dropped off the edge of the world."

"I was afraid so," Elizaveta said, adding in velvet tones, "And the other thing. Extraordinary! Almost unbelievable!"

Joshua Haleevie looked up with a self-deprecating smile from the cocktail he was concocting at the white lacquered liquor cabinet. He was almost thirty-five, and Elizaveta felt he had never been more attractive. His royal blue dressing gown and the slight frosting on his sideburns dramatized his light blue eyes. Before replying he added a measure of Cointreau to the brandy and the lemon juice in the cocktail shaker.

"Thank you, my dear," he finally said. "I do enjoy a heartfelt tribute. May I observe that your own performance was brilliant?"

"Not *that,* my beloved." Elizaveta grimaced delicately at his heavy-handed humor. "Well, yes, I suppose *that,* too. My compliments to you as well. But I was actually talking about Emily and Richard. They're terribly interesting."

He eyed her appreciatively before giving her the cue she wanted. Her blue-black hair fell loose over her shoulders in the privacy of the mint-and-cream sitting room atop the Ikra. Her eyes, the blue so deep they appeared black, were still as soft as they had been in the big bed in the next room. The crystalline light of early evening in mid-June spilled through the split-bamboo blinds and glowed on her scarlet dressing gown.

"What about Em and Dick?" Joshua asked lazily. "They seem to be getting along famously. Quite a change that."

"Precisely, my love. They used to be so tense I could almost see the sparks fly."

"What's cured them?"

"Cured? Oh, they're not really cured. This calm can't last. Only a couple of weeks ago they had a terrible fight. He walked out."

"Together again, though, aren't they?"

"I gather the fight cleared the air. They're easier together now. They told me separately. He said he'd been childish. She said it was infantile of her to take out her worries on him. Both swore—"

"Then what's the trouble? Why are you so pessimistic?"

"The sparks have vanished, Joshua. They're *too* comfortable together."

"Come now, Bess. We're comfortable together." He was deliberately dense. "What's wrong with that?"

"We shall see. You know, there are times when I'm definitely uncomfortable with you. Thank God!"

Still playing the bluff cavalry officer, Joshua muttered, "Funny thing to say, that."

Elizaveta acknowledged his buffoonery by rolling her eyes. She sipped the amber cocktail and slipped a Murad into her cigarette holder. Blowing out a plume of scented smoke, she asked meditatively, "Josh, do you ever wonder? What will it be like in twenty years? Possibly thirty?"

"Constantly, my love. And I'm terrified of growing old with Charlotte Gubbai. But I may have no choice. My father is pressing me, and, quite candidly, I don't fancy looking for another job."

Elizaveta was not offended, for she had no right to be offended. Joshua now assumed that she would never marry him. He had pleaded too often and had been rejected too firmly. He now assumed that he would in time marry the eminently suitable Jewish heiress his parents had chosen. He knew he would always love the unsuitable Russian aristocrat who was his own unalterable choice.

"Poor dear!" Elizaveta finally remarked. "Though it is the best of both worlds, isn't it? Charlotte and her shekels—with me on the side."

"Bess, you know damned well I don't want it that way. But you don't give me much choice, do you?"

"Joshua, have you ever thought"—she paused tantalizingly—"thought what it would be like to grow old with me?"

"Often, my love. I firmly intend to grow old with you—no matter who I marry."

"Then the prospect isn't utterly revolting?"

"Revolting?" He snorted. "How you can even ask such—"

"Joshua, sometimes I wonder." Gazing at the dark smoke spiraling from her cigarette, she pursued her thought. "Joshua, do you really want . . . That is, do you still want to marry me?"

"Only for the sake of poor Charlotte Gubbai." He could not take her seriously. "Only to relieve that foolish virgin of the affliction of a husband like me."

"Joshua, forget about Charlotte. Do think seriously how it would be. Married to me, I mean"

"Heaven when we're at home—sheer bliss! But outside, constant jealousy! You arouse too much admiration." He looked at her quizzically and asked, "What's this all about, Bess? Are you just testing the water? Or are you seriously considering putting a toe in?"

"I'm not quite sure, darling. I really don't know. Perhaps I'm just wondering."

Alone in the loft apartment except for Adam, Julia bleakly contemplated the dusk glowing in the high window above the rosewood table. She had sent Lao Zee away, for she could no longer bear the amah's heavy silences and profound sighs. That melodramatic sympathy hurt too much when she yearned for news of Tommy. She ached to see him again, and she feared she never would.

Somewhat to her surprise, she missed Little Pow almost as much, although in a different way. The youth had been part of her life every day for five years, as Tommy had not. She had grown even more accustomed to Tommy's absence after he left to go campaigning. Enthralled by the lingering twilight, she was turning to point out its sad beauty to Little Pow, rather than to Tommy.

But she thought only of Tommy while the evening slowly drew on night's black crepe. Her ebullient temperament kept her from total despair, although almost three months had passed since he disappeared into the maw of the city. Yet soon, perhaps very soon, it would become impossible to believe Tommy was still alive. Donald Howe would otherwise have had some further scraps of news in return for his lavish bribes and his promises of extravagant rewards.

Tommy could well have been executed among scores of captives. In the frantic days succeeding the countercoup, the rightists had processed their prisoners like a butcher stuffing suet-speckled Cantonese sausages. If he had been executed then, she would never know of his death.

How long, she wondered, should she wait before booking the passage home? How long could she wait?

If Tommy was gone, nothing any longer bound her to China, which had become detestable to her. And if Tommy was alive, what then? She was only waiting to see him, she answered herself. Then she would yield to her parents' wishes and go back to Plattsburg for a visit. Would she afterward return to Shanghai if she could? She simply did not know.

Julia was suddenly numb. Blessedly, she felt nothing. She could sometimes forget for two or three minutes that Tommy had almost certainly been immolated in the cauldron of the revolution. The return of feeling was a snake coiling around her heart, its scales cold and rasping. She would do almost anything to be sure—and anything at all to save Tommy if he still lived.

Julia grimaced wryly when she remembered her pleas to Mayling Soong. Emily had insisted that they both call on the youngest daughter of the redoubtable House of Soong. Mayling was in love with Generalissimo Chiang Kai-shek, who had just formally asked her formidable mother, Mammie Soong, for her hand in marriage. A young woman in love, Emily had believed, would sympathize deeply with the anguish of another young woman who was deeply in love. May was still dewy-eyed, although a family council had rejected the Generalissimo's suit. May *knew* she would overcome that opposition, although her mother swore that no daughter of hers would ever marry a pagan like Chiang Kai-shek. Besides, May liked Americans.

Familiar from previous visits, the Soongs' mansion on Seymour Road behind the Bund was relatively modest. A few English-language books complemented boxed editions of the Confucian classics, and ox-blood porcelain vases of the Manchu Dynasty towered above blue-and-white porcelains of the Ming Dynasty in glass-fronted display cases. Intricately crocheted antimacassars protected the easy chairs and sofa of olive-green cut plush. A big-horned Victrola squatted on a side table inlaid with mother-of-pearl.

All the clichés of middle-class American households were on display: a stack of *National Geographic Magazine*s displayed yellow-framed covers beside a bigger stack of *Saturday Evening Post*s. Topmost was a Norman Rockwell drawing of a freckle-faced boy dangling a fishing line with a bent pin for a hook and patting a shaggy dog. As Emily said, all the Soongs liked America.

May served coffee and brownies. She was, as always, totally self-possessed—and slightly condescending. Her dress of navy-blue crepe, odd for a spring afternoon, was very loose, almost baggy. The doyenne of the emancipated women of Shanghai seemed shy of showing her figure. She was apparently still swayed by the old male-dictated concept of feminine modesty.

Emerging from the enforced seclusion of the female quarters and casting off the enveloping garments that had made them appear sexless were major triumphs for Chinese women. They were now free to make themselves as attractive as they pleased. But May seemed disinclined to celebrate that victory appropriately.

Essentially serious like Emily, May was—again like Emily—a true daughter of the frivolous International Settlement. The two happily exchanged gossip while sipping black coffee from American mugs and toying with the brownies. Guiltily adding cream to her coffee, Julia looked at her closest friend as if seeing her for the first time. The glittering creature with the wide-set eyes, who concealed her laughter behind her cupped hand, was virtually a stranger—a very Chinese stranger. Emily was a wholly different person when she was with May, and Julia was momentarily jealous of their intimacy. Since neither seemed eager to get to the point, she reluctantly took the initiative and asked for May's help in finding Tommy. Rather perversely, May turned to Emily.

"What do you expect *me* to do?" She was almost petulant. "Especially when you say you've tried every possible avenue."

"May, dear, just ask the Gimo." Emily was as forthright. "He's the only one we haven't approached."

"What makes you think—" May demanded.

"Oh, we don't think he's involved!" Julia thrust in her reply. "But he can find out—if anyone can. All I ask, May, is to learn the truth."

"Well, I'll see what I can do," Mayling conceded after a pause. "Of course, Gimo's hard to get hold of. Always in and out of Shanghai. But I know how you feel, Julie. And I always liked Tommy. I'll try."

Since that afternoon weeks earlier, May had, however, provided not a scrap of hope. She returned Emily's insistent phone calls, but she had no news. She only reported that Chiang Kai-shek had, rather maddeningly, said he would try to look into the matter when he had a moment free. Julia had taken what comfort she could from the Generalissimo's reported remark "I like that young Dr. Howe."

Adam, the mastiff, placed his head on Julia's thigh, and she automatically stroked him. Reliving her fruitless quest, her thoughts began to chase themselves in circles. Incessant speculation regarding Tommy's fate had worn a groove in her brain. Like a cracked Victrola record, the unremitting litany began: *We would've heard if he had died. . . . No, they'd never tell us. . . . But he'd somehow get word to us if he is alive. . . . Yet how could he?*

With a wrench, Julia turned from that pointless round of conjecture to consider once again the common woes of all China.

Since mid-April, two antagonistic "national revolutionary governments" had been fighting each other without mercy. Never mind that the warlords were again stirring in North China. The left-wing Nationalist government in Wuhan and the right-wing Nationalist government in Nanking appeared determined to destroy each other.

In Wuhan, Comintern agent Michael Borodin raged: "We must purge our revolutionary ranks before the revolution can succeed. Forget the Northern Expedition. We must march against Chiang Kai-shek immediately."

Generalissimo Chiang was, however, already wiping out Communist organizations throughout South China. Moreover, the Wuhan regime, headed by the man called Lucifer, was itself on the verge of collapse because its supporters were defecting. They had learned that the Soviet Union, which was Lucifer's sponsor, was prepared to sacrifice his left-liberal regime in order to keep in with the dominant Generalissimo—just as the Soviets had in the past virtually sacrificed the Chinese Communists in order to keep in with the Nationalists.

Although those events were catastrophic from Julia's point of view, she preferred to think about politics and not dwell on gloomy surmises regarding Tommy. But her mind defied her will, and her thoughts again whizzed around the same groove: *Tommy isn't dead because there's no word of his death. . . . But why not even a whisper of news? . . . Why no demand for ransom and no one offering to sell information? . . . Yet it's already more than two months since he . . .*

The telephone mercifully broke in. Julia pushed Adam away and rose from the sofa. She had sat so long with the dog's head heavy on her thigh that her left leg was numb. When she lifted her foot, she felt the excruciating stabs of returning circulation. She hobbled to the instrument.

"Julie!" Emily's voice was high with excitement. "Is that you?"

"Who else, Em?"

"It's wonderful news! Just wonderful! Tommy's alive! He's really alive! No question about it! . . . Julie? Julie, do you understand?"

Julia could not reply. Clutching the table with one hand and the telephone with the other, she slid slowly down to sit on the floor. A big paw touched her arm, but she could only take in the single glorious reality: *Tommy is alive!*

"How is he? Is he hurt? Is he well?" The questions now poured out. "Where is he?"

"He's all right, but—"

"Emmy, I can't believe it! It's the most wonderful news I ever heard!" Julia broke in. "Who told you? Where is he? Why hasn't he—"

"Now Julie, just a minute!" Emily laughed. "I can't answer all those questions at once."

"Then just tell me your own way. But first tell me again that he's alive and well."

"All right, Julie. Tommy is alive and well. That's all I really know. That's all May Soong could tell me."

"May finally came through?"

"Like a lady . . . finally. He's been held . . . he's still held . . . by the garrison command, so the Gimo didn't—"

"When can he come home, Emmy? What do they want? Ransom or what? Why are they holding—"

"Give me a chance, Julie. May has no idea when they'll let him go. She can't even say for sure that they *will* let him go. And she doesn't know why they're holding him. But she promised to get after the Gimo to find out. We must be patient."

"That's crazy Em! The Gimo's the boss, isn't he? Why can't he set Tommy free?"

"The Gimo is more like first among equals, Julie. He's not the absolute boss. Not yet, if ever. So he's got to work around it."

"Oh, God, I hope so! I pray so! I couldn't bear it. Now that I know Tommy's alive, not to . . ."

36

JULY 19, 1927

Outside on the circular terrace under the faint stars, the stagnant air reeked of mildew and sweat. Even in that citadel of privilege the French Club, the slow descent of night promised little relief from the steambath atmosphere of mid-July. Everyone who could had already fled to the cool beaches of North China or the brisk hills of Central China, abandoning the stragglers to stew in their own boredom. Among missionaries, only the Jesuits still tended their flock and their observatory. Among businessmen, only raw juniors and a few unfortunate seniors remained, watchmen over a half-deserted city.

Blossoming like a parasitic tropical growth, the heat sapped vitality. The overwhelming humidity hobbled even the rickshaw coolies, whose muscles were parched oak-hard by opium. They gasped for oxygen, and their rhythmic trot dwindled to an ungainly shamble.

Husbands who had looked forward to a season of freedom from wives and children sat lethargically at the round metal tables on the terrace and longed for the summer to end. Most had for a week or two reveled in the strange perfumes and the strange textures of strange bedfellows. But the heat pressed down on libertine and virtuous alike, smothering all desire in its woolly, sodden embrace. Some contrite husbands planned chaste visits to the Olympia Cinema, which advertised a new invention that was ideal for Shanghai: air-conditioning. But most glanced enviously at the table where two men sat with three women who were manifestly not hired companions.

A number of the summer bachelors recognized Elizaveta Alexandrovna Yavalenka. Relieved of the vigilance of censorious wives, none thought her presence at the French Club untoward. Her aristocratic charm and her growing wealth would have made her wholly acceptable even without her powerful sponsor.

No one, of course, challenged Joshua Haleevie idly. His father's wealth gave him great influence, and he was playing his own hand in municipal politics. Moreover, his astute maneuvering in the booming property market was making him independently wealthy.

Joshua appeared to be no more than a nonchalant idler who happened to have a taste for culture as well as pleasure. Few knew how ruthless he was when his vital interests were threatened. Fewer knew of his commitments to the welfare of his fellow Shanghailanders: educating the promising children of coolies and servants; supporting destitute White Russians; providing artificial limbs for maimed Chinese soldiers; and sponsoring medical students. Hardly anyone knew of his vital role in intelligence-gathering.

Seated opposite him, Emily Howe twisted around her finger the yellow straw from the Tom Collins that had been brought to her by Joshua's boyhood playmate Fatty Woo, the waiters' captain. She wondered again how Elizaveta and Joshua got on so well that even their disagreements led to laughter rather than tears.

Perhaps because both had been deeply wounded: he by the Great War and she by the Bolshevik Revolution. Of course, Joshua was hardly the charming—and feckless—son of privilege he appeared. Nor was Elizaveta the callous procuress she often played to hide her vulnerability. Emily's thoughts became tangled: Liz *was* actually a procuress, and Joshua *was* a playboy in his leisure hours.

She smiled at Richard when the Filipino combo swung into "Tea for Two." He nodded toward the dance floor, but she was still snarled in her own thoughts. The masks Elizaveta and Joshua wore concealed other masks. Their complexity was not merely Byzantine but Japanese. Did their unvarying gentleness with each other camouflage a lack of passion? Richard and she were again oscillating between ecstasy and sour quarrels. Love on a trapeze was exhilarating, but it was also dangerous.

Emily uncoiled the drinking straw and leaned toward Richard to whisper, "Dance with Julie first. She needs cheering up."

Richard shrugged, and Emily read his meaning clearly: *No use trying. Julie will only beg off. She's a frightful drag nowadays.* Richard's own emotions were powerful but shallow. He was impatient with Julia's deep grief over Tommy.

"Tea for two and two for tea; it's me for you and you for me." The

Filipino singer possessed a glossy megaphone and patent-leather hair, an orange-striped blazer and white flannel slacks. "A boy for you, and a girl for me. Oh, can't you see how happy we will be."

The familiar words evoked the familiar glow. When Emily rose to dance, the top of her head was level with Richard's eyes. Her fragility was set off by a white georgette dress with a deep V in back. She shimmered under the colored bulbs strung above the dance floor. Joshua Haleevie recalled the poet's description of the execution of China's most celebrated—and most corrupt—imperial concubine: "She shone forth, lily-pale, between tall avenues of spears to die." Emily, however, looked as remote and pure as a vestal virgin.

Julia was miserable over Tommy's suffering at the hands of his Fascist jailers, but she tried for a light touch. Striving for gaiety, she appeared frenetic, almost manic in her pale blue linen dress. Laughing too loud and too long, she crammed Chesterfield after Chesterfield into her ivory holder, stubbing each out after a few drags and lighting another.

Joshua Haleevie was still trying to help, but he had little leverage in an essentially Chinese matter. Richard Hollings had not tried very hard to use his influence as the correspondent of two powerful newspapers. Other attempts had yielded no results: her Uncle Jack, One-Arm Sutton, the American consul general, and the commander of the U.S. Navy's Yangtze Patrol. Elizaveta had introduced her to municipal officers, magistrates, bankers, and gangsters. But she had learned no more.

Her comrades in the Chinese Communist Party cared, but they had too many troubles of their own. Relentlessly harried by the foreign police and the right-wing Nationalists' secret police, the Apparatus could offer little but sympathy to the foreign girl friend of a rich man's son. Itself in disarray, the Apparatus could not even locate Tommy, much less arrange his escape.

Julia was therefore besieging the new right-wing Nationalist government of Greater Shanghai, determined to win official admission that Tommy was a captive.

There was no question about her leaving before Tommy was freed. Often she felt humiliated by her vain entreaties. Yet she sometimes reproached herself for withholding the favors some gentlemen hinted could alter everything. In her black moods she feared that her strenuous efforts were making matters worse for Tommy. She was like a rescuer whose clumsy spade starts a landslide and buries trapped miners even deeper.

Julia looked up from the heap of butts in the ashtray and intercepted Elizaveta's glance. Seductive in a calf-length shift of cream lawn over a slim underdress of deeper cream pongee, the Russian had pulled her plaited black hair through a diamond clasp above her right ear. She wore no other jewelry. Amid that calculated splendor, her dark blue eyes, sometimes as cold as the Siberian tundra, were now warm with concern.

"We have in Russian a saying." Elizaveta assumed a heavy accent. "Moscow, she was not built in a day. This is meaning . . ."

"Robert Bruce and the spider," Joshua interposed. "If at first you don't succeed . . ."

"Put your nose to the grindstone." Julia hectically capped the twisted maxims. "But my poor nose is practically worn to a nubbin."

"And a charming nubbin it is." Joshua laughed. "Now Julie, I promise you, it'll be all right. They can't really keep—"

"The madam herself, as I live and breathe." The speaker was unmistakably English and unmistakably drunk. "Madame Ya'lenka, isn't it? What in the world are *you* doing here, madam?"

Elizaveta looked up with a forced smile, and Joshua looked down at his hands. She had dealt with so many obstreperous clients that the four young officers in the khaki shorts and bush jackets of Britain's Indian Army should pose no difficulty. Joshua feared that by intervening he would inflame the officers' tempers and, perhaps, force a confrontation.

"Two of your girls, I presume." The ringleader was a burly blond lieutenant. "And *what* are they doing here, madam?"

"Enjoying the cool evening, Lieutenant," Elizaveta answered equably. "Perhaps you'd leave us to it. I don't know you."

"But *I* know you. *Everybody* knows you run the best little knocking shop in Shanghai. Come'n have a dance. These little ladies, good crumpet, madam?"

"Why don't you sit down like good chaps?" Elizaveta was placatory —and evidently desperate. "I'll send you some champagne. But please don't—"

"Tart's holiday, eh? Not dancin'? Here you are. This ought to cover it."

The lieutenant fumbled a handful of banknotes from his pocket. Contemptuously counting out crumpled ten-dollar bills, he flicked them onto the table.

"There we are, all present and correct," he said. "A hundred 'n' ten Chink dollars—as near as damnit a month's pay. That'd better cover it."

Joshua was already pushing back his chair when the lieutenant grasped Elizaveta's arm and Julia's shoulder.

"Let them go, Lieutenant," Joshua directed. "Deal with me."

The truculent lieutenant blinked and drawled, "Oh, the Jewboy, is it? Well, you can't hide behind Daddy's moneybags. So . . ."

The roundhouse blow grazed Joshua's cheekbone and set him back for an instant. He stepped forward, his fists raised to protect his face, and the next blow caught him in the stomach. Gasping for air, he sidestepped and flicked a stinging fist at his opponent's eye.

"Hit me from behind!" the lieutenant bellowed. "Dirty Jewboy. Get him, lads!"

The four subalterns surrounded Joshua. His arms were bent behind him, and the ringleader drew back a steel-capped boot to kick him in the groin.

"That'll do! You're a disgrace! Call yourselves officers?"

The voice of command halted the assault. The subalterns turned to face Richard Hollings on the dance floor.

"Who's this, now?" The blond lieutenant recovered his poise. "Lads, we can cope with two of them just as easy!"

Restraint having failed, Richard stepped backward and raised his fists defensively. Seizing the diversion, Joshua tore free, whirled and drove his fist into the mouth of one lieutenant who had been holding his arms.

The ringleader roared in fury and leaped at Richard, both feet leaving the ground. He was snatched in midair and carried away by four white-coated waiters. Directed by Joshua's old friend Fatty Woo, a dozen waiters lifted the belligerent officers and carried them off.

Fatty Woo apologized profusely. Plump cheeks shaking, he snapped his fingers for a magnum of Joshua's favorite champagne: Krug 1912.

Emily was appalled by the sudden violence. Realizing how helpless the three women had been, she felt disdain for female weakness. Julia was obviously shaken, and Elizaveta trembled with humiliation.

"Is this what you want, Joshua?" she asked bitterly. "What you *truly* want?"

"Not every night, darling," he replied lightly. "A punch-up once a week is enough. Are you planning regular bouts?"

"Not quite, my dear." Smiling at his levity, Elizaveta nonetheless spoke earnestly. "Do you want to live this way? Do you really want a wife who provokes insults—and forces fights?"

"My darling Bess, I want *you.*" Joshua leaned across the table to cup her chin in his hand. "If trouble comes with you, I don't have much choice, do I?"

"You're quite sure? You've seen again how disgusting it can be."

He nodded and said, "I'm absolutely sure!"

"In that case . . ." Elizaveta took his hand in both her own. "In that case . . . I will."

With exclamations and endearments almost unintelligible to male ears, Emily and Julia welcomed Elizaveta's return to the community of respectable women. Joshua silently thanked God for the drunken subalterns and for the lottery, whose combined effect had frightened his mistress. He also thanked God that his parents had pressed Charlotte Gubbai upon him—and thus brought Elizaveta to her senses. Rather than see him marry his parents' choice, she had at last decided to marry him herself.

Joshua did not deceive himself. He saw the flaws in Elizaveta's love for him, if conventional love it was at all. She had been so battered by fate that she prized security above all else. She had been taught self-reliance so painfully that she could not permit herself to depend entirely upon any other person, not even him. The Ikra therefore represented not just independence but her only true security. If the Ikra had not been mortally threatened, Elizaveta could not have brought herself to accept his proposal.

He also directed the same clear logic upon his love for her, which he *knew* was true love. Nonetheless, he might not have persisted in his protracted courtship if she were not also his only sanctuary. The melancholy that overcame him from time to time was lightened by her presence. Since Elizaveta could dispel his near-suicidal depression, he was determined to bind her to him by marriage. She was his solace—and his joy.

Gingerly rubbing his bruised chest, the prospective bridegroom lifted his beaker of champagne. His tone was almost reverent when he said, "The bride! A toast to the bride! Now and always!"

His eyebrows knotted in concentration, Richard inserted the red Plymouth into the stream of traffic on Kiukiang Road. Despite the sluggish heat of the evening, the convertible was almost comfortable with its canvas top folded back to catch the breeze. The cramped cockpit seemed spacious to Richard and Emily after they dropped Julia at the apartment.

Julia had refused to join them for dinner. After they had left Joshua and Elizaveta, she had said she must prepare for her morning class at the Customs College. She was also very tired, and she had to be up at six to read the news on Station XMHA. Three excuses when one would do! Obviously she simply did not want to burden them with her misery.

Although Emily would have preferred a quiet meal closer to home,

Richard wanted to dine at Jeff Geoffreys's St. Andrew's Café. He had recently developed a penchant for noisy nightclubs and their nervous gaiety.

"That *was* odd," he said. "Very odd, wasn't it?"

Emily did not comment.

"Most odd, that lightning betrothal!" He cavalierly cut between a double-decker trolley and a man-drawn cart laden with cotton bales. "Who'd have thought old Joshua would be so foolish? He *is* an Old Harrovian—even if his ancestors did come from the ghettos of Baghdad."

Emily's right foot in its silver slipper involuntarily pressed down hard. The convertible's nose pointed straight at the uniformed driver of a Chrysler limousine, but Richard's suede shoe was still heavy on the accelerator. The Chrysler's brakes squealed, the driver was flung against the dashboard, and Richard triumphantly wheeled the runabout into the traffic on Nanking Road.

"Getting engaged is hardly foolish," Emily murmured. "I think it's wonderful for them both."

"Rash!" he exploded. "Devilish rash!"

"They've always been in love," Emily said. "Since the moment they met. The only surprise is that it took her so long. Otherwise, it's . . ."

Emily's voice trailed off. Her attempt to lighten the atmosphere was being met with sulky silence. Had Richard, she wondered, had too much to drink? Why else his volatile mood? Why else his testiness and his recklessness? But she could not reclaim the wheel of her own car without enraging him.

Although he loved the red convertible, he would not buy a car of his own. He could well afford one, but he said it was "just too much bother." That uncharacteristic self-deprivation was, somehow, linked to his failure to find more comfortable quarters. He preferred the large bed-sitting-room he had rented in the Hongkew apartment of a *Daily News* copy editor when he first came to Shanghai. He said implausibly, "Between the office, your flat, and traveling, I'm hardly ever there except to sleep. And not always there to sleep."

Smiling at that masculine bravado, Emily wondered again at her lover's self-denial. He was anything but stingy. His gifts to her were lavish, and he indulged himself with fine clothing, fine food, and excellent wine. Still, he was perverse. His own car and his own apartment would make his life far more comfortable, but he wanted neither.

"Richard really doesn't want a car—or a millstone around his neck," Julia had remarked. She believed that he wanted nothing to tie him down. The last thing in the world he wanted, Julia contended, was a wife, who would tie him down for good and all.

Most bachelors flinched from marriage, Emily reflected, but that normal wariness verged on paranoia in Richard. Perhaps, paradoxically, that was why he clung to her. It would explain why he grew most ardent when she withdrew and why he became elusive when she appeared receptive. No matter how Westernized, she was undeniably Chinese— and only déclassé Englishmen married Chinese. Not just a plaything, as she had feared, she was a shield for Richard. As long as he was with her, no other woman could maneuver him into marriage.

Emily felt shamed. How dare he use her like a superior call girl!

She pulled herself up. Priding herself upon her objectivity, she was being as fanciful as a shopgirl. Her dire conclusion was based on no more than Julia's offhand remark.

She must, Emily told herself, not prejudge Richard, who was neither as detached from sincere emotion nor as self-serving as he sometimes appeared. True, he had just shown himself without sympathy for either Julia or Elizaveta, insensitive to one woman's suffering and to another woman's joy. Although he might appear self-centered, he was acutely sensitive to her own moods. True, he had twice been noticeably tardy in coming to the rescue: once at the Great World and again tonight. But he had in both cases saved the situation by his intelligently delayed intervention.

"Dick, I can see your point about Joshua and Liz." Emily was briskly conciliatory, regretting the twenty-odd seconds of silence during which she had spun her flimsy web of conjecture. "It *was* a little abrupt, the way they finally decided to get married."

"Abrupt! It was unchained lightning."

"Well, it's done now." She deliberately fell back on journalistic shop talk. "Dick, is there any chance for the Wuhan government?"

"Not a hope," he said. "The Generalissimo is the only hope for China. I can't regret the departure of the Comintern's agents. But, tell me, why in the name of God has Rosamonde Sun booked passage to Moscow?"

"Dick, never forget Rosamonde used to be Madame *President* Sun Yat-sen. She'd hate to have her little sister, Mayling, queening it over her as Madame *Generalissimo* Chiang Kai-shek."

"That match isn't settled yet. Not by a long shot."

"Don't tell May that. As far as she's concerned, it's signed, sealed— and about to be delivered. Mammie Soong'll have to run a lot farther than Japan to escape her would-be son-in-law. May is really pushing him."

"Damned determined, you Chinese ladies, aren't you? If only you were determined to look with favor on my humble suit."

Persuaded by his light humor that he was far from drunk, she flirted lightly. "All right, then. I said I'd tell you when . . . and I'm doing it right now. Let's get married tomorrow. What do you say to that?"

"Wonderful, Em! I'd show you if I could let go of the wheel. You are serious?"

"I am, Dick. Tomorrow then?"

"Tomorrow . . . in principle." He paused. "But to be practical, we'll have to wait till I get back. I'm booked on the *Koryu-maru* to Kobe day after tomorrow. I hated to tell you . . . I kept putting it off. However, I'll be back soon. And then . . ."

"And then *what?*"

"And then we'll work it out. . . . We'll decide the best thing to do. . . . And when . . ."

As his voice faded inconclusively, Emily realized that he *was* drunk —very drunk! He had obviously sought in the bottle the courage to tell her of his imminent departure. For one appalling moment, she believed he had no intention of marrying her—not tomorrow or ever. An instant later, she concluded tolerantly that he had little inclination toward marriage but was not deceiving her deliberately.

Those reflections clarified her own thinking. She knew that she truly wanted to marry Richard. She could overcome her pride of race, for she loved him deeply. And she could in time remedy his few faults, above all his rootlessness.

The convertible was passing Rafferty's funeral parlor on Bubbling Well Road. Farther down, lights glinted on the hammered-brass letters: ST. ANDREW'S CAFÉ. Jeff Geoffreys's big Daimler-Benz sidecar-motorcycle stood at the curb.

"Of course we will, Richard. We'll work it all out just as soon as you get back," Emily said confidently, then paused and asked softly, "Could you please drive slower? We're going a little too—"

"Damn it, Emily, stop humoring me," he exploded. "I know that tone too well. It's bloody condescending. And you . . ."

The red Plymouth swerved violently when the black ghost of a rickshaw materialized out of the darkness. Alcohol had blunted Richard's reactions. The fender struck the rickshaw coolie and flipped him into the air. He somersaulted ten feet above the ground with grotesque grace and began to fall. Richard's foot clamped down on the accelerator.

"Got to get out of here," he muttered thickly. "Too many enemies who hate me . . . hate my honest reporting. They'll crucify me if they catch me. Not just drunken driving, but murder. They'll try'n pin *murder* on me."

Emily did not speak for fear of provoking him. She knew that he would in a moment or two turn back to see to the unfortunate coolie. If still alive, the man would need medical attention. If he were dead, common decency demanded an effort to help his family.

But the red convertible drew farther from St. Andrew's Café. After two minutes, Richard sighed with relief and said, "S'all right now. If anyone saw . . . couldn't get registration number. I pulled away too fast."

He was actually congratulating himself on his cunning—on keeping his head. He displayed no concern for the coolie and no inclination to turn back. Emily went rigid in shock and disgust. Ironically, Richard's fears were unfounded. A foreigner who accidentally ran down a coolie would be punished by no more than a *pro forma* fine. Richard was not evading danger but merely avoiding inconvenience.

"You're not turning back?" she asked, appalled. "You don't care?"

"Why should I?"

"Why . . . why to see if you've killed the poor wretch. To help him . . . help his family. It's only the decent . . ."

Richard drew the convertible to the curb, stopping by chance before the spear-tipped gates of Jade House, the Haleevies' mansion. He turned and looked at her in frank astonishment.

"Go back? And put my head in a noose? Never!"

"Richard, don't you care at all about that poor man?"

"He's probably better off dead! Put my head in a noose for a miserable coolie? Why should I?"

"Because he's a fellow human being. Because you're responsible."

"Me? . . . Re . . . responsible?" His words were slurred. "Responsible for a Chink coolie? Don't make me laugh."

"You don't really give a damn about Julie or Liz either, do you?" Emily demanded. "You don't care about anyone but yourself, do you? Not even . . . not even me. Do you, Richard?"

Enraged by his callousness and his racism, above all by his brutal selfishness, Emily flung open the door of the convertible and stepped into the dense night.

"Then you won't want this Chink girl anymore!" She turned in the yellow glow of a streetlamp. "So there's nothing more to say."

Agile though drunk, Richard sprang from the car, seized her arm, and spun her around. Emily stumbled, snapping the heel of her silver slipper, and fell hard against the fender.

"You'd better get back to your poor abused countryman, hadn't you?" In his rage, he spoke more clearly. "All you Chinks stick together, don't you?"

"You'd better go, Richard."

"To tell the honest truth, I'm happy to go. All this piety and patriotism's been getting on my nerves. I'm glad to say good-bye."

"I know, Richard!" she answered. "I know!"

Emily sat in the driver's seat, her head leaning on the steering wheel. She gulped back tears and lifted her head to watch the solitary figure stride east on Bubbling Well Road between the walls that guarded the millionaires' mansions. Although she was still trembling, she put the car into gear and very slowly turned back toward St. Andrew's Café. In the rearview mirror she saw Richard waving a gleeful dismissal.

In that moment of parting, she realized that he had deceived her for years. He was not only a racist but a scoundrel as well. He had used her physically and emotionally. He had cynically utilized her knowledge of China and her connections. He had ruthlessly exploited her—as Europeans and Americans always exploited Chinese.

She felt soiled and hollow. Yet she knew her anguish was largely her own fault. She had flouted traditional Chinese decency. She had flung herself at a barbarian to prove that she was emancipated and Westernized.

She was now free of Richard Hollings, free forever. Suddenly she was glad—very glad.

Still, she owed something to their years together. Since her car had struck the coolie, she would help him and his family as much as she could. Since the penalty for the offense might not be as light as she thought, she would not implicate Richard if she could avoid it. Her own woman again, Emily resolved that neither would she sacrifice herself to protect Richard.

JULY 26–AUGUST 1, 1927

The night of July 26, 1927, came diffidently to industrial Wuhan, the triplet cities lying on the Yangtze River at the center of China amid a lacework of streams and lakes. At nine in the evening the far bank of the river was a distant smudge beneath a glowing sunset.

Under that gaudy sky, the tall young man at the rail of the river steamer was bleakly depressed. Tommy Howe's friend Chang Kuo-tao had grudgingly agreed to this voyage. Boarding just before the gangplank went up, he had not noticed the white dollar signs on the spindly black funnels. He gazed sourly at the ideograms on the bridgehouse reading "American Vessel" and the Stars and Stripes that flapped over the boxy stern. He needed no such reminders that the only security in his anarchic homeland was provided by foreign flags backed by foreign men-of-war.

His melancholy deepened when the Dollar Line steamer swung into the channel and pointed her stubby prow toward Kiukiang, two hundred miles downstream. He looked glumly back at Wuhan, where the lights of the evening threw firefly trails across the river. The best-intentioned Chinese regime for a century was dying in Wuhan. He smoothed the short hair on his domed head, and an ode of the Tang Dynasty came into his mind. The final couplet was the distillation of sorrow: *The golden crane is flown forever, and his proud tower is desolate forever.*

It suited his bleak mood. Chronically depressed by the suffering of his native land, he despaired of his immediate mission. The message he carried could determine the fate of China for decades to come. But he carried the wrong message.

Chang Kuo-tao was further depressed by the impending departure of Michael Borodin, the senior representative in China of the Communist International, Moscow's agency for fomenting revolution abroad. Borodin's special train, now waiting at the Wuhan station, was emblazoned with crossed Nationalist and Soviet flags framing a portrait of a beaming Dr. Sun Yat-sen. The flatbed cars were loaded with the heavy-duty trucks and the touring cars that would carry the party across the Gobi Desert to the Soviet Union. After the virtual collapse of the Wuhan government under the man called Lucifer, Borodin was withdrawing to lick his wounds.

Michael Borodin was an ardent revolutionary. He was also the realist who had prevented a Communist insurrection in Canton because he knew the Communists could not hold the city. Released from Borodin's experienced guidance, the Chinese Communist Party had now decided upon an even more audacious insurrection. The man Julia had known as the dean of Shanghai Labor University was now effectively in control of the party. The dean, the author of the Shanghai Uprising, had conceived a military coup against all Nationalist factions in Nanchang, the capital of Kiangsi Province. Success would give the Communists not only their own independent army but total control over South China. The Nanchang Rising was scheduled for July 31—just five days hence.

But Moscow had just vetoed that rising, and the dean had obediently agreed to kill his own plan. Chang Kuo-tao conceded that even a successful Nanchang Rising would lead nowhere if the Soviets halted the flow of advisers, arms, and gold to the Chinese Communist Party in punishment for disobeying Moscow's orders. He had, therefore, reluctantly agreed to carry the message from the Chinese Communist Party canceling the planned mutiny.

After a bone-shaking journey in a railway carriage with broken windows and splintered seats from Kiukiang on the Yangtze River, Chang Kuo-tao finally reached Nanchang on July 30. His temper frayed by long waits on sidings while troop trains rattled past, he felt little nostalgia for his native province. Besides, he had no time for sentiment. As soon as his train halted, he was caught up in urgent discussions. These talks became heated on the ferry across the Kan River to Nanchang. The rising was scheduled for the next day.

All the conspirators assembled in a weathered brick building beside the chief inn of the shabby provincial capital. Although the oiled-paper windows and the bamboo shutters were propped open on sticks, no breeze relieved the stifling heat. Tropical humidity hung over the city, where jungle had once trailed arm-thick vines across tall palms while the monkeys howled from the treetops at emerald parrots.

The long day of squabbling in the airless room was exhausting. Personal rivalries inflamed the mutineers, and the vinegar of jealousy seasoned the cold rice of strategy. Not only rebellious military officers argued with Chang Kuo-tao but also Commissar Chou En-lai, who had been assigned to Nanchang shortly after his nearly miraculous escape in Shanghai. The men on the spot insisted that the rising must take place as planned.

Alternately mocking and affable, Chou En-lai dominated the discussions. Untroubled by the mind-numbing heat, he appeared cool in crisp khaki drill, although his comrades were flushed in sweat-soaked homespun or laborers' crumpled blue. He flatly refused to consider canceling the Nanchang Rising.

As evening approached, the senior troop commander present suggested soberly, "Perhaps we should postpone action for a time. Take more time to reconsider, as Chang Kuo-tao asks."

"The Communist Party assigned me to do a job," Chou En-lai snapped. "And I'm going to do it, regardless of second thoughts."

Outside, the cries of peddlers were supplanted by the sounds of the early evening. Where an itinerant knife-sharpener had clanged his shears, a noodle vendor trilled his bamboo flute. The squealing of pigs carried to market in wickerwork tubes had given way to the plaintive yodeling of a blind masseur. A hawker of sweetcakes cried his wares, and an itinerant storyteller pounded his miniature drum to summon an audience.

Forcing his attention back to the discussion, Chang Kuo-tao realized that retreat was impossible. Because so many knew of the plan, the conspirators would be doomed if they drew back. He therefore asked only that the rising be postponed by one day to the first of August. Declaring truthfully that he had never opposed the Nanchang Rising, despite Moscow's misgivings, he pledged his wholehearted support.

Twenty-four hours later, as the night of July 31 fell, the people of the evening clattered through the muddy streets on wooden clogs. A grove of green oiled-paper umbrellas bobbed between rustic buildings dimly lit by oil lamps. In the inn next door, musicians rehearsed. An eight-tubed flute tirelessly repeated its scales as a nine-stringed lute was tuned interminably. A ten-year-old soprano vied for high C with a two-stringed violin, and a chorus of pi-dogs keened at the ascending moon.

The scene, Chang Kuo-tao reflected, could have occurred a century earlier, even five or ten centuries. The only modern note was the eerie moaning of a locomotive on the northern shore of the unbridged Kan River. The quintessential China was medieval Nanchang on the south bank just beyond the railway's reach, not industrial Shanghai.

Apprehension crackled like heat lightning in the Communists' war room. Worried staff officers and exhausted political commissars stared intently at the wall maps and the leather-cased field telephones. The air was already rancid with the smoke of uncured tobacco, despite the occasional breeze that ruffled the moonlight.

The senior troop commander was a veteran professional soldier. His smile was a gargoyle's grimace in the blue-white glare of the acetylene lantern hanging above his head. Morning was nine hours away, and by morning they would know the outcome. If the rising had triumphed, the Communists would be on the high road to the conquest of China. If it had failed, the Communist Party would be maimed—and all the men in the room would be dead or doomed.

On the table where the city map was spread amid dirty dishes a field telephone buzzed, and every man in the room stiffened. The troop commander nonchalantly lifted the handset and listened, his smile strained.

"A dispatch by runners from our northernmost company," he finally said. "The commander in chief . . ."

Commissar Chou En-lai whispered into Chang Kuo-tao's ear: "Old Ironsides himself. Our nominal Nationalist commander in chief on this front."

". . . turned up seventy miles north of Nanchang late yesterday afternoon. He saw our troops moving south and probably suspected they were joining a mutiny. He ordered them to halt."

The troop commander lit a cigarette, and Chang Kuo-tao drew in his breath. Could old-fashioned discipline have foiled the Nanchang Uprising before it began? Chou En-lai lounged nonchalantly against a desk, but his long fingers drummed on the ebony top.

"Our troops fired a machine-gun burst above Old Ironsides' head," the troop commander resumed. "He got the idea and left smartly."

Guffaws and shouts of glee exploded across the room. First blood to the insurrection!

But events here in Nanchang tonight would be decisive. Half the military units in the city were potentially hostile to the Communists. If those troops attacked, if they even resisted strenuously, the rising would collapse.

The men in the war room were now powerless. Having made their plans, deployed their troops, and issued their final orders, the staff officers could only wait for reports and pretend that their mouths were not parched by tension.

Shortly after two A.M., a telephone buzzed peremptorily. The troop commander extended a lean hand. He listened closely for half a minute, grunted noncommittally, and replaced the handset. He studied the city map for half a minute and drew a red arrow.

"That was Detachment Six," he said. "Just reporting they've arrived at the jump-off position."

A young messenger laughed shrilly, and older men chuckled in relief. But a volley of shots in the distance hushed the war room. Shots rattled louder, and twenty seconds later, nearby rifle-fire resounded through the open windows.

Volley followed volley. A machine gun chattered, and a second machine gun answered. After twenty seconds the firing abruptly halted, and the night was silent.

The silence lasted ten seconds, then twenty seconds; it endured a half minute; it dragged its incorporeal length through the crammed room for almost a full minute. The young messenger lustily sucked a bleeding hangnail. Chairs creaked when their occupants shifted nervously. Chou En-lai yawned with tension, his jaws gaping wide. The troop commander's aide cracked his knuckles, and two officers jumped.

When a second telephone buzzed, the troop commander's fingers, which were damp with sweat, slipped on the slick Bakelite. Listening to the protracted report, he frowned. His face was mottled by anger when he slammed the handset into its case.

"Those idiots!" he erupted. "How many times have I dinned into them the proper form for a report? And the signal section isn't performing brilliantly. The telephone lines are damned scratchy . . ."

"For God's sake, man, what's happening?" Chang Kuo-tao demanded. "Let us in on your military secret!"

"The garrison here in Nanchang—about three thousand men—has surrendered," the troop commander replied. "There was a dustup. As you heard, a brisk exchange of fire. But they gave up. The city is in our hands. Now for the outlying areas. Helluva lot more troops out there."

For half an hour the instruments were silent. Amid the relieved chatter, the buzzing of a telephone was almost inaudible. The crevasses etched by strain around the commander's mouth deepened when he answered. Twenty seconds later, he smiled broadly and directed, "Disarm them first. Then we'll think whether we'll accept them into the revolutionary ranks. Yes, it's great news!"

The commander flicked his battered lighter and lit a cigarette. He coughed, then hawked with audible satisfaction before announcing with even greater satisfaction: "The Second Division reports no opposition. The fence-sitters all want to come over now!"

After the fourth similar report, the Communist commander leaned across the table and said, "That's about it. That was the cadet regiment reporting. All the police have come over. We've also made a clean sweep of all artillery units. Nothing can go wrong now."

Although several superstitious comrades shuddered, that complacent prediction proved accurate. When early dawn tinged the smoke-clouded room a pink glow, Nanchang and its environs were firmly in Communist hands.

The youthful leaders of the mutiny looked at each other with blood-shot eyes and rubbed their stubbled cheeks with grimy palms. Their faces were ashen with fatigue, and their heads ached from tension and nicotine. But they foresaw a brilliant future.

The military forces of the Communist Party had just won their first clear-cut victory; a glorious new stage of the revolution had thus begun. A mass uprising throughout the nation would inevitably follow this great victory at Nanchang, just as a prairie fire leaps from a single spark. The new Red Army, which had sprung into existence on the morning of August 1, 1927, would inevitably conquer power everywhere in China within a year—two years at most.

AUGUST 13–SEPTEMBER 6, 1927

Despite his great size, the Tibetan mastiff was still puppylike at the age of six. Rambunctious though he was, his jet-black coat with the white blaze on the chest gave him a priestlike appearance. The amah Lao Zee, who could not get her tongue around Adam, called him Ah Dee, which meant "Younger Brother."

Adam was at his most dignified that mid-August evening. His domed head turned sedately from the Atterbury Kent radio to check on Emily Howe, who was lying on the rattan settee. The street noises had somewhat subsided by eleven o'clock, and the Strauss waltz playing on Station XMHA engaged Adam's attention. Emily was musing half-asleep, her bosom moving gently under her green kimono.

She should, perhaps, have accepted her parents' invitation to join them at Peitaiho in North China, although she disliked the vulgar display Hong Kong tycoons like the Sekloongs made at the beach resort. She did not, however, wish to test the tentative rapprochement she had concluded with her parents after breaking with Richard Hollings. The wounds they had inflicted on each other still needed time—and a little distance—to heal.

Her throat still ached when she thought of Richard. Yet she had been totally sincere when she told her parents that she was through with foreign men forever. She was, however, not quite ready for a professional matchmaker to find her a good old-fashioned Chinese husband in the good old-fashioned way. She detested the thought of being hawked around the marriage-market like a brood mare. Moreover, her vanity insisted that she needed no help in getting a man.

Emily naturally preferred the freedom of the loft apartment to the stifling atmosphere of Harmony Hall. Since she could not leave Julia in the lurch, she had stayed to share both expenses and Julia's concern about Tommy. She could not leave Julia alone to wonder when—if ever—he would be released.

Emily still did not believe that her friend would return to America after Tommy was released, not even for a visit. But Julia insisted that she had to go back, if only to see her parents.

While waiting, Julia was tormented by anxiety. Emily carried the entire burden of providing consolation. Elizaveta and Joshua were little help, for they were preoccupied with each other and with keeping their engagement secret. Julia's left-wing Chinese friends were less help. When not dodging anti-Communist sweeps in the foreign concessions as well as Greater Shanghai, they were celebrating the revival of Communist hopes by the Nanchang Rising.

To Emily, who militantly supported Generalissimo Chiang Kai-shek, their jubilation appeared a delusion. Just four days after the triumph of their uprising, the Communists had been forced to evacuate Nanchang by superior Nationalist forces. The infant Red Army was presently withdrawing in disarray toward the lace-making city of Swatow on the coast, where the Communist leaders planned to establish a base for the conquest of South China. The common people showed no enthusiasm for their self-appointed liberators, who were constantly harassed by hostile forces. Emily concluded with satisfaction that the Communists' enthusiasm was not only self-deceiving but self-destructive.

A bark broke into her reverie. Adam pointed his muzzle at the Gothic arch of the radio. The Strauss waltz had stopped abruptly, and a female announcer was saying ". . . apologize for interrupting the concert." Emily heard the rustle of onionskin paper and recognized Julia's voice reading: "Reuters News Agency reports that Generalissimo Chiang Kai-shek today resigned all his offices under the Nanking Government. The dominant figure in the center-right Nationalist Administration is withdrawing from the political arena in order to break the deadlock that has set major factions within the Nationalist movement at each other's throats. With the controversial Generalissimo removed, the rival groups are expected to reunite. Supported by the Christian General, Feng Yü-hsiang, Nationalist armies are expected to march against the northern warlords very soon. Other units are expected to crush the wave of rebellions in South and Central China which the Communists have been raising under the slogan 'In autumn, harvest—and rebel!' "

The onionskin sheets rustled nervously, and Julia's voice quavered:

"The Generalissimo has already left Nanking for Shanghai, where he will see personal friends before withdrawing to his home in Chekiang Province. He will spend the next five years studying moral and aesthetic philosophy.

"We now resume our interrupted concert. The next selection is 'Tales from the Vienna Woods.' "

Julia's voice had naturally developed a nervous quaver. Emily, too, was dismayed by the Generalissimo's resignation. This time it sounded like the real thing, not just another threat made to get his own way. And he was the only man who could reunite China. His withdrawal under pressure could prove catastrophic.

The Generalissimo was, moreover, the only hope for her brother's release—the only hope, perhaps, for Tommy's survival. Cajoled by Mayling Soong, he had revealed that Tommy was a prisoner. Persuaded by Mayling, he had virtually guaranteed that Tommy would be released in time. Deprived of the Generalissimo's protection, Tommy was more likely to be shot than to be freed.

Emily lifted the telephone and gave the number of the Soongs' house on Seymour Road. Mayling might not be overjoyed at being called at ten minutes to midnight, but she couldn't help that.

"May, it's Emily. What's going on? Is this another fake resignation?"

"No, Emmy. Gimo has really quit this time. It's the only way he can bring peace. But I'm sure he'll come back to lead the reunited National-ists to victory."

"So he *is* coming back. Soon, I hope."

"I'm afraid not. Definitely not soon," Mayling responded. "Not for some time. They've got to learn a lesson, those squabbling politicians. They've got to learn they can't do without him."

"It's a risky step." Emily tested her friend's mood. "Yet you sound so happy."

"There *is* something else. You know my mother ran away to Japan. Well, Gimo's going to track her down and get her permission. He's finally getting rid of that . . . that woman, his old wife. He swears we'll be married before the end of the year."

"Congratulations, May. I'm so happy for you."

"But why're you calling at this time of night?"

"I just heard Julia on XMHA, reading the news of the Gimo's resigna-tion. Naturally, she sounded all broken up. May, what does this mean for Tommy? If the Gimo isn't around to help him . . ."

"Oh dear, Emmy, I didn't think of Tommy. I know Gimo promised to get him out. But he's been so busy lately. I just don't know . . ."

"May, you've got to do something right now." Emily sounded confident, although she was never quite sure of the volatile May. "Can you get to the Gimo tonight?"

"Hardly tonight, Emmy." Was May's voice colder? "But I am seeing him tomorrow. As always, damn it, with an old aunt as a chaperone. At my age!"

"You *must* ask him about Tommy! May, darling, please! I'll never ask you for another thing. I'll be your slave for life. You *must* get the Gimo to intervene while he still can. If it's not already too late . . ."

"I'm sure it's well within his power—even now." Hauteur frosted Mayling's voice. "But he *is* very busy. Whether he can manage anything before he leaves for the country, I just don't know."

"You will try, won't you, May? I just know you can bring him round. Oh, May . . ."

"Of course I'll try." The presumptive fiancée of the most powerful man in China was cordial again after her own power had been acknowledged. "I'll try hard. But I can't promise anything. . . . Em, I wouldn't get my hopes up if I were you."

At the end of August, Generalissimo Chiang Kai-shek disappeared into the mountains of his native Chekiang Province, which lay south of Shanghai. Like an imperial mandarin, when out of office he withdrew to the village of his birth to refurbish the tombs of his ancestors, above all his beloved mother's. Yet the couriers trotting along the hill paths between the tea bushes gave the lie to the pretense that he took little interest in politics.

No pretense cloaked his failure to help Tommy Howe. Mayling Soong only reported that her suitor had simply not had time to look into the matter. He would, she implied, have done so had he had a single free instant. Emily duly expressed her gratitude. Expressing her doubts would have mortally affronted Mayling—and not helped Tommy.

The last faint hope had failed. If Tommy was lucky, some twist of fate might someday secure his release. If he remained unlucky, he would be locked in his cell indefinitely, or he would be shot.

Even Julia, that ebullient optimist, stopped talking about Tommy. Instead, she went down to the office of the Dollar Line to book her passage to San Francisco on September 16th, two weeks later.

Emily understood but nonetheless resented her friend's abandoning her brother. At the other extreme, she felt that her father was being played for a credulous fool. Although Donald Howe was paying large sums through the Floodgate Fraternity to buy Tommy decent food and small luxuries, he still had no proof that his son was alive.

"It's costing me more than the presidential suite at the Palace Hotel," he confided to his prodigal daughter. "If only they'd let someone see him—even for a second."

"Perhaps they can't, Father." Emily did not spare him. "Perhaps Tommy's not . . . not alive anymore. They could be holding you up."

"That's always possible, Yuelin. But what else can I do?"

On a sticky afternoon in early September, Emily was drowsily reviewing the outstanding loans of the Women's Commercial Bank. Nothing more pressing required her attention. Leafing through the Ikra's file, she marveled at Elizaveta's prompt payments. She also wondered idly what would become of Shanghai's glossiest bordello when its properietress married.

Thinking of her parents in cool Peitaiho, Emily half decided to join them—and to take Julia along for one last look at China. Her friend's days were empty. Station XMHA occupied her for only a few hours a week; the Customs College was still closed for the summer; and her left-wing friends were in hiding. Nowadays Julia rarely smiled.

Emily's extension buzzed, and a sleepy operator reported that Miss Mayling Soong was calling. Since May's starling chatter about personalities, money, and politics was always diverting, Emily readily agreed to bring Julia to tea later that afternoon.

Knowing that May never asked anyone else with them, neither Emily nor Julia bothered to change her simple day dress. A dab of powder and a lick of lipstick were quite enough.

The Soongs' sitting room was, as always, humdrum with its standard Ningpo-lacquer furniture and its heaps of *Saturday Evening Post*s and *National Geographic*s. But electric fans blowing over big cakes of ice cooled the room. Though the Soongs' enthusiasm for America was sometimes excessive, they had learned to make themselves comfortable in the American way. The chocolate chip cookies were delicious, and ice cubes floated in the refreshing tea. Mayling proudly recalled that the Soongs had imported the first Frigidaire Shanghai ever saw.

She was dressed for coolness. Her cream linen smock with the scooped neckline was the opposite of the assertively Chinese *cheongsam* she wore in public as if in dress rehearsal for the role of first lady of the Republic of China. Her slender ankles were, however, set off by frivolous sandals that were no more than cobwebs of green and yellow leather strips.

Lulled by Mayling's gossip, Julia's thoughts drifted pleasantly. She heard the door bell tinkle and, a half minute later, an amah's straw sandals flip-flopping down the long corridor to the front door. The amah's unintelligible questions were answered by a deeper voice. Uninterested, Mayling poured fresh tea from a frosted-glass pitcher.

Julia looked up when leather soles sounded on the teak floorboards. A tall man appeared in the doorway. He was very thin, and his white suit was baggy. The afternoon sunlight was subdued by the bamboo blinds, but he blinked repeatedly.

Julia saw dark spirals twisting in the dense air. Annoyed at her own weakness, she closed her eyes against that giddiness. She should, she reprimanded herself, be accustomed to the close heat by now.

When she opened her eyes, Julia saw Emily's tan dress plastered against the stranger's white linen. They were embracing. Staring at the man's lean face, Julia knew she was hallucinating. Queasy and nauseated, she again closed her eyes to keep from fainting.

"Julie! Julie, darling! I've frightened you!" The English accent was unmistakable. "They just brought me here. Julie, dearest, I'm so happy to see you. I'm overjoyed, I . . ."

Julia lifted her eyelids to look at Tommy, who was kneeling beside her chair. She threw her arms around his neck and clung tight.

"Darling Tommy!" she cried. "Oh, Tommy, darling, you're back. You're really back?"

"Evidently! Julie, it's wonderful. . . . Even if I've no idea how I got out."

"You're so thin." She studied him proprietorially. "We'll have to feed you up. . . . And you're really all right? Only thinner, not sick or anything?"

"Fighting fit, though a little under my best fighting weight. Julie, I've got so much to say . . ."

Both Emily and Mayling had to have their own turn to inspect the returned prisoner before he could continue. Emily was bubbling with joy, and even Mayling was warm. When they finally settled down, Julia perched on the arm of the chair, which she had ceded to Tommy.

"Mayling Soong, you arranged this, didn't you?" Emily almost sounded accusing. "It's all your doing!"

"Not entirely!" Mayling verged upon an unladylike grin. "I didn't know he'd turn up when you were here—though I was hoping. You know I can't resist a little drama."

"They practically pushed me out the door, less than an hour ago."
Tommy's voice hardened. "Forty-five men and six women in one
lockup. I was the only one left. All the rest executed. I saw them shot.
All but me."

"Little Pow?" Julie demanded. "Where is he? They didn't shoot him,
did they?"

"Not as far as I know. In the beginning looking after him kept me
sane. Then they took him away. God knows where. . . . But, tell me,
why were they so eager to get rid of me? The pair who brought me here
were pretty sinister."

"That's their trade!" Mayling laughed. "They're the best hatchetmen
of the Supreme Lord of the Floodgate Fraternity. The Green Dragon,
Gimo's blood brother, you know."

"I begin to see . . ."

Mayling laid down the law: "You must promise never to repeat what
I tell you."

Tommy nodded emphatically. Any indiscretion would increase the
debt of gratitude his family already owed this determined young
woman.

"I couldn't keep nagging Gimo about Tommy," Mayling said. "Instead, I just *happened* to run into the Green Dragon. He was happy to do
a favor for his blood brother. A couple of . . . ah . . . persuasive talkers
called on the Shanghai garrison commander. They recalled the favors
the commander had received from the Floodgate Fraternity. They assumed the garrison commander would prefer the Green Dragon's gratitude to his displeasure."

"As easy as that!" Emily marveled, but Tommy interrupted. "They
turned me out, May. Dropped me like a red-hot coal. How come?"

"Well, Gimo tried, but he couldn't push too hard. It wouldn't do to
irritate the garrison commander. Gimo could need his support later. But
the Green Dragon didn't give a damn. The garrison commander must've
been terrified. Maybe he was afraid his opium would be cut off. So you
see . . ."

Julia was only half listening, while her eyes clung to Tommy. His
narrow scholar's face was stamped with the pallor of imprisonment, and
his eyes were wounded. Her hand slipped from his grasp to smooth his
thick hair.

Julia Pavernen, spinster of twenty-six years, knew then exactly what
she wanted. Although the turmoil of China frightened her and the
brutality of China revolted her, she wanted Tommy Howe for the rest
of her life—whether in Shanghai or in the farthest corner of his back-

ward country. Although she was exceedingly sensitive to her surroundings, she would go anywhere with him.

The intensity and the simplicity of her emotion shocked her. She wanted only Tommy. She would happily accept everything that came with Tommy—turbulence or tranquillity, luxury or hardship.

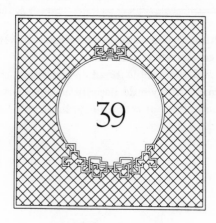

Most reckless when he believed himself most cautious, the fugitive Communist leader Chang Kuo-tao had chosen the rendezvous with his usual dash. The Majestic Café, halfway up Bubbling Well Road from the Racecourse, advertised itself as "the largest cabaret in Shanghai," and the enormous dance floor was rimmed by dozens of white-covered tables. The Majestic also advertised: 100 CHARMING DANCE HOSTESSES. But hardly a dozen couples were foxtrotting when Julia and Tommy entered through the double doors.

No one looked up. Whether slumming or working as hostesses, young foreign women in party dresses were a common sight at the Majestic. So were well-to-do young Chinese men ritually sowing their wild oats. Unobtrusive because they were exactly what they appeared to be in white sharkskin and chartreuse tulle, Tommy and Julia danced and sipped champagne. Neither noticed that it was already eleven, half an hour past the time Chang Kuo-tao had asked them to meet him.

They had come from a formal Chinese dinner for five hundred, which Donald Howe gave to celebrate October 10th, the twenty-sixth anniversary of the Nationalist revolution that had toppled the Manchu Dynasty in 1911. The host could not declare that he was, above all, celebrating his youngest son's release from Nationalist captivity a month earlier. To acknowledge that Tommy had been held incommunicado for almost five months as a suspected Communist would have imperiled the Howes' good name. They were, therefore, united behind the tale that he had been engaged on a secret mission.

"Do you know," Tommy said, "Father's had far more worries about

Emmy and me than all three of my older brothers put together. Because he sent us abroad to school, Mother says."

Naturally, Emily's resumption of filial obedience had delighted their parents. Having seen the wisdom of the old ways, Emily was admirably docile. Fearful of another rift, her parents agreed that she should, for the time being, continue to work at the Women's Bank. Nor did they immediately press her to move back to Harmony Hall when she objected to leaving Julia in the lurch.

Her mother had prevailed upon her father not to ask Emily to give up her writing. When she was married, her scribbling would provide an amusing diversion until responsibility for husband and children engaged all her energy and talents. And she would soon be married. Emily was on the verge of agreeing that her parents should commission a professional matchmaker to find her a suitable husband. She was old, already twenty-six, and her reputation was clouded. But she was the only daughter of Donald Howe, Tommy noted. The wealth and the power of the Howes would ensure a good match.

"She mustn't do it!" Julia's gaze shifted from the deserted dance floor. "But Emmy won't listen to me—or to anyone. I think she hates herself for letting Dick Hollings make a fool of her."

"Obviously, she wants to punish herself," Tommy agreed. "If only she wasn't in such a mad rush to marry. But no one can talk to her."

Glancing at the platinum blonde who had just stepped onto the dance floor with a black-bearded Russian, Julia asked with unconvincing casualness, "I suppose there's still no word of Little Pow."

"Only that he was seen alive last week." Tommy smiled at her delight in his news.

"Darling, that's wonderful! The best news since *you* walked into May Soong's living room!" She took his hand. "How do you know? From Joshua and his merry band of spies?"

"Not from Joshua. From the Apparatus, old Chang Kuo-tao's underground. The Apparatus won't say where Pow is held. Got to protect its sources. But at least the Fascists are keeping him alive."

"I'm delighted, Tommy. But since when are you on such good terms with the Apparatus?"

"I was asked to pass the news on to you," he replied. "It was more convenient to tell me."

"You're dodging the question, Dr. Howe," Julia said with mock severity. "I didn't know you were so chummy with the Apparatus."

"You know, that spell in the nick finished me with the Generalissimo and the Nationalists," he said. "They didn't mistreat me, not Donald

Howe's son, though they almost shot me. But I saw brutal executions every day. . . . Mostly working-class men and women. The Nationalists don't give a damn for the common people, whatever they say."

"So you turned to the Communists? Through your old buddy Chang Kuo-tao, I imagine."

"Yes, I tried to get in touch with old Chang Kuo-tao. Though he was away, the Apparatus sent news of Little Pow. I only heard tonight, from one of the waiters at Father's banquet. . . . But I wonder what Kuo-tao wants of us. He only just got back, you know."

"I'm sure he'll tell us—at length. Meanwhile, there's no point in speculating. Let's dance instead."

Tommy led Julia to the dance floor. Her new maturity still delighted him, though it no longer surprised him. She had learned to curb her impulsiveness and even to exercise some patience. Although she still harped on her plan to visit the United States, she was, otherwise, virtual perfection in his eyes. Her vitality and her zest struck him anew each time he met her.

The Filipino band played George Gershwin's "The Man I Love" slowly and sensually. Tommy hummed a few bars, and Julia whispered the refrain into his ear. When they returned to their table, Tommy wondered again how best to convince her that she should not leave Shanghai, not even for a brief visit to her parents in America. Plattsburg was so far away. He was thinking of a fresh approach when a bony hand thrust a small booklet at him.

He started and then grinned sheepishly at his alarm. The crone in rusty black tunic and trousers was only peddling tickets on the Chinese National Lottery. The Nanking government believed that the easiest way to get China's people to pay for building roads and airports was to offer them a flutter.

"Missy maybe catchee many dollah," the crone exhorted. "One piecee ticket no moren ten dollah. But can catchee half million dollah."

Although Tommy waved her away, she stubbornly reiterated her litany. Her persistence touched Julia's sympathy. She nodded, and Tommy dutifully laid a ten-dollar note on the table.

"Kwuh-kwuh kan . . ." the crone advised. "Look at your ticket right now, sir. Make sure it's in order."

When Tommy incuriously turned over the ticket, the hawker vanished into the gloom. Scrawled on the reverse by a thick-nibbed fountain pen were ideograms reading "Casino at 11:30."

Tommy grinned at that conspiratorial mummery. If anything betrayed him, Julia reflected as they rose, it would be his irrepressible sense of humor. Still, the struggle for social justice need not always be waged in funereal solemnity. Occasionally, it could be fun.

The back-room casino, even dimmer than the dance hall, was virtually deserted. Two Chinese men sat with four White Russian hostesses at the fan-tan table, languidly betting on the number of buttons that would finally remain as the croupier removed four at a time from a random heap. A blackjack dealer served just three gamblers.

One corner offered the China Coast version of roulette: a larger ball and a smaller wheel with fewer divisions. Alone at the roulette table sat a large young man whose sumptuous blue silk long-gown declared him the son of a wealthy old-fashioned family. Julia took the chair beside him, but he still studied the motionless wheel. Finally he told the croupier to place his stack of chips on red. When the wheel whirled, he turned away disdainfully and nodded to Tommy.

"Good to see you again," Chang Kuo-tao said casually. "The croupier is ours. Only keep betting while we talk. It's been a long time, hasn't it, Old Howe?"

"July of last year." Tommy's pleasure was obvious. "You're looking well. A bit thin, though."

"So I should be." The big man smiled thinly. "All that healthy exercise in the fresh air. I've walked across half of China since I saw you last. After the Nanchang victory, the South China debacle! As you know, the Red Army had to pull out of Nanchang four days after the rising. We couldn't take on the two Nationalist columns that were closing in. It was a retreat, even if Commissar Chou En-lai did call it an advance to a new base. And troops in retreat fall apart. Dersertion, injuries, hunger, they all cut down our strength. By mid-September we hardly . . ."

Julia was badly disappointed by the Communist leader's matter-of-fact tone. He might have been telling chance acquaintances about his summer holidays. Listening to his heavily accented Shanghainese, she slowly realized that he was relating high drama.

He did not speak of his own gradual decline within the Communist Party—from acting chairman of the First Congress to his present second-class membership in the Political Bureau. A loyal party member served gladly in whatever capacity the party directed. Besides, where else could he go? The Communist Party was his life. Without the party he was nothing.

Many of the ordinary soldiers, Chang Kuo-tao recalled, had been captured by the Nationalists. But most had either gone back to brigandry or voluntarily rejoined the Nationalists. Only one small fighting unit of the fledgling Red Army remained in existence. Some six hundred men under General Chu Teh, whom men called Red Virtue, had gone into hiding in northern Kwangtung Province to reorganize. There were also rumors of a band of peasant militia under the zealot Mao Tse-tung, but that could hardly be called a fighting unit.

"It was nerve-racking getting back here," Kuo-tao said. "I had to go through Hong Kong, then take a coaster to Shanghai. Because I'm so thin, I've been masquarading as a sick schoolteacher. I only put on this getup to meet you two."

"Well then . . ." Tommy watched the croupier's rake sweep up the hundred dollars he had perversely placed on black thirteen. "That *was* quick. Now, old friend, what do you want of us?"

"The Apparatus is in tatters," Kuo-tao replied. "We badly need your help. So I was told to renew personal contact with you. After this personal contact, you'll receive instructions through cutouts. We'll only use you for high-level work. And for propaganda, of course!"

Considering the proposal, Tommy asked deadpan, "Who's going to make up my roulette losses, Kuo-tao?"

"Just mark them down to experience!" The big man chuckled. "They'll go into our war chest. The party can use every cent nowadays. What about you, Joo-li?"

"Naturally, I'm with you," she replied. "You know I used to run errands for the underground. But I was never part of the regular Apparatus. What could *I* possibly do now?"

"Joo-li, you can do a lot," Kuo-tao said. "Your information has always been greatly appreciated. And there's a whole new field. Some day soon public opinion abroad will be very important to us, perhaps crucial. Hacks like Anna Louise Strong and Agnes Smedley are useful. But they're too obviously Communists!"

"What's propaganda to do with me?" Julia asked. "Tommy knows I can't write two coherent sentences. . . . Anyway I may not be around."

"That's the beauty of it, Joo-li." Chang Kuo-tao ignored her implicit threat. "No one will ever suspect. You will both appear to be rightists —strong anti-Communists. Joo-li, you will then work on the foreign reporters who are always drifting in and out of Shanghai. Chaps like young Vincent Sheehan. He already thinks he knows everything, so he's easy to flatter—and to steer."

"I'll have to think about it," Julia said. "I'm not going to commit myself. I'm not going to promise when I may not be here. Also, I'd like to be sure I'm doing some good."

"With two of us working together," Tommy said, "we're certain to . . ."

"Isn't there any hope of reconciliation between you Communists and the Nationalists?" Julia knew that Chang Kuo-tao might consider her incurably naïve, but she had seen extraordinary twists in political alliances during the past few years. "There are some very good people, like Mayling Soong . . ."

Kuo-tao interjected, "Just another rotten twig of the corrupt Soong clan."

"That's not fair," Julia protested. "Look what she did for Tommy. Without the Generalissimo's knowing, too. Just look at—"

Appalled at inadvertently betraying May's secret, Julia clapped her hand over her mouth. But Chang Kuo-tao showed no surprise.

"You really believe Mayling Soong got Tommy out of jail?" He laughed abruptly. "Yes, of course, I know about Mayling Soong's supposedly secret deal with the Green Dragon to free him. Half Shanghai knows."

Julia glanced at Tommy angrily. He had evidently betrayed May's confidence to the Apparatus. He was, however, not contrite.

"You actually swallowed that fairy tale, Julie, did you?" Tommy's tone was fond—and chiding. "You really believed the Gimo couldn't find out where they were holding me? That he couldn't spring me? You believed May Soong went to the Green Dragon behind the Gimo's back? . . . Even if she were that foolish, the Green Dragon wouldn't have played. He'd never take such a political action without consulting his blood brother!"

"Then why . . . why the play-acting?" Julia did not care if her question further displayed her naïveté. "Why try to mislead us?"

"That's why you two must look like rightists from now on," Chang Kuo-tao replied. "Chiang Kai-shek *wanted* Tommy held. He's purging all Communists, and Tommy looked to him like a secret Communist."

"Exactly why," Julia asked, "must we appear to be rightists?"

"You're both suspected of Communist leanings," Chang Kuo-tao stressed. "So you've got to be seen to reform. You must rise above suspicion if you're to be of real use to the Apparatus. If you're to survive!"

"I'm still confused, Kuo-tao. Why did Chiang Kai-shek suddenly let Tommy go?"

"Same reason Chiang Kai-shek didn't shoot him in the first place— his father's gold," Chang Kuo-tao replied. "Donald Howe is too rich to offend. But they'll be watching you two like a couple of microbes under a lens."

Julia grimaced, but the ugly image drove his point home. For the first time, she understood in her bones: Waging the revolutionary struggle was not fun but a deadly serious matter. The penalty for negligence was not embarrassment but imprisonment—or death!

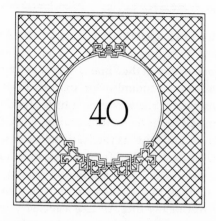

40

NOVEMBER 25–DECEMBER 1, 1927

Although Julia was now a regular agent of the Communist Apparatus, she was no longer wholly convinced that the Communists could save China—or that China could be saved at all. Her revulsion against Chinese brutality and her misgivings regarding China's future had not abated. Her present assignment differed little from her previous assignments. She was gleaning information regarding the raids on the hard-pressed Communist underground planned by the police of the foreign concessions, just as Tommy was doing in Nationalist-ruled Greater Shanghai. But she could not be as enthusiastic as she had once been.

Despite her doubts, working with Tommy made all the difference, and she did the task gladly. Yet she was no longer sure how she felt about Tommy or what she wanted of Tommy. The certainty that had flashed upon her that soft September afternoon in Mayling Soong's dowdy living room was fading amid the storms of late November.

In September, Julia had seen with brilliant clarity that she wanted to spend the rest of her life with Tommy, wherever he might go. She could not recapture that assurance in November. It was like a movie slightly out of focus. The outlines wavered, and the details were fuzzy.

It was not, Julia knew, because she was fickle. She had hardly looked at another man after meeting Tommy. Nor was her indecision a kind of delayed adolescence. Rather, she assured herself, her hesitation was a sign of maturity. She would not commit herself wholly to Tommy, which also meant committing herself to China for a lifetime, until she was absolutely certain that her love for Tommy was stable and enduring.

She was, Julia acknowledged to herself, also afraid. Above all, she was afraid of turbulent, brawling China, where all endeavors to build a better future seemed to end in the same welter of betrayal and slaughter. She was also afraid of total commitment, unready for full responsibility for another human being. She was even a little afraid of Tommy, who had now given himself to the Communist cause. The Communists could be just as treacherous and cruel as the Nationalists or the warlords. Her own future, like China's was, therefore, murky, quite unlike the beautiful clarity of the vision she had seen the day Tommy was released.

She was also anxious to see her parents before deciding how she would spend the rest of her life. All else aside, she owed them a visit after more than six years. Also, they were, naturally, pressing her even harder to come home. Perhaps a spell in Plattsburg would clarify her thoughts and, above all, her emotions. Anyway, she was a little fed up with the frenetic pace of overcrowded Shanghai.

Tommy's restraint did him much credit. He had not probed her feelings or her intentions deeply. He had obviously avoided the subject, not even urging her to stay. He had not again pressed her to marry him, although she sensed that he now wanted marriage. Julia had even had to learn from Emily that his parents were talking about employing a professional matchmaker to find Tommy a bride, though not necessarily the same matchmaker who was having difficulties finding Emily a bridegroom.

After a time, Tommy's restraint began to seem unnatural. She was, therefore, relieved when he finally confronted her over a scrubbed pine table at Jeff Geoffreys's unpretentious American-style restaurant, Geoffrey's Kitchen. She was almost glad when he said, "Emily tells me you've booked passage and actually got your ticket this time. Julie, is it all up between us?"

"Of course not, Tommy." Her first instinct was to placate him. "But I'm glad Emmy told you. I was on the point of telling you myself."

"What were you about to tell me? That we were through?"

"No, Tommy . . . I was going to tell you that I was going back to Plattsburg for a while. The *President Lincoln* sails on December third. I've promised my folks I'll be home for Christmas. After May Soong's wedding, I'll be off. Oh, Tommy, I'll miss you terribly."

"I'm glad of that," he said. "Though it is a shock—a bare week's notice. You know, I've been wondering if you were tired of me."

"Never, darling!" She laughed. "I just have to get away by myself for a while. To think things over. But I'll surely be back."

"I'm not so certain of that, Julie. Once you're back in America, it will all seem utterly different. Remember, you said as much in April, just before Pow came for me and I landed in the nick?"

"I do remember, Tommy. Maybe you're right, but I just can't help it. What can I do?"

"You could try telling me *exactly* why you feel this overwhelming need to get away from Shanghai—away from me."

Julia sipped steaming black coffee from a white china mug, almost willing it to burn her. She took a long time inserting a Chesterfield into her ivory holder, and she stubbed it out almost immediately. Perhaps she was trying to punish herself by burning her tongue and by denying her need for a cigarette. She was not callous. She felt very guilty for tormenting Tommy by leaving—and by letting him learn indirectly that she had actually booked her passage.

"All right, I'll try to tell you," she conceded. "Tommy, you've never known a fresh spring morning in upper New York State: the whole world washed clean by the rain, and the sun just peeping out. I long for the smell of cows and hay and damp earth. I'm sick of the stench of China: urine and mildew and . . . and all the other disgusting smells. I'm sick of the muggy heat and the sweat and the skin rashes. I want to go . . . I've got to go . . . where the world is still young and fresh and clean."

"I see." Tommy had never looked so grim. "Clearly, then, it's all over."

"It's not over at all, darling. It's just a short break for me. I'm sure—"

"Julie, I'm all but certain you'll never come back. If you hate China, you'll never come back. And I can't leave China. Not for good. . . . If you go, Julie, I'll probably let my parents find me a bride. I'll be thirty next year, you know."

"That would make me very sad. Not that I've got any right to talk. . . . But I'm not worth it. I'd hate to see you make yourself unhappy all your life just because of me."

"Then marry me right now. That's the only sure way to make me happy ever after . . . to keep me from making a fool of myself."

Julia tapped a fresh Chesterfield out of the white packet. Picking up her holder, she saw that a cigarette was already burning in its ivory mouth.

"Tommy, I'll still go home—whatever you say." Her voice was low. "I've got to. I know that it will tear me in half. I also know how much I love you. But love's not enough, not by itself. I've got to think about . . . about China and you and everything."

"I devoutly hope you will be back," he said. "But I doubt it."

When Tommy took Julia back to the apartment on Kiukiang Road, he kissed her lightly at the door, as if she were already lost to him. But she pulled his mouth down to hers and kissed him very hard. They clung to each other like children in a storm.

"Tommy, I do love you," she whispered. "Believe me, I hate going, but I must."

Like a nettle hidden in a bouquet of roses, the snub stung.

Emily should have been one of the four bridesmaids who followed Mayling Soong down the red-carpeted aisle between the massed flowers. Mayling had, however, explained at the last minute that the Gimo objected to Emily's inclusion in their wedding party. He would not insist, but Mayling could not displease him in the slightest on this day, regardless of her own wishes. She had therefore regretfully substituted her niece Pauline, the eldest daughter of her eldest sister, Ailing, and the banker-politician H. H. Kung.

The bride's attendants were now all blood relations. The Kung family was overrepresented: Ailing's younger children, Jeanette and Louis, were to be pages in black velvet knickerbockers and white satin waistcoats. Mayling would later be able to boast that she had been attended on her wedding day by three lineal descendants of the sage Kung Fu-tze, whom foreigners called Confucius.

The hidden nettle stung Emily again when May added, "I'm afraid the Howes are under a small cloud. Not only Tommy's imprisonment. But quite frankly, Emmy dear, also your involvement with that man Hollings. A foreigner, after all! I know that's all past. And it was innocent, so to speak. But in his position, Gimo has to be very careful."

Emily could not in decency—or prudence—retort that the Generalissimo was hardly one to make moral pronouncements. Aside from his secret-society connections, he had cut a wide swathe among the Ikra's sister establishments. He was, moreover, not quite divorced from his second wife, who had accompanied him throughout the Northern Expedition while he was writing devotedly to Mayling. Her mother had, however, accepted his promise that no impediment would exist when his new marriage took place.

The devout Mammie Soong had finally been overwhelmed by that affirmation—and by her daughter's powerful will. The matriarch, who sprang from three centuries of unbroken Christian faith, would even tolerate the groom's failure to convert. She was mollified by his promise to look into Christianity—and by his worldly power.

The Christian wedding with the pagan groom was taking place in

rivate at the Soongs' house on Seymour Road. Emily knew it should
ave been completed a half hour ago. The public wedding in the tradi-
onal style was to take place here in the great ballroom of the Majestic
lotel. Emily glanced at Tommy, who was fidgeting on the delicate gilt
hair on her left. Beside him, Julia smiled thinly. Her coolness toward
Mayling Soong, briefly warmed by gratitude for Tommy's rescue, had
ozen into dislike when she learned that Mayling had lied to her about
he circumstances of Tommy's release.

Foreigners accounted for at least a quarter of the thirteen hundred or
guests who awaited the tardy wedding party. Foreign taipans, bank-
rs, lawyers, and entrepreneurs were present in force with their ladies.
hey had turned out to pay homage to the powerful Soong family—and
honor Chiang Kai-shek. They now hailed him as their savior from
he Communist threat, which they had only lately believed he embod-
d. Under the benevolent eye of their doyen, the American consul
eneral, the Japanese, Swedish, Italian, British, and French consuls gen-
al were sleek in cutaways. The admiral commanding the U.S. Asiatic
leet sat beside the major general commanding Britain's land forces in
hina. Both wore civilian clothing in deference to the bridegroom,
lthough his nationalistic convictions had not prevented his marrying
the International Settlement, which was his bride's home.

Having made their peace with the Nationalists, the foreigners looked
omplacently at the portrait of the anti-foreign firebrand Dr. Sun Yat-
n, which hung between crossed white-sun flags over an altar table
mbowered by white flowers. Shields of red and white chrysanthemums
isplayed the double-joy ideogram that symbolized marital bliss. Above
er head, Emily saw three enormous wedding bells made of tens of
housands of white roses.

A single indrawn breath rippled across the ballroom. The foreign
and stubbornly finished playing "The Japanese Sandman" while
eneralissimo Chiang Kai-shek and his best man walked down the aisle
etween massed white flowers. The bridegroom's expression was at
nce ingratiating and defiant. His hairline mustache, his wing collar, and
he carnation in the lapel of his cutaway were all foreign. So were the
idskin gloves dangling limply in his left hand. Only his features—and
is heart—were Chinese.

Flashbulbs blinked, press Graflexes clicked, and newsreel cameras
hirred to record the social event of the year, perhaps the decade. Scores
f discarded flashbulbs popped when Mayling Soong came down the
sle on the arm of her brother T.V.

Behind her demure expression, no more animated than a porcelain doll's, the bride's eyes blazed in fierce triumph. Having won, she was magnificent in victory. Her gown of white-and-silver georgette, draped over the left hip, was accented by a train of silver-embroidered white satin. Her trailing veil of Honiton lace was secured by a chaplet of orange blossoms, while her enormous bouquet of blush-pink roses was tied with white-and-silver ribbons that matched her silver shoes and white stockings.

"Trust the Soongs!" a male voice whispered behind Emily. "They *never* let go of silver."

Eminence always attracted envy, Emily reminded herself. The Generalissimo and his bride were beyond question the most eminent couple in the land.

The marriage ceremony crowned the personal triumph of Chiang Kai-shek. Even his chief rival, the man called Lucifer, had come from the south to pledge the allegiance of the progressive wing of the Nationalists. In the north, the Generalissimo's ally, the Christian General, was on the point of driving the Old Marshal out of Peking. Moreover, the Central Committee of the reunited National People's Party was to meet in Shanghai in two days' time to restore Chiang Kai-shek to all the offices he had resigned in the spring.

As befitted the quasi-political occasion, bride and bridegroom posed for the cameramen before they bowed to the portrait of Dr. Sun Yat-sen. All of the Soongs were present except the bride's elder sister, the widow of the Father of the Nation, who had ostentatiously absented herself. Although Rosamonde Sun was again living in Shanghai, Emily knew that she could not bear to watch her younger sister's triumph.

The bride's face was indistinct behind the cloud of lace as she gravely listened to the reading of the marriage certificate. Nodding his head benevolently, the bridegroom watched the witnesses impress their jade seals on the certificate. Bride and bridegroom bowed first to each other then to the witnesses, and finally to the audience. At no time did ever their fingertips brush, for traditional etiquette forbade their touching each other.

The throbbing voice of an American baritone singing "Oh, Promise Me!" confirmed the Chinese marriage. Mayling Soong Chiang's heart raced with pride when she and her husband stood under a great bell of white roses to pose again for the photographers. She smiled graciously. The clapping of hands heralded the applause that would hail them all their lives.

While the photographers were pleading for one more shot, the bride slipped away to change into her traveling costume. Still puzzled by the strange music, the bridegroom followed. The Chiangs were to board a special train for Hangchow. The ancient pleasure resort was to be the gateway to the bright new China they were sworn to create—and to rule.

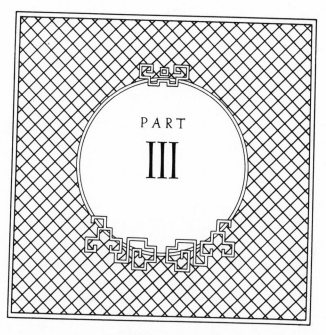

JOYS

1932–1934

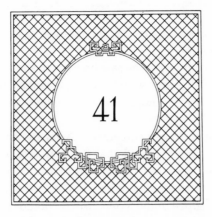

Suavely capable in all else, Joshua Haleevie was less than adroit with Elizaveta Alexandrovna Yavalenka. Normally, her presence disarmed him, although she occasionally infuriated him. He could not capture her, and he could not leave her. Early in 1932, their complex liaison still flourished because they needed each other—and because they enjoyed each other. As long as she was his alone, as she undoubtedly was, he could resign himself to the postponement of the marriage—and the children—he wanted.

Moreover, Joshua had another interest in the Ikra. Having once been a rendezvous for Chinese and Soviet Communists, the private hotel was now favored by the Japanese officers who were plotting to conquer China. Shanghai was a paradise for agents in the early 1930s, the center of intrigue for all Asia—and Joshua found the Ikra an invaluable source of information. His reports were read with respect by the Special Branch of the Settlement Police but were meant primarily for the Secret Intelligence Service in London.

Although the relationship between Joshua and Elizaveta appeared stable amid the surrounding turmoil, certain disturbing events occurred around March 3, 1932, which was Joshua's fortieth birthday. It might have been different had Elizaveta's obsession with the Ikra abated after the substantial income she had finally gained from rich globe-trotters allowed her to send away most of her professional ladies. But her obsession had not abated.

Besides, the Great Depression was hitting home by 1930. Most of the globe-trotters on whose custom Elizaveta had grown to depend were staying home. She was, therefore, forced once again to make the Ikra a house of assignation.

Joshua was unhappy when he saw how much she enjoyed that reversion. A certain raffish gleam, which had been banked, flared again in her eyes. But he had never thought she was conventional—just very difficult.

The sex lottery no longer threatened. After the first drawing closed down one out of every five bordellos, the Municipal Council had postponed subsequent drawings indefinitely. No one had instructed the council to prohibit the opening of new houses. Why, then, close houses only to see them reopen under a new name? Moreover, after the worldwide economic collapse, neither the White House nor Number 10 Downing Street was much concerned with the morals of Shanghailanders.

Having weathered the emotional storms of the lottery, Elizaveta and Joshua had sailed through sunlit waters for a few years. She sincerely looked forward to becoming Mrs. Joshua Haleevie, although her mother would have swooned at the thought of her marrying a *zhid.* But she would not set a date. She could not desert the Ikra amid the economic storms of the early 1930s. She also feared the Haleevies would cut Joshua off for marrying her, rather than the eminently respectable Charlotte Gubbai, who was their choice. Yet she was now herself well-to-do, while his commercial acumen had made him independently wealthy.

"It's getting too much, Bess!" Joshua declared forcefully early in January 1932. "I'm quite happy to chance a break with my parents. So you can't hide behind that danger anymore."

"My darling, I only want what's best for you—"

"Later, after we're married," he broke in, "I'll do what's best for me. Whatever you say! But you haven't really got the right to tell me yet. So . . ."

"Joshua, darling," she asked plaintively. "How can you say that? How can you possibly . . ."

Neither was to have the last word. Events far to the north intruded forcibly upon their lives.

The Japanese had been steadily taking over the three northeastern provinces of China, which were called Manchuria. When their warlord protégé, the Old Marshal, became too independent, fanatical officers of the Japanese Imperial Army killed him by blowing up his private railway car. His son, the Young Marshal, succeeded the warlord—and behaved even more independently. The Japanese Army therefore decided to take complete control of Manchuria.

In the summer of 1931, Japanese soldiers killed several hundred Chinese farmers for defending their land from a Japanese-sponsored seizure. Shortly thereafter, a Japanese captain traveling by train in civilian clothing on a mission of subversion was mysteriously slain. His superiors happily assumed that he had been killed by the Chinese, thus sparing them the need to invent a pretext for aggression.

In order to make Manchuria safe for Japanese settlement and Japanese agents, the Imperial Army then took over all Manchuria. Driven into exile in North China, the Young Marshal reaffirmed his loyalty to Generalissimo Chiang Kai-shek's Central Government in Nanking.

To Shanghailanders, Manchuria was far away, very cold, and supremely uninteresting. But Japanese troops attacked Chinese-ruled Greater Shanghai on the night of January 28, 1932. The Japanese hoped to divert the world's attention from Manchuria; two wrongs might not make a right, but they would make an ungodly muddle. The Japanese Army was determined to give the Chinese defenders a bloody nose and teach them to respect their betters.

It did not work out quite that way. The Chinese did not slink away but resisted fiercely.

Refugees again flooded the foreign concessions. The barking of artillery and the yapping of small arms made novel background music for smart dinner parties. It was all rather thrilling—and all a bit too close.

Conservative foreign taipans, however, convivially cheered the Japanese on. Good idea to teach the Nationalists a lesson, they said. Keep the Chinks from getting uppity.

Generalissimo Chiang was not uppity. He knew that China could not resist the major Japanese invasion that would follow a major Japanese defeat at Shanghai. He also knew that no foreign power would help him. He therefore ordered the battered defense force to pull back before it was wiped out, and he began talking peace with Tokyo.

Joshua did not cheer when the Japanese almost gave the Chinese a bloody nose. The Nationalists were asking for a say in running the Settlement and Frenchtown, and Chinese agitators were demanding that the Generalissimo take over both concessions. Joshua, however, feared the efficient, single-minded Japanese much more than he did the disorganized Chinese.

Elizaveta welcomed Japanese officers to the Ikra despite her Russian hatred for all Japanese. She *had* to be at the center of events, and they were whipping history into a gallop. Besides, it was always a good idea to keep in with the victors. However, she readily agreed to allow the Chinese secret service to mount surveillance over her new patrons. She was not committed to the Japanese.

Naturally, though, she did not demur when a certain Colonel Ishikawa requested the Caligula Suite—and two blondes. Elizaveta did not know the colonel's true name; she did know it was not Ishikawa. She also knew that he was not a colonel but a major general of intelligence who directed the subversion of China by gold, narcotics, intimidation, and assassination.

Despite her professional aplomb, she shivered when Colonel Ishikawa arrived. Even without his uniform, he was a commanding figure in gray tweed: tall and broad-chested with aquiline features. Although many women would find him handsome, Elizaveta was repelled by his flat gray eyes. She was also revolted by the tales told of him. He made a great show of his ruthlessness to terrify Japan's enemies, but he visited the torture cells only when the victim was a woman.

"This will be a very glorious night," Colonel Ishikawa declared in his stilted English. "I have escaped from my staff, and no one in the wide world knows where I am. I shall not be disturbed. It is glorious to escape all responsibility."

Elizaveta closed the heavy teak door upon Colonel Ishikawa and his two blondes, one Russian and the other Norwegian. She had performed the introductions and taken his order for caviar and *sake*. She had also reminded him that he could obtain whatever he desired by lifting the telephone concealed behind the bust of the Emperor Nero, which sneered in the bedchamber. A marble head of Caligula himself leered in the bathchamber.

Happy that she would hear no more from Colonel Ishikawa that night, Elizaveta wondered at her revulsion. Well-spoken and studiously polite, he paid extremely well for his pleasures—and his professional activities were not her concern. But he reminded her of the leeches used for bloodletting. Disgusting when shriveled and hungry, they were loathsome when swollen sleek and black with blood.

Elizaveta let down her hair for the evening, and shortly after ten, Joshua stepped out of the private elevator hidden behind the casino into her apartment. Although he was always interested in her Japanese patrons, she did not mention Colonel Ishikawa. For once she wanted to forget the Ikra entirely. For once her life appeared tawdry rather than glamorous.

She was enjoying the champagne when the internal telephone buzzed. Lifting the handset listlessly, she sat bolt upright after the first words. At length she said in Russian, "I'll be right there!"

"Trouble, Bess?" Joshua asked. "Do you need help?"

He normally avoided involvement in the Ikra's internal problems, but her tone had been urgent. After an instant, she responded, "Not if you don't want to. You know, Joshua, how you hate to . . . But you could be a great help if you really . . ."

The Russian blonde had bolted the door after telephoning. She was trembling uncontrollably, and the paper mouthpiece of her cigarette was crushed between her lipstick-stained teeth. She dabbed ineffectually with a towel at her hair, which streamed like sodden flax around her shoulders.

The Norwegian blonde was lolling in a gilt armchair, her eyes glittering with cocaine. Her sodden platinum hair was plastered into a tight cap that made her head look small, vulnerable, and curiously sexless.

The Russian blonde responded defensively to Elizaveta's sharp questions, and Elizaveta shook her head in disgust. She threw open the door of the marble bathchamber and pointed dramatically to the sunken bath. When her gaze followed her index finger, the woman of the world cowered into Joshua's arms.

"God!" she whispered hoarsely. "Thank God you're here! She said it was . . . was bad . . . very bad. But . . . this!"

The naked body of the Japanese spymaster was floating face down in the scented water of the enormous bath. His wax-yellow back was webbed with fine red lines. A whip of many hair-thin wires lay in the blood on the pale marble floor.

Without speaking, the Russian blonde turned and lowered her robe. Blood oozed from the red web on her back. She faced them and delicately, almost modestly, lifted the skirts of her robe to her hips. Her pale thighs were blotched with bruises and blood dripped from a wound the size of a silver dollar on her left hip.

"He bite hard, ver' hard!" She addressed Joshua in broken English. "Filthy pig of Jap . . . he get us in bath, Marga and me. Then he try to hold us under. . . . We cannot breathe. . . . We struggle. And then . . . he struggled, then slipped. . . . And you see!"

She led them back into the sitting room, where the Norwegian was almost insensible. Having told her story, the Russian evidently felt absolved of all responsibility.

"It didn't, you know," Joshua murmured, "it didn't happen the way she tells it. It took two strong and determined women to drown him."

"What now, Joshua?" Elizaveta's eyes were almost black in their pale caverns. "What can I do?"

Joshua terrified the two blondes with threats before sending them away. A single indiscreet word, he warned, would mean their delivery into the hands of the Municipal Police for trial—or into the hands of the Japanese for beheading.

Joshua and Elizaveta knew that they could not hush this matter up with the collusion of the Municipal Council, as they might a lesser scandal. This scandal would, moreover, provide the Japanese Army with an ideal pretext for moving against the Settlement. Colonel Ishikawa had not only been murdered, Japanese propagandists would scream, but his body had been taken to a brothel to discredit the moral Japanese officer corps. The Imperial Army might well move into the International Settlement, perhaps clashing with the other foreign powers.

Whatever else happened, the scandal would assuredly destroy Elizaveta. She would certainly face bankruptcy and imprisonment—if the Japanese did not kill her first.

"He said something about being alone." She clutched at a straw. "Something about escaping his staff. They didn't know where he'd gone. A night of freedom, he said."

"If that's true . . ." Joshua began tentatively and concluded firmly "What have we got to lose if it's not?"

Elizaveta was heartened by the word *we*. She was not alone. They stood together. Rather, he stood with her, although he had no responsibility for the disaster.

"What *can* we do?"

"If they *really* don't know, we could do the obvious," he reflected. "Get rid of him . . . just as he is. With the fighting, the corpse-collection service is picking up twice as many bodies. Another naked Oriental beaten up in a sailors' brawl. Who'd care? They'd just dump him in a common grave."

"You really think it could work?"

"My love, it's not the sort of thing I do every day—disposing of murdered men," he said. "But, yes, I'll do it. If you'll just get Wang the bartender to come up."

"Wang, the bartender? Now, why—"

"Bess, my love, you must know that Wang's been in the Communist Apparatus for years. And he's not above picking up a few extra dollars from the Nationalists. But he's always a Chinese patriot—whoever he's working for. Wang's just the man for the job. Now go back and hold the fort."

Joshua kept vigil over the drowned spymaster until three in the morning, when the pulse of the Ikra slowed. Assisted by the bartender, he eased Colonel Ishikawa's naked body into a canvas-sided laundry hamper on coasters. It fitted neatly into the private elevator and Wang pushed the hamper down the alley away from well-lit Kiangse Road.

When he turned into the side street, Joshua dropped behind. In the city that never slept, a Chinese menial could well be collecting laundry at four in the morning. A European in a velvet-collared Chesterfield would have been wildly conspicuous walking alongside the hamper. The side streets were relatively quiet, but eyes always watched through gauze curtains.

They stopped at the mouth of an alley only two blocks from the Ikra. Pushing the hamper into the shadows, they lifted the rubbery corpse and laid it on the wet pavement. One waxen foot protruded into the light of a weak streetlight, but Joshua was satisfied.

Since Colonel Ishikawa was known to frequent the Ikra, suspicion would fall on Elizaveta if he was identified. It would, however, be worse for her if his corpse were found far from his normal resorts. Joshua could not ensure that the colonel's corpse would not be identified, but he could enable Elizaveta to respond to any questioning: "Do you really think I'm such a fool I'd dump him on my own doorstep?"

After a week Joshua was satisfied that Colonel Ishikawa's body had been swept up in the regular collection of unidentified corpses from the streets. In a normal February, thirty to forty unknown vagrants might die each day of disease, starvation, and mischance. Since the Settlement was now flooded by refugees from the twilight war, violence was endemic. Among fifty to seventy corpses, many bearing wounds, the Japanese colonel's had obviously gone unremarked.

Joshua and Elizaveta were even closer after that crisis, which had bound them together with their common danger. Joshua was protective, and Elizaveta happily sheltered in the citadel of his gallantry. He marveled that a woman so fine-grained could tolerate the Ikra after that sordid incident, and Elizaveta half agreed. It appeared there could be only one outcome of their new tenderness and their new possessiveness.

Emboldened by Elizaveta's frank dependence, Joshua yielded to impulse while they were toasting his fortieth birthday on March 1, 1932. He was, he felt, young enough for new responsibilities but too old to delay an instant longer.

"You'll marry me now, Bess," he told her. "I know that. So let's set a day."

"I'm sorry, Joshua darling, but I can't." She could no longer temporize. "I'm very sorry. More sorry than I can say."

"You're . . . you're reneging?" he asked, uncomprehending. "But you agreed that we would marry. Only the time wasn't ripe. And now . . . What *are* you saying?"

"I can't marry you, Joshua. It grieves me . . . deeply. If only . . . but I can't."

"Why in the name of . . . ? I warn you, Bess, I'm not playing this game any longer. This is the *last* time."

"I wondered when your patience would run out." Her smile was melancholy. "Why can't I? All the reasons we've discussed. Your family and your circle, they'd never accept me. Besides, I *like* my present life."

"Like it? Even after . . . after Ishikawa? How can you?"

"Anything else would be too tame. I won't string you along anymore. I can't marry you, Joshua. Not now or ever!"

"Well, then, my only love!" He spoke slowly, almost meditatively. "I'll have to marry Charlotte Gubbai—if she'll still have me."

"She'd be a fool if she didn't, as big a fool as I am!" Elizaveta replied. "So you'll be leaving me? I expected that, but I hate it. . . . Will I ever see you again?"

"No, Bess," he said very slowly, "I'm *not* leaving you. I wish . . . I only wish I could. I do mean to marry Charlotte, poor girl. But no, Bess, I don't mean to leave you."

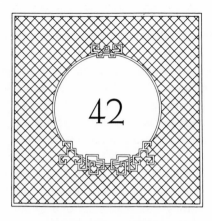

Two days after Joshua Haleevie dolefully celebrated his fortieth birthday, the Imperial Japanese Army withdrew from Greater Shanghai. Just three weeks later at a reception for two thousand guests at Jade House, Sir Judah Haleevie announced the betrothal of his youngest son, Joshua, to Charlotte Gubbai.

The previous evening the bridegroom had bade a Spartan farewell to his White Russian mistress, who was, he knew beyond doubt, the only woman he could ever love. Elizaveta wept, and Joshua was coldly courteous lest he too weep. He told her only that contrary to what he had previously believed, he could not continue to see her. That would be unjust to Charlotte. He did not tell Elizaveta that he was by no means certain he could maintain his resolution.

On May 5, 1932, a formal Sino-Japanese accord ended all the hostilities that had followed the Manchurian takeover. Generalissimo Chiang Kai-shek had made major concessions to gain that truce. His critics charged that he was selling out, but he knew that China could not yet withstand a full-scale Japanese invasion.

Just a week later, Charlotte Gubbai and Joshua Haleevie were married under the white dome of the old synagogue on Seymour Road near the first property purchased by Joshua's great-grandfather when he arrived in Shanghai eighty years earlier. The bride was petite, blond, gray-eyed, and grave in a wedding dress of cream satin embroidered with floral patterns in seed pearls. The bridegroom was pale when he crushed under his heel the crystal goblet that symbolized the destruction of the Great Temple in Jerusalem.

A thousand guests sat down to the wedding supper, almost overflowing the great dining hall of Jade House. The toasts resounded to the rafters, springing with equal zest from the Chinese and the Jewish communities. The Germans and the French strove so hard to surpass each other in sentiment and wit that even the English laughed occasionally. The bride and groom, who talked vivaciously to their neighbors at the head table, left just before midnight for their suite at the new Cathay Hotel on the Bund.

For the first time, Charlotte had insisted. She would not spend their wedding night under his parents' roof. Besides, the Cathay Hotel was convenient for boarding the Peninsular and Oriental Line's *Trafalgar,* which was sailing the next afternoon for Europe. Half the four-month honeymoon was to be spent in Paris, Florence, and London to please the bride. The groom had chosen to spend the other half in Rhodesia, Kenya, and Zambeziland, having suddenly conceived a passion for hunting big game.

Sounding her steam whistle in melancholy farewell, the *Trafalgar* began to creep among the sampans, lighters, and tenders that cluttered the murky Hwangpoo River. On the landing pontoon alongside the Bund, Julia and Emily turned, after alighting from the P&O launch, to watch the liner begin her journey to the open sea. The breeze flitting across the Hwangpoo played with their skirts and ruffled their hair. Emily shivered despite the warmth of mid-May, but Julia welcomed the cooling breeze.

"Whew!" she said. "That's better. It was dreadfully hot on the ship, wasn't it?"

"You're just not used to the heat anymore," Emily replied. "What about a cup of tea? Joshua and his champagne! It was almost too much!"

"You'd have felt a dog if we hadn't seen them off."

"Of course. But I'm glad it's over."

They threaded through the traffic that flowed in six broad lanes along the Bund. Impulsively taking Emily's arm, Julia drew her through the marble lobby of the Cathay Hotel, past the three dark teak elevator doors, and into the Palm Court. A string ensemble was softly playing songs of the giddy 1920s which already dripped sweet nostalgia in the prosaic 1930s.

"Well, Julia, you made it just in time for the big wedding," Emily said when the waiter had arranged the ornate silver tea service. "And how are your parents?"

"They send their love, Em. They're fine, except that Dad complains of stomach pains. Only nerves, Mother says."

"Julie, how long do you intend to keep trotting back and forth across the Pacific?"

"That was my last trip for a while."

"Still suffering from divided loyalties, are you? Still torn?"

"Not really, Em. I know now that my place is here."

"High time, too," Emily declared. "How Tommy's put up with it, I don't know."

"Now, Em! Tommy's an angel—but only up to a certain point. Anyway, he promised me—"

"What did he promise? You've been so close-mouthed, I can't help wondering."

"Nothing disreputable, I assure you." Julia hastily smiled and added, "Do you remember when I left in December of 1927?"

"How could I ever forget? Tommy was wretched . . . absolutely inconsolable. That stiff-upper-lip act of his completely collapsed. Why he waited a whole month, I don't—"

"You know, Em, I still feel guilty about making him break off his internship to come after me. Even though he's now made up the time."

"You know, Julie, you never told me the real story."

"There's not that much to tell. When Tommy turned up in Plattsburg without any warning, I knew immediately. Of course he looked strange in upper New York State. . . ."

Julie broke off to slip a Chesterfield into her carved ivory holder, which was growing creamy with age. She took a single long drag, blew out the smoke, looked at the burning end, and carefully stubbed it out.

Tommy, she remembered, had gotten off the Albany train and taken a boxy old taxi to her parents' house. In mid-February of 1928 the snow drifts were piled around the board porch. Ashes from the furnace had been strewn to give purchase on the narrow path of hard-packed snow that cut through to the porch. The doorbell had roused her from the chair beside the fireplace, where she was desultorily listening to George Gershwin's songs on the Victrola while listlessly flipping through the *Literary Digest*.

Julia knew she was bored but denied that she was unhappy. She told herself it was just a matter of readjusting to the United States after so long. Yes, she admitted, she did miss Tommy—badly. But she felt blue, she insisted, chiefly because she had nothing to do after her active life in Shanghai. Besides, her childhood friends seemed dull and very provincial. As soon as she found a job, preferably in New York City, and made new friends, she would be fine. Shanghai and Tommy both seemed a world—and an age—away.

"I'll get it, Mother," Julia called. "Who could it be in this weather?"

Opening the door only a crack to keep the wind from sweeping snow into the vestibule, she froze in shock. Tommy's wonderful narrow face, which she had seen lately only in her dreams, glowed with the cold above the fur collar of his overcoat. Although she could not speak for a moment, somehow she noticed that his thin-soled Oxfords were soaked through.

"Tommy!" she finally said. "Tommy!"

Julia stepped forward and, careless of the snow on his coat, pressed against him. When he put his arms around her, she knew immense joy and immense comfort.

"It's . . . like last time," she said. "The last time I opened the door to find you there . . . when you came back from Nanking. Oh, Tommy, darling!"

"Then I'm not—not unwelcome?"

"How could you even ask? You're so very welcome . . ."

Her mother called from the dining-room, "Julie, shut the door. It's blowing right from the North Pole. . . . Oh, do you have a guest?"

"Come in, Tommy," Julia said. "You'll catch your death of cold standing out there."

Everything had happened very fast after that. Julia had been poised to be swept off her feet, but Tommy seemed to have the same effect on her parents. Of course, they knew Emily and were very fond of her. They practically knew Tommy, too, for Julia had talked constantly about him. Perhaps, she reflected afterward, they had accepted the situation because they were already resigned to her marrying Tommy and living far away from Plattsburg.

Her mother was, however, unhappy about the brief time she was given to arrange the wedding. Tommy could stay with them only a few days, she said, since it was not wise to put temptation in the young couple's way. Julia smiled but did not point out that she had been tempted—and had succumbed—years earlier.

She seethed internally, but she could not object strenuously when her mother decreed that Tommy must leave Plattsburg for several weeks. Without protest, he took the train for New York City a week after his arrival. He had friends at Columbia University's medical school, the College of Physicians and Surgeons.

Just five weeks and two days after Tommy's first appearance in Plattsburg, they were married in her father's church. Julia loved her fitted grosgrain wedding dress and the clouds of net, although she momentarily felt a fraud in virginal white. The reception at her home was cheerful, despite her upright father's refusal to violate the law by serving alcoholic drinks. Although Prohibition was in the process of being repealed, not a single champagne cork popped.

That puritanical rigidity capsulized and intensified for Julia the great transition in her life. She looked around at her family and her childhood friends, and she felt sad at parting from them. But this parting was hardly more than a formality. She had, several years earlier, already left Plattsburg and the people of Plattsburg far behind her.

Standing in the familiar, shabby living room holding a glass of cold grape juice, Julia finally faced the essential dilemma that had been obscured by the excitement of the past weeks. She had left Shanghai because she could no longer bear the hopeless squalor and the incessant violence of China—and now she was going back. In her absorption with Tommy and their marriage, she had not thought about her revulsion from China until this minute. She was now, she realized with wonder, actually eager to get back to Shanghai.

Julia stood stock-still beside Tommy among the guests at their wedding party, her green eyes distant in thought. Mercifully, her shocked realization of the paradox that clouded her life was immediately followed by joyful understanding.

"I've finally got it," she said softly to Tommy. "China *is* horrible—on the surface. But China makes demands on people . . . on me . . . extraordinary demands I'd never know in a century here in stuffy, safe Plattsburg. Tommy, it's the challenge, those demands, that make life really worth living. The moments of joy, the exhilaration, show we're living fully. Do you see what I mean?"

"Very clearly!" He laughed down at her. "You could even say ecstasy, if it weren't a little pretentious. . . . And, darling, we *can* change China. It's not hopeless. Far from it. . . . I promise you can come back here whenever you please. But I bet you won't want to very often."

"Considering he gave you carte blanche, I think you've been pretty restrained," Emily said. "Only two trips in four years."

"And the last time only to show off Althea," Julia said. "Mother and Dad would never have forgiven me if I hadn't brought back their first grandchild for them to see."

"But why did you keep Tommy's promise a deep dark secret till today? There's nothing shameful about it."

"I guess I was a little ashamed of being sure I always had an escape route, particularly with you. You could've felt I didn't care enough about China . . . didn't really belong here. . . . Oh, it's hard to explain. But I guess I'm finally growing up now."

"Well, honey, don't grow up too much." Emily affectionately laid her hand on Julia's for a moment. "It could spoil all the fun we have. . . . Fun like your wedding reception here. What a difference from the one in Plattsburg!"

"Do you remember the big fat matchmaker?"

"How could I ever forget him? He took all the credit, strutted around so self-importantly we both got the giggles. Even though he had nothing to do with you and Tommy getting married."

"Well, your father wanted it that way. A big traditional wedding."

"Of course he did. And not just to make up for my defying him over . . . over Richard."

"Em, you know it really made me feel a part of China. The red satin over the altar with the incense and the offerings and the picture of Dr. Sun Yat-sen. So different . . . yet also . . ."

When Tommy and she raised their tiny porcelain wine cups with both hands, Julia had felt the action was proper and familiar—not just because she had seen Mayling Soong and Chiang Kai-shek offer the same marriage toast a few months earlier. She felt comfortable, although slightly awed, as if she had been waiting for this ceremony all her life. Tommy and she had drunk first to the matchmaker and the witnesses, next to Tommy's parents and her Uncle Jack, then to each other. Finally, they had exchanged cups and each sipped from the other's to seal their union.

The reception for two thousand in the ballroom of the Astor House Hotel had been joyful. The waiters generously pouring champagne, Julia had for a moment reflected disloyally, made up for her father's puritanical restraint. Tommy's father had insisted on that great reception—not only to show off his wealth.

Whatever Donald Howe had said to his son on their return to Shanghai that made Tommy irritable and pensive for several days, he had thereafter accepted the inevitability of the marriage with good grace. He had imposed only one condition in return for his blessing, which set Tommy's Confucian conscience at rest—and ensured the neophyte doctor and his wife a life of comfort, indeed luxury, they might otherwise not have known for many years.

Donald Howe had insisted upon bestowing his blessing as publicly as possible. After the public announcements, which included not only newspaper reports but also large newspaper advertisements, and the series of dinners that culminated in the great reception at the Astor House, there could be no talk of the Howe family's being split by a son's marriage to a foreign woman.

"You'd almost think," Emily now recalled, "that he *wanted* Tommy to marry a foreigner rather than a Chinese girl. Of course, he needed a public display of solidarity to make up for the public humiliation when I refused to marry Nien-lao. Besides, you remember, in the middle of 1928 I was still very much unmarried. And it didn't look as if they were going to find a husband for me all that easily—if at all."

Emily had, however, been striving to make up for her earlier rebellion. The crusader for women's rights had for a time almost been eclipsed by the filial daughter. She did continue her writing activities and her work at the Women's Bank, to which her parents, quite wisely, no longer objected. But she returned to Harmony Hall, leaving the loft apartment on Kiukiang Road to Tommy and Julia.

Emily advised Julia *never* to agree to move into the family mansion, "not if they offer you a wing as big as Grand Central Station." She could cope for a time with her parents' intrusiveness, but no daughter-in-law —above all, no foreign daughter-in-law—could stand up to the pressure they would instinctively exert.

Emily herself had no intention of remaining under the parental roof. She loved her parents, and she wished to please them, but she could not live with them for long. For that reason, among others, she was determined to marry just as soon as the matchmakers found her a suitable husband.

She revealed that determination to Tommy and Julia late one evening after dining at their apartment—and the conversation immediately broke down. Julia stared in perplexity at her own three-karat diamond engagement ring, and Tommy threw up his arms in an emotional display alien to both his Confucian heritage and his English public school training.

"Look here, Emmy! You'll destroy yourself if you let them fix your marriage," he warned. "God alone knows who they'll find for you. You *are* damaged goods. Only one thing is certain: whoever they dig up will be rich, elderly—and repulsive!"

Emily replied equably, "I do appreciate your worrying about me. But the sooner I marry, the sooner I'll be *really* independent. I can't stand up to the parents anymore. I used up all my resistance when I was defying them about Richard. And look where that got me! Going back to the old ways is right for me."

Supremely—and a little smugly—happy three months after she had married for love, Julia expostulated, "Em, honey, why can't you hang on a little longer? Somebody is sure to come along. We want you to be just as happy as we are. But there's not a chance if you rush into—"

"You still don't understand, Julie, do you?" Emily responded gently. "Even now, you don't understand how Chinese women are trapped."

Julia exploded, "No, Emmy, maybe I don't understand! But I do understand that you're going to destroy yourself. With all the young men in Shanghai, the stream of diplomats and foreign correspondents you meet, I'd think—"

"I could *never* marry a foreigner!" Emily declared flatly. "I learned that from my ordeal with Richard. But Chinese ladies *do* marry—and I wouldn't be happy otherwise. That doesn't leave me much choice, does it?"

"You've got all the choice in the world. Meanwhile, the Women's Bank and your writing, they're enough to fill your life until—"

"Until I'm too old to have children, Julie? Too old to be a good mother? I want children now, not at some vague time in the future. The last thing I need is romance. The best thing is to marry the man my parents choose."

Emily reached for Julia's Chesterfields, lit one inexpertly, puffed out smoke, and added, "To tell the truth, they've already found a good man. He's called Ou-yang Hsiu, and he's a well-to-do banker with a good disposition. I respect Mr. Ou-yang Hsiu—and I know I could never love him. So I'll be my own mistress."

Neither Tommy nor Julia spoke for half a minute. Their felicitations were then forced. Julia knew that her sister-in-law was deceiving herself. Emily had foolishly chosen to evade life's normal uncertainties—and life's unexpected joys as well. Apparently undisturbed by the cool reception accorded her news, Emily left shortly afterward. Regarding her fiancé she could only say that he was "an old-fashioned gentleman." She confessed that she had not met him, although she expected to see him at least once before they were married.

After his sister's departure, the normally imperturbable Tommy declared hotly: "She couldn't tell us any more because she doesn't know any more. But we can't stop her. She's set on restoring the image of a perfectly united Howe family with perfectly filial children. She besmirched that image. Now she wants to punish herself."

"To punish herself?" Julia asked slowly. "For the rest of her life?"

"There's nothing worse in Confucian morality than failing in filial piety," Tommy reminded her. "The old Sage has still got a tight grip on us Chinese, even when we pretend to be modern and Westernized. Emily's set on atoning for her treachery by making a living sacrifice of herself."

"Let's drop the subject, Tommy. It's making you unhappy."

"Spoken like a good wife. It isn't *talking* about Emmy's lunacy that makes me unhappy. It's Emmy's lunacy *itself*."

Three days later, Tommy was summoned to Harmony Hall, where Donald Howe and his four sons dined with Emily's future husband. Women were excluded from the dinner in the old way. Still, prospective bride and prospective bridegroom were permitted to bow to each other and to sit facing each other twelve feet apart in the ornate second drawing room of Harmony Hall before Eurydice Howe took her daughter away.

Tommy returned to Kiukiang Road to report to his wife, "Actually, the old boy they've lured into the net is a fairly decent type. He's even agreed to let her control her own money, keep it in the Women's Bank. She's sacrificing herself, but she's keeping her money independent—and it'll still be working for female emancipation! Talk about contradictions! You women!"

Julia let that masculine arrogance pass with a raised eyebrow, and Tommy added, "Of course, her dowry isn't peanuts. A cool half million —which is a quarter of a million U.S."

"Did your father have to *buy* her a husband?" Julia asked angrily. "Mr. Ou-yang Hsiu doesn't sound like a very nice man at all. More like a greedy pig."

"Julie, she *is* damaged goods!" Tommy explained again. "Just being seen with a foreigner spoiled her reputation."

"This marriage is the most hypocritical thing I've ever heard. . . . Tell me, Tommy, what is he really like? And exactly how old is he?"

"He's an old-style landowner, rather formal and very proper. The Ou-yang family is originally from Soochow. Himself, he seems to be a kindly gentleman of fifty-three years. . . . What're you doing?"

"Counting on my fingers, naturally. Let me see now. He would've been twenty-four when Emmy was born."

"A gulf, I grant you, but traditionally acceptable. And, at least, he *is* twelve years younger than Father. At any rate, he always wears a long-gown, and he speaks nothing but Shanghainese and Soochowese. He's very well-off, though not in Father's league. And he badly wants the connection with the Howes."

"He must have been married before. Any children?"

"Five, I'm told. And he's had two wives. One died, the other he sent back to her family a couple of years ago. Why the divorce, I don't know. But he's undoubtedly free."

"Not even a concubine?" Julia pressed. "That's unusual for an old-fashioned Chinese gentleman."

"Actually, my love . . ." Tommy looked away. "Actually, there was a little country girl. Emily said she didn't care, but Mother insisted he sent his concubine away."

"So many sacrifices just to acquire spoiled goods?" Julia's tone was derisive. "He must be a perfect angel!"

"He *is* eager. You see, he wants more children."

"*More* children? But he's got five already."

"They're *old-fashioned* children. Mr. Ou-yang Hsiu wants *modern* children for the modern age. And who better to produce them than a modern American-educated lady?"

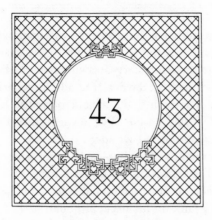

The amah Lao Zee, who fiercely guarded Tommy and Julia against peddlers, beggars, and cranks, had recently been joined by a major-domo, who was called Loo. If Lao Zee and Loo had not already gone to their own quarters, the itinerant curio dealer would not have talked his way into the big living room.

However, Tommy himself answered the doorbell at eleven in the evening, and Tommy was a pushover for the slick sales patter. The hallway was gloomy, and the intruder looked faintly sinister in the battered slouch hat and the old-fashioned long-gown worn by gunmen and toughs. Yet when he extolled his selection of Peking enamel boxes, for which Julia had a weakness, Tommy took the chains off and swung the heavy door open.

The thin curio dealer stooped under the weight of the goods bundled into the length of old silk that was slung over his shoulder. When he squatted on the floor to untie that makeshift sack, his hatbrim shaded his features. Julia and Tommy were watching his hands, which were skeletal, hardly more than skin stretched over bone. The long fingers delicately unwrapped the wares: an octagonal box with compartments for crystalized fruit and a swirling *shou*, long life, ideogram on the lid; a pair of round powder boxes painted with identical dragons; and, even more precious, a big black lacquer box sprinkled with gold flecks.

Entranced by those treasures, Julia had overlooked the strange behavior of Adam, the Tibetan mastiff, who normally bullied strangers entering his home. Adam had not barked. He had looked at the dealer curiously, rather than hostilely, and his plumed tail had wagged tentatively. As if he could not quite believe his own senses, Adam had stalked cautiously across the room to sniff at the dealer's shoes. After calling attention to the white chrysanthemum painted on the underside of the lid of the lacquer box, the dealer familiarly scratched Adam under the chin. Instead of growling, the mastiff purred in his throat.

"Damned odd!" Tommy said. "I've never seen that beast so friendly on such short acquaintance. I wonder . . ."

The curio dealer removed his hat—and Tommy recognized his friend Chang Kuo-tao. The Communist leader was haggard. The heavy cheekbones that stretched his gray parchment skin, made his face look skull-like. Long hair lay lank on his neck, although he had always worn an almost military brush-cut.

"Ni-men pu hsiang-hsin, Tan . . . Joo-li . . ." Chang Kuo-tao reached for the Chesterfields on the coffee table as he spoke "Don't you believe it's me, Tom . . . Julie?

Recovering, Julia said, "Good lord, Kuo-tao, we thought you were five hundred miles away."

"I was, Joo-li," he replied. "But I had to see the Secretariat of the Communist Party . . . what remains of it, anyway."

"Delighted to see you," Tommy said. "How on earth did you get here?"

"It's no holiday excursion, coming through the Nationalist lines. But it wasn't as bad as last year, when I left Shanghai. . . . Besides seeing the Secretariat, I also want . . . need . . . a favor from you two. So here I am."

"And very welcome, too." Slightly abashed at having been taken in by his friend's disguise, Tommy was slightly too hearty. "Take a chair. What'll you drink?"

"Just a beer," Chang Kuo-tao replied. "And would you have something to eat? Naturally, restaurants were out. I didn't want to chance even the eating stalls. Someone might've recognized me. All the workers know me from the union days."

Smiling at that pardonable vanity, Julia started for the kitchen. Before she closed the door, she heard Tommy say, "You'll stay here, of course. Too risky for you to be wandering around the city. The Settlement Police and Nationalist special agents are working hand in glove. I've never known worse persecution of progressives."

"So I've heard," Kuo-tao answered. "But I won't stay, thanks. We don't want your servants wondering about your strange guest. And I'm happier about my disguise now. If you didn't see through it . . ."

Immersed in the task because she enjoyed it, Julia chopped up scallions, added segments of garlic, sliced ginger, and tossed those ingredients into the peanut oil smoking in the bottom of a wok. After stirring with oversized chopsticks for half a minute, she turned down the flame and tipped in cold boiled rice. Then she added the honey-roasted pork she had found in the refrigerator. When the fried rice was warmed through, she tipped it into a tureen. After setting a lacquer tray with a rice bowl and chopsticks, she filled smaller dishes with the savories she knew Kuo-tao liked: pickled Chinese cabbage with chilis, boiled peanuts, and fermented bean curd, which tasted like ripe Camembert.

The big Communist leader attacked the food as if he had not eaten for two days, which was likely. He had come from the enclave in the interior north of the Yangtze called the Oyüwan Soviet Area to Shanghai to see the fugitive Central Committee of the Chinese Communist Party. Although that Soviet area was one among eight, Chang Kuo-tao was actually more like a visiting chief of state than an ambassador in the murky half world of intrigue and violence. He was also commander in chief of the Fourth Front Red Army.

"While Kuo-tao's tucking in," Tommy asked, "do you remember when he came to say good-bye?"

"More than a year ago," she recalled. "Sometime early in 1931."

"March, it was when he left Shanghai."

Daringly coming to the apartment on Kiukiang Road to say good-bye, Tommy recalled, Chang Kuo-tao had worn the stained cotton-padded long-gown and the shabby cloth shoes of a struggling rural merchant. Though he aped the rough speech and coarse manners of such a bumpkin, almost spitting on the gold Peking carpet, Tommy had not, for once, laughed at his friend's passion for disguise. Chang Kuo-tao was setting out on a long, hard, and hazardous journey, in part because he would not much longer escape arrest if he remained in Shanghai.

Tommy and Julia had learned that his name now stood at the top of the wanted list just above Commissar Chou En-lai. The Settlement Police and the Nationalist secret service knew that both Communist leaders were still at large in Shanghai. The lavish rewards offered for their capture far outweighed the modest bribes the Communists could offer for their freedom.

Sailing as a deck passenger on a foreign-owned cargo steamer up the Yangtze, Chang-Kuo-tao had disembarked at Wuhan. His merchant's disguise had carried him past the guards on the docks and the sentries at the city limits. He had taken a ramshackle rural bus.

"The young fellow at the wheel," Kuo-tao interjected, "used the horn and the accelerator instead of brakes. Only damned gadgets on that antique bus that worked."

After leaving the bus, Kuo-tao had walked more than a hundred miles to the Communist enclave. Commissar Chou En-lai, liaison officer between the Communist Party's weak Central Committee and the distant Soviet areas, had planned that route with care. Nonetheless, Chang Kuo-tao was in constant peril from informers, special agents, Central Government patrols, even corrupt provincial troops and the normally lackadaisical local police. All were alert for Generalissimo Chiang Kai-shek's fourth campaign to exterminate the Communists.

"A big fat fish like me was very lucky to slip through the net," Chang Kuo-tao interposed. "In the Soviet area things went very well for a while. But I'm now thinking of pulling out. My Fourth Front Red Army is getting too strong. So Chiang Kai-shek and his German advisers are concentrating their attack on us. I'll decide after I've talked with the comrades here."

Julia sensed that Chang Kuo-tao had already decided to withdraw from his besieged enclave. He could only go west to escape the Central Government's attacks. The local warlords, who still reigned in West China, were no match for the Red Army. Besides, they would assuredly prefer to avoid battles with the Communist forces if they were properly bribed. In the summer of 1932, many battles were still decided by silver bullets, as they had been decided in the heyday of the warlords.

Yet the general shape of China had changed strikingly. Assisted by that political chameleon, the Christian General Feng Yü-hsiang, Generalissimo Chiang had four years earlier finally taken the city called Peking, which meant "northern capital." He had hopefully changed the city's name to Peiping, which meant "northern peace." His Central Government of the Republic of China, now recognized by all the foreign powers, remained at Nanking, the southern capital. For the first time in more than two decades, only one government claimed to rule the entire vast nation.

Although the Generalissimo had brought the warlords to heel, he could not destroy them. The blatant Japanese threat was, however, muting rivalry among the opposing Chinese factions—except for the maverick Communists. It was not quite unity, and it was not quite peace.

Yet the Generalissimo had imposed greater stability than China had enjoyed for half a century. As a result, the country was moving forward economically. In the early 1930s roads, railways, factories, and schools were built despite major obstacles: feuding within the Nationalist ranks; the worldwide depression; the inherent weakness of the Central Government against the provinces; shortages of both capital and skills; and, of course, the menace posed by the Japanese and the Communists.

Tommy and Julia agreed with that ardent Nationalist supporter Emily that the Nationalists were truly beginning the Herculean task of remaking China. Yet both believed that the Generalissimo was a viper in human form. No Nationalist accomplishment could persuade them to support the Nationalist dictatorship.

Both knew that the Communists' Red Terror opposed the Nationalists' White Terror. The Red Army buried landlords to the neck and left them to die. The Nationalist Army shot all peasants it suspected of assisting the Communists. The Red Terror, Julia firmly believed, was leading to a new China, which would be just and prosperous, whereas the White Terror was atrocity for its own sake. Tommy, who could not wholly agree, did not argue with her. After all, they were now both equally committed politically.

They were also committed by friendship, a bond even stronger in China than elsewhere. Why else should they at midnight be comfortably chatting with a man who, at that moment, was avidly hunted by hundreds of police spies, informers, and detectives. If Chang Kuo-tao was discovered in their apartment, the tipoff man would be rewarded with $50,000 Mex—about $25,000 U.S.

And Tommy and herself? At best, they would be disgraced, perhaps imprisoned, for sheltering a rebel chieftain. At worst, even Donald Howe's wealth would not save them from execution.

Chang Kuo-tao wanted a service from them that he could not ask of the Communist Party. Because it was personal, the hard men of the Apparatus would consider such a request a demonstration of weakness. The task would be arduous, perhaps futile, undoubtedly dangerous. Yet how could they refuse?

"It's Lien," he explained. "I couldn't ask anyone else to find my wife for me. I've been looking for a week now here in Shanghai. She seems to have vanished. But I can't hang around any longer. You'll try, Tom? And Joo-li?"

"Tell me more," Tommy said. "I'll need something to go on."

Julia fondly remembered the quiet woman, who was equally devoted to Chang Kuo-tao and to the Communist cause. She had been restrained when Julia was first invited to the tiny apartment where Lien and Kuo-tao then lived in working-class Chapei just north of the International Settlement. It had been several years before Chang Kuo-tao invited her. He was suspicious of a foreign woman, even if she was the wife of his close friend. But Lien had taken to Julia. Their quick laughter had enlivened the political discussions that continued till dawn broke over the Hwangpoo River.

"All I really know," Kuo-tao said dolefully, "is that she's nowhere to be found. She lost contact with the Central Committee when everyone was going to ground to avoid the police. You know we sent our son back to my family in the country. So he's safe. But not Lien. She was always interested in nursing. So I thought you might've heard or seen—"

"Nothing, Kuo-tao, not a word," Tommy answered. "But I'll look around."

Despite his casual words, Tommy had just made a binding commitment. Kuo-tao, who understood, nodded his thanks and said, "Heaven alone knows exactly where I'll be. But the Apparatus should know where I am—within five hundred miles or so."

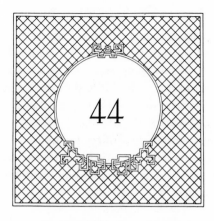

Julia conscientiously checked her diary, although she was almost as sure of the date as she was of her own wedding anniversary. On September 20,1932, it was four years to the day since Emily's spectacular wedding.

As she lifted the telephone to call the Nursery Florists she remembered a more recent event. She concentrated on her instructions to the florist to send the four dozen spider lilies that would recall Emily's wedding bouquet. But her anger had not cooled.

Only a week ago, the Apparatus had issued its arbitrary command—some two months since Chang Kuo-tao's sudden appearance at the apartment on Kiukiang Road in the guise of a curio dealer. After pleading with Tommy and herself to find his missing wife, the Communist chieftain had vanished again into the countryside.

Using great discretion, they had made many inquiries. Discretion was essential. It would be worse than pointless to find Lien if, in so doing, they inadvertently pinpointed her for the Nationalist secret police. Nor could they compromise their own cover by publicly displaying concern for a notorious female Communist. Tommy, who was acutely sensitive to the political crosswinds, also felt that Kuo-tao did not wish the Communist Party's Central Committee in Shanghai to learn of the search for his missing wife. Somehow, Tommy suspected, Chang Kuo-tao and the Communist leaders in Shanghai were not getting along.

Discreet or indiscreet, they had learned nothing. The forthright woman with the warm smile might as well have entered a Buddhist convent or have left China.

Yet they had stirred up the dust. Early on the morning of September

12, a young street-hawker had thrust a Chinese-language newspaper into Tommy's hand. Automatically handing the hawker a few coppers, Tommy had automatically suppressed his poignant impression. The youth really looked nothing like Little Pow at the same age; only his energy and his enthusiasm recalled the boy of all work, who would have been in his twenties if he had survived.

So many missing, so many sacrifices to the revolution, Tommy reflected, as he found the message written on the second page above the advertisements for herbal and acupuncture practitioners. The scrawled grass-ideograms, which only the highly educated could decipher, read: *"Cease your search for the woman immediately."*

Rage flared behind Tommy's urbane expression. He turned back to the apartment to tell Julia, who was as angry as he at the Apparatus's peremptory directive. After a few minutes, however, she pointed out that they could not openly disobey. They would have to stop looking for Lien for some time.

Although she was still angry, Julia's thoughts turned elsewhere as she hung up the telephone. She recalled Emily's wedding four years earlier.

Emily Howe was a modern woman—a militant feminist and an active supporter of the Nationalist movement. The amiable man she married was a living fossil, and their wedding was an archaic pageant.

The only concession to the times had been the use of motor vehicles. Her lavish trousseau was borne through the streets in open trucks bedizened with scarlet and gold ribbons, rather than on platforms carried by coolies. Emily herself rode behind drawn blinds in her father's emerald-green Roll-Royce Silver Ghost, rather than in a screened scarlet bridal palanquin.

Julia remembered the precise balance of modesty and ostentation in the ceremony. It would not have been proper for the wedding of Donald Howe's daughter to outshine the recent wedding of his deceased friend Charlie Soong's daughter. The solution was simple. Since the wedding of Chiang Kai-shek and Mayling Soong had been Western in almost every respect, the wedding of Ou-yang Hsiu and Emily Yuelin Howe was assertively traditional in every respect—except, of course, the motor cars.

For three weeks beforehand, Harmony Hall had been crammed with the abundant furnishings, clothing, and valuables Emily would bring with her, as well as the lavish wedding presents. The circular ballroom with the glass dome could barely contain the rolls of silk and the leather chests laden with garments, linens, and bedclothes. Those riches were laid out for inspection by thousands of friends, dependents, and the press. The *North China Daily News* was, as ever, inhibited, but the *Evening Press* in its brash Yankee way was equal to the occasion and the spectacle:

The more elaborate among the hundreds of costumes were taken out with ill-concealed pride by the family's retainers and held up for inspection [the society editor, Nina Gamewell, reported ecstatically.] And they were well worth seeing! Brocaded silks, embossed satins, and crepe de chines, as well as the most delicate gauzes, their colors ranging from the palest hues of pink, green, blue, and violet down to rich crimsons, deep grays, glowing chestnuts, and lustrous blacks—all in bewildering profusion. The jewels were shown in dozens of glass cases: bracelets, rings, buckles, earrings, necklaces, and hair ornaments. Apple-green jade was the principal stone, but diamonds, rubies, pearls, sapphires, and emeralds also shone resplendently.

"And she only exaggerated slightly!" Tommy had chortled when he read that account. "Listen to this:"

The bride's wardrobe, however, was only part of the wealth she brought to the groom. In addition there was, of course, the financial settlement, reported to exceed $2 million. Suites of furniture blocked the corridors of Harmony Hall. Huge wooden chests with gleaming brass locks stood before divans laden with coverlets, quilts, and eiderdowns. Most were of the costliest materials: flowered silks, figured satins, as well as fine cretonnes with gay prints and soft cashmeres for summer use.

The bedroom furniture was of carved rosewood, while the ornate brass bed was hung with silk curtains and silver ornaments. Embossed gold and silver teapots, ivory and jade chopsticks, crystal bowls, and silver-wire wine cups, jewelry cases, hand-painted scrolls, silk banners—all those were among the riches lavished upon Miss Emily Yuelin Howe, who is tomorrow to become Madame Ou-yang Hsiu.

"The lady reporter now gets ecstatic," Tommy had said gleefully. "It's some catalogue: 'Planned are exotic fare and sumptuous repasts—roast pigs, ducks, geese, and swans; conch, whelk, and terrapin; bear's paw, elephant's trunk, and hummingbirds!' "

"All true, Tommy," Julia had interposed, "isn't it?"

"Afraid so, my love! The last wild extravagance of old China! My poor sister! She's numb half the time—and exulting the other half. Exulting in her sacrifice, the pain that washes away her sins."

The next day the dowry and the gifts had been carried in ten trucks to the old-fashioned house in Jessfield Park that was the home of the bridegroom and his unmarried children. Although substantial, it was only a mansion, not a virtual palace like Harmony Hall.

Set within a brick-walled compound, the three-story building enclosed a courtyard roofed with glass, where two bands competed on the wedding day. Chinese musicians in soiled long-gowns picked out arias from Shanghai operas on traditional instruments, while a gaudily uniformed Filipino band rendered popular tunes. The big octagonal lanterns suspended from the overhanging verandahs trailed scarlet-silk streamers with silver tassels. Scarlet banners covered the walls, and thirty-foot runners of firecrackers hung from the eaves.

At half past two, an hour past the bride's scheduled arrival, the Filipinos grinned and played "Till the Sands of the Desert Grow Cold," humorously warning that it could be hours before she appeared. Wise in the ways of Shanghai brides, the first guests began arriving about three. Tommy and Julia honored the old ways by turning up at twenty minutes past three. Since Mayling Soong had been three hours late for her own wedding, Tommy predicted that Emily Howe would be three and a half hours late. But he began glancing irritably at his wristwatch shortly after four. Perspiration was soaking through his shirt into his sharkskin jacket.

The unseen bridegroom was enjoying the last hours of his second bachelorhood—his third or fourth, if one counted concubines—with his intimates in his private apartment. At twenty-five past four, when the mid-September heat was beginning to wane, Ou-yang Hsiu at last appeared to greet his guests. He was sleekly gray from shining silver-frosted hair to oyster-colored cloth shoes.

He chatted with Tommy but would not look directly at Julia. Embarrassed at speaking to a foreign woman, although she was soon to be his sister-in-law, he said plaintively, "I've sent for the bride three times. I've pleaded with her to come. But no bride!"

After the bridegroom parted from them with elaborate courtesies, Tommy looked again at his wristwatch and exclaimed, "It's twenty to five. Maybe she's changed her mind at the eleventh hour. If so . . ." He broke off, whistled tunelessly between his teeth, and resumed: "By God, I wouldn't've believed it. The real old way! Julie, my sweet, he's going off to snatch the bride from her jealous family."

Ou-yang Hsiu strode to the emerald-green Silver Ghost, which was conveniently waiting in the road. Four male friends piled in with him, but the Rolls did not draw away immediately. Despite the bridegroom's urgent commands, the driver waited until twenty-two Filipino bandsmen had marched out of the compound. Blaring John Philip Sousa's "Washington Post March" in jazz tempo, they crowded into one of the open trucks that had carried the dowry. As the two vehicles drew away, the refrain hung in the air: "The monkey wrapped his tail around the flagpole, around the flagpole!"

Three quarters of an hour later, the bandsmen marched again into the compound. Still blaring the "Washington Post March," their saxophones, clarinets, and trumpets swung from side to side. As they segued into Mendelssohn's "Wedding March" to a polka beat, the Silver Ghost drew up at the gateway.

Playing the role of a traditional matron of honor, Julia stepped forward to open the door of the limousine. The bride smiled blandly and clutched her bouquet of spider lilies to the bosom of her long white lace wedding gown. Her face was stark white with powder, and her lips glowed cherry-red behind her long veil.

When Emily's white satin slipper crossed the threshold of the courtyard, thunder erupted and smoke billowed from the first runner of firecrackers. Stepping forward hesitantly, Ou-yang Hsiu winced when the second runner of five thousand firecrackers began to explode. Collecting himself, he stepped forward again. Bride and bridegroom waited side by side for the joyful din to end. Dogs howled, small children cowered behind their mothers, and bigger children jumped up and down in joy. For almost ten minutes, eighty-two strings of firecrackers tolled the combined ages of bride and bridegroom by Chinese reckoning.

For some moments after the final explosion, neither the guests nor the wedding pair moved. The smoke rolling through the courtyard blinded them, the acrid fumes stinging their eyes. Peppered with red paper fragments, bride and groom advanced. They bowed profoundly to the three men standing before the scarlet-draped altar: the matchmaker and the official witnesses.

Tommy fiddled with his curved meerschaum pipe as the ceremony unfolded its apparently interminable length. Essentially the same rites had bound Mayling Soong and Chiang Kai-shek nine months earlier. Where the Chiangs had bowed once, however, the Ou-yangs bowed thrice. While the Chiangs had affirmed the marriage certificate once, the Ou-yangs did so twice. Aunts and uncles, cousins and sisters, brothers, nieces, and nephews, even sons and daughters of the bridegroom, all played small roles in the ritual.

After a full hour, Julia saw with relief that Emily and her new husband were making their final bows to Emily's parents. After honoring the father-in-law he valued above his bride, Ou-yang Hsiu lifted his wine cup to his wife. She responded with her toast to him. After they exchanged wine cups, the rite was at length complete.

Since Ou-yang Hsiu's mother had long since been dead, Emily immediately assumed the full authority of the mistress of the house. At twenty-seven she was almost elderly for a traditional Chinese bride. Most were ten to thirteen years younger. Because of her authority and her age, Emily was spared the traditional bride-baiting. She would not be teased and tormented by female relatives and finally tumbled naked into the red-curtained marriage bed.

After the ceremony, male and female guests drew apart in deference to the pretense that ladies of good family still lived apart in the seclusion of virtual harems. For half an hour, the ladies chatted and sipped sweet wines while the gentlemen gambled and tossed down strong spirits. When the servants beat gongs, all the guests sat down together at tables set under the glass roof of the courtyard. The groom presided, and, remarkably, the bride herself sat down with them.

The groom's aged uncles nodded tolerantly. She was the daughter of a man insulated from even the possibility of error by his great wealth. The aged uncles' aged wives and aged concubines were not as tolerant. Shielding seamed and tinted lips behind liver-spotted hands, they whispered severely. She was no longer a Howe but an Ou-yang, after she had bowed to the ancestral tables of the Ou-yang family. She should therefore behave with the traditional modesty of a true Ou-yang.

Emily won back a portion of the aunts' regard, which she was not so foolish as to undervalue, by punctiliously observing a new custom they believed hallowed by time. Walking three steps behind her husband, she followed him from table to table, each time raising her thimble-cup to sixteen seated guests. Completing the circuit of fifty tables kept her from consuming more than a morsel of each of the sixty-four courses.

After every second course, the bride withdrew to her chambers, where her amahs waited. With the next course, she reappeared in a new costume. Ranging from the styles of the late 1800s, which were stiff, heavily embroidered, and set with seed pearls, to the latest *cheongsams*, some daringly slit to mid-thigh, each costume was wholly different. Scarlet tribute silk set off glowing emeralds; cream-yellow satin displayed cascades of baroque pearls; and a simple tunic of black samite shot with gold framed a necklace of blue-white diamonds.

Rising with relief a little past eleven in the evening, Julia and Tommy pushed through the crush to say good-night to Emily. They saw no animation behind her mask of white powder. After looking at them without recognition for a moment, she smiled mechanically and bowed formally.

As they left the compound, Julia said abruptly, "They put on a great show. But it was hollow. What can it all mean to Emmy? What can they possibly have in common?"

"Damned if I know!" Tommy's back was rigid, and he stared straight ahead. "Not even bed, I'm afraid! Not really!"

45

SEPTEMBER 20, 1933

Emily was again enormously pregnant after a hiatus of three years. Julia had therefore happily accepted her sister-in-law's invitation to celebrate the fifth anniversary of her marriage to Ou-yang Hsiu at the mansion in Jessfield Park.

"We'll have a real hen party," Emily promised with brittle enthusiasm. "Only us and the children. Though Hsiu may make a brief appearance. Be sure to bring Persephone."

Emily's husband did not appear, briefly or otherwise. That was just as well, Julia felt, since he might have been uncomfortable. Emily's private quarters on the second floor overlooking the courtyard had an intensely female atmosphere, rather like a combined obstetrics and pediatrics clinic. Blessedly, however, the amahs, who were like well-disciplined worker ants in white tunics and black trousers, looked after the brood with no need for supervision.

Actually, there were only four children, Julia's two and Emily's two. However, the cousins together seemed like a lot more. The whole was greater than the sum of the parts.

Julia was puzzled by Emily's commanding her to bring Persephone, who was only six weeks old. Her sister-in-law only explained, "Sentiment, my dear. I want the whole family together. Very Chinese, you may say. Anyway, it's not too early for Perse to begin learning to be a social being."

That was also a Chinese sentiment, Julia reflected. Her younger daughter, however, was slumbering in Lao Zee's arms. Glancing at Persephone's fringe of black baby hair, Julia wondered whether her second daughter would go blond like Althea, her first. Tommy had consulted his old genetics textbooks late in 1930 when six-month-old Althea's hair turned light, almost platinum. Pretending suspicion, although the infant's features were unmistakably a blend of Julia's and his own, he had finally declared with mock solemnity, "You're in the clear, Julie. But only just. It *can* happen, but it doesn't happen often."

Fondly intrigued by her daughters, Julia was looking forward to watching them develop. They would, she already sensed, be quite different from each other. She was thinking about having one more child —not only because Tommy badly wanted a son. Captivated by her daughters' growth and change, she felt that a third child would be a fascinating contrast to the other two.

On balance, however, she probably would not have another. She was not frightened, although Persephone had taken sixteen agonizing hours to appear. That was unusual, Tommy had told her, for a second birth when the first had been easy. Julia vividly remembered the pain, despite old wives' tales about mothers' forgetting the pangs of childbirth. Neither was that pain the reason for her reluctance. She simply felt that they should not allow themselves such self-indulgence.

The times were hard for most. Tommy and she were, however, well off despite the Great Depression. Yet implacable Japanese pressure was forcing Generalissimo Chiang Kai-shek toward a grim decision. Very soon, he would have to fight the Japanese, which would mean a terrible war—or he would have to surrender China's independence. It was no time to bring another child into the world.

Julia was convinced that the Communists would not permit the Generalissimo to surrender. The tenacious patriotism of men like Chang Kuo-tao, his rival Mao Tse-tung, and brilliant Commissar Chou En-lai bound Tommy and herself to the Chinese Communist Party. The Communists would either force Chiang Kai-shek to fight or would carry on the fight alone. War was therefore virtually a certainty. The Japanese would never give up their ambitious campaign to conquer China, and the Communists would never give in to the Japanese.

Julia served China by serving the Communist Apparatus in secret, but her sister-in-law was playing a more public role in the struggle. As the Japanese threat mounted, Emily had been drawn closer to Mayling Soong Chiang, who was taking over direction of the weak Chinese Air Force. Mayling's dedication convinced Emily—and gave Julia hope— that the Generalissimo would in the end decide to fight. Unlike Emily, Julia was not particularly optimistic about the outcome of a new Sino-Japanese war. At best, it would be a very long struggle, a war of attrition:

Japanese efficiency and aggressiveness against China's endurance and vast area.

With the exception of a few German-trained divisions, the Nationalist forces were still primitive. The problems of preparedness were also psychological.

Mayling was now running the Air Force because her husband, trained as an officer before the Great War, was almost as ignorant of air power as were earthbound guerrilla leaders like Chang Kuo-tao and Mao Tse-tung. Nonetheless, Emily seemed to Julia fanatical in her support for the Nationalists. Emily was absolutely convinced that the Generalissimo would fight—and would win.

Emily's total commitment to the Chiangs had not prevented her fulfilling her obligations to her husband. Her swollen abdomen, almost grotesque on her slender frame, gave renewed proof of her devotion to her marital duty. Although a detached wife, Emily was a dedicated mother.

She had begun her maternal career with remarkable promptness. In mid-August 1929, less than eleven months after her marriage, she had triumphantly produced the son her husband wanted. The boy was named Jen-hsun, meaning "True Obedience," but his mother called him Jason. At four, he was perceptive and mischievous. His fond Aunt Julia believed that he showed great promise, and his mother did not disagree. Already unruly, Jason showed signs of becoming almost unmanageable. He was spoiled not only by his mother and his father but by his older half brothers and half sisters. He had no real competitor, for Emily's second child, who was born late in 1930, was a girl.

Now almost three, Patricia was dainty and docile, a little Chinese lady. Although her father loved her, he could not treasure her as he did Jason. Ou-yang Hsiu wanted more sons to carry on his name; to enrich the family by their talents; and, in the fullness of time, to venerate him as their ancestor. Girls required dowries to enrich other families.

Nor did Jason face competition from his cousins, Julia's children. Sadly, both were girls. After Althea's easy birth in January 1930, Tommy had decreed that her Chinese name was to be Tien-tsu, "Heaven's Gift." He was quite content with one child, he had said, even if that child was a daughter rather than a son. He had laughed condescendingly when his sister told him that her husband was pressing her to try for another son.

"Poor old you!" Tommy had said. "What a primitive attitude. And I thought nobody except Father still felt that way."

"Don't be silly, Tommy!" Emily had chided. "You know very well *all* Chinese men feel exactly the same. Only Hsiu doesn't dare beat me into trying for more sons."

Tommy had duly protested that he, at least, was beyond such medieval egotism. Nonetheless, he had been delighted when Julia told him in late 1932 that she was again pregnant. Although he had not been visibly downcast when Persephone arrived at the beginning of August, Julia knew he still yearned for a son.

Because she loved Tommy, she was tempted to try again—after a decent interval. She, too, might like a son. But not just yet!

As Tommy slyly pointed out, they could well afford another child. Although not yet fully qualified, he would soon be an internist, a specialist to whom other doctors appealed for a diagnosis when they were puzzled—and he would collect the appropriate fees.

Quite soon, he would no longer look to his parents for the luxuries they both candidly enjoyed. When their consciences protested so much self-indulgence, they told each other that they had to appear to be self-indulgent offspring of the bourgeoisie. The cover decreed by the Apparatus required them to show little interest in politics. When they did think politically, they had to appear inclined toward the progressive right, which nowadays meant Chiang Kai-shek's Central Government at Nanking.

"We've got lots of room for expansion," Tommy would say, still thinking about a son.

They had been happy with the loft apartment's enormous living room and two minute bedrooms until Althea's arrival demanded more space. Then they had quickly learned that a very small child required not only truckloads of equipment that ranged from diapers and bedding to cribs and scales, but, as well, two amahs of her own. Naturally, she required much space for her paraphernalia and her personal staff.

Tommy and Julia had talked of finding a house in the French Concession with a garden for Althea and the mastiff, Adam, who was her devoted guardian. Tommy's parents had again proposed that they move into a wing of their own in Harmony Hall. When Julia quailed, Tommy suggested that his father guarantee a mortgage for a house of their own. Donald Howe flatly refused. He believed that a son's place was with his parents—no matter how old the son was.

Joshua Haleevie had solved their problem. He was their landlord, having bought the building on Kiukiang Road in 1929, just after the Wall Street crash. He had offered them the remaining four floors for a few hundred Mex a year. His terms were almost embarrassingly liberal: First, Tommy was to serve as his personal physician; and second, they could buy the entire building at any time after five years.

Julia had originally believed that Joshua was amusing himself by such princely generosity, probably as a diversion from his normal shrewd, though fair, business practices. Tommy, however, wondered. His father had taught him to look very carefully for the motives behind any action that appeared excessively selfless. Under Tommy's influence, Julia, too, now wondered whether Joshua saw their house as an asset in his clandestine second occupation, which was counterespionage.

However, whether they accepted Joshua's offer or not, they could do little to divert his suspicion—if suspicious he was. Shortly after Joshua made his offer, Tommy told Julia they need not worry about Joshua's penetrating their cover. Accordingly, they happily agreed to solve their housing problem by remaining where they were and adding a roof garden for Althea and Adam.

Julia's recollections of times not so long ago were interrupted by Emily's inquiring look. She replied to her sister-in-law's implied question, "I was just thinking how lucky I was. If I'd stayed in Plattsburg . . . if Tommy hadn't come after me . . . I'd have had an entirely different life. I sometimes shiver when I think what a close call I had."

"Since you're in such a thanksgiving mood, how about a bottle of champagne?" Emily suggested. "To celebrate the good things that've happened to us both, all the good things."

"But, Emmy, I—"

"I know you think I . . . we all . . . drink too much champagne." Emily ignored Julia's mild protest. "But even you'll agree that on an occasion like this . . ."

"That's fine, Em. I guess we both have a lot to be grateful for."

Emily, who loved champagne, believed she could drink large quantities without any effect. But two glasses loosened her tongue.

"You know, Em, you can still surprise me, even after all these years," Julia accordingly said. "Whatever happened to the firebrand you used to be? What became of the crusader for women's rights?"

"Exactly what do you mean, Julie?"

Waiting for the champagne to take effect, Julia persisted. "Since you began working for Mayling, you haven't written much about women's fight for their rights. Rosamonde Sun pointed that out to me."

"Rosamonde would, wouldn't she, Julie? She's no more than a Communist apologist nowadays."

"I guess so." Julia had to pose as a right-wing sympathizer. "You know, it's not fair, what she says about you."

"What else does she say?"

"Well, Em, Rosamonde says your writing, both reporting and fiction, now only explains Nationalist deficiencies—and explains away Nationalist errors."

"Julie, I happen to believe the Generalissimo is China's only hope. Naturally I want to explain his actions . . . put them in the best light."

"Do you really want your readers to wait patiently for delivery from masculine oppression? Until the Gimo has defeated the Communists?"

"And the Japanese, Julie! The Communists and the Japanese are both threats to *all* Chinese. Not just to men but to women too."

"Frankly, Em, if your own marriage was happier, I could understand your new attitude better."

"Julie, I didn't marry for love. So I can't be disappointed, can I? Hsiu is a good husband by the parents' standards. By my standards, too. Unlike most Chinese husbands, he's not a household tyrant, so I'm satisfied."

"And you're satisfied at giving him another child?"

"Of course, Julie. I made a bargain with Hsiu and I'll keep it."

"It's not that you've found anyone else . . . even with all your freedom?" Julia realized that the champagne had loosened her own tongue —and continued, "You haven't, have you?"

"Well, Mayling keeps me pretty busy. I've also been busy producing offspring. But this will be the last. Whether a boy or a girl, definitely the last."

"So you're content, Em? No regrets at all?"

"Julie, you *still* don't understand. So don't waste your sympathy. I assure you I'm perfectly content."

Emily smiled to soften that rebuke. She poured more champagne, fumbled with Julia's Chesterfields, and inexpertly puffed out smoke. She looked reprovingly at the amahs, who were chattering loudly on the balcony, and a momentary silence rewarded her. During that pantomime of annoyance, she avoided looking directly at Julia.

"I had an ulterior motive when I asked you to come over today, Julie," she finally confessed.

"I did suspect it wasn't only to start teaching Persephone the social graces."

"I want to sound you out about Tommy. Mayling asked me to."

"What business of Mayling's is Tommy?" Julia flared. "Why can't she just leave us alone?"

"I'm surprised, Julie. I thought you had a soft spot for Mayling. She did get Tommy out of jail, didn't she?"

Julia did not answer. She did not want to lie directly about her feelings toward Mayling. But she could not tell Emily that she knew Mayling had lied about securing Tommy's release—and, perhaps, then be trapped into potentially dangerous explanations.

"It's not a personal matter, anyway," Emily continued. "It's basically a chance for Tommy to do something big for China—and to improve himself professionally. May wants him to be flight surgeon for the Air Force. It would mean training in the States for a year. You'd like that, wouldn't you?"

"Sounds interesting, Em," Julia replied warmly. "Aviation medicine is a new specialty."

"How will Tommy feel?"

Regretting her first impulsive warmth, Julia said coolly "I'll ask him, Em. But I doubt it. . . . I just don't think he'd be interested. He only needs a few months to qualify as an internist."

"This would fit right in, Julie. He'd qualify in the States—and he'd pick up the extra specialty. It's just perfect."

"I'll ask him, Em. But I wouldn't count on it."

"It's for China," Emily persisted. "Tommy is a patriot first and a doctor second. He always has been."

"Maybe not anymore, Em. He's got different priorities. Anyway, I don't think I'd like him going into aviation medicine. Too dangerous. As a matter of fact, I know I wouldn't."

"You're quite sure, Julie?"

"Of course I can't speak for Tommy. But I'm reasonably sure it's not for him . . . not for us."

"But you will ask him, won't you?"

"Of course I will, Em."

The sisters-in-law embraced when Julia left and both said all the right things. But their parting was strained.

Why, Emily wondered, was Julia so sure about Tommy's unwillingness? He might still cherish a grudge against Chiang Kai-shek for allowing him to remain in captivity, even though it was six years ago. But, Mayling had done her best for him, and he would be working directly for her, rather than for the Generalissimo.

Above all, Emily could not understand how anyone could turn down the opportunity to help China fight the Japanese—particularly not her brother, who was an ardent patriot. Yet, she reflected, Julia would not have been quite so definite if she were not sure. Why, Emily wondered, was Julia so strongly opposed to Tommy's working for Mayling Chiang?

Suspicion formed like ice on the surface of Emily's mind. For the first time, she suspected that her normally forthright sister-in-law was concealing matters of grave importance.

46

DECEMBER 21, 1934

A blue-white glow lit the sleet-scored sky as the flare drifted slowly toward the half-frozen ground. The flare died silently a minute later, and the late afternoon of the longest day of the year 1934 again hung black over the barren East Tibetan Plateau.

Only the bonfires still defied the darkness when the stars were hidden by the scudding clouds. But the fires' yellow light hardly reached beyond the sentries on the ramparts of snow the soldiers had heaped up as the pale sun descended into the great mountains. The six hundred men of the Fourth Front Red Army's reconnaissance in force were isolated and vulnerable. All around them the afternoon was pitch-black.

The image revealed by the flare remained on the retina of the commanding officer for ten or twenty seconds longer, its contrasts as crude as those of an old glass-plate photograph: the plateau stretched empty and menacing to the invisible horizon; the shadows in the hollows gleamed inky black; and the snow-draped rocks glared white. The commander lowered his binoculars. To the west he felt the loom of far higher ground, but he could not see the world's greatest mountains, the hostile Himalayas.

The commander was Chang Kuo-tao, Tommy and Julia Howe's oldest friend in the Communist movement. He listened intently, as if he had heard some alien sound under the wailing of the wind. A moment later, he issued a sharp order.

A second star-flare soared from the brass muzzle of the Very pistol and arched high, the air displaced by its passage hissing like a flight of angry geese. When the toylike parachute opened, magnesium flamed incandescent against the black-velvet sky.

Raising his binoculars, Chang Kuo-tao saw the dark shapes scurrying out of the circle of light from the sky and counted aloud, "Five, twelve, fifteen . . . maybe twenty in all. And another pack the same size. Say, forty or fifty in all. Throw more wood on the fires."

"The fires may scare wolves away," Chang Kuo-tao's reluctant companion said. "But what if the Khampas attack?"

"No fear," Chang replied. "Not as long as the flares hold out."

"And how long will that be?" his companion asked. "Another night or two . . . three at most? I'm telling you again: We must go back."

"And I'll tell you again, Chu Teh, that I will not. I know you left your command, slipped away from your First Front Army only to talk me into it. But I will not go back. I won't fall into the trap your master Mao Tse-tung has set for me."

The two men were outlined by the dying light as the star-flare drifted toward the ground. Both were powerful, and their black silhouettes were menacing against the glare when they confronted each other. Chang Kuo-tao was a head taller. The stocky general called Chu Teh, which meant Red Virtue, was not intimidated, although he was the other man's captive.

Chu Teh might listen when Chang Kuo-tao described his vision of the future of the Chinese Communist Party, which differed markedly from both the vision of Mao Tse-tung and the official line of the Soviet-oriented Central Committee in Shanghai. Chu Teh might nod at his captor's salient arguments. He might even express enthusiasm for Chang Kuo-tao's plan to unite all Chinese, leftists and rightists alike, to oppose the Japanese menace. But Chu Teh would not turn his back on Mao Tse-tung, whose vision of the future centered upon his personal domination over, first, the Communist Party and, later, all China.

Once addicted to opium and concubines, Chu Teh had been reborn spiritually through the Nanchang Rising. Working always with Mao Tse-tung, he had created the Communists' most powerful force, the First Front Red Army, and the Communists' largest Soviet area in the mountains of Kiangsi Province. Chu Teh would never abandon his political mentor, Chang Kuo-tao's rival, Mao Tse-tung.

His captor now knew that he could kill Chu Teh but could not persuade him. If he were totally ruthless, Chang Kuo-tao would execute Chu Teh. Mao Tse-tung, who was an erratic field commander, would then be at his mercy. Not even that agile politician Commissar Chou

En-lai, who had come down on Mao's side, could make up for the loss of Chu Teh's military genius. Executing Chu Teh would give Chang Kuo-tao domination over the Communist movement—and enable him to ensure that China united against the Japanese.

Thus, the amiable general called Red Virtue now stood between Chang Kuo-tao and the salvation of China. Having made Chu Teh his captive when he arrived to lure the Fourth Front Army into Mao Tse-tung's spiderweb, Chang Kuo-tao could not bring himself to inflict the death sentence. Since General Chu Teh was the darling of the rank and file, Chang Kuo-tao feared that Chu Teh's executioner would be generally hated—and would therefore be unable to exercise power effectively. Strategy rather than sentimentality, Chang Kuo-tao assured himself, stayed his hand.

The star-flare flickered out, and the antagonists faced each other in darkness. Released from the terrible scrutiny of the light in the sky, the wolves howled and drew closer. Within the bonfires' circle of warmth, adolescents quarreled shrilly, exchanging curses of nerve-curdling obscenity. Such young runners, orderlies, and buglers were called Little Red Devils. Chang Kuo-tao heard a boy sobbing, but he would not shame the homesick Red Devil by comforting him.

"It's an impasse then," Chu Teh said.

"Maybe. But I'm not giving up on you yet."

"You're not going to persuade me, Kuo-tao. No matter what you say, I can't throw over my loyalty to Mao Tse-tung. No matter what you intellectuals think, some things are more important than words. . . . So you might as well let me go."

"Or execute you!" Chang Kuo-tao threatened.

"Or execute me!" Chu Teh repeated unmoved. "Though on what possible grounds—"

" 'Stubborn persistence in leftist deviationism' would do."

"If that's what you want, why not get it over with? You've now got your own tame party Central Committee to rubber-stamp your decision."

"Just keeping up with your friend Mao, who's plotting to make himself a dictator."

"I can't believe that for an instant."

"Don't make me execute you, old friend. Surely it's better to listen than to die."

"No question about that, Kuo-tao." Chu Teh laughed. "I'd always prefer listening to dying."

Chang Kuo-tao shivered and drew tighter the filthy Tibetan sheep-skin coat he wore over his paddled jacket and trousers. Better the rancid stench of butter, urine, and smoke that permeated the half-cured hide than the bite of the wind that blew off the roof of the world. Chu Teh wore only a padded jacket and thin woollen trousers looted from some captive Nationalist officer, but he appeared untouched by the cold. He merely shuffled his feet in their double-felt boots, while his captor stamped the hard-packed snow to restore circulation.

The older man, Chang Kuo-tao concluded again, was a mountain oak —stubby, enduring, and deep-rooted. He would not bend to the pre-vailing wind like the supple bamboo, nor would he be swept away by a landslide.

When the first rifle shots sounded on the perimeter, Chu Teh did not turn. When the wolves' howls rose to crescendo before slowly trailing away into the distance, he only lit a cigarette. Almost perfectly round in its cloth helmet, his head looked like a black cannonball with a burning fuse in the faint light.

Single rifle shots rattled again around the defensive perimeter. A bugle blared, and an officer shouted, "Cease firing! Cease firing! You saw the beasts run away. Conserve ammunition!"

Even the normal noises of the encampment ceased. The silence was profound in the snowy waste. The soldiers no longer laughed or swore; weapons no longer clinked metallically; and even the Little Red Devils were silent.

After half a minute of almost unbearable peace, shots exploded again. All around the perimeter, singly and in pairs, rifles coughed in fear.

Chang Kuo-tao angrily turned to repeat his order to conserve ammu-nition. His intent altered as his lips parted and instead, he shouted, "Dowse the fires! Khampas! Khampas attacking!"

The low-pitched reports of the Tibetan nomads' old muzzle-loading rifles were unmistakable. Pushing Chu Teh down, Chang Kuo-tao fell to the ground and watched the Little Red Devils, daringly silhouetted against the glare, kick out the fires.

The flames, which frightened the wolves, drew the predatory nomads of the Tibetan Plateau. The unit's Propaganda/Agitation Section had repeatedly tried—and repeatedly failed—to convince the Khampas that the Red Army was their friend, their champion against the oppressive feudal government in Lhasa.

Chinese peasants were easily persuaded to support the Communists, who fought to overthrow the tyrannical old order. To the Tibetan horseman a Chinese was a Chinese and therefore an enemy, regardless of his politics. Besides, looting the invaders' camp would not only be more enjoyable but more profitable than trading with them.

Overhead a star-flare exploded into blue-white brilliance. Obviously faulty, it burned out in twenty seconds. In that brief time hundreds of Khampas were visible circling the perimeter. Hunched inside their cumbersome robes on their heavy-bodied ponies, the tribesmen looked clumsy. But they rode effortlessly, and they agilely fired their long rifles from the saddle.

A ripple of shots knocked two Khampas from their saddles. The soldiers still fired at the darker shapes they believed they saw in the enveloping darkness; but they could not aim accurately. Shrieks inside the perimeter proved the accuracy of the volleys the nomads fired.

Crouched behind the snow ramparts, Chang Kuo-tao spoke urgently to a young bugler. A truncated call rasped from the bugle's bell, and four star-flares hurtled aloft to illuminate the four points of the compass.

The circling Khampas were starkly lit for the vengeful rifles. Pitilessly illuminated by the flares, they galloped for the darkness beyond the circle of light. Nomad after nomad fell in that flight. They whipped their ponies harder when mortar bombs pursued them, throwing up white puffs of snow.

After ordering the flares fired, Chang Kuo-tao had not said another word. His disciplined soldiers drove off the attackers on their own. Still silent, the Communist leader watched the wolves come out.

The most daring first, then the rest in twos and threes, the pack loped into the dying light to tear at the dying men in the yellow and crimson robes. As the last flare died, the wolf pack howled a mocking requiem for the nomads killed by the men who had come to liberate them.

"Tibet won't do." Chang Kuo-tao's attention turned from the battle to the future. "We'll have to look elsewhere for a safe base."

"Tibet's also too far away. We've got to be closer to the centers of power," Chu Teh observed. "After we lick our wounds and rebuild our forces, we'll attack again."

"Obviously!" Chang Kuo-tao agreed. "If there's one thing I've learned in more than two years—"

"Two years, is it? I forgot. . . . I thought you'd been on the road only a year, like Old Mao and myself."

"Two years and two months, my friend. We crossed the Hankow-Peking Railway in October 1932 on our way west. Remember, Chiang Kai-shek's Fourth Extermination Campaign concentrated on us. I had already set up the Szechwan Soviet area when you and Mao Tse-tung finally decided you couldn't hold out against the Fifth Extermination Campaign."

"The propagandists are calling our retreat the Long March, Kuo-tao. They're already hailing it as a great victory."

"Some victory! We've abandoned all our positions in eastern and central China. And we're still fugitives without a base."

"You and Old Mao must come to terms." Chu Teh urged again. "He needs you and your army. Why do you think he sent me to talk with you?"

"If Mao and I could only agree . . . All Chinese must unite, even Communists with the Nationalists . . . unite to fight the Japanese."

"We'll have to see, Kuo-tao. First we must make ourselves secure— rebuild our power. You do see, don't you?"

"I'm not absolutely sure," Chang Kuo-tao replied. "The Japs look like a bigger danger to China . . . and to us Communists . . . than even the Nationalists. . . . But I have decided one thing: I won't execute you, old comrade."

"You know, Kuo-tao, I won't argue with you about that!"

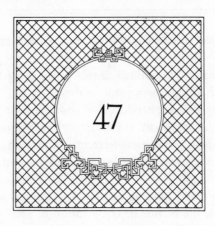

47

DECEMBER 24–25, 1934

"If you must, you must," Julia agreed. "Are you sure it's not an excuse to get out of the Pomeroys' party?"

"We'll make it to the blasted party," Tommy replied. "But I promised Mrs. Wang I'd drop in on her clinic. Christmas doesn't mean anything to her. Not that I am overfond—"

"Somehow, Tommy, I'd noticed that Christmas isn't your favorite time of the year. I can see how all the fussing—"

"I put up with the fuss, don't I? For the kids' sake—and yours, my love. You're worse than they are about Christmas."

"Well, if it's any consolation, it's already half gone. After a few hours, you won't have to put up with Christmas Eve again for a whole year."

"I don't mind the midnight service. It *is* meant to be a religious occasion. But the tree and the ribbons . . . all those transplanted German customs . . ."

"The children love it." Julia indirectly defended her own joy in the holiday. "For their sake . . ."

"For *their* sake, you do what you're dying to do—make a big sentimental to-do." Tommy laughed. "But how you can expect Persephone to take it in. She's only sixteen months old. And Emily's latest is hardly more than a year . . ."

"The little ones love it most. And Emily's latest is called Eunice. You could remember your own niece's name."

"Emily really means it this time, you reckon? No more children for Ou-yang Hsiu? No more trying for another boy?"

"She hasn't either the time or the inclination. Mayling Chiang keeps her so busy you'd think the two of them were running the war against the Communists all by themselves. Not to speak of the coming war against the Japanese."

"After waiting so long, when we finally fight the Japs, it's going to be a hell of an uphill struggle. . . . Em's constantly commuting to Nanking—doesn't that mean neglecting the children?"

"What can Emmy do? When she complains, Mayling just says, 'What are amahs for? I need you more than your children do. *China* needs your help!' "

"You know, Em could be a great asset to us. Pity she's on the wrong side."

"She'll never change. Last year, I thought she was getting suspicious about . . . about what we're up to. When you turned down Mayling's flight surgeon offer. But I'm sure she's gotten over it. She obviously thinks we're just too selfish, too dependent on our creature comforts, to make sacrifices for China."

"You can read her better than I can . . . . But in that case, perhaps we should think seriously about getting a new car. Something fitting for a fully qualified internist."

"Tommy, this toy we're riding in is hardly more than a year old. But you always . . ."

Tommy's latest automobile was an electric-blue Packard tourer with a canvas top supported by complicated stays and levers. The snow flurries of Christmas Eve had forced him to put the top up. Although she normally checked his instinctive extravagance, Julia was inclined to encourage him in this case. Julia knew only that the even more spectacular vehicle on which he had his eye was not a convertible. She was tired of alternately broiling and freezing in the open Packard.

Blessed, she reflected, was a life in which that was her worst personal problem. Politics were another matter. China was mortally threatened by the Japanese—and the Communist armies had disappeared westward. But politics aside, it was a very happy time for them.

Despite the storms of the Great Depression, their life together flowed smoothly. Any possible monotony was banished by the missions they carried out for the Apparatus, which had, naturally, forgotten its pledge to give them only high-level and low-risk assignments. They both enjoyed the gilded life the Apparatus insisted they maintain as camouflage. Amid hazards and instability, they blithely danced and partied and dined and gambled and made love and talked fond nonsense.

Julia loved her life—and she loved her husband. Yet she now took a more realistic view of both. Tommy was highly intelligent, but he was no intellectual. He joked that he had used up most of his mental capital, first, in medical school and, afterward, in qualifying as an internist. He was now, he said, living on the interest from the little intellectual capital he had left—and he could, therefore, not squander his meager intellectual income on theoretical discussion.

Most of his leisure time was devoted to the mindless amusements of the Settlement's smart set. He played tennis and rode; he loved horse races, jai alai, and rugby; and he excelled at bridge, backgammon, and charades. Often partnered by Joshua Haleevie, he competed in mounted paper chases and murderous Sunday afternoon croquet matches. Yet he was also the first to note that the Shanghai Amateur Players were putting on a new Gilbert and Sullivan operetta or that an American jazz combo was stopping in Shanghai on the way to Australia.

Tommy was sometimes so quick he almost frightened Julia. But he was not a thinker. His prop spectacles and his professorial meerschaum pipe had made him appear judicious. But he was actually quite emotional. Julia did not believe that she herself was still impulsive and ingenuous, although Emily said she had not really changed. Nonetheless, she was not as emotional as Tommy, who appeared so detached. And he was like a child about his automobiles.

"A new car wouldn't get us there a second faster in this rotten weather," Julia said. "Exactly where is this clinic of Mrs. Wang's? And what's so important it couldn't wait till after Christmas?"

"It's on the far side of Chapei, way over west," Tommy admitted. "She didn't say specifically what she wanted. I told her some time ago I was always happy to give a little talk to her midwives. Bring them up to date on modern procedures. She telephoned this morning and asked could I do it tonight."

"On Christmas Eve, Tommy? Isn't that overdoing unselfishness?"

"I told her it was an important foreign holiday. . . . She said she knew, but this was *very* important—and would I *please* be sure to come."

"Well, since there's no helping it . . ."

Less than a quarter of an hour earlier they had left the tinsel gaiety of commercial Nanking Road, where shop windows displayed heaps of imported toys, mounds of tropical fruit, and cases of wines and brandies. The red-and-green bunting that draped the lampposts and the smell of roasting chestnuts now lay behind the Packard's chromium-trimmed trunk. The Chinese Santa Clauses with white cotton beards and padded stomachs tolling their handbells outside Sincere's and the Wing On Department Store seemed figures from another world in the narrow, dark streets of industrial Chapei.

After asking directions twice, Tommy somewhat dubiously halted the Packard in front of a small dry-goods shop. The red swastika of mercy was painted on the broad wooden arrow that pointed inexorably down the alley to MADAM WANG'S MIDWIFERY CLINIC.

"You'll wait in the car?" Tommy suggested.

"No, thanks. I'll come with you. Maybe that'll make it quicker."

His hand under her elbow, they picked their way down the side of the alley. Brushing against the grimy fence, they avoided the larger puddles in the middle. Julia realized that her shoes would be ruined, but her mind was on other matters.

No matter how often she entered the lives of the very poor of Shanghai, she was always shocked and horrified afresh. Amid her distress, she was once again glad that she was fighting for those oppressed masses. When the Communists ruled China, such medieval squalor would be swept away—along with archaic foreign rule of the Settlement and Frenchtown.

At the end of the alley, yellow light glimmered through the iron bars shielding a small window. When Mrs. Wang opened the double-locked door, Julia was surprised. She had expected a thin woman with downcast eyes, a secular Sister of Mercy. She saw a full-bodied woman in a red velvet kaftan and amber necklaces. Lit by two dangling bare bulbs, the small room was divided into three cubicles by gray cotton sheets, which slid on wires overhead.

"*Dai-foo.* . . ." Mrs. Wang grasped both Tommy's hands after thrusting home three heavy bolts. "Master Physician, I'm so grateful you came. But I must apologize. There is no clinic today, no midwives to lecture."

"Bloody hell!" Tommy exploded in English before asking a little more tactfully in Shanghainese, "Then what've you got me here for, Mrs. Wang? I do have other things to do on Christmas Eve."

"I'm very sorry, Doctor. But the lady was insistent. She felt Christmas Eve was the best time. The police aren't on the prowl. Even Nationalist agents and the—"

"The lady? What lady? I hope she has a good reason—"

"She has . . . a very good reason. But I'll let her tell you herself. She's an old friend of yours."

Glancing first for reassurance at the barred door, Mrs. Wang drew aside the sheet that closed the middle cubicle. A thin woman with hands folded sat in the chair beside the examination table, her face shadowed.

When she looked up, Tommy knew he had never seen her before. She was smartly dressed in a fur-collared coat over a green silk dress, and her long hair was rigidly permanent-waved. Her scarlet lipstick matched her highly polished nails, which were, however, cut short.

"I'm sorry, madam, but I don't . . ." Tommy began when she did not speak.

"Tommy!" Julia interrupted. "Tommy, it's Lien, Chang Kuo-tao's wife, Lien. Can't you see?"

Tommy looked again at the seated woman. The Lien he remembered had been short-haired, simply dressed, and averse to makeup: the model of an austere female comrade. This was a brilliant disguise. If it fooled him, it would fool the informers and special agents who were eager to collect the substantial price placed on her head years earlier by the Nationalists.

"Joo-li . . . Tom." She smiled. "I'm so grateful you could come. I didn't want to trouble you. But when the Apparatus, too, began chasing me . . ."

"I've been looking for you, Lien," Tommy said, almost accusingly. "Every time I thought I was close, you just disappeared."

"I know, Tom," she said placatingly. "I didn't want you to find me. I was all right. . . . And I didn't want to make trouble for you. But now I have no choice. You're my last hope. I've discovered it's not only the Nationalists and the foreign police who are after me. The Apparatus also —and it means me no good. Probably something to do with Kuo-tao's political maneuvers. Yet I don't even know where he is. . . . You and Joo-li are the only ones I can appeal to now. Every other friend in the Communist movement will turn away."

Julia wanted to ask why Lien should think they would defy the Apparatus, but Tommy said, "Lien, we'll see what we can do. . . . But what've you been up to?"

"Not much, Tom. When Kuo-tao left, party headquarters here was already shaky. As you know, it later virtually collapsed. Only fragments were left. To save myself, I changed my name. I studied and became a midwife. That's how I met Mrs. Wang. . . . But it's all gone wrong. I've reached the end of my tether."

"First, we'll get you out of here. Then we'll see what's next." Tommy did not hesitate. "Have you got a nurse's uniform? And scrape that gunk off your face."

Mrs. Wang, who had been listening unashamedly found a white dress in a standing wardrobe She drew the curtain across the cubicle.

Julia was eager to speak to Tommy, but she could not say a word with the others in earshot. Tommy's impulsive generosity could not only imperil their cover but could alienate the Apparatus. Even saving Lien, the wife of their oldest friend in the movement, was hardly worth risking everything.

If their complicity in her escape was discovered, it would destroy everything they had worked for. They could be arrested by the Settlement police; they could be abducted by the Nationalists; they could even be killed in retaliation by the ruthless Apparatus. Even if the Apparatus only repudiated them, the chief purpose of their lives would be destroyed.

They missed the Pomeroys' Christmas Eve party. Tommy had made up his mind, and he moved very fast. Lien spent the night in the dressing room next to the big master bedroom on the fifth floor, but she was out of the house on Kiukiang Road before three the next morning. Even hard-working Shanghai servants were not awake before four, not even on Christmas Day.

Lien carried a small straw suitcase containing a second nurse's uniform, underclothes, a white sweater, and a few toilet articles. She carried in her head the address of the clinic for fishermen's families at Woosung on the Yangtze—and also Tommy's verbal message to his Aunt Vi, whose contributions maintained the clinic. On the letterhead of the Shanghai General Hospital Tommy had written a note to the chief nurse of the clinic. He had forged the signature of the chief of medicine at Shanghai General, who was a Nationalist hack and therefore above suspicion.

In a canvas belt under her dress Lien carried two thousand dollars in gold and notes. Tommy had given her the money at the last moment with the reiterated advice: "Catch the first train from the North Station. The police never check it. Too early for them. And remember, Lien, Woosung is only safe for a week or two. Get right away from Shanghai. Blend into the countryside."

Julia was resigned to her husband's foolhardy generosity. Almost against her will, she loved him more for it. But she was very nervous when he struck the brass gong to summon the children to the presents heaped under the big Christmas tree, which almost touched the ceiling of the cavernous sitting room. They had apparently gotten away with it, but she was still nervous when Althea and Persephone tumbled into the sitting room.

How could Tommy justify his behavior? He had put personal friendship before his duty to party headquarters, which was pursuing Lien.

Was that not precisely the bourgeois individualism against which good Communists were warned? Yet Julia was afraid she would have done the same on her own.

She turned that puzzle over in her mind while the girls strewed shiny wrapping paper on the gold Tientsin carpet. Adam, the mastiff, was mauling his present, an enormous rubber mouse with a built-in squeak, when the police inspector entered the living room. Julia smiled socially, recalling that she had recently met the young Scot called MacGillivray at a cocktail party. Obviously embarrassed, he was self-consciously brusque—and quite oblivious to her charm.

"We're acting on information received," he said formally. "One Mrs. Chang Kuo-tao, known as Lien, was seen in your automobile last night by an informant. There'll be no need for a search warrant—and no publicity—if you'll allow us to search the house."

"What's the charge, Inspector?" Tommy took his meerschaum pipe out of his mouth. "We haven't seen Mrs. Chang in donkeys' years. Though I used to see her husband occasionally in the old days. What's she done?"

"She's a notorious Communist agitator," Inspector MacGillivray said. "There's also suspicion of manslaughter in connection with a childbirth. I shouldn't tell you, but the charge was laid by Dr. Yen, director of the Wenhwa Hospital."

Tommy casually waved his pipe and said, "Help yourself, Inspector. The servants will show the way."

Julia knew that Tommy was as shocked as she was. Dr. Yen was the exception to the rule that agents of the Apparatus did not know each other's identity. Nominally a social reformer, he was spokesman for the Communists on health and welfare issues. He was always savagely critical of the Nationalists, although he never acknowledged, of course, his membership in the Communist Party.

Since Dr. Yen had laid the charge of manslaughter, the conclusion was unmistakable: The Apparatus was using its enemy, the Settlement Police, to hunt down its own followers. The revolution was not only devouring its own children; it was inciting the capitalists to slaughter its children.

Tommy offered Inspector MacGillivray a Christmas drink and, when it was refused, said, "I suppose you want to get on with it. Please go ahead. . . . By the way, was Dr. Yen also the informant who said he saw Mrs. Chang in my car?"

"Certainly not!" The inspector smiled. "That was a different . . . but you know that we can't reveal our informers."

Thus satisfied that the Apparatus was not aware of their role, Tommy and Julia chatted while the determined inspector led his constables through the house. Loo, the majordomo, later reported that the policemen had not missed a single cupboard, boxroom, or cubbyhole. Tommy laughed, but his thoughts raced in tandem with Julia's.

Suspicion was their greatest enemy. This search at dawn would inevitably arouse the suspicion of their enemies on the right: the Nationalist Secret Police and the Special Branch of the Settlement Police. Although they had been accepted for years as the pleasure-loving reactionaries they took such pains to appear, they would be under surveillance again.

Suspicion could blight their lives. All simply because Tommy had done the decent thing for an old friend. At least the Apparatus was not suspicious of them. Yet why, Julia wondered, was she thinking of the Apparatus as if it were their enemy?

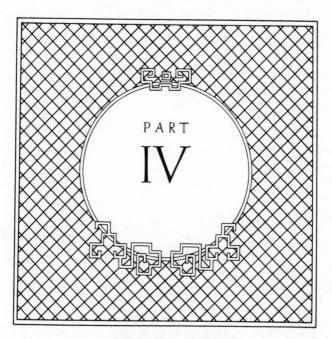

SORROWS

1937–1940

Julia would have received Richard Hollings amicably even if the Apparatus had not instructed her to offer hospitality—and guidance—to all foreign correspondents. Richard had just returned to Shanghai on August 14, 1937, ten years after stalking away from Emily's red convertible to begin a protracted tour of Asia, which led in time to a plum assignment as roving European correspondent for the *Boston Globe*. Curiosity alone would have led Julia to see him in his new role as chief Asiatic correspondent for both the *Globe* and the National Broadcasting Company.

Although she was not inclined to prolong their reunion, her duty to the Communist movement compelled Julia to spend some time with him. Richard's effrontery, which Joshua Haleevie called *chutzpah*, was even greater. He simply assumed that she was delighted to see him. He was also as casually engaging as ever—and even more attractive in his saturnine way.

Julia was not herself attracted, but she had never been. She was, however, glad that Emily was in Nanking with Mayling Chiang, who had just been formally appointed secretary general of the Commission for Aeronautical Affairs. Emily saw little of her husband nowadays. At least there would now be time to warn her to steel her heart against her former lover's insidious charm.

Julia selected the next record, silenced Richard with a glance, and spoke into the big black microphone: "XMHA is pleased to respond to the umpteenth request this week for 'Red Sails in the Sunset.' It seems listeners can't get enough of it. We'll have to send out for a new platter soon. Just tell us what you want to hear. Call Julia Howe at 95040 or write me at Station XMHA, 445 Racecourse Road. And now 'Red Sails in the Sunset' for Alma Wang and Danny Ho!"

Richard grinned at the words ". . . carry my loved one home safely to me," but did not comment. Regarding Emily, he had only remarked that he heard she was "happily married and very fecund."

Julia did not confide her own doubts about Emily's happy marriage. Yet her sister-in-law displayed no interest in any other man—and little enough in her husband. Despite Emily's frequent absences, Ou-yang Hsiu uncomplainingly enabled her to enjoy the dignity of a married woman. He also paid her considerable bills. Her own funds were given to the service of Mayling Chiang—and China.

Emily's heart appeared to be locked. But who was more likely to open it again than the man who had slammed the door?

Richard Hollings might, however, not be interested. He had discussed only politics and war after making the obligatory inquiries about Tommy and about Julia's children. Moreover, he had confided that Fiona, his wife for two years now, would join him when he had settled into Shanghai.

Otherwise, he was impersonal, saying, "Everyone knows you're a first-class source of information, insights, and gossip, I'm anxious to hear your views. In return, I'll give you my impressions of North China."

Julia was interested. Virtually occupied by the Japanese, the north was cut off from the rest of China.

"It's a whole new ballgame, isn't it?" Richard smiled and commented, "I'm learning to talk like you Yanks for my new job. . . . But it is. I've seen the true features of Japan—and I'm horrified."

Despite herself, Julia warmed to Richard Hollings. The ten years just past had obviously made him more sympathetic to China and the Chinese.

"In Tientsin the police were offering ten thousand dollars Mex for information regarding a hundred and seven corpses," he said. "All males between twenty and forty, and all found in the river. Not a mark on any of them. No sign of foul play, but all dead as mutton."

When Richard paused to take a cigarette from a round tin of fifty Senior Service, Julia held her index finger before pursed lips. She pulled her shantung dress away from her bosom and fanned herself with a record sleeve while waiting for the end of "Red Sails in the Sunset." The recently installed air-conditioning could not deal with the mid-August heat. Even her lips felt as if they were perspiring under their coral lipstick.

Into the microphone she said brightly, "So we've seen those red sails for the skaty-ninth time this week. Now we're off on another voyage. To 'Blue Hawaii.' "

Richard laughed and said: "And you're the young lady who swore she couldn't write a word. No need with that slick patter. . . . But let me go on: The police finally fished out a chap who wasn't quite dead. He was a contract laborer, and he'd been enticed to a so-called club in the Japanese Concession. All the opium and heroin he wanted, all dirt cheap. He smoked a few cigarettes—and woke up in hospital. Strychnine poisoning, the doctors said."

He pulled on his cigarette and continued: "Of course, the Japs are conducting drug warfare. In the Jap Concession in Tientsin, all the opium houses have little huts with a little window outside. You roll up your sleeve and push in your money. A jab in your arm—and there's your fix of heroin. It's all run by the Imperial Army's Special Services Section—for profit and to debauch the Chinese. The Japs are determined to conquer China by any and all means!"

Nodding, Julia wondered how to put across her own message. China is finally standing up to the Japanese, she wanted to tell him, *only* because Chairman Mao Tse-tung finally forced Generalissimo Chiang Kai-shek to fight. She had to convince him that the Communists were fighting ten times as hard as the Nationalists.

The Marco Polo Bridge Incident of July 7th, Richard Hollings observed, had fooled no one. The Japs obviously wanted to march, and they had obviously created a pretext for war.

Why else should a Japanese battalion have marched to an insignificant town overlooking the lion-head balustrades of the bridge named for the great Venetian explorer? Why else should the battalion fire the instant the garrison denied knowledge of Japanese deserters? If they were not already prepared, how could the Japanese have immediately launched the coordinated attacks that swiftly took both Peiping and Tientsin?

"You've got to hand it to them. I didn't believe Orientals were capable of such meticulous planning—or such dashing execution. I'll never look down my nose at the Japs again." He ground out his cigarette in a flurry of yellow Virginia tobacco. "Now tell me how it looks from Shanghai."

Although repetition had perfected Julia's reply to that question, her respect for Richard's shrewdness shaded her usual bold strokes. Playing on his dislike of the Generalissimo, she confided that the Nationalists were still exerting ninety percent of their military effort against the Communist-held areas—and only ten percent against the Japanese. Moreover, strong-arm men and special agents were persecuting the Communists in Nationalist-held areas, even though the Nationalists and the Communists were now nominally united against the invaders.

"So-called Communists," she added. "They're really not even Socialists. They're really agrarian democrats, social democrats."

Themselves fighting the Japanese staunchly, the so-called Communists were gradually forcing the reluctant Chiang Kai-shek to fight the Japanese. They were mobilizing public opinion against the slothful Nationalists through student demonstrations, through pamphlets, plays, movies, and posters—above all, through indignant word of mouth.

"The Generalissimo is no fool, mind you." Julia had to appear evenhanded. "Nor is he a coward. He delayed facing up to the Japs because he wanted—and still wants—to destroy the Communists first. Also, Mayling knew that war would interfere with peaceful pursuits. For the Soongs, Mayling's family, peaceful pursuits means grabbing all the graft they can—tens of millions. . . . Even the Gimo says the Japanese are a skin rash, unsightly but not a mortal threat. The Communists are a stomach cancer. If not excised, they'll kill China."

She saw that "Blue Hawaii" still had a half minute to play and continued: "You've been away a long time, Dick. But you must know that the Communists had built up strong bases in central China. They'd won over the peasants and rebuilt the Red Army. But the Generalissimo's extermination campaigns were finally too much for them: Italian warplanes and German advisers against rifles and self-taught generals. So the Communists finally pulled out. After an epic retreat . . . the Long March . . . they ended up in late 1935 at a place called Yenan. It's near Sian, which was, you'll recall, the first capital of the Chinese Empire two thousand years ago."

"And all is sweet harmony among the Communists, Julie?" Richard asked. "They were fighting among themselves like blazes when I last heard."

"Well," she conceded, "Mao Tse-tung and Tommy's old friend Chang Kuo-tao had a falling-out. Then each set up his own Central Committee. But they're getting on fine now. Mao Tse-tung is chairman of the Communist Party, and Chang Kuo-tao is chairman of the government in Yenan."

"Blue Hawaii" was not quite over. Julia waited for it to end and introduced that old favorite, "Till the Sands of the Desert Grow Cold," before clicking off the microphone.

"And the United Front Against Japan?" Richard asked. "I thought the Nationalists and the Communists could never get together."

It was, Julia said, a complicated business. The extermination campaigns had not ceased when the Communists reached their refuge in the remote northwest. In December 1936, the Generalissimo had flown to Sian, China's ancient capital, to coordinate the Sixth Extermination Campaign, which was aimed at the nearby Communist area.

One of the commanders, Julia continued, was the Young Marshal, Chang Hsueh-liang, with his formidable Manchurian army in exile. On December 12, 1936, the commanders took Chiang Kai-shek prisoner and demanded that he immediately halt all attacks on the Communists. Instead, he was to invite the Communists to join the Nationalists in all-out war against the Japanese.

The Generalissimo had raged. This mutiny, he had declared, could destroy the Republic of China. If he was discredited, the nation would fall apart. No one else could lead China.

The Communists agreed, although the little politicians and the little generals in Nanking were already maneuvering to succeed the captive hero. On December 15, 1936, Commissar Chou En-lai came from Yenan to greet his old chief and antagonist with the words "I have come to arrange a marriage between the National People's Party and the Communist Party." After much discussion, Chiang Kai-shek and Chou En-lai agreed to form the United Front Against Japan.

On Christmas Day, the Generalissimo returned to Nanking. The little politicians and the little generals cheered—and put away for another day their plans for coups d'etat.

In Yenan, as Julia thought it best *not* to tell Richard, Mao Tse-tung was only pretending to obey Nanking. The Communist-ruled territory, in theory, was now a semiautonomous region under the Nationalist government. The Red Army was now called the Eighth Route Army and was nominally under the Generalissimo's command.

Chairman Mao Tse-tung said complacently, "We are finally on the highroad to power. The United Front Against Japan is the perfect camouflage for subversion in the White Areas—and for rapidly expanding the Red Army. We are now certain to conquer *all* China!"

After mentally censoring herself, Julia declared, "The Gimo had hoped to strengthen China militarily while he stalled. But he didn't do too well. One example: Long before Mayling took over the Air Force,

Nanking made a deal with Italy to provide warplanes and training. On paper, the Chinese Air Force now deploys five hundred warplanes and a thousand pilots. Actually, it has just ninety-one fighting planes—and, perhaps, a hundred competent pilots. . . . So Mayling has just hired a hotshot American Air Corps officer called Claire Chennault to train the Chinese Air Force."

"Hold on, Julie!" Hollings held his palm up. "You still go at everything like a bull at a fence. Forget Chennault for a moment and tell me about Shanghai. There's a good girl."

To keep him from reading her expression, Julia lowered her head and let the curtain of her mahogany hair fall over her face. His elaborately casual manner was as patronizing as ever. She did not, she decided again, really like the ace newshawk Richard Hollings. In the old days she had put up with his condescension for Emily's sake. Now, she supposed, she'd have to put up with him for the sake of the Apparatus.

She addressed the wire-mesh microphone: "Next is my own choice, a brand-new record just off the boat from San Francisco. Ray Eberle, backed by Glenn Miller's band, sings 'The Nearness of You'!"

Julia clicked off the microphone and repaid Richard's veiled insolence in her own terms: "Naturally, you've looked around the streets—as any good correspondent would. You must've seen that they're crammed with refugees. Sixty thousand foreigners plus a million and a half Chinese normally live in Frenchtown and the Settlement. Another three quarters of a million Chinese refugees are now bursting our seams. They always figure they're safer here."

The syrupy melody and the saccharine words of the "The Nearness of You" was an incongruous background to her tough-minded exposition. "And, dear Richard, the signs are pretty clear. The explosion is coming. The Gimo's let North China go, abandoned Peiping and Tientsin in the last two weeks. No dependable allies there, since he finally learned he can't count on the Christian General. But he's moved the Eighty-eighth Division into Greater Shanghai. It's his pride and joy: Nazi-trained, every officer a Whampoa graduate, and great at the goose step. Also glamorous and sinister in coal-scuttle helmets."

She took the record off the turntable, then put it back and said into the microphone, "I liked 'The Nearness of You' so much I'm going to play it again." She again flipped the microphone switch off.

"The Gimo," she said, "probably hoped the Japs would go easy around Shanghai to avoid involving the other foreign powers. But the Japs are infuriated because the Chinese have dared to prepare to defend themselves. . . . And that's the background to this scary Saturday afternoon. A typhoon is hovering a few hundred miles out at sea, and the Japs are piling troops and warships into Shanghai. . . . Nothing like it since 1932. For sheer fright among foreigners, nothing like it since 1927, when everybody thought the big bad Reds were going to eat us up."

More than twenty Japanese warships, she told him, now lay menacingly at anchor in the Hwangpoo. Their flagship, His Imperial Japanese Majesty's Ship *Idzumo,* was an old battleship no bigger than a modern cruiser, which had been captured from the Imperial Russian Navy forty years earlier. Japanese marines had just reinforced the garrison in Hongkew, the old American concession that was now called Little Tokyo. Moreover, Japanese bombers from Taiwan were scheduled to make regular "courtesy flights" over Shanghai.

That display of force should have induced the Generalissimo to back down, as he had in 1932. Instead, he was reinforcing his units. The Japanese had provided the powder keg, and the Chinese had laid the fuse.

"Five days ago," Julia said, "somebody put a match to the fuse."

Early in the evening of August ninth, a Japanese navy sublieutenant had been driving westward toward the military and civil airport at Hungjao. A seaman first class was at the wheel. The black touring car was not challenged by a single Chinese roadblock. The Chinese were not aggressive, and twenty-five thousand foreign troops were prudently staying behind the barbed-wire-and-sandbag barricades that again sealed off the Settlement and Frenchtown.

Neither the sublieutenant nor the seaman first class reacted to the first shot. Both were intent on the distant warplanes on the tarmac. They could not react to the volley that followed. The big car swerved and hurtled into the ditch.

When the rear door flew open, the sublieutenant's body was flung onto the road. Six small holes marred his khaki tunic, and blood smeared his brass buttons.

Listening for the end of the melody, Julia summed up: "So the Japs had their martyrs. Nonetheless, Tokyo magnanimously guaranteed the security of the foreign concessions—*if* the Chinese would withdraw all their troops from Greater Shanghai. When the mayor refused, the good gray *North China Daily News* warned the Chinese against provoking Japan to worse excesses by resisting."

"The *News* would!" Richard interjected. "The mouthpiece of the taipans, always preaching: *Preserve trade at all costs.*"

". . . day before yesterday, Chinese employees of the telephone company cut off the Japanese consulate," she continued. "Also most Japanese firms. The Eighty-eighth Division occupied the North Station and blocked all roads. Yesterday, the skirmishing started. Friday the thirteenth, by the way."

"What about the bombing? I know the Chinese are trying to sink the warships, especially the *Idzumo*. But their planes were so high this morning I could barely hear them, much less see them."

"Maybe because it's so cloudy. No Jap pursuit planes around, but the pre-typhoon winds aren't helping."

The crooner was murmuring suggestively: ". . . not the pale moon that excites me, that thrills and delights me. Oh no! It's just the nearness of you!"

The skylight rattled, and the room trembled. The building itself seemed to sway when the petulant buzzing of aircraft engines penetrated the studio's sound-proofing.

"They're flying lower." Hollings's voice was heavy with apprehension—and with anticipation. "Can I get onto the roof? I must have a look."

"Help yourself, Dick. One flight up to the tower—and you can see all Shanghai. I'll pick you up after I wrap up the program. Another fifteen minutes or so."

After Richard's departure, Julia played four more songs. Glancing at the dog sitting rapt before the phonograph horn on the purple Victor label, she said flatly, "And now an old song that's somehow always fresh: 'There'll be a Hot Time in the Old Town Tonight.' That melody appropriately enough closes our request program for Saturday, August 14, 1937. It's almost four-thirty in the afternoon, time for me to get back to my husband and my daughters. Good-bye till Monday. Also *tsai-chien, au revoir,* and *auf Wiedersehen.* I won't say *sayonara* again until I can say *sayonara* to all the Japanese soldiers who are paying us a strange kind of courtesy call. Here it is: 'A Hot Time in the Old Town Tonight'!"

She smiled at the engineer in his glass cage and left him to close down the program. Opening the heavy door, she heard a throbbing under the music. A hairline fault in the record was producing a sound like the distant roll of drums. Though that was unprofessional, it would be worse to apologize and put a different record on.

Distant martial noises were, fortunately, as close as anyone in the International Settlement would get to the fighting in Greater Shanghai. It was faintly obscene to watch from an inviolate sanctuary while men and women were killed. But why else was she climbing the stairs to join Richard Hollings in the observation tower?

Binoculars clapped to his eyes, the correspondent was swiveling his head continuously. The big glass lenses capping the long black tubes made him look like a robot watchman against the overcast sky. Perspiration soaked his linen bush jacket; it was very muggy even a hundred fifty feet above the street.

"Can't see a damned thing!" he complained. "I can hear them, but I can't see a single plane."

Julia could not resist the gibe: "You know, Dick, this war isn't being staged for your personal entertainment."

"Really, Julie! You're gawking too."

"Well, it *is* my town."

The engines' throbbing grew higher pitched as it drew near. But the airplane remained invisible in the overhanging clouds. Julia shivered at the unseen menace and looked down at Shanghai.

The Japanese had made Hongkew northeast of Soochow Creek their fortress. Sullen beneath the leaden clouds, close-packed tenements jostled each other. Amid the wisps of black smoke curling above the rooftops Julia saw flames leap. Fires glowed bright in the brown brick buildings housing Japanese-owned cotton mills. The Chinese Air Force had not entirely wasted its bombs.

But the old battleship *Idzumo* floated unscathed in the center of the Japanese flotilla off Hongkew, a toy man-of-war with three spindly smokestacks, square gun turrets, and bright signal flags. Through the box girders of the Garden Bridge, which spanned Soochow Creek, Julia saw a ripple like an enormous white-tufted caterpillar. Thousands of Chinese in white tops and dark trousers were scurrying into the sanctuary of the Settlement.

"It's coming back!" Hollings shouted. "Look there. Over Frenchtown."

A silver shape flashed through the overcast. Stubby-nosed and short-winged, it looked like a model aircraft over a model city. The engine screamed as the warplane swooped down, the jagged white-sun of the Republic of China glinting on its wings. Two black leather heads twisted inside the Plexiglas canopy, and a rear machine gun menaced the empty sky.

"A Northrop," Richard said. "A light bomber—damned low. It's not a dive-bomber, you know."

Julia, who had not known, did not reply. She was mesmerized by the sleek modern warplane, so different from the boxy biplanes the Settlement had sent aloft to frighten away the Generalissimo and his Chinese Bolshevik hordes in 1927. Best of all, Chinese, not foreigners, now flew such American-built monoplanes.

The bomber pointed its blunt nose at the Japanese flotilla and dived low. Julia willed its bombs to hit the *Idzumo*.

"By God! *No,* it can't!" Richard pressed the binoculars into his eye-sockets. "Oh, my Lord! I can see it . . . them."

Two black cylinders were tumbling in the wake of the bomber. Free of the hand that had launched them against the *Idzumo*, the bombs drifted malignantly earthward.

To the north the defanged warplane passed unscathed through the curtain of gray-and-red explosions thrown aloft by the Japanese flotilla's antiaircraft guns. To the south the bombs vanished behind the dark buildings of the French Concession. A moment later, flame flared and black smoke rose above that low skyline. Julia heard a muffled explosion, and the tower swayed beneath her feet. Instantly, a second bomber broke through the clouds precisely where the first had appeared.

The second Northrop followed the same course as the first, but no bombs fell. The bomber floated above the smoke of the explosion, its silver flanks flashing in the light from the west. Over the Bund, it appeared to leap forward to strike its prey.

Julia saw two black bombs detach themselves. For several seconds they flew almost parallel to the bomber, rather like skipping stones on the watery gray sky.

"Leading the target . . ." Hollings observed didactically. "You see the velocity . . ."

The bombs plummeted abruptly. Released too soon to hit the Japanese flotilla, they plunged toward the Bund.

The two black cylinders disappeared behind the pyramidal tower of the Cathay Hotel, and Julia let her breath out in relief. In an instant she would see geysers of coffee-brown water. Far better for the bombs to fall into the Hwangpoo, despite the danger to shipping, than among the refugees thronging the Bund.

Smoke swirled thick above the Cathay Hotel. Julia heard the explosion first, then felt the shock wave, and, finally, saw the belated plumes of flame. Five seconds later, the terrible sequence was repeated.

"Sir Victor Sassoon won't be happy if they've damaged his nice new Cathay Hotel." After almost half a minute, the Englishman offered the obligatory jest. "I believe I'll trot over to Frenchtown to see just what damage's been done. Care to join me?"

Despite her loathing of violence, duty drew Julia to the site of the explosion. Many correspondents would be drawn to Shanghai by the violation of the previously sacrosanct foreign concessions—and the first aerial bombing of a major city since the Zeppelin raids on London in the Great War. Most of those newcomers would ask her exactly what it had been like.

Racecourse Road was deserted. Pedestrians had scurried into buildings, and wooden shutters were going up over shopfronts. Preternatural silence cloaked a city inhabited by noise-loving Chinese.

A horn hooted cheerfully. Wang, Tommy's irrepressible driver, made a dashing U-turn and flung open the back door of the Chrysler Airflow. Julia smiled involuntarily at Tommy's twin self-indulgences: the erratic Wang and the hypermodern Airflow.

Tommy insisted that Wang's skill as a driver justified both his regular disappearances and the "loans" he cadged to pay his gambling debts when he reappeared. The Airflow's massive contours were broken by neither hood nor trunk; the automobile was perfectly streamlined, a single arc from bumper to bumper. Julia thought it ugly, but Tommy the scientist insisted that it was beautiful.

Neither Julia nor Richard spoke as the Airflow rolled along virtually deserted Tibet Road toward the smoke columns rising from the plaza in front of the Great World Amusement Center. Julia heard a vast sighing, which sounded like waves breaking on a distant shore, but the clanging fire engines overwhelmed it.

When the Airflow stopped, she realized that the sighing came from hundreds of Chinese women squatting before billboards advertising Crown Cigarettes and the National Lottery. All were moaning and sobbing.

Some wore dark blue workaday tunics, and others wore lighter holiday blouses. All the garments were blackened by soot, and most were speckled with blood. Stripped naked by the blast, a plump boy of seven or eight was urinating against a tree.

Richard made for a French officer of the fire company. The pump wagon stood beside the signal tower, which the blast had stripped of its metal coverings. The traffic lights were switching from green to red and back again quite normally.

Across the plaza, the brown brick Great World Amusement Center rose comfortingly solid. A protective wall some five feet high had been erected around the hexagonal building against such a blast. Curiously mottled, the wall appeared made of many-colored sandbags.

Julia clutched her throat when she saw that buffer wall leaking red and yellow fluids. It was a wall of shattered and charred human bodies.

The soup kitchen that had been distributing rice to the several thousand refugees camped in the plaza was untouched. But the explosion had piled hundreds of refugees against the unscathed Great World— dead and dying, broken and bleeding.

Standing straddle-legged, Julia vomited into the gutter. She wiped her lips with a scrap of scented lace from her red handbag and dropped the fouled cloth into the gutter. The flowing water picked up the frivolous handkerchief and bore it away, swirling gaily on the red-veined surface.

The savory aroma of roasting flesh was nauseating. Three coolies lay unmarked beside their rickshaws, killed instantaneously by shock waves. Their flimsy vehicles were shattered. Three grotesquely compacted bundles of blue cloth had evidently been their passengers.

Tommy appeared behind her and directed brusquely: "Either help or leave, Julie! You're doing no good just gawking."

"Oh, Tommy!" She turned and opened her arms. "Tommy darling!"

He embraced her and said, "Don't go into shock. You *can* help, you know."

Beside the fire engines stood two ambulances and three of the black trucks that normally collected corpses from the streets. Doctors and nurses in incongruous whites were kneeling beside the figures strewn across the plaza. Occasionally, someone shouted to summon litter-bearers wearing Red Cross brassards, but most of those unmoving figures were clearly dead. Black-clad municipal corpse handlers dealt with them, this once not joking, but silent.

Julia helped carry the injured, forcing herself to lift charred corpses in hope of finding the living beneath them. All the rescue workers wore expressions so studiedly unemotional they were almost grotesque. They could function only by suppressing pity as well as revulsion.

Tommy touched her shoulder and said, "Sorry I had to be rough . . . only way to make you pull yourself together. But it's time for you to go home. I'll call just as soon as I can."

He did not telephone until the next morning. He did not return to the house on Kiukiang Road until four that afternoon, when the tail of the typhoon was lashing Shanghai.

"At least the wind will keep the blasted planes on the ground," Tommy said then. *"All* the flaming warplanes—our gallant defenders of the Chinese Air Force as well as the Japs."

Gulping his scotch and water, he added tonelessly: "They reckon twelve to thirteen hundred killed at the Great World. Maybe three hundred injured. Only a rough count of course."

"Richard called, Richard Hollings." Julia was glad the high window of the living room kept her from looking out on the anguished city. "He called to thank me . . . and to ask us to dinner. He's a little hard to take sometimes, though not quite as bad as you . . . we . . . thought. He said they figured seven to eight hundred killed on the Bund near the Cathay Hotel. Maybe another thousand injured."

"A good day's work for our noble Nationalist defenders!" Tommy said savagely. "God knows what they'll do when they really get into their stride."

49

SEPTEMBER 12–OCTOBER 10, 1937

Richard Hollings possessed an advantage rare for a war correspondent: he could cover *both* sides as the battle for Shanghai spread. Enjoying easy access to the Chinese positions in Chapei, he was also a welcome guest aboard the Japanese flagship *Idzumo*. The Englishman had cultivated influential officers during his protracted visits to Tokyo, and he was known to them as a "friend of Japan."

Although he condemned Japanese aggression to Julia, Richard's feelings did not color his dispatches. Almost inhumanly objective, he skillfully avoided giving offense to Tokyo. Yet Julia warmed to him because of his sympathy for her beloved Chinese. She could not read his dispatches in the *Globe* or listen to his reports on NBC; his Japanese friends could not hear his private conversations.

Richard was never delayed when he crossed the Japanese barricades on the Garden Bridge to Hongkew. All foreigners had to bow to the Japanese sentries. Some men and even women were forced to strip to prove they carried neither arms nor subversive material. The emperor's soldiers were chipping away at the façade of Western superiority in the Orient. But a "friend of Japan" was not harassed.

Covering the Chinese was harder. Although the mayor of Greater Shanghai was always good for a fiery quote, the Nationalist generals were prudently reticent. To see the men who made Chinese policy in the critical autumn of 1937, Richard had to travel 250 miles to Nanking. Whether by train or by automobile, the journey was made hazardous by Japanese ground patrols and Japanese air attacks. But no one ever had called Richard Hollings a coward, whatever their reservations regarding his character or his ethics.

He considered himself only moderately successful at forty. He had married Fiona Bradley, who was twelve years his junior, because he knew she would make a highly presentable wife and an excellent mother. She had, above all, been recommended by her father's senior position in the organization of Lord Beaverbrook, Britain's most enterprising newspaper proprietor. But the highly paid and highly visible job of chief roving correspondent for the *Daily Express,* which Richard coveted, was not on offer. He had accordingly returned—alone, for the time being—to China, determined to make his name an international byword for dramatic, daring, and penetrating reporting.

That ambition brought him to the Chinese Air Force observation post on the roof of the Metropolitan Hotel in Nanking in the early afternoon of a hot September day. The Englishman understood his host's Louisiana drawl with some difficulty.

Claire Lee Chennault, who had recently passed his forty-seventh birthday, looked as if his features were carved from seamed and pitted granite that defied time. His jet-black eyes under his hooded eyelids were set so deep that he looked almost Chinese. But no Chinese face was ever quite so aggressive.

Captain Chennault had flown pursuit planes. He preached the supremacy of the pursuit, the small, fast, agile warplane designed to hunt big, cumbersome bombers. Most military aviators, however, insisted that the bombers' machine guns would always brush aside the pursuits.

Generalissimo Chiang Kai-shek had been shopping around for an air force when Chennault was involuntarily retired from the U.S. Army Air Corps. Lured by promises of a free hand and a large salary, Chennault was now "adviser on training" to the Chinese Air Force, responsible to Secretary General Mayling Chiang of the Aeronautical Commission.

Waiting on the roof of the Metropolitan Hotel for the first Japanese bombing raid on Nanking, Chennault chewed a cigar and confided that he had ordered the attacks on the *Idzumo* that hit the foreign concessions.

"First combat action I ever initiated!" he said. "And egg all over my face! My Chinese boys are long on potential, but they've been short-changed on training."

"You were telling me about the attack on the *Idzumo,* Colonel." Hollings had unilaterally raised Chennault in rank. "Could we come back to it?"

"Sure thing, son. My bombers were ordered to bomb from seventy-five hundred feet, no lower. They were also told *not* to make their approaches over the Settlement. Nobody wanted an international incident!"

Chennault surveyed the empty sky over Nanking and continued: "Cloud cover made high-level bombing impossible. But my boys were too damned eager. They flew over the Settlement at fifteen hundred feet. Then they tried to dive-bomb."

"You know, Colonel, I didn't see a single Japanese plane."

"You'll see plenty this afternoon, son." Chennault lit his cigar butt with a wooden kitchen match. "Our early warning net's already sounded the alarm. The Chinese use runners, drums, even smoke signals —along with telephones and radio. They report maybe twenty-five bombers on the way."

All Nanking lay beneath the rooftop observation post. The eleven square miles enclosed by the massive fifteenth-century walls was still largely wasteland; it had been devastated by rebels in the last century. Although the Nationalists had built a number of modern public buildings, the people lived in cramped houses huddled around the enormous city gates. A grass airfield lay outside the walls to the west.

The field telephone rang, and Chennault thumbed the butterfly switch on the handpiece. Richard heard an excited male voice: "Bandits! Bandits! At twelve o'clock and ten thousand feet. Twenty to thirty bandits!"

"All right, Lee, don't shout. I hear you." Chennault grinned mirthlessly. "Canny little Jap bastards. I didn't expect them to circle around and attack from the north."

He drew on the ragged stump of his cigar and thumbed the butterfly switch again. "Lee? All our pursuits are waiting above the clouds? . . . Just remind them again: no one moves till the Japs turn back. . . . I know it's hard, but it's the only way!"

Chennault looked at his cigar butt with disgust and hurled it across the roof before remarking conversationally, "It's *their* precious new capital that's going to get pasted. . . . Chinese pursuit pilots could be good as any with enough training. But their training's been piss-poor." After a ruminative pause: "So I've got to let the Japs drop their bombs. Then hit them when their guard's down. It's hard on Nanking. But it's the only way to kill Japs!"

The growl of air-cooled engines on the northern horizon heralded twenty-six Japanese bombers. The sunlight glinted on their long bodies when they descended and split up to confuse the antiaircraft guns on the ground. They floated contemptuously low over the city, the blood-red suns on their wings looming enormous.

When the bombers roared down on the grass airfield, enormous gouts of earth erupted. A few seconds later, flames leaped.

The Japanese made two more passes at the airfield before strafing and bombing the city of Nanking. They then resumed formation, pointed their noses east toward their home fields, and climbed into the clouds.

Aircraft engines yammered at full throttle. Although not an airplane was visible, Richard heard machine guns chattering. After three or four minutes, the sky was silent again.

Chennault removed his cigar and picked up the buzzing field telephone. He asked, "You're certain, Lee?" Then to Richard: "There you are, son. They got eight! Eight Jap bombers are down. Let's go see for ourselves!"

A jaunty chauffeur in Chinese Air Force uniform drove them four miles into the countryside, where a pyre of greasy smoke brushed the low-lying clouds. Richard confirmed the obvious through binoculars: the burning aircraft was a twin-engined Japanese bomber.

Like a macabre paper chase, aluminum carcasses led them in the direction of the Japanese base on the island of Taiwan more than six hundred miles away. In all, they saw five shot-down bombers.

The country people stared, suspecting that these two outlanders were Japanese who had parachuted to safety. When their driver explained that Japanese looked rather different, the farmers led them across the rough countryside. They saw two more bombers, blackened skeletons with their fires burned out. The farmers also led them to two aircraft that Chennault grudgingly identified as Chinese pursuit planes. One cockpit was empty. The charred shape in the other cockpit was beyond recognition.

The eighth bomber the Chinese Air Force claimed to have destroyed was never found—not that day or ever. Chennault searched for hours before conceding: "Well, nobody counts just right in combat. Maybe they only got seven. But that'll do the trick. Look here, son, there ain't going to be but a couple more daylight raids on Nanking. We're beginning to win."

Richard Hollings left the backwoods certainties of Nanking to return to the sophisticated skepticism of Shanghai. The full-scale Sino-Japanese War was best covered from Shanghai, where the ground forces clashed head-on. The war was complex, even from Shanghai.

Although the American and British fleets combined could not have controlled the three thousand-mile-long China coast, the Japanese proclaimed a blockade—chiefly to frighten off timorous shipowners. Nationalist land forces were withdrawing from indefensible North China, which the Generalissimo had virtually conceded to the invaders. The Communists withheld the bulk of their forces, but their 115th Division inflicted the first major setback on the enemy. Since Japanese generals could not believe that Chinese would stand and fight, several enemy columns followed each other into the ambush the Communists had laid in a narrow mountain pass in the northwest.

Julia Howe rejoiced in that first Chinese victory—even more because it was a Communist victory. The Apparatus instructed her to whisper that Nationalist troops, supposedly cooperating with the 115th Division, had run away. For all she knew, the story might even have been true.

Richard Hollings was grateful for such inside information. He was also curious about Julia's sources, but he did not quiz her. She was too useful to offend.

But Shanghai was the big, exciting story. The Nationalists stubbornly held, although outnumbered by a Japanese "landing party" of more than a hundred thousand men.

Richard, however, believed that reporting facts was, at most, half his job. He feared his audience would be puzzled, bored, and, finally, repelled by reports of indecisive battles in unpronounceable places between Oriental armies commanded by generals with unpronounceable names. His obligation to his editors—and to himself—was to please the largest possible audience. Thus would the Boston *Globe* and National Broadcasting Company prosper—not to speak of Richard Hollings.

The war in the air was inherently dramatic, as romantic as single combat between armored knights. Richard, therefore, repeatedly returned to Nanking and to Claire Chennault, who had promised to choke off the Japanese air raids.

After their first raid, the bombers had returned three times in five days. They were harried by Chinese warplanes using Claire Chennault's new tactics—three pursuit planes in close formation attacking a single bomber. Although they lacked rigorous training, the Chinese pilots proved Chennault's thesis. Bombers would *not* always brush aside the gadfly pursuits.

Chennault asserted that the Japanese had lost three bomber regiments, fifty-four twin-engined aircraft in all, and remarked to Hollings, "Now for the next stage—night raids."

The Chinese antiaircraft command deployed its big searchlights in a grid the attacking planes could not escape. Impaled on the shafts of light, the crews of the night bombers could not see the pursuit planes "rocketing up the beams like a monkey on a stick," as Chennault said, exulting. During the third night raid, the Chinese shot down seven of thirteen bombers—and the raiders came no more by night.

But even Chennault, the magician from Louisiana, could not in the end overcome the massive Japanese advantages: greater numbers, better aircraft, and seasoned pilots. After six weeks, the bombers returned by day with an escort of modern single-wing pursuit planes. The Japanese pursuits shot down eleven of China's remaining sixteen obsolescent biplanes, which fell from the sky like clumsy bumblebees.

Claire Chennault smiled grimly and acknowledged, "That's the ball-game—for a while. They'll paste hell out of Nanking now. Remember, I never mentioned *escorted* daylight raids."

"And Shanghai?" Richard pressed him. "Are you writing off Shanghai, too?"

"Son, if I can't defend Nanking, there's no way in hell I can defend Shanghai. I can only fight a guerrilla war in the air. Hit the Japs where they're weak. Give me time, though, and I'll sweep the Japs out of China with air power." Chennault's black eyes dulled. "Take a while, but my boss is working on better planes and better training."

"Your boss, Colonel?"

"My boss is Madame Chiang Kai-shek. Most correspondents, first thing they want is an interview with the glamorous Madame Chiang. She does more for China . . ."

"I suppose I should see her," Richard said softly. "I used to know her in the old days. Before she married."

"Did you, by God? Son, you've got to see her."

"I suppose I've been avoiding her." Richard's voice was low. "For personal reasons."

50

OCTOBER 18, 1937

Richard Hollings was, as always, amused by the ebullient young man with whom he was lunching. When the government information officer named Jimmy Wei grinned, the dark features he called "my monkey face" twisted in a grimace.

"There goes Major Yee." Jimmy glanced out the tall window of the Metropolitan Hotel. "Who says nobody's perfect? He's a perfect idiot."

"Why so hard on him?"

"Major Yee is a disaster. So is army public relations, the worst of the . . . let me see . . . five PR outfits we've now got here in Nanking."

"Which lot of professional liars do you recommend, Jimmy?"

"My own, Dick." He grinned. "Madame Chiang herself picked Hollington Tong as vice-minister of information. Myself, I'm not University of Missouri and Columbia Journalism School like Holly Tong. But our outfit *is* reliable."

"And what have you got for me today?"

"Dick, *absolutely* off the record. For your guidance only, okay?"

The correspondent nodded. He disliked information he could not report, but it was better than no information.

"The jig's up," Jimmy said solemnly. "Know what that means?"

"Yes, Jimmy."

"Not all limeys are ignorant." Jimmy did not smile. "Well, we're pulling out of Shanghai. We failed to stop the Japs, and we've failed to suck in the Western powers. It's going to be a long war."

"Jimmy," Richard demanded, "why tell me now?"

"For your guidance, as I said. Also, I want you to remember I gave

you the straight goods." Jimmy grinned diabolically and added, "It'll
make you easier to fool next time. Also remember this: the ballgame's
not over when we retreat. We'll just be starting to fight."

"How can you ever win?" Richard pressed. "Where are the men and
the guns to come from? Not to speak of the courage!"

"We've got tens of millions of brave young men. And Uncle Sam will
give us the guns, eventually. But we've got to learn. A country can just
about survive if it's corrupt or if it's inefficient! It's doomed if it's both
corrupt *and* inefficient. We'll have to . . ."

About twenty-five, Jimmy Wei was short, tough, and mildly libertine. He was also a connoisseur of his people's food, art, and literature.
Those correspondents who knew enough about China to know how
little they really knew called him Number-One Barbarian-Handler.
Jimmy could build bridges of at least partial understanding between the
bullheaded foreigners and the arrogant Chinese.

Richard Hollings was, however, jaded after talking, writing, and, too
often, dreaming about China for several hectic months. His attention
was easily diverted from the conversation by the sophisticated tinkle of
the piano near the bar. The pianist was glissading through "The Nearness of You," which was the song of the year. Julia had played it twice
on her request program a month earlier. Fiona and he had danced to it
at the Café Royale on his last night in London.

Although she had wanted to come with him, he knew he was right
in having her wait until he was settled. In between, the war had erupted.
It was no time to introduce a new wife to old haunts and old friends.
Besides, he could not have done his work properly if he'd had to worry
about Fiona.

"It's just the nearness of you!" The refrain evoked her wide-set gray
eyes and her pale gold hair. When the orchestra played it on the P &
O liner between Suez and Singapore he had, to his considerable surprise,
realized that he actually loved Fiona. He resented being reminded anew
of his commitment to her by a pianist playing that sentimental ballad
in a hotel dining room redolent of fresh paint, new carpets, and ancient
mildew.

". . . hear what I say?" Jimmy asked patiently.

He apologized: "Sorry. I'm afraid I was wool-gathering."

Tired of professional talk, Richard was watching a small boy of eight
or nine skipping across the dining room in a khaki uniform. The elderly
amah hobbling behind was berating him in Shanghainese. The pair were
obviously not natives of Nanking, which spoke its own distinctive
dialect.

The child was beautiful. His large eyes, which crackled with intelligence, dominated his fine-cut features. His uniform bore the insignia of an Air Force major, and he wore miniature pilot's wings with the jagged white sun of the Republic of China in the center.

As child and amah vanished into an alcove, tough Jimmy Wei dissolved into sentiment. "That's what we're fighting for—the children, China's future. You know, I thought she'd gone back to Shanghai. Now there's a lady you *must* meet, even if you can't see Madame Chiang right now. She's a good story herself."

"What's she done?"

"For openers, she soloed last week. How many ladies, especially Chinese ladies, can fly a plane? She's got three kids, including that young fellow in the Air Force uniform, and she's Madame Chiang's right hand. She also does a lot of our publicity. In perfect English, not like my fractured lingo."

"Who is this superwoman? Sounds like a new Hua Mu-lan, your Joan of Arc." Richard paraded his small knowledge of Chinese history to delay the answer he believed he already knew. "She must be an amazon. A big brawny lady with thick ankles."

"Boy, have you got it wrong! When you finish your coffee I'll take you over."

The Englishman lingered over his bitter coffee. When he could delay no longer, he followed Jimmy Wei toward the alcove. Only Emily, he feared, could fit Jimmy's description.

Richard was annoyed by his own hesitation. *He* had nothing to be ashamed of. Regardless of what he had himself done, *she* had left him at the far end of Bubbling Well Road in the middle of the night ten years earlier. Besides, he was devoted to his young wife.

The crystal chandelier above the round table lit Emily Howe Ou-yang's face mercilessly. She passed that test triumphantly. Her skin was still unflawed ivory, and her eyes still shone with wit. Her full lips parted in surprise when she saw Richard. Exposed by her low-necked blouse, her shoulders appeared fragile, and he was unaccountably moved.

"Madame Ou-yang, may I present Mr. Hollings?" Jimmy Wei's formality was uncharacteristic. "I'm sure you've heard of him. He's the famous foreign correspondent who has great understanding of China. A true friend of China."

Emily forced a smile but did not offer her hand. Having also dreaded their inevitable meeting, she murmured a cool response to his proper "How do you do?"

A man laughed, and a tantalizingly familiar American voice observed, "Good God, kids, anyone'd think you'd never met before." The man rose and extended his hand. Irritated by the intrusion, yet grateful for the relief of tension, Richard found the interloper's name in his memory. "Harrison Parker Smythe, isn't it?"

Richard knew the jealousy he suddenly felt was irrational, almost ludicrous. If he was to be jealous of anyone, it should be not this brash American but the husband to whom Emily had borne three children. But he had neither reason nor right to be jealous of Emily's affections.

Harry Smythe said with mounting enthusiasm, "I've kept up my flying hours, and the Army Air Corps made me a light-colonel in the reserve. Madame Chiang wants me to lend a hand, take some of the load off Claire Chennault. That's why Emmy's being so nice to a beat-up old aviator."

That mock-modest tone was even more annoying than Smythe's normal brashness. Why should the American feel it necessary to offer an elaborate explanation of his tete-à-tete with Emily, who had not said a word after their stiff greetings?

Emily smiled levely and regarded Richard with untroubled light brown eyes. Her expression conveyed neither welcome nor antagonism. Hypersensitive to the nuances of her presence, Richard was moved again—by the casual fall of her ebony hair, evidently cut short for convenience, and by her long fingers, which lay quite still on the table. She inclined her head noncommittally, offering him no more than the courteous attention she would give a casual acquaintance.

"We have very high regard for Harry Smythe," she said evenly. "Madame Chiang expects great things of him—and I do not contradict her. We Chinese value our old friends very highly."

Emily's smile momentarily lifted her mask of cool courtesy. Richard wondered what she meant by her equivocal remark about old friends. But she reverted to banalities. "You saw my little hellion misbehaving, did you, Richard? Dear old Ven Jyeh is baby-amahing her second generation. She's really too old. She can hardly keep up with him."

"A very attractive boy, Emily," he replied conventionally. "Looks a lot like you."

"We call him Jason because he's so daring, a terrible handful. My brother Tommy thinks his Chinese name is very funny. *Jen-hsun* means 'True Obedience.' But obedience is the last thing on the little devil's mind. Though I do spoil him."

"How could you help it, Emily?"

Her lips compressed, and her teeth clenched on the words she had almost shouted: *He should have been ours, you fool, mine and* yours, *not Ou-yang Hsiu's! If only you weren't . . . weren't such a charming scoundrel, such a complete bastard, he* would *be ours!*

Emily went chalky pale, appalled by that violent outburst within her own mind. That was not how she should feel—anything but how she had *meant* to feel—when confronted again with Richard Hollings. A cool smile and a flip reference to the old days should have done it. Perhaps a polite inquiry about his new wife to show that she no longer gave a damn about him.

Why should she be disturbed at meeting her discarded lover on her own home ground? Was she not a highly regarded journalist and writer? Had she not made herself a competent aviatrix? Was she not the cherished, though wholly independent, wife of a wealthy gentleman of ancient family and the mother of three beautiful children? Had she not made a resounding success as a woman? And as a patriot? Mayling Chiang's right hand in the fight for China's future—and for China's women!

Emily despised her confusion. She resented her yearning toward Richard—and the bleak realism his presence forced upon her. She had been half aware before this encounter that she was living half a life—despite all her busyness. But she had been at peace with herself for a decade, satisfied with half a loaf. Settled and content ten minutes earlier, she had now been flung into an emotional maelstrom.

Even shrewd Jimmy Wei, who of course knew of their affair, believed she was unruffled. She had, it appeared to him, paled in surprise but immediately regained her equanimity.

". . . then I'll speak to Mayling this afternoon." Emily completed a sentence she could not remember beginning. "I'm sure she'll want a long talk with you, Richard. You're reporting for the North American Newspaper Alliance and the National Broadcasting Company, as well as the *Globe?*"

"And an occasional piece for *The Times.* The real one, *The Times* of London."

"That's fine, Richard. But, candidly, we're interested primarily in the States." Emily knew she was babbling. "Most Americans know little of China, but they all seem to have opinions on China. Naturally, Washington listens to them."

"I do have rather a large audience in America."

She rose, offered a crisp handshake, and said, "That's settled then. I must be going."

Chilled by her brusqueness, Richard was struck by the half-size Chinese Air Force pilot's wings pinned to the shoulder of her blouse. The wings were gold; the white sun in the center was seed pearls; and the blue-sky background was sapphire chips. Emily was evidently fighting a high-fashion war—rather, he mused, like Joan of Arc ordering her armor from Coco Chanel. Moreover, her self-confidence now verged upon self-assertiveness.

Deliberately turning his back on her retreating figure, Richard spoke to Harry Smythe. "I never expected to meet you here. I thought you were through with China."

"The hardest thing is getting my Mandarin back in working order," the American, who had once been a vice-consul in Shanghai, confided earnestly. "But Emily's a great help."

Richard again felt the stab of irrational jealousy, but he smiled and said: "You must be very high in the embassy now."

"I *was* first secretary in Rome, but I'm not exactly in the embassy here, Dick. . . . It's a little hard to explain. I'm on a special mission . . . on indefinite leave from the State Department."

The correspondent looked at the diplomat skeptically. That tale sounded like a cover story for a mission Washington did not wish to acknowledge officially. Yet it was hard to believe that Harry Smythe was not telling the absolute truth. His cornflower-blue eyes were candid, despite the minute crow's-feet at their corners. He looked like a sincere, albeit cheeky, altar boy.

The American was, at a guess, a few years past forty. None of them had grown younger. Richard recalled that he himself was forty. Even Emily, serene and unalterable, was just a year younger than the century and, therefore, thirty-six.

"Dick, I never lied to you," Harry Smythe persisted. "So, between us, I'm here to do a little job for President Roosevelt. He wants a first-hand assessment of Chinese capability—especially in the air."

Despite himself, the correspondent turned to watch Emily's departure. He caught his breath when he saw her rounded hips and slender torso receding through the ornamental potted palms. Behind her trailed the small boy in Air Force uniform and his aged amah. Head high, her dark hair bobbing on her neck, Emily strode across the lobby toward the main door, where a driver was standing beside an emerald-green Lincoln Continental convertible.

She did not look back. But why should she?

51

OCTOBER 27, 1937

Joshua Haleevie surveyed the late autumnal glories of his five-acre garden with satisfaction. The copper Japanese maples were a vivid background to the saffron double-chrysanthemums. The spearhead leaves of the rhododendrons were as shiny green as if polished, and the plump leaves of the azaleas flamed autumnal red. The roses climbing the pergola were still in full bloom.

Sensing that his head gardener was watching him with a stern eye, he guiltily put the pruning shears back in the pocket of his worn twill trousers. They had an inviolable agreement, Joshua sometimes said. The gardener might place small bets on horses, but he entrusted his savings to his employer for investment. In return, Joshua did not sabotage the gardener's lifework by pruning so much as the privet hedge at the back of his own garden.

Other eyes watched Joshua with approval and trust. The mastiff Adam Schall was still lively at almost sixteen, a good age, even for the hardy Tibetan breed. Adam's years were betrayed only by the gray hairs that powdered his black muzzle—and by his excessive sense of responsibility.

A week earlier, the mastiff had accompanied Julia and Tommy Howe's two small daughters to the safety of Joshua's mansion on the western edge of the International Settlement. Julia somewhat sheepishly explained that she had sent him along as "a kind of canine amah because he's so devoted to the girls." Actually, Adam, too, had been sent away from exposed Kiukiang Road for his own safety. After her husband, her daughters, and her friend Emily, Julia cared more for Adam than for any other being on earth. Sometimes, when she was fed up with Tommy's protracted working hours, the girls' antics, and Emily's fervent pro-Nationalist sympathies, Julia wondered if she did not care more for Adam than for any of them.

Althea and Persephone Howe came onto the terrace, protected from the evening chill by all-in-one pyjamas of thick gray cotton, called Dr. Dentons. Indignant at wearing those ungainly, babyish garments, they stomped down the stone steps to the velvety lawn. Adam moved protectively toward his charges and growled proprietorially when a young gardener offered them giant bronze chrysanthemums.

Walking on either side of Adam and twisting his long ears, the girls came to Joshua. Seven-year-old Althea's hair was pale blond, and her eyes were light hazel. Four-year-old Persephone's hair was jet black, and her eyes were iodine brown. Otherwise, they were very much alike, both possessing their father's pale-ivory skin and wiry physique. When pensive, they looked like their Aunt Emily; when they laughed, they were transformed into miniature Julias.

Thunder rumbled, and the fur around Adam's neck bristled into a ruff. The sky was, however, clear at dusk except for tufts of cloud and the glow on the northern horizon. Thunder rumbled again over the jagged silhouettes of the tenements near the North Station in Chapei. Adam opened his great jaws and bellowed defiance to that challenge from the heavens.

Like the Chinese, Joshua felt that dogs were useful guards, or even companions, but that foreigners foolishly ascribed more-than-human devotion to their pets. Today he envied the dog a little. Joshua was a major in the Shanghai Volunteer Corps; a renowned big-game hunter; a prime mover in Shanghai's remarkable development; a millionaire twice over by inheritance; and a millionaire ten times over by his own efforts. Yet he envied the dog, whose sole possession was a grandiloquent name. If only he could believe with the mastiff Johann Adam Schall von Bell that the rising clamor in the heavens was only thunder.

Wryly, almost ruefully, Joshua surveyed the hewn granite mansion he had built for his bride, who named it Zion. The splendor and spaciousness had seemed somewhat pointless since the specialists had told his wife, Charlotte, that she could never bear children.

The red-tiled dormer roofs were crowned by twelve chimneys, although the under-floor heating, which was regulated by electric-eye thermostats, functioned perfectly. The two-story central hall with its minstrels' gallery, which could accommodate a symphony orchestra, was dominated by an African elephant's head with ten-foot tusks. Cape buffalo, lions, giraffes, and snow leopards had all given their heads as trophies. The great granite fireplace was framed by two towering bears, one grizzled and the other brown. Their four-inch talons and saw-toothed jaws made visitors feel like naked pygmies.

When he had encountered Elizaveta, as was virtually inevitable in parochial Shanghai, she had asked, "What's become of my sensitive Jewish scholar, my reluctant warrior? . . . I'm glad you're happy with Charlotte, darling. I'm also glad you don't yet have a stuffed giant panda or a mouse-deer with glass eyes!"

Joshua did not smile when he recalled that scathing comment. He knew how greatly he had altered since his marriage. The ostentatious mansion was a symptom of his alteration, as were the eight automobiles in the garages separated from his three tennis courts by a twelve-foot yew hedge transplanted from the estate of a silk merchant beggared by cheap Japanese rayon. He used only two automobiles regularly: the black Rolls-Royce Phantom II, which had headlights as big as barrel-heads and room for nine passengers; and the fire-engine-red Packard Victoria convertible.

His sapphire Delage runabout sparkled because it was washed weekly and waxed monthly. But that jewel of the carriage-maker's art was immobilized on concrete blocks. Charlotte had jealously objected to his "tootling around town like a young blade in that bug." Since he was then still indulging her whims, he had given up that relic of his wicked bachelor days.

Besides, the twelve-cylinder Packard was more powerful, more comfortable, and more stable around the bends of the new road to Nanking. Yet few motorcars took that road nowadays. Carefree drives through the open country had been one of the first casualties of the Sino-Japanese War.

The Settlement and Frenchtown were now claustrophobic under the virtual siege the Japanese had imposed. The Japanese could not strangle China by isolating Shanghai. They might, however, succeed in strangling Shanghai by cutting the trading metropolis off from its markets in the interior of China.

Yet an explosion of prosperity was the most visible effect of the gravest threat the foreign community had known since the Taiping rebels turned back at the city gates in 1860. Julia's uncle, John Pavernen, exemplified that curious phenomenon of prosperity amid chaos. The Sino-Japanese War and disorder in Europe were making Quick Jack a rich man.

Thousands of Jewish refugees from Nazi Germany had come to the Settlement, where they could land freely and stay indefinitely. Most of them possessed funds, for they could not otherwise have bought their escape from their festering fatherland. Obviously they needed housing. John Pavernen and his partner in chicanery Gustav Vass were buying, converting, and manipulating properties. Some of the expensive dwellings they built were actually intended to last.

The real-estate bonanza, which recalled Pavernen and Vass's ill-fated Riverview Manor, was just part of the bounty bestowed by the gods of war and fortune. Quick Jack was also engaged in very profitable philanthropy.

Hundreds of Chinese industrialists had moved factories to the security of the foreign concessions to escape the Japanese threat, and they needed assistance in dealing with the foreign authorities. JPEnterprises had been revived to provide that assistance. John Pavernen had even cajoled his niece Julia into helping. Her Marxist hatred of capitalist exploiters was tempered by her human sympathy for the Chinese entrepreneurs. Besides, their activities would provide jobs for the poor.

Despite Julia's help, her uncle bemoaned the disappearance of Little Pow, who would have been the perfect agent to deal with his own countrymen. Quick Jack particularly regretted Little Pow during the complex negotiations that preceded the launching of every one of his fleet of "foreign flag companies."

The basic concept was simple. A Chinese-owned company doing business in China was subject to the depredation of Nanking's tax collectors, to the demands of corrupt officials—and to the rapacity of the Japanese. In late October of 1937, none of those predators could touch foreign-owned enterprises doing business in China. The International Settlement's register of companies now listed John Pavernen as sole or partial owner of 123 enterprises, which ranged from bakeries and flour mills through ship's chandlers and slipways to a bus line and a Ford agency.

Joshua Haleevie smiled at that bright thread in the gray fabric of recent months. But the reality of violence obtruded into the cheerless dusk that was descending around him. The conflagration around the North Station glowed scarlet against the ashen sky.

As if to propitiate fate, Joshua stooped to pat Adam's silky head and to kiss Julia's daughters, whose cheeks were as soft as the dahlias beside the gravel path. The girls giggled when he explained that many plants were not blooming because they were having a sleep like good children.

He then left Althea and Persephone with Adam and sat down to smoke a Havana cigar on the bench under the white-flowered magnolia that draped the brick wall of his small estate.

Yet his thoughts returned implacably to the encompassing crisis. The Settlement's own small army, the Volunteers, had been on active duty for months. So many refugees had joined that they formed a full Jewish Company, which one couldn't, after all, call the German Company. The official Germans, the Nazis, were still members of the international community, as, for that matter, were their close friends, the Japanese.

The German refugees had strengthened the medical profession and invigorated the community's musical life. But the doctors were now busy attending those wounded by stray shells and misaimed bombs within the previously sacrosanct foreign concessions. The musicians were carrying rifles instead of violins, for the Empire Theatre no longer presented operettas. Sandbags protected the glass doors, which faced toward the battleground of Chinese-ruled Chapei across Soochow Creek, and the marquee bore the bleak message: CLOSED OWING TO HOSTILITIES.

Shanghai's commercial ingenuity had, however, contrived substitute diversions. The International Guides Bureau advertised: *Shanghai's Most Enjoyable "War" Feature—a Trip around the Front on the Crystal Bus—including One Free Drink.* Never outdone, journalists were rushing out crisis supplements. *Oriental Affairs* had preempted the best title: "Shanghai in Torment." The *Shanghai Times* had to make do with "Pictorial Record of the Sino-Japanese Hostilities in and around the City."

Joshua Haleevie was, however, forced to acknowledge the likelihood that the unique international community faced extinction. The Settlement's existence depended upon common agreement on common interests among all the foreigners. That tacit agreement had been breached by the Japanese attack on Greater Shanghai.

Although Joshua feared that the unique way of life he cherished was just about finished, the Western powers were acting as if they expected the Settlement to last forever. Shepherded by warships, ground troops were arriving in large numbers to man the barricades. The berets of the Royal Ulster Rifles and the sola topees of the Durham Light Infantry paraded beside the pillbox kepis of the French infantry. Steel helmets flaunted the anchor-transfixed globe of the U.S. Marines alongside the jaunty scarlet pompoms of Italian sailors.

The commercial community was not reassured by the military buildup. Thousands of women and children had been evacuated to Hong Kong, and the flood of Chinese refugees into the concessions was again dammed by barbed-wire-and-sandbag perimeter fences. The Bund and Nanking Road were parapeted with sandbags, as were the show windows on Bubbling Well Road that bore the sign: THE CITY'S OLDEST VICTUALLERS AND PROVISIONERS, DOMBEY AND SON.

Although the powers' show of resolution had kept Japanese ground forces from violating the Settlement's legal immunity, the projectiles of both sides dropped on it by accident. In mid-October, the bombs of an unidentified aircraft had struck Sincere's and Wing On's, the adjoining department stores on Nanking Road, and killed more than a thousand noontime shoppers. A rain of shell fragments regularly claimed its victims, and disease flourished among nearly a million Chinese refugees. The foreign enclaves, nonetheless, remained privileged—and largely untouched—beside the carnage in Greater Shanghai.

The glow of burning Chapei shone brighter in Joshua's garden as dusk deepened. Artillery barked louder in reply to snarling machine guns. The Chinese were still tenaciously maintaining their positions in the tenements, office buildings, and warehouses north of Soochow Creek. But how long could their depleted forces hold off three times their number?

Behind the rhododendron hedge Joshua heard high-pitched yapping. Turning the corner, he found the two small girls in gray pyjamas clasping each other in pretended fear. His head level with the seven-year-old's, Adam was crouching and barking in a ridiculous forced falsetto. When he made a menacing dart, the sisters squealed in delight.

"All right, ladies!" Joshua called. "Time for bed."

He shepherded the protesting girls along the gravel path toward the house called Zion. Now guardian rather than playmate, Adam trotted behind. The black mastiff was virtually invisible in the dusk, except for the white blaze on his chest.

The sparrows were debating shrilly in the darkness when Joshua heard the metallic whine of an artillery shell. Scooping up the girls, he flung himself down on the ground. Displaced air boomed when the projectile hurtled past. As the whine receded in the west, Joshua realized that the shell had actually passed some distance away. Old instincts and old fears had deceived him.

Nonetheless, he hurriedly carried the girls toward the shelter of the house. Their arms were tight around his neck, and their warm breath tickled his cheeks. He remembered again that Charlotte could not bear children.

Why else had he married her? Why had he been such a pliable fool? Why had he not defied his parents and forced Elizaveta to marry him

—and give him sons and daughters? Despite her skittishness, Elizaveta really wanted a strong will to command her.

Extraordinary! Such vain reflections amid the sound of guns.

Above the clamor of the fieldpieces, he thought he heard the whining of trench mortar bombs nearby. Yet Chapei was too far away for any danger from mortars. Joshua froze in astonishment when he heard a mortar bomb explode at the far end of the garden less than two hundred yards away.

A second mortar bomb exploded even closer. Joshua flung himself down again, sheltering the girls with his body. Yet hugging the grass would help very little if the stick of bombs drew still closer. Shrapnel shells from fieldpieces threw fountains high into the air, but the vicious little mortar bombs sprayed their fragments horizontally only a foot or so above the ground.

When the third mortar bomb exploded, Joshua nonetheless chose to stay put rather than risk a dash for the house. He saw only the white flash of Adam's chest in the darkness, but he smiled involuntarily at the mastiff's antics. Running around in circles, Adam was barking a falsetto accompaniment to the bombardment. And dogs were supposed to be afraid of the thunder of the guns.

A fourth mortar bomb exploded, fortunately still a hundred yards away. It was the last in the stick, Joshua concluded after half a minute. The garden was suddenly still. Even the falsetto barking had stopped.

Joshua carried the girls up the stone steps, which were silver-gray in the tentative moonlight. His wife was standing just inside the French windows, and he spoke to her briefly. "No, I'm fine! Not to worry, darling. Just get yourself and the girls away from the windows. I'll be back in a minute."

Heavy with apprehension, Joshua retraced his steps across the lawn, which shone pale green in the moonlight. Near the rhododendrons lay a black mound. Knowing what he must find, Joshua trudged across the lawn with leaden steps. Adam was only a dog, he told himself, and the girls were safe.

He lifted his foot to nudge the dark shape, but drew back abruptly. He forced himself to kneel and turn the animal over with his hands. Somehow, that gesture seemed more reverent.

A ribbon of blood stretched diagonally across the white blaze like a scarlet sash. The great brown eyes stared dully, and the silver bristles on the old dog's muzzle gleamed in the moonlight.

After he assured himself that Charlotte and the girls were unharmed, Joshua's thoughts turned to the extraordinary salvo of mortar bombs into his garden. He recalled a bizarre incident that had occurred in training during the Great War. An inexperienced corporal had reversed the bearings of a trench mortar and almost killed his officers. The target lay at an angle of ten degrees from his position, but he had aimed at one hundred ninety degrees, the diametrical opposite. Only a similar error could account for the erratic volley that had killed the mastiff Adam.

Joshua could not understand why he was so stricken by the death of a dog. Deeply troubled, he climbed the stairs to the attic in the gables. Through the mullioned window he saw a brilliant red glow lighting the horizon to the north. The smoke of burning Chapei obscured the stars and the moon.

Joshua knew then why he grieved so deeply for Adam. The mastiff's death was a symbol—and a portent. Adam's death marked the end of an era in which they had all been young, happy, optimistic—and safe.

He recalled Julia's housewarming in 1922. Already fizzing with champagne, Elizaveta and he had brought along five more crates and a primitive Victrola. Later that day, Tommy Howe's friend, the Communist labor agitator Chang Kuo-tao, had delivered the black-and-white puppy to Julia.

It seemed only yesterday, but it was fifteen years ago. And fifteen years was half a generation.

He opened the small window—and recoiled from a blast of heat. The distant fires tinged his cheeks and his white sideburns with pink. All Chapei was burning. Almost five miles long, Chapei was a single sea of flame, and the sky above Chapei was the bright scarlet of arterial blood.

Amid the towers of flame, a nine-tiered pagoda rose invincible, its tile carapace gleaming vermilion. Was that indestructible pagoda another portent? Did it not signal that puny Japan could not defeat the indomitable will and the enormous expanse of China?

The next instant a gargantuan sigh rose above the fires' roar, and the pagoda crumbled into the flames.

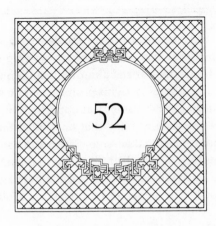

Richard Hollings was the odd man out on the American gunboat USS *Panay*. Not because he was English, but because he was cheerless. A joyful end-of-term mood prevailed, not only among the crew but among the American embassy officials and the foreign correspondents who had embarked at Nanking. Richard, however, could not rejoice at deserting the doomed city, which even the indomitable Generalissimo and Madame Chiang Kai-shek had left four days earlier for the new capital at Wuhan, six hundred miles upriver.

The Nationalist rear guard was now withdrawing, abandoning Nanking and its people to the Japanese. The last foreigners had left on the *Panay*, feeling themselves better protected by the big American flags painted on her awnings and her hull than by her six 30-caliber machine guns and her two 3-inch guns.

The Englishman stared dejectedly at the placid expanse of the Yangtze River above Nanking on the afternoon of December 12, 1937. He was depressed and exhausted by the exertions and the emotions of the past week. Above all, he was concerned about Emily Ou-yang, as he was still learning to think of her.

Since his first trip in September, Richard had visited Nanking frequently. He had seen both Generalissimo and Madame Chiang Kai-shek with no difficulty. Jimmy Wei had confided, "Your name jumped right to the head of the list because Mrs. Ou-yang . . . Emily . . . insisted."

But he had seen Emily herself only once after their meeting in the dining room of the Metropolitan Hotel. She had welcomed him politely —and distantly—to the Chiangs' suite, introduced him again to the Generalissimo, reminded Mayling of earlier meetings, and departed. After the Japanese occupied Greater Shanghai, a public figure like Madame Chiang Kai-shek could not cross their lines. Her executive assistant Emily Ou-yang could, however, slip across with false papers. But Richard's efforts to see Emily in Shanghai had been deftly turned aside. One day, Julia would welcome him as an important correspondent; the next day, she would fend him off as a threat to her sister-in-law's equilibrium.

Having last heard of Emily in Nanking, Richard hoped she was now safe in Shanghai. Alternately, he dreamed of finding her when the *Panay* finally arrived in Wuhan.

If the *Panay* ever arrived! The captain did not seem to know quite where he was bound. He had weighed anchor at eight-thirty that Sunday morning and steamed upriver, anchoring again where the Yangtze widened. He was behaving as if he had nothing to fear, although both sides were occasionally firing at neutral ships. During the afternoon, the captain allowed a dozen crewmen to visit the three Socony-Vacuum tankers anchored nearby. The U.S. Navy's prohibition of alcoholic drink did not apply aboard the tankers, which also flew the Stars and Stripes.

The captain was not perceptibly disturbed when two Japanese warplanes swooped down on the gunboat, apparently searching for the ten troop ships on which, it was rumored, a Chinese division had fled from Nanking. He was armored by his conviction of American inviolability.

"It's not real, is it?" a voice asked. "A painted ship on a painted sea."

Richard was pleased to see the Roman profile of the Italian correspondent Luigi Barzini, whose American accent and anti-Fascist views both derived from his education at Columbia University. Barzini and Richard had already formed a congenial group with Harry Smythe, who was pursuing his mysterious mission, and Norman Alley, the daring newsreel cameraman.

"Just look at her!" Standing on the upper deck, Barzini gestured at the length of the gunboat below them. "A white-and-tan warship. Like something out of an opera—a comic opera. Have you ever seen anything less warlike?"

Hollings had been turning over the same thought for the story he would write when the U.S. Navy condescended to take him to some place where he could file a cable. The white-and-tan paint that amused Luigi Barzini was intended to make gunboats so distinctive that no warlord could fail to identify them—or risk the foreign devils' wrath by shooting at them. Richard hoped that deterrent would work, for the *Panay* could not defend herself.

No ammunition filled the racks beside the three-inch guns mounted fore and aft. The after-gun was, moreover, so caged by the pipe stanchions supporting the awnings that it could not move to aim and fire. Even after six months, the Sino-Japanese War was still something of a joke to the U.S. Navy.

The anchorage the captain had chosen revealed his state of mind. His six obsolescent Lewis machine guns were loaded against snipers, although the banks of the Yangtze were distant brown smudges beneath wraiths of smoke from cooking fires. Only artillery could reach the gunboat, and illiterate Chinese artillerymen were notoriously poor shots. The *Panay* would have been perfectly secure if the year were 1914, when the airplane had only been an interesting toy.

Sixty miles to the northeast, two squadrons of the Imperial Japanese Navy's air arm were being hauled through the gray winter sky by their big aluminum propellers. The warplanes were strung out in loose formations because the pilots had sacrificed their normal precision to the race for their objective.

The naval aviators were elated at being loosed for the first time against their proper targets: ships. Reconnaissance flights had confirmed the reports of troopships carrying a fugitive Chinese division. Intent upon being first to the target, the lieutenants leading the two squadrons leaned forward to urge their aircraft to greater speed.

Harry Smythe looked up at the sky when he heard the distant growl of aircraft engines and said, "Some poor bastards're going to catch hell! The damned Japs own the sky."

"It may be selfish, but I'm glad it's not us," Luigi Barzini said. "I've had a bellyful of being bombed . . ."

"I agree . . ." Richard Hollings broke off and exclaimed, "Why the devil are they coming in so low?"

"Get down!" Harry Smythe shouted. "For God's sake, hit the deck!"

In the pilothouse near the bows, the captain, too, looked up. He did not see the bomb whose explosion flung him across the pilothouse. The flash blinded him, and the reverberation deafened him. He saw that his left leg was bent at an extraordinary angle, and pain gripped him. Nonetheless, the captain's professional eye assessed his ship. The radio shack was stove in; the foremast was down; and the forward three-inch gun had been blown off its pedestal.

Sprawled on the upper deck, Richard Hollings actually saw the two bombs that smashed the prow. When the gunboat shuddered under the double explosion, he was tossed half a foot into the air. He landed hard on the white-sanded deck, and cascades of brilliant light erupted before his eyes. Water raining down from the geyser thrown up by a near miss half-blinded him.

After blinking to clear his vision, Richard saw two dive-bombers hurtling toward the stern, the red balls on their wings enormous. Their big yellow bombs detached themselves at the low point of their dive. Both exploded in the water—and shook the two-hundred-foot *Panay* like a toy boat in a bathtub.

Richard smelled acrid cordite and heard the asthmatic wheezing of the old Lewis guns. A petty officer wearing a blue workshirt but no trousers was shouting orders at the gunners, while a nearly naked officer climbed the ladder to the pilothouse. A single sleeve, on his right arm, a single shoe, on his right foot, and the peaked cap perched jauntily on his head were all the bomb blast had left him.

Through the stench of gunpowder, the smells of China wafted across the water: frying garlic, stale cooking oil, and wood smoke; the clay scent of the laterite soil and the reek of human excrement. In the brief intervals between the gunfire wild ducks cawed overhead, and the wind carried the lowing of frightened buffaloes across the muddy water.

Afterward, Richard remembered with surprise that he had forgotten to be afraid. He remembered, too, Norman Alley standing erect and changing the magazines of his 16-millimeter camera.

Later, Richard's memory yielded other images: the radio shack behind the pilothouse hit again; an officer hobbling across the deck, blood streaming from his leg, but still shouting orders; steam roaring from the funnel when the engineer tripped the safety valve to prevent the boiler's exploding; Luigi Barzini returning from a reckless sortie below decks to report water rising fast in the hull. And constantly: the high-pitched clamor of the dive-bombers' engines; the blood-red sun flashing on their wings; the wheezing of the Lewis guns; the chatter of the warplanes' machine guns in reply.

The order was passed when the warplanes turned on the three Soco-ny-Vacuum tankers: "Abandon ship! All hands abandon ship!"

Water lapped at their feet as they waited on the *Panay*'s deck to board the two sampans that were her only lifeboats. No one was in command.

The captain was unconscious, and the executive officer, who had been hit in the throat and the hands, could no longer even scrawl brief orders with a marking pencil. Yet the abandon-ship routine proceeded smoothly. The crew took off not only the wounded and the passengers, but also medical supplies and essential stores.

"Discipline!" Harry Smythe said. "Training and discipline!"

"Beginner's luck!" Richard Hollings said. "And bloody lucky for us the Japs've gone away!"

At precisely five minutes past three, as Richard automatically noted, the last officer stepped into the motor-sampan. It was the young lieutenant whose clothes had been blown off, and he was still naked.

The survivors watching from the shore signaled frantically as the last sampan drew away from the gunboat, which was awash in the muddy water. Two barges crammed with Japanese soldiers were leaving the tankers they had been harassing to make for the Panay. As they approached, their machine guns swept the stricken gunboat.

The Japanese boarded but withdrew in haste. A minute or two later, the gunboat rolled wearily to starboard, exposed her flat bottom, which was green with long aquatic grasses and jagged with gray barnacles. Her white paint gleaming, the Panay dove, shattered prow first, into the Yangtze River. The rounded stern vanished last, leaving concentric circles of frothy bubbles.

The tough gunboat sailors could not weep, not even for the only home most had known for years. No one spoke for a minute, but finally someone said, "Well, that's it! Let's get organized."

Norman Alley wiped his soot-blackened face with the back of his soot-blackened hand and said softly, "Terrific shots! Best I ever made. They'll show the Japs were so close they couldn't have mistaken the big Stars and Stripes on the awnings. Great shots! But never again, I hope!"

Feeling themselves, as non-Americans, outsiders at a time of family grief, neither Richard Hollings nor Luigi Barzini spoke aloud. But the Italian turned to the Englishman and said very softly, "The United States is now at war with Japan. Declaration of war may be delayed, but it can't be evaded. Even if they don't know it, the Americans are already at war!"

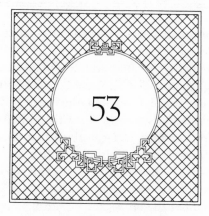

JANUARY 10, 1938

Several hundred doves fluttered in the glass-roofed courtyard of the old mansion on Jessfield Road. Dyed red, green, and pink, they swirled like confetti beneath the leaden January sky. The bamboo whistles tied to their legs trilled joyously amid the rattle of firecrackers.

The household was celebrating the betrothal of the eldest son of the wealthy gentleman Ou-yang Hsiu. But the mistress of the household, who was the youth's stepmother, was not there to see the final fireworks. Despite his desire for just one more son, Ou-yang Hsiu rejoiced in the modern family of one son and two daughters his third wife had given him. The price of a modern wife with a foreign education was, however, tolerating behavior so independent it sometimes verged on the unseemly.

Emily Ou-yang awaited her own guests in the big conservatory at the rear of the old house. If her duty to her country had been less urgent, she would not have left the family party. But Madame Chiang Kai-shek's instructions, sent by courier from Wuhan, were pressing: *Because the American people believe our defeat is inevitable, the American government is hedging —by betting on the Japs. If American opinion does not turn, even the meager assistance we now receive will cease. You must work on the Americans. You must convince them that we are fighting their fight—and that we can win. Drop everything else!*

America's own correspondents, Emily had concluded, must tell the American people that China was fighting for them and that the Japanese were America's enemy. Then the Central Government of China would get from the United States all the guns it needed to defeat the Japanese. She had, accordingly, drafted a plan of campaign with her sister-in-law

Julia, who seemed to have every foreign correspondent in China on a leash.

Julia had thrown herself wholeheartedly into the campaign—with the blessing of the Apparatus. The National People's Party and the Communist Party were, after all, formally united against the Japanese. Julia knew the Communists' chief reason for the united front but never mentioned it: Mao Tse-tung had contrived that alliance because the Communists could have been destroyed if they had not diverted the Nationalist armies from themselves to the battle against Japan.

The reception for fifty guests on the drizzle-sodden Sunday afternoon was the opening gun of the propaganda campaign Emily and Julia had planned. Consuls general were to be fed tidbits of inside information with the Shanghai dumplings. Far more than newspapermen, diplomats loved a scoop. But Emily and Julia would discuss high strategy with the correspondents. Newspapermen liked to think they were policymakers.

Despite her dedication, Emily had bridled when Julia wrote Richard Hollings's name on an invitation to the reception. She had declared vehemently, "I won't have him here. Anyway, it wouldn't be fair to my husband. Not when the other guests know that—"

"Emmy, I know just how you feel," Julia had replied. "I can hardly bear him myself. But I still see him a lot."

"Julie, how can you? He's grasping and hard."

"I just think he'll come in handy," Julia had said stubbornly. "He's a big cheese, now. Not only NBC and the *Boston Globe*. His dispatches are also syndicated by the North American Newspaper Alliance. . . . Em, are you still carrying a torch?"

"All right, ask him if you must," Emily had finally agreed. "But don't expect me to talk to him."

Natty in a soft gray flannel suit, Richard was among the first guests to brush past the scarlet poinsettias framing the doorway of the conservatory where Emily awaited her guests. She had chatted stiffly with him. When she unconsciously reached out to emphasize a point by touching his arm, she had snatched her hand back as if his sleeve were on fire. Apparently unaware of her enmity, he had chatted easily before making way for other guests.

Greeting Julia like the close friend he believed her to be, Richard remarked genially: "Emily's really gone all out. A string quartet and a strolling dumpling stand. But she seems a little tense. Hostess's nerves—"

"You didn't hear? . . . You don't know, do you, Richard?" Julia interrupted. "Em was caught in Nanking when the Japs marched in."

"Poor girl! No wonder she's jumpy! Did it shake her terribly?"

"She's tough, and I hope she's getting over it. But it's only been a month."

Richard followed her glance. Too thin, almost haggard, Emily was, nonetheless, striking in a royal-blue *cheongsam* with gold-braid trim. Her only ornament was her miniature gold Chinese Air Force wings with pearls and sapphires. Julia had, however, flouted wartime austerity because she wished to appear fragile, feminine, and a little frivolous. She wore a pink beaded dress with a round neckline. The long sleeves were secured by loops around her little fingers, and tiny gold buttons closed the skirt from knee to calf.

"Dick, she's dedicated," Julia warned. "She's working so hard for China there's no room for anything else in her life."

Emily was dressing down the American consul general, who could not take offense. The soft voice was Emily Ou-yang's, but he knew the message was Madame Chiang Kai-shek's.

"I must disagree, Madame Ou-yang." The consul general nonetheless temporized. "The United States is strictly neutral, favoring neither side."

"What about the *Panay?* The Jap aviators couldn't possibly have missed the big American flags on the awnings. Anyway, it's an open secret: Norman Alley's film—the part President Roosevelt personally suppressed—shows dive-bombers only a hundred feet above the *Panay.* They couldn't have mistaken an American gunboat for a Chinese troopship. But you Americans did nothing!"

"I don't call stiff protests nothing, Madame Ou-yang."

"Meanwhile, you're selling scrap iron and aviation gas to the Japs," she persisted. "And you're sniping at Claire Chennault and his men. Warning they'll lose their American citizenship by fighting for China."

"The law," he replied, "prohibits Americans from serving in the armed forces of foreign countries. As I said, we're neutral."

"Then, why can't you Americans act like *real* neutrals?"

"What precisely do you mean?"

"Military goods are flowing to Japan. Not guns or planes, which they don't need because they've got their own factories. But everything else. Yet China can't buy armaments from America. You even stopped delivery of obsolete rifles sold us by your own War Department. And you've forced us to unload Martin bombers in Manila—from a *Chinese* ship! You won't even sell us explosives for construction purposes. America is cracking down on China!"

"Madame Ou-yang, I shall risk being indiscreet. And you know that discretion is to a diplomat what chastity is to a lady." The consul general lapsed into ponderous old-fashioned charm. "A little unsolicited advice to you—and to your . . . ah . . . associates. Just hang on and hope for the best. Policy does change, though slowly: It won't be easy and it won't be quick, but you can look for a change."

"I'll try to hope," she replied. "But that's not easy either."

The consul general offered an almost Continental bow. He had told her very little, but he regretted even those meager confidences. He bowed again and excused himself.

"Never say die, Emmy." She heard Tommy's light tone. "It's not healthy for my favorite sister to give up hope. Definitely morbid. Bad for mental hygiene, as they call it in God's country."

"Tommy, darling!" She laughed. "You only have *one* sister."

"I suppose that's why you're my favorite," he agreed amiably. "No competition."

"Jimmy Wei, you've been leading my brother astray," Emily accused Tommy's companion. "How much have you two had to drink?"

"I assure you, my good lady," Jimmy replied, "only two or three little sips."

Jimmy Wei was elaborately courtly when he was drinking, and the pink spots above Tommy's cheekbones had obviously been produced by more than two or three little sips. Otherwise he would not have worn the ancient tweed jacket with the violent green-and-red check, which his wife hated.

Little Jimmy Wei's dark monkey-face was, however, unaltered. Having learned to drink as a reporter on the *Shanghai Evening Post,* he had become inured to liquor since joining the press office, where his chief, Hollington Tong, called him "my utility outfielder." He was today dressed in a pin-striped blue suit to play the suave diplomat.

Grasping their arms, Jimmy swept Emily and Tommy toward the bar. He demanded Black Jack Daniels from the bemused bartender, plucked a turkey leg from the buffet, and waved it like a baton to emphasize his points.

"So you want to know what it was like in Nanking after the Jap dwarves marched in, Dr. Howe?" he asked loudly.

Tommy nodded, although he had already heard the story of Emily and Jimmy's escape together. Besides, Jimmy and he had already passed beyond titles to nicknames. Drawn by Jimmy's raised voice, the guests flowed toward the bar. Those who did not know Jimmy were attracted by the novelty. The correspondents, who knew him well, anticipated another virtuoso performance.

Jimmy flourished the drumstick and said: "You know, my friends, it's not fashionable to talk about right and wrong nowadays. And we hardly ever talk about God. But Nanking made me believe in God. I saw evil —and I *knew* that good had to exist to oppose evil. God let our hostess, Madame Ou-yang, and me get away."

"Tell your story!" Tommy whispered in sibilant Shanghainese. "Or you'll lose them."

"Emily and I were trapped in the basement of the Aeronautical Commission when the Japs marched in. We were lucky. The building had been pasted by bombs and looked like a ruin. So the Japs ignored it. And we had a grandstand seat." Jimmy gulped his highball and continued: "The Jap officers held a formation in the plaza, right before our eyes. Then they turned their troops loose to pillage and kill—"

"And rape!" Emily interjected. "We had to watch. We had to learn about our enemy. . . . But . . . but what we saw!"

"They turned maybe seventy thousand men loose to sack Nanking," Jimmy resumed. "They were worse than the Mongols. *Bushido,* they call it, the way of the honorable warrior. Some honor! In the beginning, the killing was casual. The Jap dwarves were stinking drunk, and they only killed those who got in the way of their looting. Not more than ten thousand."

"Not more than ten thousand in the beginning, Mr. Wei?" the American consul general asked. "What's your estimate of total casualties?"

"Too many to count, but not less than a hundred thousand dead and injured. It started with swords and bayonets. Next they used pistols and rifles. They finished with machine guns and flame-throwers." Jimmy rubbed his eyes. "The fires burned so high the whole city was like a stage at night. . . . We watched them line up the women. From young girls, maybe eight to ten, to grandmothers—old ladies with hair pulled back so tight they were a little bald in front. You all know the type."

Jimmy shook his head as if in pain, the jester overcome by tragedy. He looked imploringly at Emily, who recounted in a monotone: "Several hundred Japanese soldiers lined up. Rough men with cropped heads and brutal faces. Great barrel chests and long dangling arms—just like gorillas. It could've been a general inspection. Many took off their trousers. Some folded them neatly. . . . But you can imagine the rest. . . . Afterward, they killed the women and girls. They hacked wildly with swords and rifle butts—like threshing rice."

"Emmy, that's enough for now." Julia stepped forward protectively. "No need to repeat every gory detail!"

"Just let me . . . just add one thing." Jimmy gulped the rest of his

highball and said: "You *cannot* compromise with them. You can*not* negotiate with them—no more than you can negotiate with a *tsunami,* a tidal
wave. Remember that, for your own sake. And remember this: We
Chinese are only the first. Like a tidal wave, Japan *cannot* stop. Japan can
only be broken . . . broken by adamant resistance.

"You are next, ladies and gentlemen. Southeast Asia, then India and
. . . God only knows what next. You may think I'm exaggerating. But
suppose I'd told you twenty years ago that a small country of sixty
million like Japan would invade a vast country of four hundred million
like China? Would you have believed me? . . . It's going to be a very
long war!"

The silence after he stopped lasted for half a minute. The diplomats
briefly withheld their ritual deploring of alarmism. The newspapermen
stared into the dark corridor of the future, which was apparently to be
lit with explosions and star shells.

"If Jimmy's right, we'll be covering wars for the rest of our lives
. . . if we live that long!" Richard Hollings did not smile at his own
unintentional jest. "Optimism isn't available in China right now."

Tommy left the guests who clustered around Jimmy and Emily, eagerly asking questions. Drawing Julia and Richard with him, he murmured, "Optimism is available—if you know where to look. Ever hear
of a place called Yenan?"

"We've all *heard,* but no one's seen what the Communists are up to
in Yenan," Richard replied. "It's impossible to get there. Anyway, the
Chinese Communists aren't fighting for China. They're controlled by
Moscow and the Communist International."

"I'm by no means sure about that, though I don't endorse their doc-
trines. Me least of all!" Tommy answered. "I get the impression that
doctrine—Marxism or whatever—isn't all that important to them, not
since the Japanese invasion. Of course, only the Generalissimo can save
China from the Japs. But Chairman Mao Tse-tung and my old friend
Chairman Chang Kuo-tao are doing great things in Yenan. They've put
the Red Army under the Central Government's control. As you know,
it's now called the Eighth Route Army. And it takes its orders from the
Ministry of National Defense."

"What about reports that the Nationalists are still blockading the
Communist areas?" Richard demanded. "Isn't the Gimo mounting a
new extermination campaign on the quiet?"

"I'm very sorry the Generalissimo still considers it necessary to contain the Communists," Tommy replied. "If he'd let up, both Nationalists

and Communists could turn all their forces against the Japanese. Mind you, I'm not criticizing the Generalissimo. But—"

"The hell you're not." Richard laughed. "But you hinted it was possible to get to Yenan."

Julia looked at him blankly. Behind the smoke from his meerschaum pipe, Tommy lifted an eyebrow.

"Tommy, you're talking like a man who knows more than he says," Richard persisted. "Is all this theoretical? Or is there some way to get to Yenan?"

When Tommy took his pipe from his mouth and nodded, the correspondent said enthusiastically, "What a story! The first eyewitness account of the mysterious Chinese Communists. Of course, if I could get to Yenan, I'd need to move round and talk to everyone—including Mao Tse-tung and your chum Chang Kuo-tao."

"Dick, you're not there yet." Julia laughed. "If you make too many conditions, even my miracle-working husband won't be able to—"

"You're not just floating a trial balloon, Tommy? . . . Julie, you really believe it can be arranged? A trip to Yenan?"

Julia nodded after a brief pause for effect, and the correspondent demanded, "Why are you two involved?"

Tommy had warned the Apparatus that openly wooing Richard Hollings could destroy their cover. The reply had been unequivocal: *It is priority one to lure an influential foreign correspondent to Yenan to refute Nationalist propaganda. Even at the risk of your own future usefulness.*

"Why are we involved?" Julia mused ostentatiously. "Well, we've been approached by an acquaintance who knows that some of our friends are foreign correspondents. So—"

Tommy broke in: "Because we believe in fair play. Because we believe in the power of the truth. As a banker's son, I don't like the Communists. But if both sides are reported fairly and honestly, it'll be best for China in the long run."

"When can I meet your acquaintance? The sooner the better."

"It's not quite that simple, Dick," Julia interposed. "We can't just order him up like a hamburger. But we'll see what we can do. And, meanwhile, keep mum."

"Naturally, Julie."

"Above all, don't tell Emmy!" Julia stressed. "That would be fatal. You'll have to pass through the Nationalist blockade, so don't tell her that—"

"I understand. Not, mind you, that I'm likely to get the opportunity to say anything to the Ice Queen beyond: 'Thank you and good-bye, Madame Ou-yang! What a nice party!' "

"My Lord!" Tommy Howe looked at the gold Rolex on his wrist. "I'm due at ward rounds in fifteen minutes. Julie, say good-bye to Emmy for me. I'm off."

"Not without me, Doctor," she said. "You haven't forgotten we promised the girls we'd be home to say good-night. And we're due at Sterling Fessenden's at eight. I'll phone Emmy tomorrow."

The Howes' victory in that skirmish in the propaganda war between the Nationalists and the Communists was marred by Tommy's misgivings. His sensibilities, Julie sometimes felt, were too tender for their secret work. She herself could not completely still all pangs of conscience, but she would not let them affect her duty.

"Bit ironic, wasn't it?" Tommy asked as they bowled past the Racecourse in the Chrysler Airflow.

"Ironic?"

"Come now, Julie," he said. "You know bloody well what I mean. Not just ironic, but a little despicable. Seducing Dick Hollings at a Nationalist party."

"Despicable or not, it's going to work," she responded. "Most correspondents would give their left arms for an exclusive on the Communist area. And Dick is hungry for fame. Very hungry."

Julia would have been less cocky if she had heard the conversation between Emily and Jimmy Wei as the guests were leaving. Jimmy, who took a benevolent interest in his friends' personal lives, was still playing Cupid. Disappointed in the results—or lack of results—after he had brought Emily and Richard together in the dining room of the Metropolitan Hotel, he was still working for their reconciliation. He knew they needed each other. Ou-yang Hsiu was a stuffed shirt, while Richard's delay in sending for his wife spoke for itself.

"You really ought to give Dick a break." Jimmy drew Emily aside. "After the *Panay*, he deserves it. Anyway, why did you invite him? Not to spit in his eye, I presume!"

"Julie invited him," she replied irritably. "Not me."

"And Julie's going to press our case with him, not you?"

"I guess so."

"It won't do, my lady. You can't trust a foreigner to plead China's case —no matter how devoted she is. Anyway, I sometimes wonder about Julie's politics."

"Don't be silly, Jimmy. I've known her since we were twelve years old. I was suspicious of her for a while, but not anymore. Anyway, Tommy—"

"Sorry, Em. But Hollings is too damned important. He's vital. The *Boston Globe's* not all that important, though it thinks it is. The power's shifting to NBC. Radio is the wave of the future. And NANA—the North American Newspaper Alliance—distributes his pieces to hundreds of papers, in the States and abroad."

"I know what NANA is, Jimmy. I do write pieces for the newspapers from time to time. Remember?"

"Sorry again, Em. But aren't you fierce today!"

"All right, Jimmy. I don't want to, but I'll have a word with Mr. Richard Hollings. What I do for China!"

Emily was still smiling at her own sally when she found Richard among the half dozen guests waiting to say good-bye to her. Her smile reinforced the false impression conveyed by the words she had to speak: "Can you stay a few minutes longer?"

Richard virtually glowed, and she hurried to add, "This won't take very long. But do have another drink."

Richard was startled by Emily's sudden warmth after five chilly months. They sat side by side on a wrought-iron bench embowered by ferns and orchids, his gray flannel sleeve two inches from her royal-blue silk. But they did not touch. Her fingers played with the Air Force wings pinned on her shoulder.

"We should have talked earlier, Dick . . . talked as friends." Emily wanted to create an amicable atmosphere before she could influence him. "It . . . whatever we had together . . . it was so long ago. It's ridiculous for old friends to stay away from each other like enemies."

"None of my doing, Emily," he replied. "I'm delighted to talk with you—as an old friend."

"And I want you to know that I bear no grudge." She was being heavy-handed, although this conversation required a light touch. "None whatsoever!"

Richard suppressed his instinctive reply. It was he who might bear a grudge, for she had turned him out. Although he did not know quite what he wanted of Emily, her awkwardness gave him hope. She would not be so ill at ease unless the conversation was important to her.

"Anyway, for old times' sake, I thought you . . . That is, I wonder if . . ." She stumbled still. "You see, I haven't written anything about what I saw in Nanking."

"You mean you haven't filed?" The correspondent was astonished. "You haven't written it for your precious *Public Ledger*—to show the Japs for what they really are? How could you sit on an eyewitness story like that?"

"Honestly, I haven't written a word, Dick. I couldn't. I could hardly talk about it. Not till this afternoon."

"That's a little hard to believe, Emily. How could—"

"You always used to tell me I wasn't professional enough. Maybe you were right. But if you're not interested, I can find someone else to . . ." Remembering Jimmy Wei's warning not to spit in Richard's eye, she amended her words: "But you're the one I want to write that story. Only you can do it full justice."

Richard's suspicion melted in the warmth of her flattery. He leaned over and impulsively laid his hand on her arm. The familiar feel of the soft skin and the delicate bone beneath the silk carried him back in time. A rush of tenderness swept over him, and his hand trembled. Finally, he withdrew his hand, having forgotten whatever he had meant to say.

Emily looked up, her eyes wide in surprise. She moved toward him involuntarily, and he instinctively lifted his arms.

Emily pulled back by an act of will, furious at that near betrayal by her inconstant flesh. Richard's arms fell, and he smiled nervously.

Emily blinked as if awakening from sleep. She folded her hands in her lap and said cheerily, "Now let's see. You do want to do the story, don't you? I can't tell any more today. Must get back to my . . . to Hsiu's party. But tomorrow . . ."

"Could we meet for lunch?" he suggested. "The French Club?"

"The French Club? It's so long since I've been there. But why not?"

There was, as yet, no need for further words about their relationship when Emily and Richard met for their first lunch together after more than ten years. Nor were there yet any words that could define their tentative understanding, which neither fully understood.

They met several times during the following week, by tacit agreement avoiding the evening hours. They pretended to themselves—and to each other—that they were refining the story of the rape of Nanking, though either one could have written that story in a single day's work. Emily told herself it was her patriotic duty to ensure that Richard's reporting was favorable to China, and Richard almost believed that his interest was primarily professional.

They had forgotten the joy of being with each other, the preternatural heightening of all sensation. During the next week, they gradually wove anew the complex strands of emotion that had formerly bound them. Despite the pressure of war, they felt no great urgency to reaffirm their still unexpressed commitment with their bodies. Yet, when they finally came together in Richard's suite in Broadway Mansions, it was the most profound pleasure either had ever known.

For almost two weeks, Emily virtually forgot the war of national survival. She had only one purpose—her reawakened love for Richard Hollings. She realized with wonder that the total impossibility of marriage had purged their relationship of all its previous abrasiveness. She could now make no demand he could not fulfill, since she could neither expect constancy nor impose responsibility. Moreover, her conscience was clear. She had already given her husband everything he required of her, and she would avoid public scandal, which was Hsiu's only admonition.

Richard could never wholly forget his work and his ambition, which were his essence. But he virtually forgot Fiona, whom he had married in England only two years earlier. He had always loved this jet-and-ivory Emily, he realized. It had not been he but she who had initiated their parting. He had never ceased to love her and to want her. The rebirth of love eclipsed all lesser emotions. From time to time he almost forgot his ambitions.

To forestall any scandal Emily imposed caution on her sometimes careless lover. As soon as they began to meet in private, they stopped meeting in public. After Richard wrote the account of Emily's experiences in Nanking, it appeared to the curious—including a disappointed Jimmy Wei—that the former lovers remained estranged.

Only Julia and Tommy, who knew them best, sensed that something was stirring. Emily looked radiant, and Richard was almost relaxed. They virtually ignored each other in public, and they vanished from view at the same time. The Howes also worried about the strain they would impose on the reunited lovers by luring Richard to the Communist capital at Yenan. That fervent Nationalist Emily considered Yenan the lair of the devil.

"Well, it's about time, isn't it?" Julia asked dully after dinner at home on the last day of January 1938. "I hate to break it up. But I'm afraid I'll have to give Richard the green light on Yenan tomorrow."

"You could put it off a bit, couldn't you?" Tommy responded. "It's your decision, after all. Not mine, thank God."

"Tommy, what is that supposed to mean?" Her tone was ominously even. "We're in this together, aren't we?"

"Of course, darling." He wanted to avoid a quarrel. "Though you're in charge of propaganda, aren't you? Or should I say liaison with the foreign press?"

"Say whatever you please, Tommy," she snapped. "Just remember, you got me into this!"

"You can always pull out," he replied. "They . . . the Apparatus . . . won't shoot you."

"I'm not so sure of that. Anyway, I don't want to withdraw. We're doing great work, essential work."

"Then what's the matter, Julie? Why are you taking it out on me?"

"I'm not taking it out on anyone. We're doing the right thing."

"Emmy hasn't been so happy in years, has she?" Tommy goaded her. "And we're about to ruin it for her."

"Not permanently. His going away for a while won't ruin it. Not if they're truly in love."

"I'm not so sure of that—" Tommy began, but Julia broke in: "I'm fed up with your pinning the blame on me."

"It was your idea to choose Dick," he retorted. "I've never really trusted him, and—"

"You agreed, didn't you? And you seem happy enough to go off to Yenan with him."

"Now be reasonable, Julie." He was alarmed by the course their quarrel was taking. "Somebody has to interpret and . . . ah . . . guide him. Somebody he trusts."

"I could do it just as well. Maybe better."

His Chinese conservatism deeply shocked, he regarded her with frank astonishment. She glared back defiantly, daring him to contradict her.

Tommy grew apprehensive. For the first time since their marriage, they had for the past year been quarreling regularly about their differing approaches to political action. Julia attributed superhuman wisdom to the Chinese Communist Party. It was not her part to question the directives of the party, she declared, but only to obey them. Tommy was more skeptical. He could not justify lying, hypocrisy, theft, and murder just because the Communist Party thought such outrages convenient.

Tommy now feared another bitter quarrel. Her glare dared him to contradict her—and, of course, he did.

"That's one of the most ridiculous statements I've ever heard," he retorted. "A foreigner? A foreign *woman* to escort a correspondent to Yenan? Preposterous! Besides, who's to look after the girls? Anyway, your Chinese isn't . . ."

She knew he meant her Mandarin, not her Shanghainese. Offended by his masculine rigidity and his racial arrogance, she nonetheless chose to take further offense.

"Lao Zee is perfectly capable," she snapped. "As for my Chinese, it's not so bad you haven't trusted me to—"

"I didn't mean Shanghainese, Julie." He was elaborately patient. "But have you ever heard Chairman Mao Tse-tung speak Mandarin? You know he's damned near unintelligible. And don't forget old Chang Kuo-tao's Kiangsi brogue. Why sometimes *I* can hardly—"

Julie's anger flared higher. Feeling guilt for imperiling Emily's new-found happiness, she naturally attacked her husband. "You think I'm a poor weak woman, don't you, Thomas Tan-ssu Howe? All right for producing children—and better kept in the nursery with the children. A stupid foreigner, to boot! Better kept away from serious matters. Okay as a stalking-horse for other stupid foreigners, a kind of decoy duck, but not—"

"Julie! Julie!" His laughter fanned her anger. "You just can't be a horse *and* a duck—not at the same time."

"Don't laugh at me. I'm not a brainless toy. . . . You think a woman . . . all women . . . are fluffy-headed fools. You really despise all foreign devils, don't you? Even me! *Particularly* me!"

"Julie, darling," he protested. "This is becoming ridiculous. Can't we—"

"Don't try to sweet-talk me, Tommy Howe. I know what you're up to. And *you* can call Richard tomorrow. I'll be damned if I will. If I can't go, I damned well won't help. Go ahead, but don't be in a hurry to come back. I'm not sure I'll want you back." She gathered herself for a final denunciation and said, "Besides, I'll miss you . . . *badly.*"

Shocked by her own words, Julia blushed like a schoolgirl and then grinned sheepishly. Against her will, she joined in Tommy's laughter.

He finally rubbed the tears of mirth from his eyes and gasped: "That's . . . that's quite the . . . the funniest thing I've heard in years. You don't want me back, but you'll miss me—*badly.*"

Julia chuckled in spite of herself, and her anger faded. But her heart still beat fast, and she was still a little indignant.

"Really, Tommy, I hate your going without me."

"Can't be helped, darling. Somebody's got to look after the girls. Do you really trust Lao Zee alone for weeks?"

"Maybe not." She was not yet defeated. "But Charlotte Haleevie would be happy to—"

"You know, Julie, it's no cakewalk, the trip to Yenan. There *is* some danger. Is it really a good idea to put both parents at risk? What would become of—"

"All right, Tommy, I'm convinced. But it's so damned unfair. A woman's always tied down."

"I'd hardly say—" he temporized, but she interposed: "Won't it blow your cover, Tommy? Our cover?"

"Certainly, if you tagged along, darling. Far too obvious if both of us went. Otherwise, I hope not. You know the Apparatus considers the mission so essential, it's happy to accept the risk."

"Thanks a lot—for nothing." For the first time Julia spoke disparagingly of their controllers. "They're happy to risk our necks. Do they also give away ice in the wintertime?"

"It's not quite like that, you know. If you're not tired of talking about it, I'll put their case again."

"Tired of talking about our survival? Hardly!"

"It's the old family-doctor act again. My chum and former patient Chang Kuo-tao is complaining of general debility . . . that period on the Tibetan Plateau during the Long March. Since we're all allied against Japan now, the Nationalists approve of giving him decent medical attention. And should I happen to run into Dick Hollings in Yenan . . ."

"Won't they be even more suspicious of us?"

"Maybe it'll work the other way. The secret police are half convinced I'm a reformed Communist . . . maybe not entirely reformed. They're thick, but not bloody thick. They'll reckon I would never go near Yenan, virtually throw away my cover, if I was still a dangerous Red."

"Why can't someone else go?"

"I *want* to go, darling." Tommy's narrow face grew grave. "Old Chang Kuo-tao's problems aren't really physical. I've told you before his problems are political. He's now clashing even more fiercely with Mao Tsetung. He's absolutely certain Mao's becoming a dictator. Nor is Kuo-tao happy with the Communist war effort either. Largely a sham, he believes. I *must* talk with him—not only for his sake, but for ours, too."

Although she still resented her exclusion, Julia's anger cooled. She no longer resented Tommy, but the unfairness of life itself. She was, moreover, deeply concerned about Tommy—and not just his physical danger. He seemed to be losing confidence in the wisdom of the Chinese Communist Party.

Life never worked out as one expected. She had for years fought to end the injustice and the exploitation inherent in the existence of the Settlement and Frenchtown. She had labored to mobilize public opinion abroad to demand the surrender of the foreigners' extraterritorial privileges, on which that existence rested. The Japanese were now threatening the concessions, and she hated the thought of their possible destruction. Yet only fear that the other powers would defend the concessions militarily kept the Japanese from closing their grip.

The dissension within the leadership of the Chinese Communist Party, which Tommy had again revealed, was even more disturbing. Nonetheless, Julia knew with perfect certainty that she would never surrender her trust in the leadership of the party.

55

FEBRUARY 13–25, 1938

Outside, the February wind whined dismally through the saw-toothed battlements of Yenan's city wall and piled the snowdrifts in front of the caves cut into the yellow cliff crowned by the nine-tiered pagoda. Seated beside Chairman Mao Tse-tung, who had overwhelmed him with courtesies since his arrival forty-eight hours earlier, Richard Hollings peered disbelievingly through the cigarette smoke that fogged the makeshift auditorium of the Yenan Academy for the Children of Senior Cadres. Elegant in a tweed hacking-jacket, jodhpurs, and riding boots, Tommy Howe was sauntering through the side door. The Englishman sprang from the rough-planed bench to greet the friend he had thought a thousand miles away in Shanghai.

"Dr. Livingstone, I presume." Richard extended his hand. "Hardly an accident, I imagine, your turning up here."

Tommy grinned and confided with disarming frankness, "Not quite. I've a patient to see, my old chum Chang Kuo-tao. But, frankly, Julie and I were worried about you. When I got the chance of a seat on an aircraft, I grabbed it."

"You came by air? What luck for you! After a week in trains and trucks, I'm exhausted. How on earth did you manage it?"

"You didn't know Emily was joining Mayling Chiang in Wuhan, did you? She was summoned to the presence just after you left. The Missimo also wanted advice from me on the Air Force's medical services. Not that you'll ever catch me in uniform again. Not if—"

"The airplane, Tommy?" Richard prompted. "How did you actually get here?"

"Oh, yes. The Sian garrison commander was in Wuhan. When I heard he was planning a visit to Yenan, I begged a lift. It appears he's carrying formal messages from the Generalissimo for the two chairmen—Chairman Mao Tse-tung of the Communist Party's Central Committee and Chairman Chang Kuo-tao of the Soviet Area Government."

"They now call it the Shensi-Kansu-Ninghsia Border Area." The correspondent shared his newly acquired knowledge. "Fits into the Central Government structure better that way."

"I see," Tommy said. "Any rate, we'll have time to talk later."

"You're staying, then? I'm delighted. It's all fascinating, but they *will* go on in Chinese. And the interpreters! You have no idea what joy a familiar face can . . ."

Tommy prudently remained silent. He had come to the Communist capital because he had a very good idea indeed what joy a familiar face could bring to a foreigner alone in China's wild northwest.

He had already digested the report of the university student whom Richard Hollings believed he had met by chance on the second stage of his train journey. The Englishman had been delighted to encounter the young man who spoke intelligible English. He had been even more delighted to learn that the student, too, was going to Yenan. It was not Tommy's business to tell Richard that his helpful guide, who had represented himself as a volunteer for the Communists' Eighth Route Army, was actually a valued employee of the border area's Public Information Department, which was, in turn, an arm of the Communist Party's Security Bureau, which controlled the secret police.

The correspondent had not for a moment been left unobserved—or unprotected—by relays of fellow travelers who concealed their knowledge of English. So far, he had displayed all the right reactions.

His journey from Shanghai to Sian had been uneventful. Although accustomed to the occasional absurdities of the Sino-Japanese War, the correspondent had jotted a note regarding the extraordinary de facto neutrality of the Chinese Post Office and the railways, which routinely crossed the fluid lines of demarcation between the belligerents. He had gone from Japanese-occupied territory back into the Nationalist-dominated areas. Finally, a smuggler's truck had carried him through the undeclared Nationalist blockade of the Communist-ruled border area—with a load of newsprint and lead type for the Communists, who evidently considered leaflets as crucial as bullets.

Richard knew that the seedbed of the Chinese nation was these fertile plains of the yellow soil called loess. The names on the land revealed the millennia-old yearning after elusive tranquility: Yenan meant "Extended Peace," and nearby Paoan meant "Protected Peace." Sian, the name of the capital of Shensi Province, meant "Western Peace." When it was the capital of all China under the magnificent Tang Dynasty a thousand years earlier, the city had been called Changan, "Protracted Peace." A thousand years before the Tang, Emperor Shih Huang-ti, the first emperor of China, had chosen that site for the first capital of a united China.

But enduring peace was clearly unattainable. The first emperor had been forced to build the Great Wall against nomadic invaders—and the Communists had only recently driven the Nationalists out of Yenan.

Richard Hollings was now to be convinced that Chinese civilization was being reborn in its original birthplace, with the Communists as the midwives. To the Chinese, who were all history-struck, that return to the source of their race was awe-inspiring. The correspondent, too, was deeply impressed, as the student had learned from their discussions during the jolting two hundred-mile truck ride from Sian to Yenan.

Tommy was gratified by the student's report. The hard journey to Yenan had suitably conditioned the correspondent. He was already salivating eagerly. And he had not yet even seen the journalistic feast of novelty and sensation prepared for him. The propagandists were busily transforming remote Yenan into a legend.

Having been a county seat, Yenan also provided the rapidly expanding Communist bureaucracy with a number of ramshackle public buildings. One such building now housed the Academy for the Children of Senior Cadres, that is, for the privileged offspring of the higher officials. The auditorium showed its age by its crumbling walls, and patches of fresh plaster emphasized its decrepitude. Like every other horizontal surface, the packed-earth floor was filmed with the powdery yellow dust of the loess soil.

Acrid with the fumes of half-cured tobacco, the long room was capriciously lit by pale winter sunlight filtered through oiled-paper windows. A few lightbulbs also glowed weakly on long wires with fraying fabric insulation. The audience wore quilted cotton jackets that made men and women look like oversized schoolchildren. Slogans hanging on the walls praised the anti-Japanese United Front, or extolled cleanliness, literacy, and discipline.

Near the faded red curtain that veiled the stage, the senior leaders sat cracking melon seeds between their teeth and sipping tea from earthenware cups. Armchairs would normally have been provided for Chairman Mao Tse-tung and Commander in Chief Chu Teh of the Eighth Route Army, the man called Red Virtue. Today all sat on rough wooden benches without backs so that Richard Hollings would see only one big happy—and equal—family. The leaders' bodyguards had concealed their pistols under their jackets, and the senior cadres had put away the numerous fountain pens that normally bristled in their breast pockets to declare their rank. The masquerade was well in hand.

After paying his respects to Chairman Mao Tse-tung and his entourage, Tommy looked for Chang Kuo-tao but could not see his friend. Tommy knew that Mao Tse-tung's presence at the public gathering was unusual. The chairman of the Chinese Communist Party was already drawing around himself the same cloak of aloofness that China's emperors had worn. General Chu Teh might foxtrot with giggling female comrades at dance parties while his pretty wife looked on undisturbed. Mao Tse-tung was more likely to seduce those awestruck female comrades in private, although he had recently taken as his fourth wife a starlet of Shanghai motion pictures.

No longer the bumptious young careerist Tommy had first seen at the National Federation of Students' meeting seventeen years earlier, Mao Tse-tung had discarded his homespun long-gown for the blue jacket and trousers of the peasants. Honed by danger and hardship, he was at forty-five no longer plump but tall and gaunt.

Chairman Mao beckoned peremptorily to Tommy, complaining in his slurred Hunan accent, "Interpreter's no damned good. Speaks English like a Cantonese talking Mandarin. Doctor, you interpret! I was telling this white-skinned barbarian about the League of Nations resolution. It proves we're going to win—that our victory is inevitable."

Tommy raised an eyebrow and omitted the racist slur from his translation. Another white-skinned barbarian was his wife and the mother of his daughters.

"Do you know about the resolution?" Richard addressed Tommy directly. "The league has just recommended that all members send aid to China. Chairman Mao is convinced it's a great victory. I'd like to ask him specifically what practical results he expects. . . . You know, I'm impressed by his grasp of foreign affairs. Should I tell him so?"

"Honest approbation is always welcome." Tommy tossed off that sententious observation in English, and then repeated in Mandarin Richard's question and compliment.

"This resolution proves that all the people of the world are united behind our struggle against aggression and Fascism." Mao Tse-tung's eyes dulled as his attention turned inward, and he continued in measured tones: "I know that the League is criticized as a do-nothing organization. Think of the difficulties the Soviet Union has met in attempting to forge a united front against Fascism through the League. But this resolution will initiate major changes in the League itself. China's fight inspires all men who love freedom and justice."

Richard began a new question, but the chairman motioned for silence. His hand rose in benediction to the ten boys and ten girls in freshly ironed blue tunics who had just appeared in front of the red curtain. The ideograms on their scarlet brassards read *Young Pioneers;* they all wore scarlet neckerchiefs; and the girls' braids were tied with scarlet ribbons. A boy clapped his hands, and they began to sing: *"Chi-lai, chi-lai, pu yüan tso . . ."*

Mao Tse-tung beamed and beat time with his fist while Tommy put the Chinese Communists' anthem into English for Richard: "Arise! Arise! All ye who hate to be bond slaves. . . . With our flesh and blood we will build a new Great Wall!"

The chorus filed off after singing four folk songs, two with new revolutionary lyrics and two unaltered. The "Internationale" normally concluded such performances, but the anthem of the Comintern was not heard that day. The stage managers directing the correspondent's reception had ruled out that avowal of solidarity with the Soviet Union.

The red curtain parted for a young man of about twenty, who read from a booklet he held in both hands: "Comrades, the staff and the pupils of the Yenan Academy for the Children of Senior Cadres welcome you." Tommy translated in a low voice. "Today we offer the instructive story of the traitor Chang Mu-tao. The scene is set in . . ."

Tommy lost the thread when Richard pulled at his arm and demanded, "Chang Kuo-tao? The *traitor* Chang Kuo-tao? What's up? You said this was a historical play."

"For God's sake, Dick, shut up!" Tommy whispered. "Chang *Mu*-tao, not Chang *Kuo*-tao. Chang Mu-tao was one of China's most notorious traitors."

In the casual tradition of the Chinese theater, the audience joined in the drama. The "oohs" and "ahs" of fond parents competed with the loud comments of self-anointed connoisseurs as the centuries-old play unfolded. Criticism alternated with cries of admiration for the silk gowns of the court ladies, the ornate armor of the generals, and the stately robes of the courtiers. The diminutive players all wore painted masks, and the audience speculated loudly on the actors' true identities.

All, however, appeared to know the child star who played the traitor Chang Mu-tao behind a villain's black mask. Tommy could see why he was a favorite. With his clear enunciation and his dramatic gestures, the boy dominated the stage.

Caught up by the virtuoso performance, Tommy hardly heard the side door open. When the light from outside backlit the newcomer in the darkened auditorium, Mao Tse-tung cackled, "This is true art! How very appropriate! An inspiration to have Chang *Kuo*-tao's son play the traitor Chang *Mu*-tao!"

Twisting on the bench, Tommy recognized the tall man whose entrance had provoked the chairman's outburst. His old friend Chang Kuo-tao stalked toward the stage, sodden cloth shoes squishing on the packed-earth floor. Stepping over the kerosene footlights, he ripped the mask from his son's face, picked up the frightened child, and strode toward the door.

"You are barbarians!" Chang Kuo-tao shouted. "It is wicked to trick an innocent child into baiting his own father! You are evil—worse than wild beasts!"

Tommy was shocked by the public clash between the two men who embodied the Communist cause. He felt great friendship and respect for the upright Chang Kuo-tao, the chairman of the Shensi Border Area Government. Yet Chairman Mao Tse-tung of the Communist Party's Central Committee represented the collective will of the party. A good Communist owed loyalty—and obedience—to the party, not to any individual. Still, it would be profoundly un-Chinese—inhuman, in fact —for Tommy to turn his back on his old mentor Chang Kuo-tao.

After that public clash, Chairman Mao attempted neither to justify himself to Richard Hollings nor to prevent his talking with Chang Kuo-tao. Eager to question the dissident leader, Richard smiled sardonically when Tommy suggested that the public confrontation between Mao Tse-tung and Chang Kuo-tao was not necessarily significant. He grinned when Tommy said his own long experience should have taught him how hot-tempered the Chinese were.

Richard did not embarrass Tommy by disagreeing aloud. Instead he suggested that, if the matter was trivial, perhaps they could ask Chang Kuo-tao himself about it?

Tommy agreed immediately. Since it was essential to make Richard believe that free public debate was normal in the border area, he could not wait to ask permission from the secret police. Besides, he was himself eager to see Chang Kuo-tao—a patient and a friend in trouble.

Tommy and Richard strode briskly toward the north gate the next afternoon, having completed the official interviews for the day. The storm had passed. Cleansed of all impurities, the clear sky appeared to extend to infinity.

The snow-covered streets were deserted except for the waifs affectionately called Little Red Devils going about their self-important errands. When two Red Devils stopped to pat a lean yellow dog, Tommy remembered the waif called Little Pow, who had vanished a decade earlier, and the mastiff called Adam, who had been killed a few months ago. The freezing wind knifing through the woollen scarf wound around his face brought tears to his eyes.

When Yenan was a Nationalist-held island in a Communist sea, the big wooden city gates had been barred against guerrillas and brigands. Since its liberation, the city's gates had stood open. The local brigands, the party declared, were now all fervent converts to the Communist crusade. Was it really conviction or was it coercion and bribery? Tommy wondered but kept his doubts to himself.

The stunted sentry shivering under the city wall looked like a brigand himself. He wore a captured Japanese army greatcoat with a thick hood; it came down to his ankles, though Tommy's and Richard's coats did not reach their knees. Even the Japanese were not as undersized as this young Communist soldier, who had probably never eaten a decent meal in his life.

Outside the gates, the blue vault of the sky arched above the white bowl of the valley. The February sun was a pale disc over the yellow cliffs. The wind had scoured the snow into enormous flying buttresses at the foot of the cliffs. Gray smoke drifted from the thatched hovels beside the frozen dirt road. The valley of Yenan appeared hostile, poverty-stricken, and virtually depopulated.

The visitors were lanced by the cold despite their blanket-thick greatcoats. Their figures cast faint shadows on the snowdrifts as they trudged toward the caves. On the overhanging cliff the nine-tiered pagoda of Yenan sparkled against the pale sky.

The placard on the terrace gouged from the cliff read: OFFICE OF THE CHAIRMAN OF THE BORDER AREA GOVERNMENT. Tommy rattled the wooden door. Getting no reply, he pounded with his fist. An unintelligible voice called out within, and Tommy shouted, *"Wo-men chao Chang Chu-hsi. . . .* We're looking for Chairman Chang."

Bolts snicked back, the door grated open, and the Communist leader stood before them. He was scowling, but he smiled when he recognized his callers.

"Come in, my friends!" he boomed. "Tom, I've been wondering when I'd see you. . . . Nobody tried to stop you?"

"Not a soul, Kuo-tao. We might have been invisible spirits, for all the notice anyone took."

"Even *he* doesn't dare, yet," Chang Kuo-tao confided. "There's still Moscow—and the world. Outside Yenan my name still counts for something. But I'm a bad host to keep you waiting."

The passageway was dimly lit by an oil lamp, and the main room was not much brighter. Tables and stools loomed formless in the gloom, and from time to time voices sounded from rooms at the rear. An oil lamp flickered on a low table that also bore a chipped porcelain teapot, four thimble-cups, a murky glass bottle, a red-and-yellow packet of cigarettes, and a battered tin ashtray.

"Our ancestors knew what they were doing, living in caves in this climate." Lit from beneath by the yellow lamplight, Chang Kuo-tao's blunt features were shadowed like a primitive mask. "Caves are warm and dry and keep out the wind. Also, there's only one way in. Nobody can take me by surprise."

With a physician's eye Tommy studied the friend he had not seen for more than five years. The big man, who was now forty, had led a strenuous life, particularly during the last six years, which he had spent as a leader of irregular troops. He was thin and obviously under strain, but he showed no sign of illness. Tommy decided that he would examine Kuo-tao if asked but would not suggest a physical examination. He suspected that his friend's messages about illness had been a ruse to bring him to Yenan.

"Tom," Chang Kuo-tao said, "I never got a chance to thank you for helping my wife, Lien. Without you and Joo-li she would have been finished. She's out, but she'll want to thank you personally."

"It was nothing, Kuo-tao," Tommy replied. "After all, nobody from the Apparatus had told me not to. . . . You haven't talked about my . . . that is, Lien and —"

"Don't worry, Tom. Nobody except us knows anything about it. . . . Now, Mr. Hollings, I'd like to tell you . . ."

Tommy had forgotten how thick Chang Kuo-tao's Kiangsi brogue became with emotion. Translating for Richard, he had to concentrate hard. He could, therefore, reply to his old friend's remarks only with occasional sympathetic grunts. But that did not matter. Chang Kuo-tao was a man with a grievance, who had long been deprived of a sympathetic audience. His indignation poured out.

"You saw what they did to the boy, a lad not even twelve years old, didn't you?" he demanded. "They're devils, demons in human form! And Mao Tse-tung is the worst!"

His big head, sand-hued in the lamplight, swung to and fro like an angry lion's. His fist smote the table, and the thimble-cups jumped. He forced a smile, but it only made him look fiercer. Belatedly, he splashed colorless spirits into the cups from the murky bottle.

"They still leave me some perks," he observed without satisfaction. "The trick with the boy, you know, is only part of their harassment. They're even worse to my wife."

He sipped the spirits and addressed himself directly to Richard: "Lien is an old Communist Party member, a leading female cadre from the beginning. When I left Shanghai, she stayed behind. When Nationalist special agents and the foreigners' police practically wiped out party headquarters, Lien escaped. But she lost contact with the party. So she went underground . . . changed her name and studied midwifery."

He emptied his thimble-cup and glared as if daring them not to drink. After refilling the empty cups, he resumed, his deep-set eyes glinting above his broad cheekbones.

"When the United Front Against Japan was formed, Lien got in touch with the Communist liaison office in Nanking, Chou En-lai's outfit. After she arrived in Yenan, we sent for our son. The three of us were together again!

"Lien has taught midwifery as well as doing political work. But Mao's rubber-stamp Central Committee won't reinstate her party membership. They said they had to investigate her conduct after she lost contact in Shanghai. She's damned upset! It's like losing her identity."

He shook his head as if tormented by gnats and looked regretfully down at his cup. After deciding against draining it, he continued in a more gentle tone. "Of course all this is just fleabites . . . trivial in the eyes of history. But the underlying issue is momentous."

Richard's lean features twisted in sympathy, and Chang Kuo-tao addressed him directly: "Frankly, Mr. Hollings, personal rivalry and personal grievances stand between Mao Tse-tung and myself. He's out to destroy me. He would have already if the Comintern hadn't stopped him. Last spring he mounted a formal Criticize Chang Kuo-tao Campaign. So that comrades would learn from my mistakes."

Fighting with his anger, Chang Kuo-tao thrust a cigarette into the oil lamp. Clamping it between his thumb and forefinger, he puffed sporadically as he talked.

"I formed my *provisional* Central Committee as the only way to get the big decisions made. We were completely out of touch with whatever was left of Party Headquarters in Shanghai. Then that dung-eating careerist Mao Tse-tung founded his own *permanent* Central Committee and bulled his way into the chairmanship.

"Again trivial, perhaps. But issues of fundamental principle divide Mao and me. Great issues: the life or death of China and the Communist Party!"

He turned and called out, *"Ehr-tzu* . . . Son, bring me my diary, last year's."

The twelve-year-old who had been carried out of the auditorium presented his father with a thick notebook, smiled dazzlingly, and vanished again into the gloom. Chang Kuo-tao flipped the volume open and read aloud: "November 1937: After three months of heroic fighting, the Central Government of Generalissimo Chiang Kai-shek was forced to withdraw its troops from Shanghai. A few weeks later, the Central Government withdrew from Nanking to Wuhan. Even warlords like the Christian General pledged to fight to the death.

"And what of the hero Mao Tse-tung? He said: 'All China will soon be occupied by the Imperial Japanese Army, and our guerrilla force will expand manyfold behind enemy lines. First, all China will fall from the hands of Chiang Kai-shek into the hands of Japan. Later, we Communists will take China back from the Japanese.' "

Chang Kuo-tao slammed the journal shut, rubbed his eyes, and said: "I was horror-struck when I heard Mao rant that way. Why does he want China to become a Japanese colony? Why isn't the Chinese Communist Party militantly supporting the United Front Against Japan? We're all Chinese together now, aren't we?"

The big man shook his head again. He was fierce yet bewildered, a wounded lion beset by jackals. Tommy's heart went out to his old friend. But what could he say? What could anyone say without defying the entire Communist movement? All Tommy could do was interpret faithfully.

"Everything Mao Tse-tung advocates helps Japanese aggression," Chang Kuo-tao concluded. "Everything Mao does mortally wounds the Communist Party and the Eighth Route Army—wounds China itself. Sometimes I wonder if Mao isn't a traitor hiding under the cloak of communism. You may feel that's absurd, but . . ."

The visitors had to leave before the early dusk of midwinter filled the valley with darkness. Fortunately, they had not brought a flashlight, which would have lit the dirt road among the snowdrifts—fortunately, because Tommy realized that he had already spent too much time with his old friend.

He had no intention of returning, above all not with Richard Hollings. He had felt almost physical pain while listening to Chang Kuo-tao's grave doubts about the direction of the Communist Party. He could not completely refute those doubts. He could, however, ensure that the correspondent took away from Yenan a picture of the Communist Party, its army, and its government that was not marred by Chang Kuo-tao's bitterness—whether that bitterness was justified or not.

Tommy and Richard returned the next afternoon to the cave of the chairman of the border region. Initially because Richard insisted and later because Tommy wished it, they returned twice more during their two weeks together in the Yenan.

Tommy, who had prudently decided not to visit Chang Kuo-tao alone, finally urged Richard to go. He had concluded that keeping Richard from Chang Kuo-tao would only accentuate the conflict between the two giants of the Communist Party. Besides, he wanted to hear more himself. The Communist Party, guided by Chairman Mao Tse-tung, was, of course, correct. But why not listen to the dissenting view?

Tommy also wanted to spend more time with Chang Kuo-tao, whatever his faults, and to cheer him in his distress. Failing to call again would only have intensified his old friend's paranoia, strengthening Kuo-tao's delusion that he was being persecuted. Besides, Tommy had to deliver the cashmere scarf and the fur-lined gloves Julia had sent. Besides, he was happy at seeing Lien again. This time he found her plainly dressed, scrub-faced, and very grateful.

Caught by Kuo-tao's charm, Tommy was appalled to find himself nodding reluctant agreement to some of his old friend's arguments. He tried to convey to Richard by his tone of voice that some statements were not to be taken at face value. As an interpreter he could not intrude his own views.

"When the war of resistance started, I swore I would put all my bitterness behind me," the old revolutionary recalled. "Otherwise, I would have had to quit the party—and destroy the purpose of my life. I even thought seriously about resigning. It was *that* bad! . . . But it's worse now! Last autumn another Criticize Chang Kuo-tao Campaign was launched by Chairman Mao." He pronounced that name with immense contempt. "Some newcomer got up at the meeting to observe that gold glittered, but not all that glittered was gold. Flies also glittered —like Chang Kuo-tao, who was a species of vermin within the Communist Party . . ."

Tommy was distressed by his old friend's ordeal, and he was dismayed by the cracks in the theoretically seamless Communist Party his old friend revealed. Above all a patriot who believed the Communists were the best hope for China, Tommy was appalled by Chang Kuo-tao's charge that Mao Tse-tung was working against the best interests of China.

Mao Tse-tung had ordered the Eighth Route Army *not* to fight the Japanese if there was the slightest risk of defeat, Chang Kuo-tao asserted. The Eighth Route Army was to increase its strength to strike against Chiang Kai-shek, not dissipate its strength fighting the Japanese. Mao had even reprimanded the general who won the first great Chinese victory against the Japanese. That victory, Mao Tse-tung had declared, was too costly.

Above all, Chang Kuo-tao charged, Mao Tse-tung was sacrificing all else to making himself a dictator. Even minor dissenters were to be purged, regardless of their value to the movement. All Communists were to obey only Chairman Mao Tse-tung.

"His hatred of dissenters is almost incredible," Chang Kuo-tao exploded on the afternoon in late February when he bade his visitors farewell. "He actually hates me more than he hates the Japanese—even more than he hates Chiang Kai-shek. His malice is turning Yenan into a sunless dungeon."

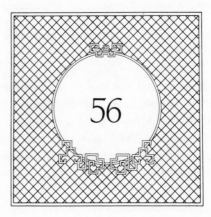

56

FEBRUARY 27–MARCH 2, 1938

Richard Hollings's tongue was normally sharp and quick; he was normally not reticent but hypercritical. He had, however, not commented to Tommy on what he had seen and heard during their two weeks in Yenan, presumably maintaining his professional objectivity. Tommy was therefore surprised when the correspondent grinned in the ruddy firelight and observed softly, "One hell of a mansion, isn't it, for the ruler of thirty million people, who is also commander in chief of almost a million troops!"

Glancing around the cave dwelling, Tommy agreed. "It's not much like Number Ten Downing Street or the White House. Can you imagine Neville Chamberlain or Franklin Roosevelt functioning in a place like this?"

Comrade Mao Tse-tung, chairman of both the Central Committee and the Military Affairs Committee of the Chinese Communist Party, was crouched before the big brick sleeping-platform, called a *kang*, which was universal in North China. He was poking the coal fire underneath to ensure that the *kang* would be warm later, and his bony features were red in the fire's glow. Beside his low bamboo stool, his ever-present cigarette smoldered in a tin ashtray. On the other side of the stool lay the quilted trousers he had just discarded.

"I can't believe it, Tommy." Richard whispered. "I just can't believe this chap is the monster our mutual friend talks about!"

Mao Tse-tung looked up interrogatively. Resuming his stool, he reclaimed his trousers and began to search their seams. He grunted in triumph, crushed a white louse between his fingertips, and flicked the tiny carcass into the coals. Turning from the pyre, he looked at Tommy again, obviously awaiting translation of the correspondent's last remark.

"Chairman, he observed that this was an extraordinary headquarters for one burdened with great responsibilities," Tommy improvised. "He marvels that you can discharge your responsibilities under such conditions."

"Tell him, Doctor, it's not necessarily by choice." Mao Tse-tung's candid smile compelled respect and invited affection. "Not that I'd want a palace, you understand. Men who live in palaces cannot hear the voices of the men tilling the fields. Sadly, the only field I have time for nowadays is my little tobacco plot."

Tommy knew that Mao Tse-tung's early life had been a determined struggle to escape from his father's farm. He was therefore not impressed by Mao's talk of longing to return to the fields. Instead, he felt a flicker of suspicion toward a man who invariably said the right thing. Yet, for all he knew, Mao Tse-tung might truly yearn for the peace of the farm but feel himself bound by duty to the tumult of politics.

"Chairman, I'd like to raise another matter." Richard Hollings's introduction obviously signaled an embarrassing question. "There are rumors of rifts in the ranks of the Chinese Communist Party. Some also say the party is not fully committed to the war against the Japanese. Some say it is split by personal rivalry. What can you tell me?"

Alerted by the tone of voice, Mao Tse-tung cocked his head and studied Richard's face while Tommy translated. He replied immediately: "You've been talking to my old friend Chang Kuo-tao, haven't you? Naturally, I know of your conversations with Kuo-tao. People tell me things even without my asking. But, you noticed, no one interfered —and no one was watching you. Still, I can make a very good guess as to what he's been telling you. Above all that I'm some kind of monster. Isn't that it, Mr. Hollings?"

Although he could not understand a word of Mao's slurred Mandarin, the Englishman nodded even before Tommy translated. Mao's expressive orator's voice had conveyed his essential meaning.

"My old friend's been telling you some strange tales, hasn't he?" Mao Tse-tung continued. "It's very sad, Mr. Hollings. I'm afraid his time on the Tibetan Plateau was too much for Kuo-tao. He's suffering from delusions. He thinks he's being persecuted."

He paused to allow Tommy to translate, and then demanded, "Do *you* think he's being persecuted? Is being appointed chairman of the border region persecution? Although his deputy does most of the work, we keep him on. The last thing I . . . the Central Committee . . . want is to humiliate a veteran fighter, an old comrade. We hope he'll soon be restored to health—and again work side by side with us. I must speak with you again about Chang Kuo-tao's state of health, Dr. Howe. Remind me, please."

Tommy was startled. Chairman Mao Tse-tung had never before that moment said a word to him about Chang Kuo-tao's health, which was obviously excellent. Richard appeared impressed, insofar as anyone could read his true reaction. He was always professionally impassive when conducting an interview.

"I'm not denying that Kuo-tao and I have our differences," Mao Tse-tung added. "Frankly, Mr. Hollings, there are many divergent views within the Communist Party. One policy finally prevails, but it is shaped in open debate. That's why I eagerly await Kuo-tao's restoration to full health, so that he can again contribute constructively to that debate. Only last year we held a full-scale campaign to reconcile his views and ours. So you can see how much we esteem him."

Could this, Tommy wondered, be the same man who had cackled about what an inspiration it was to have Chang Kuo-tao's son play the traitor? The correspondent would, of course, have noted that contradiction. But, Tommy recalled, he had been diverted by Chang Kuo-tao's dramatic entrance and had not translated that gibe for Richard. It was, of course, too late to do so now.

Nonetheless, Tommy found Mao Tse-tung's virtuoso performance not only impressive but convincing. If he had flatly denied any conflict with Chang Kuo-tao, he would not have been believed. The chairman had, therefore, candidly acknowledged their differences—and thus enhanced his own credibility. Richard would, accordingly, be taken in by Mao Tse-tung's lies regarding his rival's health, the character of the Criticize Chang Kuo-tao Campaign, and the prospects for mutual reconciliation.

It was no crime to lie for the cause. It was a grave failing *not* to lie when lies were necessary.

Mao Tse-tung presented Communist accomplishment to the best possible advantage in his talks with Richard Hollings, which took up his evenings for a week. Since the flight from Central China, the Communist Party had created an independent realm in the northwest—and had extended its underground Apparatus throughout Nationalist-controlled and Japanese-occupied areas.

Considering Nanking's bumbling pursuit, the Long March had, however, hardly been the epic victory described by Chairman Mao Tse-tung and General Chu Teh, who lent his homespun charm to the wooing of Richard Hollings. Only six thousand of an original force larger than one hundred thousand had actually reached their goal. Yet in the firelit cave in Yenan a legend was being created—the mighty myth of the Long March.

"We chose you from all those who wanted to come, Mr. Hollings." Chairman Mao mixed unabashed flattery with apparent candor. "Quite frankly, you can be useful to us. You're a brilliant writer, a keen observer—and you possess remarkable insight."

The correspondent's features twisted in genial skepticism, and he protested, "I don't flatter myself that you've read my stuff."

"Mr. Hollings, I know your work. Your dispatches have been translated for me. Dr. Howe has helped." Tommy omitted the last sentence, not primarily because it was false, but because it tied him too closely to the Communists. "I . . . we . . . wouldn't have invited you if we hadn't known your work. We have nothing to fear from objective reporting, however penetrating. We only fear inaccurate or biased reporting."

Richard Hollings betrayed no gratification but asked aggressively, "Just what do you expect of me? How am I supposed to serve your cause?"

"Please don't take offense, Mr. Hollings," Mao Tse-tung said. "We expect only that you will report fairly what you've seen and heard. No more."

Tommy watched Richard as he spoke those words. The correspondent's mask of indifference slipped, and he looked almost worshipfully at Chairman Mao. So much for journalistic detachment!

"I am a student of world history." The chairman was expansive. "And I have come to one conclusion: America will dominate the future—until the imperialist powers destroy each other in war, so that the Soviet Union and a Soviet China take the lead of all mankind. *Don't translate that last bit, Howe!* You, Mr. Hollings, represent the press of America. Quite frankly, we need friends in America—and we deserve friends in America. I believe you will help us win millions of friends in America!"

Mao Tse-tung stood beside the elementary-school map of the world hanging on the wall of the cave. Placing his palm on the pale blue shape of the United States, he declared, "We are fighting America's battle here and now. America will not have to fight tomorrow if she supports us today."

The chairman's fingers traced the outlines of the Japanese islands and moved west to encompass the expanse of China. He turned and said, "Good-bye, Mr. Hollings. You've listened patiently to the rambling of an ignorant countryman. But you undoubtedly have other pressing engagements. And I must attend to my duties. Good-bye, Mr. Hollings."

The correspondent would not take his dismissal without a final question: "What about communism, Mr. Chairman?"

"Communism? I don't understand. What of communism?"

"For China, Chairman? What of communism for China?"

"No one can say when, Mr. Hollings. Most of us believe communism will arrive someday. Some among us doubt it. We are not now working for communism. However, some day in the future . . ."

Richard Hollings already knew that the weeks in the border region were the most important of his life. The untold story of the Chinese Communists could be his springboard to greatness—if he performed adroitly. Nor was he completely taken in by Mao Tse-tung's flattery. Even a politician less astute than the chairman would have preferred the correspondent of the *New York Times* to himself. Richard assumed that he had been chosen because the Communists believed the solidly conservative convictions of the *Times* would prevent its publishing a detached—much less a favorable—account of the border region.

Besides, the *Times* correspondent might have declined the invitation because he feared it would imperil his relations with the Nationalists. Despite the United Front Against Japan, the Generalissimo would hardly be happy about a foreign correspondent's consorting with the Communists behind his back. Richard made a mental note: he would have to mend his own fences with the Nationalists.

He moodily paced the perimeter of the airstrip, hardly aware of his surroundings. He had come to say good-bye to Tommy, who was leaving in the Boeing monoplane of the Nationalist area commander. He was by no means sorry to see Tommy go.

They had been together too much not to rub on each other's nerves. Besides, Tommy had showed signs of unpleasant curiosity regarding his relationship with Emily. Fortunately, brotherly concern had not quite overcome the reticence bred in an English public school.

Nonetheless, Tommy had been getting too close to the bone—close to asking about his intentions toward Emily. As if a happily married man could have any intentions beyond mutual affection and mutual pleasure toward a married woman who was the mother of three young children.

The Boeing lifted off, circled the valley, and pointed its silver nose south. He would himself have to endure the bone-cracking ride in a supply truck to Sian the next morning.

Tommy and he had already agreed to keep their association in Yenan a secret. Tommy's standing as a fashionable physician would be damaged if he were suspected of being a Communist sympathizer. Richard did not want his journalistic competitors to know that the Howes could provide a passport to the border region. He wanted no one to know of his sojourn in Yenan until he was himself ready to reveal it.

The hammering of air-cooled engines in the west penetrated Richard's self-absorption. Looking at the sky, he saw a small transport aircraft in the distance.

A Cadillac ambulance appeared on the rough road from the town. Donated by the Chinese restaurant owners of New York City, it was used by Mao Tse-tung for personal transportation. The big ambulance stopped beside him, the chairman poked his head out the window, and the interpreter who had been dismissed when Tommy appeared stuck his head out beside the chairman's.

"Yes, Chairman?" Richard asked in his rough Mandarin.

"You must make promise, Hollings," Mao Tse-tung directed in the interpreter's rough English. "You must not write up this airplane. I will tell you it comes from a Soviet air base where Soviets train Nationalist pilots. Some old comrades return, some not seen for many years. We are very happy. But, Hollings, you will not mention this."

"Can you say why, Chairman?"

"You English, you are so stubborn." Mao Tse-tung's forced laughter was menacing. "Stalin and Chiang Kai-shek have signed a treaty, you should know. The Soviets should only fly to Nationalist areas. Hollings, you not want get pilot into trouble. So don't write about Soviet planes coming to Yenan.

"More better, do not write anything about Soviets. They have no influence here. My Communist Party is only a Chinese party."

57

JUNE 7, 1938

Emily was not looking forward to the gala reception to celebrate the redecoration of the private hotel Ikra. She was even less enthusiastic about the "small gathering of old friends" to which she had been asked by the note written in mauve ink in a finishing-school backhand. *Countess Elizaveta Alexandrovna Yavalenka* had been slashed through on the embossed invitation and replaced with the single word *Liz*. Emily was touched despite herself.

The invitation crackled as she slipped it back into her evening purse. Lifting the mirror from the vanity case in the armrest of the limousine, Emily inspected herself. Unnecessarily retouching her lipstick, she was struck again by the contrast between her fragile appearance and her innate competence. The tiny dimples still flickered beneath her cheekbones, and her expressive eyes were unclouded by time. She would do, Emily decided.

She glanced at Nanking Road. The traffic was heavy, although the anti-Japanese war was almost a year old in early June of 1938. The war had actually created lucrative opportunities for the greedy and the unscrupulous, Chinese as well as foreigners. A mile from the gutted battlefield of Chapei, shopwindows displayed the greatest abundance of luxury goods Shanghai had ever seen. The Settlement was booming while China bled.

Emily was almost ashamed of the Phantom VI, the latest of her father's Rolls-Royces, each one bigger and more ostentatious than the last. She had, however, borrowed it to overawe both the Japanese-protected thugs who plagued the Settlement and the arrogant Japanese sentries on its borders. The White Russian bodyguard who sat beside the old driver would not hesitate to use the automatic pistol in the black leather holster belted over his white tunic.

The Howes had recently gone back to carrying a bodyguard, the practice that had astonished Julia on her arrival in 1921. Troubled times bred kidnappers and assassins, particularly in the foreign-ruled concessions of Shanghai. The International Settlement and the French Concession were jewels glittering amid the squalor of war, although, perhaps, not for long.

Emily shifted uneasily on the split-hide seat and pulled her *cheongsam* away from her thighs. Mid-calf in the latest fashion, the dress was a film of white lace over a silk slip. Yet the humidity made even those wispy garments oppressive. Regardless of the heat, silk stockings were also essential for a formal occasion. She yearned for the freedom of the wartime capital. In Wuhan she wore sensible slacks, which required neither the ladylike stockings with their binding garter-belt nor a ladylike mincing walk.

She glanced out and met a beggar's malevolent gaze. His eyes were red-rimmed, and the crimson scar that pulled up his lip revealed broken teeth. Hunger had wasted his broad peasant face, and his skin was gray. With horror she recognized on his filthy tunic the badge of the crack 88th Division, which had so valiantly defended Chapei. His slashed trousers revealed cushions of inflamed purple flesh where his legs had been amputated above the knee. He sat on a board mounted on roller-skate wheels, presumably the 88th's parting gift.

And she had been yearning for the freedom of the wartime capital. Emily was shamed by her own frivolity. The freedom of war! Some freedom!

She spoke to the old driver through the speaking-tube. One more scrap of human jetsam would now be saved when the Rolls took the maimed veteran to the Haleevies' rehabilitation clinic.

The traffic was already clotting on Kiangse Road; Elizaveta had apparently asked half Shanghai to her gala reception. Emily would have come even if the firmly penned *Liz* had not touched her. Emily was on duty. The reception at the Ikra was perhaps not precisely the kind of occasion Mayling Chiang had in mind, but it should prove fruitful.

May still refused to allow her to come to Wuhan to stay. Not because the Japanese were implacably closing on the provisional capital; May expected her associates to display the same contempt for danger she herself did. But May believed that Emily was more valuable in Shanghai.

Jimmy Wei's office could deal with normal liaison with the press, and the efficient secret service could provide routine intelligence reports. But only Emily could convey to China's first lady the spirit of the cosmopolis. And only Emily could convince Shanghai's influential Chinese that their distant government would overlook neither patriotic sacrifices nor unpatriotic crimes. Something between a tattletale and the voice of conscience, Emily enjoyed neither role.

When the emerald-green Rolls was halted by the crush of vehicles, she decided to walk the last few hundred yards. Even though she was wearing fragile silver evening slippers, that was no hardship for one who had hobbled out of burning Nanking disguised as an old country woman with bound feet. Annoyed when her White Russian bodyguard insisted upon accompanying her, she was grateful when he cleared a way through the throng gawking at the rich at play. She felt vulnerable in her flimsy *cheongsam* amid the jostling crowd in serviceable workers' blue. Seventeen years after her return from the United States, she was still not completely at ease in a Chinese crowd. Like Mayling Chiang, she could face danger with equanimity, even zest, but she abhorred discomfort.

Her bodyguard saluted at the entrance and promised to wait in the kitchens. Even denser than the throng outside, the throng inside induced the same claustrophobia. But it smelled better. The expensive fragrance of perfumes combined with the expensive aroma of Havana cigars. The scent of new wool carpets mingled with a hint of fresh paint, testifying to the Ikra's redecoration.

Although she was five foot seven in heels, Emily caught only glimpses of the new splendor. The corridors were too crowded. Giving her name to a red-coated footman, she found herself looking into the small elevator tucked under the stairs. The cut-glass windows and the heliotrope satin curtains had been superseded by ultramodern rhomboid mirrors and jet-black pendants.

A rotund footman ploughed a path through the crowd for her. The former saloon bar was now identified as the cocktail lounge in angular black letters on a mirrored background. The restaurant, previously red plush, had been transformed with swatches of tangerine, dove-gray, and lime-green satin. The semicircular ballroom, however, was hardly altered. Only the woodwork shone whiter; the gilt Ionian columns gleamed more golden; and the velvet curtains glowed a deeper scarlet.

The Edwardian ballroom was the heart of the reception. The choker-collared tunics of American naval officers gleamed white beside the loosely cut khaki twill of their Japanese counterparts. The two groups were warily cool six months after the *Panay* incident. Some of the Italians wore the black shirts of Benito Mussolini's Movimento Fascismo, whose musclemen beat up any Shanghai Italian who resisted the dictator.

The Germans were better behaved, because the Nazis' machinery was still weak in Shanghai. Having withdrawn their advisers from the Nationalist army only a few weeks earlier, the Germans were not quite sure where they stood. Only one field-gray Wehrmacht uniform was visible —and not a single swastika. However, the horizon-blue of the French and the scarlet of the British set off the rainbow-hued evening gowns of the ladies and the more presentable courtesans. Neither group of women was disturbed by the others' presence—as both would have been only ten years earlier. Most civilians wore dinner jackets, though a few diehards were in tails.

A certain raffishness had crept over even respectable Shanghai in the tumultuous 1930s. Always avid for gain by any means, fair or foul, the foreign community had, nonetheless, previously preserved a façade of starchy respectability. The exigencies of war now justified the collapse of standards—as if Shanghai had not known war in the past.

Only Soviet Russians were excluded from the reception, in deference to the handful of White Russians, whose ancient cream uniforms made them appear the attendant ghosts of the dead czar. Elizaveta hated the Soviets even more bitterly after discovering how they had manipulated her in the 1920s. She was, therefore, flirting with the Japanese. Although they were the hereditary enemy of Russia, the Japanese were now the particular enemy of the Bolsheviks. She was also tolerant of the Nazis and the Fascists because they, too, were enemies of the Bolsheviks.

Joshua Haleevie was not happy about his former mistress's involvement with the Nazis, who cruelly persecuted Jews, among others. Most of the German refugees in Shanghai could earn their own living, since almost all possessed professional skills. Gritting their teeth at the newcomers' touchy arrogance, members of the established Jewish community were trying to help their coreligionists.

Joshua had not objected when his father, Sir Judah, suggested three months earlier that his wife, Charlotte, should investigate the possibility of resettling refugees in Australia and America. Joshua had, however, evaded the suggestion that he might accompany her. His interests and his affairs in Shanghai, he had declared, were in need of close attention. Sir Judah had wisely refrained from asking precisely what kind of interests, affairs, and attentions his son meant.

Joshua's primary interest in Shanghai obviously merited the closest attention, Emily reflected with light malice, though she did not know whether Elizaveta and he had resumed their affair. Joshua was apparently not concerned that his presence at the reception must become known to Charlotte. His tentative approach to Elizaveta was, after all, only a little more dangerous than his recent foray against the tigers of Nepal. Besides, Charlotte was intelligent; she avoided demands and recriminations equally.

Dazzling in his white sharkskin dinner jacket, Joshua was strolling among the guests, evidently seeking information. Emily had almost overlooked his other role. He was not only a highly successful entrepreneur but one of the best-informed men in Shanghai. Nationalist secret-service assessments had recently bolstered her belief that Joshua was the brains of the International Settlement's intelligence service—and probably more.

He stopped to chat with a man almost as tall as himself, who wore humdrum rimless spectacles and a little black mustache. A senior editor of Domei, the official Japanese news agency, Roland Yamaguchi was very valuable to his employers. He had acquired a continental gloss from his European mother—and colloquial American from the University of Missouri. He was highly intelligent and an excellent source for other correspondents, always ready to trade information. Emily found him a formidable antagonist in the propaganda war between China and Japan.

Both Joshua Haleevie and Roland Yamaguchi were looking down, addressing a third person Emily could not see. When the crowd eddied, she glimpsed the shorter man. Gregory Hardin was the antithesis of the popular impression of a Texan. He was compact, trim, and shy, rather than tall, bulky, and loud. A tenacious and meticulous observer, he had recently joined the *New York Times.* Gregory Hardin's thoroughness was almost a match for Richard Hollings's flair.

After looking in vain for Richard, Emily drifted instinctively toward the trio of Hardin, Yamaguchi, and Haleevie. Abruptly, she turned away. She was very fond of Joshua, and she liked Gregory Hardin. She almost liked Roland Yamaguchi, but she could entrust neither her temper nor her dignity to a public conversation with a Japanese.

Emily looked around the ballroom again. She did not like being alone. Madame Chiang Kai-shek's personal representative in Shanghai should, for political effect, be surrounded at all times by an aura of power, which meant supplicants and admirers. Regardless of that rationalization, she felt just as she had at Bryn Mawr freshman dances. Somehow it was demeaning—and a little frightening—to be a woman alone at a party.

Roland Yamaguchi put his hand on Joshua's arm and drew him toward the bandstand, which was a gigantic pink scallop shell. The move was obvious, indeed blatant. Yet it was adroit. The astute Japanese had made it appear that the influential Shanghailander and he were exchanging confidences, while the *New York Times* correspondent was left alone to wonder what important news he was missing. But Gregory Hardin, apparently unperturbed, smiled his welcome when Emily joined him.

"What's new?" she asked automatically. "What am I missing?"

"We were only chewing the rag," he replied. "Talking about Dick Hollings's copy from Yenan, Mrs. Ou-yang."

"Do call me Emily!" she chided. "You make me feel like my own mother-in-law when you say Mrs. Ou-yang."

"Anyway, Mrs. . . . ah . . . Emily, it wasn't important," Hardin said. "Just shoptalk—a little bitchy as always. Tell me, how was the Missimo . . . ah . . . Madame Chiang last time you saw her?"

"Now, Greg, you know I haven't seen her in months." She wondered why he had abruptly changed the subject. "She's fine as far as I know."

"You know there's talk of her going to the States for medical treatment?"

"There's also talk of a rift between her and the Generalissimo. Just nonsense! *All* China's enemies don't wear Japanese uniforms or carry guns. Rumor is a powerful weapon." Feeling she had reacted too strongly, Emily returned to the original subject. "What about Dick Hollings's copy?"

"Well, Mrs. . . . ah . . . Emily . . ."

Gregory Hardin paused in evident embarrassment, and she was pleased. Reluctant to criticize Richard directly because he knew of their past affair, the sensitive *New York Times* correspondent had obviously heard no gossip about the affair's resumption. Otherwise he would not have criticized Richard even indirectly. She would press Greg Hardin further if necessary. It was important professionally, as well as personally, that she know how his colleagues felt about Richard's six articles on the border region. Those articles had initially puzzled her and ultimately, she supposed, not displeased her.

The series had taken an inordinately long time to appear, in part because Richard was in no hurry to file. "It's more important," he'd insisted, "to get it just right." Swearing her to secrecy regarding his scoop, he had not even cabled the exclusive stories. He had, instead, frugally confided them to the new trans-Pacific airmail service provided by the four-engined flying boats Pan American World Airways called China Clippers. Since the series had not come clacking onto the teletype, his editors had been equally leisurely in publishing them. Only during the past week had clippings trickled back to Shanghai.

"Don't you think, Emily, that his stuff was a little bland?" Gregory Hardin phrased his criticism delicately. "He had a terrific opportunity. Anybody would give his left arm to get to Yenan. But Dick made it sound like Boys' Town. His pieces were as bland as rice pudding. A raisin or a jujube here and there. But, otherwise, pretty tasteless—though very sweet."

"If I may intrude on this culinary discussion." Richard Hollings appeared at Hardin's elbow, lean and dark in a cream silk dinner jacket. "Madame Ou-yang I would hardly expect to approve—regardless of what I wrote. But you, Gregory . . ."

"That's not true, Richard." She was glad of the public challenge, for he had in private avoided discussing his reportage. "I don't disapprove. To the contrary, I think your pieces are reasonably fair—as far as they go. Naturally, though, I'd like more bite."

"Bite, Emily?" he replied airily. "We seem trapped in culinary metaphors. What do you mean by bite?"

"The bite of truth, Richard. Truth has sharp teeth."

"So we've moved from cookery to dentistry. Do tell me . . . us . . . what you mean."

"Richard, we Chinese know the Communists far better than you can. You only had a few weeks with them." She wanted to say certain things to Richard—and a public quarrel was the best smokescreen for their private life. "But you lived in Shanghai for years. Obviously you didn't learn as much as you should."

Richard prompted: "Do go on, Emily."

"The Communists are all liars. They actually boast about lying. Whatever they told you was mixed with lies. They're out for power by any means. Killing, torturing, raping—it's all the same to them."

"I don't quite see where all this is going." Richard was defensive—and patronizing. "What's the point?"

"You wrote about the Communists as if they were just another political party. A nonviolent political party like the Democratic League. That's totally misleading."

"Since the United Front Against Japan, the Communists are just another political party—all working with the Central Government to resist the invasion. Yes, they have their own territory—just like an American state. The Democrats hold power in Washington, but the Republicans hold certain states."

"A political party with its own army?" Emily protested. "Two armies in fact: the Eighth Route Army and the guerrillas of the New Fourth Army. Some political party!"

"I hear, Dick," Hardin cut in, "there's more to be said on the Communists' side than you reported. How come you held off?"

That quiet question, Emily realized, was more damaging than her frontal attack. For once, Richard looked daunted.

"Why don't we drop this?" She was immediately protective. "We're not getting anywhere."

"No, Emily, I'll answer that one." Richard passed his handkerchief over his forehead despite the air-conditioning. "Just give me a second or so."

While Richard considered his answer, Emily glanced around the scarlet-and-ivory ballroom. Waiters in embroidered Russian blouses were weaving through the throng with silver salvers of champagne and vodka or large trays of smoked sturgeon and fresh caviar. The twelve-piece ensemble on the scallop-shell bandstand was playing the latest hit, "Thanks for the Memory." A Filipino baritone was crooning, "You may've been a headache, but you never were a bore. . . . So thank you so much."

How appropriate, Emily felt when she glimpsed Quick Jack Pavernen talking with Elizaveta. He was sleek in a midnight-blue dinner jacket. She was stunning in a ballgown that was obviously new, though it could have come from her mother's Edwardian wardrobe: buttercup slipper-satin cascaded from a nipped waist into a swirling skirt; the minimal bodice was barely held up by silk-skein shoulder straps.

What, Emily wondered, were they up to now? They were a pair: John Pavernen loved shady enterprises, and Liz loved the thrill of danger.

Richard was, however, finally offering the apologia over which he had agonized: "Greg, I suppose I didn't want to be *too* kind to the Communists. It wouldn't carry conviction. Besides, why alienate the Nationalists even more? . . . Emily, you've also got a point, a small point. Not your hysterical attacks on the Communists as murderers and rapists and God knows what else. I did write that there were disagreements within the Communist ranks. But that wasn't a testimonial to their democratic devotion to free debate . . ."

"Exactly!" Emily interposed. "They're anything but devoted to free speech."

"Maybe I did pull a punch or two. I'm not completely satisfied. I want to go back to Yenan and get to the bottom of the Communist story. The point is—"

"Very laudable!" Emily gibed. "Protect your access—even if you delude the reader."

Ignoring her, Richard continued: "You see, the Nationalists won't bar me from their territory. They're too dependent on foreign goodwill to bar correspondents. But the Communists only have to hold back their invitation. So it's just good sense to keep on their good side until I've got to the bottom of—"

"Porco Israelita!" The shout rang across the ballroom. Near the scallop-shell bandstand, Roland Yamaguchi and Joshua Haleevie were staring in amazement at a stout blond man who wore the black-and-silver dress uniform of the Italian Fascists, complete with ceremonial dagger. The company stared, and the Italian repeated his taunt in English: "Swine! Jewish swine! Capitalist Jewish swine!"

Joshua glanced around the room, smiled at the bystanders, and shrugged contemptuously at the Fascist. Still smiling, he slapped the man's ruddy face with his palm and on the return stroke with the back of his hand.

He then turned away, smiling apologetically as if to say: I'm terribly sorry, but it had to be done.

He had taken two or three steps when the Fascist bellowed in anger. Joshua disdainfully walked on. Roland Yamaguchi uttered a sharp warning, and Joshua half turned. The Fascist was charging like an infuriated rhinoceros, his dagger held before him. A woman screamed, and a man laughed in embarrassment.

Caught off balance, Joshua raised his left hand in defense. Yamaguchi clutched the Fascist's shoulder, but could not halt the charge. The dagger pierced Joshua's upper arm, and the assailant pulled back for another blow.

Yamaguchi's arm snaked around the man's throat and jerked hard. The Fascist slumped against a gilt pillar. Materializing as if from the walls, a pair of White Russian guards in white tunics dragged him away, boot heels drumming on the dance floor. The younger Russian, Emily saw, was her own bodyguard.

Elizaveta ran to Joshua, tears of rage in her eyes. Blood oozed through the rent in his sharkskin sleeve. Her arms went around him, careless of her yellow satin ballgown. Into the shocked silence, he ruefully remarked, "Sorry, Bess! Afraid I've been misbehaving. And just look at the jacket. Damned well ruined."

Elizaveta did not speak, but instinctively crooned consolations. She held him close, scarcely looking up when Roland Yamaguchi bowed deeply before them.

"I am fearfully sorry!" the Japanese apologized. "It is disgraceful that such a thing should happen!"

"It's not your fault!" White with delayed shock, Joshua spoke slowly. "Nothing to do with you!"

"That sort of thing is very bad!" the Japanese murmured. "With allies like that, how can Japan . . ."

As if himself at fault, Roland Yamaguchi bowed again and walked stiffly toward the door. At the reception desk he saw Tommy and Julia, who disapproved of Elizaveta's ostentatious redecoration and her extravagant party when China was struggling with the aggressor. Unable to bring themselves to snub her, they had deliberately arrived late, planning to go directly to her private apartment.

Julia wore a *cheongsam* of pale green crepe de chine, which pointed up her mahogany hair and her green eyes. Tommy was not happy with her wearing the Chinese-style dress to proclaim her support of the Chinese cause. Unlike the less emphatic Chinese figure, her assertive breasts and hips were shamelessly voluptuous in a *cheongsam*. Himself resplendently colonial in a cream linen suit, Tommy was checking his Gladstone bag with the receptionist when Yamaguchi broke stride to advise, "Better hang on to your bag, Doctor. Your friend Haleevie's just picked up a nasty stab wound. He's in the ballroom."

Tommy pushed through the crowded corridor. Behind him, Julia cursed the tight *cheongsam*, which hobbled her despite slits reaching three inches above the knee.

At the door of the ballroom, Jack Pavernen smiled in relief and said, "You heard? She's taken him to her apartment. Sent for Dr. Rosenberg."

"No need for amateurs!" replied Tommy, who had not touched a needle or a suture since the accidental bombing of the Great World the previous year. "The demon surgeon has arrived."

In the small rear elevator, Julia observed testily, "You're very jolly, my dear, considering we don't know how bad it is."

"But I do, Julie lamb. No blood on the floor and no panic among the guests. Not so bad, you see, as it may've looked at first."

It looked bad enough. When the elevator reached the sixth floor, they found a chalk-pale Joshua lying in his shirtsleeves on the mint-green settee. Elizaveta was kneeling beside him, holding a towel to his arm. Several red drops flecked her cheek, and blood oozed through the towel.

"Dr. Rosenberg's not in. And they can't seem to find any other . . ."

she said dully before recognition kindled in her eyes. "Tommy! . . . Oh, thank God! I was just . . ."

Tommy gently stripped the towel away. The wound was shallow, four to five inches long, and weeping blood. He replaced the towel and said to Elizaveta, "He'll be fine. Nothing to worry about. But you're needed below. . . . You can't just abandon your guests."

"Tommy," Elizaveta pleaded, "I must . . . stay with him. To help."

"You'd be more hindrance than help," he replied with calculated brutality. "Julie, get the smelling salts and give her a whiff before she faints. Then help her get tidied up and send her down."

Tommy cleaned the wound, disinfected it with alcohol, sprinkled iodoform, and sutured the edges. In a few months, Joshua's fair skin would show only a faint red line, which would fade to whiteness within a year.

"A couple of codeines and a brandy will fix you up nicely." Tommy cocked his head and admired his work. "What the devil have you been up to, chum?"

"Playing the chump, Doctor!" Joshua answered as he sipped the cognac Julia had poured. "I've been allowing myself illusions."

"A canny old trouper like you?" Julia laughed. "Impossible!"

"Old, yes. But canny? Not necessarily."

Tommy pressed: "Who was trying to carve his initials on you?"

"Giancarlo Poletti, our local Mussolini." Joshua smiled sheepishly. "And he pricked my illusion, too. I've been annoyed at the new influx —all those arrogant German Jews. Of course, I helped them. I had to. But I wasn't Jewish, I told myself, not the way *they* are. I was British. So I am, but I've discovered I'm also Jewish. Then, I'm afraid, I lost my temper."

"With that windbag?"

"Afraid so, my boy. Poletti is unusual for an Italian, but he was more vehement than Hitler about the subhuman Jews. I took exception. Very mild exception, you understand. Then he swore at me, and I had to slap him. You see the result."

"It couldn't have happened in the old days!" Julia was mock-solemn. "That's what my father-in-law always says."

"And my father," Joshua agreed. "Ladies and . . . ahem . . . professional hostesses at the same reception. Comic-opera Italians with stage daggers. My word!"

Emily put her head around the edge of the door. Finding Joshua sipping brandy and joking with her brother, she opened it wide. Behind her, Gregory Hardin was unobtrusive in his tan nankeen suit. He had asked Elizaveta why she was suddenly inviting him to join the gathering of old friends, and she had replied, "We're getting old and stuffy, Gregory. We need new blood." The correspondent was still wondering whether he was new blood or fresh blood.

Emily's white lace *cheongsam* blended with the white carpets and walls, and Julia's green crepe de chine blended with the green upholstery and curtains. When they kissed each other, they eerily vanished into that background for an instant. Seating herself on a green-cushioned chair, Emily reappeared and announced: "Liz says she'll be along just as soon as she can. Meanwhile, we're to broach the champagne."

The Krug 1932 popped discreetly, and the door opened. Richard Hollings entered with John Pavernen, whose patent-leather hair was obviously dyed, although his green eyes were still piercing. He was drawing luxuriously on an Upmann panatella, and the rich blue smoke wreathed his head. In his late fifties, Quick Jack was trim, except for the incipient potbelly beneath his white dinner jacket.

"Champagne, is it?" His baritone voice was resonant for his slight frame. "Well, there's lots to celebrate."

"Really?" Hollings cocked a patronizing eyebrow. "My dear Jack, that fact has escaped me. Aside from the Ikra's new furniture, I really don't see . . ."

John Pavernen strolled across to the white-lacquered liquor cabinet to kiss his niece roundly and take a goblet of champagne from her. He nodded cordially to Emily, whose nod in reply was restrained.

"Lots to celebrate, boys and girls." He raised his goblet in salute. "Not just the facelift for the old Ikra. Though that's pretty snazzy when you consider that Liz was just another poor White Russian taxi dancer only a few years ago." His insensitivity was legendary, and he added: "I also propose a toast to peace in China. Chiang Kai-shek can't keep turning down *every* peace offer. The Japs are reasonable, but he won't even be a Japanese puppet if he doesn't come to terms soon. He'll just be a grease spot. He's got to make peace. Let's drink to peace!"

John Pavernen raised his glass amid frosty silence. Emily and Julia glared at him, while Tommy assumed his impassive Buddha expression. It was not for him to clash in public with his wife's uncle, who was the senior member of her family in Shanghai. Julia was about to speak when Gregory Hardin softly interposed a question: "Are you speaking solely as a businessman, Mr. Pavernen? Or as an American?"

"As an American businessman, Greg." John Pavernen was happy to expound. "Above all, China needs law and order. The Japs are the boys for that. Business needs peace and stability to make profits—and pull

China up by its bootstraps. Only the Japs can provide that security."

"You seem to've done pretty well," Hardin interjected, "considering there's been no peace in China for three decades."

"I'm not denying it. For a country boy, I've done pretty well. But why kid ourselves? The Chinese have been trying since 1911, but they can't set up any government that lasts more than a couple of years. I've done pretty well out of Chinese feuding. But it's now time for peace, time for the Japs to clamp down."

"Uncle Jack, I can't believe I'm hearing you right," Julie burst out. "Are you really serious? As an American?"

"I sure am, Julie. What interest have Americans got out here except business? The sooner the Japs bring the Gimo to heel, the sooner we can get on with business."

Julia was too angry to reply, but Gregory Hardin snapped, "If you're speaking as a *legitimate* businessman, Mr. Pavernen, you're an ostrich. The Japanese will impose their kind of order on all business dealings. They won't put up with any competition—only businessmen who're useful to them. Pull your head out of the sand, Mr. Pavernen. Or, at least, stop talking through the part that sticks up in the air when you bury your head in the sand."

John Pavernen filled his glass and laughed. "Now, Greg—"

"You're talking dangerous nonsense," Hardin continued implacably. "Do you think the Japs will be satisfied with China? Sure, they'll lie down for a while to digest China, like a python with a pig in its stomach. But afterwards? Southeast Asia is next—oil, rubber, and tin. Ever hear of the Greater East Asia Co-Prosperity Sphere, Mr. Pavernen? Besides . . ."

Gregory Hardin looked in apparent surprise at the goblet of champagne in his hand and automatically sipped. No one else spoke, not even John Pavernen.

"There is something more important than business or even national interest." Hardin's Texas drawl was hard. "Justice and morality! The Chinese are fighting for justice, not only to preserve their country. The Japanese militarists stand for the rule of naked force . . . return to the Dark Ages. Mr. Pavernen, I pray we don't get into this war. But the Chinese are fighting *our* fight."

Gregory Hardin rubbed his upper lip with his forefinger, apparently abashed at his own eloquence. He feared that his youthful zeal had embarrassed the urbane company, for no one uttered a word. After ten or twenty seconds, however, Joshua Haleevie lifted his glass and said, "Hear! Hear! A most eloquent statement."

Evidently unmoved, John Pavernen drained his goblet, looked at his watch, and declared, "Well, I can't wait all night for Elizaveta. I've got business to attend to."

As he strode toward the door, he was stopped by a murmur from Gregory Hardin: "Mr. Pavernen, I apologize for any personal references. But everything else I said stands."

"I understand, Greg. We all get het up sometimes. No offense taken."

Beneath his joviality, John Pavernen was angry at being reprimanded by a man thirty years his junior. Pausing with his hand on the door-knob, he asked, "I'll be seeing you next week, Julie, the way we planned, won't I?"

After a perceptible pause, Julia replied, "Yes, Uncle Jack. Of course."

That grudging assent from his amiable niece shocked John Pavernen. With the door half-open, he took his hand from the doorknob and turned to face the silent condemnation.

"Maybe you wondered why the countess invited me to your cozy little confab." His tone was jagged with resentment. "Particularly since I'm not an old buddy like you folks, but more of a business acquaint-ance. You see, folks, we're still in business together, Liz and me. If Mitsubishi and the Imperial Army's Kempeitai—the thought police—are good enough for the countess, I guess they're good enough for me."

He looked accusingly at his niece and concluded: "But I can see I'm not good enough for you fine folks. So I'll be going. Tell my partner in crime good-bye for me."

"I have to survive, Joshua! Survival is always first for me!" Elizaveta was rarely less than dramatic. "I've told you many times. I've never made any secret of it. Why are you shocked now?"

Joshua did not reply. Some color had returned to his face, but his lips were pale and his eyes were distant. He did not like Elizaveta's evasive response to his direct inquiry as to why she was collaborating with the Japanese. He almost disliked her when she talked such nonsense. Be-sides, he should have known from his own sources what she was up to. He would have known if he had not allowed affection to blind him—even during their years apart.

After five years of separation, Elizaveta felt that even a carping Joshua was far better than no Joshua at all. No longer fearful about his wound, she was light-headed with joy in her new Ikra and her old Joshua.

A pity, however, that her intimate party had gone flat. Even Julia was reserved, though she normally bubbled with gaiety on festive occasions. John Pavernen, someone explained, had been called away on business.

Although she had ordered a lobster supper, her friends had all left after drinking the obligatory toast to the new Ikra. They had drifted away, and their farewells had seemed forced.

When she asked him why, Joshua had told her baldly of John Pavernen's revelations. He had then virtually demanded an explanation. Although that explanation was obviously unsatisfactory, he now said gently, "Tommy warned me against getting fussed. But I can't swallow your argument. You're very well off. How can you talk about survival . . . use it as an excuse?"

"Oh, Lord, Joshua, I *am* sorry." She was remorseful. "I almost forgot your wound. I'm evil: self-centered, grasping, rotten, and selfish."

"Don't go to the other extreme, Bess." Joshua grinned. "But, I warn you, I'll come back to the subject in the morning."

"In the morning? You mean you'll spend the night? How wonderful!"

"Not that wonderful, dear. You've got an injured forty-five-year-old on your hands."

"Your bloody uncle takes the flaming cake," Tommy exploded. "The gold-plated copper-bottomed award for shit of the year!"

"Sorry, darling," Julia murmured. "It's only an accident of birth that I . . ."

She switched her attention away while Tommy finished swearing and assessed the loft living room, to which they had returned from the Ikra. The new rosewood settees and chairs were upholstered in glowing turquoise. She had gradually disposed of the original furnishings, leaving only the big old rosewood chair and the leather Ming Dynasty chairs Tommy prized.

Tommy regularly complained that the new furniture was too grand. He said he hated to sit in it. He was, however, now lolling on the settee, his feet on the new cushions.

"You know, pet," Tommy finally said, "it was really Joshua's fault . . . getting stabbed."

"I thought the Italian, that Fascist Poletti, had—"

"Even so, Joshua has only himself to blame. He needn't have hit Poletti. He's getting touchier all the time."

"At least, he showed no sign of leaving the Ikra." Julia sighed luxuriously. "If this brings Joshua and Liz together again, it'll have been well worth it."

"Julia, my love," Tommy said quizzically, "your moral standards are becoming very elastic!"

"Why Tommy Howe!" She did not pretend not to understand him.

"You're the one who got a foolish virgin into bed long before any wedding."

"*Before* a wedding. Not *after* a wedding with someone else."

"I see what you mean, but—"

"First with Emily and Hollings—and now with Joshua and Liz— you're positively encouraging extramarital affairs. Glorying in immorality."

"Now Tommy, you know that's not so." She knew he was leading her on. "As far as Em and Dick . . . I haven't seen Em so radiant since . . . why since they broke up years ago. And you know that Hsiu doesn't care as long as there's no public scandal. Em and he understand each other. Tommy, she's happy again."

"So happiness is all. Will Liz make Joshua happy?"

"In the long run, I doubt it. But Charlotte and he never had a real marriage. Even on their honeymoon he dragged her off chasing lions and tigers. No children, either. That's no marriage. Only an alliance between the Haleevie and the Gubbai families. So why shouldn't Joshua . . . Anyway, he can't stay away from Liz. That's a fact of nature, not immorality."

"You win, Julie." Tommy laughed. "You've persuaded me. . . . But your uncle's babbling about his . . . and Liz's . . . dealings with the Japs is another matter. If Hardin talks . . . or Hollings, with his Japanese connections . . ."

"Greg Hardin won't talk, I assure you. As for Dick, you can judge better than I."

"I don't know, Julie. I still can't make Dick out."

"Tommy, I've been wondering. How bad would it be if Uncle Jack's outburst got back to the Japs?"

"It could hurt us, the Apparatus. The Japs might change their arrangements for shipping arms to their puppet Chinese warlords. And that could mess up our surveillance of those shipments. Most are now shipped as American merchandise by JPEnterprises, an American firm. The wealthy anti-Communist Countess Elizaveta Alexandrovna Yavalenka provides additional financing, if anyone asks. It's a sweet deal, as Quick Jack would say."

"Suppose the Japs do make changes."

"Watching arms shipments to puppets—or potential puppets—provides vital intelligence, Julie. We now know just where the guns are going. We therefore know exactly which warlords the Japs are suborning—or attempting to suborn. And that tells us where the next Jap thrust is aimed. Armed with that information—"

"Yes, I know. The Eighth Route Army and the New Fourth Army then take countermeasures. Maybe a preemptive attack . . . maybe a political counterthrust. At worst, they capture the arms."

"Got it in one, Miss Einstein. So, you see, it would be damned awkward if the Japs caught on and changed their arrangements. You're certain Hardin won't gossip?"

"No, Tommy. He'll either shut up or write the story. But I'll drop a word, steer him away."

"On *those* terms already?"

"Not *those* terms at all, you smug beast," Julia said. "Someday, I will have an affair with one of my dashing foreign correspondents. I simply find Greg honest, hardworking, and idealistic. He finds me amusing, useful, and reliable—honest, in fact."

"I hope he's never disillusioned." Tommy's jests about their clandestine activities were strained nowadays. "Hollings I can manage. Maybe I'll hint that Yenan could bar all correspondents for American publications if Chairman Mao learned that American-flag companies were smuggling Jap guns. Dick is desperate for another trip to Yenan."

"Well, he hasn't *offended* anyone by his pieces."

"Nor pleased everyone either. Though he's certainly trying hard. You know, he asked old Mao Tse-tung about communism for China. And Mao said, 'Certainly not now. Not tomorrow or the next day either. Not even in the foreseeable future.' So the ace political correspondent reports that they're not Communists at all. Just social democrats with rural interests—agrarian democrats, in fact."

"They'll laugh at that in Yenan, won't they? But I'm using the line myself. What better way to win friends than to convince foreigners that the Communist Party of China isn't really Communist at all?"

"Julie, I told him! I explained carefully to Hollings that communism is an ideal for the distant future. Nobody expects perfect justice in a perfect society for decades. That's what Mao meant, not that we weren't working for communism. I didn't want Hollings to lose credibility. Who'll believe a word he writes if he makes such fundamental errors? He'll look a perfect chump."

"Everybody'll believe every word, Tommy. Never underestimate the ignorance of the average reader. You expect too much from people, dear. Your telling him obviously made no difference. Either he didn't understand or he didn't want to understand."

"Perhaps it's beyond Hollings. Some agrarian democrats!"

"Of course they're true Communists." Julie agreed absently and added, "Darling, I've been wondering. Wouldn't it be nice to have another dog? The girls would love a puppy. And it's almost a year since Adam . . ."

Tommy sensed that Julia was approaching some delicate issue obliquely, but he replied evenly, "Not a ruddy mastiff. Something smaller, a real *shih-tzu* this time. Though it's odd to be thinking about dogs in the middle of a war."

Julia was relieved by that equable response. She was ostensibly talking about a new dog, but Tommy must know she was also thinking about his old friend Chang Kuo-tao. The Communist leader, who had enlisted them both in the Apparatus, had also brought the puppy Adam from Peking years earlier.

"I still can't believe it!" Tommy murmured. "Kuo-tao quitting the party! I just can't believe it!"

Tommy and Julia had just received full information on that spectacular defection. Julia was disturbed to learn that Chang Kuo-tao had resigned from the Communist Party and had left the Border Region. But her faith in the party's leadership rested upon bedrock; her faith was firm, though perhaps shallow. Appalled by his mentor's defection, Tommy faced a fundamental crisis of belief in the Communist cause.

During the first week of every April, the Central Government of the Republic of China offered symbolic sacrifices at the tomb of the first emperor of China. As chairman of the Border Region Government, Chang Kuo-tao had naturally participated in the veneration of the common ancestor in nearby Nationalist-held Sian. He had afterward not returned to the "airless dungeon" of Yenan.

Commissar Chou En-lai had then pleaded in vain with him to reconsider. Refusing, Chang Kuo-tao was publicly censured. Both the Chinese Communist Party and the Comintern declared that he had not resigned but had been expelled. On May 20, 1938, he had replied with a devastating "Open Letter to My Countrymen."

"The *only* purpose of the Communist Party is now to conserve and expand its own strength in order to seize power over China," he wrote. "Support for the war of resistance against Japan and the United Front with the Nationalists are only propaganda devices to that end. The Communist Party actually works unceasingly to destroy *all* other anti-Japanese elements in order to clear its own road to power."

"He *must* be wrong," Tommy whispered. "He's only one man."

"His whining about deception is absurd." Julia staunchly declared.

"Remember, Lenin himself said it was a revolutionary duty to deceive the enemy—by all possible means."

"Particularly when the enemy begs to be deceived. Like your chum Hollings."

"That reminds me, Tommy." She tried to divert him from his brooding. "The Soviets have been after the Apparatus. They know of our existence, though not our identity. And they want us to do some chores for them. Make some specific inquiries. I guess we should, don't you think?"

"Never, Julia!" Tommy exploded. "Whatever I'm doing, I'm doing for China. Not for the Kremlin, the Soviet Union, or the Comintern. The Russians can get stuffed."

58

JUNE 8, 1938

Joshua had underrated either himself or her. Perhaps he had underrated both of them, Elizaveta concluded smugly the morning after her reception. Despite his wounded arm, their coming together again had been blissful.

Elizaveta languorously surveyed the debris of their breakfast in her bedroom. Joshua was propped up in the seven-foot bed, happy but pensive. Was he repenting his betrayal of his childless—and loveless—marriage? Or was he brooding over John Pavernen's revelations and her own involvement with the Japanese.

"Bess, darling, you're more enchanting than ever." He intuitively answered her questions. "And the other thing you're wondering about, my marriage? God knows, I tried. But it faded away, whatever it was —and it was never much. No fault of Charlotte's. All my fault—and yours. Bess, you're champagne to a man thirsting in the desert."

She leaned over and kissed him, gratified as much by what he had *not* said as by his flattery. He's not going to worry me about Quick Jack's spilling the beans, she assured herself. He's now got pleasanter things to think about.

"You're very eloquent, my love," she said happily. "Now you're not to worry about anything. You're only to rest and pamper your arm."

"Oh, I almost forgot. Young Hardin asked me to tell you he's going to ring you. Wants to finish your talk, he said. You used to be frantic to keep your name out of the newspapers. What's up?"

"He wants to talk about my children."

"Your children? Don't be absurd, Bess."

"Not precisely *my* children. Not fruit of my womb, worse luck. Still, four hundred are a pretty big responsibility."

"Four hundred? What are you running, woman, a baby farm?"

"Not quite. Actually, a crèche and a school for lost children, the debris of war. Most never knew their parents. It takes money—loads of money. Also, I desperately need the goodwill of the Japanese."

"So that's why you've been playing the Japanese game. This does make that business look different. But still . . ."

"Also, Joshua, fundamentally I'm on their side. Bad as the Japanese can be, they're a lot better than the Bolsheviks. And they're always getting into border clashes with the Soviet Red Army. So you see why . . ."

"You're playing with fire," he exclaimed. "Have you forgotten 1932? Colonel Ishikawa, how he died?"

"No, darling, I haven't. And neither have the Japanese. They've a pretty good idea I was mixed up in his disappearance. That wretched Rumanian tart—the devil himself couldn't keep her from blabbing after two drinks. They don't know about you, though. The Rumanian didn't recognize you . . . thought you were just another . . . ah . . . patron."

"So the Japs are blackmailing you? How the devil I didn't know . . . didn't find out . . . I can't understand."

"Only a slight case of blackmail. The occasional bit of information. Also, my appearing as the legal originator of certain arms shipments. They do pay well."

"Yes—out of their earnings from their opium and their heroin. Bess, it won't do. You're hurting a great many people to help a few hundred children."

"Come see my orphans, Josh, and you'll understand."

"Look here, if it's the money, I'm sure the Haleevie charities could find—"

"Thanks, darling. But can you imagine the Japanese letting me carry on if I defied them?"

"We'll work out some way."

"Never forget the Japs are anti-Soviet. I'd make a pact with Satan himself to attack those devils who took away my Russia. Yes, the Japs are sometimes beastly. Still . . ."

"Methinks the lady doth protest too much." Despite the light-hearted quotation, Joshua's expression was grave. "I can't believe you've told me everything."

"There's an old Russian saying: Only a foolish woman tells her man everything!"

Elizaveta's voice assumed the heavy Slavic timbre she affected when she was clowning. She inclined her head in mock-submission and veiled her blue-black eyes with her long lashes.

Joshua smiled, but persisted: "And what else ties you to the Japs?"

"This may sound silly. Remember going to the Great World just before the Generalissimo took Shanghai? Emmy took me to see a fortune-teller. Everything that's happened since proves the fortune-teller was right. She said that I'd have many children, but none of my own. As I do now. . . . Also that I'd be admired by many men, but never possess the one I want. I don't possess you, do I, darling? . . . The other predictions I'm not so sure about. That I'd be very happy. Who can tell about happiness till the end? That I'd live a long time, which is nice. But not always where I chose, which isn't so nice."

"Any more predictions?"

"The last is already true: that my enemies would be my friends. So I've got to go along with the Japs. They're the enemies of my friends, but they're also the enemies of my enemies."

59

JULY 18, 1939

Richard Hollings propped himself on his elbow and took an emotional inventory of the slender body that lay beside him under the scarlet canopy of the carved and gilded bed. Emily Howe Ou-yang was thirty-eight, and maturity had made her more beautiful. Ripe physically, she was also ripe in sensibility and intellect. With her eyes closed and her face devoid of cosmetics, Emily was as serene as a time-polished ivory statuette of Kwan Yin, the Goddess of Mercy. Tenderly, Richard surveyed her from the high forehead, which was framed by blue-black hair and dewed with perspiration, to the narrow feet with the incongruous crimson toenails.

Her small breasts were minutely fuller, and the pink nipples were a shade darker. Although her waist was almost as slim as it had been when they became lovers fifteen years earlier, her hips were now more rounded and their bones were sheathed. Her shoulders no longer looked so frail that a feather's weight would bruise them. The lean-muscled grace under her apparent fragility was more apparent.

Richard brushed a lock off his forehead. He was forty-one, but his skin was taut and his dark brown hair was untouched by the drabness of time. He was, rather remarkably, not concerned about himself that hot afternoon.

He was almost obsessed with the woman beside him. He had last seen her half a year earlier in Shanghai, a thousand miles away. They had this day just met again in Chungking, the new provisional capital of the Republic of China, which lay far up the winding, gorge-choked Yangtze River, battlemented by mountain ranges. Beyond the reach of Japanese ground forces, Chungking was apparently secure. In July of 1939, two years after the Marco Polo Bridge Incident precipitated total war, the Nationalist Government had retreated far from Shanghai. Generalissimo Chiang Kai-shek's back was against the wall.

Emily and Richard had come together passionately, almost violently, the urgency of wartime inflaming the urgency they felt after their long separation. There had been little time for words, but Richard knew on that humid afternoon that he loved Emily profoundly and irrevocably. He castigated himself for the searing quarrels and the wasted years. And he thanked his hearty Anglican God for the revelation of love, however belated. He also thanked God that she lay, vulnerable and trusting, beside him in the summer pavilion of the hillside compound overlooking the gray city.

Unbidden, a vivid image floated before him; he saw the pale face and the blond hair of his wife, Fiona, who was eight thousand miles away in London. He thanked his accommodating God that she was childless, since he now knew that he would fight to keep Emily beside him all his life. Not that he did not love Fiona, although her father had helped his career not at all. Quite simply, he loved—and had always loved—Emily so much more.

A dog barked, and Emily's eyes flickered open. She smiled, momentarily surprised, and reached up languidly to touch his face. Suddenly she sat up, unperturbed by her nakedness, and asked in alarm, "What was that?"

"Only a dog," he answered. "Startled you, did it?"

"My God, yes! . . . You don't know, do you, Dick?" Suddenly aware of her nakedness, she pulled her blue lace peignoir over herself. "Barking dogs mean air raids in Chungking."

"Good Lord, why? Are dogs supposed to have extrasensory perception . . . or to hear the Japs' engines before we do?"

"No, my clever friend! You see the fog is so thick from October through April that the sun never shines through. So dogs bark when they see the sun—as if it were an intruder, a burglar."

"I'm dense today. I still don't see what dogs barking has to do with raids."

"Simply this: Jap bombers can't fly when there's fog. Even in July, when the sun shines, the dogs bark. And that means it's good flying weather. So we get bombed."

Her arms snaked around his neck and drew him down. His breath quickened and mingled with hers.

"God, Dick," she whispered into his mouth, "every time I see you, I just . . ."

Her mood abruptly altering, she pushed him away and sat up against the scarlet bolster. Luxuriously prolonging the moment, she shrugged into her peignoir, primly buttoned it, and took a cigarette out of his packet of Lucky Strikes.

"Enough of this!" she commanded. "We haven't talked at all. You know it's more than six months since you left Shanghai! Three months later Mayling finally let me come to Chungking. In May, just in time for the first air raid. Here on the hill, outside the city, my children are reasonably safe. But I'm talking too much. I always babble when I'm happy." She paused and whispered, "I *do* love you, Richard. God help me."

"Emily, I . . . Em, I just . . ." Richard was hobbled by the inhibitions of his class and his nation. "I just wanted . . ."

"Yes, darling!"

"I love you, too. Deeply. More than I can say. I just realized how much. I swear to you . . ."

"Don't swear anything. Tell me often, please, but don't swear anything. . . . Now, tell me everything that's happened since you left. You were on your way to London . . ."

"I've been in perpetual motion. A few weeks in London seeing old friends and talking with chaps in the Foreign Office. Then to the States."

Richard did not mention his wife, who had accompanied him to America—and pleaded to return with him to Shanghai. He knew Emily would not ask about Fiona.

"The Yanks are frenetic . . . talk business day or night. I rushed around, seeing all the big men. Of course, the editor of the *Boston Globe* and the people at NBC. Also President Roosevelt and Cordell Hull, the secretary of state. Hull calls the Japs pissants, whatever pissants may be. Yes, Washington is deeply concerned with Asia—above all with China."

Emily took a long drag on her Lucky Strike, coughed, and asked, "What do they think about China? Where are their sympathies?"

"There's no question about it. Everybody's cheering for the Chinese, from the president to the truck driver and the pullman porter. Except in the Middle West, where they're only interested in the next harvest. And the women are all collecting for China Relief."

"It sounds very good. Then it's just a matter of time!"

"Until what?"

"Until we get the help we need—and deserve. No more pettifogging to keep us from getting warplanes and arms. You see, it's only a matter of time, isn't it?"

"Sorry, Em, no! First, the Americans are determined to stay out of war. And second, Japanese propaganda outdoes yours, despite the sympathy for China. What's *most* important, after all, is that China trade is drying up because of the fighting. But the Japs will buy anything: oil, scrap iron, grain, even soya beans. The profits are fat, and the Yanks go along."

Emily was appalled by that picture of the United States, which was utterly different from her own memories. Drawing on her cigarette, she insisted, "The presidential election is next year, and—"

"And Roosevelt's already running for a third term. . . . He's throwing out promises to keep America out of all foreign entanglements."

Disturbed by that unsatisfactory report, Emily resorted to self-parody and muttered, "But we're not here only to talk."

She leaned across to Richard, her manner wanton. He unbuttoned her peignoir and took her in his arms, dismissing both the immaterial past and the evanescent future for this real moment. Real—and overwhelming, he concluded muzzily later, when they sank again into sleep.

The wailing of sirens awakened them.

Glancing at her wristwatch, Emily set her feet on the red tile floor. She opened the filigree wooden shutter and observed, "An hour or so to twilight. I told you about the barking. The Japs'll be here in about half an hour . . ."

"Shouldn't we . . ." He realized that he had no idea what one did in Chungking in an air raid.

"They never hit this hill. You'll have a grandstand view, looking right down at the city."

She poured tea from a cylindrical pot and offered a plate of crisp dried pork.

"Fatty Huang taught the Szechwanese to air-dry pork the way he likes it," she said. "You must remember Colonel J. L. Huang, Mayling's all-purpose factotum—and the leading gourmet in a nation of gourmets. And what food in Chungking! Not only Szechwan chefs, but refugee chefs from Peking, Shanghai, Canton, Hunan, and God knows where else. It's fabulous."

"For the rich!" he observed.

"I'm afraid so. But we can't fight all the good fights at once. Till we drive the Japs out, I'm forgetting about social justice—even about women's rights." Truly contrite, she nonetheless changed the subject: "What kept you in the States so long?"

Richard leisurely lit a cigarette before replying, "Everyone wanted to talk about China. And I did some lecturing and some special broadcasts. All very lucrative. Also . . ."

"Also what? Don't be coy."

"Also . . ." He grinned at her impatience. ". . . it seems I've written a book. About China, though I know it's presumptuous. Any rate, Boni and Liveright want to publish it in the States. Also Victor Gollancz in the U.K."

"Richard, how wonderful!"

Emily flung her arms around his neck, kissed him hard, and asked, "When does it come out? What's it called?"

"And I thought you were only interested in my body." He laughed. "Early next year, probably February. The tentative title is *Yellow Earth, White Sun, and Red Star.*"

"Do you *have* to mention the Communists in the title?" Her pleasure was clouded. "They're not really that important, you know. And you've only just gotten to Chungking. Will you be able to add a chapter on the new war effort from the new capital? Otherwise your book won't be complete."

"I should think so, darling. I've still got months. I want to see everything. And I'll need your help."

Richard did not intend to deceive Emily, but only to please her. Besides, he honestly did not know at what point the text of his book could no longer be altered. Since a newspaper could correct a story in ten minutes, he assumed that book publishers, too, could make changes at almost the last minute.

"It's been chosen as a main selection by the Book-of-the-Month Club," he added. "The publisher is terribly pleased."

"I *am* impressed."

"I'm told it means a fair amount of cash, so if we ever . . ." He let the hint hang in the air, though he knew she would not pick it up. "It also means a new status for the author. Boni and Liveright are begging for another book very soon. Apparently I'm now a respected author, not just a hack correspondent. Or so they tell me."

Richard's embarrassment was unfeigned. Although he was avid to advance himself, it was bad form to praise one's own accomplishments.

"*Yellow Earth, White Sun, and Red Star.*" Emily tried the title out, in part to turn the conversation from the hint that had made him sound like a suitor, which was unthinkable. "Why not just *Yellow Earth and White Sun?* It's shorter, punchier—and says all you need to say."

"Sounds good. I'll give it some thought."

Sirens wailed urgently—louder, shriller, piercing. They sounded like human sentinels shrieking warning of peril rather than brazen-throated machines.

"Ching-pao! Ching-pao! . . . Air-raid alarm!" Emily laughed edgily. "Even the sailors off the foreign gunboats now know that much Chinese. That's the second warning. We have another fifteen minutes."

"You know bombers scare me stiff."

"Darling, you'd better learn to live with them. We've averaged two raids almost every day since April. . . . But tell me, did you see Tommy and Julie in Shanghai?"

"Of course! I was in a great rush—shifting from the trans-Pacific liner to the coaster for Hong Kong, where I could catch the Chungking flight. Shanghai's beginning to wither on the vine, you know."

"And Tommy and Julie?" Emily pressed. "How are they?"

"They seemed fine," he answered airily. "What else can I say?"

"A great deal, I'd think. If you're trying to spare me, Dick, don't. Your tact has already alarmed me. What's wrong with them?"

"To be perfectly honest, Em, nothing I can put my finger on. They're both in good health, outwardly cheerful, and working hard. The girls are fine, too. Though your niece Althea, the fair-haired one, if I'm not mistaken, she's a bit of a handful."

"Richard, you're still being evasive. Tell me what you know—or suspect. Otherwise, I'll imagine something worse."

"If you insist. . . . I could be wrong, but I got the impression Tommy and Julie weren't getting along." He explained: "A little friction is normal for you and me. But friction is unusual for Julie and Tommy. He goes into trances, doesn't talk. She doesn't laugh as much—or as spontaneously."

Emily's eyes were insistent, and he added defensively: "Devil take it, Em, it's probably my imagination. The war's moved on, but life in Shanghai is still a strain with the Japs all around. It's like being in a cage in the zoo with the Japs always peering in."

"Why they don't come to Chungking I can't understand," Emily mused. "Or go to the States. . . . But you know Tommy. He'd never leave China. Yet why stick in Shanghai?"

She leaned across him to stub out her cigarette, and he stroked her hip suggestively. She smiled, shook her head, and leaned back against the bolster to muse further. "I think I'll write and ask Julie point-blank what's wrong. Worst she can do is tell me to mind my own business."

Emily slipped off the high bed, leaving the ice-blue peignoir crumpled and flat like a snake's shed skin, and walked across to the chest where her hastily discarded clothing lay. Richard watched with delight the play of her taut buttocks, her tapering thighs, and her slender ankles. Looking over her shoulder, she intercepted his gaze and—to his aston- ishment—winked. This was a new Emily, self-possessed and occasion- ally ribald. As she shook out her flimsy undergarments, her cream silk blouse with the jeweled Air Force wings, and her beige cotton slacks, he concluded that there was, after all, something to be said for war.

While he pulled on his shirt and trousers, she asked, "Dick, when can I see your manuscript? I'd love to read it."

"I'm sorry, Em." He slipped the strap of his binoculars over his head. "They make so much fuss about not weighing the aircraft down. The long and the short of it is I left my only copy in New York. Just as soon as I get the book . . ."

"I'll hold you to that." She slipped her arm through his. "Now shall we go see the war?"

Richard Hollings had paid little attention to his surroundings earlier that day, when the sedan-chair coolies carried him up the narrow hill- path to the stone-walled compound where the Ou-yang family was established in comfort remarkable for wartime refugees. The bamboo chair had repeatedly swung over the edge of the precipice, and fear had distracted him from the view. When Emily led him out of the compound at twilight, he looked down at her gleaming hair, not at distant Chung- king. Enthralled by the line of her cheekbone, he was hardly aware of his surroundings until they stepped onto a rocky outcrop that looked across a river at the city.

Emily pointed down and said, "Extraordinary sight, isn't it?"

The center of Chungking, a name that literally meant "Many Felicita- tions," lay at the point of the triangle formed by the meeting of the broad Yangtze and the narrower Chialing River. Within the crenelated city walls stood squat buildings with drab tiled roofs, and a sprawl of new construction covered the hills to the west. Stone stairs climbed hundreds of feet from the river's edge, where grimy wooden shacks perched on stilts like gray herons on skinny legs. Every ounce of water and every grain of rice was carried up those stairs on men's backs. On the ridge above its river moats, the fortress-city was almost impregnable to attacks on the ground.

It was naked to attack from the air. Through his binoculars, Richard saw the black scars that incendiaries' conflagrations had branded on the city's face. Chungking's antiaircraft batteries were hardly more effective against the bombers than the dark sentinel pines on the hills that cupped the medieval city. The Chinese Air Force, Emily confessed, was impotent—virtually destroyed. Claire Chennault was striving to rebuild the Air Force from scratch in Kunming, four hundred miles to the southwest. The Japanese bomber fleets were based at Yochow, four hundred miles due east.

The bombers came out of the southwest, having flown around the city to take the antiaircraft gunners by surprise. Storming out of the sunset, the silver squadrons stretched from horizon to horizon. They swept overhead in precise V's like wild geese, the discs on their wings blood-red.

"Never so many before," Emily said somberly. "This must be the biggest raid ever."

Shocked by the immensity of the attack, Richard counted forty-six Mitsubishi twin-engined bombers. The squadrons swept over the defenseless city, flying wingtip-to-wingtip. The searchlights on the ground made them glitter like sequins against the dark sky.

All the bomb-bay doors opened simultaneously. Swarms of small incendiaries swam downward through the searchlights' beams like fat guppies, followed by the big heavy-explosive bombs like predatory pike.

Richard put his arm around Emily's shoulders and felt her tremble. Stripped of bravado, she buried her face in the crook of his neck.

Fires blossomed scarlet in the dark wedge of the city. Seconds later, the big bombs thundered. Leaping high, the flames glowed red on the bombers' silver bellies.

Fearful of being highlighted by the fires, Richard pulled Emily down to the ground. The great silver shapes passed directly overhead, their immense wings eclipsing the stars.

A torrent of red tracer bullets streamed down at them, striking the rocks ten feet away and popping like oil bubbling in a pan. Lit by the conflagration, the air gunner floated within his Plexiglas enclosure as if alone in the dark sky. He thumbed the triggers of his twin machine guns again, and his round goggles glared like the eyes of an enormous and malevolent fly. Remarkably, neither Emily nor Richard was touched.

When the armada had passed, Emily exclaimed, "A small miracle. He didn't get us! My rule is simple: Always be cheerful! Be cheerful or you'll cry! . . . But this is the worst I've seen, the worst Chungking has endured."

The north wind bore the fires' stench to their nostrils as they walked slowly back to the compound: burning kerosene, burning wool, and burning flesh.

Her composure restored, Emily touched Richard's arm and said, "You'll have to spend the night. Not with me, unfortunately, but in the guest pavilion. Hsiu is tolerant—up to a point. I don't try him except when you're around, darling. And that hasn't been very often."

"Not by choice," he declared. "If it were only up to me . . ."

"Maybe someday it will be." She offered him that first tentative hope casually. "Perhaps when the war is won . . . But this is stupid talk. Your wife, after all . . ."

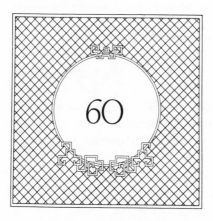

60

Waking the next morning under the ghostly mosquito net, Richard remembered the evening with a shrug of distaste. When Emily and he returned to the main house, they had found Harrison Parker Smythe III lolling in an easy chair. He was rakish in suede chukka boots, chino trousers, a brass-buckled bush jacket, and a campaign hat with a leopard-skin band. His cornflower-blue eyes beaming innocence, he had only grinned when Emily exclaimed, "I thought you were with Claire Chennault in Kunming!"

If he had not seen Emily's surprise, Richard would have suspected a put-up job. During dinner, Emily and Harry had worked together so smoothly they might have rehearsed their lines. Remembering how Smythe had pursued Emily in Shanghai years earlier, Richard was again jealous. The American was obviously enamored of Emily, and her ease of manner with him bespoke intimacy. With an effort, Richard thrust away his suspicion, which was not only unworthy but irrational.

His thoughts returned to the conversation at the dinner table. Emily was well stocked with scotch, bourbon, and brandy, which sold on Chungking's black market for seventy-five American dollars a bottle. She had said that her chief, Mayling Chiang, made sure her liquor cabinet was always full. Across town, Commissar Chou En-lai, the chief representative of the Communists, gave regular tea parties for foreign correspondents, where liquor and propaganda flowed. Emily was, she acknowledged, assigned to counteract the damage Chou En-lai did by entertaining the correspondents just as lavishly—"and," she said, "telling them the truth."

Her truth, Richard felt, was heavily weighted in favor of the Nationalists. Speaking alternately like a very lively Greek chorus, Harry and Emily had extolled the brilliant strategy of Generalissimo Chiang Kaishek.

Retreating before greatly superior Japanese firepower, particularly tanks and warplanes, the Nationalist armies had battled for every inch of soil. The Generalissimo's purpose, Harry had stressed, was to exhaust the Japanese, much as the Russians had exhausted Napoleon when he was foolish enough to invade another vast land. Emily nodded solemn agreement, and Richard refrained from pointing out that the Generalissimo was still tying up his best troops to checkmate the Communists. She would only have replied, with justification, that the Communists were husbanding their forces to hurl against the Nationalists when the war against Japan was finally won.

Richard had kept his temper then, but he had flared at the next passage in the duet Emily and Harry were obviously singing for his benefit. First had come a dish called Ants Climbing Trees, which was pungently spiced minced meat on a bed of translucent noodles. She did not, Emily had said, know where the name came from. But there had been nothing obscure about Harry Smythe's attempt to enlist Richard in the propaganda campaign.

In return for inside information on the war in the air, the American wanted the correspondent to give the American people the old message with a new twist: The war against Japan was already America's war; America should therefore supply the warplanes needed by the Chinese, who were already fighting that war. Moreover, China might well need American pilots to fly those warplanes.

After Richard told Harry he could not be bribed, the two had glared at each other. Finally, Emily had cajoled them into a show of amity and had offered her own contribution: figures drawn from captured Japanese documents.

The enemy claimed to rule six hundred thousand square miles of China's territory and seventy million of China's people. That, Emily had said smugly, left three million square miles and three hundred and thirty million Chinese outside the Japanese grasp. The Japanese, she had added, themselves recognized their mortal dilemma: the deeper they got into China, the slimmer were their chances of victory. Seven million Chinese soldiers were luring a million-odd Japanese into the biggest trap in the world—the vast expanse of China. "We cannot advance," a captured Japanese Imperial Staff Report had concluded, "and we dare not retreat."

When the dinner ended with small Szechwan tangerines, Emily had excused herself. Pleading exhaustion after a strenuous day, she had told Richard, "Harry'll show you where you sleep. Maybe lend you a razor, too."

She had then kissed him lightly on the lips, leaving him surprised by that casual display of affection before an outsider. Later, turning on his hard wooden bed, he had told himself he would never understand female behavior. Smiling at that banal conclusion, he had fallen asleep.

After breakfast, Emily advised patience, although Richard was anxious to get back to work and Harry Smythe had business at the Ministry of Defense. No public sedan chair appeared at the gate, although two or three normally waited there for fares. Surmising that all able-bodied men had been pressed into clearing the rubble left by the greatest raid of the war, Emily offered her private sedan chair.

When Richard said he would walk rather than dispossess her, she directed her chair-bearers to the Aeronautical Commission. She preferred not to provoke Mayling Chiang by tardiness, although her old friend would have been happy with the excuse that she had lent the sedan chair to a correspondent. Despite her increasing hauteur, Mayling never forgot the overriding importance of American public opinion.

Mayling's preeminence derived largely from the American connection. She was not only her husband's interpreter but his collaborator in dealing with the United States, largely because of her popularity with the American people. Since that popularity depended upon the American press, she would do almost anything for correspondents—even, sometimes, tell them the truth.

While Emily's sedan chair swayed down the precipitous path to the ferry across the Chialing River, her houseguests scrambled a few hundred yards behind. Burdened though they were, the chair-coolies steadily drew farther ahead of the two foreigners.

Harry Smythe stopped on the downward path to study Chungking's latest scars. The thick smoke rising from burning buildings was the funeral pyre of hundreds of men, women, and children. A brisk wind chased the lamb's-fleece clouds across the sky and prevented the smoke's forming a funereal pall over the tormented city.

The clear skies were foreboding. Heavy smoke cover would have hampered the Japanese aviators who were at that moment being briefed for the next attack.

"You're not," Harry asked, "in a great hurry, are you?"

"Not frightfully," Richard replied, "though I should see some people."

The American hooked an arm around one of the dark pines beside the trail and said meditatively, "Szechwan they call it, Four Rivers. China's most fertile province—and most heavily populated. Much of the romance of Chinese history started here."

Richard realized that he was listening to a declaration of love for the inchoate nation-continent called China. His jealousy of Harry Smythe's closeness to Emily was, he realized, misplaced. Harry did love Emily, but as a daughter of China, not for herself.

"Szechwan is also the end of the line." Harry glared down at the bomb-scarred city. "The Gimo is cut off from the outside world. Since the Japs dominate the coastal provinces, he's got no outlet to the sea except the narrow-gauge railroad through French Indochina. An occasional plane lands from Soviet Central Asia or flies over the Himalayas from Calcutta. He mostly depends on broken-down trucks dragging themselves through the mountains on the Burma Road. More than half their load is their own gasoline. Not great, is it?"

"How do you square that with the optimistic picture you drew last night?"

"Dick, an entire nation is at bay on this plateau. More than twenty million Chinese have swarmed into Szechwan, the ones with guts and imagination! And they're still coming—despite disease, starvation, accidents, and bandits!"

Gazing at the peaks on the horizon, Harry said softly, "I've seen the mass migration of a people. By ramshackle buses. By bicycle, oxcart, and horseback. In jalopies and antiquated trucks held together with string and chewing gum. Thousands came on junks through the Yangtze gorges—and a privileged few by plane. Most came on their own legs. Toddlers and grandmothers with bound feet. Solid bourgeois from the treaty ports and soldiers from Manchuria. Mule drovers from Shansi and tea merchants from Amoy. Marine engineers from Canton and electricians from Tientsin."

The American wrestled a cigarette from a limp pack of Camels. His chromium-plated Zippo lighter threw a flame three inches high. Blowing out the smoke, he looked down at his cigarette in apparent surprise and dropped it.

"Got to cut down," he reminded himself absently. "It's going to be a long war."

"Harry, this is all very inspiring," Richard interposed. "But mass migration is *not* winning the war."

"I got carried away," the American confessed. "Dick, it *will* win the war. Mechanics and engineers have brought their factories along—on men's backs or man-pulled carts. They can make everything from matches and textiles to cement and guns. The heavy machinery came on junks. Or by flatcar to the end of the tracks and then manhandled over dirt mountain roads. You can't beat a people like that."

Abashed by his own emotion, the American turned and trotted down the trail to the riverbank. Waiting for the sampan that sculled men and beasts across the placid Chialing River to Chungking, Richard pondered his first report. The first sentence sprang into his mind: *The Chinese people are capable of anything—except surrender.*

He rejected that adulatory lead. It was ridiculous to make such a sweeping judgment so soon after arriving. He had hardly spoken to anyone except Emily and Harry, who were both vehement champions of the Nationalists. He would have to make his own assessment. Besides, it could be awkward waxing lyrical about *both* Chinese regimes.

The two foreigners jumped from the ferry onto the muddy foreshore —and into the reality of Chungking on the morning after the war's most savage air raid. Many pedestrians held crumpled cloths soaked in vinegar to their noses. The city's stench gripped Richard's throat like a giant hand, and bile rose bitter in his mouth. The nauseatingly sweet odor of putrefying flesh overpowered the stench of excrement, sour rice, and fermenting chillies. Gagging, Richard choked back the bile.

Harry Smythe extracted a flask of eau de cologne from his jacket pocket and wet down his own handkerchief before offering it to Richard. The cloying cologne intensified the sweetness of corruption. The stench was palpable—almost animate. It clogged Richard's mouth with filth and almost stopped his nostrils. Although he had endured the stenches of Asia for many years, he felt as if he were suffocating.

"I'm going the other way." Harry Smythe clapped him on the arm. "For the press hostel just follow that road. . . . Don't let it get you down, buddy."

Sampans were carrying heaped corpses to the far bank for mass burial, while men and women searched among the dismembered corpses on the muddy foreshore. Fragments of human beings spilled across the foul black mud like the leavings of a cannibal feast. Eyes stared imploringly from bloodied faces, and bony hands clutched the merciless air. A shapely leg severed neatly above the knee still wore an immaculate beige silk stocking and a high-heeled pump.

The searchers turned the bodies over like monks and nuns atoning for their own sins by carrying out the grisly task. It was the least—and the most—they could do for their dead. Confucius had enjoined all Chinese to preserve unmutilated the bodies given them by their parents. Richard realized with horror that the searchers hoped to reunite disjointed limbs and severed heads with their original torsos so that the dead would go entire into the afterworld.

He turned away from the shambles and took the road to the press hostel. Despite the broken streets, the gutted buildings, and the burnt-out shrines, Chungking was vibrant with life—and hope. Workmen squatting among the rubble knocked mortar off bricks and stacked them for future use. Boys and girls carrying slate tablets covered with a hundred repetitions of the same ideogram trudged uphill to school, skylarking and laughing. Hawkers of food and drinking water cried their wares, and dogs barked defiantly behind bamboo palings.

In the busy lobby of the gray-tiled press hostel, the musty smell of mildew contended with the aroma of fresh paint. Opened a week and a half earlier, the hostel was already showing hairline cracks in its plaster walls.

Jimmy Wei popped up to greet Richard, his dark monkey-face warmly welcoming. Overwhelmed anew by Jimmy's ebullient personality, Richard finally broke away. In his room, which was somewhat larger than a monk's cell, he rolled a sheet of paper into his Hermes portable, typed the heading—and sat staring at the malevolent white surface for almost a quarter of an hour.

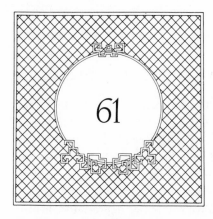

While Harry Smythe and Emily Ou-yang maneuvered to draw Richard Hollings into their schemes to gain American support for the Nationalist Government, the Soviet Union acted. The dictator Joseph Stalin promised arsenals of weapons and battalions of military advisers to Generalissimo Chiang Kai-shek, whom Soviet propagandists had instantaneously transformed from a "feudal despot" into a "democratic hero."

Stalin's reasoning was brutally simple. Japan was his dangerous neighbor in the Far East, and the Chinese Nationalists were more likely than were the Chinese Communists to kill many Japanese soldiers. Impressed only by power, Stalin made the more powerful Nationalists his protégés. He also planned to regain the Soviet influence, which had been lost in 1927 when the Chinese Communist Party was scattered and the Comintern's agents were expelled. Naturally, he hedged his bet by continuing his secret support for the Chinese Communists.

The paranoid first secretary of the Communist Party of the Soviet Union further graciously advised the Generalissimo: "You must make sure there is no treachery or disloyalty behind your back. The best way is to shoot at least four and a half million people. Once a suspect enters the gates of the Soviet Ministry of the Interior, there are only two exits: Siberia or the grave."

By instinct a conciliator rather than a dictator, Chiang Kai-shek did not act on that advice. Besides, he felt that his secret police were already brutal enough. For his part, Joseph Stalin sent no more than a trickle of war matériel to supplement his large military advisory mission. The

Nationalists disregarded the advice of the Russians, whom they called the hairy barbarians, as distinguished from the Japanese dwarf barbarians and the Western oceanic barbarians.

The pealing of the doorbell six flights below was repeated in the roof garden Julia Howe had created above the loft sitting room of the house on Kiukiang Road. The Howes liked to have advance notice of visitors in these troubled times, although they were weathering the storms of war better than most in late August 1939. Although the commercial beat of Shanghai was slowing, that decline had hardly touched them. While Donald Howe's holdings depreciated, his son's practice had expanded.

Tommy's public school accent attracted the conservative British, and Julia was a lodestone for the Americans. Wealthy Chinese felt less apprehensive about submitting to the exotic perils of Western medicine when it was practiced by one of their own. Although they had taken over the entire building on Kiukiang Road to gain room for Tommy's offices, Julia was hardly burdened by household cares. The number of servants seemed to increase twice as fast as their duties.

The amahs would have spoiled nine-year-old Althea and her six-year-old sister, Persephone, if Julia had allowed them to. She was proud that her daughters spoke Shanghainese well. She would have been ashamed if, like some American children, they saw their parents so infrequently that they barely spoke English. But, because she was afraid of smothering the girls with her attentions, she continued to present her record-request program every other day on XMHA.

It was curious, Julia reflected, but her life somehow seemed more normal than it had for some time—aside from more frequent and more abrasive disagreements with Tommy on political questions. It was odd to consider invasion and partial occupation a kind of normalcy. Yet most of her life in China had passed amid tension and danger. Even the blessed years from 1931 to 1937 had been stalked by war and revolution, although those threats had seemed far from the charmed city.

Julia looked at Tommy with concern when the doorbell pealed impatiently a second and a third time. In residential Shanghai, unlike bawdy Shanghai, an unannounced caller at half past eleven in the evening was unusual. To the Howes it was mildly alarming. Their secret work for the Apparatus gave their lives deeper meaning—and exposed them to danger. They feared the Japanese Kempeitai, the Settlement Police, and also Nationalist special agents.

"I'll go." Tommy pulled his dressing gown about his lean frame. "Not likely to be a patient. They'd telephone, not come by. I wonder who would . . ."

He descended the spiral staircase to the cavernous sitting room and opened the glass-and-mahogany door that now served where steel plating, folding grills, bolts, and chains had once kept two young women safe. The hall, which had been dingy, was now bright in lavender and yellow. He heard the elevator already rising in its silver-grilled shaft.

Tommy told himself to relax. Loo, his majordomo, would not admit a stranger this late without inquiring on the house telephone. He consciously relaxed his tense neck muscles—and marveled at the irony. Why should a man such as he have to force himself to relax in his own home?

When the elevator arrived, Tommy swung the door open and a vision appeared: Countess Elizaveta Alexandrovna Yavalenka wearing a stole of white Siberian fox over a Cossack-inspired black silk kaftan in the eighty-six-degree heat. A large wicker hamper burdened her. Where, Tommy wondered, was the uniformed White Russian footman who rode in the front seat of her twenty-two-foot-long Hispano-Suiza? She had recently acquired that limousine from an up-country warlord, in part as a return for services rendered by the Ikra—and in part for machine guns.

"Tommy, darling!" Her embrace was scented with Mitsuoko perfume and Hine cognac. "Be a pet and help me."

"Do your own lifting and carrying now, do you?"

"I'll explain when we're safely inside," she whispered. "I don't want anyone to know. The servants are all spies, of course."

Amused by her melodramatics, Tommy bundled the wicker hamper up the spiral staircase to the roof garden. Soon the two women, jet-black head and tawny head close together, were seated on a settee beside the gilt statue of Kwan Yin, the Goddess of Mercy and the patron of women.

Elizaveta extracted two chill-dewed bottles of Taittinger *blanc de blancs* from the hamper and directed: "Don't just stand there, pop one."

Julia asked happily as Tommy attacked the cork, "What're we celebrating?"

"No one must know, my darlings. The Japanese have their spies everywhere."

"The Japanese?" Julia was amazed. "But you're working *with* the Japanese?"

Elizaveta raised her glass and proposed: "A toast! To General Georgi Zhukov! And to his gallant soldiers! They have driven the Japanese invaders from the Russian Motherland."

"But, Liz," Tommy said, "only last week you were praying for the Japs to beat the Bolsheviks."

"A lady can change her mind, can't she? After all, blood is thicker than vodka. General Zhukov has driven a Jap tank army from our sacred Siberian soil after a three-month battle. The news just came through."

"Sweetie, I'll drink to any Japanese defeat! But I don't like drinking to Bolshevik murderers." Julia automatically reinforced her right-wing cover. "You, of all people, Liz, should know—"

"I'm a realist, Julia. The czar will never reclaim his throne. Hateful as the Bolsheviki are, they have united Great Russia. And they are standing against the Japanese aggressors."

Tommy was thunderstruck by Elizaveta's change of heart—and by her calling herself a realist. She had, he was convinced, never faced reality in all her life, not even during her terrible years in Siberia. Moreover, her faith in the restoration of the czars had never before wavered.

"The sacred soil of the Motherland!" She proposed another toast. "Forever inviolate!"

Setting his goblet down on the side table Tommy observed wryly, "If you look hard, you'll find your sacred Siberian soil is really Chinese. Your czars stole it from us at cannonpoint. But I'll drink to the defeat of the Japanese."

"I must fly." Elizaveta flipped open the jeweled lid of her wristwatch. "Must get back to the Ikra to keep the peace. The Japs'll be insufferable tonight, morose and quarrelsome."

After dropping kisses on their cheeks, she floated down the spiral staircase to the elevator. Tommy shook his head and Julia poured more champagne.

"You see, darling, it's true," she said comfortably. "Everyone sees the light in time—even a hardened reactionary like Liz."

"What a performance!"

"Tommy, forget about China's old imperialist boundaries. Liz is delighted because it's Russia that's won. And I'm delighted because the Japs got their comeuppance from the Soviet Union, which is China's best friend."

"I'm not so sure of that, Julie." Tommy fished in his pocket for his old meerschaum. "Almost all Soviet aid—what there is of it—is going to the Nationalists. Stalin obviously doesn't give a damn for the Chinese Communist Party. In 1927, remember, Moscow bloody well abandoned the party. It could happen again."

"Darling, please don't be morbid. This is an entirely new day, and we must be practical. China has no other friend."

"Julia, I've been thinking." He lit the meerschaum, and a cloudlet of pale gray smoke screened his face. "I'm worried about Shanghai. Anything could happen. I've asked several times—and I still don't see why you won't take the girls to visit your parents. Just till we see what's going to happen. It's about time the girls saw their grandparents again."

"Darling, how many times do I have to tell you? I won't leave you here alone."

"My dear girl, you know I can't leave China. Certainly not now. All the reasons that make it imperative for you to go make it imperative for me to stay."

"Tommy, I do my share for the Apparatus. A little more than my share because of your practice. If I go, you'll be hamstrung."

"True enough. But the time I now give to the family I could devote to the Apparatus. It would even out."

"Do you *want* to get rid of me, Tommy? . . . I resent your implication that I'm expendable. It's just as important to the Apparatus for me to stay as for you to . . ."

The telephone on the marble side table rang imperatively, and Julia snatched up the handset in annoyance. Listening intently, she twice asked, "Are you sure?" She finally asked, "And that's all it said?"

Very slowly she replaced the handset. Her crimson lipstick was a garish scar on her chalk-white face when she turned to her husband.

"That was Billy Wang down at the station . . . XMHA." Her voice was flat. "He knows I'm interested in politics, so he rang me. . . . Oh, my God! I can't believe it! Moscow and Berlin have signed a nonaggression pact. Stalin has concluded a treaty of friendship with the Nazis!"

"A pact with the devil!" Tommy was surprised, but he was not shocked. "What about the Japanese? They *are* the Nazis' allies, after all."

"Nothing about the Japs. Billy Wang would've told me. Tommy, maybe I've got hold of the wrong end of the stick. Maybe it's a Soviet plan to split the Germans and the Japanese."

"I doubt that," he observed. "Perhaps we should call your friends in the Soviet consulate. Ask if they're going to make common cause with the Japs."

"Tommy, you know that's impossible. The Soviets could never—"

"Just as impossible as a Soviet pact with the Nazis!"

"Joseph Stalin *must* have a good reason." Julia's faith was reviving. "A very good reason."

"I'm sure Comrade Stalin has a good reason—or thinks he has. But I also wonder: Is he right? And is it good for China?"

"If it's good for the Soviet Union, it's good for us," Julia affirmed. "Without the secure base of the Soviet Union, the progressive movement would be impotent. Therefore, the highest priority must be given to the welfare of the Soviet Union, which is the fatherland of workers everywhere."

"End quote, the dean," Tommy riposted savagely. "Julia, please spare me the half-baked rationalizations of Shanghai Labor University. How any decent Chinese could justify toadying to Moscow—"

"You can be as sarcastic as you want, Tommy." Her expression was set; her small square chin was thrust out; and her small competent hands were clenched in her lap. "But I'm absolutely certain of one thing."

"And what, my dear, might that be?"

She did not answer immediately. Most of their intense quarrels of recent months had arisen from her conviction that they should work directly for the Soviets. Tommy would not even respond to the feeler from the Soviet consulate general. He had, however, never before today addressed her with cold, contemptuous sarcasm.

"And what is that, Julie?"

Although his tone was less hostile, she still did not reply. Instead, she twirled a Chesterfield into her ivory holder and studied him through the smoke. He was still a very good-looking man. The two faint lines reaching from his cheekbones to his mouth made him appear scholarly, almost ascetic, but the faint wrinkles at the corners of his narrow eyes relieved that severity.

"I was just waiting for you to simmer down," she finally said. "You know very well that the Communist Party of the Soviet Union *must* put its own interests first."

"Thank you, Julie. I'm grateful, for the insight."

"Whatever forced Moscow to make this treaty," she said, "it's all the more reason for us to work with the Soviets directly. You've been stalling far too long. How much longer can you defy party discipline? How do—"

"The Communist Party of the Soviet Union is not *my* party!" He spoke through clenched teeth. "And it never will be."

"That's evading the issue, Tommy. And you know it. Moscow is our only hope. Moscow is China's only hope, the world's only hope for peace and progress. How can we refuse—"

"Never mind, Julie," he said wearily. "I do wish you'd take Althea and Persephone home till this blows over. Julie, you're out of your depth here. The game's getting too dangerous."

"Don't take that world-weary tone with me, Tommy!" Her voice rose uncontrollably. "Danger be damned! I'm not some little fool you've got to get out of the way as soon as serious matters come up. I've done as much as you have for the Apparatus, for the cause—maybe more. So I have the right to speak. I tell you again: we *must* work with the Soviets."

"You're like the animal trainer who picked the wrong end of the python." His tone of light amusement infuriated her. "He talked to the tail, stroked it affectionately until he was sure the python was devoted to him. But the front end threw its coils around him and crushed him."

"What is that rigmarole supposed to mean?"

"The Soviet consulate here in Shanghai is the tail of the python. The head is in Moscow. No use making friends with the tail. . . . Go home, woman! For everyone's sake, go home!"

"What an imagination! You should have been a novelist, not a doctor," she replied. "But you're not getting rid of me. Shanghai *is* my home. I'm staying. And I'll make contact with the Soviets without you, if necessary."

"Go home, woman!" he shouted: "Go home before you get us all killed with your foolishness! How I ever . . . why I ever thought you could . . ."

Despite his fury, Tommy's movements were tautly controlled. He tapped his pipe out, rose, and placed his foot on the first rung of the spiral staircase. Abruptly he wheeled to face her, scarlet splotches of rage glowing on his cheekbones. Tommy hurled his meerschaum pipe at the marble side table. The cream-white bowl split.

"I'm going to the hospital!" he shouted. "I don't know when I'll be back."

It was by far their worst fight. Tommy had always exercised steely control over his deeply emotional nature. If his self-control had finally snapped, something was fundamentally wrong between them. Whatever it was, it went far beyond their clashes over political differences.

Julia shivered. She was suddenly afraid, mortally afraid. Was it, she wondered fearfully, some failing of her own that had set off the explosion? Or was it some profound dissatisfaction within her husband? Was he resentful because she did not kowtow to him as Chinese wives—at least in public—kowtowed to Chinese husbands? Had she wounded his masculine pride by assuming what seemed quite natural—her own equality?

Despite the muggy late-August atmosphere, Julia drew her scarlet housecoat around her and retied the fringed sash. Unthinking, she lit a Chesterfield and unhappily unrolled her thoughts.

Tension was inherent in every relationship between female and male. Successful marriages kept that tension under control, and the most successful marriages utilized it. Her own marriage, however, incorporated another source of tension: her husband's innate conviction of racial and cultural superiority.

Any Chinese was bound to develop some defensive racial prejudice in Shanghai, where Chinese were treated by foreigners as inferiors, although Chinese *knew* themselves to be immeasurably superior. When Tommy and she disagreed, did his racial prejudice focus upon her? Did he then regard her as an uncultured foreign devil? Did he hate her because she came of the race that had repeatedly humiliated his country?

Unwontedly introspective, Julia assured herself that she had no racial bias. Anyway, it was not a Chinese she loved, but Tommy, who was a unique human being. Besides, he had never showed any physical distaste. Quite the contrary!

"The hell with it!" she exclaimed aloud. "The hell with the whole business—male arrogance and Chinese superiority! Forget about subtleties, my girl! He was a bad-tempered spoiled child tonight! Stubborn and infuriating!"

It was a typical Tommy touch: the roses began arriving at noon. He had known that, numb with emotion, she would take a pill and sleep late. She awoke shortly after the golden roses arrived. Her amah Lao Zee brought them with her breakfast tray to the bedroom that occupied half the fifth floor.

Lao Zee was clearly skeptical about the note Julia had written in her clumsy ideograms: *Do not wake me before twelve. Doctor had to go to hospital.* Lao Zee sniffed so expressively she might just as well have said aloud, "It's been years since Doctor was so junior he had to spend the night at the hospital. I know you two have got up to some nonsense. Spoiled babies!"

The golden roses came first, a dozen tied with a vermilion ribbon; and two hours later, two dozen roses the color of heart's blood, tied with a golden ribbon. Tommy himself arrived at four with three dozen white roses tied with vermilion and golden ribbons. Having sent the girls off to the hospitable Charlotte Haleevie, Julia was waiting in the enormous sitting room wearing lounging pyjamas. The yellow roses and the red roses were glowing in crystal vases when Tommy pushed the door open.

"Lao Zee told me I'd find you here," he said sheepishly. "How are you feeling?"

"Just fine!" she answered. "Tip-top! Couldn't be better!"

"All right, Julie." He offered her a rueful grin. "I take your point."

"How do you expect me to feel? Like the Queen of the May?"

"I'm very sorry. Whatever the merits of the . . . ah . . . argument, there was no excuse for losing my temper." He had evidently rehearsed his conciliatory speech. "It was a filthy trick!"

"I shouldn't have goaded you," she conceded. "I'm sorry, too, darling. Sorry I egged you on. But you did frighten me."

The stately gavotte of mutual apology and mutual forgiveness led to reconciliation. Yet they had agreed not on the issues but only on the futility of quarreling over those issues. Tommy remained obdurately opposed to their working for the Soviets—and was determined that Julia and the girls must leave the dangers of Shanghai. Julia remained implacably opposed to leaving—and was determined to collaborate with the Soviets. Nonetheless, they passionately sealed their reconciliation in the big bedroom.

"Maybe we ought to fight more often," Julia suggested dreamily. "It's such fun making up. Who'd think an old married couple like us . . ."

"Not so much of that *old* stuff, pet. That was a most satisfactory demonstration of youthful vigorous . . ."

"Who'd deny it, Doctor? Certainly not me."

"Julie, maybe we could get away for a couple of weeks. We could both do with a change of scenery."

"What a lovely idea. Where shall we go?"

In the end, they went nowhere because there was nowhere to go for a week or two from beleaguered Shanghai. North China, their normal summer resort, was dominated by the Japanese. Japan itself was obviously out, as were Japanese-occupied Korea and Taiwan. Resorts in the interior, like Kuling on Mount Lu, were barred by the disorder, as was even the river beach at Woosung only fifteen miles away. Manila, Hanoi, Singapore, and Bali all were too far away—and no cooler than Shanghai.

"Only Hong Kong's left," Julia observed disconsolately. "But nobody in his right mind would go to Hong Kong in August."

If they had been traveling, they might have been out of touch with the news at the tumultuous end of August 1939. After the signing of the Russo-German Treaty of Nonaggression, Europe was erupting. And the Howes were again arguing bitterly.

Tommy maintained that the cataclysmic events in Europe were a direct result of the Berlin-Moscow treaty. He contended that Adolf Hitler had marched into Poland only because Nazi Germany was certain of the Soviet Union's benevolent neutrality. Tommy did not share Julia's pleasure when the Soviet Red Army took over eastern Poland. And he was appalled by her delight when Britain and France reluctantly declared war on Germany on September 3, 1939.

"I hate seeing more people killed," Julia said. "But you can't make an omelette without breaking eggs. Stalin's strategy is brilliant. After the Nazis and the capitalists destroy each other, the Soviet Union will be the most powerful nation in the world. Then comes the triumph of the progressive cause! The nonaggression pact was a master stroke."

"Sometimes, pet, you sound rather like a propaganda play," Tommy replied perversely. "You know the Chinese tale about the man who sat on the hillside to watch the tigers fight. He got eaten! Anyway, you forgot the bloody Japs."

"The Soviet Union will take care of the Japs. When the time is right, Uncle Joe Stalin will join China—and together we'll devour Japan."

"Who will your Uncle Joe join, Chairman Mao or the Generalissimo? The way he's acting, it looks like the Gimo. If I were Mao Tse-tung, I'd be worried stiff."

The next day, a secret message from Yenan reached the Howes, having been delayed en route. The Chinese Communist Party had issued urgent instructions to the regulars of the Eighth Route Army, the guerrillas of the New Fourth Army, and the subversive Apparatus. All Communists were to virtually disregard the Japanese in order to concentrate on driving all Nationalist forces out of North China and the Yangtze Valley.

Little maggots of doubt gnawed at Tommy's faith in the Communist Party, but Julia's faith grew stronger. Because their emotional reconciliation had not reconciled their increasingly divergent political views, the friction between them again grew painful.

That same week, Tommy picked up the *China Weekly Review*, which declared in a cover headline: JAPANESE-AMERICAN WAR IMMINENT! That was the title of a book by a Japanese general that had just been published.

The jacket showed the United States Pacific Fleet being destroyed by torpedo planes and dive-bombers of the Imperial Japanese Navy.

Tommy was gravely pleased at the prospect of the United States' being compelled to become China's ally in battle. Julia was dismayed. Working and, occasionally, praying for a Japanese defeat, she had not believed her own country could become involved directly. Tension rose still higher in the house on Kiukiang Road.

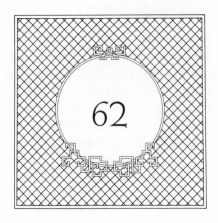

62

OCTOBER 3, 1939

"You can't write that," Harry Smythe commanded.

"You can't stop me," Richard Hollings rebutted. "But what's wrong with my lead?"

"Just about everything." The American read aloud from the typed sheet: " 'President Roosevelt's confidential envoy is committing the U.S. to hostilities with Japan by his aid to China—both legal and illegal.' Do you really want to ruin my mission—and my career?"

"Not to worry," Richard replied. "I could write instead: 'The United States is already at war with Japan in subtropical Kunming in China's extreme southwest. Predictions of inevitable conflict from Tokyo have been confirmed by events: Former American service aviators are training the Chinese Air Force—and, occasionally, flying combat missions themselves.' "

"Please, don't scare me that way, Dick. You've already taken years off my life." Smythe's face was actually pale under its constellation of freckles. "Do you want to give me a heart attack? Destroy all our work?"

"It's absolutely true—and I hate to give up a good story. But for you, chum . . ."

"I should've known you were kidding, old buddy."

"It's damned hard to do what you want me to," Richard pointed out. "Not without treading on your toes."

He looked across the grass airstrip of the Kunming Flying School from the thatch-shaded verandah of Claire Chennault's office and added, "The only way I can put across your message is by editorializing, like this: 'The United States will soon have to fight Japan openly because it is already fighting Japan covertly. The U.S. should, therefore, get in as many licks as it can before formal hostilities begin. Above all, it must supply China with the aircraft and aviators China desperately needs.' "

The American offered a grimace of grudging approval, and the Englishman reflected on the skill with which Harry and Emily had handled him. Even his own Emily, to whom he had two weeks earlier pledged eternal devotion—and meant every word.

Smythe played the bully, while Emily was sympathetic. That obvious variation on the tough-cop/friendly-cop routine alternately amused and irritated Richard.

He had, however, been proud when Emily took the controls of Claire Chennault's Beechcraft for the flight from Chungking to Kunming. He had also been terrified when the light aircraft rolled down the sandspit airstrip in the middle of the Yangtze River to take off between overhanging cliffs. But that was only for a minute.

Richard was still irritated by Harry Smythe's casual intimacy with Emily. Yet Harry was happily occupied with his "French teacher," a reed-slender young Vietnamienne who had traveled six hundred miles to Kunming on the rickety railway from Hanoi to collect debts owed her wine-merchant father.

In the three days since their arrival, Emily and Richard had found Kunming an extraordinary blend of nineteenth-century France and medieval China. The railway with the miniature locomotives, which Emily called Toonerville trolleys, was unoccupied China's only rail link to the world outside. The narrow-gauge tracks wound through mountain passes to Haiphong on the Gulf of Tonkin. In early October the ornate houseboats on Kunming Lake had already been deserted by the French families who took refuge there in the summer. The beige roofs and jalousied windows of French villas peeped through the peeling trunks of eucalyptus trees.

Under pepper trees dropping their green pellets, the streets were thronged with small dark men of the mountain tribes wearing faded blue turbans and their women wearing beaded black aprons over knee-length skirts. Pack mules that had struggled over the Himalayas with simple manufactured goods were loaded in the noisy marketplace with tin, salt, and opium. Rickshaws with tinkling bells wove among water buffalos and sway-backed swine. From time to time the "peanut whistles" of the miniature locomotives shrilled a lament for distant Europe.

"Helluva place for a flying school!" Claire Chennault had remarked while they were finishing their breakfast coffee on the verandah. "Right out of the Middle Ages. Wouldn't surprise me if Marco Polo's ghost turned up for flying lessons. He came right through Kunming, I hear. It's as far as we can get from Jap bombers. Sometimes it's not quite far enough."

When Chennault grinned, his seamed cheeks curved like supple old leather. After years of weathering in open cockpits, his face was the swarthy mask of a Pawnee medicine man. Yet he bowed with the grace of his Louisiana French ancestors and offered Emily his arm.

The incongruous pair then disappeared into his office: he heavy-set in U.S. Army suntans without insignia; she slim in the beige silk blouse and leaf-brown slacks that were her own wartime uniform. Both wore the Chinese Air Force's gold wings, and both worked for Mayling Chiang. The Missimo, as the Americans called her, had sent Emily to placate Claire Chennault, who was once again loudly discontented with the support given him in creating a new Chinese Air Force.

Mayling had happily agreed to Richard Hollings's accompanying Emily. Publicity was vital for the Air Force—and for Mayling. She had smiled, unbending with Emily as she could with no one else, and had added in her soft southern accent, "Now, Em, you're not to exhaust the gallant correspondent. Leave him some strength for his work. And for pity's sake, pretend you take Claire's threats seriously. . . . But only I can accept his resignation—and I *never* will."

Emily now understood that admonition. The man at the rattan-and-plywood desk before the aeronautical chart of South China was no longer the gallant gentleman who had found her an ashtray before taking his own chair. His lips curved downward; his iodine-black eyes were narrowed; and his head drooped sadly on his powerful neck.

"I'm afraid there's no other way!" His normally robust voice was reedy. *"This* time it's really too much for me, Madame Ou-yang. You see—"

"Emily," she interrupted, "was good enough five minutes ago."

"Emily, it's a sorry thing to lay my worries on the shoulders of a beautiful young lady."

"I'll bear up, Claire. I'm not all that young either, you know."

"To me, you are." His sorrowful expression contrasted so sharply with his gallantries that Emily smiled. "But if you don't take me seriously—"

"I take you very seriously. All Chinese do." Her emotion was sincere. "We are all in your debt."

"That makes it even harder, Emily." He paused histrionically. "You see, I've got to resign. When I'm hunting in the bayous, I'll be thinking of my friends in China. But Madame Chiang can easily find another broken-down old pursuit pilot to run this place."

"I have full powers . . . almost," Emily broke in. "I can meet any reasonable request. But I *cannot* accept your resignation. . . . Only Madame Chiang can. And she's going to be very busy for the next three months. So you may as well soldier on. Unless you're ready to desert."

A reluctant smile creased Chennault's thin lips, and his thick-set body twisted in its chair. Finally, he threw back his head and chortled.

"All right, Em, honey, you win," he conceded. "But you've really got to do something about tires. Otherwise, I *will* have to close up shop. Stones on the runways are cutting tires up something terrible."

"We've got two gross in the pipeline, Claire. We do read your memos."

"Another thing." His face darkened. "I've had to wash out seventy percent of the new class. Find me men with *no* flight training, instead of these dodos who think they're hot pilots. Also, for God's sake, find me good liaison officers. Not grafters and useless—"

"We can always shoot the worst cases, Claire. Make an example of—"

"What good does shooting do? Just find me better men. . . . Or else I'll—"

"You'll resign again, Claire?" She smiled sweetly. "You'll give up flying?"

When he failed to respond, Emily pressed her advantage: "Mayling told me about the hour you spent telling the Gimo exactly what was wrong with the Chinese Air Force. Chapter and verse, pointing out every dishonest, incompetent, or disloyal subordinate. And he said—"

". . . he knew everything I told him," Chennault interjected. "He knew even worse things about those men."

"So you asked why he didn't get rid of corrupt and inefficient officers. Even shoot them!"

Claire Chennault grinned and recalled: "He said the Chinese are the only people he's got to work with. If he got rid of everybody who was at fault, who would be left?"

"So there you are," she said. "We've got to do the best—"

"The hell we do!" His palm slapped the desk. "Not for the Air Force. We've got to get other people—preferably Americans."

"What's wrong with Chinese pilots?"

"I hate to tell a Chinese lady, Emily, but you asked for it. Your men could make great pilots—if we had all the time in the world to groom them for flight training. Educated young Chinese won't work with their hands. We've got to give them a feeling for machinery—the love and respect American kids develop for jalopies before they're fourteen. If the war lasts long enough, we'll produce great Chinese aviators. But we need real pursuit pilots right now to turn back the Japanese."

"I don't like it, Claire," Emily admitted. "In the long run, we've got to have a Chinese-manned Chinese Air Force. Even if we have to train ten-year-olds from scratch. But in the short run, I guess you're right. We need American pilots, not just American planes."

"I hate to end this love fest, Emily, but I promised Hollings I'd have another talk with him."

When Claire Chennault set out to be charming, he was overwhelming. No longer authoritarian, the backwoodsman gave way to the courtier.

Richard Hollings listened in silence. He had concluded that public opinion was as important in the new geopolitical warfare as were weapons, strategy, and courage. Heroes had always fought villains. Today, for the first time in history, the struggle between good and evil was reported to the entire world within minutes of battle's being joined. Public relations could, upon occasion, be even more important to a military commander than tactics.

Chennault was demonstrating his instinctive mastery of public relations. With almost Chinese finesse, he had not yet mentioned his near obsession: the absolute necessity to oppose modern Japanese aircraft with modern American aircraft. Instead, he was reminiscing about the early days of the flying school in Kunming.

"When the first two Curtiss Hawk squadrons landed here, more than half cracked up. I had to go all the way up to the Gimo for authority to give every so-called pilot a basic flight test—and to wash out the hopeless ones. . . . Luckily, they can find the field. Old Baldy over there's some landmark. Of course, for the Japs too."

He pointed at the hill range beyond the amethyst waters of Lake Kunming, where the houseboats danced. Landslides had ripped all the soil from the highest peak, and it shone rust-red in the morning sun.

"Long way from Nanking in 1937, when we knocked those bombers down, isn't it, son? The Japs are arrogant now. They even landed pursuit planes on Chengtu Airport, a hundred and sixty-five miles *west* of Chungking. The pilots jumped out and set fire to our planes on the ground, while the other Japs circled overhead to keep the ground defenses pinned down. Helluva thing, isn't it?"

Richard made a note and nodded.

"The Japs make three or four passes over a city before letting go their bombs. To show who owns the air. And to make the Chinese people feel resistance is just plain futile."

"No Chinese resistance at all, Colonel?"

"Well, son, you couldn't really call it resistance. Most of the good pilots are dead. And the rest . . ."

Emily looked pained, and Harry Smythe looked upward at the thatch roof over the verandah. Emily bit her lower lip. She hated Chennault's belittling Chinese pilots, even though that harsh judgment emphasized the need for greater American assistance.

"Well, things're looking up," Chennault observed. "My boys can now take off and land every time without splattering themselves over the landscape."

He looked eastward suspiciously. He cocked his head as if his eardrums, thickened by the roar of engines in open cockpits, had, nonetheless, picked up vibrations inaudible to the others. Finding nothing in the pale sky above the hills, he resumed: "It's also a matter of equipment. Our new pursuit, the P-40 *might* match the Jap's old Nate. I don't know about the Zero, their new pursuit. Anyway, tactics are going to be as important as planes."

He looked at the sky again and frowned. He squinted at the clouds and glanced toward the thatch-roofed operations shack.

"Something's up," he said. "I can't . . ."

A lanky Chinese lieutenant loped out of the operations shack. When he came into earshot, he called: *"Ching-pao,* sir. About forty bandits closing from the northeast. Estimate arrival in twenty-four minutes."

"Both squadrons to scramble in exactly fifteen minutes," Chennault commanded. "Mr. Adair and Mr. Alison to command. They know their orders: total radio silence."

The lieutenant saluted and trotted away. Chennault observed, "If they were all like young Lee we'd practically have the war won. Incidentally, Mr. Hollings, Adair and Alison are Chinese names for today. My American boys aren't supposed to fly combat. Now, in half an hour, we're going to be taking a hell of a pasting."

"The big ambush you were planning, Claire?" Harry Smythe asked.

"You can see the dummy planes on the field. With a little luck, we'll have us a turkey shoot."

"I've never heard of a reporter seeing an air battle from above," Harry said. "How does that strike you, Dick?"

Richard smiled at the preposterous thought. But Harry Smythe, the old Jenny pilot, was obviously eager to take him up.

"Fine with me, Harry." Chennault was offhand. "I want *all* aircraft in the air, including trainers. Only dummies on the field."

Richard forced himself to say cheerfully, "Then I suppose we'd better get going, Harry."

"I'm not your pilot, Dick. I'm not checked out on those Fleet trainers."

"Well, in that case . . ." Richard was disappointed—and relieved.

"I've got so many hours in that trainer," Emily volunteered, "I can fly it blindfold."

Richard knew he could not reject her offer. She was so touchy about masculine condescension that he could not even hesitate.

"Where's the aircraft, pilot?" he asked. "I'm ready whenever you are."

"You'd think somebody'd ask me," Claire Chennault said. "I'm only the fellow running the show. Take Baker Oboe-three, Emily. She's the only trainer with a radio. Go up to ten thousand feet and stay there. Don't descend and get mixed up in the dogfight. Also, total radio silence. Not a peep out of you!"

"The first time I ever kissed the pilot before a flight."

Richard laughed into the intercom microphone and craned his head around to smile at Emily. Framed by the leather flying helmet, her face was very small; it was further diminished by the round goggles and the big earphones. She pursed her lips in a kiss.

"Love you, my darling!" she whispered into her microphone, and added, "We'd better not talk, though. Might miss something on the radio."

The biplane spiraled toward ten thousand feet, the postage-stamp airdrome green beneath it. In the front seat of the tandem cockpit, Richard found his view obstructed by the lower wing. But he could sweep the horizon by swiveling his head.

Neither Emily nor Richard could acknowledge to the other a sudden desire to be back on the ground. He feared implying lack of confidence in her. She was determined to prove herself a dauntless aviatrix.

When the trainer passed through the first sprinkling of cloud at six thousand feet, both relaxed. Despite the proven efficiency of the ground warning network, they had both feared being attacked by the Japanese armada while they were climbing and exposed. The white-sun rondels on their wings looked like bull's eyes, and they were alone in the sky. The two squadrons of Hawk pursuit planes that had taken off just before them were invisible in the layers of cloud above ten thousand feet.

When the trainer leveled off in the lower fringe of those clouds, the cold pierced their flying suits. Although it seemed hours, Emily's gold Rolex read 11:32. Just nineteen minutes had passed since the young lieutenant reported the air-raid warning. The Japanese should be over the field in five minutes.

The Fleet trainer flew great circles through the hanging fringes of the clouds. With a minute to spare Emily pulled the joystick back, and the trainer climbed four hundred feet.

The enveloping clouds trailed clammy tendrils across their faces. Richard swore at the cloud cover. If he could not see the action, the danger they ran was criminally stupid. Before he could ask Emily to go lower, the clouds parted. Craning his head, he could see the airfield among the patchwork fields. Rifts continually opened and closed in the clouds beneath him.

Despite his close-fitting earphones, the trainer's air-cooled engine was so loud that he could hear nothing else. Suddenly, the trainer's fabric vibrated to the reverberation of many aircraft engines. A sprinkling of black specks appeared on the horizon and rapidly grew into a multitude of silver airplanes.

The Japanese drew close, implacable as time and apparently as invulnerable: forty-two twin-engined Mitsubishi bombers like heavy-bodied killer whales and twelve Nate pursuit planes as their pilot fish. The armada circled, contemptuous of the smoke puffs of the antiaircraft guns.

Bomb-bay doors hanging open beneath their bellies, the Mitsubishis made a pass across the field. But no bombs fell. The twelve Nates circled protectively above the bombers. But no Chinese warplanes appeared in the sky.

On the ground below, a Hawk darted from a sandbag revetment, streaked down the grass runway, and hurtled into the air. High above, Richard envisioned the derisive smiles of the Japanese aviators when the Chinese fled at treetop level.

That break for safety was Claire Chennault's final dramatic touch. The scenery was already in place. Imperfectly camouflaged Hawks were scattered among three Northrop bombers and a brand-new DC-3 transport. If he had not seen them on the ground, Richard would have been deceived by the bamboo-and-fabric dummies with oil-soaked rags and firecrackers stuffed into the cockpits behind their cellophane windshields.

In V formations of seven as precise as if guided by wires, the Mitsubishis thundered across the field. Bombs saturated the barracks and the hangars. Smoke rolled over the runway, and ground explosions flared.

The cloud banks above the armada were unbroken. When, Richard wondered in impotent anger, would Chennault call the Chinese pursuit planes down upon the raiders? When the wind whipped the ground smoke, Richard saw that some of the dummy airplanes were still intact.

The bombers swooped lower, ignoring the tracer bullets from the ground machine guns. The air-gunners sprayed the field, and a dummy pursuit plane erupted into flame. Firecrackers sparkled like machine guns, and viscous smoke mushroomed from the oil-soaked rags. Across the field, two more dummies exploded.

Richard was straining tensely against his shoulder harness, marveling at the patience of the Chinese pilots who were still circling above the clouds. How long could Chennault wait?

The Nates broke off their protective patrol and strafed the field. The bombers assembled in six V's for the homeward flight, and the escort formed up as if for a ceremonial fly-past.

"Now!" The word crackled in Richard's earphones. "Now, Tigers. Go get them! Good hunting!"

The blunt-nosed Hawks dived out of the clouds before that final "Good hunting!" Flashing past Richard, they looked like models: the pilots' leather-encased heads anonymous behind their windshields; the Nationalist white-sun rondels shining on their wings; their fixed undercarriages bulbous with wheel spats. The tails of the two leading Hawks were painted with three white stripes. Led by their American instructors, whose contracts forbade combat flying, twenty-four warplanes of the Chinese Air Force swooped on the enemy.

Still diving, the squadrons split into three-plane echelons in order to concentrate their firepower and provide mutual protection. Chennault disdained old-fashioned dogfights where individual aircraft challenged each other.

The Japanese were droning eastward, unaware of the Hawks. Streaking past the astonished Nates, the Hawks did not fire their machine guns until they were within a hundred yards of the bombers.

Within seconds the Mitsubishis began to blow up. The Chinese three-plane echelons twisted through the debris of burning bombers and, clawing for height, soared into the sun.

Their wings flashing, five bombers fell from the sky. Two spiraled, but three plunged straight into the ground. All but one exploded on impact. The fifth pilot managed by a near-miracle of airmanship to make a belly landing, and Richard saw black ants scurry away from the wreckage.

The clouds closed beneath the trainer, and the correspondent for the first time heard in his earphones the cries of Chinese pilots interspersed with terse commands in English. When the clouds parted again, the Japanese Nates had turned against their tormentors. Surprised and outnumbered, they undoubtedly regretted the ammunition and fuel they had expended attacking the ground targets. Three Nates abruptly broke eastward and fled, easily outdistancing the slower Hawks.

The remaining nine Nates evidently had just enough fuel to meet the Chinese head on. They did so, and after twenty seconds, three Hawks fluttered toward the ground.

The Japanese pursuits broke out of their loose formation in a challenge to individual combat—and the three-plane Chinese echelons chewed them up. Five Nates spun into the ground.

Their exhausts blue against the sunlight, the remaining Nates followed the retreating bombers they had failed to protect. The Hawks were still chewing at the bombers, but the chase broke off abruptly. Chennault's recall echoing in their earphones, the Chinese pilots hurled their aircraft into victory rolls over the smoking airfield.

The Fleet trainer still circled, and Richard assessed the fallen. He counted nineteen Mitsubishi bombers, as well as the five Nates and the three Hawks he had seen fall. Emily looked at her Rolex. It was 11:46, just thirteen minutes since the Japanese armada had appeared on the horizon.

"Congratulations!" Richard spoke into his microphone. "It's a splendid victory!"

"They'll have more confidence now," Emily said. "Our boys."

Her voice was flat, quite devoid of elation. He twisted in his seat to look at her. Behind her goggles, Emily's face was contorted as if she were weeping.

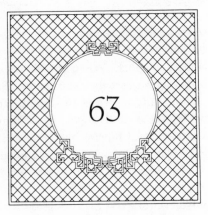

63

NOVEMBER 26, 1939

The rickshaw coolie's vein-knotted legs were bare in the dank chill of late November, when even beggars cocooned themselves in filthy garments. The coolie's feet were blue-white with the cold in rubber-soled sandals made from old tires. His footfalls threw up white puffs from the overnight snowfall. In the ten blocks from Kiukiang Road, Julia had with macabre fascination counted forty-six corpses under that thin white blanket. Shanghai had not lost its primeval power to surprise and, occasionally, revolt her.

She still disliked rickshaws, but she did not wish to arrive at Kai Ming College in the Lincoln Continental convertible that was her husband's latest toy. Such flamboyantly bourgeois camouflage was not really essential to his work for the Apparatus. Capitalist luxuries could, moreover, undermine one's values. Since Tommy had grown up in luxury, he should be immune to corruption. Nonetheless, she was worried about him.

Since the defection of his mentor Chang Kuo-tao, Tommy's ardor for the Communist cause had diminished perceptibly. He still served the Apparatus, but he had major reservations about the policies of the Communist Party.

The coolie's rubber-tread soles braked the rickshaw before an enormous mansion. The four stories visible above the brown brick wall were plastered with ideograms declaring it severally: a college, a middle school, a kindergarten, a clinic, and an orphanage. Fifty colleges, two hundred middle schools, and a thousand primary schools were now operating in the Settlement and Frenchtown, for refugees from China had doubled the concessions' population. Joshua Haleevie believed that more than three million human beings were now crammed into those eleven square miles.

Marveling at the number of people who must live in that one building, Julia absently counted out seven Mex, about two dollars American. The coolie instinctively lifted his hand to tug at her sleeve. Thinking better of it, he stuffed the coins into his waistband and fled. The tail of the yellow rickshaw flicked around the corner as if pursued by ten thousand demons.

The coolie's train of thought was obvious: If not a mistake, the munificent payment must be blood money, atonement for the luxury she enjoyed amid misery. If it was a mistake, she must be so wealthy she would never miss it. And if it was conscience money, it would be no kindness to return it.

Following the arrow on the sign reading *Kai Ming College, President's Office,* Julia idly counted twenty-four windows in each of the five stories of the left wing alone. The mansion must possess more than sixty bedrooms, as well as many reception rooms. She was glad of her utilitarian wartime garb: padded jacket, woollen slacks, comfortable low heels, and a bright yellow oilskin rainhat. Damp would have penetrated every cranny of the old-fashioned building. Central heating—or more than two bathrooms for all those bedrooms—would be considered spendthrift luxury.

Most Shanghai bourgeois believed that money spent on display was money well spent. But central heating and bathrooms were not seen from the outside. An ostentatious show attracted business by demonstrating how good business already was. Unobtrusive comforts would, if revealed by chance, demonstrate reckless self-indulgence and thus drive customers away.

Her husband had enunciated that social theory some time ago. The witty, high-spirited Tommy she married had laughed loudest at the foibles of his countrymen and had smiled at the foibles of foreigners. Nowadays, he sneered at the foibles of foreigners and lamented the foibles of his countrymen. The war had made him so Chinese she could no longer anticipate his reactions. When she might have expected him to laugh, he was grave; when she might have expected concern, he laughed bitterly.

Their quarrel about her teaching at Kai Ming College showed how volatile he was. Worried that she might be bored, he had in the past encouraged her to work. Yet he had exploded when she told him two days earlier she was going back to teaching. He had warned she was imperiling their cover because the college president, a former student of hers at Shanghai Labor University, was a secret Communist activist on the educational battlefront.

Tommy was accustomed to finding her at home whenever his erratic professional schedule allowed him a moment of leisure. Unlike the frivolous Chinese wives he admired nowadays, Julia could not devote her days to gossip, mah-jongg, beauty parlors, and entertaining. She had finally decided she must look to her own needs, since she could not understand his new needs.

Guided by the signs, Julia climbed a broad staircase with a dust-furred banister. The high ceilings and the ornate plaster moldings were all for display. So were the enormous bedrooms visible through open doors, with their three-color marble fireplaces, gilt mirrors, and ornamental gas jets.

On the third floor, she found herself in a jam-packed tenement. The corridor was littered with the paraphernalia of domesticity. Pots, pans, kettles, and tureens were strewn around terra cotta braziers. Bundles of kindling lay beside heaps of vegetables; tubs of washing nudged chamberpots; and two sandlewood coffins lay along the wall. Through half-open doors Julia heard the manic clatter of mah-jongg tiles and the ritual cries of the men playing the game.

Women froze over corrugated-wood washboards to stare at the foreign woman with the jaunty yellow rainhat. Babies gaped—babies snug in baskets, babies slung on their mothers' backs, and babies fighting pet dogs for scraps. Young boys and girls looked up from slates on which they were painstakingly inscribing ideograms. Two elderly men playing Chinese chess did not lift their eyes, but their liver-spotted hands were motionless. There were only two young men. Shifting sacks of coal, they were for an instant as still as a statue symbolizing virtuous labor.

On the fourth floor the arrow pointed down the corridor. When Julia opened the door of the office, a neat woman in a padded *cheongsam* looked up from her desk.

"Mrs. Howe? I'm very sorry. The president was called away suddenly. He hopes you'll go ahead with your class in half an hour."

Julia accepted a cup of tea and glanced at her watch. The big brass doorknob turned slowly, and the door opened to admit a short man in a padded long-gown. He dragged his left leg, and his features were obscured by the brim of his black fedora. Seeing Julia, he turned and slipped out of the office.

If he was part of the Apparatus, his fear at seeing her foreign face was easily understandable. Although safer in the foreign concessions of

Shanghai than anywhere else outside their own rural bases, Communists were still persecuted by the foreign police. The secretary did not comment upon the man's fleeting appearance, and Julia could not question her.

Julia was nagged by a sense of familiarity. Had those large eyes flickered in recognition? The set of the shoulders was also hauntingly familiar. The man, she realized with a cold thrill, was rather like Little Pow. But Little Pow had been dead for more than a decade. If he were alive, he would certainly have been in touch with Tommy and her.

Casting off the past, she found the classroom. The smell of chalk dust recalled to Julia her happy days at Shanghai Labor University, as did the kerosene heater she suspected was a concession to foreign frailty. The blackboard on the wall awaited the diagrams illustrating the complexities and perplexities of English grammar that the literal-minded Chinese students loved.

Julia realized how much she had missed the interchanges with eager young minds. The Apparatus had instructed her to play the corrupt social butterfly, but she had never felt comfortable in that role. She was delighted that the Apparatus now permitted her to teach again.

A new class was, however, taxing. All that potential still unplumbed. She decided to gauge the class's ability by a dictation exercise followed by discussion. She had translated a passage from the Communist *New China Daily*, which was published in Nationalist Chungking because the two rival groups were still nominally joined in the United Front Against Japan.

"Certain divisive tendencies have recently become apparent within the Nationalist-Communist United Front for the anti-Japanese war of resistance," she read aloud slowly. "Rogue Nationalist elements have repeatedly attacked elements of the New Fourth Army, the Communists' guerrilla forces in enemy-occupied areas. A particularly vicious attack was launched by infantry and secret Special Agents on November 11, 1939. More than two hundred wounded soldiers and their dependents were brutally slaughtered and . . ."

Julia's mind strayed. Actually, the current wave of fighting had begun a year earlier, when Communist units attacked and dispersed a Nationalist regiment. Although the Communist Party had explained that the Nationalist unit was secretly collaborating with the Japanese, the politically unsophisticated found it hard to understand why the Eighth Route Army had struck first. Since then, clashes had usually been initiated by the alert Communist guerrillas to forestall attacks. Occasionally, however, the treacherous Nationalists had struck first.

After a flurry of questions, the class earnestly corrected its transcriptions. Lulled by the warmth of the kerosene heater, Julia almost dozed off.

Through the crack in the sliding doors that divided the improvised classroom from its neighbor she heard an assured female voice. Bursts of English were interspersed with a foreign language that was at once guttural and melodious.

Dismissing that minor mystery, Julia began the class discussion. Pretty Miss Lee, who spoke English best, obviously came from a well-to-do family. Her hair was permanent-waved, and her long nails glistened scarlet. Her shaggy camel's-hair coat with the mink collar was spread open on her chair to show off her saucy figure in an opulent orange silk *cheongsam*. Her flimsy pumps and sheer silk stockings displayed neat ankles.

Julia's frivolous side warmed to the vain Miss Lee. She was not, however, amused when the young lady declared pertly that she had understood every word of the dictation, but not its meaning.

"It doesn't make sense, Mrs. Howe," Miss Lee insisted. "If the Communists started the fighting, it must be their fault."

A rather plain Miss Chang replied: "You've got every right to protect yourself if you know I'm planning to steal from you. If you don't, you're helping me commit a crime. There's an English expression . . ."

"Acting as an accessory," the delighted Julia supplied.

"Thank you, Mrs. Howe," Miss Chang continued smoothly. "You are acting as an accessory. So, you see, it is your own duty to stand up to me. Even using force to stop me stealing . . ."

"What are the police for?" Miss Lee asked.

"But no police are higher than the political parties," a young man said. "Who would stop this crime if Eighth Route Army does not."

Pleased with the homely analogy about stopping a thief, Julia beamed on Miss Chang, who was the precise opposite of the coiffed, curled, and cosseted Miss Lee. Her hair was plaited in two plump braids tied with red ribbons, and she wore a padded blue cotton long-gown on top of another long-gown. Against the chill of the old mansion, she also wore a bulky cardigan, thick lisle stockings, and bedroom slippers with pink pompoms.

The reactionary Miss Lee was undeniably more attractive than the roly-poly rag doll with the flat unpainted face that was the progressive Miss Chang. Julia reproached herself for that thought. Not only Tommy but she herself was still tainted by bourgeois values.

Leaving the classroom, Julia saw another woman who was even less concerned with wartime austerity than the self-obsessed Miss Lee. The woman was quite tall, and her black hair was caught in a chignon. She wore a tailored suit of stiff yellow silk. The jacket flared over her hips, while the tight skirt tapered its hem to a few inches below her knees. The seams of her gossamer silk stockings emphasized sleek calves and ankles. Flung negligently over her arm was a sable coat.

The fashion plate turned, and Julia smiled at her own obtuseness. Only Elizaveta Alexandrovna Yavalenka possessed the height, the wealth, and the daring to wear that extravagant costume. She had obviously been teaching Russian, the mysterious language on the other side of the sliding doors.

"Julie, darling, I've been waiting for ages." Elizaveta embraced her. "Do you want a ride or is the dashing Tommy picking you up?"

The light snowfall that swirled on the streets in the morning had melted by late afternoon, and the dead bodies that defiled the streets in the morning had been carted to a common grave by the corpse collection service. The early dusk created caves of darkness beneath the walls of Jessfield Road, and Julia's imagination tenanted them with men and women suffering torture, disease, and starvation. She still loved Shanghai deeply. But she now loved Shanghai for the suffering it endured, rather than for its spurious glamor.

Heads turned when Elizaveta's black Hispano-Suiza rolled east on Bubbling Well Road. The twenty-two-foot-long limousine with the enormous headlights was conspicuous even in a city where the aging Donald Howe still painted his Rolls-Royce emerald-green.

Having that morning endured the discomfort of a rickshaw, Julia settled with a sigh into the luxurious automobile. She ran her fingertips over the glove-leather upholstery and inhaled the fragrance of the hot-house roses in the cut-crystal vases. She was dedicated, she told herself, but she was not so fanatical as to hate comfort.

"You never expected to see *me* at Kai Ming College, did you?" Elizaveta asked complacently. "It's a long way from Kiangse Road!"

"Liz, dear, you never lose your ability to surprise me. Particularly when you're being virtuous."

"It's all Joshua's idea. He felt in his own clever way that I was in danger of becoming boring. Worse, in danger of boring myself. He decided that only good deeds could save me. Since the orphanage alone wouldn't do the trick, I volunteered to teach a little Russian. My students are ragged, but they're not as mucky as the babies."

Julia chuckled at the absurdity of her old friend's protestations and observed lightly, "Liz, honey, you're getting just like Joshua. You two will never convince me that you do good deeds only for selfish reasons. By the way, how is he? It's been ages since I saw him."

"He hasn't come back to me—not entirely. But he spends a lot more time with me now."

"I asked about Josh, not you, darling." Julia wondered why she was being so persistently—if lightly—malicious. "Well, I suppose it comes to much the same thing. How does he manage with Charlotte, if it's all right to ask?"

"All right to ask? I'd be astonished if you didn't, my dear. . . . He manages by telling the truth when his . . . his wife . . . is in town. That, fortunately, isn't very often. Russian peasants revolted against absentee landlords, which my family never were. Charlotte is rarely in Shanghai, and Joshua has revolted against an absentee wife."

"Whom he drove away in the first place, Liz. But, since you're in a mood to confide, tell me why you would never marry Joshua. For a time, we all hoped—"

"It wouldn't have worked, Julie. He's not . . . I'm not . . . the sort for formal obligations. This way, he'll cling to me. . . . Joshua's like me. He gets bored very easily. The worst thing would have been children, though sometimes . . ."

Julia made an understanding noise.

"Any child of ours would've been a mess: Joshua's fits of depression, almost melancholia, and my black moods, my Slavic gloom. What a heritage for an innocent baby! Joshua's worse now, you know."

"Why, Liz?"

"Because he loves the Settlement, the ideal of government by all nationalities. I think he loves it even more than he loves me. Without the Settlement, he'd be another stateless Jew, although a wealthy, charming, and able Jew. The last few months he's just about despaired."

"Why just now? Things have been bad for years."

"Lucifer, Julie. The wretched opportunist Dick Hollings nicknamed Lucifer long ago when he was the Generalissimo's chief rival. Lucifer collaborated with the Communists, and now he's collaborating with the Japanese."

"And he'll be formally heading up a Jap puppet government in a couple of months," Julie agreed. "He's already doing the job without the title. But everybody knows he's a has-been."

"Darling Julie, everybody knows Lucifer is a has-been—except the Japanese and those Chinese who want a quiet life at any price."

"You're a chameleon, Liz, always changing color. Not so long ago you were rooting for the Japs against the Bolsheviks. Then General Zhukov whips the Japs—and, suddenly, you're a Russian patriot. Now, you sound as if you hate the Japs. Bit of a quick change artist, aren't you?"

"I have had to be in my . . . ah . . . profession, darling." Elizaveta's face was a white oval in the dim interior of the limousine. "But just look at the international city Joshua loves. Not far from Kai Ming College, Lucifer has his little secret police headquarters. You've heard what goes on at number 76 Jessfield Road: kidnapping, torture, extortion, murder. Almost *anything* you can imagine to break the will of Chinese patriots who want to hold out against the Japs. Anything to force them to join Lucifer and work with the Japs. Joshua's model settlement has become a nest of stinging vipers—all under the cloak of extraterritoriality."

"Also the Fascists . . . that Italian with the dagger," Julia mused. "And the disgusting Nazis. The German-Jewish refugees thought they were safe here, but they are intimidated, slandered, and beaten up. Shanghai's the center of Nazi propaganda and espionage for the Orient. . . . Shanghai's becoming a cesspool. I know exactly how Joshua feels."

"I'm not sure you do, Julie. None of us can know *exactly* what it's like for Joshua. His wonderful city dying, already rotting . . . What's that fuss up ahead?"

Julia stared in surprise at the crowd blocking the intersection leading to the Laoza police station, where the May Thirtieth Incident had occurred in 1925. Despite the protests of her White Russian bodyguard, Elizaveta ordered the chauffeur to stop. Impelled by curiosity as well as her new commitment to civic responsibility, she was determined to learn why so many pedestrians were staring at the lamppost that lit the intersection.

The two women plunged into the crowd behind the uniformed bodyguard, who flourished a long flashlight, which was also a formidable weapon. On the curb, a Chinese man was lying just inside the edge of the cone of light cast by the lamp, so that they could see only his head. His chubby cheeks and brilliantined hair showed that he was no street vagabond.

The bodyguard shone his flashlight on the man—and Julia's fingernails dug into Elizaveta's palm. The man's head, neatly severed at the neck, was propped against the lamppost. Blood was still trickling onto the curbstone.

"Look!" A woman exclaimed in broad Shanghainese. "Head just cut! Look! See drops of sweat on forehead."

Julia forced herself to move forward step by step. She could not just stand and gape like the foreign men and women in evening dress who had joined the crowd. Unlike those parasites, she was a living part of tortured Shanghai.

Her neck rigid with strain, Julia forced herself to look at the grisly spectacle. She knew the young Chinese, who had evidently been killed on the spot a few minutes earlier. He was a reporter and occasional columnist for the respected Shanghai *Shun Pao,* the oldest newspaper in China. Recoiling from his paralyzed grimace, her eyes moved to the crude ideograms on the yellow paper pasted to the lamppost:

Warning to all editors: This just punishment, meted out by angry patriots, will befall all who sabotage the formation of the government that will make honorable terms of peace with the Japanese Empire and restore prosperity. This man was a traitor to China and a lackey of the warmongering usurper government of Chiang Kai-shek. He dared to write against the salvation of the country. Be warned by his fate!

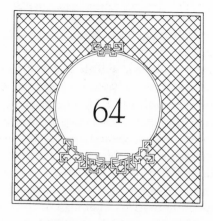

Richard Hollings feared a cool reception on the afternoon of December 20, 1939, when he took up the standing invitation to all foreign correspondents to Commissar Chou En-lai's weekly reception, which offered tea, whisky, and propaganda. He feared the Communists would be displeased by his close ties to the Nationalists. Since it was the best-informed group in Chungking, Yenan's delegation to the Central Government undoubtedly knew about his association with not only Emily but also Harry Smythe and Claire Chennault. He had, he reflected as his rickshaw jolted through potholes, been unwise. He should not have written so enthusiastically about the war in the air and the campaign to secure American planes and pilots. The Communists would, obviously, not wish the Nationalists to create a powerful air force; that weapon was as likely to be used against them as against the Japanese.

The correspondent was particularly apprehensive about meeting his host again. As chief of Yenan's delegation to Chungking and deputy minister of the all-powerful National Military Council, Chou En-lai ranked first among the many Communists—open and secret—who held offices in the Central Government. Richard had known him since the mid-1920s in Shanghai. He had reported the commissar's miraculous escape from Generalissimo Chiang Kai-shek's countercoup in 1927, and they had conversed amiably during his stay in Yenan. Nonetheless, Richard found the volatile Communist leader slightly intimidating. He could never quite tell what Chou En-lai was thinking.

He was, however, greeted like a long-unseen disciple. Beaming goodwill, the commissar trotted out his makeshift English to recall their brief meetings in Yenan.

"When," he asked jocularly, "will the Generalissimo let you come back and see us? We are very pleased to greet you, always."

"Any time you wish, Minister," Richard replied. "I'm longing to see all my good friends. That is . . . I hope we're still good friends."

"Dear Dickie, we are such great friends," Chou En-lai affirmed. "Chairman Mao sends his chin-chins."

Chin-chins indeed! Richard was startled by that strange China Coast term meaning "regards." He was bemused by a vision of the sometimes genial—but always authoritarian—chairman of the Communist Party, Mao Tse-tung, smiling coyly and wiggling his fingers in greeting like a Westernized dandy in Frenchtown. Anyone less likely to send chin-chins than Mao Tse-tung was hard to imagine—unless, perhaps, it was Chiang Kai-shek.

Richard was nonetheless delighted to learn that he stood well with the autocratic Chairman Mao. Their last conversation had ended with a warning not to reveal that Soviet airplanes landed at Yenan—in violation of agreements between Chiang Kai-shek and Joseph Stalin. Although he had naturally not done so, he remembered Mao Tse-tung with some trepidation.

"Please present my respects to the chairman." Richard was calculatingly indiscreet. "I'm delighted by your welcome but, I must confess, also a little surprised. Candidly, I was afraid you'd think I was too close to the Generalissimo's group."

"Because of the charming Madame Ou-yang?" Chou En-lai reverted smoothly to the services of his Cambridge-educated interpreter. "My dear chap, that's your affair. We Communists don't apply outmoded bourgeois moral standards to the relations between men and women. Marriage is no more than a bourgeois contract to preserve private property. And property is theft!"

"You're refreshingly straightforward as always, Minister."

"If that's my reputation . . ."Chou En-lai laughed. "I might as well live up to it."

Affectionately grasping the correspondent's elbow, the commissar led him toward a window niche. They avoided the huddle of newspapermen, all of whom were drinking scotch or bourbon rather than tea.

"We like your candor and your accuracy," Chou En-lai declared. "If we had written your book, we could have avoided some errors. We would also have omitted some criticism. And that might have been a mistake. All in all, we are well pleased by *Red Star and Yellow Earth.*"

Flustered by so much praise, Richard said: "I haven't seen the finished book myself. . . . *Red Star and Yellow Earth?* That must be a mistake. The title is *White Sun, Red Star, and Yellow Earth.*"

"I haven't seen the book, Dickie," Chou En-lai said, twinkling. "But I have seen a fifty-page summary. Most detailed. I assure you it's called *Red Star and Yellow Earth.* A better title . . . forward-looking."

"On second thoughts I do like the new title better. More punch! But they might've told me."

"I *am* telling you, Dickie. I'm also telling you we won't hold your gravest error against you. Chairman Mao was quite annoyed, but I talked him around. . . . We told you over and over again that we were Communists, true Marxist-Leninists. Yet—"

"I said almost as much in the book."

"But not quite. You almost convinced *me* that we are not Marxist-Leninists at all." From anyone less authoritative, Chou En-lai's laugh would have been a giggle. "So, it appears that we are agrarian reformers. At worst, Socialists, good-hearted Social-Democrats. Mao Tse-tung was livid at that insult. He felt it was the same as accusing him of bourgeois sentimentality . . . lack of revolutionary ruthlessness. But he finally agreed that, for the time being, that is just the image we require. I tell you this off-the-record."

"I appreciate your candor, Minister. You know it sounds as if someone did a lot of editing behind my back."

"Not to worry, old chap," Chou En-lai said. "I can assure you that your editor in New York hardly touched a word. All your own work, I'm pleased to report."

When Gregory Hardin approached, Richard thanked his host and left the party. He was puzzled by Chou En-lai's enthusiastic reaction to his book. He truly believed that his reportage had been even-handed—by no means a hymn of praise to the Communist regime.

Waiting for a rickshaw, Richard recalled a strange incident two days earlier. He had met Tommy Howe's old friend Chang Kuo-tao in the compound of the Ministry of Information. The big Communist, with whom he had spent so many hours in Yenan, had ignored his outstretched hand and looked through him. The renegade must have had access to the report on *Red Star and Yellow Earth*—and must now hate its author for failing to air his personal grievances and his malicious allegations against Chairman Mao.

That omission had proved wise. *Former* Chairman Chang Kuo-tao of the Border Region Government was no longer even a minor star in the constellation of power. The red star of Chairman Mao Tse-tung, however, now shone almost as bright as the white sun of Chiang Kai-shek, which it might in time eclipse.

But could Chang Kuo-tao have seen the confidential summary Chou En-lai mentioned? Yet all things were possible in Chungking, even amicable private communication between former intimates who castigated each other in public.

Could Emily, too, have learned of the report? Again, anything was possible, though in this case it was most unlikely. He could, of course, explain the awkward business of the altered title. She too knew at first hand the caprices of editors and publishers.

Chungking was a thousand miles up the meandering Yangtze River from Shanghai. As 1939 drew to a close, the retreating Chinese had worn down the Japanese armies, imposing a near-stalemate. The Nationalists and Communists were more interested in fighting each other than in fighting the Japanese. Chungking was, nonetheless, the capital of a nominally united Republic of China. Not only Chou En-lai but the Christian General and other warlords worked in ostensible amity with the Generalissimo. Yet Chungking remained a backwater.

The great events were occurring elsewhere, chiefly in Europe. Long before this day in late December of 1939, the Nazis had crushed Polish resistance. The Soviets had, moreover, reoccupied eastern Poland, which had once belonged to the czars.

At the Ikra, Elizaveta Alexandrovna Yavalenka toasted "the reclamation of the sacred soil of the Russian Motherland," despite the derision of her lover, Joshua. In the six-story house on Kiukiang Road, Julia Howe rejoiced at "the strengthening of the workers' fatherland, the heartland of peace and democracy," despite the skepticism of her husband, Tommy.

At the press hostel in Chungking, Richard Hollings restively checked his pigeonhole for messages. The world's attention was focused on Europe, although hardly twenty shots a day were fired on the stalemated western front. As the first Christmas of World War II approached, a Paris seething with gaiety called it *drôle de guerre*, a joke of a war. Neutral Americans read about the "phoney war." What little attention they could spare from their own affairs was directed toward Europe rather than Asia.

Richard was anxious to move on to that big story. In Europe, he could raise higher the edifice of his new fame. He was no longer a mere foreign correspondent but an authority on world affairs—or he would be, just as soon as *Red Star and Yellow Earth* was published in mid-February 1940.

Besides, it might be wise for him to be away from Chungking when
Red Star came out. He accordingly decided to leave China immediately
after New Year's.

Because Emily sentimentally treasured her memories of their New
Year's Eves together in Shanghai, he had promised they would celebrate
the arrival of 1940 with all the gaiety Chungking could offer. But that
was the limit of his stay in China.

He had not yet told her he was leaving. Yet she would know that he
could not linger in a backwater like Chungking while the world awaited
his dispatches from the major fronts. He could probably wangle a seat
to Calcutta on China National Aviation Corporation, though he would
prefer going to Hong Kong. The night flight to the Crown Colony over
territory tenuously occupied by the Japanese was not as hazardous as
the flight to India over the white-fanged Himalayas, which pilots called
the Hump.

Although eager for his tryst with fame elsewhere, Richard found
himself reluctant to depart. Having persuaded his joint employers that
he should go, he did not want to go. Of course he hated to leave Emily.
When he got back to England, he would set in motion his divorce from
Fiona. And the sooner he left, the sooner he could return a free man.
He could not in honor formally propose marriage to Emily until he was
free of Fiona.

Richard realized with some surprise how attached he was to China.
He had derided the devotion of old hands to the country. China was to
him no longer just a fascinating political and social laboratory—or a
springboard to fame. Sensitive to the English language even after two
decades in journalism, Richard shuddered at that mixed metaphor. Yet
China had got her claws into him. Breaking free would be painful.

Emily's reaction to *Red Star* worried him. She had obviously not yet
learned of the new title nor seen a summary of the contents; she was
too straightforward to remain silent if she had. However, she had not
said another word about the book after extracting his promise to give
her the first copy he received.

The pert youth who distributed the messages in the press hostel
tugged at Richard's sleeve and pressed the familiar blue-and-white
envelope of the Chinese Government Radio Administration into his
hand. Opening the cablegram, he read, first with dismay, then with
elation: NATBROCAST CONCURS BEST YOU REMAIN CHINA TILL MARCH STOP TERRIFIC
JOINT EUROPEAN ASSIGNMENT THEN AVAILABLE BEST REGARDS DAVIDSON GLOBE

He wanted to tell Emily immediately, but she did not like him to
telephone when she was with Mayling. In any event, the telephones

were out again. But he had to tell someone. From the bar he heard Jimmy Wei's assertively American accent. Assuming an expression of sardonic amusement, Richard sauntered toward the bar.

A number of correspondents were gathered around the irrepressible Jimmy Wei. Despite their derisive remarks, he stood unperturbed and natty in a pin-striped blue suit. He held aloft one of the undersized, thin-shelled eggs produced by Chungking's long-legged, yellow hens.

"You'll never do it, Jimmy," a Dutch photographer jeered.

"Impossible, my good chap," contributed the Reuters correspondent, a Chinese who was fearfully Anglicized. "No matter what you say."

"My dear old thing," Jimmy said, "the day before the winter solstice is the only day it's sure. That's tomorrow, but we can give it a go today. Pity you don't know our ancient Chinese lore."

Jimmy Wei was inspired by the foul gin labeled Chungking D., which the correspondents called Chungking Death. Yet he managed to be assertive without being offensive.

"Any more bets the egg won't stand on its small end? Step up, gents, and be relieved of your dough."

The only bettors were a visiting French correspondent and an Irishman noted for his shifting journalistic affiliations and his constant thirst. The others knew Jimmy too well.

He held the egg lightly between the extended fingers of both hands, intoned an ancient incantation, and placed the egg on the bar.

The small egg wobbled for a few seconds, teetered, and almost fell over. Miraculously, it recovered. After five tense seconds, the egg stood firmly on its small end.

Someone applauded, and others joined him. The Irishman protested, "Fraud!" But he was silenced by scornful stares. And the egg stood complacently on the table.

"Fifty dollars says you can't do it again with *my* egg," the Dutchman proposed.

Jimmy appeared nonplussed. His dark monkey-face frowned, and he shrugged elaborately.

The incantation was even more protracted, and the transfer from his fingertips even more precarious. Yet the second egg soon stood on the bar beside the first, hardly trembling at all.

"Wait'll I get my box," the photographer demanded. "Damned odd business. Worth a picture."

The next hour passed in the most innocent entertainment the press hostel had ever seen. Jimmy Wei stood eggs on tables, on chairs, on stairs, counters, and shelves. Driven outside by the photographers' need for better light, he stood eggs on the verandah, the paving stones around the banana plants, and, briefly, the hostel manager's bald spot.

Finally, seventy-eight eggs were standing on their small ends in defiance of Newtonian physics. The hostel manager then instructed his waiters to recover tomorrow's breakfast.

"All in ca—ca—cahoots!" the Irishman protested. "They'll not be letting us have a look at them eggs."

Despite such skepticism, which Jimmy disdained to refute, the great egg-stand became a major story abroad. Jaded correspondents were delighted after months of cables advising "briefest coverage." *Life* magazine's Christmas issue featured a full-page picture of an enigmatically smiling Jimmy Wei surrounded by a gross of standing eggs.

Even Richard Hollings, who felt he was not paid to cover such frivolous—and probably fraudulent—nonsense, was dragooned by peremptory cables from NBC. With good grace, he produced an extremely funny seven-minutes of mock scholarship, which strayed from flamboyant Jimmy Wei's psychology to the alteration in gravity in Szechwan at the winter solstice.

Jimmy steadfastly refused to acknowledge—much less reveal—any trick. He would only repeat: "Ancient Chinese wisdom, gentlemen. Not comprehensible by barbarians. Also the China story of the year."

He was absolutely right. Richard was chastened, although he still did not like covering trivia like the great egg-stand. He was just past forty and finally established. An advance review of *Red Star and Yellow Earth* in *Publishers Weekly* had hailed him as "a diamond in the crown of American journalism—one of our five most distinguished foreign correspondents."

Boni and Liveright, his American publishers, had airmailed Richard the clipping along with a letter that did not allude to their arbitrary alteration of his book's original title. Almost rhapsodic over the impetus given to *Red Star* by the Book-of-the-Month Club, as well as widespread newspaper serialization, the letter concluded: "Hollywood is interested. But, candidly, unless progressive elements on the Coast swing all their influence behind it, I'm afraid we haven't got a Chinaman's chance of a movie. Sorry, I couldn't resist that."

Richard replied: "I am delighted at bringing to world attention the epochal changes in China—the new society rising from the ashes of mankind's oldest culture. I am humbled by all those printers printing, reviewers reviewing, and, above all, readers reading."

The news from England was almost as good. The publisher Victor Gollancz had told Richard of triumphs in a letter carried by a second secretary joining the British embassy in Chungking. Gollancz's own Left Book Club, whose books were distinguished by yellow dust-jackets with bright red lettering, had naturally snapped up *Red Star and Yellow Earth*. The Book Society had somewhat warily expressed interest, and there was a prospect of serialization in the *Manchester Guardian*. *The Times* had asked Richard for regular columns in the future—and had informed him that it was "planning a good notice." That was the equivalent of an American newspaper's cabling: "Running rave review."

Fearing Emily's reaction to the new title, Richard did not immediately share those triumphs with her. But he decided during the last week of December that he could no longer conceal the alteration from her. Accordingly, he showed her the letters from New York and London with the prefatory remark "I'm afraid they changed the title, Em. They're calling it *Red Star and Yellow Earth*."

"I know what editors are like, darling," she responded almost negligently. "Don't worry about it as far as I'm concerned. But let's not kid ourselves. It's going to be embarrassing explaining what happened to the Nationalists' white sun. Of course it doesn't make any difference to me . . . to us. I won't let it!"

Choosing not to hear the undertone of desperation in that brave assertion, Richard wondered why he had been reticent about the new title. Emily was realistic about the vagaries of the editorial pencil—and she would fight to preserve their love in a hostile world.

He did not know that Mayling Chiang had a week earlier remarked, "Emily, I've seen some disturbing reports about your Richard Hollings's book from our embassies in London and Washington. Sounds almost as if he's gone over to the Reds."

"No," Mayling had acknowledged when Emily pressed, "none of the informants has actually seen the book. The diplomats are, as usual, relaying political gossip."

"Yes," Mayling had agreed, "we should withhold judgment. After all, he is convincing the Americans that China desperately needs American warplanes and aviators."

Emily knew she was fighting a rearguard action when Jimmy Wei's boss, Hollington Tong, confided that he, too, had received alarming reports regarding *Red Star and Yellow Earth* from officers of his China Information Service abroad. From Singapore, George Yeh, who was an expert on Elizabethan poetry, reported leafing through an advance copy sent to the *Straits Times* for review.

"I had to content myself with a quick once-over." Emily translated Dr. Yeh's elided cablese into normal language; the two American-educated Chinese officials communicated in English. "What I did see made my hair stand on end. This pernicious book will do our cause immense harm. Mr. Hollings has gone over lock, stock, and barrel to the Communists. He portrays Mao Tse-tung as a mixture of George Washington, Oliver Cromwell, Abraham Lincoln, and Jesus Christ. Nationalist resistance to the Japanese is minimized, while the Communists are depicted as battling valiantly against the Japanese. Mao and his henchmen are shown creating an earthly paradise.

"According to Richard Hollings, a new era has dawned for China. The novelist Ting Ling is lovingly depicted as the embodiment of the magnificent new Chinese woman. On military matters, Hollings is remarkably . . ."

Tears of rage blurred Emily's vision. Heaven alone knew what went on in Yenan, where all decency had been cast aside! She could not believe that more than smiles had passed between Richard and the woman called Ting Ling. Knowing both her man and the promiscuous left-wing writer, Emily amended her thought: Anything could have happened!

She was furious. That Communist slut, that drab fanatic, to epitomize Chinese womanhood. What of Mayling Chiang? What, if it came to it, of herself? Such praise for Ting Ling was an insult to every decent Chinese woman.

However irrationally, Emily now assumed that Ting Ling and Richard had been lovers. Why else his praise?

She also saw a degrading parallel between her own role in Richard's life and Ting Ling's role. The Communist woman, who possessed a certain waiflike charm, the allure of the pathetic, had probably made love to Richard to win him to her cause. Had she herself not done the same, she Emily Howe Ou-yang, who prided herself on her integrity?

No, that was not true! She had slept with Dick not for China's sake but for her own. She loved him deeply, and she had loved him for years. Only when she was depressed by the chaos her love affair was making of her life did she console herself that she made love to Dick for love of China. Anyway, patriotism was no excuse!

Only love could justify her hazarding her position and the regard of her peers. War was delaying the bill, but it would soon have to be paid in full. Her *only* justification was her love for Richard, and she would defend that love with all her might—whatever he had done.

Young girls dreamed of a grand passion, the overwhelming love that set the world at naught. It was ridiculous to be overcome at thirty-eight like a giddy virgin of eighteen. But she had lost her freedom of will.

Everything else appeared trivial: her work, her achievements, her family, even her country. No matter what, she would not let Richard go! Neither, however, would she make the deadly error of telling him how he dominated her life. If she did, he would devour her. She could not make herself a part of him. She could not totally surrender her individuality to become an appendage, however cherished.

On the last day of the fourth decade of the twentieth century, Chungking was joyless under gray fog. The deprivation natural to war was even more austere because of the Generalissimo's puritanical New Life Movement. "Not Strength Through Joy, like the Nazis"—Emily herself laughed—"but Strength Through Abstinence." Drinking, even dancing, was forbidden. Besides, the true Chinese New Year, the Lunar New Year, was still more than a month away.

The foreign community was restive. Most diplomats, officers, and correspondents were as superstitious about this New Year's Eve as the Chinese were about every Lunar New Year's festival, when all humans were reborn and all debts, spiritual or material, were settled. Since their own countries were now at war, the foreigners knew that the coming decade would determine their fate, as well as the fate of the Chinese. Since the foreign community needed an outlet, a New Year's ball was to be held at the British embassy. The British were unrivaled for parties and ceremonies, whatever muddle they might make of policy. Because the embassy was legally British territory, it was under no compulsion to obey the Nationalists' puritanical laws.

The head of chancery had himself informed the Chinese Foreign Ministry that the embassy proposed to hold a gala ball, at which it further proposed to broach its hoarded stock of champagnes, wines, cordials, and liquors. If the Chinese government so desired, Chinese citizens would not be invited thus to breach wartime austerity. Such exclusion might, however, smack of discrimination—even, perhaps, of foreigners' extraterritorial rights at Shanghai, which the Chinese government found abhorrent.

The director of protocol had smiled and declared that the Chinese government saw nothing amiss in the proposed entertainment. His government was, in fact, pleased that its foreign guests could thus amuse themselves amid the rigors of wartime. He actually said "tickled pink," being, like Rosamonde Sun, a proud graduate of Wesleyan College in Georgia. On behalf of the Chinese government, the chief of protocol agreed that excluding Chinese citizens might recall old antipathies best forgotten. Speaking for himself, the director was delighted—"really tickled pink again"—to accept the personal invitation of the head of chancery. Finally, the Chinese government would be obliged if the embassy would again convey to London the urgent need for prompt renunciation of extraterritoriality to cement Allied Solidarity.

As a leading British correspondent, Richard Hollings was naturally asked to the ball. The British ambassadress confided to her husband, the ambassador, that she anticipated New Year's Eve with the same queasy ecstasy as she had her first grown-up dinner party. She was, however, delighted by Madame Ou-yang Hsiu's promise to come. Since Madame Chiang Kai-shek could not attend such a frivolous gathering, her executive associate was the next best thing. The ambassadress's sentimental heart was, moreover, wrung by Emily's tragic romance with Richard. Despite the ambassadors, the ministers, the generals, and the admirals who were invited, the ambassadress considered Emily and Richard her prize guests.

"Certainly your star turn," the head of chancery had agreed, having spent too much time in Washington as a second secretary. "The fellow's already famous—even before a single copy of his book's got to Chungking."

The head of chancery was misinformed. Six copies of *Red Star and Yellow Earth* had arrived in the provisional capital three days earlier on a flight over the Hump.

Richard Hollings had ruefully canceled the cocktail party he had originally planned to show off his own two copies. Admiring the yellow dust jacket with the five-pointed red star superimposed over his own name, he had prudently decided to tell no one that the books had arrived. And he had smiled wryly at his naïve hope of laying the very first copy in Emily's lap.

Yet he found very little he would alter or omit—and much to admire —when he read his own words, which were, as Chou En-lai had said, virtually unedited. Perhaps, he concluded, he might have added a paragraph or two clarifying the defection of Tommy Howe's friend Chang Kuo-tao. But nothing more.

Richard was unaware that Hollington Tong had pressed upon Emily one of the four copies sent by his New York office. Fortunately, Mayling Chiang was preoccupied with her plans to fly to Hong Kong to be treated for a persistent skin inflammation. She was also planning to see her elder sisters, Madame H. H. Kung and Madame Sun Yat-sen; she hoped to persuade them to return to Chungking with her. Otherwise, Mayling would have pounced on the book—and precipitated a crisis.

Emily had only glanced into the preface to assure herself that Richard had deleted the thanks originally accorded her. She had then secreted his book in a drawer filled with chiffon scarves and other fripperies she rarely wore in Chungking. She could not evade the ordeal, but she would read *Red Star and Yellow Earth* in her own time. Holly Tong could not press her too hard, but Mayling was certain to demand a reckoning in time. Emily had apprehensively sworn that she would read *Red Star* when the holiday season was over, after both the Western and the Chinese New Year had passed.

Blessedly, her husband, Hsiu, was no immediate worry. Since Hsiu did not know what foreigners thought of Emily's public appearances with Richard, he could not be disturbed by their opinions. Nor would he have cared if he had known. For Ou-yang Hsiu, foreigners were clever beasts that made ingenious machines. He was no more interested in their moral judgments than he was in his watchdogs' views.

Hsiu did, however, care greatly about the judgments of his peers, the solid, wealthy, old-fashioned Chinese families transplanted to wartime Chungking. Such families, however, knew little of Emily's behavior. Anything out of the way they ascribed to the exigencies of war. She had to associate with foreigners, and foreigners considered fantastic behavior normal.

Besides, Hsiu had told Emily at the beginning that he would not object to her behavior as long as she did not bring public scandal down upon the family. An honorable man, he would keep his word as long as Emily kept hers.

She had dutifully produced three children, and she was diligently fulfilling her responsibilities to those children. Now not quite eleven, Jason wanted to enter the cadet program of the Chinese Air Force, but Emily dutifully told him that the sons of good families did not enter military service. Patricia, who was nine, and Eunice, who was six, were already displaying the traditional feminine virtues, docility, above all. Fortunately, they displayed none of their mother's fiery independence.

For the moment, all was well, Emily felt, although she could not be certain that Hsiu would never protest. If he had not spent so much time at a Buddhist monastery on Omei, the sacred mountain two hundred miles west of Chungking, he might already have become difficult. But she could deal with Hsiu; he needed her more than she needed him.

Casting off all fear of the future, Emily entered the ballroom of the British embassy on Richard's arm. Lit by hanging lanterns with vermilion tassels, the walls were hung with bright silks and glowing Persian carpets. The company was just as colorful, for the ambassadress had asked her guests to come in fancy dress. Emily was delighted that she could in conscience not wear a *cheongsam,* which Richard called her full-dress uniform. Her scarlet chiffon evening dress with floating panels and plunging neckline was strangely set off by Richard's gray cassock and pectoral cross, both inveigled from the papal nuncio so that Richard could play the Gray Eminence.

Emily was Ginger Rogers in *Flying Down to Rio.* Although she would hardly dye her hair, she had lavishly combed in henna powder. Her natural vivacity was just right, as were her slightly garish makeup and her swirling skirts. Her brief scarlet bodice was tight over her small, high breasts.

The design was Elizaveta's and, like Elizaveta's own evening dresses, was unashamedly derived from her mother's pre-1914 gowns, which she still possessed. Elizaveta had pressed the dress upon Emily when she left Shanghai, saying, "I had it made for you. There'll come a time when you yearn for—desperately *need*—something totally frivolous there in the backwoods."

On New Year's Eve, Emily truly needed the dress, which was the color of joy. In Richard's arms she shimmered like a flame around the ballroom. Champagne flowed in profusion, astonishing when every replacement bottle had to come by narrow-gauge train from Haiphong or by overburdened airplane from India. Most embassies had, however, foresightedly laid in stocks by the last steamers and gunboats to sail up the Yangtze from Shanghai. All were now eager to make the night bubble with gaiety. No one knew where he would be next New Year's Eve.

Not for years, Emily suddenly realized, had she been so unreservedly happy. Not, in fact, since she had broken with Richard and contracted her foolish marriage.

Only briefly was the enchantment marred. An earnest lieutenant off the USS *Tutuila,* who held her like a fragile Ming vase, remarked without malice, "Your friend Mr. Hollings, we've been hearing a lot about him lately. Folks're saying he's written a wonderful book about China. I guess, though, you've read it already."

"Sorry, sailor," Emily replied shortly. "I haven't read it either."

She thanked God that Harry Smythe was still in Kunming, for he would not have been put off so easily. Nonetheless the music, the perfumes, and the champagne restored her joy. She was radiant when couples came together again a few minutes before midnight.

Floating in Richard's arms for the last dance of the year 1939, she looked up and saw that his beard, shaved only hours earlier, was again asserting itself. Behind his half mask, his eyes were actually darker than her own. He looked down at her straight center part, where her scalp shone pearly white dusted with red henna.

"Darling!" he whispered. "Always, my darling!"

She smiled, almost afraid to speak, and whispered, "Forever!"

They did not hear the countdown to the New Year swell around them, and the midnight gong was remote. Unmasking, they kissed lightly once—and once again.

"All will be well!" Richard assured her. "All will be well beyond doubt . . . always!"

"Of course!" she echoed. "Always!"

Around them the party was singing "Auld Lang Syne." They kissed again more urgently. And both were suddenly afraid.

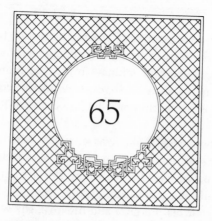

65

FEBRUARY 3–MARCH 6, 1940

Against her will, Emily's eyes would return to the bottom drawer, where the unopened copy of *Red Star and Yellow Earth* lay under her scarves. She felt that a time bomb was concealed under the frothy silk. If she tampered with it, the bomb could explode prematurely. In any event, explode it would in time.

On a damp, chilly afternoon in early February when she could delay no longer, she opened the drawer. Holly Tong had been demanding her opinion of Richard's book. She could hardly continue to plead that she had not found time to read it when even Jimmy Wei rolled his eyes. After locking her bedroom door, she fumbled with the pages.

Normally a fast reader, Emily took a full week to plod through the book's 416 pages. Her initial reaction swung wildly from approval to horror. Although she knew she wanted to approve, she found some passages strikingly accurate—and she was pleased by Richard's insights into China.

Most of his book she read with mounting bewilderment. Since she knew Richard was not blind to reality, she was forced to conclude that he had deliberately distorted reality. From her talks with Tommy's friend Chang Kuo-tao she also knew the stark truths that underlay the bright and specious picture Richard had painted. She further knew that Chang Kuo-tao had discussed those truths with Richard at length.

Emily's chief reaction to *Red Star and Yellow Earth* was, however, incredulity; she simply could not believe Richard's account was as biased as it appeared. She therefore put it aside for a week and then forced herself to read it again.

The distortions were even more glaring the second time, and the few redeeming passages seemed thin. Richard, she concluded sorrowfully, had done irreparable harm to China—in order to promote himself. He would become famous, she saw, for discovering the wonderful world of Mao Tse-tung—as he would not if he had depicted its true and unattractive face.

During the three weeks she was engaged with the book, Emily refused to see the author. Her excuses were almost deliberately transparent, but she dared not talk with him. Besides, she wanted him to suffer a little while she was suffering so profoundly. Desolate because she was deprived of his presence and his love, she was furious at him for forcing her to a harsh decision.

It was not primarily being compelled to choose between Richard and China, though that choice loomed large. It was not even being compelled to choose either Richard or her present work, as well as all her friends and associates, though that choice galled. It was, above all, his compelling her to choose between him and her self-respect.

Before reading his book, she had decided that she would, if necessary, sacrifice her work, her reputation, and perhaps even her children to be with him. However, she had further decided that she could not sacrifice her existence as an independent human being.

She now knew that choosing Richard would be a betrayal of all the purposes of her life. Having agonized and delayed for weeks, she knew she must break with him—this time, permanently.

Too much of her being was, however, entwined around the man she still loved. She dreaded the confrontation with Richard as she had dreaded nothing since she sailed for America at the age of ten. If she were only a little more cowardly, she would tell him in writing that it was all over. If she loved him a little less, she would end it with a brief note. But she could not spare herself by hiding behind an impersonal typewriter.

She must see him soon, Emily told herself, although her long silence should already have spoken for her. Richard must have concluded that she was avoiding him because she had read his book—and despised it. Her reasoning was clear: By late February he must have received the author's copies, and he had promised to give her one. He would have failed to do so only because he knew that she would hate *Red Star and Yellow Earth*. Of course, if he had not yet received any copies, he would have told her so.

Emily knew that she must act, but she still hesitated.

Richard had not pressed to see her. Was it tact or fear of rejection that led him to again visit Claire Chennault in Kunming? Yet, perhaps he simply did not feel strongly enough to demand that she allow him to plead his case. Perhaps the ardent lover of New Year's Eve had given way to a coward who was afraid to see her.

Emily was again furious. Not her withdrawal, she told herself, but his cowardice was keeping them apart. It would serve him right if she let him go off without another word.

Still, perhaps she had already punished him sufficiently. Perhaps he had really been deceived by the Communists, who were brilliant propagandists, which meant convincing liars. Herself a seasoned propagandist for the Nationalists, Emily respected the enemy's skill. Perhaps Richard had not fully realized how damaging his hymn of praise to the Communists would be to the Nationalist government.

Emily was still searching for excuses for Richard when he returned to Chungking in the first week of March. Anticipating her reaction to *Red Star and Yellow Earth,* he had gone to Kunming to gather new material. He hoped to balance the scales—and to allay her anger—with a laudatory book about Claire Chennault, who was talking about forming a pursuit unit to be called the American Volunteer Group. An American foreign legion of the air in China would make brilliant copy.

On his return, however, Richard found a cablegram, sent with reckless disregard for expense by his literary agent: I CAN NOT REPEAT NOT PREVENT YOUR DOING BOOK ABOUT CHENNAULT. NO ONE CAN STOP YOU EXCEPT YOURSELF. BUT PLEASE BEAR THIS IN MIND: YOU ARE ABOUT TO BECOME INTERNATIONALLY FAMOUS AS THE WORLD'S LEADING AUTHORITY ON CHINA—AND A MAJOR AUTHORITY ON INTERNATIONAL AFFAIRS. BONI AND LIVERIGHT WANT ANOTHER BIG REPEAT BIG BOOK, NOT REPEAT NOT A LITTLE ADVENTURE STORY ABOUT A JOHNNY REB BIRDMAN FOR SCHOOLBOYS. BONI FEEL SUCH A MINOR SUBJECT WOULD IMPAIR YOUR STANDING, WHILE A BIG THEME WOULD SOLIDIFY YOUR REPUTATION. I AGREE.

FOR EXAMPLE, THE SOVIET UNION'S ROLE IN THE WORLD AND THE WAR. SURELY, YOUR FRIENDS IN YENAN CAN HELP YOU THERE.

BONI PREPARED TO PAY THREE-THOUSAND-DOLLAR ADVANCE FOR CHENNAULT, OWING HIGH REGARD FOR YOU. THEIR INITIAL OFFER FOR SOVIET BOOK IS FIFTY THOUSAND, AND I CAN PROBABLY GET TEN THOUSAND MORE. IT'S ENTIRELY UP TO YOU. CORDIALLY, MOSS.

Richard winced at that aside about his friends in Yenan, which would have been read with interest by the Nationalist secret police. He was also sad about killing the Chennault book. But his agent and his publisher were absolutely right. He could not allow himself the luxury of mending his fences with the Nationalists; he had to strike while the iron was hot. Wincing again at the mangled metaphor he decided: If they wanted the Soviet Union, they'd get the Soviet Union.

A pity he couldn't placate Emily with the book on Chennault. But she was professional enough to understand that he had no choice. Perhaps he could do that book later.

Knowing that he was working for their future together, Emily would also understand that he had to move quickly, rather than linger in China. He had almost forgotten her long, angry silence. But all that nonsense would blow over when he gave her the good news of the new commission from his publishers.

Whistling cheerfully between his teeth, Richard drafted a telegram to his agent accepting the offer of fifty thousand dollars for a book—implicitly favorable—on the Soviet Union. Victor Gollancz in London would certainly snap it up.

His Hermes portable cheerily clicked out two more telegrams. Almost identical, they pointed out to the *Boston Globe* and to the National Broadcasting System that the China story had, for the time being, petered out, while the Soviet Union was the key to the war—and, therefore, the key to the future of mankind.

Having briskly disposed of not only the future of mankind but his own immediate future, Richard was in no mood to tolerate feminine caprices any longer. They had very little time before his departure, and they had to make the most of it. Having virtually expunged their tacit quarrel from his own mind, he simply assumed that Emily had gotten over whatever was bothering her.

Briskly, he boarded a sampan ferry across the Chialing River. Just as briskly, he scrambled up the path toward the Ou-yang compound, ignoring the reproachful obscenities of sedan-chair coolies done out of a fare.

Emily received him in the formal sitting room. She had almost convinced herself that she was unjust in her condemnation of *Red Star* and its author. Richard saw that she had lost weight she could not afford to lose—and her wide eyes were suspiciously liquid.

"You took your own sweet time, didn't you?" She evaded his embrace. "Anyone would think I had leprosy."

"I thought you wanted . . ." His brisk self-assurance was taken aback by that female illogic. "I thought you wanted time to yourself, Emily. And you could have sent me a word."

"I did need time. Maybe I still do." One instant assertive, the next instant she asked plaintively, "Richard, how could you do it to us?"

"What have I done, Emily?" He delivered the response as he had rehearsed it. "Whatever it is, I didn't deserve to be cut off by you. . . . I've come to tell you I've got to leave—very soon. I'll be back, of course. But God alone knows when we'll see each other again. Time is precious —and you're wasting the little time we've got left together."

She neatly rearranged the crocheted antimacassars on the red plush sofa before saying, "You sound as if avoiding you was only a whim on my part."

"No, dear, not a whim. Far too protracted for mere feminine caprice." Because he was perturbed, he spoke ornately. "I'd consider myself fortunate if it were no more than a whim. You do realize, don't you, that you've kept us apart for more than six weeks?"

Emily smiled tensely at the nervous pomposity that was so unlike his normal breeziness. She finally sighed, "Oh, that mine enemy would write a book."

"And what precisely is that cheapjack biblical quotation meant to convey?"

"If *you* don't know! Primarily, I suppose, that you did write a book and—"

"And a damned good book, too," he exploded. "But I'm not here for literary criticism."

"I'm not so sure about . . . about that!" Her voice rose ominously. "Oh, Richard, how *could* you *possibly* do it? Did you for an instant think of *us?* What it would do to me? Or only of *yourself?* You've betrayed me . . . betrayed everything! How *could* you do it to us?"

Striving to remain calm, he replied in perplexity: "Look here, Emily, I gather you're unhappy about *Red Star.* Maybe some parts are a little over the top. But it's not the end of the world. After all, it's only a book."

"*Only* a book!" Emily erupted. "My God, you might as well say *only* a life! *Only* the lives of millions of Chinese men, women, and children! My God in heaven, *only* a book!"

"Steady now, Em!" He fell back on banalities. "Let's not go overboard."

"Overboard? What do you expect—the reserve of an English gentleman? I'm not English—and I'm not a gentleman. To hell with reserve. . . . My God, don't you *know* you've ruined everything we had?"

Richard fumbled a cigarette from his crumpled packet of Camels. Three wood-sliver matches snapped in his finger before he lit the cigarette with the fourth. He took a deep drag and expelled the smoke viciously.

"Emily," he finally said, "I reported it the way I saw it. And I would again. I love you . . . love you profoundly. I've tried to tell you that . . . Perhaps I already have, but I'll say it again: I want you to marry me. I want to divorce Fiona and marry you. . . . But no matter what, I can't let you tell me what to write. You can see that, can't you?"

"No, Richard, not really," she replied shrilly. "Not when you're writing lies, lies that could destroy the Republic of China . . . pave the way for a Communist takeover. You're discrediting the Generalissimo and exalting Mao Tse-tung. You'll ruin our chances for American aid. Why you've as good as condemned millions of Chinese to slavery."

"Isn't that a bit hysterical, Emily? You're drawing a wildly distorted picture. . . . Is that what you mean when you say I've ruined it all?"

"That too." Her voice sank lower as she fought to control her violent emotion. "And myself. The pressure I've been under . . . from Mayling, Holly Tong, even Jimmy Wei. . . . You never thought of the consequences. I can't go on with my work if I keep seeing you. Nobody would trust me."

"If only I could take you with me . . ."

"Well, you can't. I have three children—and I do love them. And they need me. So . . ."

"So it's not just the book, is it? I don't know whether that makes me feel better or worse."

"It *is* the book. All else aside, anyone who could write a book like that . . . I don't *know* that person. I don't know you at all. How could I ever trust you again . . . about anything? If you're ready to twist and distort and lie—"

"Steady on. *Red Star* is true—just as true as I could make it. Even the best reporting shows a few mistakes. But, over all, it's a true picture and—"

"My God, I'm afraid . . . afraid you really believe what you're saying! Yet you're not a fool."

"A knave or a fool?" His voice was flat. "Is that it, Emily?"

"What else can I say? When I look at the difference between what I know to be true and what you wrote, what else can I possibly think?"

"You might try thinking that *you* don't know everything," he retorted. "Being Chinese doesn't mean you know everything about China. For a change, why don't you look at the inefficiency and corruption on your own side? Except for your precious Gimo, everybody's got his snout in the trough. Why don't you—"

"Nobody says the Nationalists are perfect, certainly not me. But we can talk about it. Correspondents can write about it, and they do. On the other side, you describe a rustic paradise. You *must* know that's nonsense. Nobody can disagree in Yenan. Mao Tse-tung is an out-and-out dictator. Why Chang Kuo-tao—"

"Chang Kuo-tao is a turncoat—a traitor and a renegade. If you're going to listen to the ravings of every defeated politician—"

"Richard, this is becoming pointless. Why don't we drop it?"

"I'm all for that, Emily." He was again conciliatory. "That's why I came here today. Let's drop politics. . . . We don't have much time. We can discuss all this calmly and coherently when I come back. But for now—"

"You really mean that, don't you? You really believe it's possible! Love conquers all!"

Emily took a Camel and clenched it between her lips. She nodded her thanks for the proffered match as if they were casual acquaintances at a cocktail party.

"You can still surprise me, Richard," she said softly. "You still can. You really believe we can just forget the issue. . . . It's not only your self-absorption. It's your *massive* insensitivity."

"Emily, is that really fair?" he protested. "How can you say—"

"You still don't understand what you've done to us, do you? To think I was in love with a creature I invented. You never cared enough for me . . . for us . . . to think for a single instant about the consequences."

Richard had been battered into silence. Staring levelly at him, Emily picked a shred of tobacco from the tip of her tongue.

"Richard, there's no point . . . no point whatsoever." She ground her cigarette out. "There was never any point, not really. At least you've always been a gentleman . . . in your own way. Now go quickly—like a gentleman."

66

MARCH 29, 1940

The red ensign of the British Merchant Marine shielded the small coaster from the warships of the Imperial Japanese Navy blockading the China Coast. Nonetheless, the twin four-inch guns of the destroyer *Tatsuta* moved to follow the coaster's entrance into the Yangtze River from the South China Sea. Plodding up the Yangtze to the Hwangpoo and Shanghai would take several hours, and Japanese guns would track the coaster all the way.

"Just intimidation," the ship's captain told Richard Hollings. "No one's got a shell in the guts yet. Bound to happen some day, though."

The correspondent filed that remark in his memory. It summed up the mood of Shanghai even before he saw the queen city of the Far East again. Apprehension cloaked by bravado surely must dominate the metropolis that was slowly expiring in Japanese hands. Although the invaders had not dared march into the foreign concessions, their grip was stifling the trade by which the great port lived.

Richard had come back to write a farewell series on the Shanghai no one would ever see again—regardless of the outcome of the Second World War. His foreign audience was, naturally, far more interested in the foreign-oriented cosmopolis than in remote cities inhabited only by Chinese or in battles fought entirely between Orientals. He planned to deal with Shanghai expeditiously and then take up the roving assignment in Europe his joint employers had given their new star.

Since the waves were whitecapped, the dark brown Yangtze was a river of coffee topped with whipped cream. Richard's heart no longer responded to the junks on the water and the pagodas on the banks. He had seen too many rivers in China—and far too much of China. But he was almost done with China.

An era was ending for Richard. He had come back to Shanghai to close the circle of his life in China where he had begun it. Moreover, the right introduction to the Soviet Union was worth traveling thousands of miles to obtain, since it could mean tens of thousands of dollars. He already knew the title of his new book, *The Bear at Bay*, but he had to get his foot into the Kremlin's door.

He had in Chungking, of course, spoken to Chou En-lai, who promised to vouch for him—after denying any special influence with the Soviets. He had also paid a courtesy call on the Soviet ambassador. But the Soviet consul general in Shanghai was far more influential than the ambassador in Chungking. The consul general was the master spider at the center of the network of Soviet espionage, diplomacy, trade, and subversion throughout Asia. Foreign correspondents' gossip, which was usually accurate in such matters, described him as a personal protégé of Joseph Stalin and a major general in the OGPU, the security and intelligence service. His word could open the gates of the Kremlin.

Richard had cabled Tommy Howe his time of arrival. After Yenan, he had no illusions about Tommy and Julia's political position. He was convinced that Tommy was very important in the Apparatus and, accordingly, close to the Soviet spymaster. If Tommy vouched for him, he could hope to attain the same privileged access in Moscow that he had enjoyed in Yenan under Tommy's sponsorship. After seeing the Soviet consul general, he would be off.

So many arrivals and departures! It seemed to Richard that he had been traveling continuously since he left Shanghai in 1927 with Emily's denunciation of his selfishness ringing in his mind.

He sternly put Emily out of his mind. His wife, Fiona, still in England, was always delighted to see him; she was always grateful for his sparing her the time. And Fiona never railed at him. She never analyzed his shortcomings, never denounced his sins.

But why did he spend so much time away from Fiona? Despite himself, his thoughts turned to Emily again—and he realized again that he was truly happy only when they were together.

Richard would not believe that his second dismissal was any more final than his first dismissal had proved to be. He knew Emily had been constantly swinging from fury to grief before his departure. Harry Smythe had told him so—with savage satisfaction at making him suffer because she was suffering so terribly. He had himself wandered around Chungking, unable to work, until he was unexpectedly offered a seat on a special China National Aviation Corporation flight to Hong Kong. Suspecting that Emily had pulled strings to get him out of Chungking, he had, nonetheless, accepted immediately.

He had not written her a farewell note. After much agonizing, he had, instead, sent her a copy of *Red Star and Yellow Earth* inscribed: *To Emily from the author with all his love forever. In the hope that she may some day want to read it again and, perhaps, change her mind.*

Recalling that dignified and civilized inscription had somewhat consoled Richard on his journey to Shanghai by way of Hong Kong. The journey had begun when a sampan ferried him to the sandspit in the middle of the Yangtze that served as Chungking's airport.

Two worlds met. The shore was thronged with sedan-chair coolies, lantern bearers, horse grooms, messenger coolies, and food hawkers—all of them following essentially medieval occupations. On the sandspit, the twentieth-century airliner loomed huge, its silver flanks red in the sunset. The newly delivered Douglas DC-3 was the pride of China's national airline: it could carry thirty passengers 1,400 miles at almost 200 miles an hour.

The cabin lights were off when the transport rolled down the sandspit at dusk to twist through the surrounding hills into the open sky. When the DC-3 reached cruising altitude, even the navigation lights and the safety beacon were turned off. After five hours of flight through Japanese-controlled airspace, the DC-3 had sideslipped into Hong Kong's Kaitak Aerodome. When he disembarked, Richard had seen why the airline had risked the special flight.

The glow of the interior light in the Daimler limousine on the tarmac silhouetted three women. Richard recognized Mayling Chiang when she leaned forward. Since the family resemblance was unmistakable, the others were surely her elder sisters: Ailing, called Nanny, who was Madame H. H. Kung; and Chingling, called Rosamonde, who was Madame Sun Yat-sen. Therefore the fuss and the secrecy. Mayling was now returning secretly to Chungking after undergoing medical treatment in Hong Kong. She had evidently persuaded both the fearful Nanny and the haughty Rosamonde to join her.

Rosamonde had previously preferred to snipe at her brother-in-law's Nationalist Government from the security of British Hong Kong. Her visit to Chungking would please Chairman Mao Tse-tung. In combination with Chou En-lai, she would undoubtedly enchant the foreign press and further gild the Communists' image.

Standing on the tarmac at Kaitak Aerodome, Richard had congratulated himself on picking the winning side. He congratulated himself again when he stepped off Municipal Pontoon Six onto the Shanghai Bund after disembarking from the coaster that had brought him from Hong Kong. He saw Julia Howe waiting at the end of the gangplank in the yellow cone of a streetlamp. They were practically partners now; even before himself, she had picked the winning side.

Julia's costume made no obeisance to wartime austerity. Two long tassels hung from the apple-green pillbox cocked on the side of her head, and the mulberry linen bolero that matched her slim skirt flaunted the padded shoulders popularized by Joan Crawford, the Hollywood star of the year. Julia looked glowingly happy.

She had reason to be happy. The prolonged war, a quagmire for the Japanese and the Nationalists, was proving a splendid opportunity for the Chinese Communists. They were energetically expanding their territory and their armies. Moreover, the Soviet Union was the only victor in the continuing phony war in Europe. After their victory in Poland, the Germans still faced the French and the British. But the Soviets had painlessly extended their power. Julia must be delighted.

Contemptuous of appearances, she pressed against him and kissed his lips. Her impulsive welcome was far warmer than he had expected or had ever received before. Julia had in the past never quite forgiven him for jilting Emily—and flinging Emily into the aging arms of Ou-yang Hsiu. Julia's first words revealed why he was back in favor.

"You're looking great, Dick," she bubbled. *Red Star and Yellow Earth* is a terrific book. Tommy and I loved it. And how's Emmy? I'm delighted you're back together again."

"Emily is very well. But I'm afraid we're not quite back together at the moment. She's not at all pleased with me or my book."

"You could hardly expect her to *like* it, could you? And I guess she couldn't forgive you for leaving. But lovers' tiffs soon blow over."

Requiring Julia's goodwill, Richard preferred to leave it at that. He had told her the truth. She could interpret it as she liked.

"And yourself, Julie?" he inquired. "How are Tommy and the girls? All thriving, I trust."

"Absolutely thriving, Dick. We're all just fine. And very optimistic about the future: for China and the world. It's all working out just right."

The only undiluted truth in that sunny affirmation was Julia's optimism about political events, which her husband did not fully share. All the Howes were not thriving. Ten-year-old Althea was afflicted with asthma, which her father ascribed largely to Shanghai's perpetual dampness. Althea's parents were enduring the unhappiest hours they had ever known together. More than a decade of harmony had given way to acute disagreements over personal as well as political questions. Tommy scorned Julia's Pollyanna optimism. She detested his dour pessimism regarding his nation, his city, and his family.

Like Joshua Haleevie, Tommy was deeply depressed by the decline of their beloved Shanghai. The trucks of the corpse-collection service now picked up more than a hundred unidentified bodies every morning —and two hundred new refugees arrived every day. Women with matted hair led ragged, starving children in an endless hunt for scraps of food. Boarding houses, hotels, derelict mansions, and schools were crammed, but tens of thousands slept on the streets. The overburdened charities could not sustain the horde of refugees.

The Settlement and Frenchtown were also tormented by criminals, who were protected by the Japanese and their Chinese puppets. Generalissimo Chiang Kai-shek's chief rival in the past, the man Richard had years earlier nicknamed Lucifer, was now a public traitor to China. After the first beheading that shocked Julia and Elizaveta, political murder had become commonplace. The Supreme Lord of the Floodgate Fraternity, the Green Dragon, could no longer control either narcotics or violence. His secret-society battalions were outnumbered and outgunned by regiments of free-lance thugs.

Julia had reserved Richard's old suite at Broadway Mansions, just north of the Garden Bridge in Hong Kew. Since he was reluctant to talk about Emily, she told him about the breakdown of law and order while sipping a mint-sprigged Tom Collins mixed by the room boy.

"As you've seen, Dick, downtown is practically a no-man's-land. Special constables patrol with their revolvers in their hands. You couldn't miss the armored cars and tanks. More guns bristling from more pillboxes than even in 1927. Only this time, it's no false alarm."

"You're staying on, Julie, you and the girls? Isn't it a bit foolhardy for you to—"

"Tommy keeps harping on that, Dick. He wants me to take the girls back to America. My parents are getting old, he says. There's also Althea's asthma and the danger. She must find a better climate, and the international situation is so uncertain. He's afraid we'd be trapped here if war comes. So you see—"

"Slow down, Julie." The Englishman raised his palm peremptorily. "You're going too fast. Tell me, what does Tommy plan to do? Will he go with you to the States?"

"Sometimes he says yes, sometimes no. Even if he could cut through the red tape and practice medicine in the States, he finally says, his place is here in China. But he wants *me* to go into exile."

"Julie, a lot of couples are going to be parted as this war gets bigger. Hundreds of thousands already are. It is not a family picnic, you know."

"So Tommy keeps telling me. He says the girls won't get proper schooling with the crisis here—and it could go on for many years. . . . But I'm damned if I'll go. I've got my work: XMHA and teaching and . . . and other important work. But Tommy says cholera and typhoid are already widespread and will get worse. Also, malaria, with the waterways blocked and stagnating. It's hard to argue with him, Dick."

"Julie, I admire your spirit but not your logic. Have you ever thought how much you could do in the States just now? For China and for . . . ah . . . the progressive movement."

Having read *Red Star and Yellow Earth* with delight, Julia was now convinced that Richard Hollings was, at the very least, a Communist sympathizer. She was now encouraged by his using that code term, "the progressive movement," to mean the Communists and their allies throughout the world. Still, she could hardly tell him that she and Tommy were quarreling bitterly about her wish to work directly for the Soviets. She could hardly confess to a journalist that she was a spy, no matter how sympathetic he was.

"Can Tom join us for dinner?" Richard lit her Chesterfield. "I can't wait to see the old rascal."

"Fat chance!" Julia drew in a deep draught of smoke and accepted another Tom Collins. "Tommy is off healing the suffering rich. There's *so* much illness among the wealthy, particularly the glossy Shanghai ladies. *All* the Chinese ladies love Tommy. Just as long as he's only *healing* them."

"What about you, Julie? Are you free for dinner? If Tommy doesn't mind."

"He won't mind as long as I leave a message like an obedient little wife. He's just as happy not to have to worry about me."

Realizing that she had drunk a little more than she should, Richard decided they would dine in the suite. Though he had been looking forward to the superb Russian food of the Renaissance Café on Avenue Joffre, Broadway Mansions could produce the delicacies he had been longing for: fresh caviar, smoked salmon—and porterhouse steaks. After a few drinks, he recalled, the cosmopolitan Julia was apt to revert to rather basic American taste in food.

Her bitter remarks about Tommy disturbed Richard. Their apparent rift was troubling to one who had until recently believed—and who still hoped—that he would become their brother-in-law. Both Howes were provoking, Tommy apparently as much as Emily. They were virtual fanatics in their dedication to China. He still could not quite fathom why Emily objected so strenuously—and so personally —to *Red Star.*

Richard did not mention Tommy during dinner, preferring to answer Julia's questions about Chungking and to refresh himself from her inexhaustible well of gossip about Shanghai. But his thoughts reverted to the infuriating sister and brother when Julia led him onto the terrace to look upon the fairyland radiance of Shanghai at night.

Perhaps we'd both be better off if we'd never met the Howes, he reflected, neither Emily nor Tommy. They've got such high standards, other human beings can't possibly live up to them.

Julia looked at him strangely. Fearing he had spoken his thoughts aloud, he impulsively observed, "They can be terribly provoking, the Chinese, can't they?"

"Can they not!" she affirmed. "Sometimes, Dick, I feel like saying the hell with them. The hell with *all* Chinese!"

Julia leaned back against the railing and stared at him. The lights of the Bund, glittering across Soochow Creek, cast a halo around her tawny hair. On her left, Nanking Road streamed westward like the brilliant tail of a comet.

When she leaned back farther, he grasped her arm and cautioned, "Careful now. It's a long fall."

"Fall to where, Dick? Sometimes, I swear, I wouldn't mind falling."

Julia's speech was too precise, too carefully enunciated. The meal had obviously not sobered her. Burgundy had followed the Tom Collinses, and they were now swirling liqueurs in balloon glasses: Cointreau for her and brandy for him.

"Exactly what did you say a minute ago?" she demanded after a prolonged pause. "About Tommy and Emily? I swear I heard you say something."

"I only said the Chinese could be provoking. What else did you hear, Julie?" Teasing her, he realized that he was not dead sober himself. "What did you think?"

"I thunk . . . I think . . . I was thinking about Tommy and Emily. You know, sometimes they're too good for ordinary mortals like you'n me. Too hard to get 'long with. So pure . . . so patriotic . . . so logical . . . so . . . oh, hell, so superior and . . . and so Chinese!"

"Don't be bitter, Julie. It'll be all right, I promise you."

"It's not all right with you and Em, is it, Dickie? Not gonna be all right? Little Julie's no slouch. I can hear it in your voice."

"No, my dear, it's not quite all right," he confessed. "She's miffed at me again. To tell the truth, about *Red Star* . . ."

"What'd you expect, Dick?" For a moment she spoke crisply, almost mockingly. "A medal from the Gimo . . . the order of the White Sun and Blue Sky? Lord's sake, you knew exactly what you were doing, didn't you? And some people're proud . . . very proud . . . of you, Dick. Me for one."

"I did try, Julie. I tried very hard to get the message across. I'm so glad you feel I've succeeded."

"Succeeded? That's an understatement. From what I hear, you've changed the course of history. The reviews, I've rarely seen such raves. And the commentaries, even the editorials. Richard, my boy, you're a one-man Agitprop team."

"I'm so glad you liked it, Julie. After the static I've been getting, I must say it's a nice change. You're not just flattering me?"

"Richard Hollings, just come a little closer so I don't have to shout." Julia quaffed her Cointreau recklessly. "No need to let the whole world in on it. That's better. Now I'll just whisper . . ."

Setting the balloon glass down on the railing, Julia stood on tiptoe to whisper into his ear. She swayed slightly and leaned against him to support herself. He felt the soft weight of her breasts upon his arm and the warmth of her thighs against his leg.

Turning toward her, Richard told himself he was not really being unfaithful to Emily with her closest friend. He could not deprive Emily of that which she had already rejected. And Julia obviously knew exactly what she was doing—after twelve years of the fidelity that had scandalized hedonistic Shanghai.

Considering their relationships with the brother and sister, it was almost incestuous. But who else in the world could offer the other revenge as exquisitely sweet?

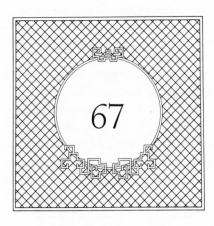

APRIL 3–20, 1940

Joshua Haleevie was amused by the cartoon from the London *Daily Express*. The broad penstrokes of David Low depicted Adolf Hitler and Joseph Stalin meeting to sign the Russo-German Nonaggression Pact, which had precipitated World War II. Both the jackbooted and bemedaled dictators were smiling amiably and lifting their peaked caps courteously. As he bowed to Stalin, Hitler remarked, "The scum of the earth, I believe!" Stalin, also bowing, replied, "The bloody assassin of the workers, I presume!"

Although the Russians and the Germans were in cahoots in Europe, they did not even meet in Shanghai. Although their consulates stood side by side in Hongkew, they avoided each other, as they had when they were avowed enemies. Was that continuing antipathy feigned, Joshua wondered. And if so, why?

The anonymous director of the anonymous intelligence service of the International Settlement made a note in his pocket diary: *Ivan and Fritz?* He would have to look into the apparent antagonism between those allies.

Shanghai was a fertile field for intelligence, sprouting tendrils that led to major developments elsewhere. The foreign powers therefore ran their espionage operations in the Far East from the concessions. All except two: the Americans had no intelligence operation, and Britain's Secret Intelligence Service worked out of Singapore. Joshua Haleevie, however, communicated directly with London.

He was already following up an intriguing lead regarding the Nazis. Elizaveta had casually remarked on the great funds at the disposal of the cultural attaché of the German consulate, one Johannes Witzer-Weidemann. He was hail-fellow-well-met not only with the Japanese and the Italians but also with diplomats and merchants of lesser countries. And he regularly gave parties at the Ikra that cost more than five thousand dollars. Elizaveta was happy with his patronage, but suspicious of his activities.

Like any well-brought-up daughter of the Russian aristocracy, she spoke French, German, and Italian, in addition to English and her native language. She did not parade her linguistic accomplishments. It was vulgar to boast—and it was often useful to understand without being known to understand. The proprietress of the Ikra had to listen discreetly, so that she would know everything that went on under her roof.

Always voluble, the free-spending Herr Witzer-Weidemann became garrulous after a few drinks. She had seen him nudge the embarrassed German consul-general and had overheard him remark, *"Die Maisache kommt hervorragend an....* The May business is coming along splendidly."

On another occasion, Witzer-Weidemann and a visiting brigadier general of the German general staff had repeatedly toasted each other. Afraid to draw too close, Elizaveta had nonetheless heard two words repeated: *Maibaum* and *Maibowle.* The Maypole and the May punch were apparently innocuous. But why such concentration on the month of May?

Growing curious, Joshua had resorted to the hidden microphones he had planted in the Ikra when the internal telephone service was installed. The bartender called Wang, who had helped him dispose of the corpse of Colonel Ishikawa, regularly changed the spools on the wire-recorder. Wang would, of course, report the electrical eavesdropping to either the Nationalists or the Communists, perhaps both. But Joshua did not care, since he was only fishing for information.

Though inconclusive, the wire-recordings led Joshua to suspect that he had hooked a big fish. He ordered constant surveillance of Witzer-Weidemann and called in an informant who was the senior Chinese clerk of the German consulate.

The surveillance revealed that the cultural attaché had many unlikely friends in most unlikely places, "people who probably think culture is a new machine gun," as one report sourly observed. The chief clerk believed that Witzer-Weidemann was the kingpin of Nazi espionage in the Far East. The cultural attaché spent much time in the radio room communicating with outlying posts—and with Berlin.

Routine instructions were given to the Chinese clerk, whose new sixteen-year-old concubine had expensive tastes. He was to obtain carbons and/or discarded copies of Witzer-Weidemann's incoming and/or outgoing messages. He would be liberally rewarded if he turned up anything significant. But no one was particularly optimistic.

Joshua now stared at the flimsy papers on his desk with incredulity. It should not have happened; it could not have happened; but it had. Witzer-Weidemann had sent messages to seventeen agents, all different and all in unbreakable code—except one. Extraordinary good luck, or perhaps the Nazi's arrogant carelessness, had put into Joshua's hands not only the coded text but the rough draft in plain language of one message: *Confirm hereby decisive action first ten days of May. Remain alert for instructions regarding exploitation.*

The figure 37490, which must stand for May, appeared in every message. Further, a fragment of a coded message from Berlin repeatedly displayed that figure.

Marveling that the Germans used the same code inward and outward, Joshua whistled speculatively through his teeth and took a Havana panatella from the humidor on his desk. Herr Witzer-Weidemann evidently possessed information of far more than routine significance. Just as clearly, the Nazis were scheduling a major—perhaps decisive—action for early May. It was imperative to discover exactly what the cultural attaché knew.

Joshua drafted a cablegram informing London that he was pursuing a major lead and requesting authority to bring Witzer-Weidemann in. The risk was low, since the kidnapping would appear to be the work of Chinese gangsters. If he were skillfully questioned under drugs, the German would, afterward, not even recall what questions he had been asked.

Expecting no prompt reply, Joshua was not surprised to be still waiting three days after dispatching his urgent inquiry. There was in early April probably still a margin of safety, still time to counter whatever action the Nazis planned for the first ten days of May. He decided to give London two more days before sending a scorching reminder—or acting on his own.

Joshua then relegated the Witzer-Weidemann affair to the back of his mind. When not occupied with business or with his balancing act between his wife and his mistress, his thoughts reverted to the enigma recalled by the cryptic note in his pocket diary: *Ivan and Fritz?*

Why, he wondered, did the totalitarian allies—the Soviets and the Nazis—ostentatiously avoid each other? If their apparent antipathy camouflaged actual cooperation, they were very skillful at hiding it. Not a hint of collusion had been turned up, neither by telephone taps nor by the loose surveillance maintained by the Special Branch of the Settlement Police on the staffs of the two consulates.

The new concubine of the Chinese senior clerk at the German consulate was, however, *very* expensive. It was lucrative but neither arduous nor dangerous for the clerk to forget his newspaper at his favorite teahouse—and to pick up the newspaper left behind by his counterpart in the Soviet consulate general. The same afternoon that Joshua resolved to wait only two more days before abducting Johannes Witzer-Weidemann, the two chief clerks exchanged newspapers.

As Joshua expected, Wang, the bartender, had reported the electrical eavesdropping to the Apparatus. After a week, the Apparatus had concluded that the information was of little value—and had therefore passed it on to the Soviet consulate. After brooding for another week, the Soviets had decided to give the information to the Nazis.

Johannes Witzer-Weidemann's immediate response to that belated news was to request the Soviets to find out who was so interested in him. Further delays occurred while the Soviets asked the Apparatus and the Apparatus pressed Wang the bartender. But the answer finally reached the German: Joshua Haleevie was responsible.

The Nazi's request immediately bounced back to the Soviets: *Esteem great favor your arranging final disposal of the interfering Jewish swine. For obvious reasons, we prefer not to take direct action ourselves.*

Julia found the late afternoon traffic on Bubbling Well Road of no compelling interest. Shifting uncomfortably on the hot leather seat of the Lincoln Continental, she toyed with her cigarette holder. She was determined not to light another Chesterfield until her wristwatch showed precisely five o'clock. She would just have to last another twelve minutes without nicotine.

If Joshua had not entered the shop of Dombey and Son, Victuallers, by that time, she had permission to end her vigil. Soviet Vice-Consul Pavel Egorov had, however, assured her that Joshua would make an appearance.

"He *always* goes to Dombey's on alternate Tuesdays to look over their new selection of cheese," the Russian had stressed. "You understand, Mrs. Howe, we only ask of you an introduction."

She had nodded impatiently, annoyed by the sun in her eyes and by the slats of the bench cutting into her back. Their rendezvous, tryst, as Egorov melodramatically called it, had been in Garden Park on the Bund opposite the British consulate. The only Chinese in that park were gardeners. No fear, therefore, of Special Branch detectives disguised as coolies or clerks. Their conversation had been strained because he held the *North China Daily News* before his face, while she had pretended to be immersed in a copy of *Gone With the Wind.*

"You will accost Mr. Haleevie as if by accident and detain him in conversation," Egorov had directed. "When Mr. Slavinsky comes by, you will introduce them and take your departure."

He had turned a page of the newspaper before emphasizing: "You *must* leave immediately. And you must *not* interfere—no matter what happens."

"Why all the hocus-pocus?" she had demanded. "And how am I to know this Mr. Slavinsky?"

"You will know Mr. Slavinsky by his white panama hat. . . . I can tell you: Slavinsky has problems with the Municipal Council. He believes Mr. Haleevie can help him. Slavinsky is a goddamned *White* Russian. By such help we are winning over the goddamned émigrés. But, Mrs. Howe, the reason for the meeting is not your business."

He had then folded his newspaper and walked away, leaving Julia to brood on Soviet manners. It was not the first time Pavel Egorov had reproached her. When she brought Richard Hollings to the Soviet consulate, he had said, "Mrs. Howe, you must never—never under any circumstances—come anywhere near this building again. Never!"

He had talked to Julia as if she were vastly his inferior, like a chambermaid in a third-rate provincial hotel. When her anger cooled, she had seen that it was for her own protection. It would be disastrous if anyone learned that she was close to the Soviets, and the consulate was under intermittent surveillance. It would be catastrophic if Tommy learned that she had six months earlier anticipated his inevitable agreement—and had placed herself at the disposal of the Soviets.

She had, so far, only passed on information acquired from her uncle regarding Japanese troop movements or arms shipments, as well as tidbits regarding American arms sales to the Nationalists. Leaving notes in garbage cans at the Columbia Country Club hardly made for intimacy. But she knew the Soviets were grateful. She had returned the five thousand dollars in old notes they left her, rather than sign the accompanying receipt. She was not serving the cause for gain.

The tryst in Garden Park was the first time she had seen Pavel Egorov since he received Richard and her at the consulate. Why, she wondered, should the press attaché be involved with favors to White Russians? Yet he was responsible for propaganda, and winning over his semi-Fascist countrymen would certainly make effective propaganda. Besides, someone had to undertake the unpleasant tasks of espionage if the Soviet Union, the fatherland of the workers of the world, was to be safeguarded against capitalist plots.

Egorov had also introduced Richard to the consul general, who promised to smooth the correspondent's entrée to Soviet leaders. Richard had left Shanghai elated.

Richard, indeed! Julia had not yet solved the problem of conscience Richard posed. Perhaps she never would. She smiled reminiscently and assured herself again that she did not regret her single indiscretion.

And Tommy? She prayed she would never know exactly how Tommy would react.

Without thinking, Julia lit a cigarette, although it was only nine minutes to five. Tommy would be livid if he learned of her night with Richard. He would go berserk if he learned that she was working for the Soviets. One night was, conceivably, forgivable, but six months of deception was undoubtedly beyond the limits of his tolerance.

She tapped her fingernails on the steering wheel and surveyed the traffic again. No sign of the big red Packard Victoria by which all Shanghai knew Joshua Haleevie.

Julia leaned across to tap her cigarette into the ashtray and was struck by her reflection in the rearview mirror. Her own eyes regarded her with an appraising green stare. Or were they mocking?

She stubbed her cigarette out and fumbled in her purse for her hand mirror. She might as well salvage what she could from the interminable wait by touching up her lipstick. If Joshua turned up, she would see him in her mirror.

What, she wondered again, had impelled her to make love to Richard? He had, above all, been so woebegone. He was deeply wounded by Emily's rejecting him, though he had tried to smile it off. Yet it had not really been her responsibility to make up for Emily's cruelty—or to take Emily's place in his bed.

She had, of course, been a little tight after gin and burgundy and Cointreau. She had also been resentful of Tommy. No question about that. But that was hardly an explanation and it was certainly no justification. In fact it was rather frightening. She was naturally monogamous, innately faithful.

She followed Marxism-Leninism, but not its puerile theories on love and marriage. The act of love no more significant than a glass of water when thirsty? Horsefeathers! Marriage only a contract, an agreement to provide domestic and sexual services in return for bed and board and trinkets? What piffle!

Julia's lips curved in the mirror. Too much analysis, Joshua had once observed, was the death knell of spontaneous feeling. How right he was! And where was he?

She turned to scan the rush-hour traffic, but could not see the white canvas hood of the red Packard Victoria. Her critical eyes returned to her own reflection. Though her forehead was virtually unlined, she moistened her index finger and rubbed the minute indentation between her chestnut eyebrows.

Grinning in self-mockery, she pushed her hair off her forehead and looked up to see that the big red Packard convertible with the white-sidewall tires had just parked in front of her Lincoln Continental. Joshua was strolling toward the recessed doors of Dombey and Son. They might, she saw as she got out of the Continental, have dressed for the occasion. His linen suit was the same off-white as her linen dress. But he had clearly seen neither her nor her distinctive automobile.

"Joshua!" she called. "Joshua!"

He turned and smiled warmly when he recognized her. Then his light blue eyes looked beyond her, and concern ruffled his tanned features. Yet his expression cleared so quickly that Julia felt she had imagined his concern. Grasping her shoulders lightly, Joshua kissed her cheek.

"Julie!" he said. "What're you up to here?"

"I've heard so much about Dombey's new shipment of cheese," she improvised, "I thought I'd see for myself."

"We're on the same errand. May I take you in?"

She had obviously been mistaken when she thought he was troubled a moment earlier. He was in high spirits, gallant and playful.

Julia slipped her hand into the crook of his elbow. When she heard her name called, she turned. Dazzled by the declining sun, she saw the bulky man waving at her as a black silhouette. But his white panama hat was unmistakable.

"Oh, Mr. Slavinsky!" Julia began the mummery. "I haven't seen you in ages. How are you? Still studying English?"

"Ya, but you was my best of all teacher." Neither the Russian's accent nor his syntax did credit to his teacher. "I am so glad to meeting you again."

Prattling a reply, Julia saw out of the corner of her eye that Joshua was grinning at her embarrassment. She would have to put up with a lot of teasing from him later. But it was in a very good cause.

"Mr. Haleevie," she said automatically, "may I present Mr. Slavinsky? A former student of mine, as you've gathered."

"Mr. Haleevie, I have so long admired . . ."

Julia wondered how soon she could leave. The White Russian would not discuss his purpose while she was present, but she could not follow Pavel Egorov's curt instructions to leave immediately. How could she abandon an old friend with a stranger to whom she had just introduced him? That would look precisely the put-up job it was. Sometimes the Soviets were very impractical.

The White Russian was tall, robust—and clearly an innocent. His blunt features were honest, and his hazel eyes were trusting. She had evidently done a good turn for a hard-pressed human being, as well as for the furtive Pavel Egorov. Anyway, Egorov wasn't important, only the cause he—and she—served.

Julia stood between the two men, who were facing each other. The White Russian was curiously tongue-tied after finally gaining an introduction to the man who could solve his problems. To fill the gap, Julia told of a funny incident in the classroom, casting the reticent Slavinsky in the leading role. She would remember an urgent engagement in another minute and leave them alone, as Pavel Egorov had directed.

Her eyes were drawn by the movement of Slavinsky's left hand, which Joshua could not see because she was in the way. Clenched on a long leather handle, Slavinsky's fist was inching out of the side pocket of his jacket. Paralyzed by astonishment, Julia watched the shining blade of a knife slowly draw free of the pocket.

Her thoughts moved faster: Pavel Egorov had obviously ordered the attack. Why else instruct her to leave immediately—and on no account to interfere? Whatever his motive, Egorov was mistaken. Joshua Haleevie was not a foe of the Communists, but a foe of the Japanese. Communists and non-Communists were united against Japan's aggression. She had to prevent a horrible mistake.

The blade was already thrusting underhand at Joshua's stomach. Julia threw her weight on the Russian's forearm and screamed: "Look out! A knife!"

She felt flame arc across her thighs as the blade was pulled back. Joshua was apparently untouched, though his jacket was ripped. Julia fell forward to the pavement, landing painfully on her hands and knees. Looking over her shoulder, she saw Slavinsky strike again. Joshua stepped aside, and the assassin overbalanced.

The next instant, his arms were pinioned by two burly Chinese in workmen's blue jackets. Simultaneously, Joshua scooped Julia up and carried her to his red convertible. Without a word, he tumbled her through the door and slid into the driver's seat. After stamping heavily on the self-starter, he swung the Packard into the stream of traffic.

"You know," he remarked evenly a half minute later, "if it hadn't been for you, Julie, I believe that chap would've done for me."

Fumbling in her purse for a cigarette, Julia could not answer immediately. She was buffeted by remorse, fear, and anger. At least Joshua was unhurt, although his jacket was ripped. Looking down at the rent in her skirt, she saw a thread of blood.

But the wound was slight. Above all, she was appalled by her own actions. She had only by chance escaped being utilized as an instrument to kill a close friend. How could Egorov have been so stupid—and so ruthless? He had almost murdered a staunch enemy of the Japanese. Besides, only luck had kept her from blowing her cover. She flicked her lighter and drew smoke deep into her lungs.

"Also, my dear Julie, if it hadn't been for me," Joshua continued in the same light tone, "one of that lot would have got you!"

"Got me?" she asked. "I'm desperately sorry, Joshua. That man Slavinsky must be mad. I'm so sorry I introduced you. But he was after you, not me, wasn't he?"

"So *he* was," Joshua agreed genially and turned a corner. "But *all* the others were interested in you. Not only the Special Branch, who, thank God, reacted so quickly. *I* don't rate an escort of plainclothesmen. So it was you they were following. Obviously *not* to protect you but to keep a suspicious eye on you. I also saw a couple of lads I know to be Nationalist special agents. And if my eyes didn't deceive me, three thugs from the Apparatus as well. All in *your* honor, my dear."

"My honor?" Julia was shocked. "Why should they care about me?"

"Why, indeed? Julie, you've obviously offended a lot of people by your . . . ah . . . activities. It's lucky for me the Special Branch was tailing you. But it doesn't bode well for your future welfare, does it?"

Turning into the driveway of his mansion, Joshua murmured reassurances. But he ignored her defensive questions. Instead, he took her to a small room lined with books and told his majordomo, "Give Mrs. Howe a large brandy."

Joshua returned after ten minutes, having changed his ripped jacket. Julia had found the lavatory and washed her torn hands and knees. She had renewed her makeup but could only pin together the slit in her skirt. A fine red line disfigured her right thigh.

"Well now, Julie," Joshua asked, "what *are* we going to do with you?"

Since the question was obviously rhetorical, she smiled shakily over her drink. Even medicinal brandy was served in crystal balloons in the Haleevie household.

"Tommy's on his way," Joshua added. "He said he was afraid of something like this. . . . Julie, he agrees. You're leaving tonight for Hong Kong. The *Chusan* sails at ten, so there's just time to—"

"Leaving?" she protested. "That's madness! Why should *I* leave? You're the one who's in danger. They . . . he . . . was after you, not me. I don't see—"

"Julie, I can now look after myself very well, thanks to you. Your Soviet playmates won't catch me napping again. I'm indebted to you . . . deeply grateful! You've also cast light on some other matters that have been puzzling me. But you, my dear, are definitely leaving."

"Joshua, don't joke." She laughed unconvincingly. "I simply don't see any reason—"

"Julie, the time for fun and games is over," he cut in. "Among others, the Soviets will now be after you for spoiling their game. Also the angry Nationalists and the Apparatus, which will feel betrayed by your carrying out an assignment for the Soviets. That's a pretty collection of enemies, isn't it? Not to speak of Special Branch. You've got to leave, madam—right now."

"I'm not saying you're right about my . . . ah . . . activities, Joshua. But even if you are, what's the rush? Surely a few days longer, if I am well protected, won't—"

"I *can't* protect you indefinitely from the Settlement Police, my dear. Particularly not after this incident, which I'll have to explain. That's why I whisked you away so fast . . . to keep you out of the clutches of Special Branch. Do be realistic. You're now a liability—a danger to Tommy and to your little girls."

She gestured in feeble protest, but he overrode her: "You used to be a shield. The Nationalists have good reason to be suspicious of Tommy, but they wouldn't touch him. Not with an American wife who was so well in with the foreign press. But, now, you attract danger. All bets are off as long as you're still in Shanghai. Afterwards, Donald Howe's son and Donald Howe's granddaughters will still enjoy Nationalist tolerance. But not . . . not if their mother remains here."

"Joshua, aren't you being a bit melodramatic?" she asked faintly. "You make me sound like Typhoid Mary . . . bringing disaster wherever I go."

"Except that you're not immune. You haven't already forgotten today's little melodrama, have you? Would you like to attend the opening night after the botched dress rehearsal?"

Wheels skidded on gravel, and a half minute later Tommy entered the room. He was carrying a small suitcase and her beige cashmere coat. He appeared calm, but the corners of his mouth were white.

"Joshua's right, darling," he declared. "You'll have to go. Tonight! Now, Josh, if Julie and I can have a moment alone . . ."

When the door closed, Tommy said no more. He took her in his arms and pulled her close. He kissed her forehead and then her lips.

"My darling!" he said. "Darling, daring, brave Julie! I do love you! And I'll miss you fearfully. But it's—"

She kissed him fiercely, drawing reassurance from his lips. He held her so tight her ribs hurt.

"Julia, I love you very much. If you'd only told me about you and the Soviets. You know, I could be very angry . . ." He broke off and resumed gently: "Everything will be all right. You'll be away a while and then we'll . . ."

She could not believe it would be so simple, but she nodded. He stepped back to arm's length to look hard at her face and noticed the rent in her skirt.

"I almost forgot," he said professionally. "Now let's have a look at that cut."

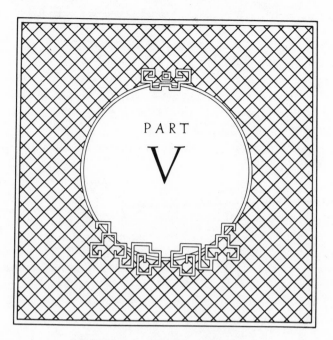

PART

V

DEPARTURES

1946–1949

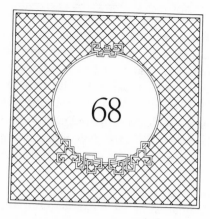

JUNE 15, 1946

The Imperial Hotel in Tokyo did not seem a real building to Julia, but more a natural growth than human handiwork. The yellow brick structure crouched near the gray stone walls of the emperor's medieval palace as if it had sprung from the earth rather than the genius of the American architect Frank Lloyd Wright. Otherwise remarkable for luxury and taste, the Imperial's bedrooms were all defaced by signs reading: DO NOT SMOKE IN BED! The U.S. Army had stenciled that injunction on the back of every door—as was its undeniable right.

In June of 1946, Tokyo itself was slightly unreal. The arrogant Japanese, whom Julia had seen strut and pillage in China, were now the docile servants of the Allied Army of Occupation. The emperor still reigned, but the nation was ruled by the supreme commander for the allied powers, General Douglas MacArthur, from the Dai Ichi Building, which faced—and greatly overtopped—the palace.

Julia and Tommy had been bemused since their debarkation in Yokohama two days earlier. Their daughters, Althea and Persephone, were excited at finally being en route to the birthplace of which they had heard so much—and remembered so little. The girls were fascinated by the Tokyo, first Oriental city they had seen in almost six years. Julia and Tommy were jubilant, yet aghast—equally ashamed of their horror and their gloating.

They found it difficult to take in the simple but overwhelming reality: Japan, the power that had only recently humbled Europeans, Americans, and Chinese, was now itself humbled and devastated. They had felt grim satisfaction when they first drove through the charred ruins that had been the metropolis of Tokyo. Enormous firestorms had followed the incessant air raids mounted by hundreds of American Superfortresses. Later, they were appalled by the suffering of the Japanese people, who had really had little more choice between war and peace than had the Chinese people. Revenge did not taste as sweet as they had believed it would during the dark days when it appeared that Japan would not only conquer China, but would also drive America out of the Pacific.

Victory had, however, not turned to ashes in their mouths, for they rejoiced at the humiliation of the Japanese militarists. But the victory was not complete. The decisive struggle for China was now beginning in earnest, and they were returning to play their part in that struggle.

Tommy had a mission in Japan first. His assignment from the Apparatus was the true reason for the Howes' stay at the Imperial Hotel en route to Shanghai, although they had ostensibly come for a medical conference. They had been admitted to Japan on the authority of the Nationalists' Central Government, a formality that Emily had easily arranged. They had entered the defeated country not on visas issued by the Japanese government but on the big, round entry permits stamped in their passports by Supreme Allied Headquarters.

Tommy's true mission was diplomatic—and secret. He was to win a beachhead for the Chinese Communists in Japan.

Because it had no international standing, the Yenan government of Chairman Mao Tse-tung was not represented in Japan. However, both Generalissimo Chiang Kai-shek's Republic of China and the Soviet Union maintained missions in Tokyo. Both were counted among the five Allied Powers. Chairman Mao naturally distrusted the Nationalists, who had been his formal allies in the struggle against Japan. He did not entirely distrust the Soviets, who were still his ideological allies. But he could hardly expect the Soviets to represent Yenan's interests.

Since Tommy could readily gain admission, he had been sent to establish close relations with the All-Japan Association of Democratic Physicians. From that initial base, the Chinese Communists planned to extend their influence throughout the defeated country. Commissar Chou En-lai, who directed Yenan's foreign policy, wanted a connection distinct from the obvious connection with the Communist Party of Japan, whose leaders had spent the war in Yenan. And Chou En-lai wanted that connection to be invisible, for the time being at least.

Slightly sheepish at the melodrama, Tommy had, therefore, slipped out through the underground arcade of the Imperial Hotel wearing worn and stained workclothes. He did not really look Japanese. But another shabby Asian should pass unnoticed in the bustle of the Kanda Ward, where the Democratic Physicians had their one-room office behind a scientific bookshop.

He was right. No one showed any interest in him. His meeting with the secretary also went very well, in part because the two leftist doctors discovered that they had both studied in capitalist England. When he emerged into the black-uniformed student throngs of Kanda, he was, however, unmasked.

The man who accosted him was so tall that he, like Tommy, over-topped the students by a head. Otherwise, he appeared nondescript with his small mustache and his rimless glasses.

Like his country, Roland Yamaguchi had fallen on hard times. The former senior editor for Domei, Japan's official wartime news agency, was very thin, and his gray flannel suit was very worn. But his manner was unaltered: amiable and aggressive. When he hailed Tommy he was also suspicious.

"Dr. Howe," he said. "And in a damned queer getup. . . . Working on new contacts for your masters?"

"Yamaguchi, isn't it?" Tommy ignored the challenge. "Good to see you. . . . I was always sorry we couldn't talk in Shanghai. But the war's over, thank God."

"I'm glad the killing's stopped," Yamaguchi responded after a moment. "You know, I never did think we could win. . . . Otherwise, there's not much for me to thank the gods for. Try living in a defeated country sometime, Doctor. Maybe it's good for the soul, but that's all."

Puzzled by the newspaperman's abrupt shift from open aggression to implicit appeal, Tommy did not reply.

"Look here," Yamaguchi suggested, "let's have a coffee. I'm sure you can afford it—even if you are masquerading as a downtrodden worker."

The Japanese was alternately cordial and resentful when they were seated in a minuscule coffee bar behind purple cheesecloth curtains. He appeared to enjoy the syrupy liquid that tasted to Tommy like roasted wheat kernels sweetened with caramel. In his own wry fashion, Yamaguchi was evidently happy to meet anyone who recalled his days of glory in Shanghai, even a former enemy.

"Look, Doctor, let's not beat about the bush." His gentle tone contrasted with his implicit threat. "I know the Kempeitai and Imperial

Army Intelligence were both suspicious of you in the old days in Shanghai. They knew you had Communist connections. They suspected you were an agent of the Apparatus. But they couldn't be absolutely sure. So they decided to let you run, largely because they wanted to watch you run down your contacts."

Tommy, who had in the old days of which Yamaguchi spoke been watching the Kempeitai and its arms-smuggling, remained silent.

"When I find you in this weird getup emerging from a notorious Communist bookshop in Tokyo, there's little doubt left in my mind," Yamaguchi declared. "I'm now certain you're a Communist agent."

"You've built a house of cards on no foundation whatsoever, Yamaguchi," Tommy finally countered. "I have my own reasons, personal reasons."

"Do you really expect me to believe that you're swanning around Tokyo in that disguise just to cheat on the gorgeous Julia? I'm hurt, Doctor. Do you really think I'm that dumb?"

"You've got it all wrong, Yamaguchi. But you could have a certain nuisance value."

"A pretty fair nuisance value, I'd say. It would ruin you if I whispered to American counterintelligence that you'd been a Communist agent."

"All this on your unsupported word?"

"Remember, Doctor, the Americans have now got all the Kempeitai's files. It's only a matter of telling them where to look."

"Just what do you want?" Tommy asked abruptly.

"Look, I'm not as badly off as you think. I've got a job. I'm working for the Associated Press of America."

"You work for the Americans? And you're planning to rat on them?"

"I work for the Americans. They don't own me. Also, Doctor, the AP is not official, not like the old Domei agency. . . . So I don't necessarily have to blab."

"And the price?"

"A loan, Doctor, a loan in installments. Let's say a hundred U.S. dollars a month for a year. Then we can review the deal. Perhaps increase my allowance. Perhaps end our arrangement."

Tommy agreed immediately. The price was just low enough so that it would be foolhardy to defy the blackmailer. Later, when he told Julia of the encounter, she reassured him: "Yamaguchi is basically an honest man, Tommy. I learned that in Shanghai. But it's certainly a warning to us. We're not fireproof . . . not immune to discovery."

"A damned stiff warning, Julie," he replied. "Altogether, the next few years are going to be very tricky: nasty and dangerous. Still, as you say, Yamaguchi, at least, is honest—by his own lights."

With that comfort they had to content themselves, after deciding that it would be pointless and, perhaps, risky to tell the Apparatus of the misadventure. They also decided to leave just as soon as Tommy had completed his mission. In Shanghai they knew far better than they did in Tokyo the unavoidable perils created by their dual lives—and the best precautions against those perils.

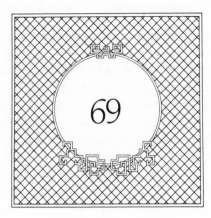

The SS *President Wilson* steamed up the Yangtze River cautiously. In late June of 1946, almost a year after the end of the war in the Pacific, the captain was still fearful of unswept mines. Julia stood beside Tommy in the bow, their daughters beside them. Still disturbed by their near scrape in Tokyo, she vividly remembered her last departure from Shanghai six years earlier. In mid-1940, when the *Chusan* carried her out of the reach of the enemies she had made through her assignment from the Soviet consulate general, Julia's emotions had been in even greater turmoil than they now were on her return.

The cramped cabin of the *Chusan,* all shiny yellow varnish and thread-bare puce carpet, had depressed her during her three solitary days before reaching safe haven in Hong Kong. Two weeks later, the staterooms on the SS *President McKinley* crossing the Pacific were roomy and attractive. Julia had, however, tired of repeating her implausible tale. She could not really expect her fellow passengers to believe that she had first gone to Hong Kong to say farewell to a dying friend and had then returned to Shanghai so that her daughters could join her on the *McKinley* for the voyage to the United States.

Shepherded by an increasingly cantankerous Lao Zee, ten-year-old Althea and seven-year-old Persephone had been as sunny as the Pacific Ocean itself, after recovering with disheartening rapidity from the shock of leaving their father and their home. The twelve-day voyage to San Francisco had, however, been marred by superfluity: too much food, too much time to think, and too much of the company of the ten

American wives who had followed the consulate's advice and removed themselves and their children from the war zone.

Julia had missed Tommy desperately. They had been able to snatch only a half hour alone on the boat deck of the *McKinley* while Lao Zee settled the girls in their cabin. Thank God, there was only Tommy; he had sensibly concealed her second departure from her friends as well as her enemies. Tommy had been at his best. Not a word about the mess she had made, no reference whatsoever to her keeping secret from him her work for the Soviets.

He had pledged his love again, and he had promised either to send for her "just as soon as this nonsense blows over" or to join her for a time in the States. They would not, he had said confidently, be separated for more than six months. In the meantime, the change of climate would help Althea's asthma. Besides, both the girls and their maternal grandparents would be happier for meeting each other again.

Things had not worked out as they planned while the *McKinley* tugged at her buoy and the gulls mewed around her stern. The tedious voyage across the Pacific Ocean had been the prelude to several years apart from the two beings Julia loved most: Tommy and Shanghai.

She had originally been so confident that her stay would be brief that she had only subleased a furnished apartment on Morningside Heights in Manhattan, rather than take a long lease on a better apartment. Her parents had agreed that she would be happier in New York City, where she could meet congenial new friends in the neighborhood of Columbia University, and the Horace Mann School offered the girls a first-class education. By September 1940 they had been settled in a spacious apartment overlooking the Hudson River, which even those fiercely loyal Shanghailanders Lao Zee and Julia acknowledged was more beautiful than the drab Hwangpoo.

In late October, a letter from Julia crossed a letter from Tommy. She had asked when she could return to Shanghai. He had instructed her to confirm by telephone the graduate fellowship in chest medicine offered him by Columbia's School of Physicians and Surgeons. She was to cable that confirmation to him, for he was tired of waiting for the academic bureaucrats to send their formal invitation.

Tommy himself had arrived on Christmas Eve of 1940, two weeks later than he would have liked because Julia had enjoined him not to entrust himself to airplanes. He had been greeted not only by an exultant wife but by two nearly delirious small daughters. Even dour Lao Zee had bubbled. Julia's subsequent welcome in private was uninhibited;

Tommy had complained with a straight face that he was exhausted by emotion—and exertion—when he began his work at Physicians and Surgeons in mid-January.

The fellowship had, however, almost seemed no more than a pretext for his coming to the United States. He gave his family far more time than he could in Shanghai. He had, further, promised that he would not go back until they could all go together. Discovering New York in Tommy's company was a joy for Julia, and the girls were just the right age to appreciate its gaudy splendors.

In late September of 1941, a cablegram had shattered their idyll: Donald Howe had suffered a stroke, and the prognosis was not good. Tommy had then entrusted himself to airplanes. He vanished, it had seemed, between one moment and the next, leaving a closet full of clothing, a spare razor, and a yawning hole in their lives.

Tommy had cabled when Donald Howe died in mid-October. His father, he later wrote, had departed from the world in peace at the venerable age of seventy-eight. His mother, Eurydice, who was five years younger, wished to retire to a Buddhist convent near their native village in the countryside. He would remain in Shanghai until the estate was settled. Although he had complete faith in his three elder brothers, he wanted to be on hand to ensure that his father's bequests to charities were properly handled. That responsibility he could not in conscience leave to his brothers.

Tommy had in subsequent letters promised to be back in New York by mid-January of 1942. He reported further that he had smoothed over Julia's indiscretions, placating the Apparatus himself while Joshua squared the Settlement authorities. The entire family could therefore return to Shanghai in the summer of 1942, when the girls would have completed their school year and their father his interrupted fellowship.

The shock was so overwhelming that Julia had not immediately thought of the personal consequences when the news bulletin interrupted the Philharmonic Orchestra's concert to report the surprise Japanese attack on the American fleet at Pearl Harbor on December 7, 1941. After that, news of a minor naval action at Shanghai was buried among reports of spectacular attacks on Singapore, Manila, and Hong Kong. Finding two paragraphs about the Shanghai incident at the bottom of a page in the New York Times had, however, concentrated Julia's thoughts on her own predicament. She had then concluded bleakly that she faced a long stay in the United States—and a very long separation from Tommy. The war was now total.

A cablegram from Elizaveta Alexandrovna Yavalenka, received on New Year's Eve, had advised Julia that Tommy was well and had concluded cryptically: GONE AWAY FOR HIS HEALTH. After months of agonizing silence, Julia had finally received a letter from Tommy on a single sheet of coarse brown paper. Forwarded by Harry Smythe in Kunming, it concluded: *Do not worry if you don't hear from me. I am not likely to be able to write again for some time. And regular correspondence will be impossible. You will hear if something untoward occurs. You must, therefore, not worry about silence, which will mean that all is well. I love you always.*

All the world was now at war, and the war was not going well. In the Pacific theater, the Americans, the Dutch, and the British were numbed by repeated blows. Attacking the concentrated targets that had evaded them in China, the Imperial Japanese Army and Navy appeared invincible. If Julia had not seen the Japanese staggering through the military quagmire created by China's vast size and enormous population, she would have despaired.

The defeats in the Pacific were shattering, but the German sweep in Europe had been devastating. France had collapsed while Julia was steaming toward San Francisco on the *President McKinley* in the early summer of 1940. France might not have fallen quite so ignominiously, Julia felt, if Britain's Secret Intelligence Service had given a whit of attention to the reports of its unpaid agent in Shanghai, Joshua Haleevie.

After the debacle, it was obvious that German Cultural Attaché Johannes Witzer-Weidemann had been privy to the secret plan whose fulfillment made screaming headlines on May 10, 1940. The "business of May," which Witzer-Weidemann had toasted, was clearly the *Blitzkrieg*, the lightning German attack against the Low Countries and France. If Joshua had been allowed to extract that secret from Witzer-Weidemann, the battle might have gone differently. Forewarned, the French might, at the least, not have collapsed so quickly.

Yet, Julia had even then reflected, all the warnings in the world would not really have altered the outcome. France had actually been forewarned repeatedly during the years between the wars but had not awakened to her peril. A society honeycombed with moral corruption could no more reform than its people could change the color of their eyes. Innumerable warnings had also failed to avert the inevitable fate of the International Settlement and the French Concession in Shanghai.

Julia had learned of "the last days of Shanghai" from Elizaveta. Technically neutral because Russia was not involved in the Pacific war,

Elizaveta was unobtrusive because of her obtrusive profession. Her racy letter, carried to New York by a neutral friend, had pronounced the epitaph of the unique international community on the Hwangpoo.

"It was a race between the Limeys and the Yanks to get away first," she had written. "Right after the U.S. Marines pulled out, the last of the American gunboats, bar one, disappeared downriver toward Manila. And the last of the British flotilla, bar one, churned off to Hong Kong.

"Joshua spent the night of Sunday, December 7, at the Shanghai Club. He said he wanted to be near the action. Actually, he wanted to be near me. His wife was of course away—either in Sydney or Washington. And Joshua was proceeding by easy stages toward a berth at the Ikra. He would have arrived in another day or two.

"About four a.m. on Monday, the night erupted. The Bund was rocked by exploding shells, and I was awakened on Kiangse Road. I could only see the flare of explosions over the Hwangpoo against the sky, but Joshua had a grandstand seat. From his window, he saw tracers flaring over the river and Jap fieldpieces firing at ships. To the north he saw the old Japanese flagship *Idzumo* exercising her ancient naval guns."

Reading the letter, Julia could almost see Elizaveta insert a Murad into her cigarette holder and write: "All the British and American warships were gone, except two. The *Idzumo*'s targets were two wee gunboats: HMS *Petrel* and USS *Wake*. Both were manned by skeleton crews, and the *Petrel* was commanded by a sixty-three-year-old Naval Reserve lieutenant. So, my dear, the *Petrel* burned—and the Japs swarmed over the *Wake*. The war for Shanghai was over.

"When he walked out onto the Bund, Joshua found his way barred by Japanese sailors with fixed bayonets. Rather than argue with the inevitable—and with cold steel—he went back to sleep. First, though, he telephoned me. The phones and the utilities were all working. The Japanese wanted to take over a going concern.

"Next morning Jap soldiers poured into the concessions. Since resistance was impossible, the little men marched in unopposed. They posted proclamations telling us what we already knew: a state of war now existed between Japan and the allies—Britain, Holland, and the U.S. The posters urged everyone to carry on his normal business.

"*My* business was all right, despite competition from local amateurs and imported Japanese tarts who called themselves geishas. But who else could do business? Most people could only mark time until the crackdown: confiscation of the property and internment of all enemy nationals. Your Uncle Jack refused an offer of liberty in return for working for the Japs."

Julia, who was not surprised, read on: "Joshua had previously arranged to disappear when war came—and he did. With his chum, the head waiter from the French Club, Fatty Woo, he drifted into the interior. Extraordinary, those two! They fought with the guerrillas, and they rescued aviators shot down over Jap-occupied territory.

"I stayed with my orphans. I still had some unfinished business with the Japs. So I stayed put for the time being."

Elizaveta's fate—and China's—had, however, been determined as much by apparently obscure events in the interior as by those dramatic Japanese actions. Early in 1941, Nationalist-Communist relations had broken down, and the United Front Against Japan had ceased to exist, except in name. The break had been precipitated by the clash called the New Fourth Army Incident. Julia recalled discussing with her students at Kai Ming College the first clashes between Nationalist military units and the guerrillas of the Communists' New Fourth Army in 1939.

Since that time, the New Fourth Army had been growing stronger—and more independent behind Japanese lines. Exasperated by the Communists' constant insubordination, the Generalissimo had finally ordered that guerrilla army to move north. Rather than give up the Yangtze Valley, the Communists had mutinied. After the Nationalists captured the Fourth Army's commanding general early in 1941, the Communists had appointed a new commander—and had consolidated their positions near Shanghai. With the United Anti-Japanese Front now hardly even a pretense, Commissar Chou En-lai had left Chungking—not to return for several years.

While the Communists expanded their power behind the fluid Japanese lines, the Nationalists had taken to the air. Harrison Parker Smythe III had grinned with satisfaction when he told Julia on a flying visit to the United States: "Claire Chennault really got going in the spring of 1941, after he received orders from the Generalissimo to buy a hundred American pursuit planes. Just as well our publicity campaign had prepared the people and the Administration. We'd finally convinced the American people that the Chinese were fighting their fight. All legalistic obstructions were swept away—and Chennault was allowed to recruit pursuit pilots from the U.S. Army and Navy."

By late 1941 the American Volunteer Group had been flying Curtiss-Wright P-40s. Unfortunately, the small, swift, and agile Japanese Zero was proving a better pursuit plane than anything the United States yet produced. Chennault had, however, drilled his volunteers in his three-plane tactics, which gave them an edge. He also paid a bonus of U.S.

five hundred dollars for every Japanese plane shot down. The Americans had painted grinning teeth on their engine cowlings—and had inevitably become known as the Flying Tigers.

Stranded in the United States, Julia had fought her own war, which she considered minor and regrettably free from danger. In 1942, the new American propaganda agency, the Office of War Information, had welcomed her enthusiastically and posted her to San Francisco. Although she had warned that she could hardly write one original sentence, her radio experience, her knowledge of China, and her association with foreign correspondents were considered ideal qualifications. Her covert association with the Chinese Communist Party was evidently a further, perhaps decisive, recommendation. Staffed by gifted amateurs, the Office of War Information on the West Coast focused its propaganda primarily on Asia—and secondarily on the American people's perception of Asia.

San Francisco was very pleasant. Althea and Persephone had avidly discovered America, and Lao Zee had found in Chinatown a family that spoke Shanghainese. If it had not been for Tommy's absence and Julia's constant anxiety about him, San Francisco would have been delightful.

In October 1942, her desk chief had introduced her to a white-haired Chinese who taught sociology at Stanford University. Professor Han's courtly manner amused her, but the message he carried had ruffled her. The Apparatus had formally directed Comrade Julia Howe to place herself at the disposal of a Soviet controller. They were all on the same side now, Professor Han reminded her. The Chinese Communists, the Soviet Union, and the United States were all fighting a common enemy. Since Yenan lacked Moscow's chain of consulates and front organizations in the United States, she was to work directly for the Soviets.

Having already been used by the Soviets as a cat's-paw against Joshua Haleevie, Julia had protested. Serving as a Russian spy was no part of her commitment to the struggle to liberate China; and the Russians were not fighting Japan, but only the Germans. Professor Han had replied, "You have received your instructions. It is not up to you to debate, but to obey."

Julia had not obeyed. After debating with herself for a week, she had simply ignored her appointment with her Soviet controller. To her surprise, she was subjected to no great pressure. Professor Han had smiled coolly and declared, "The Russians are, of course, the Russians —Communist or not. We understand. But just remember: never defy *our* assignments!"

After several colleagues at the OWI made extended trips to Chung-king, Julia had felt it was her turn. She could see Emily, whom she missed greatly. She could strive to find Tommy and, perhaps, arrange a vist to Yenan. The girls would be happy with their surrogate mother, Lao Zee. Julia's own mother, who was vigorous at sixty-three, had volunteered to come to San Francisco to look after the family.

"It'll do the old fellow good to get away from cold upper New York State to balmy California," she had written. Julia smiled. Her father was exactly eleven months older than her mother, who knew that San Francisco was not balmy but foggy.

Julia had then waited for formal approval of her journey. She was confident of approval because her desk chief was enthusiastic. What better tale to bring the human realities of the war home to the American people than a wife's seeking her Chinese husband, who was fighting in Japanese-occupied territory? What better way to touch the heartstrings of the Chinese people than the devotion of an American wife to her Chinese husband?

Bureaucratic delay was to be expected of any government organiza-tion, even one run by gifted amateurs. Julia had, nonetheless, been indignant when her chief told her of further delay "for reasons they won't tell me." A visit from the courtly Professor Han had clarified the matter—and aroused her to fury.

"It has been decided by the Apparatus, that you can be of greater service here than flitting off to Chungking," he had told her. "What do you want with those reactionaries anyway?"

When her fury subsided, Julia had been forced to recognize that her personal wishes could be thwarted at will by the revolutionary conspir-acy to which she had given her total allegiance. She had made herself the pawn of men who had no regard whatsoever for either her wishes or her welfare.

That sacrifice was, however, still justified in her eyes. She would, she reflected, be a sorry sort of human being if she could not give up her selfish personal desires to further the struggle for the future of China and mankind. Nonetheless, she swore again that she would *not* serve the Soviet espionage machine—not because it was so ruthless, but because it could blunder so disastrously, as Press Attaché Pavel Egorov had blundered in ordering the assassination of Joshua Haleevie. She hated the Soviets for deceiving her.

Still seething at being kept from going to China, Julia had been delighted when Emily telephoned from Washington, D.C., in May 1943 to announce her impending arrival in San Francisco with Mayling

Chiang. Julia could not go to Chungking, but Chungking was coming to her in the person of her sister-in-law.

They had met at the reception at the San Francisco Press Club, where Vice-Minister of Information Hollington Tong waxed garrulous. By the Press Club's tradition, the statuette of a black cat standing before him guaranteed that his indiscretions would not be reported—neither his bitter criticism of the Chinese Communists nor his slurs on the "left-wing intellectuals who dominate the American press."

Afterward, it had been like being back in the dormitory at Bryn Mawr following a long weekend apart. Julia's daughters were fast asleep after rediscovering their Aunt Emily, as was Lao Zee after a tear-stained reunion. Snug in quilted dressing gowns, Julia and Emily looked down from Telegraph Hill at the swirl of fog where the lights of the Golden Gate Bridge shone in peacetime. They had talked the night out, naturally dwelling on the topic that had also fascinated them at Bryn Mawr —men.

Emily had brought a long letter from Tommy, which began: "My own darling Julie," and closed: "Forever, my love." His letter would be her talisman in the uncertain future, but his news was already stale. Since the direct route across the Pacific was blocked by the fighting, Emily had taken nearly a month to reach New York. She had flown three quarters of the way around the world from Chungking to Calcutta, then through the Middle East to Africa, and, finally, across the Atlantic from Portugal.

"In Lisbon," she said, "I just managed to avoid Richard Hollings. No doubt, he was up to something shady."

Emily only shook her head when Julia asked, "And in all this time, still no one else?" No point in pursuing that topic. A woman of formidable constancy, Emily was completely—and pointlessly—faithful to her lost love.

Julia did not praise Richard's new book, *The Bear at Bay*, which had established him in the front rank of serious journalists. She had her own reservations about the Soviets' operations abroad, but her sister-in-law had become a fanatical anti-Communist. Emily would have sneered at Richard's wholesome picture of the Soviet Union united against the Nazi invaders. Nor did Julia confide that the OWI expected Richard to call into San Francisco in two weeks' time en route to the Pacific Theater.

"It'll be a new world when we go back to Shanghai after the war." Emily had inevitably turned to the world situation. "It's only a couple of months since the British and the Americans renounced extraterritoriality. They hated to give up their privileges, but they knew they couldn't turn the clock back after the war. Even I shed a tear for the end of the Settlement and Frenchtown. Anyway, old Shanghai is finished forever."

In July 1944, Sir Judah and Lady Haleevie had come to San Francisco from New York, where they had been living since buying their way out of Shanghai. Almost as much as she loved her own parents, Julia loved the old couple, who were a living link to the sunlit past. Joshua's estranged wife, Charlotte, who accompanied them, was delighted to have her entertain them. Even dutiful Charlotte needed an occasional respite from her demanding parents-in-law. Julia spent hours talking with them about the old days; the Haleevies had not only watched Shanghai grow but had themselves built a good part of the metropolis on the mudflats.

Living in princely exile in an apartment occupying an entire floor of the Fairmont Hotel, Rachel Haleevie had still treated Julia like a giddy twenty-year-old. Julia had not been greatly surprised, when Rachel mused on the futility of afterthoughts—and confessed with the candor of age: "My dear, I'm very sorry I stood between Joshua and his Russian lady. It was another age . . . But even so. This marriage with Charlotte, it hasn't turned out so well, has it?"

On a chilly October afternoon, Julia had found the Haleevies' servants milling frantically in the enormous apartment. Immured in his bedroom, Sir Judah was a remote presence. Only seventy-one to her husband's eighty-three, Rachel Haleevie had died in her sleep an hour earlier. When he received Julia, Sir Judah was a grieving Old Testament prophet with silver hair.

"It's better for Rachel." His voice was steady, although his eyes were red-rimmed. "She wanted to go first. She was afraid of being left alone. But, Lord, why did she leave me without saying good-bye?"

In accordance with Mosaic law, Rachel Haleevie had been buried the next day. Her eldest son, Jeremiah, had arrived the following day, having performed the miracle for wartime of chartering a Lockheed Stratoliner. In the interim, Julia and Charlotte had sat with Sir Judah. All the curtains were drawn; all the mirrors were covered; and Julia was constantly on the verge of tears.

"We keep vigil for a week—so that the survivors won't brood." Sir Judah's composure had still been unbroken. "To keep them busy, particularly the women, looking after the guests. But for an old fellow like myself virtually alone! It only gives the servants something to do. If we were in Shanghai, hundreds would be calling!"

Jeremiah Haleevie had not had to make another hurried journey. On the fifth morning after Rachel's death, the valet called him to his father's bedroom. Even more like an Old Testament prophet in his old-fashioned nightshirt, Sir Judah lay serenely against his pillows. A smile still lit his worn features, although his blank eyes revealed that he had rejoined his wife.

As 1944 slowly closed, Tommy had contrived to write almost once a month. Julia could reply in care of Harry Smythe, who was, as he himself said, "colonel, senior aide, chief cook, and bottle washer" to Claire Chennault, now a major general commanding the U.S. Fourteenth Air Force in China.

Tommy and Julia had to phrase their sentences very carefully because their letters could be intercepted. Harry Smythe would put out his eye before he read them, but other Americans—and, of course, the Nationalists—were hardly as scrupulous. Tommy wrote that he now truly appreciated the field work Kit Marlowe had done for Frank Walsingham.

Confirming her recollection of Elizabethan drama with a quick shuffle through an old textbook, Julia had learned she was being informed—and warned. The playwright Christopher Marlowe had been an agent of the first Queen Elizabeth's spymaster, Sir Francis Walsingham. Tommy's service to the Communist cause patently still involved espionage.

The suave Professor Han had stood smiling narrowly in the doorway when Julia answered the bell of the apartment on Telegraph Hill the Sunday before Christmas of 1944. After taking the best armchair and happily accepting the brandy that was grudgingly offered, he had said, "The Apparatus has not, my dear Mrs. Howe, sent me with further unpalatable news, only new instructions and a review of the situation so that you will be more effective in your work. Dr. Howe requested that you be fully informed."

Julia had felt a glow of pleasure at Professor Han's being required to come to her on Tommy's instructions. She had nodded and settled down to nurse her scotch and soda.

"The Nationalists are doing the job for us by their vile deeds. They are strengthening our friends' support and driving our enemies into our arms." Professor Han had declared complacently. "Very soon China will drop into our lap like a ripe peach. We must still struggle hard, but the outcome is certain."

That autumn, he explained, the first major Japanese offensive in years had been beneficial. The large-scale attacks called *Ichigo*, Operation Number One, had driven the Nationalists out of most of South China, captured the forward bases of Claire Chennault's Fourteenth Air Force, and even threatened Chungking. After clearing a wide corridor from Manchuria to Indochina, the Japanese had stopped in exhaustion. But Operation Number One had savaged the Nationalists while leaving the Communists virtually untouched. It had also precipitated the inevitable break between proud Generalissimo Chiang Kai-shek and his acid American chief of staff, General Joseph Stilwell.

"Stilwell behaved like a fool—much to our benefit," Professor Han had continued. "How he could possibly think that he could force Chiang Kai-shek's hand! Another arrogant foreigner who thinks he knows China.

"I beg your pardon, Mrs. Howe, but you know what I mean. Stilwell demanded that Chiang Kai-shek withdraw the Nationalist units blockading our Border Region. He wanted to use those four hundred thousand men against Operation Number One. . . . And he threatened to cut off American supplies if Chiang Kai-shek did not comply. When the Generalissimo issued an ultimatum, President Roosevelt had no choice but to relieve Stilwell."

Julia bridled her impatience. Professor Han's confidences had all appeared in the State Department dispatches from Chungking she regularly read—and regularly passed on to the Apparatus.

"That leaves Chennault the most influential American in China," he had resumed. "He's a great man—in the air. But not on the ground. He's leading the Generalissimo down a blind alley by arguing that the Nationalists can defeat the Japanese—and the Communists—with air power alone. But his Fourteenth Air Force couldn't even halt the Japanese assault on its own bases. Victory will be won on the ground. I pray every night for Chennault's good health."

Professor Han had lifted his empty tumbler suggestively, and Julia had happily refilled it. He had sipped appreciatively and observed, "The Americans are disgusted with Nationalist corruption. Chiang Kai-shek's brother-in-law, Finance Minister H. H. Kung, insists that the Americans pay one dollar U.S. for twenty Chinese dollars. The black market rate, the *realistic* rate, is eight hundred Chinese to one U.S. And how much of the profit goes into H. H. Kung's own pocket?

"Chiang Kai-shek still can't control his own Central Government. And he still can't bring the warlords to heel. He's like a juggler with too many bowls and glasses in the air. When exhaustion forces him to stop, the whole lot will smash."

Professor Han had smiled with satisfaction and declared, "Chiang Kai-shek is simply not ruthless enough. Comrade Stalin told him he must exert iron control . . . execute millions to ensure his complete control. But he didn't."

"And my role?" Julia had asked.

"As you know, we *never* deny that we are Communists, dedicated Marxist-Leninists," he had replied. "Still, many Americans have convinced themselves that we are really agrarian nationalists . . . revolutionary reformers, whatever that means. All to the good . . . Mrs. Howe, have you a pencil and paper? You might take some notes."

Amused at being treated like a student, Julia had complied when he continued, "You will in the future concentrate on the Nationalists' failings: their corruption, cruelty, ineffectiveness. Also, their avoiding fights with the Japanese, even collaborating with the Japanese. Regarding our side, you will stress our patriotism, moderation, idealism. Also, our total dedication to the war against the Japanese and our constant readiness to negotiate with the Nationalists—on *equal* terms."

Since Commissar Chou En-lai had just walked out of negotiations with the Nationalists for the third time, that last point rang somewhat hollow even in Julia's sympathetic ears. Generalissimo Chiang Kai-shek had declared that talking with the Communists as *equals*—and recognizing their Border Region as autonomous—would mean the Central Government's renouncing sovereignty over the Communist-occupied areas of China. Chairman Mao Tse-tung contended that the Communists were only a political party, but insisted that the government of the Border Region in Yenan was equal to the government of the Republic of China in Chungking. The split was irreconcilable.

"Professor Han, I take it that the battlefield for public opinion is now primary." Julia had spoken with the formality the issue merited. "Do I also take it that we can win on that battlefield?"

"Never, Mrs. Howe!" He had obviously been shocked. "In some circumstances, public opinion can be decisive. We must always attend to public opinion. But, in China today, propaganda can no more win alone than guerrillas can win alone. Both are the handmaidens of conventional military forces. The big battalions will bring us to power. And the day of reckoning is very close!"

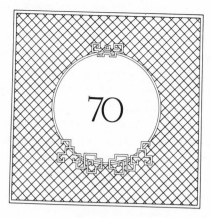

When the Howes stepped again onto the Bund on June 21, 1946, Julia saw that Shanghai, a little worn and a little scarred, was still Shanghai, only grown older. Although the Republic of China now ruled both the International Settlement and the French Concession, neither the city's shape nor its tough, wise-cracking natives had changed. Something fundamental had, however, changed—something fundamental, but not readily apparent.

Julia puzzled over that elusive change while she and her family were borne down Nanking Road in Joshua Haleevie's Rolls-Royce Phantom, which had been preserved through the Japanese occupation behind a false wall in his garage. Coming ashore in the launch from the SS *President Wilson,* she had found the Bund wholly unaltered—as always, ponderous, crude, and assertive. From Jardine's and the Chartered Bank at the northern end to the Shanghai Club and the Bank of China at the southern end, the temples of Mammon had suffered little. The old Japanese flagship *Idzumo* no longer dominated the Hwangpoo, but the American destroyer with the big white *246* painted on its bow was a welcome replacement.

When the Rolls was halted by a traffic policeman, Julia's daughters leaned out the window. The elder's pale blond hair was a striking contrast to the younger's jet black. Self-consciously blasé at sixteen, Althea nonetheless showed her curiosity about the birthplace she had not seen for six years. To thirteen-year-old Persephone, Shanghai was enchanted. The sisters gaped at the crowds swirling on Nanking Road and at the profusion of silks, jades, furniture, and delicacies displayed in shop windows and on curbside counters. Although shabby in mid-June 1946, almost a year after the Japanese surrender, Shanghai was herself again: hectic, materialistic, and ostentatious.

Tommy, too, leaned forward for a better view. The city's pulse had quickened in the six months since his departure for New York to resume his interrupted fellowship at the College of Physicians and Surgeons—and to reclaim the wife and daughters he had then not seen for almost five years. Julia was still nagged by the fundamental alteration in Shanghai, which she could not put her finger on. When the Rolls was released by the policeman's wave, she found her answer.

The Settlement Police had been natty in their crisp summer khakis. The police were now sloppy in crumpled cotton uniforms and ill-fitting visored caps. The policeman at the busy intersection slouched, and a cigarette drooped from the corner of his mouth.

Rather than the heavy traffic on Nanking Road, he might have been directing the sparse traffic of a Chinese city. Julia smiled at her own lapse. He *was* directing the traffic of a Chinese city.

For the first time, the reality of the concessions' new status came home to her. Because America and Britain, later followed by France, had renounced their extraterritorial privileges during the war, the International Settlement and the French Concession were now part of Chinese-ruled Greater Shanghai. Although she had worked hard for that change, Julia was saddened by the demise of that gorgeous anomaly, the multinational metropolis. Being within the old boundaries of the Settlement yet not being in the Settlement was eerie, rather like being a ghost at one's own funeral.

Lao Zee, Tommy observed softly, would not have liked this new Shanghai, which looked exactly like the old Shanghai. A great snob, the amah had been proud of the Settlement's foreign administration. She would have hated a Shanghai that was ruled just as the Nationalists ruled other Chinese cities—inefficiently, corruptly, cruelly, and capriciously.

Julia took Tommy's hand. Lao Zee would be coming home a little later, when her coffin was unloaded from the hold of the *President Wilson*. After the only Shanghai family in San Francisco's Chinatown moved away, Lao Zee had pined. Although she described China as "very dirty country with many bad men and many wicked mandarins," she had made them promise that her bones would be returned to that dirty country.

When the Rolls stopped before the house on Kiukiang Road, Julia felt she was meeting an old friend who had suffered greatly, but survived triumphantly. The doorway and the windows were obviously new, and the crescent of pale bricks reaching from the third to the sixth floor was a fresh scar against the weathered old bricks. Tommy had told her of the damage inflicted late in the war and the repairs that were almost complete before his own departure. The work could not have been done with half the speed—or half the skill—in New York for twice the price. The old Shanghai spirit was still alive.

The red Packard Victoria with the white canvas top parked before the house obviously belonged to Joshua, whose automobiles apparently bore charmed lives. He had sent a note with the chauffeur of his Rolls suggesting that the Howes might prefer to disembark and look again on Shanghai undisturbed by a welcoming party. He would, he added, await them at Kiukiang Road.

Behind the Packard stood twenty-two feet of coal-black Hispano-Suiza gleaming as if just out of the showroom. Sometime countess Elizaveta Alexandrovna Yavalenka was also waiting for them. The Cadillac Fleetwood limousine a shade longer than the Hispano-Suiza was unfamiliar, as was the metallic-silver Cord coupé with the boxy body and the headlights sunk in the mudguards.

"Em's new runabout." Tommy pointed the stem of his pipe at the Fleetwood. "She doesn't like driving herself any more. What with her children and visiting firemen, she says, she really needs a decent-size motorcar. Almost indecently large, I'd say."

Julia smiled with exaggerated sweetness and waited for him to continue. When he looked guilelessly at her, she asked, "The Cord, Tommy? You always wanted a Cord, didn't you?"

"Did I? Of course it's not much, that one. Practically an antique—more than ten years old."

"I hope you and the Cord will be very happy together. At least it's not as hideous as that Chrysler Airflow."

"Hideous? Why the Airflow was beautiful. And it's still very advanced technically—even after ten years. Do you know . . ."

Julia turned to her daughters, who were staring in disbelief at their home.

"Gosh, it's only a brick house," Althea marveled. "Mom, I always thought of it more as a castle."

Emily embraced them all in the cavernous sitting room that was a cave of memories. She was wearing not her wartime uniform of blouse and trousers but the form-fitting *cheongsam* that she had, with some reluctance, adopted as an affirmation of her patriotism. Julia was disturbed by Emily's strained expression. She was so thin that her pelvic bones were little peaks beneath her orange *cheongsam*. When she smiled, her translucent skin made her appear ethereal, but the line between her eyebrows remained.

Tommy kissed his sister, frowned, and declared, "I don't like the way you look, Em. I've got a good man I want you to see. David Chen'll give you a going over and—"

"Don't fuss, Tommy," she protested. "Julie hasn't seen my children since . . . Althea and Perse, how you've grown. I know it's not the thing to say, but . . ."

Dark-haired Persephone threw herself into the arms of her glamorous Aunt Emily, the daring aviatrix she had always worshipped. Despite the natural reserve of her sixteen years, Althea, too, yielded to her aunt's formidable charm. She glanced with ostentatious lack of interest at the youth and the two girls standing behind their mother.

"Jason, Patricia, and Eunice," Emily directed, "say hello to your Aunt Julia and Uncle Tommy. By the way, Hsiu asked to be forgiven. He wasn't feeling . . ."

They were not to hear how Emily's absent husband was feeling at seventy-two, for her voice trailed away. No one expected Hsiu to appear except at formal family functions. Instead, Julia and Tommy assessed Emily's children, who were Ou-yang Hsiu's "modern family." Dutiful and embarrassed, their nieces kissed them. Their nephew offered a half bow, a handshake, and flutes of champagne.

Watching Jason over the rim, Julia felt a rush of affection. Although his round head was like his father's, the seventeen-year-old was in manner, physique, and features uncannily like the young Tommy Howe. Tall and thin, he moved with engaging awkwardness. His stance, his shy assurance, and his gentle smile all recalled the Tommy she remembered meeting twenty-five years ago.

Jason's crumpled cotton trousers and stand-up collar tunic were, however, the clothing of a junior clerk. Somewhat defensively, he explained that he was to attend a student meeting that evening and did not want to appear different.

When Tommy and Emily looked at each other, Julia knew they too were recalling student meetings in the 1920s. Jason, his mother explained, was demonstrating solidarity with his fellow students at American-oriented Yenching University in Peiping. Since the war had affected his education, he needed a thorough grounding in English before transferring to an American university.

Wondering idly why Emily had explained at such length, Julia turned again to her nieces. Patricia, who was fifteen, and Eunice, who was thirteen, were attractive in striped cotton dresses and saddle shoes. Their heads were long like the Howes', but their features were small, neat, and bland like the Ou-yangs'.

"You've got to see the roof." Jason shooed his miniature harem up the circular staircase. "Let's go up and let the grown-ups play."

Humor, Julia noted, as well as gentle charm. He would be devastating in a few years. Where, she wondered, had he acquired that understated self-assurance that was so like Tommy's or Joshua's? And where had Joshua himself got to?

She heard a man's voice and looked up to see Joshua and Elizaveta. She was sweeping down the staircase wholly unchanged, as if time had no power over her. Even her dress was rather Edwardian, the style she had always favored. Her blue linen skirt swirled just above her ankles, and her waist was tiny. Of course, Liz would! The New Look they were talking about in Paris featured long skirts, nipped waists, and full bosoms. That erotic, ultrafeminine style was the opposite of the skimpy, rather mannish clothing women had worn during the war.

"My darlings!" Elizaveta hugged Julia. "My favorite American and my own guerrilla doctor. It's so good to see you together again!"

Julia felt her eyes prickle in response to that Russian warmth. She did love Liz—and it was uncanny how Liz had not altered. Close up, however, Liz's skin was suspiciously taut along the jawline and around the eyes. She had evidently had a face-lift.

Elizaveta swept around to coo over Tommy, but Joshua had not yet reached the foot of the spiral staircase. Stumping down step by step, he planted his left foot in its gleaming black oxford on the next tread and swung his right leg on the prop of a Malacca cane. When he finally reached the bottom of the stairs, his forehead was damp with sweat. When he came toward them, his right foot dragged slightly on the gold Tientsin carpet.

"I see it did have to come off," Tommy murmured. "You might've let me know."

"Shout the good news from the housetops, Doctor?" Joshua's smile was unchanged. "I felt that news could wait. . . . My dear old Julie, how are you?"

Julia put her arms around Joshua and hugged him tight. Tommy had only told her that the compound fracture of his leg, unheroically sustained when an ox cart overturned, had not knit properly. They had also had a cheery letter from Joshua at the London Clinic. He had not mentioned amputation.

"It's wonderful to see you, Joshua," Julia exclaimed. "Just like old times. . . . You poor dear, is it still painful?"

"Only hurts when I walk." He grinned. "Elizaveta also got some adjustments made, some mysterious female thing. The best quack for that was also at the London Clinic. Chap called Wolfe."

Elizaveta threw her lover an irritated glance, and Tommy suppressed his smile. Hereward Wolfe was a superb plastic surgeon who had perfected his skill remaking the faces of Royal Air Force pilots trapped in burning aircraft. Julia impulsively kissed Joshua again.

"Restrain your passion, my dear," he urged. "Not in front of your husband. Just as well that my wife's in Palestine with my sister Sarah doing good deeds."

Elizaveta nodded imperatively, and he proposed: "A toast! To immortal Shanghai! And to us! Not quite immortal, but trying hard."

The war years had engraved deep lines on Joshua's face and turned his hair gray. Although his hand trembled minutely, he was still a gallant figure in his white linen bush jacket.

Emily lifted her glass again and proposed: "To Shanghai! To China!"

Evidently embarrassed by so much emotion, Tommy asked, "Did I ever tell you about visiting Shanghai General Hospital the week the war ended? No? I thought not."

Filling his pipe, he continued: "Several wards were full of Japanese soldiers. When we entered them, every man Jack sat up erect—at attention. Except three encased in plaster and one in a coma."

He lit his meerschaum with a wooden kitchen match and asked rhetorically, "Why? I don't really know. Respect for authority, perhaps. Not toadying . . . not the people who blew themselves up rather than surrender. But imagine scores of wounded, sick, and dying—all sitting at attention for the enemy."

Julia joined Elizaveta on the rosewood settee, whose cushions had been recovered in the original orange Thai silk. Shanghai's material abundance amid poverty was even more striking than it had been before the war. All things were available to those who had the money, particularly the eager services of those who did not. The house actually looked fresher, more sparkling, than it had when she left six years earlier.

"The Japs are odd . . . damned odd." Elizaveta lit a Murad with a lighter just like Jack Pavernen's gold-plated cartridge. "They did the damnedest things."

"Tell Julie how you got out of Shanghai," Tommy urged. "I told her a little, but I don't know the details."

"After I closed the Ikra," Elizaveta recalled, "the Japs were aghast. . . ."

No more gilded playground for brass hats. But I was tired, and I'd lost most of my . . . ah . . . staff to internment, repatriation, and war marriages. Besides, it was no longer fun, so I decided to—"

"Getting out of Shanghai, Liz," Tommy reminded her. "You were telling Julie how—"

"How could he reward me, the Japanese garrison commander asked, how repay my great services? Without thinking, I said I wanted to get the blazes out of Shanghai, but I couldn't go without my remaining orphans, a hundred or so. To my surprise, he immediately agreed to help. The orphans, he said, were the future of China—and they would remember the kindness of the Imperial Japanese Army when they were older."

Scented smoke spiraled from her lapis lazuli holder, and she said, "The general talked himself into it: sending the orphans to the country-side would greatly advance Sino-Japanese amity. So I got in touch with Joshua and the guerrillas in the usual way.

"Led by Japanese MPs under a white flag, the convoy took the Soo-chow road. Their motorcycles glittered, and the Hispano-Suiza gleamed like a diamond. My chauffeur and my footman were both in white uniforms. Then came five Imperial Army buses carrying the children. We unloaded them at the rendezvous, and the Japs duly left us. After an hour or two, the guerrillas turned up. The Japs never knew that every one of the amahs and coolies who were looking after the orphans was a Chinese agent badly wanted by the Kempeitai."

Emily's laughter at the hoodwinked enemy froze in her throat, and she said in wonder, "The prophecy, Liz! Remember the soothsayer at the Great World. Her prophecy, most of it has come true. So the rest is certain. You will live a long time, she said, but not always where you choose. Liz, you *will* live a long time—judging by the way you look. And you would hardly have stayed two years in the hills with the guerrillas if you'd had a choice. You *have* been admired by many men—just as she predicted. I won't ask about possessing the one you really love. I don't really know what possession means in that context."

Julia looked with concern at her sister-in-law, who was continuing frenetically: "Many children, but none your own. Right on the button. And your enemies *were* your friends—the Japs. Above all, you look very happy, just as the soothsayer said. I think it's wonderful."

Julia decided she must very soon have a good old-fashioned gossip with her sister-in-law, who was closer than a real sister. The three years since they had last met seemed to have taken a heavy toll of Emily. Why was she so frenetic about a fortune-teller's lucky guesses?

Emily was, however, reasonably detached when conversation turned to the Nationalist administration of Shanghai. The city was today even more prosperous and even more pleasant for the rich and the privileged, as Joshua and Elizaveta confirmed, but it was, undeniably, far worse for the poor and the powerless.

"I think, Julie, you call them carpetbaggers in America," Elizaveta said. "There are hundreds of carpetbaggers from Chungking. They've expropriated everyone they could accuse of being a collaborator—and, naturally, they've taken over all Japanese property. How do I manage? One can get around anything with enormous bribes. The Ikra is reopening soon."

"Give the Nationalists a chance, Liz!" Emily pleaded. "It's just teething pains. Excesses have undoubtedly occurred—and there will probably be more. But we are making progress. Things are getting better. Just give us a little time. We've never run a cosmopolis like Shanghai before."

When Tommy turned the light off, Julia moved closer to him in the big rosewood bed. His lips brushed her hair as he leaned over to kiss her good-night. She slipped her hand into his and within two minutes heard the regular breathing of sleep. Unable to tamp down the excitement of the day so quickly, Julia lay on her back watching light glimmer ghostlike across the ceiling whenever an automobile passed five stories below.

Curiously, no one had said a word about the civil war between the Nationalists and the Communists. It was almost as if they were afraid to mention the spreading conflict that dominated their lives. Since the beginning of 1946, the rivals had again been fighting viciously. The global war that killed tens of millions had been only an interval in the Chinese civil war, no more than a distraction to Generalissimo Chiang Kai-shek and Chairman Mao Tse-tung. Despite the conciliatory efforts of American General of the Army George Catlett Marshall, the two were again at each other's throats. Battle now ranged from the grassy plains of Manchuria to the paddy fields of the south, from the back alleys of Shanghai to the campuses of Peiping's universities.

Julia's thoughts leaped about: from the ocean voyage to the shape of Shanghai; from Emily's apparent strain to Jason's charm; from Elizaveta's unchanging beauty to Joshua's mutilation; from her daughters' diffident reunion with their birthplace to their future.

She also recalled the past. Civil wars had been the backdrop for the first party she attended in Shanghai, the reception for Eurydice and

Donald Howe's thirtieth wedding anniversary. China had at that time already endured a decade of civil war. And civil war had continued for another sixteen years, until the Japanese threat briefly united the Nationalists and the Communists. As it had in the past, civil war today appeared the normal condition of China—though, she hoped, not for much longer.

Despite her startling discovery of a prostrate Japan, Julia did not fully appreciate the scope of the changes wrought by the war until she had been back in Shanghai for several months. She understood intellectually that she was living in a new epoch, but she did not understand emotionally. She felt that she was still the same person, still living in the same place, old Shanghai, that was dearest in all the world to her. As Tommy pointed out, she had no instinctive feeling for the new realities because she had been so far away while those realities were hammered out on the anvil of war.

She had expected to slip effortlessly back into her familiar ways in the familiar places. Instead, she was ill at ease in the city she loved. She should have been delighted that the former territory of the International Settlement and the French Concession was now under Chinese rule. She should have been concerned above all to hasten the transfer of all authority in China from the corrupt and futile Nationalists of Generalissimo Chiang Kai-shek to the idealistic and dynamic Communists of Chairman Mao Tse-tung. Yet she was not, not entirely.

Julia's unease drove her to reexamine her basic principles; she and Tommy talked long into the muggy August nights. Whatever else might be amiss, she was joyful because their rapport was now completely restored. Prolonged separation had made each realize that the other was the most important thing in life.

Tommy readily acknowledged that, as Julia suspected, he was no longer convinced that the Communists' coming to power, now virtually inevitable, would necessarily bring universal stability, prosperity, and happiness. Of course, he added, the Communists could not be worse than the Nationalists. Actually, they were certain to be a lot better. The Generalissimo's government was now almost bankrupt financially and militarily, as it was already totally bankrupt morally. Although he wondered about Communist rule, it was, Tommy said, the only hope.

"You're saying that we have no choice?" Julia asked. "No other place to go?"

"That's the way it looks to me, darling. . . . If we care about China, about ordinary people, we've just got to carry on."

"Tommy, I'm certain it'll be wonderful. But that's not much comfort to you, is it? You seem so disillusioned, my darling."

"No, Julie, just grown-up. I'm finally growing up. I now know there are no perfect solutions to the problems men and women make for themselves. Just bad solutions—and slightly better solutions."

"You're Job's comforter, darling. You know I don't agree. . . . Though you were so right about not working for the Soviets."

"That's over and done with. Forget it."

"The Chinese *are* different, aren't they?"

"Of course. Whatever his faults, Mao Tse-tung isn't a paranoid homicidal maniac like Joe Stalin. Julie, I'm just shying at ghosts. China will be all right with Old Mao at the helm."

"And us, Tommy? Will we be all right in the meantime?"

"What do you mean?"

"Our cover, Tommy. Isn't it worn pretty thin?"

"If anything, it's better than before. We no longer have to pretend to be so far to the right. Attitudes have changed. Being in the middle is good enough camouflage now."

"Tommy, I'm not only worried about our cover. I'm terribly concerned about our safety—and the girls'. If the Nationalists really catch on to us, if the American or the British do . . ."

"Julie, I'd like you to take something on faith," Tommy said slowly. "Just for now."

"I'll try, Tommy." She laughed. "Even if it goes against my nature."

"Believe me, darling, we're in no real danger from the Nationalists. Not as long as Emily is so close to Mayling Chiang—and we watch our step. It wouldn't do to get too friendly with, say, Rosamonde Sun. You heard that she's coming back to carry on her anti-Nationalist propaganda? But, aside from such a blatant—"

"Emily can't pull the wool over the eyes of the Americans and the British, Tommy. Why she doesn't even know she's protecting us from the Nationalists."

"Doesn't she? I sometimes wonder. Anyway, Julie, not to worry about the foreigners. Joshua will take care of them."

"Joshua? Why should he possibly—"

"Julie, you said you'd try to take it on faith."

The Apparatus was, of course, unaware of the Howes' misgivings. Counting them among its oldest and most reliable agents, the Apparatus flung them into the vicious political skirmishing that was leading to "the final battle for China." They were assigned to recruiting new followers, as well as to espionage and propaganda. They were, however, instructed not to compromise their cover by going anywhere near the Communist-sponsored public demonstrations that were eroding Nationalist power.

This once, Tommy was inclined to defy that prohibition, as, naturally, was Julia, the perennial rebel. They were determined to see the protests against the civil war. The Nationalists were not the only villain. The Americans had been transformed by Communist propaganda from staunch allies of the Chinese people to brutal imperialists preying on the Chinese people.

The biggest demonstration Shanghai had yet seen was mounted on V-J Day, September 2, 1946, the first anniversary of Japan's surrender. Tommy and Julia wanted to be inconspicuous when they watched the spectacle. Not that they would stand out among the crowds, but because they did not want the Apparatus to learn of their disobedience.

Fortunately, Joshua asked them to join him at the Shanghai Club. The parade was to end with a popular rally before that bastion of foreign power. No outsider would look for leftists in the capitalist stronghold. The club servants, who all knew them, believed that Dr. and Mrs. Howe were good-hearted, although confirmed reactionaries.

Before the war, Chinese had not been welcome at the Shanghai Club. Now the chief steward, who was, of course, himself Chinese, welcomed Tommy and led them to a favored position on a settee beside a window. Before the war, patriotic demonstrators had faced well-disciplined British-led Settlement constables, rather than the aggressive Nationalist riot squads. Shanghai was today truly a new world.

Joshua joined them, saying, "Glad you got drinks. When does the performance start? Are they holding the curtain for us?"

"Nothing much yet," Tommy answered. "Only a few dozen rather quiet demonstrators and a few squads of police. Nasty-looking brutes."

In addition to the revolvers in their holsters, the riot police were armed with three-foot ebony truncheons. Tensely rapping their truncheons against their palms, they stiffened when a roar rose from a side road. An officer wearing mirror sunglasses spoke sharply, and the ranks came to casual attention. Behind them, seagulls wheeled over the muddy Hwangpoo River.

Heralded by that roar, demonstrators streamed onto the Bund after marching unscathed from the Racecourse. First in tens, then in hundreds, and finally in thousands, waves of young men and women lapped against the temples of Mammon on the Bund.

The riot squads did not move. In their crisply starched shirts and blouses, the students were plainly not the children of the poor. The Nationalist police would not lightly attack the offspring of privilege under the eyes of foreigners. They were further restrained by Chinese reverence for the learning that the students exemplified.

The breeze off the Hwangpoo carried the salt tang of the sea and the stench of night soil. The muggy atmosphere stirred, and the gulls fighting for scraps from the ships soared higher. When the slogan-painted banners above the crowd flapped in the wind, the reports reverberated like titanic hands clapping.

END FRATRICIDAL STRIFE, one banner exhorted in pompous English. RESIST THE KUOMINTANG MURDERERS, another commanded in Chinese. AMERICANS, LEAVE CHINA ALONE, in English again and beside it, DEMOCRATIC YANKEES MUST NOT SUPPORT KUOMINTANG FASCISTS.

"Covering the waterfront, aren't they?" Joshua remarked. "Naturally, they're thickest around the *Daily News* building so the correspondents'll have a good view."

"The sooner we . . . ah . . . they crack down on this nonsense the better!" An anonymous American spoke among the group at the next window. An English voice added, "But they're right. The sooner the fighting ends, the better for business."

Depressed by memories of three decades of similar interchanges, Joshua smiled wearily at Tommy, who shrugged his shoulders. Julia threw them a fleeting glance, and her eyes returned to the scene on the Bund.

They looked so young, those bright idealistic faces, so young and so vulnerable. At their age, she too had believed she could remake the world. Although she now knew how hard it was to make even the smallest change for the better, Julia was profoundly moved by their dedication. The new China was marching before her eyes.

The students were not only courageous but ingenious. Two youths wearing U.S. Army suntans and aviator's leather helmets were throwing small bomb-shaped objects into the crowd of spectators. The banner carried on long poles above them implored in English: YANKEES, STOP

GIVING BOMBS FOR KUOMINTANG TO KILL CHINESE BABIES. Three young women in long skirts, high-necked blouses, and gray kerchiefs, who presumably represented colonial America, shouted unintelligible slogans under their banner's cryptic exhortation: YANKEES, REMEMBER YOUR OWN REVOLUTION!

"Good Lord!" Joshua pointed. "Those two take the cake!"

The male figure was a veritable Uncle Sam: tall and thin in red-and-white striped trousers, claw-hammer coat, and white-starred waistcoat. An enormous papier-mâché nose protruded beneath the red-white-and-blue top hat that hid his features.

The female figure beside him was even more extraordinary. She wore an intricately draped green dress that swept the ground, and she carried a flaming green torch. Green greasepaint coating her face, she was the image of the bronze Statue of Liberty. Somewhat incongruously, she wore a blond wig. The sign above that all-American couple declared: UNCLE SAM LOVES MISS LIBERTY—AT HOME!

Behind them strutted a young man costumed as General of the Army Douglas MacArthur, even to oversize sunglasses and a peaked cap festooned with gold braid. His hands were red with a fluid like blood. Two men with bloated stomachs wore waistcoats covered with dollar-signs. In his top hat one displayed a placard reading: WALL STREET BLOODSUCKER. The other's read: IMPERIALIST LEECH.

"The party's getting rough," observed the American at the next window. "No question who set up this show. The goddamn Commies!"

The demonstrators were now chanting: "Americans, have a heart! . . . Stop support to Nationalist killers! End the civil war!"

The riot police still waited. A ripple ran through their ranks, and truncheons twitched in sweaty hands when the students taunted them: "Running dogs of the imperialists! Chinese faces and barbarian hearts!"

A truncheon flicked at a student's head—and the police lunged at their tormentors. But a sharp order from the officer with the sunglasses halted them. No policeman took up the students' invitation to cast off the chains of servitude and join the patriotic masses.

Uncle Sam had clambered onto the top of a green Pontiac that was imprudently parked on the Bund. Stretching out his hand, he helped the Statue of Liberty climb up beside him. Students handed a microphone to Uncle Sam and formed a cordon around the Pontiac.

Julia nodded in approval. That maneuver had been well planned, as had the positions of the four loudspeakers, each protected by its own cordon of students. Considerable preparation had clearly gone into this demonstration.

"Only a matter of time," the American at the next window gloated. "They'll get that fresh kid. Serve him damned well right. Some nerve . . . screaming about Yankee bloodsuckers."

The cordon protecting Uncle Sam broke, and the police surged over the green Pontiac. Hard hands clutched Uncle Sam's ankles and dragged him from his perch. A club knocked off his top hat, and blood welled from his cheek. The police gallantly helped the Statue of Liberty down from the car. Curiously, the riot squad did not beat the disheveled Uncle Sam or the weeping Miss Liberty, but simply closed ranks around them.

"Gonna make'n example of 'em," the American declared with satisfaction. "So they don't wanna muss 'em up too much. Look better in court unmarked."

Tommy exclaimed unintelligibly, rose, and thrust his way through the group surrounding the window. Julia stared for another instant at the features half-revealed by the tear-smudged green greasepaint—and followed him into the violence on the Bund.

Tommy's white linen jacket ripped from cuff to shoulder when a student grabbed his sleeve. But his forearm clubbed those who stood in his way. Julia followed in his wake, clutching her pearl necklace. Her floral print dress was bright among the drably dressed throng.

"Ho-ping! Ho-ping!" The chant rose ironic over the melee. "Peace! Peace!"

A head taller than the crowd, Tommy fought his way toward the police cordon that now surrounded some two dozen prisoners. The stench of sweat and fear filled his nostrils. Swearing students struck at him, then turned to hurl cobblestones, bricks, and bottles.

Tommy battled through the demonstrators to confront the enraged riot squads. Ebony truncheons flailing, they charged. A moment later, three policemen lay on the cobblestones, blood trickling from their wounds. A truncheon glanced off Tommy's shoulder and flung him aside. As if he believed himself invulnerable because he was a doctor and not a student, he stepped forward again.

"Traitor!" A thickset student shrieked and yanked him back. "Never surrender!"

His blood up, Tommy turned and smashed the assailant with his fist. Finally seeing that Julia had followed him, he grasped her hand and made for the gap between demonstrators and police.

"We must get to them!" he shouted.

Ignoring the eccentric foreign woman, two policemen closed on the respectable-looking Chinese man who had joined the rebels. A truncheon tapped Tommy's ribs—softly, it appeared, almost playfully. The blow almost knocked him off his feet, and two policemen wrenched his arms behind his back. Bent double, he was propelled through the cordon surrounding the prisoners.

Julia hurled herself at the policemen who held Tommy. Startled, one released his hold and turned to confront her. Tommy pulled free when he saw Julia thrown to the cobblestones, her flowered dress incongruously gay. He brought his fist down on the policeman's neck, sorry he did not have a stick.

"Hold it, you mother screwers!" The bellow froze both Tommy and his opponent. "Just hold it right there!"

"That's better." The officer with the mirror sunglasses continued, "Now what've we got here? By God, I thought so. Dr. Howe isn't it? Wasn't your father . . ."

Tommy nodded. His father's fame as an old Nationalist supporter had evidently bought him a respite.

"You don't remember, do you, Doctor?" the squat officer asked. "You fixed up a wound for me years ago. . . . And everyone knows of your father's contributions. You a Communist? What a ridiculous idea! You're not hurt, are you? Your lady, is she all right?"

Startled by that abrupt alteration from violence to deference, Julia heard Tommy reply, "Thank you, Captain. We're both all right. But we do have a problem."

Tommy stretched out his hand, a green fifty-dollar bill visible between his fingers, and said, "Two of your prisoners . . . Just high-spirited kids, after all. Badly misguided, but that's a matter for family discipline. You see, my nephew and my daughter . . ."

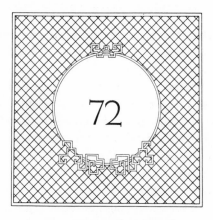

NOVEMBER 6, 1946

"We commit to the earth this husk, which was our brother. Ashes to ashes and dust to dust!" The American minister intoned the last words into the cold dusk and dropped the last clod onto the mahogany coffin. The damp soil crumbled on the gold-plated plaque, which was inscribed: *John August Pavernen, January 6, 1877–November 3, 1946.*

The tattered gravediggers of the Shantung Road Cemetery were eager to escape the raw wind and the dank fog. But the last mourners lingered around the open grave. They, too, were eager to be gone, but they were loath to go.

Weeping unashamedly, Gustav Vass lifted his silver hip-flask and drank a solitary toast to his partner in construction and chicanery. Elizaveta Alexandrovna Yavalenka lit her Murad with the gold-plated cartridge-lighter John Pavernen had given her—and let it fall glittering into the grave. Expensively bundled against the cold in a cashmere greatcoat lined with mink, Harrison Parker Smythe III blew his nose loudly. His cornflower-blue eyes were moist.

Old and stout, the dead man's Korean mistress concealed behind a black veil the ravages her tears had inflicted on her gaudy makeup. She was rich, for he had left her all he possessed. But she was bereft.

Quick Jack Pavernen had returned to Shanghai late in 1945, delighted, as he said, "to get back to civilization, business, and decent service." He had died of influenza a year later at the age of sixty-nine. His ingenuity had only begun to exploit the opportunities for shady dealing offered by Nationalist corruption, massive American relief supplies, and spreading civil war.

He was buried after services at the Union Church, which were attended by a hundred foreigners and twice that many Chinese. The foreigners had cherished him because he was an engaging rogue. Even when he was at his most sanctimonious, they had felt that he was laughing at himself—as well as at them. The Chinese had loved him because he was their silent benefactor amid their constant tribulations. Even the coolies who carried the enormous floral tributes left their own small wreaths on the grave. A stunted coolie, apparently half blind, stumbled over a shovel as he turned away. Above all, John Pavernen had been consistent. He had never slackened in his quest after the dishonest dollar, not even when he could have made many more honest dollars with less effort.

Across the grave, the eyes of Julia Howe met the eyes of Emily Ou-yang—and both hastily looked away. Julia nodded coldly and returned to her own macabre thoughts. Although she was accustomed to the abrupt cessation of human life in China, nowadays there seemed to be more deaths. The generation just senior to her own was dropping away, leaving great rents in the lives of the survivors.

Julia raised her head and again met Emily's eyes. Ashamed of her previous coldness, she smiled tentatively. Emily returned her smile, and they turned in tacit agreement toward the lane where the automobiles waited. When they met at the foot of the grave, Emily leaned over and kissed Julia. Their gloved hands clasped, they walked toward the automobiles.

Walking ten paces behind his wife and his sister, Dr. Thomas Howe also smiled. It was time to repair the breach with Emily that had opened after he snatched the children from the cold embrace of a Nationalist jail. When they took the unrepentant sinners to the house on Kiukiang Road, Julia had given way to her anger at Jason for involving Althea. She was implacable because Althea's asthma, virtually cured by the years in America, had flared up again.

Althea had, however, been bruised chiefly in her pride. They had put her to bed and sent Jason home. The chauffeur carried a curt note to Jason's mother, for Julia had refused to telephone Emily.

"Let Emily find out from Jason that he's safe—thanks to you," she said. "Let Jason explain what he was up to with *my* daughter. Let him do the talking. . . . *If* he can find his mother, that is. She's probably off in Nanking hobnobbing with that frightful Mayling Chiang. Ultimately, of course, the Generalissimo is to blame for it all. But I blame Emily almost as much."

"I won't press you to ring her," Tommy had replied. "We should have known, though. We were forewarned."

"Don't be silly, Tommy. How could we have known?"

"Remember last night? You told me you'd overheard a conversation between Althea and Perse."

"More of an argument than a conversation. About Aunt Emily. Persephone is devoted to her glamorous aunt. There may be trouble there someday, Tommy. Love auntie, love her politics."

"We'll face that when we have to, Julie. Perse is only thirteen."

"It's amazing what you don't know about girls of thirteen—or sixteen. 'Aunt Emily says.' That's Perse's constant refrain. The girls almost came to blows when Althea said Emily was a right-wing harpy preying on the Chinese masses."

"We should've guessed where that came from. I myself never . . ."

"Nor I ever. I guess I've been afraid that giving them political guidance would endanger our cover. Besides, in the States, there was no immediate need . . ."

"We'll have to see about that. . . . Of course, that line about right-wing harpies came from Jason. His *student* meetings! Yet he seems to love his mother."

"Darling Tommy, he can very easily love his mother and hate her politics. You know, he's convinced Althea that she is China's Joan of Arc. If it hadn't been for you . . ."

"I'd like to know what particular swine recruited my nephew," Tommy interrupted. "I'd never have done so myself."

Julia smiled mischievously, and Tommy grinned sheepishly. He had just denounced some unknown comrade for doing precisely what they were doing—recruiting young men and women for the Apparatus.

"Though it does seem ruthless," Julia said. "Innocent children. Seducing them and flinging them into the political struggle. They're too young to be involved in so much danger."

Tommy replied with grave irony, "It *does* look different, doesn't it? It's quite different when it's your own child—even your own nephew."

"I'm not sure whether I'm angrier at Emily for her carelessness or for her stupid reactionary politics. Probably her carelessness, though. How could she *not* know what Jason was up to?"

"In the abstract, you approve of what he was up to. But not when your ox is gored—your daughter is at risk."

"I just don't want the kids dragged into it. But the Communists are the only answer for China."

"Unquestionably, darling. We *must* carry on with the Apparatus, but . . . but . . ."

The repetition of that small *but* encapsulated Tommy's doubts. Nursing his scotch and water, he sat brooding in the rosewood armchair until Julia demanded, "But *what*, Tommy? You were going to say . . ."

After taking a long sip, he said slowly, "What would you think, Julie, if I told you there was another way? Another approach, at least."

"I'd listen—as I'm listening right now. You know, darling, you mean more to me than any politics or—"

"And you to me. Which makes us bad Communists, more like bourgeois individualists. It's this way, Julie. During the war, it seemed only the decent thing, just natural, to work closely with Joshua. We were all allies, and I do have fond memories of England."

"You sound as if you were also working for the British."

"In a way. Actually a fairly active way. You know, darling, it *still* seems the decent thing to cooperate with the British. Our primary quarrel, yours and mine, isn't with the British or the Americans anymore. Not since they gave up extraterritoriality. Our enemy is Chiang Kai-shek. After Mao Tse-tung's victory, China should have good relations with Britain and America. To counterbalance the Soviets, you see."

"You *have* been thinking ahead. Yes, I see that. Otherwise the Soviets could—"

"I thought you'd agree."

He smiled over her detestation of the Soviets, which he shared. Their reasons were, however, divergent. Julia hated the Soviets because they had deceived her and used her to identify Joshua Haleevie to an assassin. Tommy disliked them because he believed they were carrying on the imperial Russian tradition of exploiting China.

"I've also been doing it for our own sake—yours and the girls," he resumed. "Some day we may need Josh and his British connections."

"As a kind of lifeline?"

"Perhaps. Anyway, it still seems the decent thing to keep on working with Josh, giving him—and the Secret Intelligence Service in London— information and assistance. For China's sake—and for our own."

Tommy paused in thought. He had told Julia almost everything. Yet he wondered whether he could reveal the last page in the catalogue of deception. The realities of postwar Shanghai had, however, made Julia more thoughtful and had curbed her impulsiveness. Having always trusted her heart completely, he knew he could now trust her discretion.

"Julie, there's only one more thing," he said. "You wondered about our cover. You once asked, 'Isn't it worn thin?' Of course you're right. But we're safe from British and American counterintelligence. Joshua protects us and—"

"Tommy, you've told me that already. But you didn't explain what you meant by taking it on faith."

"I couldn't risk Joshua's neck then. However, now . . . it's simply this, Julie: Suspicious questions *have* been asked about us. But Joshua has been able to block further investigation and to quash suspicion. He only tells the truth. Dr. and Mrs. Howe, he says, are his agents, double agents, and he takes full responsibility for them."

Tommy's revelations did not quite quell Julia's fears. She had rarely in the past been deeply frightened by the danger inherent in their work for the Apparatus. In good part, she had simply assumed herself beyond the reach of Nationalist vengeance in the impregnable Foreign Settlement. She had been terrified upon occasion, above all when she was forced to flee from Shanghai in 1940. But she had never been dogged by day-in and day-out fear.

That illusion of security was now shattered. Extraterritoriality no longer existed, and Tommy had just told her they might some day need a lifeline. Brutal Nationalist vengeance would undoubtedly follow if they were unmasked. She might escape with prison or deportation, but Tommy would not evade a bullet in the back of the neck. Since they were not playing a game, they could not quit when they wished. He had, therefore, taken what precautions he could for his wife and himself— and for his country.

Tommy's attention returned to the scene in the cemetery, which was bleak in barren winter. His wife and his sister were walking arm in arm, evidently patching things up.

Julia had been very unhappy about her quarrel with Emily. Her Uncle Jack's sudden death had shaken her, and she had, for the first time, not been able to turn to Emily for comfort. She had loved the rogue—and her father, his elder brother, could also go soon. Her guilt at not spending more time with her parents was deepened by their hearty affirmation that they were happy as long as she was happy, even if she did have to live ten thousand miles away to be happy.

Julia and Emily waited arm in arm beside Emily's enormous Fleetwood. Emily had come alone, not even bothering to convey her husband's inevitable regrets. The Howes gladly accepted her offer of a lift and sent their own car home.

Somehow, the women could not relax in the perfumed dimness of the Cadillac. They chatted lightly about fashions, friends, books, and children—carefully avoiding the Jason-Althea imbroglio. Tommy felt himself an intruder. If he had not been present, they would probably have had a jolly time dissecting husbands. Emily declined their invitation for a drink but bade them farewell warmly.

Standing just off the Bund on Foochow Road, the American Club always amused Tommy because it was *so* American. Six four-square stories of dark brick relieved only by white stone lintels over the windows, the building was a marked contrast to the very British and very ornate Shanghai Club on the Bund—with its cupolas, pillars, and canopies.

Harry Smythe was waiting in the dining room, which was also very American with its blond maple furniture and its bright print curtains. Harry, too, looked very American in his blue blazer, gray flannel trousers, burnished cordovan loafers, and button-down blue oxford shirt. Tommy had warned him that they would not have too much time. His office hours began at two-thirty, and he liked to look over his patients' records beforehand.

"Seeing you're in a rush, Tommy, I won't beat about the bush." After ordering, Harry plunged into business. "We'd like you to join us."

"You do get right down to it, don't you?" Tommy sipped his dry martini. "Tell me, though, who are *we?* And why am I so honored?"

When Harry grinned, he was again the insouciant vice-consul. He extricated the toothpick from his Gibson on the rocks, nibbled the pearl onion, and said, *"We* are Claire Chennault, a fellow called Whiting Willauer, and me—among others."

"What can I possibly do for such a distinguished group?" Tommy signaled for a second dry martini. "You know, I thought you were working for General Marshall, the great peacemaker."

"The great peacemaker is getting nowhere. Why should I tag along? I'd rather throw in with Claire Chennault. He gets things done."

"What's he getting done now?"

"Claire's starting an airline, nothing less. He's really going to do something for China."

"So many people are doing so much for China," Tommy murmured. "We're inundated with foreign carpetbaggers. And most of them are doing very well by doing good. But Major General Claire Chennault must be taken seriously, as must Harrison Parker Smythe III. Do tell me what I can do for you."

"We want you to be chief flight surgeon. Not only keep your eye on the aviators, but on health conditions wherever we fly."

"Harry, where's your airline coming from?"

The waiter placed a dry martini before Tommy and a Gibson on the rocks before Harry. He then served them creamy clam chowder in red-banded cups.

"All right, I'll take it from the top." Harry chewed his second pearl onion. "You know Chennault came back to China at the beginning of the year. He was appalled by the terrible suffering, and he wrote to a number of us."

Harry pulled a creased sheet of paper from his inside pocket and smoothed it on the tablecloth. After popping tortoise-shell half-glasses on his nose, he said: " 'I have,' Claire wrote, 'retraced my steps upriver from Shanghai through Nanking and Wuhan, to Chungking—the same route we all took during the war. I was shaken by the devastation, disease, and starvation I saw. Every city in the interior except Changsha was completely destroyed—just black rubble. Only half of Changsha was in ruins.' "

Harry gulped his Gibson, lit a Camel, and continued, his voice deliberately flat. " 'This isn't just a passing famine caused by a single crop failure. It is *permanent* disaster—and no help in sight. The Japanese stripped the countryside bare of food and killed all the pigs and chickens. The Chinese are eating bark and boiled weeds, and, as a delicacy, rice-straw bulked out with clay. The Japs swept up all oxen and buffaloes. Men and women now harness themselves to heavy wooden plows. But the Japs took even the seed-corn.' "

"Not only the Japanese," Tommy murmured. "Also the local warlords —and both the Nationalist and the Communist armies. They all pillaged. No choice if they were to survive. I saw the countryside while you were reveling in the luxury of Kunming."

"Some luxury!" Harry smiled warily. "Anyway, Claire wrote: 'The Yangtze Valley is almost a desert—and it used to produce half China's rice. More than half the river shipping has been sunk, and there is no timber to build anew. Railroads are wrecked; roads are mostly potholes; and few trucks are still running. Airlift is virtually nonexistent—only forty medium-sized civilian transports for all China. The hundred and twenty transports the U.S. turned over to the Central Government at the end of the war are all flying troops and supplies to the Nationalist armies in the field.' "

Harry gulped the rest of his Gibson, stubbed out his cigarette, and said, "So Claire concluded: 'Lack of modern transport is pushing China back to the Stone Age. Both trade and aid are paralyzed. Millions are dying of starvation and disease—four million this year in Hunan Province alone—while trade goods and relief supplies pile up in coastal warehouses.' "

The sandy-haired American carefully folded the sheet of paper and returned it to his inside pocket. He slid the half-glasses off his nose and slipped them into his breast pocket. Placing his palms flat on the table, he looked at Tommy and said softly, "Sure, Claire wants an airline of his own. He likes his toys. His new Flying Tigers for peacetime—if you can call this peace. But he's also desperately concerned about China. I know it's now fashionable to make fun of Claire Chennault. But, by God, he does care about China."

"No contest, Harry. Very few Chinese mock Claire Chennault, not even the leftists. I'm with you so far."

"Claire decided an airline was desperately needed. The United Nations' China National Relief and Rehabilitation Agency has been pouring in food and supplies. But there's no way to get the stuff to the needy. Now, CNRRA has agreed to advance two million U.S. dollars to buy airplanes. And the Central Government's just given the go-ahead."

"The transport aircraft, where do they come from?"

"The airplanes? Whitey Willauer's bought them."

"He simply popped down to the neighborhood shops and bought them?"

"Whitey Willauer is . . . was . . . war surplus property administrator. He sold them to Claire."

"And to himself, Harry? How enterprising!"

"It *was* a good deal. A few thousand dollars a plane—and we'll pay it off with the receipts from CNRRA shipments."

"And what do you call this airline?"

"CNRRA Air Transport, CAT for short. Claire is chairman, Whitey is president, and I'm a vice-president. Can we count you in?"

"As a consultant. I won't give up my practice. But in principle I'm with you."

The waiter replaced the soup cups with enormous T-bone steaks. Tommy waved away the French fried potatoes, and the waiter placed a bottle of Châteauneuf-du-Pape on the table.

"It's not a bad burgundy." Harry raised his glass. "To a long and fruitful association."

"To CAT," Tommy duly responded. "And now tell me why you're disillusioned with General Marshall."

"The general's going home right after the New Year, as you've heard."

"Only because President Truman wants him to be secretary of state.

No one's said anything about the whole truce mission's packing up."

"They wouldn't, would they? But Washington's definitely getting out of the peacemaking business."

"Why the rush for the exit? Why is General Marshall going home so angry?"

"As you know, he's gotten the Nationalists and the Communists to the conference table a number of times. Every time, one or the other broke it off—and then blamed the U.S. Neither wants peace through compromise. They're both talking to gain time—and the upper hand on the battlefield. So the denizens of the Temple of the Thousand Sleeping Colonels have concluded."

Tommy chuckled at the nickname for the headquarters of the U.S. Truce Mission in Peiping and prompted: "But why now?"

"The general's tired of taking all the shit. No matter what he does, it's wrong. The Nationalist propaganda machine in the States screams that Marshall—and the president—are practically Communists. Chairman Mao Tse-tung charges the U.S. is *entirely* on the Nationalists' side. Do you blame Marshall?"

"Harry, doesn't the U.S. understand that it has vital interests in China? You Americans are like a schoolboy taking his ball and bat home when the game doesn't go his way."

As if he had been waiting for the question, Harry answered immediately: "I call it the Two Unwillings, Tommy. The U.S. won't give up such idealistic goals as creating perfect democracy and building a modern industrial economy in China. But the U.S. is equally unwilling to pay the cost of attaining those goals." He refilled his wineglass. "Only a massive commitment of American weapons and a substantial commitment of American troops can halt the Communists. Chiang Kai-shek can't do it alone. But the U.S. won't make the commitment."

"So," Tommy mused, "the U.S. tells itself the game isn't worth playing."

"That would be sensible. American policy isn't sensible. We won't make the commitment, but we won't give up the goals. So we're left with the worst of all possible worlds."

Tommy was elated when he left the American Club. He had valuable information for his controllers—for both the Apparatus and London. American vacillation would ensure a Communist victory. The United States would maintain a presence in China and would continue to give assistance to the Nationalists—but neither its presence nor its assistance would be substantial enough to affect the outcome decisively.

Five days after John Pavernen's funeral, Emily telephoned Julia to say that she wanted to drop in for a chat. Knowing her sister-in-law's fierce candor, Julia was not surprised when Emily declared without preliminaries, "I've come to beg your pardon. Jason's behavior was inexcusable. . . . To involve a child like Althea in his political stupidities."

"Althea could have told me what they were planning." Julia relented considerably. "She was pretty irresponsible, too. And she's hardly a child. Not nowadays at sixteen. Em, you must be frantic about Jason's antics. It's so dangerous and so embarrassing!"

"I've tried, but I don't know what more to do, short of sending him to the States right now. And I'm afraid he'd get just as involved there. The Reds are very active among Chinese students in the States."

"He is courageous," Julia conceded. "Though how he can believe the Communists' promises, I don't—"

"You've been away, Julie. *All* the kids are true believers now. They believe everything the Reds tell them—and nothing their own parents say. Althea was pretty courageous, too."

"I simply can't forgive her for not telling us. Besides, a well-brought-up girl should never under any circumstances in public—"

"You know, dear, you've still got a female slave mentality." More confident of their reconciliation, Emily spoke with her normal candor. "Tommy may be the ideal husband, but that's no reason to become his docile handmaiden. Of course, you're so traditional—a better Chinese wife than I've ever been."

"Not so traditional, Em, not in politics." Julia had given much thought to the precise public alteration in her political position necessary to preserve her credibility—and her cover. "After seeing what's going on in Shanghai, I'm afraid the Generalissimo's not the answer."

"*What* is going on in Shanghai?" Emily's voice was edged. "Exactly what do you have in mind? And if not the Gimo, then who? Chairman Mao Tse-tung?"

"Heaven forbid! Not the Communists. But somebody's got to do something when the Chinese dollar drops from from eight hundred to sixteen hundred against one U.S. dollar. How many people will starve when their money becomes worthless? I had the Third Force in mind. It's the only hope."

"Are you on that kick, too, Julie? The non-Communist opposition? Take it from me, dear, those well-meaning liberals'll never amount to anything . . ."

The conversation became surrealistic. Accustomed to dissembling, Julia now intentionally revealed some of her true feelings. Emily was a strong Nationalist supporter and a doctrinaire anti-Communist. But she was neither fanatical nor self-deluding. Emily would have been suspicious of Julia's motives—or doubtful of her sanity—if Julia had continued to spout a hard right-wing line in the face of all the objective evidence. Still it was a very complicated dance.

Julia was forced to deny some of her beliefs, while affirming others. Out of her own direct experience she wholeheartedly agreed with Emily about the danger of Chinese Communist involvement with the Soviets, but she had to say naïvely: "Maybe Mao Tse-tung isn't so close to the Kremlin. You remember, Dick Hollings saw no sign of . . ."

"He *reported* no major Soviet influence!" Emily said hotly. "His reporting is always selective and self-serving. Don't talk to me about *that* man."

Julia could hardly confide to Emily that Tommy, who was an insider, was deeply troubled by Soviet influence over the Chinese Communists. No more could she acknowledge that the Communists stage-managed the "spontaneous" demonstrations that were systematically eroding Nationalist prestige and power.

Nonetheless, the discussion was good for Emily. She could speak her mind, as she could not with her reactionary Nationalist associates. The flush on her cheeks and the vigor in her voice were good signs. She was speaking freely, and she no longer appeared quite so strained. Thanks were also due to the iron tablets prescribed for the anemia her doctor had diagnosed.

"I must apologize, too." Julia turned the conversation. "I'm sorry I lost my head about Althea and Jason. It was cruel . . . stupid . . . to cut you off. I've been acting like a ninny."

"Politics makes fools of us all, Julie. . . . You know, I think Jason will have to go to the States. But how can we keep him away from the radical Chinese students? There must be—"

The telephone's ringing rescued Julia from an ironic dilemma. Was she, of all people, to advise on keeping her nephew away from Communist influence? A little ashamed of her dual role, she lifted the handset.

"Julie? I *am* the lucky chap today . . . getting on to you first crack out of the box."

She glanced at Emily, who was stealing one of her Chesterfields. Knowing the answer, she asked, "Who is that?"

"It's me, Richard Hollings, as you very well know, pet." He was no less cocksure for the passage of the years. "When can we get together? Are you and Tommy free for dinner tonight?"

"I . . . I don't know. I'll have a look at my diary."

His unqualified assumption that she wanted to "get together" galled. She would not otherwise have declared self-importantly that she must consult her engagement book. Her hand shielding the mouthpiece, she counted to fifty while Emily stared in amused speculation.

"I'm afraid we can't make it," Julia finally said. "You'll have to excuse me now. There's someone here."

Quite unabashed, the Englishman said conspiratorially, "I fully understand, Julie. A worthy and boring someone, no doubt. I'll ring back later."

Emily blew out a cloudlet of smoke and asked, "Who was that who wouldn't be put off?"

"You're not going to like this, Em. Naturally, I couldn't talk with him. Not with you sitting there. It was Richard, Richard Hollings, your old beau. You do—"

"Julie, darling, I *do* remember Richard Hollings. The name hasn't completely escaped my memory. Even though that torch burned out years ago."

"Are you quite sure, darling?" Julia responded in kind to the heavy sarcasm. "Are all the ashes dead? No glow at all?"

"Not an ember. Do you know why?"

"No, but I'm fascinated."

"He never loved me. Never!"

"Never?"

"Julie, he didn't try very hard to make me change my mind. He hardly tried at all. He went off like a little lamb when I got him onto Mayling's special flight to Hong Kong. If he really cared, he would never have left me *just* because I told him to. He would have moved heaven and earth to *make* me take him back."

Even with all Shanghai under Chinese rule, it was convenient to be a foreigner. Much safer, too. The Nationalist police were far kinder to foreigners than they were to Chinese. Everything had apparently changed in Shanghai, but little had really changed.

Richard Hollings and Julia Howe were therefore safe, although they were the only non-Chinese among the thousands of street hawkers demonstrating in front of the police station. Julia nonetheless felt conspicuous and exposed in her own city.

Richard's head swiveled within the turned-up collar of his trenchcoat like an amiable jack-in-the-box. Although he was approaching fifty, he looked youthful. His lean features were only a shade more saturnine than they had formerly been, while his temper had clearly improved. He was neither quite so cutting nor quite so obsessed with self-advancement. Success had improved him.

He was, however, just as persistent, constantly cajoling Julia to intercede with Emily on his behalf. His former mistress, however, refused to see him.

Julia wondered momentarily why she had agreed to interpret for him today. It was not because of his charm. She had wanted to see this latest among the mass protests that were slowly destroying the Nationalists.

"Doesn't this remind you of anything?" Richard shouted above the clamor of the mob.

"It's like watching the same movie again," Julia agreed. "We saw all this back in 1925—the May Thirtieth Incident."

His reply was drowned out by the crowd's roar: *"Kang-yi! Kang-yi! . . .* We protest! We protest! The Nationalists butcher innocent working people!"

Protest demonstrations twenty years earlier had also been dominated by masses of blue-clad workmen and by many fluttering banners. However, the inevitable slogans now denounced the brutality of the Nationalists, rather than the foreigners' brutality. Chinese military police had two days earlier killed seven among the throngs of hawkers demonstrating against new ordinances that barred them from many districts.

A modern municipality, the mayor declared, could not permit hawkers to cry their wares anywhere they pleased and turn affluent residential districts into Oriental bazaars. The hawkers were naturally infuriated by that threat to their rice bowls—and the Apparatus had naturally stepped in to organize the demonstrations. As if on schedule, the military police had lost their nerve, fired, and killed the seven. Martyrs were not essential for successful agitation, but martyrs were very useful.

PUNISH THE GUILTY, one banner read, and another, CHINESE MUST NOT KILL CHINESE. Although the demonstration had nothing to do with American intervention in the civil war, a banner in English exhorted: END FOREIGN INVOLVEMENT IN CHINA.

The mob was now surging toward the police station, screaming like headhunters for their enemies' blood. The time for speeches was past.

Behind barbed wire, the military police waited. They wore American field-jackets and varnished American helmet-liners. Their American M-1 carbines were loaded.

Swearing that no one would do business if they could not, the hawkers invaded the few shops that were still open. Smoke rose from the automobiles they overturned. The crash of shattering glass and the groans of splintering shutters rose above the mob's shrieking. Waves of demonstrators rolled toward the police station, thrust against the barbed wire by the pressure of those behind.

Military policemen nervously checked their ammunition. The riot was already more ferocious than the May Thirtieth Demonstration.

Screams rose shrill when the mob crushed the barbed-wire barriers and rolled forward. Forced against the brown brick building, the MPs lifted their carbines.

The first shots cracked above the heads of the mob. The reports of the light weapons tore through the shrieking like a ripsaw through plywood. For several seconds, the demonstrators stood in silence. Then blood anger exploded. The furious mob engulfed the MPs in its midst.

A second volley rattled from the police station, and Julia saw a youth crumple. The red bandana around his neck grew darker, and the gray-haired man shouting beside him stared in astonishment. But the youth was held upright by the pressure of the crowd. When his neighbors drew back in horror, he flopped to the pavement.

A third volley sounded, and the mob began to turn. The MPs advanced with flailing carbines. Individual shots punctuated the continuous screaming as the MPs trapped within the mob fought their way clear. When their shiny green-and-white helmet-liners formed a ragged rank, their carbines rose.

Richard gestured toward the intersection behind them, and Julia turned to follow him.

"Time to get out of harm's way." His words barely carried over the din. "We've seen this before. Same act under different management."

"That's the only difference," she agreed. "Chinese are now giving the orders to kill Chinese. You can see a little riot somewhere in Shanghai almost every day. The Nationalists are losing control even before the Communists arrive. It's all crumbling."

While Tommy and Julia were dressing to go to the first pre-Christmas ball at the Cathay Hotel a few days later, she said: "The Nationalists are fools. Twelve dead and more than a hundred thirty hurt in the hawkers' riot. Well, it's all grist to our mill."

"Aren't you a bit harsh, dear?" Tommy squinted at the mirror and knotted his black bow tie. "The Nationalists don't start the riots. And they don't *want* the deaths."

"I'll *never* get used to the deaths, Tommy. I'd make a rotten agitator. I'd be shattered by every martyr I created. At least it's better in Peiping. The student demonstrations there, nobody's been killed so far."

"There will be. If only because our comrades are afraid there won't be."

"I'll scream," she interjected, "the next time anyone says 'You can't make an omelette without breaking eggs.' "

"Somebody's bound to get killed, what with the demonstrations and riots spreading so fast, all the way from Chungking to Manchuria. Still, in Peiping no pretext was needed. That poor girl was undoubtedly raped by a half dozen American soldiers."

"You really believe that, Tommy?" Applying lipstick, Julia looked up from her mirror in surprise. "Really?"

"What do you mean, Julie? You know bloody well that student at Peking University . . . What was her name? Yes, Shen Chung. Of course she was raped by drunken GIs. Just because you're American . . ."

"Darling, it has nothing to do with my being American. I know that soldiers can behave atrociously. But I'm sure Miss Shen made it up— or asked for it. Tommy, she's lying."

"And just how do you reckon that?"

"No Chinese woman—lady or slut—would ever complain in public. Not about rape, especially by barbarian soldiers. She wouldn't cry rape unless she was getting something out of it. Justified or not, a public protest will destroy whatever reputation she possesses. Won't it, Tommy?"

"You're not completely wrong. So?"

"So Miss Shen Chung, who's probably no better than she need be, must have a good reason for screaming the house down. Isn't it remarkable that this terrible fate struck the one woman who *would* make a public fuss! So it makes little difference whether she was raped or not —though I doubt it. She—and the Apparatus—had a very good reason indeed for creating a public issue. Miss Shen Chung's shame is to be the nation's salvation."

"It's working, isn't it, Julie? The anti-American movement is sweeping the country. Everyone is demanding that the Americans stop supporting the Nationalists. Demanding that the Americans get out of China."

"So American correspondents report that a wave of anti-Americanism is sweeping China. Then the American people, naturally want to get out of China. It's good tactics. Old hat, but effective."

"Do I detect a note of unhappiness?"

Julie studied her face in her hand mirror, smoothed an unruffled eyebrow, touched the perfume bottle's glass stopper behind her ears, and confessed, "I know I should be delighted. But, Tommy, deliberately creating martyrs. Isn't it a little like trading in human flesh?"

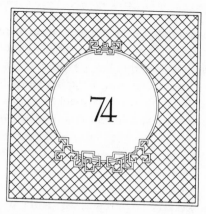

JANUARY 2–SEPTEMBER 8, 1947

The man on the bicycle was a living barometer of Shanghai's decline in the year 1947. He pedaled eastward, toward the Bund, on Kiukiang Road at seven-thirty on weekday mornings, and he returned westward at six-thirty in the evening. Julia never learned where he worked or slept, nor even his name or age. But she concluded from his venerable black Raleigh bicycle and his threadbare respectability that he was a clerk in an old-line foreign trading house.

She knew, however, that he was cautious. Whenever he stopped to patronize the small tobacco shop on the corner of Honan Road, he first clamped padlocks on both the handlebars and the drive chain and then secured the Raleigh to a lamppost with two more chains. Despite the alarming rise of theft, it seemed excessive caution when he also detached the brake pads and pocketed them.

Julia had first noticed the bicyclist between showers of icy sleet when, muffled in an ancient tweed coat, he was pedaling homeward on the first Friday in January of 1947. From the Raleigh's handlebars hung a sausage-shaped string bag about six inches long, which was stuffed with ten-dollar banknotes bearing the portrait of Dr. Sun Yat-sen. She surmised that he had just exchanged the regular bonus that many foreign firms paid valued employees in U.S. dollars. On the Bund, a dozen illegal money-changers brazenly conducted their black-market transactions in front of the official Bank of China. He was evidently taking the cash home. Julia assumed that his wife would use it to buy staples as quickly as she could—before it lost much of its buying power.

The string bag grew all through the spring as the currency declined in value. At the beginning of March it was about eighteen inches long. At the end of March two long bags full of banknotes hung from the handlebars. The clerk was getting ten to twenty times as much Chinese National Currency in exchange for a foreign currency bonus that remained unchanged. Inflation was so virulent that the Chinese dollar was losing its value against the U.S. dollar at a hundred and fifty percent a week.

By early summer, the string bags on the handlebars had been exchanged for a small suitcase strapped to the luggage rack. By midsummer, it was a large suitcase. By late summer, the large suitcase was supplemented by two very large string bags slung like saddlebags over the rear fender—and the bicyclist was making his cash run twice a week. By early autumn, he was returning home every day with a conspicuous load of banknotes.

Although cautious, the bicyclist obviously did not care who saw him carrying around millions of dollars. Shanghai's swarms of thieves, who would steal a bicycle in an instant, were not interested in cumbersome bales of cash. The banknotes bought too few goods.

With faith in the future falling as fast as the Chinese dollar, Shanghai was becoming pathetically shabby. Routine maintenance was virtually suspended by hotels, apartment houses, and even the self-confident foreign clubs. Drab streetcars became ramshackle, their seats splintered, their paint peeling, and their motors clanking dismally. Untended roads were punishing obstacle courses for automobiles. Axles snapped because of deep potholes, and passengers jounced like water on a hot griddle. While awaiting its fate, Shanghai was running down.

Not even Joshua Haleevie would put additional capital into the doomed city. The flow of capital was the other way—outward. His beloved Shanghai was dying, and he was helpless to save it.

Tommy's older brothers were smuggling their funds to Hong Kong, New York, and London. Customs officials and bankers were easily bribed to ignore the Central Government's stern regulations against sending foreign currency abroad. Besides, cabinet ministers, senior civil servants, and generals were the worst offenders. They shipped gold bars and U.S. dollars as official baggage. It all came down to a resounding vote of no confidence in the Nationalists' Central Government.

Julia was afraid to look too closely. Individual suffering was frightful—and the years had not completely inured her to Shanghai's hideous contrast between the pampered rich and the tormented poor.

Sing-song girls in sheer stockings and fur coats still haggled with bony rickshaw-pullers for half a cent—only the stockings were now nylon from the American PX. The haggling had, however, taken on a new edge. Once good-natured, virtually a sport, it was now a fight for survival. The contenders were like starving rats slashing at each other on a garbage heap.

The plight of the children was heart-rending. Thousands of families spilled into the streets when inflation made it impossible for them to pay vastly inflated rents. Their sons and daughters offered their bodies for the equivalent of a bowl of rice—beginning at the age of six or seven. They were the lucky children.

The crippled, the scarred, and the ill-favored were debarred from prostitution. They gathered in ragged packs at the doors of restaurants to beg from well-fed patrons. At the back doors, they fought for the scraps the waiters and dishwashers considered too mean to take home to their own hungry families.

The ordeals of the waif Little Pow in the 1920s now seemed almost minor. Small children followed coolies carrying rice sacks, hoping to find a few spilled grains. Others shooed the sparrows away from the undigested oats in the steaming manure dropped by the few horses that still served the city. Despite municipal ordinances, hawkers everywhere cried wares ranging from fountain pens and tangerines to pornographic photographs and condoms. They had few customers, since even their prices were soaring.

Julia became almost ferocious, which was not like her. When Tommy told her in mid-July that the Communist Party was planning on several more years of civil war to wear down the Nationalists, she exploded: "They *can't* wait! They *musn't!* It's getting worse every day. God alone knows what Shanghai will be like in a couple of years."

"We're not ready yet," he pointed out. "We must be certain of victory before we launch the final offensive."

"Tommy, I'm certain that tens of thousands of children will die in the meantime—in Shanghai alone. When I think of our own kids in the same . . . But there's one good thing. Nothing could be worse than this. I *know* we picked the right side years ago."

Tommy agreed. She was right, regardless of his own doubts about the Communist Party. Nothing could be more appalling than the Nationalists, who compounded brutality and callousness with rapacity and ineffectiveness. He was ninety percent convinced that Chairman Mao Tsetung would bring peace and prosperity to China. But that ten-percent doubt nagged him like a sore tooth.

"You know, it's a funny thing," Julia resumed. "I haven't seen my money man on the bicycle for a week now. That's a bad omen!"

. . .

Now as close as they had ever been, Emily and Julia naturally wished their children to spend more time together. Emily felt that no harm—and perhaps some good—would come of exposing her children, particularly Jason, to the strong American influence exerted by Althea and Persephone. Julia knew that Althea liked masculine company, and Jason was safe because they belonged to the same family. Moreover, his idealism would be good for her bourgeois daughters. There was nothing fundamentally wrong with Jason's politics. He was just a little too zealous.

The cousins were, however, bored by long days at the wholesome Columbia Country Club and occasional evenings at the cinema. Since Jason had sworn to his mother that he would involve neither his sisters nor his cousins in the student movement, time passed slowly. The impasse was broken by an invitation from the aged Howe aunt who maintained a mansion she called a cottage on the Yangtze River at Woosung, some fifteen miles from Shanghai.

Auntie Vi, who would not have a telephone, wrote that she would be delighted to have her nieces and her nephew come and create as much tumult as they wished, for as long as they wished. In addition to fishing, she offered them swimming, sailing, tennis, and horses.

"Besides," she wrote, "it will do the American girls a lot of good to see the *real* China." Smiling at that description of his aunt's estate, Tommy agreed heartily.

The recluse Ou-yang Hsiu nodded benevolently when his daughters Patricia and Eunice returned, under the protection of Auntie Vi's aged majordomo, two weeks later. The girls were suntanned and bursting with tales of their innocent adventures in the countryside. They did not immediately speak of their absent brother. But Persephone Howe had already told her parents, "Althea and Jason were spoilsports. Always saying they were bored. I'm glad they left early."

Tommy nodded automatically, and Julia said, "That's nice, dear. You must tell us all about it after—"

"What did you say?" Tommy exploded. "Jason and Althea left early? When?"

"Why, nine or ten days ago, Daddy. They said you told them they could leave if they got bored. Where—"

The telephone broke in. Emily was on the line, frantic at her daughters' report.

"Tommy, *where* are Jason and Althea?" she demanded irrationally. "You must know."

"I don't, Em, but I'll find out bloody quick. And get your friends in the Nationalist police busy."

He hung up briskly, his adrenaline surging. He was ready for action, but he had little idea what to do.

Ten days was a long time for two youngsters to be missing. If they had been kidnapped, he should already have had a demand for ransom. Besides, they had set out of their own will, after lying about having his permission to do so. On their journey back to Shanghai, they could, of course, have been abducted or injured. But that was unlikely. He had to assume that Althea and Jason had deliberately run away.

Tommy began his inquiries in Woosung, recruiting farmers and fishermen to search the district. He also asked for help from the Apparatus. Perhaps some comrade had seen the two youngsters where they should not have been.

Tommy assured the distraught Emily that he was making every possible inquiry. Her aged husband came to the telephone to demand that no effort be spared in the search for his youngest son. Curiously, the father, who had three other sons, sounded even more alarmed than the mother, who had no other son.

Tommy grew gloomier by the day. The search of the Woosung area proved unproductive, and no word filtered through the Apparatus. Julia was irritable, and Emily was no help. She appeared and disappeared at odd hours, always dashing home in case her Nationalist sources had turned up some information.

On the fourth day, a grubby envelope came in the mail. Posted from Soochow, the letter read: "Dear Elders, Please do not worry. We are with the New Fourth Army, and we are serving China. Jason is old enough to carry a rifle, and Althea can roll bandages or assemble hand grenades—even learn to carry a rifle. It is glorious to make our contribution to the inevitable victory of the people's cause."

Under her neat signature Althea had written: "P.S. Mommy and Daddy, I'm sure you'll understand. We were afraid it would all be over before we could join."

Tommy erupted: "I only understand that bloody Jason's practically kidnapped her. Soft city youngsters like them will collapse . . . fall apart . . . under field conditions."

Julia was so relieved to know they were alive that she could even laugh at Tommy's indignation over his daughter's and his nephew's doing just what he himself had already done twice: joining the army in a time of national peril. She even toyed with the idea of letting her daughter suffer for her ideals for a while. But Tommy was still swearing at his nephew for seducing his daughter to the political cause he had himself served for decades. Besides, he said, there was no reason for his daughter to endure primitive hardships and perform hard manual labor. There were plenty of peasant girls for that sort of thing.

Julia mischievously remarked, "I suppose we should really be proud to give our daughter to the revolution."

"Pride be buggered!" he swore. "And bugger the revolution, too! But *how* do we get her back? I can't ask the Apparatus. They'd laugh themselves sick."

"Quite properly, too. You're quite sure you want her . . . them . . . back?"

"Don't be a fool, Julia. Of course, I'm sure . . ." Taking in her mock-innocent expression, he laughed. "God, I'm so glad they've turned up. Now what do we—"

"Let's go see Rosamonde Sun, Tommy. We owe her a visit anyway. Not that she gets lonely. Half the press corps is sitting at her feet . . . as if she were some kind of goddess."

Madame Sun Yat-sen held open house for the young liberals of Shanghai, foreign and Chinese. She also conveyed to foreign correspondents the information and views that the Chinese Communist Party wished to make known unofficially.

Since Tommy had never warmed to Rosamonde, Julia took the lead. She drew aside the woman she so greatly admired and spoke softly for almost ten minutes. Rosamonde's doll-like features crinkled in agreement, and she impulsively kissed Julia's cheek.

"I'll do what I can," she said, patting Tommy's hand. "Your motives are estimable."

After leaving the big house in the former French Concession, Tommy pointed the Cord's long hood homeward and asked, "What did you tell her about my motives? Blessed if I know exactly what they are myself."

"I told her we were, naturally, disturbed—as parents. As patriots, however, we were very proud to have our daughter and our nephew serve in the New Fourth Army. Certainly they were old enough, I said. So many others served when so much younger. We couldn't completely suppress our fears for their safety, but would strive to overcome that weakness."

"Sod it, Julie, do you *want* them to stay with the peasants? Have you gone mad? They wouldn't last six months."

"No, darling, I don't and I haven't—though I am a little ashamed of our selfishness. However, I didn't think Rosamonde would take kindly to a tearful plea to get our poor innocents out of danger. Not when so many are fighting and dying."

"What *did* you say? What's all this guff about my estimable motives?"

"I told Rosamonde I'd been reluctantly persuaded by you—because you have a cooler head. Both of us were very proud, but you wondered if the kids wouldn't be wasted. Not everyone can carry a gun. But very few speak English—and even fewer have the chance to be educated abroad to serve the revolution even better. As Rosamonde herself has done."

"Clever you. I never could have been that smooth. She'll pass the message on, then? Nothing now but to wait."

Considering the guerrillas' poor communications, their wait was remarkably short. On the evening of the ninth day after their visit to Rosamonde Sun, the elevator discharged two travel-worn and unrepentant sinners into the big sitting room of the house on Kiukiang Road. Crestfallen, yet self-important, Althea tearfully kissed her parents. Eighteen-year-old Jason was stiff-lipped. But he clasped his Uncle Tommy's hand hard, and he hugged his Aunt Julia.

"We swore to tell *only* you, Uncle and Aunt," he confided solemnly. "Comrade Chou En-lai *himself* directed us to return to Shanghai and resume our normal lives."

"Chou En-lai himself?" Tommy echoed. "How very strange!"

"Daddy, Comrade Chou knows everything that goes on," Althea said. "Even about two unimportant little soldiers like us."

"And, Uncle, he wrote directly to us. He instructed us to think of the future—not only of the present. Many brave young men and women can carry rifles or assemble hand grenades. But very few have the opportunity to educate themselves abroad to better serve the nation."

"How wise!" Julia exclaimed. "Did he say anything else?"

"Also, we are not to associate with leftists any more. Some people, Comrade Chou En-lai instructed, must learn to wait—and to serve in silence."

Why, Althea's mother wondered, had Chou En-lai responded so handsomely to their plea? To repay Tommy for his assistance during the White Terror of 1927? Or to recompense them for their years of silent service? Perhaps Chou En-lai had simply done the sensible thing from his own point of view. Educated youths were truly too rare a resource to be squandered.

Relieved and decisive, Emily directed: "We've got to get the kids out of town immediately. If the Nationalist special agents learn the truth about this latest escapade, they'll both be in danger. And I won't be able to hold the agents off for long. I can't protect them—not with Mayling in her present mood. They've both got to be on the next boat to San Francisco."

Two days later, Althea and Jason stood on the deck of the *President Wilson*. The Blue Peter fluttering on the foremast signaled that the liner would depart within the hour. Patricia and Eunice, who were not sailing, clung to their heroic big brother, their eyes wide in worship. Persephone, who was sailing, tearfully blew her nose into a grubby handkerchief.

Both Emily and Julia touched their eyes with their handkerchiefs. Tommy was self-consciously poker-faced at being so soon again deprived of his daughters. Ou-yang Hsiu was, as usual, not present.

Emily explained that her husband's absence was not this time by his own wish. He had been distressed by the youngsters' flight to the Communists, and, at seventy-three, he was suffering the consequences of that distress. He had been bedridden for a week with acute indigestion and muscular pains. His condition was alleviated by neither his traditional herbal doctor nor by his friend, the equally elderly Doctor Chee, who had completed his medical training at Heidelberg in the 1890s.

"I don't like the sound of that." Tommy retreated in relief from paternal emotion into a professional problem. "Did Old Chee take an EKG?"

"Doctor Chee wouldn't know an EKG from a boa constrictor." Julia laughed and explained to the puzzled Jason: "An electrocardiogram, dear. It measures the activity of the heart."

"I'll see to it," Emily declared. "Shall I call that nice David Chen who found I was slightly anemic last year?"

"Do that, Em," Tommy urged. "Just to clear the air. Though Hsiu's a tough old bird."

"Now, you've got it straight, haven't you?" Emily admonished the three voyagers. "The consul general will meet you in San Francisco. And Aunt Julia's cousin Bob, who is your distant cousin, will look after you in New York."

"Yes, Mother. Don't worry." Jason was blasé. A Pacific crossing could not faze the patriot who had crossed enemy territory to join the New Fourth Army. "We'll be all right."

"You won't forget!" Emily persisted. "Bryn Mawr will certainly take Althea—even at the last minute. I've sent them a cable. And the

George School has already admitted Perse. She's just a term early. But, Jason . . ."

"Yes, Mother, I remember. General Sun Li-jen is a distinguished graduate of the Virginia Military Institute. And General Sun has cabled VMI. So, it's virtually certain the VMI will admit me. But I'm not to mention communism or joining the Fourth Army. I'm to be on my best behavior for the selection board. And I'm not to have anything to do with leftists—not that I'd want to. Is that okay, Mother?"

"Yes, dear, it's just fine." Emily kissed him. "And do try to write regularly."

"It's okay, Mother." Jason turned away to hide the tears that started in his eyes. "I won't forget anything. Can we go down to the cabin now and drop our things off? This topcoat's killing me in this heat."

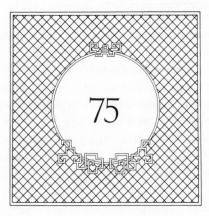

OCTOBER 16–DECEMBER 20, 1947

Ou-yang Hsiu died in mid-October, shortly after the cautious Dr. David Chen declared that he had "turned the corner." He was apparently recovering from minor heart seizures, which had initially appeared to be indigestion, when a massive attack carried him off. Mercifully, he died quickly. Fully conscious almost to the end, he complained, "It feels like ten razors cutting up my chest."

His wife, who was twenty-seven years younger than he, had faced his mortal illness with calmness, almost, it appeared to her brother and her sister-in-law, with detachment. Emily, who thought she knew her own heart, was herself surprised by her desolation after his death. She had expected to feel bereft, for she had come to love her husband in her own way. She had not expected to feel that the framework of her life had collapsed.

Emily had believed that light, although strong, affection bound Hsiu and herself. But she felt lost without the male figure who had for nineteen years been the single fixed point in her life.

That deprivation coincided with a period of involuntary quietude in her public life. With victory over the Japanese, the great crusade had come to an end. Like Mayling Chiang, Emily found that her knowledge of the United States was not as much in demand when all the guns were turned on the Communists. The Nationalists had never needed the United States more, but the old guard were sourly suspicious of all foreigners—particularly the brash Americans. When Herculean efforts should have been devoted to defeating the Communists' propaganda offensive in the United States, the Nationalists were almost paralyzed.

Some American missionaries and some congressmen spoke up for the Nationalists' Free China, as did a few journalists and a few business-men. A much greater number espoused the Communist cause—moved primarily by revulsion from Nationalist corruption and brutality. When the Nationalists' champions were dubbed the China Lobby, the battle was almost over. That name was its own condemnation. In any event, the men and women who shaped American public opinion preferred rosy Communist promises, which they barely understood, to the harsh face of the Nationalists, which they had come to know too well.

At the beginning of the bleak and empty December of 1947, the irrepressible Jimmy Wei urged an apathetic Emily: "You've got to start living again. You—"

"And how do I go about that, Jimmy," she interrupted. "There's no great demand for my talents."

"You can make our case to the U.S. better than anyone else. You've got to get back into the mainstream."

"Well, I guess I have sort of cut myself off."

Emily saw no need to confide further in Jimmy. She could not tell him that she now deliberately avoided those circles in which she might meet foreign correspondents because she was afraid of running into Richard Hollings. She believed that she never wanted to see Richard again. She knew that, above all, she did not want to see him when she was desolate and vulnerable after her husband's death. She did not want his pity.

Wryly, she recognized that she also did not want to see him because she feared she would yield to his attraction. She had always been a one-man woman, and Richard was her man. Nonetheless, her pride in her own integrity kept her from him.

However, she no longer condemned him as absolutely as she had in Chungking. Emily had matured, intellectually and politically, as well as emotionally. Despite her devotion to Mayling Chiang, she now saw that the Nationalists had major—perhaps even fatal—flaws. For that reason, as well as family solidarity, she would never breathe her growing suspi-cion of the role Tommy and Julia were playing. If she had not acknowl-edged that the Nationalist crusade was flawed, she could not have brought herself to deflect inquiries from the secret police regarding her brother and her sister-in-law. She would, moreover, have been unable to bring herself to block all investigation by affirming that they might behave strangely because they were doing "clandestine work of na-tional importance" for Madame Chiang Kai-shek.

Emily's conscience did not reproach her for that deceit. She had come to put human values above political values. She would support the

Nationalists to the death, but she no longer saw the civil war in China as a battle between absolute evil and absolute virtue.

"Let me do some spadework in Nanking," Jimmy was saying. "The best thing would be a tour of the States: lectures, interviews, broadcasts —the whole shooting-match. In the meantime, why not get to know the correspondents again. They're not *all* hypnotized by the Reds."

"God knows the job badly needs doing. Even talking about it makes me feel more alive."

"You might start by dropping in on Madame Sun Yat-sen's soirées for the press. You know, tea and Red propaganda."

"I couldn't, Jimmy. I despise her."

"If we could only shut her up. But persecuting the sacred widow of the Father of the Country. Forget it!"

"Jimmy, I really don't see how—"

"Well, you *are* an old family friend of the Soongs', aren't you? Why don't you act like one?"

When the telephone rang, Tommy Howe was shuffling through the file of clippings his secretary kept for him. He had to keep abreast of events, but he was hard-pressed to do so. In addition to his practice, he was serving as CAT's chief flight surgeon and, of course, carrying out the missions assigned by the Apparatus.

Julia answered the telephone and mouthed the single word "Emily." While she talked to his sister, he reread two items that together said it all:

November 12—The general offensive of the People's Liberation Army captures Shiachiachwang on the Peiping-Hankow Railway, the first major city in North China to fall to the Communists. [It had all begun for him, he recalled, with the strike by the workers of that same railway.]

December 8—Washington gives the Nationalists 140 warships, including a heavy cruiser and several destroyers in exchange for American naval bases in China. [Perhaps too much, he concluded, but unquestionably too late.]

Hanging up, Julia told him that his sister wanted to venture into the camp of her enemies. But Emily was a little timorous. Would they, she asked, come with her to Rosamonde Sun's?

Like Julia, Tommy was delighted that his sister was shaking off her lethargy. He did not, however, share Julia's hope that she could be brought to see the light as they saw it—and he wondered at her sudden interest in the left wing. But naturally he would help her.

A week before Christmas of 1947, Tommy rang the bell of the big house in the old French Concession. An enormous holly wreath with a red bow hung on the door.

"I'd almost forgotten Rosamonde was a good Christian." Julia smoothed her mink. "As the only believer among us three, I'll be right at home."

Carols were sounding from a portable record-player, and someone had mixed a bowl of Christmas punch. Emily assumed that the guests had provided those bourgeois fripperies; Rosamonde Sun was reputed to be above such frivolity. Since she had last seen her hostess very briefly in Chungking some seven years earlier, Emily could not properly assess the legend, perhaps myth, of the self-sacrificing and compassionate Madame Sun Yat-sen. Her reputation appeared excessive—but saints always appeared excessive to their contemporaries.

On the record a choir was singing "Adeste Fideles." A small fir tree was hung with miniature Chinese lanterns whose red silk tassels swayed when the old floorboards flexed and creaked. Tobacco smoke eddied; the conversation was intense; the liquor flowed; and voices were raised. Emily was bemused by the familiar atmosphere, just like every gathering of newspaper people anywhere.

"First some punch, my friends," Rosamonde directed. "Then you must meet the interesting people. Gregory Hardin over there you surely know already. Everyone does. He's been with us so long."

Emily waved to her favorite newspaperman. Favors or promises, even threats, could not influence him. It was a pity that a correspondent noted for his integrity was reporting more favorably on the Communists every day. Of course, he depended largely on second-hand reports, since he was virtually barred from the battle zones.

"The correspondents don't speak Chinese," Hollington Tong, the perennial chief of propaganda, always explained. "Unfortunately, I can't always spare a member of my staff to accompany them."

A stupid policy, Emily felt. Even Jimmy Wei was starved of authentic information by the Nationalists' diehard reactionaries, who despised all foreigners, particularly newspapermen. Such obstructionism left the field open to hardy pro-Communist campaigners like Rosamonde Sun. She could always provide the latest information, and her information was always favorable to the Communists.

Taking a cup of punch, Emily saw how right Jimmy Wei was. A lot of work was needed. But could anyone hope to reverse the tide? Yet any effort was better than none. She would strive again to bring the truth about China to the outside world. Her sunny smile belying her bleak resolution, she turned toward Gregory Hardin—and felt Rosamonde Sun's hand cold on her arm.

"Emily," Rosamonde said, "I believe you know Richard Hollings."

Emily just kept herself from replying that she knew Richard Hollings too well. Her smile no longer sunny, she murmured, "Good evening, Dick."

Richard, who had obviously arranged the encounter, exclaimed, "Emily! I only got back just from India yesterday. What luck running into you."

No need to tell him that since his return to Shanghai a year earlier, his every arrival and every departure had been reported by Julia, who nonetheless denied that she was trying to promote a reconciliation. Despite Emily's resolve not to give him an opening, the barbed words slipped out: "Are the harpies of the press gathering for the feast, Dick? Or should I say carrion crows?"

"Correspondents may be queer birds, Emily, but we're not totally perverted," he answered easily. "If there were no wars and no revolutions, we'd happily dine on other meat . . . more agreeable meat. Anyway, I'm getting too old for these capers."

He was about fifty, she calculated rapidly. The gray that had spread from his sideburns to his temples aged him only slightly and gave him an air of authority. The crease between his eyebrows and the crow's-feet at the corners of his eyes made him look weathered—yet tempered, more than worn. His eyes were, however, tired.

"I didn't mean you started the wars," she replied. "Just that you preyed on wars. Well, don't you?"

"A partial apology, which is *rather* uncharacteristic," Richard ruminated. "After a personal attack, which is *wholly* uncharacteristic of the cool Miss Howe. . . . I *am* sorry. I mean Madame Ou-yang. What can be the reason?"

"Don't flatter yourself, Dick. It's not you. . . . But everyone will be eager to talk with you if you just got back from India. Don't let me keep you."

"Perhaps I'm not eager to tell them, but only you. . . . Incidentally, did Julie ever tell you about my wife? You remember my mentioning Fiona?"

"Quite!"

"Her divorce, the final decree, came through a month ago. She's been fed up with me for ages. I was never there, she said, and I was always thinking of somewhere else when I was there. So she finally decided to get rid of me."

"How nice for you! No responsibilities at all now. But why tell me?"

"It's important that you know." Richard's brown eyes were grave. "You're the only . . . the only one I've ever cared about . . . at all. From the beginning, it's always been you. No one else ever! And I still hope that . . ."

Emily's pulse raced despite her resolve to remain detached. She could not continue to be casually unkind after that declaration, no matter how she despised him. But did she really despise him as she had in Chung-king?

She had sent him away because of his book *Red Star and Yellow Earth.* They had broken over politics. All the other issues, she now saw, had been minor. She also saw that *Red Star,* though misleading, was not as distorted as she had thought at the time. With her recognition of the Nationalists' flaws had come recognition that even the Communists possessed some virtues. *Red Star* had focused on those virtues, while glossing over the Communists' many faults.

Emily still believed that the Nationalists were China's only hope. She feared the Communists, but she no longer despised them. She could, therefore, now see that much of Richard's reporting had been honest. She still disagreed strongly with his thesis, but she no longer despised him. She certainly no longer hated him, if she ever had.

"Emily, I said I still hope . . ." He let the sentence trail off. "You could at least smile . . . say something. I want to tell you—"

"Don't say any more, Richard, not just now." The implicit encouragement escaped of its own accord. "I haven't really been up to scratch since Hsiu died. . . . Oh, you didn't know?"

"I'm so sorry, Emily," he said very slowly. "No matter what others may think . . . what you may have thought . . . I know how important he was to you. I'm terribly sorry."

Emily looked at him in surprise. She did not, she realized, truly know him, even after all the years. Not merely to sense the depth of her feeling for her elderly husband, which she had concealed even from herself, but never to have charged her with dereliction of affection when they were lovers. Richard was by nature jealous, but he had remained silent for her sake.

"Richard, I . . ." Emily knew she must be cautious because she was disarmed, but the words again slipped past her guard. "You know, Dick, we can't just pick up where we left off."

"I never hoped for that much." He smiled ruefully. "But, Em, we're both free now. Shall we give it a whirl?"

"And have more dreadful fights over politics? I wonder, Dick, I really do."

"Politics isn't everything, Em. Damned near everything nowadays, but still not quite. Why can't we begin the experiment by having dinner tonight?"

"I came with Tommy and Julia," she responded weakly. "It wouldn't be right to—"

"All the better. They can chaperone us. Do say you will, Em."

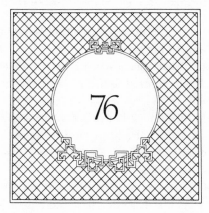

Nothing in the world was quite like American coffee laced with thick cream. Coffee never tasted quite the same anywhere else in the world.

Julia poured herself another cup and lit her second after-breakfast Chesterfield. Her daughter Althea frowned across the room-service table when Julia poured cream with a liberal hand.

"It's all right, darling." Julia anticipated the rebuke. "I'm careful about my figure when I'm at home. Traveling, a little leeway . . ."

"It's not just the cream, Mom," Althea said. "All those cigarettes. You know they make you cough. If you're speaking today, you don't want—"

"There, then." Julia stubbed out the cigarette. "Is that better?"

"Much better. But you really should cut down. I heard you coughing all night."

"The way you talk, anyone would think the Commodore Hotel was going to throw me out for disturbing the guests. Have I really become a public nuisance in my old age?"

"Now, Mother, don't try to make a joke of it. You really must . . ."

Althea had become so officious since entering Bryn Mawr that Julia felt as if their roles were reversed. It was like having her own anxious mother around, rather than her daughter. Still, Althea meant well.

Besides, Althea had freely chosen to join her in New York for the conference on "China in Crisis," sponsored by the Committee for a Democratic Far Eastern Policy. Persephone had preferred to spend the entire Easter holiday of 1948 at the mansion in the Virginia hunt country loaned to her Aunt Emily by a wealthy Nationalist sympathizer. Persephone, who adored her glamorous aunt, shared her aunt's devotion to the Nationalists. Althea was now very discreet on the instructions of Commissar Chou En-lai himself, but she was dedicated to the Communist revolution.

Still, they would all be together in a few days at Emily's borrowed mansion. Since Jason would also be in Virginia, nothing could have kept Althea away. She was, however, fascinated by the conference—and absurdly proud of her mother's role.

Julia had not, of course, confided to Althea that both her parents were active Communist agents. Despite the child's dedication, that confidence would have been too dangerous. The Nationalists still ruled Shanghai, and the vengeance they exacted in the guise of justice was quick and gory.

Like any nineteen-year-old, Althea was as fascinated by New York as she was by the conference. A morning with a classmate in the big city was too exciting to miss, but she left in a flurry of promises to return that afternoon.

Julia's speech was to be called "A Conservative Looks at China." She had been told that it was time for her to speak out against the Nationalists. The objectives of the conference were to halt American assistance to the Nationalists and to swing American support to the Communists. As directed, she was to assist by speaking of the recent opening of her own eyes to the true situation, after she had blindly supported the Nationalists for years. She would point out: "Even Americans who want to keep the Nationalists in power are now reluctantly forced to admit that the so-called Communists are winning. There is no possible way to make American aid to the Nationalists effective, much less ensure a Nationalist victory."

She would conclude with a ringing appeal: "Isn't it time we Americans stopped helping the wrong side? Isn't it time we stopped throwing tinder on the bonfire of civil war? Isn't it past time we stopped encouraging the bankrupt Nationalists to keep fighting—and to kill additional hundreds of thousands? Isn't it time to give the other side a chance to show what it can do? As you know, they're not really Communists, but national revolutionaries."

She would not, however, give credit to the author for that masterly misdirection of truth. Richard Hollings, who had invented the misleading term "national revolutionaries," was known as a champion of the Chinese Communists. The ostensibly academic conference on China in

Crisis, which was sponsored by the newly created front organization called the Committee for a Democratic Far Eastern Policy, was ostensibly independent. Deeply concerned scholars, journalists, labor leaders, and businessmen were discussing China's problems, ostensibly without prejudgment or political pressure. Of course, they would, after much thought, *independently* reach the inevitable conclusion that the Nationalists were finished and the Communists were the hope of the future.

The telephone broke into Julia's thoughts. She lifted the handset eagerly. A number of friends from the old days at the Office of War Information were coming to the conference. Besides its vital purpose, it should be fun.

"Madame Howe? Madame Julia Howe?" She could not immediately identify the voice, though the suave pseudo-English vowels were familiar. "Do you remember the friend who often brought news of your husband during the war? . . . A bellboy is bringing an envelope to your room. Please do not overlook it."

What was Professor Han of Stanford University doing in New York? Julia smiled at her own naïveté. He would, of course, be present, although he was evidently still under deep cover.

She gave the gray-haired bellboy a quarter, which was probably too much. She was a little apprehensive, for Professor Han always brought unpleasant tidings. She ripped the heavy manila envelope open, almost breaking a nail. The crisp bond paper bore neither salutation nor signature, but only the message in green ink:

The sponsoring committee has been informed that you will *not* deliver a speech. You will, however, attend the sessions. You will express skepticism regarding the speeches, just enough to demonstrate that you remain a reactionary element.

It would be dangerous for you to support the revolution publicly. You will, therefore, not reveal yourself even as a well-meaning liberal.

After victory, you will, however, publicly proclaim your discovery of your past errors—*after* seeing the reality of the New Democracy created by the Chinese Communist Party. Owing to your wide acquaintance in journalistic circles, your dramatic conversion will be highly effective. Destroy this immediately.

Julia tore the paper into small pieces, which she flushed down the toilet. Although angry, she smiled at the fantasies of the thriller-writers, whose heroes burnt incriminating letters before consigning them to the sewers. A waste of time, she had been taught. Besides, the smoke and the residue of ashes could arouse suspicion.

Julia smiled, although she was deeply disappointed. She had hoped to throw off some of the tension of her secret work by revealing her true position and her true views—at least as far as she was authorized to do by the Apparatus. Now, she would have to play her double role for some time to come: professed reactionary and secret Communist. She would also have to feign laryngitis for Althea's benefit.

On reflection, being forbidden to speak was a great honor. The Apparatus no more hesitated to discard an agent than she hesitated to discard a used Kleenex. But it seemed that Tommy and she were too valuable to be used and discarded. The future role for which she was reserved was far more important than adding another American voice to the tirades American voices raised against the Nationalists at an American conference.

She could now acknowledge to herself that she had not looked forward to speaking. An audience of several hundred was different from the impersonal microphone of XMHA. She was actually relieved—and pleased that she was not yet required to discard even part of her cover. She had feared a violent reaction when Emily learned of her denouncing the Nationalists. At least the danger of a breach with her sister-in-law was now postponed.

Aside from her persistent political backwardness, Emily was in fine form. During the three months since their meeting at Rosamonde Sun's, she and Richard Hollings had attained a tentative reconciliation. Julia assumed they were again sleeping together, but that was not the heart of the matter. Although essential, sexual satisfaction would not determine whether they could stay together. They had to forge an emotional link strong enough to withstand the friction of two strong—sometimes abrasive—personalities.

Richard was determined to marry Emily. He contended that marriage would ensure a permanent relationship. Pointing to the failure of his previous marriage, Emily contended that only a permanent relationship could ensure a lasting marriage.

To that irrefutable wisdom, Richard gaily replied, "But aren't you glad that marriage didn't work? I am—profoundly. Otherwise I couldn't offer you my hand, soiled though it may be."

Since they could not avoid politics entirely, they skirted political disagreement, sometimes dangerously. Yet Emily was open-minded— for a supporter of the Generalissimo. Richard was, as ever, mercurial. But he would never force a confrontation on an abstract issue, political, moral, or intellectual. He was not the kind to sacrifice himself for a cause —or to inconvenience himself excessively.

The ties that bound Emily and Richard were already strong. Since she was determined to spend several months in the United States in order to see her son and to campaign for the Nationalist cause, he had, for the first time in memory, subordinated his career to his affections. He had arranged to join her during the final month, having convinced his employers that he must reacquaint himself with American attitudes.

Richard had not told the *Boston Globe* or NBC that he also needed treatment for a respiratory complaint, which defied even the miraculous new antibiotics. Tommy had referred him to the Presbyterian Medical Center in New York, which was affiliated with his beloved College of Physicians and Surgeons of Columbia University. Taking his ailment seriously, Richard had actually stopped smoking.

If he could give up cigarettes, he could, perhaps, even persuade the skeptical Emily to marry him.

Julia's husky whispers convinced Althea that her mother had suddenly fallen victim to laryngitis. Although disappointed, Althea was still fascinated by the conference. For the first time in her life, she confided a little tremulously, she was in the same room as "men and women who make the world go round, really important people." She was also delighted by the setting: the ornate red-and-gold ballroom of the Commodore Hotel. Perching on her gilt, red velvet chair, she craned her head like a child in fairyland. She was enthralled by the oratory, and she believed every word.

Julia automatically sieved the half truths and the untruths from the rhetoric. Deceit was, of course, often necessary, as she was deceiving her daughter about her laryngitis. But Althea was drinking in too many distortions, not to speak of outright lies. She would have a word with Althea that evening. A little frankness would actually strengthen her cover, just as the Apparatus had directed.

Julia knew some of the Chinese present as fellow travelers; the unknown were probably secret comrades. The most important Chinese was, however, the most conspicuous person in the ballroom.

His gray worsted suit stretched perilously over his heavy frame, Feng Yü-hsiang, who was called the Christian General, sat uneasily on a spindly ballroom chair with his enormous hands splayed on his thighs. He had for decades been popping in and out of power like a jack-in-the-box. He had connived with warlords, monarchists, and the Japanese;

with missionaries, Nationalists, and the Soviets. He was now seeking an arrangement with the Chinese Communists.

The Christian General was taking advantage of his involuntary exile to find new allies. Generalissimo Chiang Kai-shek had sent him on a world tour, "to study water conservancy measures," when his intriguing became intolerable. He now sat in the ballroom of the Commodore Hotel trying to ingratiate himself with the distant Chairman Mao Tse-tung by nodding his watermelon head in ponderous approval of speeches in English, which he did not understand. That performance was, Julia supposed, no more bizarre than his earlier baptizing entire regiments with fire hoses to win over missionaries so that their home countries would provide him with armaments.

Yet Feng Yü-hsiang was, at least, a Chinese who had been involved in Chinese politics for a generation. Aside from the few Chinese students from universities, the handful of Chinese fellow travelers, and the sprinkling of unknown Chinese comrades, the participants were conspicuously non-Chinese. That was, of course, quite normal at an American conference, and almost half the speakers were associated in some way with China. But the rest had no connection whatsoever with China.

"The usual bleeding hearts," she had heard a round-faced young man with heavy spectacles remark at the press table. "They turn out for every worthy cause—worthy in Uncle Joe Stalin's eyes, that is."

Julia resented the glib orators who were innocent of any knowledge of China. She was virtually certain, too, that the Soviets had recruited them. Soviet involvement was, however, her own particular bugbear. It would disturb few others.

The white-haired president of the Pullman porters' union had obviously not been selected because he was either a China specialist or a moving orator. He was, however, black. The Soviet racists were always anxious to parade as many members of the colored races as they could.

The Filipino who demanded removal of all American bases and businesses from his native islands was a more plausible speaker. Although he naïvely confessed that he knew nothing about China, he was at least an Asian. And he spoke with authority about American atrocities—a theme the audience loved. Particularly eloquent regarding America's misdeeds was a large Indian lady in a purple-and-pink sari, who seemed unaware that America had never colonized India.

After such highly seasoned fare, Julia feared boredom by the white "labor leaders, progressive political figures, and democratic personages," as the chairman introduced those who had nothing to do with Asia. But their oratory was fiery and moving.

Fervent applause from the audience and occasional tears promised enthusiastic approval of the prepared resolutions. The conference responded with shame and anger to American perfidy in supporting the "Chiang Kai-shek remnant clique." It responded with cheers to the promise of an imminent Communist victory in China.

"How you could possibly attend that . . . that shameless farce!" Emily exploded before Julia could touch her drink. "Even Richard stayed away. My old *Red* Hollings stayed away. But you went."

Julia ignored the attack and sipped her drink. Shocked by her sister-in-law's vehemence, she knew they would quarrel savagely if she replied in the same tone. Yet Emily's second sentence pleased her greatly. If she could laugh at Richard's political leanings, they must have come a long way toward resolving their differences.

"Julie, sometimes I really do *not* understand your actions." Emily persisted, almost as if she wanted a quarrel. "And to take an innocent child—particularly with Althea's record. I saw the list of speakers. They're a bunch of Communists."

"We were just trying to learn a little, Em." Julia did not succeed in being wholly conciliatory. "It might do you some good to come down from your ivory tower occasionally."

"Ivory tower? Me? Chungking and Kunming weren't ivory towers, my dear. But some people who spent the war in San Francisco—"

"Ladies, let us have peace." Richard somewhat nervously intervened. "No need to fight the Chinese civil war here in Virginia."

"Even though it's being lost next door in Washington?" Emily subsided sulkily. "But really . . ."

"Peace, Emmy?" Julia smiled and slipped into her role of skeptic. "You know, in a way, you're not so far wrong. The way they went on, you'd think the Generalissimo had a forked tail and hooves. But they painted Chairman Mao Tse-tung as an archangel—at the very least."

"And they complain about the Nationalists' China Lobby," Emily observed. "The Americans, especially the American press, talk as if we were all devils—just as you said, Julie. But they ignore the tricks and the lies of the other side."

"Em, the war's going to be won or lost on the battlefields of China," Julie interposed. "Not in the pages of American newspapers."

"Maybe it can't be won in the newspapers, but it can be lost in the newspapers. If Congress cuts our aid any more—"

"If the Gimo used the aid better, he could win. And Washington wouldn't cut aid so much if he were winning. Americans love a winner, you know."

"Julie, I nearly forgot," Richard interposed. "There's a letter for you. It came special delivery this morning. I'll fetch it, shall I?"

"You Americans don't know a winner from a loser." Emily ignored the interruption. "You don't even know your own best interests."

"Em, I'm the last person to want the Communists to win." Though the flat lie was not new, Julia was a little ashamed of herself. "But even you've got to admit the Gimo is primarily to blame."

"He's not perfect. But who could've done better? If he had executed *all* the Communists when he should have, the Americans would have raised a terrible outcry. Maybe not you, Julie. Though most educated Americans seem to want the Communists to win. But the people, the simple people who are the backbone of this country, they see it clearly. They're for us Nationalists because they fear communism. They know we're fighting their fight."

Julia's temper rose, and the words escaped: "Emily, if you Chinese would just stop blaming other people for your own failings, you'd be a lot better off. I'm getting sick of everybody always blaming everything on the Americans. And you used to admire this country."

"Julie, experience has taught me a lot. I've learned that Americans cannot be trusted. Not even the best of them. Not even you, Julie. They seem open and frank, but they're not what they seem. They smile—and grab whatever they want!"

Emily stopped abruptly, evidently shocked by her own words. Her sister-in-law was appalled. This quarrel could rupture decades of intimate friendship and split the family. Emily obviously knew more than she was saying.

Which of her own apparent betrayals, Julia wondered anxiously, had Emily discovered? Was it her secret life in the Apparatus—a discovery that could, quite literally, prove fatal? Or had Richard Hollings sealed their reconciliation with a full confession? Her one rather unsatisfactory night with him had occurred years ago. But Julia knew Emily would find even that single lapse unforgivable.

"Here's your letter, Julie." Richard reappeared. "Hope it's good news."

Happy for the respite, she unfolded the brief note. She read it quickly and then reread it slowly.

"I'm afraid I'll have to leave, Em," she said. "Mother writes that my father is not very well. No cause for alarm, she says. That's why she wrote, rather than telephoning. But I'd better get up to Plattsburg. I can leave the girls here, can't I?"

As she and her bags were bundled into a car, Julia realized that before today she would not have asked Emily's consent to her daughters' staying on. Before their friendship had altered radically fifteen minutes earlier, she would have assumed that consent.

77

SEPTEMBER 5, 1948–JANUARY 8, 1949

A week after Julia's much-delayed return from America in early September of 1948, Tommy was still inventing reasons to leave his consulting rooms on the ground floor in order to see her for a few minutes during office hours. Julia discovered an excuse to intrude into his consulting rooms every time she left the house. They had been six months apart, their longest separation since the war, and they had celebrated their reunion in bed for almost twenty-four hours.

The servants were delighted and amused. They were also skeptical of Julia's claim that she had to rest after too rapidly traversing too many time zones. They would not believe it had taken her only sixty-five hours to fly from San Francisco to Hong Kong in Pan American's China Clipper.

Loo, the majordomo, almost overstepped the line. They had always thought of him as old, although he was only five or six years older than Tommy. Shortly after Julia's return, he had asked slyly, "Doctor, have you got more medicine to make old men act young? You haven't taken it all yourself?"

Flattered, Tommy had tossed him a bottle of multivitamin capsules. To Julia he remarked, "At least vitamins won't do him any harm. Nor cost anywhere near as much as rhinoceros horn and ginseng. If he believes they will, the vitamins might even work for him."

"Is that how you do it, darling?" she had asked. "Vitamins?"

"No need," he had replied. *"You* do it to me."

Tommy was, all in all, a most satisfactory husband, Julia complacently concluded again. While she was delayed in the States, he had telephoned repeatedly. Getting those trans-Pacific calls through, he later boasted, had been a greater feat than harrying the Japanese with the guerrillas. Julia had been able to give him little hope of her speedy return until mid-August, when her mother intervened.

"Darling, he is your husband—and he obviously needs you," she had said. "Your father will miss you, but there's little you can do for him. I need you, too, but I'm not going to be a selfish old woman. He could live another six weeks, Dr. Creeke says, or another six years. Your father will understand. Go home to your husband."

Julia was torn, but decided to leave when Tommy confirmed the uncertain prognosis. His professional integrity would not allow him to misstate her father's prospects, no matter how much he might wish to. Tommy had told her that bowel cancer could spread rapidly or, almost as likely, go into remission. Unless she planned to remain at her father's bedside for months, perhaps years, she really should return to Shanghai.

Julia had already spent so much time with her daughters that they were getting on each other's nerves. Four women alone were not much fun, particularly when they ranged in age from her mother's sixty-eight to Persephone's fifteen.

The girls had spent half their summer holiday with Emily and Richard, enjoying the companionship of Patricia, Eunice, and, of course, Jason. In response to her sister-in-law's coolly polite invitation by telephone, Julia had coolly declared that she could not leave her father. Besides, she had added, the children could look after themselves. Anyway, Emily would hardly want her around when she was worried about Richard.

The correspondent was resting. He was also writing his memoirs, an endeavor Julia thought rather pretentious for a man only a year older than her husband. When she expressed surprise, his laughter had snaked through the telephone lines. He had pointed out that he was accustomed to working hard, rather needed the money—and was for the moment physically debarred from doing anything else.

The radiologists at Presbyterian Medical Center had found something they described vaguely as "a spot on the lung." With a faint air of embarrassment, the chest specialist later told Richard that he was suffering from tuberculosis, which prosperous white males simply did not contract in the enlightened 1940s. The new antibiotic, streptomycin, had virtually tamed the disease once called galloping consumption. Social embarrassment aside, tuberculosis was rarely fatal nowadays. Still, a long rest was indicated—and an immediate return to China was impossible.

The chest specialist had sent Richard off with a clap on the back and the assurance that he probably need curtail his activities for no more than a year. Richard's question about going back to China had restored the specialist to good humor. He had almost forgotten the protracted sojourns in that unhygienic country that explained how his patient had contracted a disease that was no longer fashionable, or even prevalent, in the West.

After she returned to Shanghai, Julia regretted not having stopped to see Emily and Richard on her way home. Emily was staying in America to be near her children, to continue her propaganda campaign, and above all, to be with Richard. Their promised return next year seemed a long time off.

Julia had, however, not particularly wanted to see her sister-in-law before leaving the United States. She had been distressed by her parting from her father—and eager to see Tommy. Besides, not she but Emily was chiefly responsible for the coolness between them that had lasted for longer than any previous disagreement. Julia hesitated to make overtures that were likely to be rejected.

"Julie, where are you?"

Tommy's voice startled her, for she had not heard the elevator. When he entered the sitting room, she saw that he looked tired. The air-conditioning was balking again, and the house was very hot. What else, however, did ninety-nine percent of Shanghai's people endure in early September?

"Darling!" he called again. "Oh, there you are. Bloody hot, isn't it?"

She nodded and lifted her mouth for his kiss. After mixing gimlets for both of them, he fussily lit his meerschaum pipe. Although he had been at her to cut down her smoking, the meerschaum was his constant companion.

"A funny business," he said. "The Christian General is dead."

"But I saw him only a few months ago in New York," she answered, unthinking. "He certainly didn't look ill."

Julia smiled penitently. Her husband had once pointed out that everyone said the same thing on hearing of the death of an acquaintance —as if their having seen him last month, last week, or even that morning should somehow have fended off death.

"He was only sixty-seven, and he wasn't ill," Tommy answered. "Or, at least, illness didn't kill him. It was a fire on a steamer in the Black Sea. Did you know he was going to Russia?"

"It's not surprising. I told you the Soviets practically ran the conference on China in Crisis. How did the fire start? Were many killed?"

"Now there's the mystery, my love. No one else was so much as singed. It seems the old boy was a photography buff, very keen. That's news to me, but no matter. All his inflammable film somehow caught fire, presumably by spontaneous combustion. Presto, no more Christian General."

"That's very fishy, Tommy."

"When you remember that film has been pretty fire-resistant since the thirties, it's *very* fishy. But maybe not Soviet film."

"They got rid of him, didn't they? I wonder why."

"Presumably because they were afraid he'd queer their pitch in China. Or maybe just tidying up the past. Maybe, Julie, on behalf of our own masters, the Chinese Communist Party. You know from your own experience how obliging the Soviets are in that way."

Flowing out of the north, the great tide of the Communist People's Liberation Army was flooding Nationalist defenses. On the map, the Liberation Army's advance looked like a vast blot of red ink spreading very rapidly. First Manchuria and the northwest, then North China, and, finally, most of Kiangsu Province north of Shanghai—all fell to the big Communist divisions. They were not guerrillas but well-equipped regular forces. The red tide halted for a time on the far bank of the Yangtze River, not quite reaching Nanking or Shanghai. But it would obviously roll on very soon.

"It's not quite panic yet," Tommy observed a week after Julia's return, "but people are on the verge of panic. They could go over the edge any time. Personal concerns are neglected. Everything else is trivial when a dynasty is falling."

The trivial aspects of that collapse were often tragic and macabre. Occasionally they were funny.

On January 31, 1948, three hundred taxi-dancers and sing-song girls had marched through the streets to protest the decree that closed down *all* the nightclubs of Shanghai, with no nonsense about drawing lots. They were supported by hundreds of musicians, waiters, and lavatory attendants. Two days after that demonstration, the Ministry of Social Welfare had reiterated the decree and had, further, prohibited all social dancing, private as well as public.

On the same day that moral purity was thus affirmed, military police had put down a strike of Shanghai cotton-mill workers, killing three and wounding more than sixty. During the next few months, students and teachers throughout China had struck "in support of the anti-hunger and anti-oppression movements." Shanghai students had actu-

ally discovered a new issue, rioting against American revival of Japanese
militarism. As if to celebrate July Fourth, hundreds of students from
Communist-occupied Manchuria had clashed in Peiping with Nationalist police. Eighteen were killed, and twenty-four were seriously
wounded.

"The litany," Tommy said wearily, "goes on and on and on."

"I never thought it would happen this way," Julia replied. "I envisioned a mass uprising—not great armies marching."

"The great armies *are* marching. But starvation, disease, and disorder
are marching faster. So is inflation. While you were away, the cost of
living sometimes doubled in twenty-four hours. Some shopkeepers
changed their prices every other hour. Others closed down in despair."

"The rich are on a buying spree," Julia interjected. "I've already seen
that. A simple dress costs dozens of basketfuls of Chinese banknotes.
But a couple of U.S. dollars will buy practically anything, even furs and
jewels. Chennault's people use the CNRRA commissary. China's Nice
Relief and Riches for Americans, they call it. A can of baked beans from
the commissary will buy a pair of beautifully made-to-measure shoes
at Kow Hoo's. It's the same for the military and diplomats—anyone
who can get into the PX. It's rotten, Tommy, just rotten!"

"Not for long, now, darling. Whom the gods would destroy, they first
make mad."

He fanned out on the table a number of back copies of *The China
Weekly Review,* the American-edited journal that had been the bible of
liberal foreigners since it began publication in 1917.

"Just look at the prices," he directed. "They really bring it home."

The magazine dated March 1, 1941, bore the price 80 cents CNC,
which was in Chinese National Currency then equivalent to 15 cents
U.S. On February 2, 1946, after wartime inflation, the *Review* had cost
CNC$150, and on July 10, 1948, it was CNC$300,000. The last issue
dated September 4, 1948, cost 60 cents gold *yüan,* exactly 15 cents U.S.

"Remarkably consistent," Julia commented dryly. "In American
money *no* change over seven years. In Chinese currency a mammoth
increase! You know, I still don't understand exactly what a gold *yüan* is
supposed to be."

"It's the latest panacea that's meant to solve all economic problems:
Stabilize the currency. Banish inflation. Control prices and wages. Restore confidence. Create work. Et cetera, et cetera."

"Is it working at all, Tommy? Or is that a stupid question?"

The gold *yüan,* Tommy recalled, had recently replaced the ludicrously
inflated Chinese National Currency. It was nominally backed by re-

serves of actual gold; and Chinese citizens were required to exchange all their gold, silver, and foreign currency for gold *yüan*—at four *yüan* to one U.S. dollar. The economic czar appointed to enforce those measures was General Chiang Ching-kuo, the Generalissimo's thirty-nine-year-old son, who had spent his formative years as a hostage in the Soviet Union. Taking office in Shanghai on August 19, 1948, Chiang Ching-kuo had enforced the regulations with great vigor.

"Ching-kuo's like Joe Stalin," Tommy summed up. "He believes the more people he kills, the more stable the country will become."

Two days later, Julia strayed into the horrors of Chiang Ching-kuo's reforms. Driving in the Cord coupé to Rosamonde Sun's house, she was halted on Avenue Edward VII near the Great World by an officious policeman who said "All traffic must stop for fifteen minutes. Until after the punishment. You must wait."

An American-made army truck halted, and its tailgate dropped to reveal fourteen men squatting under the American M-1 carbines of military police wearing varnished American-made helmet-liners. The prisoners' faces were bruised, and blood stained their torn shirts. Prodded by the carbines, they alighted painfully. Their hands were tightly bound, and their ankles were hobbled by chains.

The prisoners were forced to kneel on the gritty cobblestones. Handwritten placards tucked into filthy headbands proclaimed their individual crimes.

Above the slack lips and the bloody cheeks of the nearest man, the placard read: COMMUNIST BANDIT. A thin man beside him displayed the pinpoint pupils of the opium addict and the verdict: SECRET MONEY EXCHANGER. A well-fed youth wearing the shreds of a Western-style silk shirt was labeled: GOLD HOARDER.

Julia could not look away. As Tommy had said, the Generalissimo's son was fighting economic collapse with mass executions. Yet, despite Nationalist inefficiency, some of those men might be her comrades-in-arms in the secret war for freedom and justice. Julia shivered but stared in terrible fascination.

An MP officer wearing wrap-around aviator sunglasses unholstered his pistol. The Colt .45 was standard American army issue, and the initials U.S. were embossed on the brown leather holster.

The MP stood behind the slack-lipped COMMUNIST BANDIT, holding the Colt two inches from his head. Flame spurted from the muzzle, and blood and bone gushed where lips had drooped an instant earlier. A single .45-caliber bullet could stop a charging buffalo. The man's head had exploded, leaving nothing recognizable as human above the stump of the neck.

Julia closed her eyes and leaned her forehead on the hard steering wheel. Although the Cord's cramped cockpit was hot, she shivered again. Shots sounded staccato. She smelled cordite, and bile rose coppery in her throat. Fighting faintness, she opened her eyes again.

Ten of the fourteen men lay on the cobblestones. The MP officer was pushing a fresh clip into his pistol, and the remaining prisoners were staring straight ahead in terror. Apparently dissatisfied, the officer removed the clip, pressed the bullets down, and snapped the clip back.

The pistol prodded a stout man whose placard declared: ECONOMIC SPECULATOR. Fear had not totally wiped the good humor from his bluff features. Julia recognized him with new horror. He was Joshua Haleevie's childhood friend, the sometime headwaiter at the French Club called Fatty Woo, who had fought beside Joshua and Tommy with the guerrillas.

Julia closed her eyes again and saw a vision of Tommy in the same position. By Nationalist standards, her husband was a hundred times more culpable.

The fatal shot should already have sounded. Several seconds had passed since the MP raised his pistol to Fatty Woo's head. Julia glanced up fearfully. Fatty Woo was on his feet, solicitously supported by two MPs. They led him stumbling to an old Ford sedan, and he climbed awkwardly into the back seat.

A single shot sounded, then two more close together. Three more men lay in death on the cobblestones. The MP officer stood behind the last victim, reholstering his pistol. The sun glinted on his sunglasses, transforming him into a robot with photoelectric cells for eyes.

Julia remembered that she had been on her way to Rosamonde Sun's. She started the motor, but revulsion flung her back against the leather seat. She trembled for almost two minutes before she could put in the clutch and flee to the sanctuary of her own home.

When she told Tommy, he listened in silence, interrupting only to freshen her scotch and water. When she told him of the curious reprieve of Fatty Woo, Tommy smiled for the first time that evening and said "I knew Joshua was worried. Fatty's life cost Joshua two thousand U.S. A fortune nowadays. But it worked."

"Tommy, it could have been you."

"Not a chance, darling. We've got the wherewithal. We could pay two *hundred* thousand U.S. If necessary, Joshua would lay out two million. And who could resist that? You can get away with murder if you've got the cash. Even get away with . . . ah . . . sedition. If you don't have the cash? Well, you saw it."

Sitting at his desk, Tommy reflected that there was no need of a soothsayer to see the future clearly. By November 1, 1948, the gold *yüan* had fallen from its official value of four to one U.S. dollar to ten thousand to one. The Generalissimo's son had resigned "with deepest apologies for . . . intensifying the people's suffering." On December 1, the People's Liberation Army had taken strategic Hsüchow three hundred and fifty miles north of Shanghai after the Generalissimo squandered his best remaining divisions by appointing commanders who were only political hacks. On the same day, sixteen million U.S. dollars' worth of American arms arrived in Shanghai. It was the last delivery to the Chinese mainland. The Generalissimo had asked that all further shipments be diverted to the island of Taiwan.

By Christmas of 1948, the shape of the future was unmistakable. Setting the seal upon the imminent end of Nationalist rule, the staunchly anti-Communist Joshua Haleevie had remarked on Christmas Eve when he stopped by for an eggnog, "You know, Tommy, it's about time we told London what it should do to get on good terms with a Communist regime. Besides recognition, what else will Chairman Mao want?"

Tommy had duly passed the inquiry on to the Apparatus. He did not expect a quick reply. Even the farsighted Chou En-lai would not be primarily concerned with foreign affairs when the Communists were rolling up the old map of China.

On that map, the Nationalists still appeared to have some prospect of surviving. South of the Yangtze River, China was largely free of the red inkblot of the People's Liberation Army. But the Nationalists had lost the will to fight. Their leaders were either preparing to make their separate peace with the Communists or stealing more public money to ensure comfortable exile. The white area south of the Yangtze was, therefore, hardly more significant than the white speck in the red north where the old warlord called the Model Governor stubbornly held Taiyüan, the capital of Shansi Province.

Tommy picked up the files of the patients he was to see that morning. Notwithstanding Christmas, civil war, and the impending change of regime, personal illness still struck. Most of his patients were now genuinely ill. He had weeded out the hypochondriacs, in the process also weeding out his most lucrative patients. He was, as always, treating many who could not pay.

Money mattered little nowadays. Very soon Shanghai would be liberated—and he would have no use for personal wealth. He would practice medicine as he had once dreamed, free of all pressures except the patient's needs. Whatever his misgivings about the major domestic and foreign policies Chairman Mao Tse-tung might pursue after his victory, Tommy was confident that conditions for a relatively nonpolitical endeavor like health care would be virtually ideal in practice.

The telephone buzzed, and his secretary advised, "Mr. Smythe on line two, Doctor."

"Tommy, old pal, good to hear your voice." The American was, as always, jovial. "How would you like a scenic flight this morning? We've got a problem in Taiyüan: a DC-3 down and a pilot hurt. . . . No, I can't find another doctor. Otherwise I wouldn't ask you. . . . It'll mean an overnight stay."

Tommy agreed to meet Harry at Hungjao Airport in half an hour. Leafing through his patients' files, he found nothing urgent. After instructing his secretary to refer any emergency to Dr. David Chen, he took the elevator to the fifth floor to change into warm clothing. Since Julia was out, he left her a brief note.

The engines hammered when the Curtiss Commando lifted off the slushy runway, and the bare aluminum tube of the fuselage reverberated tinnily. Overcrowded, grimy, and licentious, Shanghai dwindled beneath the silver wings. The engines labored as the airplane struggled for altitude. Uncomfortable on the canvas bench hung along the side, Tommy huddled into the sheepskin coat Harry had tossed him at takeoff.

Despite heavy woollen socks, his feet were already losing feeling on the bare metal floor. The slush scraped off boot soles had run into the grooves of the floorboards, where it was freezing again. Reaching under the bucket seat, Harry produced a pair of sheepskin-lined boots. Tommy smiled his thanks, but even with his feet in those cocoons, he could not feel his toes.

Harry mouthed a question, and Tommy shook his head. The engines' roaring and the wind's keening made it impossible to hear. When Harry lifted his cupped hand to his mouth as if drinking, Tommy nodded. Anything hot would be very welcome.

The American clambered up the incline of the fuselage like a toddler climbing a slide, and Tommy peered through the small porthole. Beneath them the Yangtze River flowed lethargically through the severe winter landscape. He saw puffs of gray smoke on the northern bank, followed seconds later by flashes on the southern bank. Communist artillery was firing across the river that cut China in half. That was presumably why the pilot was climbing high. More than eight hundred miles to the northwest, Taiyüan was a minuscule islet in the red ocean of the People's Liberation Army.

Harry returned with paper cups after the Curtiss Commando leveled off. Although the noise level was slightly lower, he shouted into Tommy's ear, "Hope you like cream and sugar."

Tommy did not even like coffee, but he nodded again. Clutching his cup, he stooped to tuck his worn Gladstone bag under the canvas bucket seat. Leaning back, he contemplated the spectacle of an overloaded CAT airplane in flight.

All the green boxes stacked in the forward area bore the legend: *Ammunition, ball, .30-caliber, U.S. Army.* At the rear, where the fuselage tapered, heaped-up hay bales fenced livestock intended to feed the defenders of Taiyüan. A rooster crowed, shrill above the din, and hens clucked in their wicker baskets. The hay barrier slipped, and a gray billy goat pushed through it. His scimitar horns swaying, his tiny black hooves picked their way around sacks of rice, baskets of vegetables, and earthenware jars of preserved eggs. Poking his head through the green curtain that cut off the flight deck, the billy goat contentedly oversaw the pilots.

The Commando also carried five young Chinese men. They were setting up a mah-jongg game on one of the twenty padlocked U.S. Army footlockers secured along the center line of the fuselage. Wondering what those footlockers contained, Tommy glanced at the long, bulky object tied down with wire rope under a tarpaulin.

An ever-reliable CAT DC-3 had been raked by machine-gun fire while dropping rice to Taiyüan. The long object was a replacement for the DC-3's damaged engine, and the five young men were mechanics. The transport's pilot had also been hit. Tommy was on the flight because Harry Smythe would not trust his fliers to Chinese military surgeons.

Although the twin engines were revving more slowly at cruising altitude, the Commando's thin aluminum shell still clattered metallically against the protruding aluminum ribs.

"Everything all right, Tommy?" Harry half shouted. "It'll be four . . . maybe four and a half hours."

"Fine, Harry. Though I wonder what those footlockers are in aid of."

The American grinned enigmatically and replied, "Why don't you ask the captain? I'd be interested in his answer. Meanwhile, what do you know about our Taiyüan operation?"

"Very little."

"For five months now, CAT's been keeping Taiyüan afloat in a Red sea. The Gimo flew in the day after the siege started, and then gave Chennault his orders: *Drop everything else if you have to, but keep Taiyüan supplied.* We've brought in tens of thousands of tons of food and ammo. First time ever. Never been a besieged city supplied from the air for so long."

"And how much longer?"

"We can keep bringing the stuff in indefinitely." In the freezing interior of the millimeter-thin fuselage at eight thousand feet, Harry's breath was thick, white vapor. "How much longer really depends on the troops—and the stubborn old Model Governor."

He rose and gestured toward the flight deck. Tommy stepped gingerly over the lashing wires and nudged the billy goat aside. An American with pale lashes framing light gray eyes sat in the captain's chair on the left. A peaked cap was cocked rakishly over his ear; its badge was a grinning tomcat. In the copilot's seat, a grizzled Chinese was speaking into a hand microphone.

"Welcome to my office," the captain said. "Sorry the heating's on the blink back there."

He spoke in normal tones, and he was in his shirtsleeves in the heated and insulated cockpit. Adjusting with difficulty to the lower noise level, Tommy offered the conventional response when Harry said, "Captain Wessex Hakluyt Johnson. Everybody calls him Wex. Johnny Wang I think you know."

"Anhwei Province is down there under the clouds," the captain said. "At least, I hope it is. . . . There's nothing much to see now. Why don't you come back up here when we land, Doctor? It could be interesting."

"What number strip's this one, Wex?" Harry asked.

"Don't recall for sure, Harry," the captain replied. "Johnny?"

The grizzled copilot hung up his microphone and counted on his fingers before replying, "Dr. Howe, every time the Communists get too close, the governor builds a new airstrip closer to the city. I'd say this is number six."

"Then the siege ends," Tommy asked, "when there's no more level ground for a new strip?"

"I guess so, Doctor," the captain replied. "Though we could support it with airdrops—for a while."

After the two passengers had reluctantly left the warm cockpit to huddle again on the bucket seats, Harry remarked, "Tommy, old buddy, you didn't ask Wex about the footlockers."

"I may be thick, Harry, but I'm not bloody thick. I won't be your cat's paw."

"I just wanted to hear what Wex would say. As you know, U.S. dollars will buy anything, including money, in Shanghai. Well, U.S. dollars will buy twice as much Chinese money in isolated Taiyüan, so the crews bring in fat rolls of greenbacks to exchange for Chinese banknotes. Back in Shanghai, presto, they sell the notes for twice as much in green. It's a sweet racket. Though I'm not supposed to know those footlockers will go back packed with banknotes."

"You don't mind?"

"Why should I? Worse things happen in Shanghai every day. And I've always got volunteers for the Taiyüan flight, which isn't exactly a piece of cake. Sometimes it's very hairy. Only Taiyüan is left. A year ago, there were ten to fifteen cities on the brink of falling to the Chicoms. All good pickings for my fly-boys."

"And for you, Harry?"

"It's not my act, Tommy. I can't see holding up people who're desperate to escape on a plane."

At 3:18 the copilot leaned through the curtain and beckoned. Tommy took the folding jump seat behind the captain and snapped his safety-belt. Through the numerous glass panes that made the cockpit like a greenhouse he saw a dark winter landscape sparkling with occasional fires.

"All settled, Doc?" the captain asked. "Here we go then."

The bulbous nose dipped, and the Commando descended so rapidly that Tommy's ears popped repeatedly. The big airplane stood on a wing end in a sharp turn, then settled into an even steeper descent. The captain turned the wheel and pulled it back. As the Commando climbed sharply to the right, a string of flaming spheres rose from the ground.

"Goddamn them boys," the captain swore. "I heard they got themselves some flak guns. Goddamn!"

Two parallel rows of yellow lights flared in the darkness ahead, and the captain pushed the wheel forward. The Commando hurtled downward, and a minute later the wheels threw up showers of gravel that drummed against the aluminum skin. The big airplane bounced high. As the wheels touched the ground again, the captain was pumping the brakes.

Tires squealed, and gravel spurted from the landing strip. The night was lit in flashes as the copilot flicked the landing lights on and off. When forward motion stopped, the captain pointed toward the rear.

"Move fast now, Doc," he said. "You never know what surprise the Commies have got for us."

Gripping his Gladstone bag, Tommy slid down the small aluminum ladder hooked into the open doorway. He saw by hanging kerosene lanterns that the Commando had stopped in an enclosure of sandbags roofed with corrugated iron. Outside, mortar bombs exploded.

"Welcome to Taiyüan!" Harry Smythe grinned. "Your patient will be in the dugout."

The stricken pilot was a slight American known as Walrus Reilly. Tommy set his broken arm but left the machine gun bullet in the flesh of his thigh for hospital attention.

Stepping outside when the shelling that greeted their arrival subsided, Tommy saw the medieval battlements of the walled city of Taiyüan against the moonlit sky. Within the revetment, the mechanics worked all night on the damaged engine. Relieved to find no need for a complete engine change, they only replaced damaged parts with parts from the spare engine. They were obviously as eager to leave as the captain had been to reach Taiyüan.

The Commando was ready for takeoff at dawn, Harry Smythe flying as copilot. The repaired DC-3 was to follow an hour later, to avoid offering the alerted Communist gunners a second target in quick succession. Tommy was to fly on the DC-3 with his patient on a stretcher and grizzled Johnny Wang at the controls. Watching the Commando being loaded, Tommy would almost have preferred to remain in besieged Taiyüan, rather than board that overburdened aircraft.

The cannibalized DC-3 engine was the biggest single item, but the double-padlocked footlockers were heavy with Chinese banknotes. In the space left at the rear by the departed livestock stood a mound of chests, carpets, and trunks. The military cargo having been unloaded, cloth-wrapped bundles, canvas valises, and great wicker baskets filled every cranny, right up to the green curtain of the flight deck.

"How you're going to take off," Tommy remarked to Harry, "I don't really—"

"This is only the beginning, pal," Harry replied. "Just you watch."

Standing in front of the aluminum ladder, Captain Wex Johnson and four military policemen were engulfed by a wave of human beings. When truncheons flashed, the throng recoiled. Reluctantly lining up, still jostling and swearing, the passengers produced large red tickets. The captain painstakingly examined each one.

"You're collecting fares?" Tommy asked. "Who issues the tickets?"

"We've got a little office in town," Harry Smythe replied. "But Wex Johnson is looking for a special chop. Every one of those people has ponied up. Not just our fare, but old Wex's special fare. He takes only greenbacks or gold bars. Same for the baggage. Every piece pays a tariff to Wex. He's going to be a very rich man when this is all over. I figure, after expenses and payoffs, he's clearing ten to fifteen thousand U.S. on every turnaround."

Tommy was beyond being surprised by his native land or its friends. Julia would have seethed, but he only counted. When eighty-five men, women, and children had been crammed on top of the abundant luggage in an airplane designed to carry no more than fifty, Harry Smythe laid a restraining hand on Wex Johnson's arm. The double cargo doors clattered shut, and the captain climbed a tall ladder to the flight deck.

Before following him, Harry rather formally shook hands, and Tommy asked, "You're not really going to fly in that overloaded whale? It'll never get off the ground."

"Old Wex'll get off the ground all right." Harry was nonchalant. "He's got too big an investment not to. So long, pal. See you in Shanghai."

While Harry climbed up to the flight door, the engines sputtered in the cold dawn. They coughed into life, and gray smoke billowed through the sand-bag enclosure.

Behind that curtain, the engines' scream rose higher until it seemed they must throw their pistons. When the slipstream cleared the smoke, Tommy saw the Commando pushing furiously against its wheel chocks. The engines' screaming dropped, and Wex Johnson leaned out from the glass-enclosed cockpit to signal with a raised thumb.

When the engines screamed louder, Tommy put his palms over his ears. Coolies jerked the chocks away, and the Commando shot out of the enclosure like a pebble from a slingshot. The wheels hardly touched the gravel runway, it seemed, before the transport rose ten feet into the air. The next instant, it pancaked onto the ground, badly straining the undercarriage. At the very end of the runway the Commando rose clumsily, hastened by the puffs of exploding mortar bombs.

Tommy gulped cold air. He realized that he had stopped breathing during that laborious takeoff.

The Commando rose slowly over the walled city, a gleaming intruder above the crenellated battlements and the high watchtowers of an earlier age. The climb was painful, and the Commando wallowed. Lumbering through the air, the heavily laden transport slowly gained altitude.

Tommy turned to his patient, whose stretcher was propped on wooden ammunition boxes.

"Look, Doc! Look at her!" Walrus Reilly shouted. "She's too heavy. Not answering the controls. Wex hasn't got her in his hands yet."

The glass panes covering the nose caught the morning sun when the Commando dropped abruptly. The wounded pilot dug his nails into the canvas stretcher. The Commando recovered and climbed again toward the folded brown hills.

"He's too goddamned close to the ridge," Walrus Reilly agonized. "But he should make it. Just! . . . Oh, no! Oh, my God!"

Bright against the pale dawn, a stream of tracers licked at the laboring aircraft. The nose dipped lower, but lifted again just before it would have smashed into the ridge. Rising triumphantly, the Commando cleared the hill.

"It's okay now, Doc," Reilly said. "By God, he scared me."

One silver wing dipped inexplicably, barely clearing the second ridge. The Commando jerked in the air as if checked by brakes. The wing dipped again, and the airplane appeared to halt in midair.

The next instant the big transport cartwheeled. It tumbled over and over, revolving ever faster, a silver cross flashing against the pallid sky. A wingtip caught on a ridge, and the transport crumpled into the rocks of the hill.

"Oh, my God!" the injured pilot repeated monotonously. "Oh, my God!"

Tommy saw flames flicker in the broken silver carcass. Seconds later, a pyre of black smoke rose from the stricken Commando.

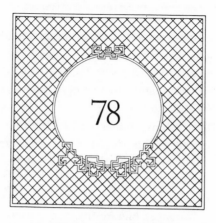

78

APRIL 27, 1949

The baby grand had been lacquered black and set with hexagonal mirrors to go with the new ultramodern decor of the dining room when the Ikra was completely redone a decade earlier. Although now scratched and dented, the piano still sparkled under the subdued lights. And it responded nostalgically to the long-nailed fingers on the keyboard.

"The dear old thing's a night creature like me," Elizaveta Alexandrovna Yavalenka observed. "Not meant for daylight—or for Bach. But it'll do this last time."

The piano player twirled his drooping mustache, settled his dinner jacket over his paunch, and absently stroked the keys. No distinct melody emerged, but, rather, a euphonious tinkling like the gentle clashing of a chandelier's crystal pendants.

Two bone-lean Chinese sing-song girls in long scarlet *cheongsams* were undulating before the upright microphone planted on the minuscule dance floor. Their mouths were shiny scarlet ovals, and their hollow-cheeked faces were painted to make them modishly skull-like. The rhinestone bracelets that garlanded their stick-thin arms glittered in the blue spotlight. Their cobralike undulations were growing slower. Slitted eyes opening a crack wider in appeal, they looked hopefully over their shoulders at the piano player.

The tinkling resolved itself into a melody, and the piano player nodded their cue. The duo began chanting in a minor key. The plaintive tune reminded Julia of children retorting to taunts with the singsong doggerel "Sticks and stones will break my bones, but names will never harm me." Brave defiance did not quite conceal the fear beneath.

"Maskee!" The skull-women trilled the unique Shanghai expression. *"Maskee! Maskee!"*

"Can't be cured, must be endured!" Tommy insisted upon translating it. Julia felt that the resignation to an unjust fate was better conveyed by "What the hell, it doesn't matter!"

Maskee! starving rickshaw coolies declared with a grimace. *Maskee!* feckless amahs protested with grins at once servile and insolent when they could not hide a broken plate. *Maskee!* soldiers said, turning in helpless anger from a dying comrade.

The melody concealed within the piano player's spare rendition seeped into Julia's awareness. Her mother had crooned the lullaby when she was an infant. Yes, of course. It began "Hush, little baby, don't you cry." Then it offered consolations ranging from diamond rings to ponies. It closed with the promise that, despite all disappointments, "You'll still be the cutest little baby in town."

In sibilant pidgin English, the duo was actually shrilling:

> Me no worry,
> Me no care,
> Me going to marry a millionaire.
>
> And if he die,
> Me no cry,
> Me going to get another guy.

The poor sad little things, what would become of them? Millionaires were a diminishing, not to say vanishing, asset in Shanghai in late April of 1949. Rapidly going out of fashion, millionaires would soon be as popular as skunks. The mindless jingle nonetheless caught the mood of the feckless city in its last springtime under capitalism.

The People's Liberation Army had swept across the Yangtze River on April 21, meeting no organized resistance, but only sporadic resistance from the demoralized Nationalist forces. The west wind that alone threatened the Communists' armada of sampans and junks had, at the last auspicious moment, shifted. The Communist New China News Agency reported that the boatmen said, "Chairman Mao Tse-tung borrowed the east wind for the crossing."

On April 24th, Nanking had fallen to the Communists. The liberators were now regrouping to take Shanghai when they chose.

And Shanghai itself? Shanghai waited, and Shanghai still played, despite the puritanical decrees of the expiring Nationalist regime. Shanghai also watched those who could depart do so in haste.

Generals and politicians naturally led the exodus, though some lingered to extract the last ounce of gold from the stricken city. Many Chinese capitalists followed their smuggled capital to Hong Kong, but many remained.

Those who were loath to go placed their trust in the Communists' promises that they would be permitted, indeed encouraged, to carry on their businesses. Neither communism nor even socialism would be instituted after liberation, Chairman Mao Tse-tung had pledged, but a transitional system he called the New Democracy. Private business would thrive when economic activity was no longer hamstrung by corruption, disorder, and brutality.

Some foreigners had left, but not the greater number. To most, Shanghai was their home, their native place, as surely as it was home to the settled Chinese community. Many foreigners felt themselves bound by their obligations to their Chinese staff. Others still believed themselves impregnable to the slings and arrows of Chinese strife.

The refugee communities were, however, very nervous. Most Chinese refugees had nowhere else to go, and the helpless White Russians were aghast at facing another Bolshevik conquest. As edgy in Shanghai as they had been complacent in their native Germany, the European Jews were bolting. The members of the old, predominantly Sephardic Jewish community were, of course, not refugees. Some had, however, departed to watch developments in Shanghai from a distance before committing themselves. Joshua Haleevie's eldest brother, Jeremiah, who was now the head of the family, had gone no farther than Hong Kong, where most of the Haleevies' liquid assets were now concentrated.

Joshua himself remained. Distinguished in his white dinner jacket, he sat opposite Elizaveta and tapped out the beat of the artless ditty with a patent-leather pump. His wife, Charlotte, had drifted away more than a year ago to make her own life in New York and Jerusalem. But that no longer had much to do with him. He could not leave the city that had given him life, he had told his mistress, when that city faced its greatest trial. Should the Communists behave well, he would look a fool if he scurried away. Should they behave badly, he would look a poltroon for running off.

In 1927 Joshua had been frightened away by neither Commissar Chou En-lai and his popular rising nor by Generalissimo Chiang Kai-shek and his army. He had stood firm before the Japanese in 1932 and again in 1937. He had left Shanghai after the Japanese attack on Pearl Harbor in 1941, but only to fight elsewhere. Why should he behave differently in the face of the present threat, which might be illusory?

When she forgot to be vivacious, Elizaveta was pensive. When her lover laughed without apparent care, tears started in her midnight-blue eyes. Her vision was no longer veiled by self-deception. She had a few days earlier realized that Joshua's love for her was not unlimited. Believing that he would never leave her, she had often treated him cavalierly. She had been confident that he loved her just that fraction more than she loved him. She was now devastated by unmistakable evidence that her own love was marginally greater than his.

He had formerly taxed her with loving the Ikra better than she loved him. Yet she had now sorrowfully concluded that Joshua loved Shanghai more than he loved her.

Why else should he have peremptorily declined to join her on the SS *Anson,* which was sailing for Hong Kong in the morning? He could always return to Shanghai, she had pointed out, just as she would return if his optimism proved justified. He had finally given up urging her to stay and test the Communists' promises along with him. But he had obdurately refused to join her in the safe haven of Hong Kong.

"It won't be the same thing if I have to come crawling back." His explanation had rung hollow in her ears. "The Communists are Chinese. They'll remember who stayed to welcome them. Besides, I've made some overtures—and I must be here to receive their answer. . . . No need for dramatic farewells. You're not going forever, whatever you think. You'll be back, or I'll drop down to Hong Kong after a month or so. But what about the Ikra?"

"It's not so hard to give up the Ikra, darling," she had replied. "But I can't bear the thought of giving *you* up."

"You'll never have to, Bess. You've finally made your choice, it seems. Either the Ikra or me! And it's me! I'm overjoyed . . . even if you left it a little late."

"Then you will come with me on the *Anson?* Oh, Joshua, I'm so—"

"Bess, I'm afraid that's out." He was not brusque, but he was rather matter-of-fact. "I must be here . . . whatever happens. Darling, I promise I'll get away just as soon as I can. We'll take a cruise around the world. Whatever you want. We'll marry, if that's what you want. A divorce from Charlotte is only a formality. Though nowadays, people seem to think that marriage doesn't make much difference."

"No difference, Josh?" Her vehemence surprised him. *"All* the differ-

ence in the world. If we had only married years ago, *everything* would've been different. Of course I'll marry you."

"Bess, you're making me very happy." His voice faltered minutely. "In Hong Kong, then, in a month. Sooner if things settle down here."

With that commitment, Elizaveta had to content herself. But her chest ached with despair. Not so much because she was leaving Shanghai, which had become her true home. Not at all because she doubted Joshua's promise. He *always* kept his promises, unless it was flatly impossible. She despaired because she knew in the core of her being that he would not be able to come to her. The Chinese Bolsheviks would see to that. She feared that enemy so profoundly that her own great courage had failed.

She knew she was losing Joshua, but she could not stay. Joshua did not love her as she now knew she loved him. No other woman was her triumphant rival, but the hot-eyed and cold-hearted slut called Shanghai.

Elizaveta felt her fixed smile grow rigid on her lips. She lifted her goblet of the Krug 1936, the last of her vintage champagne. That gesture sealed the farewell that all the company, except herself and one other, were gaily pretending was only a brief parting.

She could no more envision the Howes' leaving Shanghai than she could the Bund's floating out to sea. Tommy looked almost as distinguished as Joshua in his cream silk dinner jacket with the light blue bow tie Julia had coaxed him into substituting for somber black tonight. He had that piercing look again. That look made Elizaveta feel he knew her every shameful secret, yet was not shocked, only fondly amused.

Seated between Julia and herself, Jimmy Wei looked like a wise old monkey in his old black dinner jacket. No one had actually invited Jimmy, but everyone had assumed that he would appear. He grimaced and tapped his fingers to the player piano's tinkling rendition of "The Anniversary Waltz." Opposite him an empty chair stood before an untouched place setting. His sprightly wife, Mary, would have been seated in that chair if she had not already left for the Nationalists' offshore refuge on Taiwan. Jimmy was himself to rejoin the Generalissimo on that island, after he had, as he said, "finished saying good-bye to Shanghai."

Three more chairs were empty before complete place settings. Had they been filled, their occupants would have completed the party that Elizaveta had joined at Jeff Geoffreys's St. Andrew's Café in June 1921.

A champagne goblet was upended before one of those chairs. Harry

Smythe would never again lend his brash assurance to any gathering. Although his Curtiss Commando had crashed out of reach behind Communist lines, Joshua had established "from private sources," which meant Tommy's contacts in the Apparatus, that there were no survivors. No one had mentioned Harry Smythe that evening, and no one would. The upended goblet was monument enough.

The remaining chairs were reserved for Richard Hollings and Emily Ou-yang. Or was she Emily Hollings by this time? Perhaps it really didn't matter, after so many years, whether they had finally married. They were together in Washington, and they had finally accepted what everyone else had known from the beginning: they might fight bitterly and feel ill-used by each other, but they would be miserable without each other.

Although Richard's health still kept them from coming to China, he had repeatedly telephoned to gather material for the column on foreign affairs he was now writing twice a week. He could not trust Emily's judgment, he only half joked, because of her ridiculous prejudice against the so-called Communists. She was also angry at the Nationalists amid her sorrow at their ignominious retreat. "But she's just too doctrinaire an anti-Communist," Richard said only half-jokingly, "to offer any useful thoughts on the future."

Richard would have written about China in any event, but, in fact, he had to write about China because the United States was fascinated by China. Emily was, therefore, riding high professionally despite the collapse of her cause. Exemplified by the Generalissimo and Mayling Chiang, the plucky Nationalists, bravely standing up to the Japanese monsters, had been the darlings of the American people until the Communists usurped that sentimental affection for China. Few Americans rejoiced unreservedly at the imminent Communist triumph. But attention was focused on China by the spectacular collapse of a regime that had only four years earlier been hailed as one of the five great Allied powers.

That intense interest worked greatly to Emily's benefit. Her stories about Chinese women, although initially addressed primarily to Chinese women, had become the object of a virtual cult in the United States. Translated by the author into English even more evocative than her original Chinese, the episodes were strung on a single narrative thread. The novel, provocatively entitled *Tales from a Chinese Harem*, was taken up by the Literary Guild after it became a best-seller by word of mouth. Emily had already contracted to write a second volume using the same material. Afterward, she planned a raw novel on the Flying Tigers, though it might disappoint readers who expected only cozy women's fiction from her.

Initially resentful at being labeled a "women's writer," Emily now considered that label a distinction. She was again fighting hard for female emancipation, although she was also determined to tread the greater literary stage, where the author's sex was not all-important. Yet she had been born into an era when the struggle for women's rights made justifiable—and often overriding—demands upon whatever talent she possessed. Contentedly settled with a man for the first time in her life, she was again preoccupied with the problems of women.

To Emily's great relief, Richard had accepted her success gracefully—indeed with pride. He had admitted his initial surprise at his lack of envy. Considering his ambitious, competitive nature, Richard had concluded, his delight must prove how deeply he loved her. Emily still wondered if he would feel quite the same way if, rather than fiction, she was publishing reportage, which was his field.

So much Julia knew from Emily's letters, which had virtually bridged the rift between them. She missed Emily keenly, but she was glad Emily was not in Shanghai to see the Nationalists' tawdry end. Naturally, Julia was herself bubbling with excitement and anticipation. She almost betrayed herself, but she remembered the assignment for which Chou En-lai had reserved her. Concealing her jubilation, she feigned resignation to the Communists' imminent victory.

Elizaveta, who was a past mistress of illusion, had conjured up an atmosphere of hectic end-of-term gaiety: not only the decadent piano player and his scarlet sing-song girls, but the balloons and streamers hanging from the mirrored chandeliers. She made them feel like a privileged few, rather than the last survivors in a deserted hostelry.

In rakishly formal Shanghai, the men of course wore dinner jackets. Having commanded Julia to put on her most spectacular evening dress, Elizaveta had appeared in a Schiaparelli creation—no lesser word would do—that combined her beloved Edwardian elegance with Victorian romanticism. A cloud of white organdie appliqued with gold and silver flowers floated over the pleated bell of pink silk that was the skirt. The brief organdie bodice, which was almost an afterthought, admirably displayed Elizaveta's snowy shoulders.

Julia was not outshone. Her figure, which had hardly altered over the years, was outlined by a sheath of burgundy moiré. The stylized pagodas embossed on the fabric were the same as her six-tiered gold earrings. Relieving the severe cut, the skirt flared in back in two stiff pleats.

Julia was still glowing with the memory of her tailor's tribute: "Only perfect shape can wear such dress." She might not be the most effective spy in Shanghai, she told herself, but she was almost certainly the most glamorous.

"You men all are so smug." Elizaveta perversely addressed the one man who was patently not smug. "All such optimists."

"Doesn't strike me that way right this moment," Jimmy Wei replied dolefully. "What've you got in mind?"

"I've run away only once in my life," Elizaveta declared. "Twice, actually, not counting the time the Japanese escorted me out of Shanghai. Both times when I was much younger. Both times from the Bolsheviks—first in Russia and then in Siberia. But, here in Shanghai, I've stood firm."

Elizaveta was not inebriated, not even slightly. She was, however, a trifle manic.

"This time I'm not waiting for the Bolsheviks to expropriate me," she continued. "Months ago, when Peiping was sold out, I knew it was all over. The Bolsheviks can have my poor old Ikra—but not me. I'm no longer an aristocrat. . . . I'm middle-class. The Bolsheviks hate the middle classes worse than poison."

"Liz, do you know where the gold *yüan* stands today?" Tommy was uncharacteristically sharp. "Six million to one U.S. dollar. Remember when all Chinese were forced to turn in their dollars, their gold, and their silver for gold *yüan?* Remember when the Nationalists were shooting the holdouts? And do you remember the rate? Yes, four *yüan* to one U.S."

"We all know that," Joshua interposed protectively. "Why pick over those dead bones again?"

"Liz says the Communists hate the middle class. What about the Nationalists? The Nationalists stole the middle class blind. Stripped clean everyone who turned over foreign currency and precious metals for gold *yüan*—which are now worthless. Yet the Nationalists have always claimed to be pro-capitalist and anti-Communist. With such friends, why should the middle class fear its so-called enemies?"

"We Nationalists always appear even worse than we really are." Jimmy Wei did not look up. "The way it's ending . . . no dignity. The Gimo resigning. Worse, flitting off to Taiwan after eleven days of fantasy, when he thought he could hold Shanghai, make it his last bastion. And the garrison's disgusting behavior. Two hundred thousand soldiers acting like wild men—raping, pillaging, and killing. I'm too old to change my loyalty, maybe too stubborn. But it's undeniably disgusting. Why the Shanghai garrison—"

"The garrison commander had to have his reward," Joshua interjected. "And he had to reward his troops or they would've mutinied. After all, he did ship the government's gold to Taiwan. Tens of millions . . . and only a few millions stuck to his fingers. . . . So he let his troops play. What are a few thousand rapes and some wholesale looting when the world is ending?"

Jimmy did not respond, but Tommy bristled. "Just don't say it's the old Chinese way . . . that it always has been and always will be. Whatever else, the Communists don't act that way. Never mass misbehavior. Not like these animals in uniform here."

"Tommy, we only know what the Communists choose to let us know," Joshua replied. "Or what foreign correspondents write about them. You, of all people, know just how doubtful some of that reporting—"

"Gentlemen! Gentlemen and ladies!" Jimmy Wei's manner was fierce. "I sense a myth being born. Like most myths, it's got a basis of truth. I'll give you an example. The Gimo, everyone says, is personally honest but has bad advisers and crooked subordinates. True enough on both counts. But the Gimo didn't have to tolerate *every* murdering crook who pledged loyalty to him. As long as we Chinese live by myths, we'll never—"

"Jimmy, what myth is worrying you?" Tommy's voice was gentle. "We don't *know* it's a myth about the Communists' good behavior."

"My good doctor, that's not what I had in mind. I'm worried about the stab-in-the-back myth. Also the who-lost-China witch-hunt. Both are already starting in the States. Those myths will poison the air for decades. . . . But I'm talking too much."

"Jimmy, be a dear and say exactly what's on your mind," Julia coaxed. "Among friends."

"Among friends? Why not? If I can't trust you, who can I trust? I might as well be a lying Communist . . . never trusting anybody."

Jimmy did not look at her, and Julia did not wince visibly at his oblique condemnation. Instead, she prompted: "Please tell us what you mean."

"All right, I will. . . . The United States hasn't lost China. The Americans never had China, so how could they lose China? Generalissimo Chiang, God help him, didn't lose China either. Even he never had China to lose. He wasn't a dictator. He was more like a chairman of the board who couldn't fire a single director. He couldn't even fire a foreman. The Gimo never ruled China, so he never lost China. But he did hold things together. No one could've done more. His so-called supporters ranged from Confucian monarchists and illiterate, feudal robber barons to wild-eyed Socialists and Trotskyites. How could anyone rule China with a gang like that?"

"What about America, Jimmy?" Julia was intrigued. "What about America's losing China?"

"I can see the stab-in-the-back myth growing. Yeah, I know *Comrade* Chou En-lai sometimes joked that Richard Hollings would conquer China for *Comrade* Mao Tse-tung." He pronounced *comrade* as if it were a curse. "Old Red Dick Hollings and his buddies in the press would conquer China for the Communists. Uncle Holly Tong believes it, too. But it's just not true. Sure, their reporting helped turn off American support. But they didn't decide the fate of my country with their little typewriters. . . . Do you want to know who really lost China?"

"Please, Jimmy." Tommy was respectful of his enemy's agony. "Do go on."

"I lost China, Tommy. *I* did because I didn't do enough to save China. Inefficiency and corruption lost China. Those who knew, those who cared, we didn't fight the graft and the sloth—not enough to change them. We went along. So no matter what anyone wrote in the papers, we would have lost anyway. The fate of China was decided in China—nowhere else."

Unashamed, he wiped his eyes with a linen handkerchief and then said, "Sure, the Yanks kept sticking their noses into our business, which they don't understand. Claire Chennault didn't help by preaching clean, easy victory through air power. Even last autumn, he was still telling the Gimo he could win with maybe fifty bombers. Not just win a battle, but turn the tide of the civil war!"

Jimmy Wei gulped his champagne and delivered his closing words to his empty goblet: "Despite all that, American interference was never crucial—not really decisive. The issue was decided before the Yanks ever got into the act. You want to know who lost China? I'll tell you again. *I* lost China!"

At the beginning of May, Julia was forced to recognize that Tommy's elation did not match her own at the moment when his country stood at the threshold of a wonderful new era. Once again, the detached scientist in Tommy was restraining the ardent patriot. That was not a bad thing. The revolution needed ardent heroes and also men who could remain cool amid the heat of crisis.

Tommy confessed that his misgivings had grown. Not just general apprehension before sweeping change or even his old doubts about the Communist leaders. He was deeply troubled by recent events.

From Peking, once more called the Northern Capital, Chairman Mao Tse-tung had on the eve of victory issued a declaration regarding foreign policy. Let there be no mistake, he had told the world. The new China would "lean to the side of the Soviet Union."

Tommy and Julia had expected as much, though both had grave doubts about unreserved cooperation with the Soviets. They were not alone. An influential group within the Chinese Communist Party was wary of drawing too close to the Soviets. Like Tommy and Julia, that group remembered Soviet arrogance, Soviet slights, and Soviet opportunism—beginning with the First Congress of the Communist Party in Shanghai in 1921.

But Chairman Mao was assuming near-imperial grandeur in the rosy dawn of victory, and those dissenters were powerless to prevent his cutting China off from the West. By the late spring of 1949, the United States had become *the* chief enemy in the Communists' public statements. The Apparatus had, moreover, failed to respond to feelers like

Joshua's, which were designed to improve British relations with the new regime. Preoccupied with the violent transition of power over the world's most populous nation, the Communist leadership was almost absentmindedly committing China entirely to Moscow.

Shanghai was waiting anxiously for the People's Liberation Army to end the dreadful suspense of that protracted transition. Unlike Julia and Tommy, most of the city's millions waited in fear rather than expectation. For the Howes, the gradual Nationalist withdrawal heralded the new era for which they had so long fought. For most Shanghailanders, that withdrawal closed an era that was familiar, however harsh.

Even Julia's joyful anticipation was, however, broken by reminders that the globe still revolved while Shanghai waited. Since Western Union and Cable and Wireless were both functioning superbly on the edge of chaos, Shanghai was still in touch with the outside world.

In early May, a yellow Western Union envelope yielded a message from Washington. Frugally sent by the cheaper, night-letter rate, it was extravagantly wordy: BLESS US COMMA BROTHER AND SISTER EXCLAIMER WE WERE MARRIED AT FOUR PEEYEM SATURDAY MAY SEVENTH AND IMMEDIATELY BEGAN LIVING HAPPILY EVER AFTER STOP LONG EXPERIENCE THUS CONFIRMS THAT COMMA ALTHOUGH RIDICULOUSLY BELATED COMMA OUR DECISION WAS AYE HUNDRED AND TEN PERCENT CORRECT STOP CAN HARDLY WAIT SEE YOU TWO STOP YOUR CHILDREN AND OUR CHILDREN JOIN IN SENDING VAST QUANTITIES OF LOVE STOP EM AND DICK

Although long overdue, that was very good news indeed. Julia telephoned Tommy, who expressed his delight and promised to open a bottle of champagne when he got rid of his last patient. Their pleasure was obviously shared by their majordomo.

"Look, Missy, have got one more piece telegram," he caroled a day later, lapsing into pidgin. "Maybe b'long more good news."

Julia took the blue-and-white Cable and Wireless envelope eagerly. With some surprise she saw that it was addressed to her alone, unlike Emily and Richard's message. It might be bad news after all. Although her father's cancer had apparently gone into remission, he was not a young man. Suddenly apprehensive, she opened the cable, which came from Hong Kong and covered five telegram forms.

APOLOGISE DEEPLY FOR DISTURBING YOU [it began] BUT PRESUME YOU WOULD WISH TO BE OF ASSISTANCE STOP IF SUPPOSITION IS INCORRECT OR TASK IS TOO DAUNTING COMMA PLEASE ADVISE AND I SHALL TELEGRAPH DIRECT STOP NONETHELESS THE ENTIRE FAMILY WOULD BE MOST GRATEFUL IF YOU COULD UNDERTAKE THIS DISTRESSING TASK ON OUR BEHALF STOP

Disturbed and puzzled, Julia flipped to the last page to read the signature: JEREMIAH HALEEVIE. Recalling that Joshua's elder brother had taken charge of the family holdings in Hong Kong, she felt a chill of fear and read on.

SS ANSON DOCKED KOWLOON TWELVE HOURS AGO BADLY BATTERED BY ENCOUN-
TER WITH FREAK TROPICAL STORM BEATRICE IN THE STRAITS OF TAIWAN STOP SINCE
ALL PASSENGERS HAD TAKEN TO THEIR CABINS ON THE CAPTAINS ORDERS COMMA
NO APPREHENSION WAS FELT UNTIL DEBARKATION STOP A SEARCH OF ENTIRE SHIP
THEN YIELDED NO SATISFACTION STOP

THE CABIN OF COUNTESS YAVALENKA WAS UNDISTURBED COMMA INDICATING
THAT SHE HAD NOT RETURNED AS DIRECTED STOP COUNTESSES AMAH SUBSEQUENTLY
CHECKED AND FOUND ONE RAINCOAT AND ONE SET OF NORMAL GARMENTS MISSING
STOP I MUST REGRETFULLY CONCLUDE THAT COUNTESS YAVALENKA WAS CARRIED
AWAY BY A WAVE BEFORE SHE COULD REACH HER CABIN STOP

I SHOULD BE PROFOUNDLY GRATEFUL IF YOU WOULD BE KIND ENOUGH TO GIVE THIS
APPALLING NEWS TO JOSHUA YOURSELF STOP IF ANY MESSENGER COULD ALLEVIATE
HIS SHOCK AND SORROW COMMA IT WOULD BE YOU STOP FOR YOUR INFORMATION
TO IMPART AS YOU JUDGE FIT COMMA CHARLOTTE HALEEVIE IS ALSO BEING INFORMED
STOP PLEASE GIVE HIM ALL OUR LOVE AND ALL OUR SYMPATHY

Shocked, Julia neatly folded the message and tidily returned it to its envelope. Unaware, she lit a Chesterfield. When a fit of coughing shook her, the meaning of the message struck home.

Elizaveta was dead, Elizaveta the survivor. An inconsequential thought intruded: the soothsayer at the Great World had been wrong in predicting that Elizaveta would have a very long life. The next instant, Julia saw starkly that Elizaveta had courted her fate. She had not committed suicide, but she had, with Slavic fatalism, flirted with death.

It must have begun when Joshua demonstrated that he loved Shang-hai more than he loved her—and Elizaveta felt herself deprived of the obsessive love that had sustained her almost all her life. Aboard the coaster to Hong Kong, she must have known hours, even days, of total desolation—the overwhelming, black Russian melancholy. A refugee once again, she had irretrievably lost her most precious possession, the Ikra. She must have believed in her despair that she had also lost Joshua.

No one would ever know precisely what aberration had driven her to the rail of a ship in a typhoon. Yet Julia knew beyond doubt that Elizaveta had not embraced death, although she had recklessly courted death.

Julia lifted the telephone again. The handset was very heavy, and her fingertip slipped weakly in the holes of the dial. She hoped irrationally she hoped she would fail to reach Joshua. Anything to put off the fearful task his brother had put upon her. But Joshua himself answered on the second ring.

"Hello, sweetie," she began. "I wonder if you've got time for a drink this afternoon. . . . Yes, here. . . . No, nothing in particular."

The three weeks that passed between those telegrams and the arrival of the People's Liberation Army should have been lit by elation. Instead, sorrow for Elizaveta and pity for Joshua clouded those weeks.

Joshua had aged before Julia's eyes when she told him of Elizaveta's death. He had not spoken, at first, but had shrunk into himself. His light blue eyes filmed over, his smile became a grimace, and his face grew ashen.

"I should have gone with her, Julie," he finally said. "If I had, this never would have happened. If I had done other things earlier . . . Who knows?"

Joshua said no more that afternoon beyond automatic courtesies. He sat silent for a long time. He said no more until he thanked her for telling him and wished her good-night.

The next morning he telephoned Tommy to talk about protecting their employees from the rampaging garrison troops. Later, he came round to assess the few snippets of information they could pass on to British intelligence. After a few words of commiseration, Tommy did not speak of Elizaveta—and Joshua did not mention her. He remained optimistic regarding relations with the coming rulers of Shanghai, and he spoke confidently of new building projects. From time to time, however, he lost the thread of a sentence—and stared in mute appeal.

Joshua and Tommy had almost nothing to pass on that London could not have gleaned from the newspapers. The Apparatus had only informed Tommy that liberation was imminent. He was instructed to reassure all his associates—as best he could without breaching his cover—that the New Democracy was a threat to no one except the imperialists and their henchmen, the bureaucratic capitalists. He could, moreover, promise that the city would experience no immediate changes except, perhaps, emergency measures to alleviate public suffering. Therefore, no patriotic businessman need feel threatened.

"Finally it's certain," Tommy declared on Saturday, the twenty-first of May. "Liberation's only a matter of a day, maybe hours away."

"How do you know?" Julia laughed. "Secret dispatches from the front?"

"Better than that," he answered. "The last CAT flight is leaving Hungjao Aerodrome right now. As usual, CAT is the last plane out. As usual, overloaded with refugees and gold bars. Julie, your American pilots have got more courage than brains or scruples. . . . Still, it was very decent of them. CAT Operations called to say they were holding two seats for us."

"What did you tell them?"

"Only that we were Shanghailanders—and would stay."

All Saturday afternoon and all Sunday they heard shellfire from the southwest around the airport. Throughout Monday and Tuesday, sporadic small-arms fire sputtered amid intermittent shelling. The tempo was leisurely; the volume was light; and the explosions were muted by distance.

"They're just seeing the Nationalists off," Tommy said on Monday with the authority of a veteran of two wars. "Hurrying up the lads we've seen straggling toward the river with their loot. There's no serious fighting, believe me."

Tommy and Julia locked up the house on Kiukiang Road at six on Tuesday evening. Tommy himself oversaw the shooting of bolts and the securing of chains to be certain that no member of the household would endanger himself by violating the curfew. They went to bed early, almost exhausted by the tension of expectation and by the faint melancholy that clouded their jubilation. Old Shanghai had been their life, and old Shanghai was perishing.

They fell asleep in the twilight of Nationalist rule—and awoke to the dawn of Communist rule. The People's Liberation Army had marched into Shanghai during the night. By six on Wednesday morning, when Julia and Tommy climbed the circular staircase to the roof garden, the remaining Nationalist soldiers had exchanged their uniforms for workmen's faded blue clothing and vanished into the tenements of Chapei. At six-fifteen, the scouts of the Liberation Army entered Kiukiang Road.

Their stained cotton uniforms dark against the ruddy brick buildings, the vanguard of the liberation advanced warily into the sunrise. Two by two for mutual protection, but strung out against surprise attack, the soldiers darted from doorway to doorway. They clutched their rifles and their submachine guns, ready to reply to hostile fire. But the morning was deathly still except for the chirping of the sparrows on the rooftops.

After half an hour, the liberators' confidence grew. Loose columns of farm boys in baggy green tunics moved eastward toward the Bund and the Hwangpoo River. All were young, many no more than sixteen or seventeen. Most were bare-headed, though a few wore crumpled caps bearing faded red stars.

The country boys gawked in amazement at the tall buildings and the shiny automobiles. Identifiable only because their tunics had breast pockets, the officers did not reprove such unmilitary curiosity. The young officers, too, gaped at the opulent façade of the wicked metropolis.

The big wooden wheels of horse-drawn supply carts creaked in the hushed dawn, and the small steel wheels of man-drawn machine guns squealed as they jolted on rough road surfaces. The first tentative columns swelled into mass formations, which filled Kiukiang Road.

Most of the soldiers of the People's Liberation Army wore canvas shoes with rubber soles, but some still wore straw sandals. They did not march in time, but each at his own pace. Thousands of soft soles scuffed on the hard city pavements like a great wind sweeping across an endless grassland. That immense and implacable shuffling was the loudest sound on the bright May morning when age-old rural China reclaimed Shanghai.

EPILOGUE

MAY 2-6, 1952

The gray-mustached porter glided into the velvet-curtained compartment of the train on cloth soles, and poured green tea for the foreign woman. His tread was further cushioned by deference. It was only prudent for an ordinary man to serve the cadres of the new People's Republic with downcast eyes, just as he had served the mandarins of the Manchus' Great Pure Dynasty more than forty years earlier. Though excessively considerate, the foreign woman was clearly a personage of importance.

The premier himself had escorted her to the platform. When she leaned out the window, the premier had taken her hand as if to keep her from leaving. Further hallowed by the farewell tears of Madame Sun Yat-sen, the foreign woman traveled under the protection of the young man and woman from the premier's bodyguard in the adjoining compartment.

Protection, the old porter wondered, or surveillance? Really, it came to much the same thing today, as it had in the past.

As the train wriggled out of the hard shell of the city, tile-roofed, brick factories employing twenty-five to fifty workers gave way to shacks with corrugated-iron roofs, where three or four men beat out ploughs for peasants and sprocket wheels for bicycles from scrap metal. The countryside thrust its green tentacles into the industrial suburbs and gradually engulfed the city. Water buffaloes wallowed beside sampans in the creeks that drained the marshy Yangtze Delta, and trading junks lowered their masts to scull under humpbacked bridges. Aside from the cobwebs of telegraph and electricity wires against the horizon, the scene had been the same a thousand years earlier.

Julia leaned her head against the back of the worn velour seat and tore open a red-and-gold packet of Gate of Heavenly Peace cigarettes. American cigarettes had not been available in Shanghai for two years. Slipping the paper cylinder into her ivory holder, she lit the yellow tobacco with a sliver-thin wooden match. A moment later she chuckled. Somewhere along this stretch of track stood an enormous billboard which had before liberation extolled Chesterfields. Anticipating that advertisement, she had automatically lit up.

Still not habituated to the harsh Chinese tobacco, she coughed and ground the cigarette out in the cut-glass ashtray on the folding table under the window. Her eye was caught by the cornflowers growing beside the gravel roadbed, and she glimpsed a column of farm boys marching under the orders of a green-uniformed recruiting sergeant of the Liberation Army: more conscripts for the Chinese People's Volunteers fighting the Americans in Korea.

The giant billboard took her by surprise. She had been looking for a brightly colored picture. Instead, she saw a white expanse with two blocks of scarlet ideograms. On the left: OPPOSE THE U.S. AND AID KOREA! BUY BONDS AND COLLECT SCRAP METAL TO RESIST AMERICAN IMPERIALISM! And on the right: ADVANCE THE CAMPAIGN TO CRUSH THE FIVE EVILS! EXPOSE THE CRIMES OF BUSINESSMEN WHO STEAL THE PEOPLE'S PROPERTY!

Presumably, those exhortations were more wholesome than cigarette advertisements. But not necessarily. The war in Korea was killing hundreds every week. And the civil engineer Liu Zoongyee had two hours earlier flung himself under the premier's limousine to protest the methodical extinction of all the entrepreneurs China desperately needed.

Slowing arthritically from its leisurely twenty-five-mile-an-hour pace, the train jerked to a halt. Ancient airbrakes huffing and puffing, it flung its passengers forward and backward. This first stop was Kashing, where the Communist Party of China had concluded its First National Congress forty-one years ago. The deserted platforms were funereal. Half the lightbulbs were dead, and the rest flickered with the feeble current. The resort town on the South Lake had evidently been badly hurt by the Communists' brutal campaign to destroy the entire bourgeois class and seize all private enterprise.

They called it the Campaign Against the Five Bourgeois Evils. China's new masters were determined to extract every last ounce of gold—and, if need be, every last drop of blood—from every industrialist, every shopkeeper, and every master craftsman. Such entrepreneurs were to be whipped into submission, and the workers were to be driven like mules. Even less than the Nationalists did the Communists spare the lash.

When the train pulled out of Kashing, the foreign lady gazed through the half-open window into the night. They had called her *wai-kuo tai-tai*, the foreign lady, for so long that she almost thought of herself in those words. She felt neither tired nor restive, neither happy nor sorrowful; she was neither angry nor cowed, neither hungry nor sated. She was for the moment, totally detached.

Julia gazed into black velvet darkness broken occasionally by the flare of a fire. The immemorial smells of rural China drifted to her nostrils: woodsmoke, freshly turned earth, pungent nightsoil, fetid pigsties, and musty mildew. Aside from those haunting smells, she might have been traveling alone through unpeopled blackness.

Julia rose mechanically and undressed for the night before removing her makeup. She slipped on her nightdress and creamed her face with automatic motions. After brushing her hair, she drew the light coverlet over herself and stared at the ceiling.

With its lights extinguished, the compartment was indistinguishable from the enveloping blackness.

Tommy had loved the dark mysterious night in the interior of China. He had always said, "It's like another planet, except that the inhabitants speak my language . . . just about."

She would not sleep if she thought about Tommy. If she was to get through this final journey unscathed, she must not think too much about Tommy. Closing her eyes, Julia listened to the voices of the train: the high-pitched chatter of the wheels and the deep bass creaking of the carriage.

"Leaving China!" The wheels condemned her. "Leaving China! Leaving Shanghai!"

"Forever!" The carriage groaned. "Leaving forever!"

The porter's timid knock startled Julia out of her revery. She was glad of the fresh tea he brought, though irritated by his obsequious manner. A day after departure, the train was threading through the crumpled foothills of a mountain range. She asked the porter where they were.

"Quite a bit south of Nanchang," he replied. "Nothing worth seeing around here. Even Nanchang's just a wide space in the hills. . . . Will the great lady condescend to discuss the menu for luncheon?"

His exaggerated deference grated, and Julia replied shortly that there was nothing to discuss. A bowl of noodles would do—no more than a bowl of noodles.

The old porter was an original. Not only did he address her with titles suitable for a Manchu princess, but he was unaware of the significance of the city of Nanchang. How could any adult in New China be ignorant of the Nanchang Rising, which had given birth to the Chinese Red Army?

She glanced out the window to see dense smoke. The train was laboring up a steep incline at ten miles an hour. Going downhill, they rocketed along at a dizzying forty. Never faster, because the engineer did not trust the ancient airbrakes at a higher speed.

They were leaving the bare, dun mountains of Kiangsi Province for the great Central China Plain where lay Hunan, the native province of Chairman Mao Tse-tung. Julia's spirits lifted. She had been depressed by the bleak hills, which barely tolerated human habitation. The single-track railway twisted through ravines hewn from raw rock, almost scraping the jagged, seamed cliffs. Those wounds on the earth inspired Chinese folktales of gigantic dragons battling to the death. Gnarled Kiangsi Province was as deformed as the broken bones of those ancient dragons.

A far pleasanter aspect of the many-faced country Julia loved lay just ahead. The great rice bowl of Central China glowed golden in her memory. Yet it was ridiculous to travel from the port of Shanghai to the port of Hong Kong by going five hundred miles inland. China's railway system remained backward—and three years of Communist rule had seen further decline.

After a courtesy knock, the door opened for the old porter, who had a damask napkin draped over his arm. Startled by the intrusion upon her thoughts, Julia looked blankly at him. He stepped back and almost upset the tray carried head-high by the waiter behind him. His face chalky with anxiety, the porter lifted his eyes imploringly. Julia smiled an apology, and his face cleared.

"Hsieh-hsieh!" he whispered. "Thank you!"

He was genuinely grateful to her for relenting from her unprovoked rudeness. Subservience was ingrained, hardly to be altered by three brief years of egalitarian rule. Theoretically egalitarian rule. Premier Chou En-lai in a Zil limousine was no more like the common man than was an Imperial Grand Secretary in a golden palanquin. Less, actually. Who had ever committed suicide by flinging himself under a palanquin?

The porter waved the waiter into the compartment with a flick of the napkin. On the silver tray, ivory chopsticks and sterling silver spoons flanked a silver-gilt tureen.

Cupped in pale green leaves, transparent vermicelli was intertwined with pearly sharks' fins and translucent skeins of swallows' nests. For sharks' fins and swallows' nests Chinese aficionados gave great sums, and these were the finest. On that costly bed lay petals of whelk, rounds of conch, tiny oysters, rosy shrimp, and miniature lobster tails.

She had ordered a simple bowl of noodles, and she had been served a culinary extravaganza. It was like being presented with a diamond-studded Patek Phillipe when one expected a Mickey Mouse watch.

She smiled her thanks, and the porter confided proudly, "It's called Dragons Mingling Amid Pearls in the Clouds. A dish created for the great Empress Dowager!"

Reluctant to mar the perfection with intrusive chopsticks, Julia meditatively, almost timidly, twined a strand of vermicelli around a minute oyster. The subtle flavors awakened her hunger, but she prolonged the pleasure by taking only a morsel at a time. She was enjoying the dish too much for haste. She was, after all, leaving China—and such food—by her own choice.

Outside, flooded fields thrust their silver fingers into the foothills, and smoke rose from huts with straw roofs. Worn brake-shoes squealed; air-lines coughed; and the ancient carriage lurched. Groaning piteously, the train halted and stood softly whimpering to itself.

The porter knocked, opened the door, and stuttered in consternation, "Apologies, Gracious Lady, profound apologies. It is required that all passengers alight. I protested, but even the noble lady herself must condescend to alight."

Touched by his concern, Julia was herself unconcerned. Train journeys in China were always punctuated by unscheduled halts, whether for water buffaloes, missing sections of track, or barriers erected by desperate men, who also looted trains and held passengers for ransom. Such outrages were, however, unlikely since the People's Liberation Army had imposed rough order on the countryside.

Inconspicuous in rumpled blue cotton tunics, Premier Chou En-lai's young security man and security woman followed ten feet behind as Julia stepped down to the gravel roadbed supported by the old porter's hand. Hampered by the tight skirt of her yellow suit, she was conscious of the frivolousness—and the fragility—of her white pumps and sheer nylon stockings. In the hot sun, a trickle of perspiration crept down her spine. They were roughly as far south as Miami.

Why, she wondered, the abrupt halt near the cluster of tumble-down farmhouses she had earlier glimpsed? Following the other passengers around the bulbous nose of the ancient sixteen-wheel locomotive, she saw hundreds of men and women in patched work clothing squatting beside the tracks. Three men sat on stools behind a battered table set on a rough platform. They wore quasi-military peaked caps and relatively new blue cotton jackets. "They say they're very proud, and they want us to see." A man spoke in rapid Shanghainese, showing off his understanding of the slurred Hunan dialect. "You'd think they'd offer us a cup of hot water no matter how poor they are. Such courtesy isn't capitalist. It's just Chinese!"

Julia craned her neck but could not identify the speaker. Only an official secure in his authority would dare to criticize the "great mass of farmers," who were, along with the "industrial workers," hailed by the Communists as the new masters of China. He must be very sure of himself to imply that not all the old customs were bad. The old ways were everywhere under attack. In the cities, officials were being punished for succumbing to bourgeois temptations. In the countryside, land was being summarily redistributed. It was, to say the least, imprudent for anyone to question that transformation.

Feeling perspiration soak into her beige silk blouse, Julia slipped off her jacket. Her bright skirt was unfortunately conspicuous, but she could not, in any event, make herself inconspicuous. Her tawny hair and her green eyes would set her apart even if she wore the drab tunic now prescribed for women as well as men. Despite her Chinese name, she was irretrievably foreign in appearance—and, probably, in character. She was also blatantly bourgeois in the pretty yellow suit she had chosen that morning to lighten her depression.

For the first time, Julia felt uneasy. Her friendship with the grandees of the new regime would not protect her if the ignorant farmers—or the ignorant leading cadres who controlled them—should decide that she embodied their hated enemy: foreign imperialism. Even a farmhand from the next county was considered an intruder in the depths of rural China. Even the Chinese train crew and passengers drew together for mutual protection.

The farmers hardly looked at their reluctant guests. Since they could not offer even cups of hot water, the last courtesy of the impoverished, it would be rude to show their curiosity regarding the alien beings from Shanghai. Nonetheless, several farm wives stole glances at the women among the outlanders.

The country people's fear was even stronger than their curiosity. They stared fixedly at the three cadres in blue tunics behind the table hung with slogans. The senior cadre, who sat in the center, revealed herself as a woman when she adjusted her cap. Julia saw twin black braids, once the emblem of virginity.

The farmers stank. The wind carried the stench of old sweat and decay. Julia smelled rotting teeth and festering wounds. When the wind blew from the paddy fields, the human excrement that made the rice grow seemed wholesome after the feral stench of the farm people.

Even those women who had dared to look at the intruders from another world swiveled their heads when two figures shambled forward between files of young men with red armbands and old Japanese rifles. The militiamen thrust the middle-aged man and woman onto the platform. Julia saw that they were plump and apparently still self-confident. But their cheeks were bruised, and their mouths were bloody.

"Sha! Sha! Sha Low Ti-chu!" Hundreds of farm people screamed in their barbarous accents, "Kill! Kill! Kill Landlord Low!"

After waving the throng into silence, the female cadre spoke in Mandarin, her accent of the north. Years earlier, Julia had learned at Shanghai Labor University how to drill witnesses for such public trials. Manipulated by the agitators, the farmers would believe they were spontaneously erupting into fury at the landlord who had exploited and oppressed them all their lives.

"Comrades, we share your bitterness!" The female cadre spoke again in a high, sweet voice. "But revolutionary justice gives even swine like these a hearing. You will all get your chance to testify. When the last witness has spat out his bitterness, the masses will pronounce their verdict on these bloodsuckers!"

The twin braids of maidenhood swinging saucily as her head turned, the leading cadre searched the crowd. The first witness should already be springing up. She frowned and waited.

Unless the peasants participated actively, it was pointless to parcel out the landlord's holdings. Above all, the process was designed to force the farm people to make a political commitment. The cadres would thus break down the "slave mentality" of the old social system—and clamp absolute Communist control upon the hamlet.

These peasants were, however, passive, almost sullen. Halting the train had not been such a brilliant stroke, for the shy country folk were obviously inhibited by the alien audience. They were overjoyed at the prospect of owning the land for whose use they had formerly rendered the landlord the greater part of their meager crops. But they were still too timid to speak against him.

"Hao-la! Ni-men yao fang . . ." Such simple language the peasants must understand. "All right! You want to let them go—bloodsucker Low and his vicious wife? All right then, the revolutionary masses are the boss. Landlord Low will be given back his holdings. You farmers are very kind! To pardon the Lows for stealing . . . torturing . . . raping . . . exploiting . . . enslaving . . . murdering . . ."

The high voice, clear as a sing-song girl's, tolled the landlord's crimes, and the peasants squirmed. To be thus accused implicitly of cowardice and explicitly of unrevolutionary magnanimity was an indignity. To be accused by a young lass was a humiliation. Even worse than losing face, they were losing their newly acquired land.

Shouting hoarse imprecations, a young man with a purple birthmark pushed toward the platform. But a small woman with seamed cheeks pulled herself erect on the twisted willow branch that served her as a crutch and shrilled, "I want to spit out my bitterness!"

The leading cadre beckoned forward the gnomelike woman, although she had evidently not been rehearsed as the first witness. Women, the Labor University had taught, were a powerful force for destroying the rotten old social order that had kept them in subjugation.

The dwarfish farm wife was soon screaming. Her thick accent made her almost unintelligible. Julia could distinguish only a string of unconnected words: ". . . daughters . . . beat . . . sty . . . strangled . . . bean curd . . . raped . . ."

The same male voice she had earlier heard among the passengers explained in concise Shanghainese: "The women's daughters were taken by Landlord Low as maidservants—and as playthings. His wife beat them and made them sleep with the pigs. In a fit of rage, Low's wife strangled the younger daughter, who was ten. The elder, who was thirteen, was given nothing but watery rice gruel, not even a sliver of salted cabbage or a morsel of bean curd. When she complained, the landlord raped her. He then gave her to his strong-arm men to play with . . ."

Julia could see only the man's back. He had turned abruptly and, limping slightly, made for the caboose at the end of the train. Yet there was something familiar about the way he carried himself, the set of his shoulders at once proud and vulnerable.

Landlord Low and his wife undoubtedly deserved what was coming to them. Julia should not have been disturbed by the brutal destruction of their personalities as the cadres drew from witness after witness lurid accounts of usury, extortion, rape, torture, and murder. Landlord Low and his wife undoubtedly merited their fate. They had certainly committed all—or most—of those outrages.

Local despots like Low not only owned almost all arable land, but loaned money, monopolized trade, and collected taxes. They were also, in practice, judge, jury, jailer, and executioner. Through war and revolution, landlord families like the Lows had exercised tyrannical power everywhere in rural China.

Most of the witnesses wept. Many of the women were barely audible. Ashamed of speaking about sexual matters, they were appalled at speaking in public. Men shrieked in rage, their faces red and their fists raised against the cloud-flecked sky.

The young militiamen halfheartedly fended off the infuriated peasants who attacked the landlord and his wife. Bleeding from jagged scratches, the Lows crouched defensively. They were held erect when the female cadre asked the People's Court for its verdict.

"Sha! Sha! Sha Low Ti-chu!" The same roar had greeted the Lows' arrival: "Kill! Kill! Kill Landlord Low!"

When the youthful militiamen relaxed their grip, the landlord's wife slumped. Two struggled to hold her up on her knees. Her parchment-gray face lolled on her shoulders, and her tongue protruded. She hung in their hands, shapeless as a half-empty rice sack.

The female cadre's command was drowned out by the throng's shrieking. When the peasants surged toward the platform, the cadre gestured imperatively.

Two militiamen gingerly took old Mauser pistols from their wooden holsters. Blinking nervously, they placed the muzzles against the Lows' necks.

Julia saw the twin smoke-puffs an instant before she heard the shots. As Landlord Low and his wife crumpled onto the platform, the farm people recoiled. The souls of those executed, just released from their bodies, could wreak terrible vengeance.

But the mob's fury did not abate. Having been inflamed by the cadres, the peasants would not relinquish their rage. The militiamen and cadres were helpless when the mob turned on the train. One fired a rifle, but he might as well have tossed a pebble. The old porter gasped, "They think we're the enemy! These moronic dirt-farmers hate all outsiders!"

"Sha! Sha! Sha wai-ti!" The chant resumed: "Kill! Kill! Kill the foreign imperialists!"

Julia shrank back against the carriage as if its dust-streaked sides could divide to take her in and shelter her.

"Sha wai-jen!" The shriek was like a blow. "Kill the foreigners!"

No consolation that the Chinese passengers were also foreigners to the maddened peasants. Julia would not close her eyes. She would not go blind to whatever fate . . .

Shots crackled close by. A volley seconds later was obviously fired by disciplined troops with semiautomatic rifles. The mob recoiled, suddenly voiceless, except for the women's sobbing. When a second volley crashed into the sudden silence of the late afternoon, the mob turned and ran.

Julia looked for her saviors and saw a squad of Liberation Army soldiers drawn up before the caboose. Their trim tan uniforms and the semiautomatic American rifles they handled with accustomed authority marked them as crack troops.

"Cease firing!" The elusively familiar voice commanded in Shanghainese. "Cease firing and entrain. All passengers entrain immediately!"

Secure again in her green plush compartment, the carriage wheels rattling comfortingly, Julia shivered with delayed shock. So much for Tommy's taunt that she scooted over the surface of his country like a water fly on a pond. She had descended to the depths of primeval China, and she was terrified. She was also conscience-stricken because she had so long served the political movement that incited and delighted in such brutal spectacles.

She abruptly pulled the window shade down to hide the rice fields and pushed the ivory call-button. When the porter appeared, she asked, "That Shanghai man . . . the Shanghai man with the limp who commanded the soldiers. Do you know him? Who is he?"

" 'Nother passenger, Missy." The walrus mustache trembled, and he retreated into pidgin. "B'long only 'nother passenger. Me no savvy, Missy."

Julia did not press the question. She would have the truth out of him in time, if he knew it. She smiled at the myth of Chinese impenetrability so many old China hands repeated to explain their inability to understand the people among whom they lived. One Chinese had certainly penetrated her, she reflected bawdily.

Her mind strayed to some memorable occasions of Sino-American communion, which Tommy exuberantly called "passages of high venery and low lust." Was that, too, all over for her forever? Was the fever of the blood never to rise again? If only Tommy had not . . . If she only knew . . . But such thoughts were unbearable.

She met the porter's uneasy gaze and flushed slightly. Still, he could hardly have divined her thoughts. She crossed her legs the other way and pulled the yellow skirt down over her knees. She then spoke with the imperious confidence of a Chinese matriarch, which almost made foreigners' arrogance seem fawning.

"If you won't give me information, you can at least get me something to drink! Scotch whisky with ice and mineral water. But I suppose that's impossible. Brandy, then. You're sure to have brandy. Commissars or compradors, they all love brandy."

"Nat'chly, Missy." He clung stubbornly to pidgin. "What kin' wanchee?"

"Not J&B." She continued in Shanghainese. "I'd like something with more body. What about Johnny Walker?"

"Can do, Missy! Chop-chop, Missy."

When the porter withdrew, having reproached her hauteur with his ludicrously broad pidgin, Julia grinned sheepishly. He had made her feel an absolute bitch by accepting her bad humor so amiably. It was hardly his fault that she felt trapped on this apparently interminable journey.

After ten minutes, the door drifted open on oiled hinges. The old porter stood behind a silver trolley like those on which pretentious restaurants offer selections of appetizers or desserts. Ashamed of her bad temper, Julia smiled her thanks.

"Quite like the old days, isn't it?" Speaking Shanghainese again, he beamed forgiveness. "A delight to serve you, madam."

On the trolley, cut-crystal goblets clustered around a crystal bowl filled with ice cubes. The damask tablecloth was so heavily starched it crackled as the train swayed, and five unopened bottles clinked gently against each other: Cutty Sark, J&B, Johnny Walker Black Label, Chivas Regal, and Ballantine's Twenty-four-Year-Old. Only the slight twitching of the porter's walrus mustache revealed his pleasure in putting the foreign lady in her place. After serving her the Ballantine's, he wheeled the trolley out smiling beatifically.

Julia laughed, feeling herself humbled. She sipped the smoky Scotch, and her expression darkened.

Why, she wondered, had Premier Chou En-lai commanded such splendid treatment for her? Neither his gratitude for her past services nor their old friendship could entirely explain her being pampered like a princess of the blood royal. Could it be a mute apology for Tommy's disappearance? Or was he trying to ensure that she continued to praise the Communist regime when she could speak freely outside China?

Since she would never know, she sipped her drink—and waited with no great anticipation for her dinner. She was tired of inactivity and fed up with being crammed with food like a prize goose.

After dinner, she gave up trying to force herself to be cheerful. Resignedly, she slid open the door of the miniature washroom and removed her makeup with coarse Chinese cotton wool. After sponging herself with a washcloth dipped into the doll's-house washbasin, she applied cologne liberally and drew her quilted scarlet dressing gown over her thin nightdress. The night air could be cold on the Hunan Plain. In somewhat better spirits, she pushed the call-button. She would take a turn along the corridor while the porter made up her bed.

Julia set out briskly, her mules swishing on the green carpet. The long corridor was lit only by lamps glimmering at either end. The doors of the compartments that lined one side were all closed, and the windows on the other side were pitch-black. Darkness hung like a curtain before her eyes; she felt she could reach through the window and stroke the black velvet of the night. A pinpoint fire flared orange in the distance for a moment. Afterward, the darkness seemed even thicker.

The black night seeped through the windows into the carriage. Before her astonished eyes, the corridor grew darker. Annoyed at the delusion, Julia stepped into the slightly wider vestibule at the end of the corridor. The overhead lamp was very dim, so feeble it barely lit the translucent glass panel in the door leading to the next carriage. Not intrusive night, but erratic Chinese electricity was creating the gloom.

Tentatively, then with more authority, Julia ran through the warmup positions of Tai Chi Chüan, the stylized Chinese shadowboxing. Her right hand extended before her, she prolonged the stretching movement called Grasping the Bird's Tail. After pulling back slowly, she pushed both hands forward and swung into the threatening posture called the Single Whip. Her right hand was poised as if to swing a lash.

The overhead lamp flickered, died, and flickered on again. The vestibule was even darker. Julia resolutely ignored the illusion created by her own fears. The outlines of the black shape on the other side of the door were distorted by the translucent glass panel. The shapeless figure expanded and contracted like a jellyfish in the wavering light.

Determined to banish the illusion, Julia swung into the Tai Chi Chüan posture called Playing the Fiddle. Her hands were extended like a violinist's, and her chin was cocked high. She stared through the glass panel and saw that the phantom figure had not vanished. It appeared to be grasping the brass doorknob, which was slowly turning.

As the door opened a crack, she heard a noise behind her and glanced over her shoulder to see the reassuringly burly porter. The door crashed shut. The black shape had no more been an illusion than had the slow dimming of the overhead light.

Angry at her own fear, Julia wrenched the door open. The sinister figure was just slipping through into the next carriage. He slammed that door behind him, and the bolt snicked shut.

"Must lock up ver' good, Missy!" The porter reverted to pidgin at the door of her compartment. "Have got many bad men about these days!"

Gravel rattling on a corrugated-iron roof awoke Julia. She slipped her watch from under the pillow and was startled to find it already ten. Raising the window shade, she saw that heavy rain was pounding the carriage. When the downpour lifted for a moment, she saw that the train was inching through a narrow valley. The river foaming beside the tracks was obscured when the rain descended again. She pulled down the shade and pushed the call-button.

Since they were running through mountains again, they must be in Kwangtung Province. Perhaps three hundred miles separated them from Canton, a journey of twelve to sixteen hours. That metropolis of the south was only a way station for her. Hong Kong was again her destination. Hong Kong was to be the first staging post of her second exile from China, as it had been for her first exile. She would, she supposed, then return to the United States—for want of any other place to go.

At least she need not worry about money. Tommy's brothers had moved most of his funds to Hong Kong and New York with their own.

Nor would she be alone, for the girls would greet her. Althea, at twenty-two, would then do as she wished. Still coltish at nineteen, Persephone would be good company until she finished Bryn Mawr—and took up her beloved Aunt Emily's invitation to spend "a few weeks, a year, or more in Taiwan," the green island where the Nationalists had taken refuge.

Throughout the world politicians and journalists were still busily explaining—or explaining away—the Nationalists' defeat and the Communists' victory. Some called it the Communist conquest, as if Mao Tse-tung and Chou En-lai were alien invaders, rather than native sons of the yellow earth. Many Americans were railing at the American culprits they blamed for America's "losing" China. Americans believed they had given more to China than had other peoples. They therefore expected more of China. They were now lamenting the loss of China —and looking for scapegoats to blame and punish for America's losing what America had never possessed.

But the gentle knock must be the porter. Having double-locked and bolted the door, Julia had to dismantle her barriers against intruders in the night. She could almost see again the figure in the glass panel change shape as it scuttled away. She hesitated before sliding the last bolt open, but smiled at her own timidity.

The porter waiting outside in his crisp white jacket was the epitome of all the decent ordinary Chinese men she had known, from coolies and carpenters to bankers and merchants. Pleased at returning to an everyday world of irreproachable solidity, Julia smiled and asked for: "Coffee, toast, and orange juice, if you have it."

"Of course we have orange juice, Madame Howe!" The porter's smile virtually challenged her to ask for something truly exotic, perhaps softshell crab or filet of moose.

After dressing, Julia fought her desire for a cigarette. She should no longer need the consolation of nicotine before breakfast. It was all over now. She was on her way out of China. The decisions—and the perils —lay behind her. Regardless of the phantoms her imagination had conjured up last night, she was safe because she was unimportant.

Brakes squealed, and the train slowed to crawl around a hairpin turn. Looking down when she smelled smoke, Julia saw that she had lit a cigarette. She stabbed the long butt into the cut-glass ashtray, and pressed the call-button. The porter had already kept her waiting almost half an hour. When he knocked, she called, *"Lai! . . .* Come in!"

Backing awkwardly into the compartment with the big silver tray, the porter appeared to have shrunk. His shoulders looked narrower within his white jacket, and he seemed much shorter. Besides, his hair was no longer pepper-and-salt, but glossy black. The clumsiness of a new porter had obviously delayed her breakfast.

His left foot scuffing the heavy-pile carpet, he swung the tray on the pivot of his slight body. A smile lit his large eyes, and his triangular face was like a benevolent jack-o'-lantern.

"Hsiu-jyeh!" the new porter said. *"Pa-vay-nan Hsiu-jyeh!"*

Not Madame, but Miss. Not Madame Howe, but Miss Pavernen. Julia stared uncomprehending. His spare face altered before her eyes, growing plump. Her vision clouded, and the compartment became hazy. So much for cigarettes on an empty stomach.

Wiry fingers grasped her wrists and pulled her erect. The aroma of coffee helped revive her, and she automatically took the hot cup in her hands. After a moment, she lifted her head to look at the apparition.

"Pow . . . can it be?" she asked in wonder. "Little Pow? Is it really you, Pow? But you've been . . . It's so many years. We thought you were dead. How can—"

"Pa Hsiu-jyeh . . ." The familiar light voice was hardly altered. "Miss Pavernen, I'm very sorry I frightened you. But it was the only way. It's so good to see you, Miss."

"Pow! Little Pow! It *is* you!"

Julia grasped his wrists and drew him to her. He returned her embrace, and when she set him free, he stood beaming at her.

"Sit down, Little Pow, sit down!" she commanded. "Coffee? A cigarette? Oh, Pow, why didn't you tell us? All these years and you never—"

"Joo-li Hsiu-jyeh . . ." He took a cigarette and spoke more familiarly. "Miss Julie, I wanted to . . . so many times. But it was judged not necessary for you to know. So I had no choice."

Julia nodded, for she understood perfectly. The Apparatus had decided that its agents Thomas and Julia Howe need not know that its agent Little Pow still lived. Personal emotion did not matter, only political necessity.

"And you, Little Pow?" She could not refrain from the question. "You didn't mind?"

"Of course I minded. What other family did I have except you, the doctor, and Master Jon? But what could I do? You didn't see me at Master Jon's funeral, did you?"

"Of course not. If I had—"

"I was the fourth coolie bringing flowers—my own flowers. And you didn't know me when I came into the president's office at Kai Ming College. I turned and left—even though my heart ached to see you and not speak."

"Oh, Pow, I'm overjoyed. It's wonderful . . . just like a new life. . . . What do they call you? What have you been doing? What do you do on the train? A porter? A waiter? Surely with your knowledge of English . . ."

"That is enough for questions." He spoke one sentence in stilted English before reverting to Shanghainese. "Miss Julie, I'm not a waiter or a porter. And they don't call me Little Pow, though I hope you will still. . . . But for others? Pow means bubble. Am I a bubble bobbing on the tide? Pow was thought unsuitable. I am now called Lee Teh."

Julia offered her lighter to the wiry man who was thumbing a cigarette and grinning at her. Few in the Communist movement did *not* know of Lee Teh. The slender man in the waiter's jacket, no more than five foot two, was legendary. Pow was just forty, she calculated, and Lee Teh had been a noted guerrilla leader for two decades. He was also famous for his intelligence coups against both Japanese and Nationalists. Disguised as a coolie or a scullery boy, he could blend into any crowd and penetrate any stronghold.

"It's hard to believe. . . . So hard to believe, Little Pow. That *you* are Lee Teh. Such great deeds! I'm so proud of you, Pow!"

The veteran guerrilla blushed like a schoolboy. Pinching the cigarette between his thumb and forefinger, he took a deep drag.

"When you disappeared, when Tommy couldn't find you," she continued, "we thought you were dead."

"Commissar Chou En-lai looked after me. I've been with him on and off over the years. You might say I'm his man, the premier's man."

"And he never told us. . . . Pow, are you married? Any children?"

"Fu shi, Joo-li . . ." More relaxed, he no longer called her Miss. "No, Julie. I never had time. The revolution is a jealous mistress. I've had close

comrades-in-arms, and I've had lovers. But no other family. Only the doctor and you."

Julia's uncle John had saved Little Pow from starving on the streets of Hongkew. Afterward, Tommy and she had been his father, his mother, and his teachers. In family-centered China he would naturally claim them as his family. And he would give them his loyalty—second only to his loyalty to the Communist Party.

"But why reveal yourself now, after all these years?" she asked. "Only because of longing and love?"

"Unfortunately not, Julie, though I couldn't let you leave China without saying farewell. But there are . . . ah . . . problems that must be dealt with. Some questions, you see, that . . ."

He looked down at the green carpet in embarrassment, evidently torn by a conflict between fundamental loyalties. He should not even have made himself known to her, although he said fiercely that he could not let her leave China without saying good-bye.

"The premier told me to look after you . . . to protect you." Pow struggled with his conscience. "He didn't specifically forbid me to speak to you. So, I—"

"Protect me? Why should I need protection on a public train?"

"Julie, I must have your complete cooperation if we are both to . . . to come through this." He ignored her question. "I'll explain as much as I can, when I can."

"Pow, I'm so . . . so excited at seeing you I can hardly think straight. But why the mystery? Why not explain now?"

"I'll get some more coffee."

He slipped out the door. While she waited, Julia's joy gave way to more complex emotions. She was a little frightened by his words. She was also relieved to learn that she had not necessarily conjured up the phantoms of the preceding night.

"I wanted to check on your bodyguards, though they don't know me," Pow explained when he returned after ten minutes carrying a silver coffee pot. "They're good watchdogs . . . always obey the last order they receive. They're now obeying the premier's orders—or seem to be. But they didn't move very fast when those wild peasants. . . . I wonder! Could Kang Sheng have—"

"Pow, please tell me what this is all about." Julia was chilled by his reference to Kang Sheng, the Communists' cold-blooded chief of public security, who was nicknamed the Executioner. "I didn't imagine that business last night, did I? The black figure and the nice porter coming to my rescue?"

"Julie, that black figure was me. I was uneasy about the porter. After he saw me, he wouldn't have dreamed—"

"You mean the porter was out to harm me?"

"I don't really know, but I had to scare him away. He'll be all right now. He's frightened half to death. Also, last night I hadn't decided when to speak to you. Perhaps just before the border, I thought."

"Well, you've now done it, Pow. So please tell me what's going on."

"All right, Missy." His grin faded as he spoke. "The problem is, first, what you know about China and, second, what you're going to say when you're out of China. Kang Sheng the Executioner and his crowd say it's idiotic to take a chance. They wanted to liquidate you . . . to eliminate any risk. Premier Chou En-lai blocked that. He said: 'Don't be negative! Think of the good she can still do us—not the harm!' But the premier hasn't really made up his own mind. That's why I'm here. To make sure nothing happens to you before he's decided . . . and to help him decide."

"As I understand it," she replied, "my old friend Chou En-lai hasn't quite decided whether to let me go free or to dispose of me."

"I'm ashamed to say that's about right, Julie." He gazed at the intricate pattern his toe was tracing on the green carpet. "Chou En-lai could decide to eliminate you. I don't know whether I can allow that to happen. You are to me my mother and—"

"Pow, this is a nightmare," she burst out. "Why in the name of heaven would they, the premier himself, want to . . . to . . . kill me?"

"Because of what you might say, Julie. They're afraid you'll be very critical."

"How absurd, Pow!" Her laugh sounded forced to herself. "Anyway, what does it matter what *I* say? Not that I have any intention—"

"No intention now, but, later, who can tell?" he said. "As you know, Julie, we Communists are determined to restore the Motherland's good name. The People's Republic of China must be seen to be powerful—and just. We must regain the face China has lost. So we're spending millions to entertain foreign delegations—and to deceive them when necessary. Millions for fares, hotels, banquets, and transportation. More millions to coach every person the foreigners might possibly see. Also to build phony villages and factories. You know how it's done."

"I still don't see what all this has to do with me."

"Now, Julie, you've heard Chou En-lai with a few drinks inside him. Remember what he says about your friend Richard Hollings and his book *Red Star?*"

"I've heard him, Pow. Richard Hollings, he says, conquered China for

Chairman Mao by conquering world opinion. But it's only a joke, Pow. All the support of all the opinion in all the world couldn't have won China if it hadn't been for—"

"Yes, it's a joke. But *not* only a joke. We know it's not that simple. But world opinion is still crucial for us. Julie, you did wonders for the cause with the foreign correspondents. And later, in the American— what do you call it?—War Information Bureau."

"Office of War Information," she supplied automatically.

"Thanks." He took one of her cigarettes, lit it, and resumed: "After liberation, when you proclaimed that direct experience had convinced you—despite your reactionary bias. Living in the People's Republic had shown you how wonderful it was. You convinced tens of thousands, didn't you?"

"Perhaps," she agreed reluctantly. "But the analogy isn't—"

"Analogy be damned!" Little Pow exploded in his anxiety. "Julie, just think. You're now famous as a great champion of the new China. If you let loose a blast against us, it would hurt us badly. You also know too damned much about the inner workings, the seamy side. You'd be damned convincing. So you can see why Chou En-lai is having a hard time fending off the Executioner. And why I can't guess how he'll decide himself. So, you—"

"Pow, what happened to Tommy?" Julia demanded. "I'm certain you know. You *must* tell me, Pow."

"I did what I could for him, Julie." Frowning in concentration, he stubbed his cigarette out. "I can hardly say any more."

"Where is he, Pow?" She was implacable. "Is he alive? You know, don't you? Even if I can't see him. I don't care so much about myself. Only—"

"You *must* care about yourself, Julie," Little Pow advised. "For his sake . . . for the doctor's sake, you must get away!"

"Then he *is* alive. Thank you, Pow, thank you!" She could not pause to rejoice but persisted, "Now you must tell me *where* he is."

"Julie, I swear I'd tell you if I could. But I can't. I can only tell you to be hopeful. Don't ever despair about the doctor . . . or about yourself!"

They sat no more than three feet apart, but Little Pow's words came to Julia thin and faint, as if spanning a great distance. She knew only that her life could begin again.

She had always refused to believe that Tommy had been killed in his flight from Shanghai last summer. But she had not *known*. Now Little Pow had as good as said Tommy still lived—and had implicitly acknowledged helping him escape.

She still did not know whether Tommy was wounded or ill. She did not know whether he was safely holed up somewhere or was constantly pursued by the vengeful chief of public security, who was for good reason called the Executioner. She did, however, know that Tommy was in grave danger anywhere in China.

After she left China, Julia realized, stricken, she might not be able to help him. Yet she had been wholly unable to help him during the past year. She had not even been able to find him. She had been completely cut off, a virtual pariah until the day a month ago when Premier Chou En-lai came to tell her he had decided to grant her an exit visa.

No, she could not help Tommy by staying in China. When she crossed the Hong Kong border, she would no longer be a helpless hostage—and she would, perhaps, be better able to help him.

Little Pow was a powerful ally. The revolutionary hero was evidently chafing under the stern discipline of the Communist Party, which had been his home since he was fifteen. His emotional loyalty had turned again to Tommy and herself, who had virtually adopted him a quarter of a century earlier. But when would his ingrained loyalty to the party reassert itself?

Little Pow shook another cigarette from the red-and-gold packet. Turning away from Tommy, he reverted to his original topic: "Julie, you do understand? Premier Chou En-lai hates the idea of throwing you to the wolves. But even Old Chou's hand can be forced. In twelve hours we should know his verdict."

"Twelve hours?"

"When we reach Canton. I can then use the military telephone line to speak to the premier in Peking. If I can't get through, my orders are to hold you."

"I see!" Julia felt her new ally was somewhat less than ardent. "And, of course, you'll obey your orders?"

"Many know my name, but few know my face." He evaded her question. "Your security watchdogs are here to watch you, as well as to watch over you. They must not know me unless it's essential. And, of course, the Executioner's gang. I don't know for certain that they're on this train, but they must not know that I . . ."

Little Pow's voice trailed off, and he stared at the window, which was still obscured by sheets of rain. Scowling and rubbing his left thigh, he said, "It always hurts in weather like this. But without Tommy I'd have no leg. I probably would have died in 1927. So I'll do everything I can to . . ."

When his voice again trailed off, she glanced at him sharply, and he erupted: "All right, Julie, if you *must* know! You've become a shuttlecock between rival factions in the Communist Party. Kang Sheng the Executioner is outwardly worried only about the danger you represent. Really, though, he wants to get at Chou En-lai through you. You've been the premier's protégé, and he's decided to let you out. If Kang Sheng gets you, it's one in the eye for Old Chou."

"After all these years, still factional struggles? Even after liberation, just as vicious?"

"Julie, it's worse than ever." He laughed sourly. "And you're right in the middle of this battle."

Little Pow limped to the door, muttering about making sure the old porter was frightened into total silence. Julia did not begin shivering until he had been gone for a minute. Her forced composure endured until she looked down and saw her hands shaking in her lap.

Above all else in heaven or earth, Tommy was alive! Little Pow had encouraged her to hope that she would see him again, perhaps quite soon. She trusted the tough-minded little general totally. She knew she would see Tommy again—by God's grace, very soon.

Her own peril? She had acquired a staunch ally. If she were just a shade more confident that he would defy the Communist Party to save her, she would no longer worry. Little Pow was bone-loyal. But to whom? Yet he had already compromised himself by helping Tommy—and by revealing that help to her.

Dusk came more quickly to Shaokwan than to Shanghai, which was seven hundred miles farther north of the equator. At six in the evening, when the train shuddered to a halt, the semitropical twilight already half-obscured the station's wooden sheds. Nonetheless, Julia decided to stretch her legs on the cracked stones of the platform. Shaokwan would be the last long halt before Canton, where Pow was to telephone Chou En-lai to receive his final orders: either to detain her or to let her go free to Hong Kong.

Julia stepped warily into the steambath heat. Little Pow had told her she could get out for a time at Shaokwan. He had also warned her to avoid her fellow passengers. There was only himself to protect her.

When Julia asked about the soldiers who turned back the enraged peasants, Pow had replied shortly: "They're gone, Julie. They're a crack squad recruiting for the slaughterhouse—finding men to die under American bombs in Korea. We need a few real volunteers to leaven the regular divisions we've poured in. Anyway, they got off at Hengyang to put on their show."

Watching the fiery sun subside behind the purple hills, Julia calculated coolly that the odds were slightly in her favor. Little Pow would almost certainly choose her welfare over party discipline—*if* he was confronted with a split-second choice so that his instinct ruled. Given time to reflect, she feared, he would take the easier way of following orders.

The familiar bustle of a provincial railway station in China diverted Julia, who feared she was seeing it for the last time. Squat baskets stuffed with protesting chickens were being heaved onto a flatcar by bony coolies. Intelligent pigs squealed in terror in the long wicker tubes that confined them. Big earthenware jars scrolled with yellow dragons and packed with preserved duck's-eggs also awaited loading for Hong Kong. China's own people were hungry, but the British Crown Colony paid in hard cash. The People's Government badly needed foreign exchange—in good part to pay for Soviet armaments for the war in Korea.

Several coolies were arguing loudly under the flickering kerosene lanterns. When not toiling, coolies were always either arguing or gambling.

A small, wiry coolie emerged from the station shed, jaunty despite the big baskets of white cabbage suspended from the ends of his bamboo carrying-pole. He dragged his left leg, but his singlet revealed powerful shoulders. Little Pow was watching over her disguised against their enemies as a coolie.

He shrugged off the heavy carrying-pole and, unhooking the baskets, bent his head to set them down. An unladen coolie darted from the shed, almost stumbling over Julia. His coolie's carrying-pole arced gracefully against the purple sky. Gilded by the sun's last rays, the heavy bamboo swung down.

"Pow, get down!" Julia screamed in Shanghainese. "Duck!"

Little Pow dropped to his knees, and the pole whistled viciously through the air where his head had been an instant earlier. He hooked his foot behind his assailant's ankle. The burly coolie almost fell on Pow, who squirmed aside. The coolie then lay still, apparently winded.

Pow's back was to the second coolie who attacked him. Julia saw a knife gleam.

"Chiu-ming! Chiu-ming!" she screamed. "Help! Help!"

Julia snatched up a basket of squeaking chickens and hurled it at the second coolie. Startled rather than hurt, he drew back. She raised a big egg-jar high, gasping at its weight. The yellow dragons appeared to writhe in the sun's dying rays when she brought it down on the coolie's head. Appalled, she dropped the jar.

When the first assailant tried to rise, Little Pow flicked his own carrying-pole at the man's head. The impact appeared glancing, but it thudded like a smashed melon.

Hands grasped Julia's elbows from behind. She instinctively brought her high heel down on her assailant's foot. Twisting in his grip, she screamed again, *"Chiu-ming! Chiu-ming!* . . . Help! Help!"

"Madam, it's all right." An anxious female voice said in Shanghainese. "Please don't shout, madam. You're safe now."

Julia turned and saw that the male bodyguard had pulled her out of the melee. His female partner calmed her while the crowd gaped at the mad foreign woman.

"Why in heaven's name interfere between coolies fighting?" the security man asked. "You could have been hurt . . . badly hurt."

"I thought . . ." she stammered. "I thought he was trying to . . ."

"Now, Madame Howe, nobody will hurt you," the woman assured her. "Not while we're here. We'll get you home safe and sound."

Julia allowed herself to be bustled back into the womb of her compartment. An hour after the train left Shaokwan, she heard a muffled knock, and a small voice called, "Tea, Madame Howe. Hot water for your tea."

When she unbolted the door, Little Pow slipped into the compartment. His mouth was cut, and his limp was more pronounced. Clearly chastened, he was, however, not badly hurt.

"My thanks, Julie," he said softly. "My great thanks."

"And my thanks to you, Pow. We make a great team. We could appear at country fairs."

"They must be on to me," Pow said. "The real enemy, the Executioner's men, not your tardy bodyguards. But have they connected the coolie with the porter?"

"We've got to assume they have. We're under siege, aren't we, Pow?"

"Looks like it." He fished in the pocket of his white jacket. "I brought a pack of cards so we can play rummy. You never could beat me."

The carriage rocked violently as the train clattered over the junction, and the fan of playing cards slid toward the edge of the table. Julia checked their slide, studied her own hand, slapped down a ten of spades, and happily declared, "Gin!"

They had been beleaguered in the compartment for almost seven hours, and this was her first win. Little Pow only nodded abstractedly and peered around the edge of the window shade.

"It's not right, Pow," she teased. "When you win, you make a big fuss. When I win, you practically ignore it."

"Sorry, Julie." The small Communist general buttoned his stained workman's jacket over his grimy singlet and mustered a worried smile. "That was the junction for the city. Maybe a quarter of an hour now to Canton Main Station."

"Where the charade begins."

"Where the charade begins. . . . And we'd better make it good. No chance of rehearsing. It's the real thing."

Perspiration ran down Julia's back beneath her blue cotton tunic, and the coarse trousers chafed her thighs. Her palms were clammy with tension. Pow's fate, as well as her own, could depend on her convincing her hostile audience. As he said, there would be no dress rehearsal—only the single performance for which she was already in costume.

An hour ago, Pow had summoned the two bodyguards from the adjoining compartment, revealed his identity, and given them their orders. After banishing the men, Julia and the female bodyguard had exchanged clothing. The young Chinese woman was delighted to wear the foreign-style dress, the sheer stockings, and the high-heeled pumps. Since her performance would have to be at least as good as Julia's if Little Pow's stratagem was to work, it was as well that, at least, the flame-red dress fitted her reasonably.

The hardest part was, of course, their features. Only concealment could make the double impersonation convincing. The security woman had applied lipstick, rouge, and powder liberally. No point in mascara or eyeshadow. The wide brim and the fine-meshed veil of Julia's black straw hat should, however, hide her Chinese eyes. Julia blessed the sentimental impulse that had moved her to pack that hat, which she had last worn for her uncle Jack's funeral.

Little Pow's solution to the problem created by her own conspicuous nose and her green eyes was ingenious: a two-foot straw cartwheel with a hole in the center for the top of the head. The strips of black cloth hanging from the brim to keep off the sun would effectively hide her foreign features. Wearing the characteristic headgear of a Hakka woman meant that Julia would have to carry luggage, as those hard-working women did. But that was all to the good.

"We *want* the Executioner's men to suspect that something is fishy," Pow observed. "If we divert them with an obvious fake, they'll be sure you're hiding something. But they won't know what *you're really* hiding. When they figure out that the security woman is disguised as a Hakka laborer, they won't wonder whether the foreign lady in red is the right lady in red."

"And the security man?"

"He'll be got up as a coolie . . . obviously disguised. You and he will shadow the lady in red, and I'll carry her bags. I'm pretty sure they're on to me. They know me as a coolie, and they know I won't leave you, Julie. So they'll be certain she is you."

"Why should the bodyguards want to disguise themselves?" she asked. "Wouldn't that look *too* fishy?"

"Anyone who's spent most of his life in the underground thinks it only natural for agents to camouflage themselves. Especially Kang Sheng's mob. They're not called the Secret Executioners in fun. . . . First time you're *against* the Apparatus, isn't it?"

She nodded. Rattling across successive switches, the train was rapidly bringing the ordeal closer. She dared a glance around the window shade but saw only dimly lit houses.

"Another few minutes and I've got to leave you," Pow said. "The Executioners'll break their backs to get me if they suspect anything."

"You're really sticking your neck out for me, aren't you, Pow? More than I knew—"

"Julie, it was bound to happen sometime. This isn't just another big quarrel inside the Communist Party. It's practically a civil war. The split is . . ." The train slowed before halting. "No more time. The bodyguard'll take you to a safe place. I'll see you soon . . . I hope."

Little Pow turned abruptly and limped into the adjoining compartment. A minute or so after the train stopped, the woman in red stepped onto the platform. Little Pow followed, Julia's leather suitcase dangling from one end of his carrying-pole and her crocodile train-case from the other. The security woman teetered on the unfamiliar high heels, and her waist was too thick for the dress. Nonetheless, she stepped out with the assurance of a foreigner for whom Chinese throngs had always made way.

"Our turn now, Mrs. Howe," the security man said. "Time for you to carry some luggage. Why you foreigners need so many bags I can't understand."

Julia smiled at the familiar Chinese directness and followed him, stooping submissively. She carried a crocodile suitcase in her right hand and a small Gladstone bag in her left.

Although it was past one in the morning, a gust of sound struck Julia when she stepped onto the platform. The Cantonese were, as usual, transforming still night into noisy noon. She lowered her head and followed the bodyguard up the ramp to the concourse. The flat heels of her cloth shoes made walking awkward, and the black pennants on her hat obscured her vision.

"Close, but not too close," the bodyguard whispered while they waited to check the luggage. "Show more confidence. They must believe we think our disguise is impenetrable."

With an effort, Julia inhaled slowly. She had been betraying her tension by breathing shallowly.

"They're watching us," the bodyguard muttered. "Look at them if you want to. It'll make us seem clumsier, as the comrade general wishes."

Three men were chatting near the exit to the street. Their well-cut and neatly pressed jackets of fawn tropical worsted identified them as privileged officials. They politely stepped aside when Julia and her bodyguard started for the trishaw rank outside. Two of those three-wheeled vehicles, which were propelled by a man pedaling, were receding down the street. The lady in red sat stiffly in the first. In the second, Little Pow balanced the two pieces of Julia's luggage they had not checked.

"Shameen Island!" the bodyguard directed loudly. "Shameen Official Guest House."

Julia twisted on the hard seat to glance nervously behind them. Having heard their destination, the men in fawn tunics were chatting nonchalantly. They were obviously not interested in a Shanghai security woman transparently got up as a Hakka working woman. Their quarry was the foreign woman in the flame-red dress—and they were now doubly sure that she had gone to earth on Shameen Island in the Official Guest House, which had once been the Victoria Hotel.

The Communist regime had evidently not yet succeeded in imposing on Canton the drab conformity that blanketed Shanghai. Lights still blazed in late-night restaurants, and the clatter of mah-jongg tiles was a cheerful obbligato to high-pitched conversations.

"Heung jaw-been . . ." the bodyguard directed in clumsy Cantonese. "Turn left here. . . . Never mind Shameen, just turn left . . . and right again . . . next left . . ."

The trishaw threaded a maze formed by houses whose upper stories leaned companionably across the narrow alleys.

"Ho-la!" the bodyguard finally grunted. "That's fine!"

When the trishaw had pedaled away, its red reflectors dwindling in the distance, the bodyguard led Julia down a lane. Turning and twisting, they walked for five minutes before he pulled her into a shadowed doorway. He tapped lightly, and a small woman carrying a candle immediately opened the door.

"Good-bye, Mrs. Howe," the escort said. "I'll see you tomorrow at the station."

The small woman was very friendly—and completely unintelligible. Pressing tea and cakes on Julia, she chattered merrily in harsh Cantonese. When Julia replied in Shanghainese, her broad face crumpled into an incredulous smile seamed by a thousand wrinkles. When Julia tried Mandarin, she chortled with laughter at a ludicrous foreigner speaking the ludicrous northern language.

The woman cocked her head, apparently hearing a distant knock. She laid her small hand on her guest's sleeve and beckoned. Julia followed her to a back door, where Little Pow waited with a cheap cardboard suitcase and a small straw valise at his feet. He lifted the cases and sidled into the shadows cast by the overhanging upper floors before striding away. Julia shuffled after him.

"No need," he said, "for the bodyguards to know where we really are."

"I haven't the foggiest idea, Pow."

"All the better." He grinned. "Anyway, the security woman will stay in her . . . your . . . room at the guest house, and the man will stand watch outside her door until tomorrow evening. By that time, we'll be safe— or we'll be dead."

"Don't you trust them, Pow?" Julia lengthened her stride to keep up with him. "After all they've done tonight?"

"They'll be fine until they liaise with the Foreign Affairs Bureau here. Then, if they learn that Chou En-lai has changed his mind, as he may well . . . But we'll get across the border somehow."

"We? You're coming with me, Pow? Sacrificing everything? Pow, you mustn't—"

"Suppose he says no, Julie. What then?"

Silently, she followed him through the pools of darkness that lay before the windowless ground floors. They saw no other pedestrians in the medieval alleys. But light streamed through cracks in doors, and the exchanges of shouts that the Cantonese consider conversation resounded from open windows.

Little Pow stepped abruptly into a courtyard, fumbled with a key, and led Julia up a steep staircase hardly wider than his shoulders. The odors of fried garlic, dark vinegar, and burnt sugar contended with mildew. After checking the window shutters, he lit a kerosene lamp to reveal plush chairs set around a table inlaid with mother-of-pearl. After pouring tea from a gallon thermos, he lifted wicker-and-bamboo steamers of plump Cantonese dumplings from an even larger thermos.

"Eat first." He picked up bamboo chopsticks. "Then talk."

"Eat and talk at the same time," Julia countered. "Pow, where do we go from here?"

"To the station to catch the six o'clock train, the first train in the morning. There's a dress for you in the bedroom. You must make yourself look as old as you can. So slather on the makeup as if you're hiding a raddled face."

"Little need to pretend," she said wryly. "But why, Pow?"

"You're crossing the border as Miss Ethel McMurtry Phillips, an aged English missionary from a village in the Kiangsi mountains, who has just been expelled. I'm crossing as a baggage coolie, as usual."

Julia smiled uncertainly and asked, "Where on earth can you get a passport for Ethel McMurtry Phillips?"

"Tommy took care of that detail a week ago." He casually popped a dumpling into his mouth. "Reckoned we might need one for you. So he sent it across. Even fudged a photo from an old picture of you."

"I see," Julia responded sensibly. "So that explains ... You said *Tommy* sent it? Then he is ... is ... all right?" Her voice rose. "And he's in Hong Kong? Oh, Pow, is he really—"

"Calm down, Julie, or we'll have the police around our ears. I'm sorry. I shouldn't have surprised you that way."

"Pow, darling, you can surprise me that way any time you want." She leaned across and kissed his cheek. "I knew it. I knew it when you told me to be hopeful. And he *is* all right? Pow, I'm so delighted I ... But why didn't you tell me earlier? Why in the name of God keep me in suspense?"

"It's part of a very complicated arrangement, Julie. I really shouldn't have told you even now. . . . It's a long story."

"We've got lots of time. It couldn't possibly bore me."

"It's almost two o'clock, Julie. I've got to get through to Chou En-lai right away. I'll tell you all about Tommy afterward. And, Julie, pray that Old Chou gives us the right answer."

"You can assure him that I won't talk when I get out. How could I?"

"And convince him? How am I to do that, Julie?"

Pow slipped out the door, and his cloth soles sighed up the staircase. A minute later, she heard his voice raised as if speaking to an operator. Annoyingly, she could hear bursts of talking but she could not make out a single word.

Alone for the first time since Little Pow had confirmed his hints about

Tommy, Julia gave herself wholly to joy. She now *knew* her husband was alive. Tommy was alive in nearby Hong Kong, and she would see him tomorrow! Nothing else mattered. When she crossed the border, she would not be closing the best part of her life as she had believed only yesterday. She would be resuming her life.

Julia found herself praying, as Little Pow had suggested only half in jest. A word from her old friend Chou En-lai would mean that she was virtually safe in Hong Kong. She had no doubt regarding Pow's ability to get her across the border in any event. But what if Chou En-lai directed him to detain her? Pow might already be torn by conflicting loyalties in the room above her head, where he was still shouting on the telephone to Peking.

The shouting finally stopped. Her breathing suspended, she listened to him shuffle down the stairs. His expression was noncommittal, and he did not immediately speak.

"Well, Pow," she demanded. "What did he say?"

"I finally got through. But Old Chou is out. I said I'd try again in an hour."

If it were her decision, Julia concluded bleakly, she would *not* go free. Far safer to detain her or eliminate her, rather than stake so much on her promise to remain silent. From Chou En-lai's point of view, letting her leave China might be like turning his back on a ticking time bomb. Gratitude for her services to the revolution might move Chou En-lai to spare her. But gratitude was a highly perishable commodity.

"So we wait, Pow," she said. "Nothing else to do, is there?"

"We wait, Julie. And I try to make up my mind. What am I to do if I can't reach him?"

"Obey your last orders, Pow," she urged. "Get me out before Chou En-lai's enemies strike at him by . . . by disposing of me. Pow, they could even grab me and make me speak out against him. It's not so hard to make someone say what you want nowadays, is it?"

"Very easy, Julie," he agreed. "Especially nowadays."

"Meanwhile, please tell me everything about Tommy. Maybe it'll help make up your mind."

"I'm sorry, but we had to keep you in the dark. And Tommy agreed. When the crunch came, you had already started your performance. You were testifying loudly to the glories of the new China—and enjoying the limelight. So we couldn't tell you anything."

"Tommy couldn't tell *me?*" Julia was shocked. "But he knew I would never—"

"Also, it wasn't his secret to reveal. A group in the Communist Party is struggling to keep open our channels to the outside world. To keep China from becoming totally dependent on the Soviet Union—a Soviet colony, a danger to itself and the entire world. Little Teng Hsiao-ping, the new vice-premier, he's one of our leaders. Premier Chou En-lai can't throw all his weight on our side—not openly. The Executioner Kang Sheng and his faction are strongly pro-Soviet—with Chairman Mao's backing. It's major, a decisive struggle over policy. It's also a struggle for power—and the premiership is the prize."

Little Pow refilled their minute teacups from the big thermos and took up the thread again. "The Executioner's mob was suspicious of Tommy from the start. His association with Joshua Haleevie, for one thing. Also, his release by the Generalissimo in 1927 and his sister's rabid pro-Nationalist activities. Not to speak of his American wife. But you get the idea. . . . Yet Tommy was under Chou En-lai's wing. So they pecked away at him, that way also pecking away at Old Chou himself. First, they got rid of Haleevie. That was easy, you'll recall. All foreigners were being expelled except those who, like you, were working for us. They kept Haleevie on a string . . . forced him to pay great sums to settle phony debts and imaginary back salaries. As well as atoning for his family's criminal exploitation of the Chinese masses."

Little Pow waved his hand as if dismissing a banal subject and took another one of Julia's cigarettes.

"You know all that. It was standard treatment for foreigners. . . . Tommy was a harder nut to crack. Even if they could prove his connection with British intelligence, he could always claim he was acting on instructions. And the premier would back him up. If Old Chou repudiated Tommy, he'd be striking a blow at himself. . . . So the Executioner took the long way round. Framed Tommy for trumped-up violations of Communist Party discipline. Invented charges of corruption in his practice and in administering the remaining property of the Howe family."

"And then Tommy disappeared," Julia interjected. "And I knew absolutely nothing after that. Not even how he disappeared."

"It was simple, Julie. The old guerrilla network still functions well when it's needed. I got Tommy over the border to Hong Kong. I reckoned he could do more for China there. We needed a man in Hong Kong whom the British would trust. It was my decision—and I'd do it again. But we couldn't tell you. You do see, don't you?"

His defensiveness did not bode well for herself. If he had to justify rescuing his co-conspirator, he would assuredly balk at smuggling her across the border against express orders. She had no claim on his political loyalty. Nonetheless, she *was* his surrogate mother.

"I've made up my mind, Pow." Her decision took shape as she spoke. "I won't talk about the seamy side of the New China when I get out. I'd only look a fool and a turncoat." She had to convince him that he must help her. "Instead, I'll work with Tommy . . . as always."

"Julie, *why* did you decide to leave?" Little Pow probed gently. "I don't mean now. You've got no choice now, not with the executioners after you. But why leave China in the first place? You didn't know about Tommy when you decided."

"Frankly, I thought I was leaving him behind me. But there was no more I could do for Tommy by staying on. I hoped I could do more abroad." She gave Little Pow an oblique smile. "Somehow, I knew I had to go when they changed the name of Avenue Edward VII to Yenan Road. Understandable, marking the end of an era. But it was also a gesture of exclusion . . . of isolation. I knew then I could do no more to help. It was up to the Chinese. Foreigners were only in the way."

"What about those who've stayed on? There must be several dozen foreigners. And they must believe they can help."

"Pow, I couldn't surrender my mind. I couldn't become a marionette, dancing when the party pulled the strings and speaking only from the official script. Besides, I could no longer justify policies that were obviously bad for China, policies like the Campaign Against the Five Bourgeois Evils. Honest businessmen had been repeatedly promised they wouldn't be touched. Yet they were expropriated and driven to suicide —or like Tommy to flight. Intervention in Korea also stuck in my craw. I know General Douglas MacArthur was dangerous. But committing more than a million Chinese fighting men was folly. And then to invade South Korea! China is Moscow's cat's-paw—and cat's-paws get burnt. This Korean business has set back economic progress—and increased Soviet influence. It's going to be hard to shake off the Soviet yoke when the time comes. How can anyone convince Chairman Mao that leaning to the Soviet side is the biggest mistake he could make? But we must all work toward . . ."

Little Pow raised an admonitory palm and said, "Enough, Julie! You've convinced me your motives and your intentions are pure. Now I've got to convince Premier Chou. I'd better try again."

Little Pow was gone almost half an hour this time, but Julia could hear only a low murmur. Evidently the connection was better. She was initially cheered by his long absence. At least, he had not been peremptorily directed to detain her. Yet why was it necessary for him to spend so much time pleading with the premier?

Little Pow's expression was glum when he returned, but he shook his head to allay her anxiety.

"Old Chou's not to be found anywhere," he said. "I'll try again before we leave. But we can't waste much time."

Julia did not ask what had taken him so long but smiled to put heart into him—and went off to transform herself into Miss Ethel McMurtry Phillips. The baggy tan cotton dress she found on the bed in the next room owed more to the tentmaker's art than to the couturier's.

The Secret Executioners were waiting when Julia's trishaw drew up before Canton Main Station at four in the morning. Their fawn tunics were immaculate, and their cheeks were freshly shaved. But their eyes were red-rimmed when they openly looked her up and down.

She was hideously exposed, and she had never felt more lonely. Yet she had to make this last stage of her journey alone. However disguised, Little Pow would have been a giveaway. The Executioners were looking for a foreign woman accompanied by an undersized Chinese man. By herself, she could blend with the other foreigners now being expelled from China. Three nuns in blue habits entered the station just after her, and a White Russian couple carrying coats of Manchurian squirrel were waiting at the passport-control counter.

Julia stooped to tighten the rope tied around the battered cardboard suitcase that had replaced her expensive leather case. Her crocodile train-case had also been jettisoned, its cosmetics transferred to the cheap straw valise in her left hand. Her other bags would be left behind in the checkroom. Glancing up from the suitcase, she saw a fourth Executioner hovering near the checked-luggage counter.

How could she even think about luggage when his dull eyes scrutinized her? Yet he must have been informed that the foreign woman was still asleep in the Official Guest House.

The unworldly Ethel McMurtry Phillips would undoubtedly be very nervous, but Julia had no need to pretend. Sighing aloud, she awkwardly picked up her luggage and made for the passport-control counter.

The Executioner stepped across and peremptorily took her new English passport from the immigration officer. He contemptuously flicked the gold lion-and-unicorn seal on the cover before studying the blurred photograph inside. For half a minute his eyes shifted repeatedly between her face and the photograph. As became a meek missionary spinster, Julia lowered her eyes for an instant. Then she lifted her head and stared directly into the Executioner's eyes—as became an arrogant foreigner.

Presumably the Executioners possessed a good photograph of her. All to the good! They would be looking for similarities. The only visible similarity between the smart Julia Pavernen Howe and the dowdy Ethel McMurtry Phillips was that they were both foreign and female. Otherwise, they were wholly different. The sacklike dress draped her like a tarpaulin, almost covering her ankles, which were thick in lisle stockings. Her old brogues, which Tommy called stout British walkers, completed the graceless costume, and a faded blue cotton scarf covered her hair.

Ethel McMurtry Phillips was, further, losing her dogged battle against the onslaught of age. Her face was plastered from hairline to collar bone with pancake makeup so thick it was cracking. Behind her prim glasses, her eyelashes bristled with mascara. Small cupid's bow lips of greasy crimson were Julia's best inspiration. The discs of crimson rouge on her cheekbones completed the portrait of a repressed spinster who still yearned after storybook romance.

The Executioner stared unblinking back at Julia. She saw in his eyes the respect for age no Chinese could quite shake off. She also saw hatred for a foreigner and disdain for a woman. When he returned her passport to the immigration officer, Julia was chilled by his contempt. He had judged her beneath notice, which was exactly what she wanted.

Lifting her baggage with another weary sigh, she entered the next stage of the bureaucratic maze that led to the train for Hong Kong. She passed without incident through currency control, customs examination, and the security police checkpoint. Weighed down by her suitcase, she walked awkwardly down the ramp to the platform on legs wobbly with relief.

The grimy second-class carriage was a purgatory after her luxurious compartment on the Shanghai–Canton express. Each time the local stopped, she was jolted violently on the wooden seat—and it made twenty-four stops on its ninety-mile route. Gnawing on the tangerines she had bought at Sekloong Station, she gratefully gave a few coppers to the slovenly attendant who poured fresh hot water onto the cloud of green tea-leaves in her murky glass.

Yet she dreaded arrival at Shumchon, the last stop, which was scheduled for 3:53 P.M. She would have to pass controls at the border even more stringent than those at Canton. Finally, she would have to carry her bags some fifty yards across the covered bridge to British Lowu.

Since liberation, all passengers had to change trains at the border.

That was a political decision. The pigs and vegetables she had seen loaded yesterday would cross unhampered. That was a matter of business.

The last border guard in baggy green uniform with red collar-flashes casually waved Julia on. Behind her lay the numbing formalities of departure from China, which had taken almost two hours. Every garment in her luggage had been pawed, fortunately by male customs officers, who could not see the great differences in quality between the dress she wore and the dresses she carried. She herself had been pawed by a female customs officer to make sure that she was concealing no contraband on her person.

Julia glanced back at the border guard. Standing beneath the scarlet flag of the People's Republic of China with its five yellow stars, he was idly fingering the submachine gun slung from his shoulder. At the other end of the covered bridge across the shallow Shumchon River, she saw the Union Jack flapping over a square, whitewashed building. Beside that building stood two Hong Kong constables spic and span in khaki shorts and shirts, black leather revolver holsters on their belts.

Julia looked back again, determined to imprint that last sight of China indelibly upon her memory. Through sudden tears, she saw the border guard languidly waving on a coolie who wore rusty black trousers, a stained singlet, and rubber sandals. His flexible carrying-pole bobbed under the weight of the five big leather suitcases suspended from its ends. Behind the coolie's grin, she recognized the triangular face and the big eyes of Little Pow.

She had known he would not let her go without saying good-bye. He had not said good-bye when he bundled her off in the trishaw after failing for the third time to reach Premier Chou En-lai by telephone. She had known then that he would himself see her safe across the covered bridge to Hong Kong.

Loping to catch up with her, Little Pow grinned but did not speak. When they were almost halfway across, he glanced back at the bored Chinese guard and said softly, "Drop the little case, Julie. Let it spill."

She obeyed automatically. Bottles, tubes, jars, and brushes rolled on the splintered boards and tumbled into the trough between the railway tracks.

Kneeling to help her sweep up her belongings, Little Pow said, "I had to say good-bye, Julie. Heaven knows when we'll meet again."

"You're not coming over? . . . Of course not. There's no need now.

You weren't specifically told to keep me. . . . You never did speak to Chou En-lai, did you?"

"Julie, it's not that simple." He let two curlers spurt through his fingers and roll away. "I did speak to the premier's chief of security. He told me to hold you. That's another reason I came—to make sure you got across. I was afraid those damn bodyguards would get the word at the Foreign Affairs Bureau. But you're safe now."

"Pow, will you be all right?" she asked. "Won't you be in trouble for disobeying? Shouldn't you come with me?"

"I take orders from Premier Chou—and nobody else. No jumped-up cop is going to tell me what to do." He glanced at the complacent border guard. "Julie, I've got to go back. Things are still getting worse in China, but someday they'll get better. I've got to go back and hurry that day along. In the long run, our revolution will prove the best thing that's happened to China in two thousand years. On that day, you and Tommy will return as honored guests. Until then, I must say good-bye. But I'll be seeing you."

He swept the last of her cosmetics into the straw valise and handed it to her with a courtly little bow. She could not kiss him in public view, but their eyes met for a prolonged moment.

Little Pow saw the commotion at the Chinese end of the bridge while Julia was still lost in an emotional revery.

"Run, Julie, run!" he shouted. "They're on to you."

Sweeping up her bags, Julia saw the premier's security man race past the border guard. Drab again in blue cotton, the woman followed. Behind her, two border guards were unslinging their submachine guns.

Julia ran toward the haven of the British border post. Six Hong Kong constables emerged from the whitewashed building and trotted toward her. She heard Little Pow shouting apologies for hampering her pursuers with his carrying pole and its burdens.

She caught her toe in a crack between the boards and stumbled. The constables were drawing close, led by a tall man whose face was obscured by the black visor of his cap. Julia almost regained her footing, but the suitcase dragged her off balance. When she began to fall, the tall policeman stretched out his arm to catch her.

Julia fell heavily against him, shocked for an instant by the impact. When she raised her eyes, Tommy was looking down at her, his features rigid. He was clearly too moved to smile—or even speak.

"Tommy!" she at length murmured. "Tommy, darling! I knew you'd come!"

"It's all right, Julie, everything's all right," he finally replied. "You're safe . . . finally." He paused. "Can't kiss you here, not in this uniform. But I thought I'd better see you across myself."

"I knew you would, darling, I always knew . . ." she began, but then demanded guiltily, "And Little Pow? What about Pow?"

The Hong Kong constables had formed a khaki rank across the bridge. Two border guards in rumpled green were shouting at them, while a third gripped Little Pow's arm.

"Don't worry about Pow," Tommy advised. "He'll talk his way out of it. Undoubtedly persuade them he was trying to stop you. It helps to be a general."

A constable swept up Julia's bags, and she walked beside Tommy toward the shelter of the Union Jack. A red-faced English police officer waved them into the whitewashed guard post. The cool cube inside was sparsely furnished with a yellow-shellacked desk and two rattan chairs. A small radio was playing softly.

Tommy put his arms around Julia and pulled her close. She clutched him and pressed against him. He kissed her very hard.

"Julie," he murmured. "Always you!"

Julia's guard was completely down for the first time in a year. No longer needing to control her emotions, she gave way to them. Tears came to her eyes, and she clung to Tommy. She tried to respond to his words, but she could not speak. To her utter surprise, she found that she was trembling. The tremors became stronger, and the next moment she was shaking uncontrollably.

"Tom . . . Tom . . ." she finally stuttered. "It's all over. . . . All we believed . . . our work . . . and China. All . . . all finished."

Fearing the onset of hysteria, Tommy grasped her shoulders firmly. But her tremors became more violent.

"Stop it, Julie. Just *stop* it!" he commanded. "It's not all over. Not by a long shot."

He had caught her attention, but her involuntary spasms continued. Anything to divert her, since he could not force himself to slap her. He turned the radio to full volume, and the song reverberated in the white-washed concrete cube: ". . . love to get you on a slow boat to China, all by myself alone."

"Listen, Julie!" he commanded. "Just listen to what they're playing. 'Slow Boat to China.' "

She smiled blearily and said, "Thank God, I've found you. . . . But it's finished, Tommy. We'll never go back."

"We will, Julie. We certainly will. Slow boat, slow train, or fast plane —we will go back to China!"

ROBERT ELEGANT, author of the international best sellers *Dynasty, Manchu,* and *Mandarin,* was a correspondent in Asia for almost twenty-five years, reporting primarily for *Newsweek* and the *Los Angeles Times/Washington Post* News Service. He has won many professional prizes, including the Sigma Delta Chi Award for distinguished foreign reporting and three Overseas Press Club Awards for best interpretation of news from abroad. He holds a Master of Arts from Columbia University in Chinese, which he speaks and writes, and has published six nonfiction books on Asia, as well as six novels. Born in New York, he now lives in England.